THE
REBEL OF THE FAMILY

Eliza Lynn Linton

edited by Deborah T. Meem

broadview literary texts

National Library of Canada Cataloguing in Publication Data

Linton, E. Lynn (Elizabeth Lynn), 1822-1898
    The rebel of the family

(Broadview literary texts)
Includes bibliographical references.
ISBN 1-55111-293-0

1. Women's rights—Great Britain—History—19th century—Fiction.
I. Meem, Deborah T. (Deborah Townsend). 1949–   II. Title.   III. Series.

PR4889.L5R4 2002   823'.8   C2002-900674-0

Broadview Press Ltd. is an independent, international publishing house, incorporated in 1985.

North America:
P.O. Box 1243, Peterborough, Ontario, Canada K9J 7H5
3576 California Road, Orchard Park, NY 14127
TEL: (705) 743-8990; FAX: (705) 743-8353;
E-MAIL: customerservice@broadviewpress.com

United Kingdom:
Thomas Lyster Ltd
Units 3 & 4A, Ormskirk Industrial Park
Burscough Road
Ormskirk, Lancashire L39 2YW
TEL: (01695) 575112; FAX: (01695) 570120; E-mail: books@tlyster.co.uk

Australia:
St. Clair Press, P.O. Box 287, Rozelle, NSW 2039
TEL: (02) 818-1942; FAX: (02) 418-1923

www.broadviewpress.com

Broadview Press gratefully acknowledges the financial support of the Book Publishing Industry Development Program, Ministry of Canadian Heritage, Government of Canada.

Broadview Press is grateful to Professor Eugene Benson and Professor L. W. Conolly for advice on editorial matters for the Broadview Literary Texts series.

PRINTED IN CANADA

Contents

Acknowledgements

I would like to thank the University Research Council of the University of Cincinnati for enabling me to travel to England and review the first edition of *The Rebel of the Family*; Janet Reed, chair of the Language Arts Department in University College of the University of Cincinnati, for supporting released time from my heavy teaching load and thereby allowing me to prepare the text; Tapati Bharadwaj, for outstanding editorial assistance; The Center for Women's Studies at the University of Cincinnati, for assigning Tapati to me during Spring quarter 1999; and finally, my partner Michelle Gibson, who by now knows far more about Eliza Lynn Linton than anyone needs to.

Deborah T. Meem
University College
University of Cincinnati

Introduction[1]

The Rebel of the Family was the twelfth of Eliza Lynn Linton's twenty novels; it appeared serialized in *Temple Bar* in 1880 and was published complete in three volumes late that same year. It is an early "New Woman" novel, raising a number of controversial issues, some familiar and some new and, for contemporary readers, outrageous: mercenary marriage, "democracy" or the mingling of social classes, enforced idleness for gentlewomen, feminism, lesbianism. Typically for Linton, she problematizes these ideas in ways that have confounded both her contemporaries and readers today. Well known in her periodical journalism as at least a social conservative, and at most a reactionary misogynist, Linton complicates that view of herself in her novels.

The Rebel of the Family tells the story of Perdita Winstanley, middle daughter of a genteel but impoverished family. Perdita, as her name implies, is "lost" in her widowed mother's home: a democrat in a family of aristocrats, an intellectual in a family of shallow thinkers, a plain and bespectacled young woman in a family of beauties, a passionate emotionalist in a family of cool and calculating marriage marketeers. Perdita repeatedly embarrasses her mother and sisters. For one thing, her plainness and outspokenness not only limit her own marriage prospects but, as her elder sister Thomasina says, reduce the other sisters' chances as well: "You are not such good style as I am, and not so pretty as Eva; and we are both more likely to get married than you; but you do what you can to spoil our chances, having none of your own, by what you call your honesty—that is, by professing the extraordinary opinions you have got hold of, no one knows how or where—by dressing unlike everyone else—by making yourself ridiculous and unconventional in every direction." Worse even than "professing ... extraordinary opinions," however, passionate Perdita practices what she preaches. She claims to believe that middle-class women should be allowed to work; and through the intercession of Thomasina's rich suitor, she goes out to work at the Post-office Savings Bank. She claims to believe in democracy, by which she seems to mean class mixing; and she strikes up a friendship (later a romance)

---

[1] I would like to thank the University of Chicago Press for permission to use a portion of my article "Eliza Lynn Linton and the Rise of Lesbian Consciousness" which appeared in *Journal of the History of Sexuality* 7:4 (April 1997), pp. 537–60. Copyright © The University of Chicago Press. All rights reserved.

with druggist Leslie Crawford. She claims to believe that middle-class women ought to exercise some control over their own lives; and she becomes involved with the West Hill Society for Women's Rights and its "Lady President," Bell Blount.

Perdita's mother and sisters punish her for this improper behavior; she is ridiculed, scolded, ostracized, and ultimately banished from the house. But the author does not punish rebellious Perdita. In the course of the novel Perdita grows from a condition of "chronic humiliation" at the beginning to a confident recognition of "human worth and the truth of things" at the end. Her love-match with Leslie Crawford ends up allowing her sisters to seal their mercenary arrangements as well. At the same time Perdita learns that Bell Blount and her feminists are really hypocrites. So, one asks, where does Eliza Lynn Linton really stand on these issues?

Even contemporary reviewers (see Appendix A) of *The Rebel of the Family* noted the inconsistencies in Linton's point of view. *The Academy*, for instance, panned the book, noting that the author appeared to write "without any fixed moral basis," and the result was that "what [she] means us to infer from [*Rebel*] we know no more than she does herself." *The Saturday Review* found the book to have some "intrinsic merit," but admitted that a reader's main interest might lie in "an ardent desire to find out whether what seems at moments the author's advocacy of strange views is serious or not, whether she means to sympathize with or to laugh at her heroine's convictions and inconvenient theories." If one judges Linton's real views according to her periodical journalism, one would have to assume the latter. Since the appearance of her "Girl of the Period" essays in *Saturday Review* in 1868 (see Appendix B.3), Linton had made a name for herself as perhaps *the* most virulent antifeminist in England. She criticizes the G.O.P. as the antithesis of the "fair young English girl" of the past. This outrageous modern maiden sported outlandish hats, dyed her hair, and used vulgar slang—in short, she undertook an "imitation of the demi-monde in dress" and even in attitude. She wished to go everywhere and do everything, and her boldness was an affront to conservative elements of her age, such as Eliza Lynn Linton's *Saturday Review* persona. But perhaps worse than her sluttish public image was her willingness to sell her own person, to engage in "the legal barter of herself for so much money ... that is her idea of marriage."

In *The Rebel of the Family*, this attack on women would seem to hit both Perdita and her sisters. Perdita is certainly bold in thought and speech, unconventional in dress, and insistent upon a certain freedom of movement and activity. At the same time, however, she scorns the idea of mercenary marriage. She cries out passionately against genteel Thomasina, "I would rather break stones on the road than marry ...just for a settlement, and without caring whether I loved the man or not!" In *Rebel* Linton displays considerable personal sympathy for Perdita, if not for all her causes. Certainly this sympathy arises in part from Perdita's similarity to the youthful Eliza Lynn, nearsighted and "not a handsome woman ... even when I was young and slight, and with my 'wealth of golden-brown hair'" (letter to Gulie Moss 1892, quoted in Layard 29). In addition, as Andrea Broomfield argues (see Appendix C), Linton's misogynistic *Saturday Review* persona was just that—a persona, spouting opinions that would sell magazines but did not necessarily jibe with the author's own. The journalistic persona was at least consistent; the *Rebel* point of view is less so, at least as regards Perdita and her eccentricities. The book similarly wavers in its point of view towards Bell Blount, arguably the most interesting character in *Rebel*.

By the time she wrote *The Rebel of the Family* in 1880, Eliza Lynn Linton knew Balzac, whose 1834 novel *Esther Heureuse* ("Gay Esther") introduced many British readers to "l'amour sapphique." She also knew "Carmilla" (J.S. LeFanu's 1872 lesbian vampire ghost story) and probably also *Lesbia Brandon* (Swinburne's unfinished novel). Perhaps even more significantly, Linton had lived since 1876 in Italy, escaping from an ill-advised relationship with a woman whom she names "Katie Pender" in *The Autobiography of Christopher Kirkland* (1885). Nancy Fix Anderson thinks that relationship at least "aroused strong lesbian feelings" (156) in Linton, whether or not she and "Katie" were sexual together. At any rate, she fled England with a young friend, Beatrice Sichel; the following year they spent time in Rome with well-known lesbians Harriet Hosmer, Matilda Hays, and Adelaide Sartoris. These friendships seem to have influenced Linton's writing. Her 1879 novel *Under Which Lord?* contains a subplot describing an intense attraction between two young women who, hopelessly tangled in crises both moral and familial, convert to Catholicism and become nuns. Then in 1880 she created Bell Blount, the first fully realized "modern" lesbian woman in English literature. Bell is first described as a "handsome but bold and confident-looking woman ... nearer fifty than forty" dressed expensively but vulgarly in "a kaleidoscopic arrangement of colors that was simply barbarous." Before we know anything about Bell, Linton's strategically placed "but" directs us to suspect her of unwomanly "wildness"—and such indeed turns out to be the case. Bell woos the ingenuous Perdita with her "caressing voice," ostensibly to the cause of women's rights, but apparently also sexually. Passionate innocent Perdita is at first attracted to Bell, and feels "as if about to be initiated into those hidden mysteries where the springs of human history are to be found." Immediately, however, Perdita recoils, "chilled and repelled ... [by] something in Mrs. Blount's face." Perdita is at once "bewildered and shocked ... [and] fascinated and attracted" by Bell's proposal. Bell's world, where women work and love each other, beckons invitingly to Perdita, who feels unloved and ridiculous at home. So she agrees to accompany Bell to her house; at this "Mrs. Blount's face flushed vividly" and she "startled Perdita by suddenly taking her in her arms and kissing her with strange warmth." Lest we miss the point concerning Bell's inverted sexuality, when the two women arrive at Bell's house, Bell is greeted by "a little woman, darting up from the sofa and flinging herself into [Bell's] arms." This is Connie Tracy, Bell's "good little wife," as she explains to Perdita, who "was everything that one woman could be to another." Connie is immediately (and rightly) jealous of Bell's new interest in Perdita, and as the novel progresses it becomes clear that Bell's intended seduction of Perdita is indeed both political and sexual. The story comes down to a prolonged battle between the lesbian Bell and the "manly man" Leslie Crawford for the soul of Perdita Winstanley. Perdita is susceptible to Bell's advances partly because of her loneliness and her sense of living a "purposeless life," and partly because she is, as she admits to herself, a woman of "shameful passion." For Perdita, who had always wished to be a boy, Bell represents the possibility of "manly freedom [from] ... feminine fetters." At the same time, Bell represents something "monstrous" and unnamable; in her innocence Perdita can only conceive of Bell as a "handsome hybrid" or a "living enigma." Perdita, like Queen Victoria,[1] is ignorant of lesbianism, and fearful of "initiation ... against her will," but she knows when she is being courted. Bell writes her love letters, then takes her to a women's rights meeting, the closest equivalent to a lesbian gathering at that time. Bell Blount's vampire-like power very nearly overwhelms Perdita. When Bell begs her to "leave that prison which you call your home, and come to me, your truest friend and safest lover," Perdita trembles ("she scarcely knew why"), and Bell's "passionate emotion gained on [her] so far that she returned [Bell's] caress

---

[1] In 1885, when Queen Victoria was asked whether the Criminal Law Amendment Act outlawing homosexual acts between men should also apply to women, "she is supposed to have expressed disbelief that such acts between women were physically possible" (Terry Castle, *The Apparitional Lesbian: Female Homosexuality and Modern Culture* [NY: Columbia UP, 1993], 66).

with gratitude and affection." Only the unexpected arrival on the scene of jealous Connie Tracy prevents who-knows-what from happening!

Bell Blount ultimately fails to win Perdita. For one thing, Perdita, it turns out, is not a real lesbian. She is rather "essentially a man's companion, friend, and lover." Moreover, Perdita "had the natural woman's instinctive admiration for masculine strength—the loving woman's instinctive glory in acknowledging her own comparative inferiority." But at least as significant as Perdita's own inborn heterosexuality is the gradual revelation of Bell's moral weakness. For Bell, we learn, is a hypocrite. She rails against marriage as the sanctioned selling of women, yet she herself "keeps" Connie Tracy, who is "as much Bell Blount's creature as if she had been a man's mistress ... giving body and soul for maintenance in the present, and the hope of a permanent provision in the future." In addition, Bell's feminism is designed to benefit only upper- and middle-class women; she does not appear to "recognize sex as a category that cuts across class lines" (Ardis 25). Hence Bell advises Perdita "not to make friends out of your class. We must respect social degrees as we find them ... and the emancipation of woman does not include democratic equality or communistic mishmash in any form." Finally, as Perdita comes to realize, Bell's sweet words of love merely mask her desire for control, and Perdita develops a justified fear that "Bell Blount would take her by main force." In short, Bell is the vampire lesbian on the prowl.

Eliza Lynn Linton's creation of Bell Blount represents a milestone in the literary representation—and the popular understanding—of lesbianism during the last third of the nineteenth century. While Linton cannot name—no one could in 1880—what Bell *is*, there can be no mistaking the nature of her desire. In addition, Linton shows herself to be aware of the beginnings of an urban lesbian subculture, spurred by increasing opportunities for education and independence for women. In *The Rebel of the Family* Linton criticizes Bell Blount harshly, connecting her lesbianism with extreme man-hating feminism, with sexual coercion (and implied perversion), and with hypocrisy. Yet at the same time the ingenue heroine Perdita finds Bell attractive to a nearly irresistible degree, and readers of *Rebel* are meant to pick up on that magnetism as well.

If those readers were reviewers, the magnetism escaped them utterly. *The Saturday Review* praised Linton for drawing Bell Blount "with complete fidelity," but understood that the "scenes in which Bell Blount figures cannot possibly be pleasant" and, moreover, that these scenes "deal with somewhat risky matters." Not daring to speak the name of lesbianism, *The Saturday Review* contented itself with dismissing those inferences in *Rebel* as "worse than absurdities." *Academy* agreed, describing Bell as "a character too odious, and the scenes in which she appears too repulsive, even for comment." (See Appendix A.)

But if those readers were male literary figures, their opinion was much more positive. Swinburne wrote to Eliza Lynn Linton in January 1881 that her "noble books" were "the most heroic in temper since the Brontës', and of so much wider intelligence than theirs" (188). And Henry James, with whom Linton corresponded off and on for a decade, modeled his 1886 novel *The Bostonians* after *Rebel*. Like Linton's novel, *The Bostonians* introduces a gifted ingénue who is befriended by an older, obviously lesbian, feminist. Into the picture strides a "manly man" who takes an interest in the ingénue. Both plots turn on the outcome of the extended struggle between the lesbian and the man for the affections of the attractive young woman. In both cases the heterosexual imperative is irresistible, and the ingénue chooses the man. If there is a difference between how Linton and James treat their literary lesbians, it is that Linton creates in Bell Blount a far more radical and sexually desirable lesbian, and having done so, is required by convention to discredit her in the end and portray the successful male suitor Leslie Crawford as supernaturally strong and noble. James, by contrast, draws a more sophisticated, more intelligent, and less overtly sexual lesbian in Olive Chancellor; he is therefore able to depict the male rival Basil Ransom as flawed, and the eventual heterosexual coupling as somewhat less than either inevitable or wholly satisfying. Both books—Linton's and James's—describe the rebellion of their ingénue heroines as only temporary. At the end Perdita Winstanley and Verena Tarrant renounce their flings with feminism and lesbianism and are "catapult[ed] ... back into domesticity" in a characteristic plot pattern that Ann Ardis calls a "boomerang" (98). In books of this type a rebellious New Woman heroine is "boomeranged" back into respectability and conformity; thus Perdita and Verena end up safely married and with their wild notions somewhat muted by their lapse into a conventional life pattern.

As a man, and with a man's license to explore the less proper side of life, James could muddy the moral waters of *The Bostonians*. But Linton was already known by Dickens and others for straying too close to "the sexual side of things" (qtd. Anderson 66); she was also well aware that her old nemesis George Eliot had more than once been castigated for presenting themes that no "female novelist can touch on without leaving a feeling of hesitation, if not repulsion, in the reader" (Rev. of *The Mill on the Floss* 471). In taming the rebellious Perdita Winstanley, Linton nods (not for the first time, as Anderson's and Broomfield's articles in this volume attest) to Mrs. Grundy. She follows her own oft-repeated pattern: toying with scandalously progressive ideas; redeeming those ideas with an overlay of conservative antifeminism; finally leaving the reader with the unresolved notion that the redemption might be worse than the scandal.

Reviews

Victorian literary reviews tended to include, in addition to critical judgment and analysis, considerable plot summary and occasional excerpts. The selections I have chosen for this volume (Appendix A) have been edited to exclude the latter elements.

Periodical Journalism

During her long and prolific literary career Eliza Lynn Linton wrote hundreds of articles, several of which ("Mature Sirens," "Modern Man-Haters," "The Shrieking Sisterhood") she refers to directly in *The Rebel of the Family*. In choosing which to include here, however (Appendix B), I have operated on the principle that the present edition is likely, for some time at least, to represent the only Linton work in print. Therefore I have chosen four articles spanning Linton's career, so that a reader new to the author will have at hand several important and representative pieces of her journalism.

The earliest chronologically is the most progressive politically. "Mary Wollstonecraft" appeared in the radical journal *The English Republic* in 1854. Here Eliza Lynn Linton refuses to judge Wollstonecraft for cohabiting with a man outside of marriage, she praises *A Vindication of the Rights of Woman* as "one of the boldest and bravest things ever published," and she rails against "the slavish submission of Englishwomen" in her own time. Building on these ideas, her 1856 "Marriage Gaolers" makes a strong statement in favor of married women's property reform. "The Girl of the Period" (1868) began a new era for Linton. Here she takes to task modern young English girls, whom she sees as materialistic and immoral. This article became Linton's hallmark, and for the rest of her career she clung stubbornly to the carping and misogyny first introduced in it. In "The Wild Women as Social Insurgents" (1891) she has moved on to attacking feminists, now focusing on women who, in the name of politics or fashion, choose to blur established boundaries of gender and social class. This article may interest today's feminists as a footnote: here for what may be the first time in literary history is a reference to a "butching" woman, a female butcher. While I assume that the word "butch" existed in underground slang speech prior to 1891, Linton's use of the term to describe a "hard-fisted woman of the people" is quite new.

Critical Articles

The four critical pieces in this volume have been selected, like the periodical articles, on the assumption that they will aid a reader encountering Eliza Lynn Linton for the first time. Nancy Fix Anderson, author of the standard biography of Linton (*Woman Against Women in Victorian England*, 1987), here offers a biographical essay based in part on new sources (Appendix C). Andrea Broomfield then examines (Appendix D) the relationship between the adaptive techniques Linton learned as a journalist and the development of her fiction. Constance Harsh's essay (Appendix E) focuses on Linton's later antifeminist novels, in which the figure of the New Woman (of whom Perdita Winstanley in *The Rebel of the Family* is an early example) is held up for punishment or ridicule. Finally, Valerie Sanders discusses the various reasons Linton "has remained so stubbornly outside the feminist canon" and makes a case for her inclusion now (Appendix F).

Works Cited

Anderson, Nancy Fix. *Woman Against Women in Victorian England: A Life of Eliza Lynn Linton*. Bloomington: Indiana UP, 1987.
Ardis, Ann. *New Women, New Novels: Feminism and Early Modernism*. New Brunswick NJ: Rutgers UP, 1990.
Castle, Terry. *The Apparitional Lesbian: Female Homosexuality and Modern Culture*. NY: Columbia UP, 1993.
James, Henry. *The Bostonians*. NY and London: Methuen, 1886.
Layard, George Somes. *Mrs. Lynn Linton: Her Life, Letters, and Opinions*. London: Methuen, 1901.
Linton, Eliza Lynn. *The Autobiography of Christopher Kirkland*. 3 Vols. London: Bentley, 1885.
Rev. of *The Mill on the Floss* by George Eliot. *Saturday Review*, 14 April 1860, IX, 470–71.
Swinburne, A.C. *Letters*. Vol. 4, 1877–82. Ed. Cecil Y. Lang. New Haven: Yale UP, 1960.

Eliza Lynn Linton: A Brief Chronology

1822   Born 10 February in Keswick, England, twelfth child of Rev. James and Charlotte Alicia Lynn. Charlotte Lynn dies in July, age 39, leaving eldest daughter Charlotte Elizabeth in mother role.

1823   Charlotte Elizabeth Lynn dies.

1835   Eliza's favorite brother Edmund drowns in Derwent River.

1837   Writes secretly to Richard Bentley, editor of *Bentley's Miscellany*, then sends a story for consideration. It is not acknowledged.

1843   Eliza Lynn becomes infatuated with "Adeline Dalrymple," an older married woman.

1844   Two poems, "A National Convention of the Gods" and "A Wreath," are published in *Ainsworth's Magazine*.

1845   Eliza Lynn moves to London, living in a boarding house on Russell Square and working in the reading room of the British Museum.

1847   Eliza Lynn's first novel, *Azeth, The Egyptian*, is published. She meets poet and classical scholar Walter Savage Landor, with whom she establishes a loving "father–daughter" relationship.

1848   Second novel, *Amymone*, appears. Eliza Lynn is hired by the *Morning Chronicle*, the first woman journalist in England to draw a fixed salary.

1848–49   Eliza Lynn is romantically involved with Edward MacDermot, a young Irish Catholic doctor. They never marry because Eliza refuses to convert to Catholicism.

1850   Meets George Eliot, the beginning of a long and vexed relationship.

1851   Novel *Realities* appears, and receives very negative reviews. Eliza Lynn is so deeply disappointed that she does not publish another novel for 14 years, instead earning her living as a journalist and short story writer.

1854   Publishes a feminist article, "Mary Wollstonecraft" (pp. 403–09 this volume), in William Linton's radical journal *English Republic*. Also publishes an antifeminist article "Rights and Wrongs of Women" in Charles Dickens' *Household Words*.

1858   Marries William Linton, radical engraver and publisher, a
        widower with seven children. Refers to herself from this
        time on as "E. Lynn Linton."

1864   Because of vast differences in personal habits, social class,
        and political persuasion, Eliza Lynn and William Linton
        separate.

1867   *Sowing the Wind* published.

1868   "The Girl of the Period" (pp. 412–17 this volume) appears in
        The Saturday Review. It causes an immediate sensation, and
        Eliza Lynn Linton's essays on women continue to appear
        bimonthly in *SR* for a decade.

1872   *The True History of Joshua Davidson, Christian and
        Communist* published, causing public outrage for its
        assertion that if Jesus lived now, he would be a
        communist.

1874–75 *Patricia Kemball*, one of Linton's most successful novels and
        the first to be serialized in a magazine, appears in *Temple
        Bar*.

1876   Linton leaves England for Italy, at least partly because of a
        traumatic "estrangement" from a young woman. She is
        accompanied by another woman, Beatrice Sichel, and
        does not return permanently to England until 1884.

1880   *The Rebel of the Family* appears.

1885   *The Autobiography of Christopher Kirkland*, Linton's
        fictionalized autobiography (using a male pseudonym), is
        published.

1889   Linton signs a public anti-woman-suffrage petition.

1891–92 Linton publishes three antifeminist essays in *Nineteenth
        Century*: "The Wild Women as Politicians," "The Wild
        Women as Social Insurgents" (pp. 417-27 this volume),
        and "The Partisans of the Wild Women."

1893   *The One Too Many* is serialized in *Lady's Pictorial*,
        denouncing university education for women.

1895   *In Haste and At Leisure* appears, castigating women for
        taking on the characteristics and privileges of men.

1898   Eliza Lynn Linton dies on 14 July.

1899   Memoir entitled *My Literary Life* published posthumously.

1900   Linton's last novel, *The Second Youth of Theodora Desanges*,
        published posthumously.

A Note on the Text

The text of *The Rebel of the Family* included here follows the first (1880) Chatto & Windus edition. Chapters are numbered according to the 1886 three-in-one edition (also Chatto & Windus) to avoid the confusion of the multi-volume format. Linton's sentences tend to be exceedingly long, stitched together with what would today be called highly idiosyncratic punctuation. I have standardized Linton's punctuation of dialogue, but otherwise in general I have retained her punctuation intact, supplying or changing marks only where there is a clear error in the first edition, choosing among other available editions (including also the 1880 pirated American edition).

THE
REBEL OF THE FAMILY

BY

E. LYNN LINTON

AUTHOR OF

"PATRICIA KEMBALL,"
"THE ATONEMENT OF LEAM DUNDAS,"
"THE WORLD WELL LOST,"
"MY LOVE!" ETC.

A NEW EDITION

LONDON

CHATTO AND WINDUS, PICCADILLY

THE REBEL OF THE FAMILY

CHAPTER I.

THE SEAMY SIDE.

WITHOUT question it was poverty; but it was genteel poverty and there was no shame in it. The seamy side was terribly to the front in these hard latter days, but the substance of the garment was velvet; and in the estimation of some people a skimped length of frayed silk is better than the most comfortable wrap of honest homespun, or the freshest little frock of daisy-patterned print. Mrs. Winstanley was one of these people. The widow of a major who had had nothing but his pay, and the daughter of a bishop who had died as poor as if he had been an archaic fisherman, she was proud of her position as one of the socially safe; and though she had infinite difficulty in keeping up appearances, and was reduced by her comparative poverty to somewhat ignominious straits, yet she held up her head as superbly as if her pence had been pounds, conscious that her name was borne on the *Libro d'oro*[1] of inherited respectability and that if her purse was poor her blood was rich. Indeed, had she been asked, she would have said that she preferred her impecuniosity with her gentle birth to wealth and a doubtful grandfather. Born in the velvet, she clung to her stately rags as to a talisman that gave her honour, if not sufficiency; and the pivot of her whole existence was, that she was essentially a lady, of whom neither debt nor cheese-parings could make anything else.

But how poor she was! and what a hard fight of it she had! No one but herself knew the severe shifts to which she was put in her daily life; and even her daughters, for whose sakes she buffered, were not told all. She let them know only just so much as would check unnecessary extravagance; but she thought it politic to keep the worst in the background. The discretion of the young is not always to be trusted; and they might by chance disclose things which she was doing her utmost to conceal, and make the world free of the rents and patches which she spent days and nights in devising how to hide beneath artistically arranged folds.

---

[1] The Golden Book.

And as she practised a good deal of formality with her children, even that outspoken Perdita, who despised tact and held it for hypocrisy, was systematically drilled into reserve on certain matters, and did not venture to ask what she was not voluntarily told; while Thomasina, the eldest and wisest of the three, and naturally the one most confided in, saw no more than it was intended she should see and discreetly held her peace on the rest. Little Eva, the youngest—playful, caressing, kittenish little Eva, who never could be got to understand the value of money, but who would buy brooches and porte-bonheurs[1] as recklessly as if her mother counted her income by hundreds where she reckoned units—little Eva, with her blue eyes and fuzzy golden head, her flower-like face, soft red ripe lips, small hands, jimp waist, and that sweet lisp which suggested kisses—lovely little Eva who won all hearts at a glance, she, of course, was out of the question as a confidante on grave matters or a participator in troubles when she could be lightened of her share. The child, as she was sometimes called, was too fresh and artless to be associated with any of the perplexities of life; and even Mrs. Winstanley—an astute woman— accepted this theory of her youngest daughter's ingenuous innocence, and often said to Thomasina, how cruel it would be to sadden such a joyous nature as the child's by the knowledge of pecuniary difficulties and the practice of self-denial! Born of the sunshine, she must live in the sunshine; and the shadows darkening so many corners of the family tabernacle must not be suffered to fall on her.

As things were, she was the life of the house; and, being the most beautiful of the three, was the best investment of maternal hopes and the family future. It was only wise then to pet and cherish her; to dress her prettily and give her more than her strict share of dainties; to keep her well in body and serene in mind, that her sleek skin should not lose its softness nor her complexion its purity, her face its bewildering brightness nor her manners that bewitching insouciance, that freedom from care which Mrs. Winstanley reckoned as equal to the repute of some hundreds per annum more than she possessed. She was the best fly in the maternal fishing-book; and it was only common sense to keep her in good trim.

But neither was Thomasina a losing concern. A tall, graceful, dark-haired girl with a small head and a swan-like throat, a full head and shoulders above little Eva who was the exact height of the Medicean Venus and modelled after the same pattern. She was not so handsome

---

[1] Charm bracelets.

perhaps, as good style; more elegant than picturesque; and less critically beautiful in face than charming in manner. Her manners indeed were absolutely perfect, and her smile was one of the finest bits of facial artistry to be found within the four seas. It was a smile that never degenerated into a grin nor lost itself in the exaggeration of a laugh; a smile that did not narrow her eyes nor show the nascent tracks of future wrinkles, but that brightened still more her large, deep, lustrous orbs, and rounded off the contours of her face without distorting the muscles or deepening the lines. It was a smile that counted for beauty, like a good complexion or a fine figure; and this and her manner and her style made the best assets in her personal treasury. When she heard a new-comer say in a loud whisper to his neighbour: "What a charming smile Miss Winstanley has!" or: "What wonderful style there is about her!" or: "What a graceful person she is, and how delightfully well-mannered!" then her soul was satisfied because her existence was justified. She had done her duty to herself, her mother, her future and the family fortunes. She had therefore earned her right to be well-dressed and taken out into society, as fairly as a workman, who has laid his tale of bricks, has earned his pint of beer and his stipulated week's wage. Her mother thought so too; and rewarded her as munificently as was in her power. The dinner might be meagre and the butcher and baker might be left unpaid, but Thomasina was always beautifully attired, and never stinted in those amusements which were of any probable social value or which might contain the magic ring. She and Eva, and Mrs. Winstanley herself, were noted for their dress; and no one, to see the handsome triad, would have suspected the presence of that Black Care which sat so heavily on the Mother's still comely shoulders and sometimes threatened to strangle her outright; no one would have suspected the unsubstantiality of all this brave appearance, or that the fairseeming of the ladies of No. 100, West Hill Gardens, was no more real than the beauty of the Ellewomen.[1]

Things were different with Perdita. In one sense her mother's cross, she was in another her relief. A very poor investment indeed, so far as future matrimonial return on any present outlay of dress and pleasure went, she cost considerably less than either of her sisters and was of but little account in the family inventory. She was not beautiful like Eva nor graceful like Thomasina; her face was too sad when in repose, too tumultuous when excited, for a civilization which deifies quiescence and blasphemes enthusiasm as "gush;" and her list of personal charms was small.

---

[1]   Mermaids (see Hans Christian Andersen, *Danish Tales*, 1870).

Certainly she had an abundance of auburn hair of the true Venetian colour, long, thick broadly waved and silky—but her nose was blunt and her skin was freckled; she had a sensitive, generous and handsome mouth, and she had large soft hazel eyes—but though the orbit was fine and the lids well cut, they were too convex for real beauty, and she was short-sighted and wore spectacles. Her figure was good—but she took no pains with herself and never made the best of her "points." In bearing she was shy, abrupt and uncertain; now silent and timid, now blazing like a flame of fire, impassioned as a Pythoness, her self-hood lost in her subject. She had none of her mother's worldly wisdom, and scorned the theory of keeping up appearances with nothing at the back of things to give them reality; so far indeed from this, she held truth before all things, and thought honest poverty better than sham sufficiency. She said what she thought, however much it cost her; for though her mind was bold, her temperament was sensitive, and she suffered a moral martyrdom when she was flouted and condemned for having spoken the truth.

And she said a great deal that she called truth but that shocked all reasonable people, and caused her to be looked on by them as mad, or bad;—which was not an agreeable alternative. She had a whole store-house full of objectionable flags and held every wrong opinion that a virtuous young lady could hold; besides being everything that she ought not to have been. She stood to lose all round. A stoic to pain and personal inconvenience; of savage simplicity in taste; indifferent to finery, to luxury, to the ordinary amusements of polite society; intolerant of all shams and an iconoclast of all clay-footed idols; murderously direct in thought and daring to give an opinion on matters whereon young women of properly constituted minds have no opinions at all—she crowned her iniquities by taking an interest in politics and having views of her own. She, only just twenty-one at this date, had the presumption to talk about Bismarck and Gambetta, the Nihilists[1] and the trades-unions, as if she understood what she was saying—she had the impiety to regard kings and queens as so much political finery good only for the childhood of society—she dared to say that the land should belong to him who tilled it, and that a titular landlord, eating up the largest share of the profits, was a crime—that the game laws were infamous and that

---

[1]   Prince Otto Fürst von Bismarck-Schönhausen (1815–98), known as the Iron Chancellor: architect of the German Empire, credited with the 1871 unification of Germany. Léon Gambetta (1838–82), French republican leader, opposed the Second Empire of Napoleon III, helped create the Third Republic after 1871. Nihilists: Russian radicals and revolutionaries during the reign of Alexander II, 1855–81.

the fish of the rivers should be as free to all as the birds of the air or the little brown beasts of the field; that the poor had rights and the rich had duties; and, in short, she was one of that objectionable class—a young person with principles—and those principles such as good society has agreed to taboo and ladylike mothers to regard as crimes.

A republican in theory, she was as a democrat in practice, and was always doing something maddening to a well-bred conventionalist like Mrs. Winstanley. She had been seen carrying a fat, sleepy, dirty baby through the street to ease a fragile little child staggering under the overpowering burden; she had been known to give a hand to hectic and consumptive washerwomen coughing and panting over their baskets; she had been caught picking up a carter's whip and a cabman's hat; she sympathized to the extent of sixpences with ragged little urchins who had broken mother's eggs or father's beer-bottle, and were sitting on the doorstep with their knuckles in their eyes and their plebeian little hearts almost bursting with terror and despair; she could not be broken of the degrading habit of speaking to the maids not only as courteously as if they had been ladies but as affectionately as if they had been sisters; and she once wanted to teach an ignorant little Buttons how to read. When she was rebuked for her misdeeds, she dared to quote the Bible in self-defence and put forward the life of Christ as her example; and she was just the most worrying, unsatisfactory, and perplexing kind of thing that could be imagined as making one of the Winstanley family. A rebel and a democrat—and her mother the widow of a major and the daughter of a bishop!

Small wonder then, things moral and material being as they were, that Perdita was left on the outside of that mother's heart. For though this again is one of the shocking truths which the world has agreed to deny—all mothers do not love their children; and of those who do almost all make a favourite of one and comparatively an outcast of another. And Perdita was the outcast here. She was set aside in the family calculations and treated less as a daughter than a poor relation who must needs be suffered but is never adopted—more as an excrescence on the bole than as a branch of the family tree. Indeed, some of the less intimate among the visitors at West Hill Gardens thought that she was probably a portionless niece whom Mrs. Winstanley, good creature! had brought up for charity; and others that she was Eva's companion and governess. She had an intelligent face, they said, and was almost ugly enough to be clever.

Mr. Brocklebank, for one, thought this until he asked Miss Winstanley directly who that silent, shy, unconformable young person was, with her marked simplicity of dress, her wonderfully swift changes of colour, her extraordinary enthusiasm for freedom and the rights of man—the sacred duty of insurrection against tyranny—and the heroic sublimity of the republican form of government as contrasted with the degrading self abasement of king-worship. When Thomasina said sweetly: "That is my sister Perdita, the genius of the family," Mr. Brocklebank lifted up his eyebrows and repeated with a dry smile: "The family genius! Ah, is it so? Good for how many loaves in the art of breadwinning, I should like to know?"

"Not many, I fear," said Thomasina with her best-bred air. "Genius is so seldom practical!"

And after Mr. Brocklebank had said sententiously: "The only rational test of genius is—what can it perform that the world desires and will pay for?" and she had smiled sweetly and answered vaguely, "Yes," the conversation dropped, and Perdita became for the moment non-existent.

This Mr. Brocklebank was an important item in the Winstanley social inventory, if not yet what it was hoped he might be made eventually. Not exactly a snob, the wealthy owner of furnaces and pigs was not exactly a gentleman, according to the classification of those born in the purple. His father, who had conquered fortune from the original starting-point of a puddler, had never been able to overcome his difficulties with the English language nor to master the relative uses of his knife and fork. But Benjamin, his son and successor, now well on to fifty, had been helped over these initial stiles at a comparatively early age; and though his bearing wanted that last subtle polish of inherited good-breeding, he was not actively offensive, and, as he used to say of himself, might pass in a crowd without disgrace. He was fond of long words and involved sentences; would have scorned to say 'begin,' as much as he would have scorned to wear fustian and a billycock,[1] but clung to 'commence' as the sign of a scholar who knew his syntax and what was due to polite society and himself. He was never known to 'go on' with anything nor to 'end' it, but he 'proceeded' and 'progressed' as religiously as he had commenced; and he 'concluded,' when all was done, in the stately fashion belonging to an English gentleman of good style and breeding. With these little weaknesses of form, he had that solid kind of character and business-like way of dealing with difficulties which are of such inestimable value in a family of lone women who can be 'bluffed' and bullied to any extent, and deceived as easily, for all their natural sharpness and suspicion, as a hawk can be hoodwinked by

---

[1] Fustian: a strong cotton and linen fabric. Billycock: a Derby hat.

a falconer. He was fairly well-educated, though by no means ranking as a scholar. He was, however, a good historian and geographer; he knew the latest applications of practical science; and he was well up in the political movements, home and foreign, of the present moment; but he was shaky in classics and knew nothing of mathematics; he was of doubtful taste in art, though a patron and a picture buyer; and he was full of contempt for the life of the days which are dead and done with. Best recommendation of all—he was magnificently rich and could spend his money at times royally, if, in the main, he was close-fisted and demanded full value for every sixpence with which he parted.

Taking, then, the good with the bad, Mrs. Winstanley and Thomasina wisely decided, without confession of motives, that the former outweighed the latter; and that Mr. Brocklebank was an acquaintance whose visits were to be encouraged, whose interest in the family history was to be kept warm, whose habits were to be studied and whose prejudices were never to be shocked.

In person he was largely and heavily framed; his hair was short, straight and grizzled; his face was clean shaven; his eyes were small and deeply set beneath heavy overhanging brows, but they were singularly keen and quick; he had a thin and resolute mouth; his speech was slow and clear; his manner, masterful yet kind, was destitute of grace, even when wishing to be most courteous never shaking off its clumsiness and always traversed by a thin line of unconscious brutality.

He was a Liberal in politics—of that school which would curtail the prerogatives of the Crown and reduce the influence of the aristocracy, but which would also keep down the working man with a strong hand and a hard heel—"his nose to the grindstone, sir, and strikes and unions made illegal"—while throwing the balance of power into the hands of the middle classes, more especially the merchants and manufacturers, these being of most use to the community. He was in some sense too a Woman's Rights man, in so much as he would give women full liberty to work, and would open for their benefit fresh avenues of industry; but he stopped short at the vote. He did not desiderate to be governed by petticoats, he said with disdain; though he thought it a shame that men should have to support the unmarried and consequently useless and unproductive among them; and for his part he would compel the idle to work. He had a profound contempt for sentiment which would not bear the test of practical good sense, and was of no value if weighed against money. Sensitiveness which stood in the way of self-interest— super-subtle delicacy which would not wash when put into the great cauldron where the forces of society jostle each other and the strong destroy the weak, he looked on as a mild kind of madness; and people who preferred their feelings to their pockets were, according to him, fit for Earlswood.[1] He respected only industry, good sense, endurance, the main chance and that coarse callousness which can give knocks and bear them without making a blare or taking the world into its confidence. And the one great object of life with him, both for himself and others, was to go ahead, make money and conquer circumstances.

Such as he was, however, he had lately become a frequent visitor at West Hill Gardens; and he evidently admired Thomasina, to whom he paid open court. A shrewd observer might have seen that he also watched little Eva with more than common interest; and that of late he had begun to study and draw out Perdita, the rebel and the democrat. For all that, he was essentially Thomasina's admirer; and by common consent was assigned to her as her special and peculiar property. She thought him so herself; and neither of her sisters disputed her prize.

Mrs. Winstanley and her daughters were sitting in the drawing-room at this house of theirs, No. 100, West Hill Gardens. It was a beautiful spring day; but the blinds were down and the windows shaded in muslin and lace, as if the sunshine were man's worst enemy and human beings were like those plants which grow best in the twilight. The mother and Thomasina were sitting by a small occasional table, working. Mrs. Winstanley was making a flounce of modern point; Thomasina was embroidering a length of silk in artistically designed marigolds, as a trimming for her new ball-dress. Eva was lying half across the sofa playing with a little black kitten; and Perdita was behind the curtains, sitting in the bay of the window, reading.

The four had been sitting thus for some time in unbroken silence, save for Eva's conversation with the kitten, when a note from Mr. Brocklebank, addressed to Thomasina, was brought in, requesting that he might have the pleasure of presenting her with a ticket and escorting her to the flower-show next Wednesday. His sister, Mrs. Merton, had just returned from Paris, and she would accompany them. He hoped that Miss Winstanley would respond by an answer favourable to his desires. This was the commencement of the flower-shows of the year, and he would be pleased to pay this mark of respect to the amiable family who had honoured him with their friendship and to whom he returned the homage of his admiration. His servant had orders to wait for Miss Winstanley's response, which

---

1   An "Asylum for Idiots" near Redhill, Surrey.

he made bold to conclude beforehand would be in the affirmative. Then, with a flourish, he was hers obediently, Benjamin Brocklebank.

To this note Thomasina despatched a short but graceful little acceptance; and then, taking up her embroidery again, began with her mother an anxious discussion as to ways and means.

"It is a great nuisance! I dislike so much multiplying my gowns in this manner—they take up so much room and are so soon out of date," said Thomasina in a perfectly unruffled voice, looking at her mother; "but I am dreadfully afraid I cannot make what I have serviceable for next Wednesday. You know how dreadfully particular Mr. Brocklebank is; and of course I must look up to the mark when I am with him and his rich sister. Mrs. Merton, just from Paris, will be resplendent!"

"So far as that goes, your simplicity is better style than Mrs. Merton's magnificence," said Mrs. Winstanley. "Not that I mean by this to raise any objection to a new dress for you, Thomasina. It was merely a remark."

"Yes, Mrs. Merton does overdress tremendously," returned Thomasina. "But the worst of it is, these human peacocks have the art of making one look mean and poor, unless one can turn the tables and make them look vulgar by one's own elegance. Unfortunately elegance is as expensive as magnificence!"

"And you really have nothing that will do?" asked Mrs. Winstanley, into whose cheeks had come two hard red spots—the sure sign that she was worried. And indeed that abominable person the butcher had sent an insolent note to-day, demanding at the least part payment of his long-standing bill; and the March rent was still unpaid.

"Oh, wear your dead-leaf, Ina!" said Eva, in a tone of entreaty and child-like admiration.

By the way, she was the only person in the family or out of it, to whom was allowed the familiarity of this contraction. Both Mrs. Winstanley and Thomasina thought pet names foolish and bad style; and none but 'the child,' who dared everything and was permitted as much as she ventured, would have presumed to thus shear off the two most important and distinctive syllables of Miss Winstanley's name.

"I have worn my dead-leaf so often, I cannot go in it again," Thomasina answered, affably.

"But you look so lovely in it, Ina! It suits you so well! You put me in mind of that beautiful creature in Tennyson who did something wicked to the old man. You never had any dress that you looked so nice in; and you know how nice you always are!"

Eva spoke with generous enthusiasm.

"Thank you, dear," returned Thomasina with her charming smile. "It is very kind of you to admire my poor old wardrobe so much; but I am afraid, little Eva, it must be renewed for this occasion."

The sisters were always delightfully polite to their mother and each other. It was the tone of the house, extending even to the cat. Nothing roused Mrs. Winstanley's anger so much as brusqueness of behaviour or the crude statement of unpalatable truths. Ladies should be ladies all through, she used to say; and good breeding was not a thing like old point and diamonds, to be worn only on grand occasions and put away as too fine for family use. From the first, when they were quite little creatures, she would allow no nursery squabbles, and always punished the one who made an uproar, whether originally in fault or not. It was unladylike to cry, to vociferate, to resist; and she chastised the want of good breeding in the outbreak rather than the injustice, the tyranny, the greed, that had caused it.

But while Thomasina and Eva, the eldest and youngest, had apparently the sweetest tempers possible, and proved the excellence of her theory, it must be confessed parenthetically that Perdita, the unlucky sandwich, offered but an indifferent example and seemed morally unable to rise out of the awkward squad which is always being drilled and is never fit to appear on parade. She would speak the truth and put things as she saw them. And what worse quality could be possessed by a member of a family where keeping up appearances was the eleventh commandment, and the uncovering of the seamy side the unforgiven sin?

"I am sure if you, who look such a princess in what you have now, want a new dress—"

"Gown," interposed her mother.

"—A new gown, I do too!" then cried Eva. "I am frightfully shabby! Mother, you will give me a new gown if Ina has one, won't you, dear darling mumsey?"

"My dear Eva! You are not going to the flower-show," remonstrated Mrs. Winstanley.

"Why not, mother?" said Eva. "If Ina goes, I do not see why I should not too."

"And Perdita?" asked her mother blandly.

Eva laughed. Her laugh was as musical as a bird's song and when she threw back her head and opened her mouth she showed two full rows of the loveliest little sharp white teeth that can be imagined—very small, very even; but for all their beauty, teeth that somehow suggested the eating of flesh.

"Poor old Per! Fancy funny old Per at a fête!" she cried, immensely amused by the oddity of the idea. "She would not know what in the world to do with herself; and with those blundering old eyes of hers would go peering into the nettle beds when she wanted to find the azaleas."

"My dear Eva, poor Perdita's misfortunes are not to be made the subject of ridicule," said Mrs. Winstanley. "She cannot help being short-sighted; and you ought to pity rather than laugh at her."

"Eva can laugh at me if she likes," said Perdita a little hotly, looking up from the "History of Greece," where she was poring over the story of Thermopylae wishing that she had been born in those days and had been shield-bearer to Leonidas.[1]

"Oh, you dear, delightful, funny old Superior Person!" laughed Eva. "You are the eagle and I am the midge; and the eagle is far too grand to be annoyed by the midge. Is it not so, magnificent old Per?"

"Perhaps, if you like to put it that way," answered Perdita with constraint.

"My dear Eva, I cannot have Perdita called old. Where have you learnt such an objectionable epithet?" said Mrs. Winstanley, again remonstratingly. "Besides, if Perdita is old, what is your sister Thomasina? and what am I? The inference is not very polite, Eva."

"What is Ina? a youthful princess; and you, mumsey?—a queen in the prime of life!" said Eva. "And both are centuries younger than poor old Per who was born old. I am sure she read before she could talk; and when she did talk, she spouted. Now didn't she, mumsey?"

"My dear Eva! how often am I to tell you that I extremely dislike all these personalities? especially among sisters with whom it is such a strict family duty to make the best of what they have and to hide each other's faults! Perdita's unfortunate character is to be dealt with as tenderly as her personal blemish; and if I am willing to put up with her odd habits, so ought you."

"But, mother, what odd habits?" cried Perdita energetically.

She was doing nothing to justify this sudden attack on her, only reading about Leonidas and Thermopylae; and she blazed up with indignation at the wanton injustice of the onslaught.

"My poor child!" said Mrs. Winstanley with a compassionate smile, followed by a tender sigh. The question was one of such obvious mental darkness that she could not choose but smile for pity and sigh in regret.

---

[1] In 480 BC at Thermopylae, King Leonidas I and 1400 Greek soldiers died in their attempt to stop a Persian invasion from the north.

"Come here to me," she continued, "and I will show you a little what I mean."

Perdita laid down her book and went up to her mother. She had the awkward bearing of a sensitive person tutored by snubbing and always under sentence of condemnation—that kind of resentful depression which belongs to the ugly duck of a family made to feel an outsider and the blemish of the household.

"Let me look at your hands," said Mrs. Winstanley.

She was quite mild and ladylike, but Perdita visibly trembled as she held out her long, thin, nervous hands.

"What is this?" her mother asked, pointing with the tip of her scissors to the thumb and first two fingers of the right hand.

"Ink," answered Perdita, as guiltily as if she had said blood.

Her mother slightly shrugged her shoulders.

"As usual!" she said in a hopeless voice. Then, looking at her critically, "Where is your collar?" she asked with the same hopeless accent, as if no amount of delinquency could go beyond her expectations.

The girl put up her obnoxious hands to her denuded throat.

"I have none, mother," she said; "the last was such a mere rag, I was obliged to throw it away."

"I am afraid then that you must go bare if you destroy your things in this manner," said her mother quietly. "You had some new ones lately, I think? and I really cannot afford so much extravagance. Evidently you are not so careful with your things as you might be; and I fear that you must learn how to make the best of your wardrobe by experiencing the inconvenience of going without when you have been negligent and careless."

"No, mother, they were not new. They were some old ones of Thomasina's and more than half worn out when I had them," said Perdita with a tendency to tears.

It was a very little thing to cry about; and with her fatal indifference to dress, it was really too absurd to make a trouble of a few linen collars. But it was the spirit of the thing, not the thing itself, that struck her so painfully; it was this new evidence of her mother's injustice and not the denial of a little feminine adornment that humiliated and dissatisfied her. Thomasina and Eva might have dresses which would cost pounds and were not absolutely necessary; and she must not have what would not cost as many pence, and what was, according to custom, absolutely necessary. Not that she grudged them, or coveted a new dress for herself. Not the least in the world; but she did not like to feel always on the outside of the home nest, and she did honour justice. So she thought, standing there with flushed face, lowered eyes and her full lips twitching nervously.

"Surely you are not going to cry about a few linen collars, Perdita?" said Thomasina with courteous rebuke. "I have plenty and can always lend you as many as you want."

"Thank you," returned Perdita, with fiery ingratitude. "I do not like borrowing; and if I cannot have my own things, I will not have any."

"Now you are unladylike, my child," said Mrs. Winstanley: "and I do not suffer rudeness in my drawing-room. You will find your place in the schoolroom till your temper has cooled."

On which, Perdita, accepting her sentence of banishment as one used to it, went into the schoolroom, which was the only place where she felt at home and safe; and after one brief fit of bitter despair, lost the consciousness of linen collars, flower-shows, sisters, mother and herself in the pages of that thrilling story which sets forth how men should live and die for liberty and country.

And while she was feeding her fiery heart with this stimulating food, those sisters and their mother were deep in sweet discussions of costume and material—and how it would be possible for little Eva also to be taken to the fête without costing her mother more than the new dress—which would be a possession.

When the scanty meal which went by the name of dinner was announced and Perdita was summoned, she went in such heat and preoccupation of thought—such haste of body and forgetfulness of all table proprieties—she was so flushed and tumbled and unkempt and untidy, so reprehensible altogether—that Mrs. Winstanley, looking at her for a moment critically, stopped midway in the dining-room and took hold of her shoulder to arrest her tumultuous passage to the table.

"My dear Perdita, no one dines at my table in the state in which you are," she said with perfect suavity. "Oblige me by going back to the schoolroom. I will send your dinner there; and you can eat it in the manner most congenial to you."

"I am so sorry, mother!" Perdita began with disorderly zeal.

"Do not begin a harangue, Perdita," said her mother, interrupting her and making a sign with her hand to the door. "When you have learnt to respect yourself, my poor child, you will know how to respect your sisters and me. Till then you must be content to live in seclusion. Say grace, Thomasina; and, Lovell, take Miss Perdita's dinner to her in the schoolroom."

"How I wish I was a boy!" said Perdita to herself as she went back, humbled and subdued, to what was essentially her prison if also her home. "If I were a boy I would leave home to-night and never come back again till I had made a name and my fortune! Oh, what a dreadful thing it is to be a girl and a poor lady!—neither able to earn money nor live independently. I am of no use here; I am only an encumbrance. Mother does not love me; and they are all ashamed of me because I am awkward and ugly and don't care for dress and have to wear spectacles. We are horribly poor; and I am just a burden on them all. What can I do! what can I do! If only there was a civil war and I might disguise myself as a man and enlist on the side of the people!—if only I could go out into the world and do something for myself! This home life of ours is horrible! We are so poor and we pretend to so much! Everything for show and no real comfort—fine dresses for the girls, and the tradespeople not paid! What a dreadful state of things! How I wish I had been a boy and could end it, at least for myself!"

The heart and soul of all poor Perdita's lamentations and day-dreams was always this wish—that she had been born a boy and could go out into the world to make a name for herself and a fortune for her family!—always this same impatience with her womanhood, of which she had not yet learned the noblest use nor the best development! The *Sturm und Drang*[1] period with her was severe; and, seeing how the current of modern thought goes, it was an even chance whether it would end in some fatal absurdity or work through its present turbulence into clearness of purpose and reasonableness of action.

CHAPTER II.

AMONG THE FLOWERS.

THE day of the flower-show broke without a cloud and the brilliant sunshine of the sky was repeated in the perfect harmony and unruffled smoothness of things at No. 100, West Hill Gardens. The monster establishment in High Street, which supplied everything necessary to civilization—from tin tacks to salt pork—from the cake and trousseau to a

---

[1] German "storm and stress" literary movement (1765–85) that arose in reaction to traditional authority and the formality of the prevailing literary style.

bride at a pinch, and an Archdeacon to say grace—that world-renowned emporium of goods, hard and soft, had fitted out the Winstanley girls handsomely, on credit; and their new costumes showed the charms of each to perfection. Thomasina, in peacock-blue, looked like a maiden Juno, as was her ideal; Eva, in cream and azure, like a school-girl Venus, as was hers; and Mrs. Winstanley was Demeter in a lustrous black silk before that dark and gloomy Dis had carried off Persephone.

Some benevolent *deus ex machina* had come down from the clouds at the right moment to help the fond mother with her youngest born, and had sent Mrs. Winstanley a couple of tickets for the fête; so that while Thomasina was given over to the valuable care of Mr. Brocklebank and his sister, the still handsome mother and Eva beat the preserves on their own account, and soon gathered round them a small party of friends of whom Mrs. Winstanley could say with pride, All were select; not a detrimental among the bachelors nor a spotted peach among the women; all of the strictest order of respectability, and eligible to a man!

It was such a party as consoled her for weary nights and anxious days, when she racked her brain to devise means how two and two could be made to do the work of five or even six; a phalanx of solid social worth which made her believe for the moment that her hollowness was substantiality and her impecuniosity sufficiency, if not wealth.

Every now and then she and little Eva, with their friends, crossed the path of Mr. Brocklebank and his two ladies. But they did not coalesce. Mrs. Winstanley had unbounded confidence in her eldest daughter's discretion; and she thought that probably the ironmaster would take this whole-hearted surrender as a compliment to his patronage, and the recognition of his friendship.

She was just not clever enough to think that he might take it as a skilful cast with a very brilliant fly at the end of the line. Whether he did or not, no one could tell. He was all that was courteous and pleasant to Thomasina; not tender, perhaps, for tenderness was as little in his way as indiscriminate almsgiving or paying his hands a shilling if he could screw them down to elevenpence three farthings; but he was undoubtedly 'nice' and with that subtle manner of mastership and possession which some men have towards women even before they have declared themselves as lovers—that manner by which they keep off intruders yet do not commit themselves.

One characteristic of Mr. Brocklebank, from which he did not seem able to free himself, was the pertinacity with which the habit of business clung to him. When he was not an ironmaster he was something else that was commercial and mercantile; and when he was not scheming for his own benefit, he was working out the fiscal problems of the nation and vexing his soul over this falling off in the exports and that decline in the imports. He could not take his pleasure idly; and even to-day, with the beautiful Miss Winstanley by his side, he spent more than half his time in jotting down the names of such flowers as pleased his fancy, with the addresses of the growers and the probable price of seeds or roots—so much percent discount for so much quantity and cash down. But he always asked her opinion before he booked his own; anxious to hear if she thought such and such a plant would look well in those magnificent houses and grounds of his, which only wanted a well-bred, handsome, lady-like woman, with style, to make perfect.

And once, when she demurred to his choice and for her own preferred a certain "Lady Clare," as more beautiful than his "Miss Julia," he said in the nicest way possible, "Then Lady Clare it shall be;" and, what he would have called 'inscribed' the name in his bulky pocket-book with a smile; adding, "I will name the plot, Miss Winstanley's."

"That *is* a concession! you *are* favoured, Miss Winstanley!" said his sister, Mrs. Merton, pleasantly. "I never knew my brother Benjamin to alter his mind before nor to give any one the credit of his own work."

"You have never known your brother Benjamin to possess the advantage of such counsel as Miss Winstanley's before," said Mr. Brocklebank.

His gallantry was a little heavy and oppressive, not to say clumsy; but it was gallantry; and that was something!

Mrs. Merton smiled with that soft-breathed, purring way of hers which made her look the very embodiment of good-nature. As indeed she was. Set full in the sunshine, not a grief had been bequeathed to her and she took care not to make one for herself. She fought off worries as she would have fought off wrinkles; and neither trod on other people's toes nor put her own in the way of being trodden on. Rich, under forty, handsome, a widow and without daughters to rival or sons to ruin her, she acknowledged herself, what all the world agreed to call her, the happiest woman in London. She had a fine house and three well-appointed carriages—one for each kind of occasion; she dressed like a duchess and had as many diamonds as a queen; her digestion was perfect and her nerves were either seated more deeply than other folks', or were in sheaths of extra toughness, for she was as insensitive morally as she was hardy physically. And she never realized the pain of others, because she was almost as impossible to wound in her own person as if she had been a pillow of down or a caoutchouc doll.

To her brother she was always genial and complaisant. Had she but consented to live with him and be the mistress of his house rather than of her own, he would have been perfectly content and would have put aside all thoughts of matrimony for ever. But Clarissa preferred her liberty to his companionship; and laughed off the proposal as a joke, which would be anything but a joke for either of them, she said, if taken seriously. If her happiness had been in any way dependent on him—had she had expectations from him or had she derived part of her income from his generosity—things would have been different. Then she would have been his docile creature, careful only to keep her place warm and influence unbroken. But as matters were, she, wanting naught from him, gave up to him nothing that she cared to hold, and did as he desired only when it did not interfere with her own pleasure.

She was anxious that he should marry, because he would then leave off asking her to live with him; and he himself would be happier with a wife than he was now without one. Hence she was ready to lend her countenance to any nice-looking, well-dressed girl whom he chose to favour with his attentions. Perhaps her complaisance would have been strained had she been asked to chaperon a dowdy or a fright; but a girl like Thomasina, say, carrying Lady written in every feature and stamped on every gesture, was thoroughly acceptable—for all that she had not a penny for her dower and would probably place her mother and sisters as pensioners on the books of Armour Court.

That, however, was her brother's affair, not hers, she thought wisely enough; and so far as she was concerned, he might marry whom he would.

Her whole action with him was like a pleasant, faintly-heard little symphony accompanying the leading strain. She never made herself prominent and never discordant. What he liked, to that she agreed; what he discarded, that she did not retain; yet for all this, she kept the threads of her own life perfectly clear and never let him dominate nor interfere in things pertaining solely to herself.

It was the kind of nature that exactly suited Mr. Brocklebank; and when he wished to express his admiration of a nice woman, he used to say "Something like my sister Clarissa, but not quite so sweet."

Of all the fancies in the way of young ladies which her brother Benjamin had taken up as possible and laid down again as unsuitable, Thomasina Winstanley was the most congenial to Mrs. Merton. Though their temperaments were entirely different, each lady came to the same point, held the same principles, followed the same practice insomuch as each agreed to make the best of things as they were; to abjure all unnecessary excitement and annoyance; to live in perfect tranquillity of mind as the state most favourable to their digestions and complexions; never to meet trouble half-way; and to make their health, good looks and wardrobes the main objects of their care. This was the only kind of life worthy of rational women, they thought; anything else was silly according to Mrs. Merton, inartistic according to Thomasina. Hence it was that, when Mr. Brocklebank flattered the bishop's grand-daughter as he did just now, Mrs. Merton smiled with that pretty soft purring way of hers which made her friends feel as if she were a lump of vitalized swan's-down, and which charmed Thomasina herself as the very perfection of gentleness and receptivity, of complaisance and concordance.

"You are very kind," Thomasina said, in answer to the ironmaster's gallantry and with a graceful smile to Clarissa. Her clear-cut face was animated to just the proper degree—the pleasure expressed on it by no means broadly or hilariously shown—only to the point becoming a lady who, while respecting herself, was gratified by the homage of her companion.

"I should be charmed to have Miss Winstanley's opinion on a great many concerns at Armour Court," then said Mr. Brocklebank, turning to Thomasina.

He had this odd way of using the third person when addressing ladies. He thought it pleasantly familiar by its very formality; and it had, besides, that grave kind of jocularity in which such men as he delight.

"I should be very glad to give you my opinion on anything, if it would be of use to you," said Thomasina with charming acquiescence.

"Suppose then, we arrange for a visit to my poor place from Mrs. Winstanley and her young ladies? Clarissa would accompany us; and we should have a good time, as our cousins across the herring-pond say. What verdict does Miss Winstanley pronounce on this proposition? Does she think it can be managed?" asked Mr. Brocklebank, looking down on his ladylike companion with a satisfied smile.

"I think it would be very nice," answered Thomasina.

"And you, Clarissa?"

"Yes, delightful! I am sure we should all enjoy it."

Mr. Brocklebank took out his pocket-book.

"Suppose we name this day week, then? Euston Square; ten o'clock; to remain over Sunday and return to town on Monday week by the express?"

He wrote down the dates and figures.

"I ought to be at the Works on business next Wednesday," he continued. "Suppose we nail it now at once, if quite agreeable to Miss Winstanley?"

"Quite agreeable to me, but I must first speak to my mother. I could not arrange a thing of this kind without consulting her," said Thomasina, with a rapid mental survey of present gaps in their personalities which did not signify at home but must be filled up if they went out on a visit.

"Let us lose no time—let us look for her," said Mr. Brocklebank in his swift, brief, business-like way, turning abruptly from the tent and leaving the second half of the flowers unseen.

He was a man who boasted of his promptness and decision; and perhaps he was not sorry to a little exaggerate these qualities, which to him represented superiority and success, that he might pose himself favourably before Thomasina. He had never yet been sated with praise and admiration; and he had had a good deal of it in his time—as was but natural with those reputed millions in his pocket.

Presently they came on Mrs. Winstanley and her friends sitting in a picturesque group under the trees. Their coming made a commotion; and the young men rose in a body and gave up their chairs to the two ladies.

"Oh, do come and sit down in the cool, Ina!" said Eva, drawing her dress as if to make room for her sister on the chair just vacated by the most eligible young man of the party. "You look so hot and fagged— and it is so delightfully fresh here!"

"Thanks, dear," said Thomasina quietly. "I will take this chair, instead. You are sitting in a cross light; and" —to Mrs. Merton— "a cross light is so terribly trying to the eyes."

"Yes," said the rich widow, with a passing wonder whether this little passage had been as innocent as it seemed or had been an underhand bit of sisterly sparring—attack and defence in due form and with the customary salute.

As by this time half a dozen young men had dived into the crowd for more chairs, and Mr. Brocklebank's broad shoulders had forced his passage through the thickest of the throng, where he saw two or three seats without owners, the little difficulty was arranged to the satisfaction of all concerned; and as the most eligible young man—for all that he was engaged to a certain Miss Maud Disney—one Hubert Strangways of Strangways, came back to his former station, Eva's pretty little face lost that somewhat strained look of forced hilarity which had come into it and smoothed out into more natural expression of kittenish content.

Then Mr. Brocklebank in a rather loud voice made his formal proposal to Mrs. Winstanley, and clinched the matter by saying with friendly insistence: "I will take no denial."

"Nor do I wish to give you one," returned Mrs. Winstanley with graceful acquiescence. "The pleasure is too great to refuse."

"You will all come," said Mr. Brocklebank; "your other daughter too—whom I have not the pleasure of seeing here today"—looking round; "she too will form one of our party on this occasion."

"Thank you very much for your kindness," said Mrs. Winstanley with that kind of smile which means: "you are talking amiable nonsense." "But my second daughter is, as perhaps you know, an original, and does not go into society. I am waiting to see how she will develop," she went on smoothly but rather rapidly, as if to prevent comment. "She has splendid talents and ought to make something of herself; so I give her perfect freedom to live the life that best suits her, hoping that some day her genius will find its fitting expression."

"Oh, she must come for all that!" said Mr. Brocklebank with a positive air. "I have a library at Armour Court where she may run loose if such is her desire. We will lock the door on her if she prefers total solitude and only let her out at meal times—ha! ha! But we must include Miss Perdita, we must, indeed."

Mrs. Winstanley smiled; so did Thomasina. Eva laughed.

"We will think about it," said Perdita's mother. "But no one out of the family knows how fearfully shy she is, and how difficult it is to get her to show herself."

"Oh, I'll tame her!" said Mr. Brocklebank, squaring his shoulders; at which Mrs. Winstanley smiled again; then faintly sighed and turned the conversation on to the beauty of the rhododendrons and the perfection of the cut roses.

Soon after this they all rose to fulfil the ostensible purpose of the day and strolled back towards the flower-tents.

As they were going up the Broad Walk, they met, coming from the conservatory, a tall, handsome young man of about twenty-six or so, walking with a lady who was evidently his mother. Each had the same flat, broad forehead; the same sunken eyes and contracted orbit; the same high, keen, handsome nose; the same thin, loose, sensitive lips; the same blueblack hair and long, lean, nervous form. They were manifestly run in the same mould, differenced only by sex.

When they came near, the young man stopped and said: "Halloo, Strangways!" familiarly; then took off his hat and offered his hand to Mrs. Merton.

Her still, fair, personable face became a deeper pink as she laid her plump, well-gloved hand in his, and said cordially: "How do you do, Sir James?"

She only bowed, slightly and distantly, to the lady, his mother, without speaking.

The handsome face of the young fellow whom she called Sir James brightened with unmistakable pleasure; his mother's darkened with unmistakable annoyance, as she returned that slight and distant bow with one yet more reserved, and seemed to think even this too great a concession.

Rich Mrs. Merton, the widow of a city tradesman, was not in Lady Kearney's set; and she disliked these exotic intimacies which her son was so fond of making. They seemed to betoken a certain democratic tendency which, should it be true, would be to Lady Kearney next thing to a crime and the bitterest sorrow of her life. But she was becoming mournfully aware that she could not control, as heretofore, this beloved son of hers who once had been her second self. Since his father's death and his own accession to the baronetcy, four years ago now, he had taken the bit between his teeth and carried things with a higher hand than once she would have thought possible. From his childhood upward he had been emphatically her boy, not his father's; and she had managed him by indulgence. Now her teaching reacted against herself, and he opposed her wishes because he would not withstand his own. And as the society of Mrs. Merton pleased him, and her soft swan's-down kind of nature soothed him when he was more than ordinarily rasped by his mother's nervous irritability and incessant interference, he had cultivated the acquaintance of the rich widow until it had ripened into a friendship that was the seed-ground of more than one thorny brake of gossip and stinging weed of scandal. Some said she was doing her best to hook him and his title, and would succeed, though she was thirteen years his senior; others that he was not such a fool as he looked, and take care the biter was not bitten! Some said even more than this; and others opened their eyes and ears and took it all in as gospel which needed no proof to corroborate. Mrs. Merton was eminently of the order of Mature Sirens;[1] and do we not all know that these are the most dangerous women on the list? Everything then might be expected from her; and no one thought it necessary to examine into the truth of anything that was said.

Lady Kearney was cool to repudiation in her manner to Mrs. Merton, and Mr. Brocklebank was insolently glacial to Sir James. The ironmaster

---

[1]   Linton refers here to her own piece "Mature Sirens" (*Saturday Review*, 9 January 1869, 46–47), in which she describes the attractive middle-aged woman who "knows what she has and what she can do" and who is "always beautiful, because always in harmony."

had a fund of natural pride—heavy, bovine, self-sufficient—pride that disdained the petty weakness of class ambition, and preferred to be a king among sparrows rather than, as he once said, a kittiwake flying at the tail of eagles. If a fossilized old Tory like Lady Kearney, with her craze about blood and pedigree, chose to consider him and his unfit for her association because they had made their money in business and had never a grandfather to their backs, let her. He would not balk her humour, nor seek to bridge over the gulf which she had ordained should separate them. And he wished that Clarissa would see the thing as he did. But even the best of women are unreasonable creatures, as he often said; and no power on earth can hammer rational views of life into them. They are the human moths ever caught by glare and glitter. A little sets their imagination in a blaze and their blood in a flame and finishes the day's work there and then. For his own part he preferred £ s. d.[1] and the consciousness of his own important aid in the commercial grandeur of his country to the barren honour of intimacy with a lot of haw-haws who do not know a cog from a ratchet, or the piston of a steam engine from its safety-valve.

He had always girded at this friendship with Sir James; but his sister, the soul of compliance in all that related to himself, was sweetly inflexible on certain matters wherein her own pleasure only was of account; and her acquaintance with the young baronet was one of these matters. What was to be the upshot of it all, her brother could not foresee; nor did he know what she wanted with a tame cat about the house at all! She had always declared, since old Seth Merton died, that nothing short of a dukedom should make her marry again; and she evidently enjoyed her liberty too well to part with it, save for a sufficient compensation. Hence he was sure that she was not angling for a husband; and, as Lady Kearney would not endorse her—would not, indeed, have anything to do with her at all—it could not be for admission into that *huis-clos*[2] of exclusives among whom my lady was such an influential member. Nevertheless, the thing was plain, if to Benjamin Brocklebank and some others the reasons were not forthcoming: Sir James Kearney was Mrs. Merton's favourite friend—to be found in her pretty blue satin boudoir at times when no one else was admitted—always present on her "days," often with her in public, and rarely absent from her five o'clock tea. And the why and wherefore were the riddles which the sphinx of incongruity flung to society to answer.

---

[1]   Pounds, shillings, pence (British currency).
[2]   Closed circle.

All of which did not prevent Lady Kearney from showing by her manner that she disapproved of the acquaintance, nor Benjamin Brocklebank from showing by his that he resented her disapproval.

As a set-off, my lady was cordial to exaggeration to young Hubert Strangways and looked almost humanely at Mrs. Winstanley and Thomasina. Her quick eyes discovered that they were good style, and born in the splendour of inherited velvet.

Neither was Sir James so deeply fascinated by his widow that he could not see any one else when she was by. On the contrary, he had a keen admiration for a pretty face, wherever found, and a perception of style as quick as his mother's. His critical eyes took in the "points" of the group at a glance, and approved as rapidly as they discerned. Mrs. Winstanley and Thomasina were evidently "safe;" and Eva—

"By George," said Sir James to himself, "that little girl is the most beautiful thing out!"

But he did not ask to be presented, nor did he linger long. He pressed his fair friend's hand with fervour; for the second time lifted his hat; said to Hubert: "Come and see me tomorrow, will you, old fellow?" and gave his last look to Eva; then strolled off with his mother, hating his filial obligation of attendance and angry that good manners forbade his turning round and looking once more after that Venus in cream and azure.

Unable to do this, he relieved his mind by rebuking his mother for her evident animosity to Mrs. Merton; to which she returned a cross-fire of rebuke for his too evident cordiality. The Kearneys of Hibberton were *la crème de la crème* of English life; but that did not prevent a great deal of domestic wrangling carried on in unexceptionable English, with the most correct pronunciation and an entire absence of gross words or vulgar phrases.

"What a handsome man and what a poker of an old lady!" cried Eva before they were well out of earshot.

"Lady Kearney and Sir James? Yes, they are very aristocratic-looking, both mother and son," said Mrs. Merton. "But I fancy Lady Kearney would not care to be called an old lady, Miss Eva!"

"Why, she must be ever so old!" cried Eva, opening her large blue eyes in surprise. "She must be more than forty; and what is that but old!"

"Eva!" remonstrated her mother with indulgent rebuke. "What a terrible little chatterer you are!" she added with a deprecating smile.

"Poor little me! I am always getting into trouble," said Eva, turning to Hubert Strangways with a puckered, troubled face. "I shall never be made into a woman of the world—never! Thomasina is; but I am not;

and never can be! There are so many things that I do not understand and cannot learn! I cannot make out why one may not say what one thinks, without feeling that one has been naughty. What harm is there in calling the mother of a great tall man like that 'old'? Lady Kearney can't be young to be his mother at all!"

"Don't learn the ways of the world, Miss Winstanley," said Hubert with admiring fervour.

"I'm Eva, I'm not Miss Winstanley," put in the child simply.

"Don't let any one change you," he continued, flushing with strange pleasure at her sweet rebuke and looking as if she were Eva indeed, and something else, to him. "You are perfect as you are, Miss Eva. You could not be changed for the better."

"How nice of you to say that!" said Eva gratefully. "I shall always think of you as my friend after that."

"Do," he answered, looking full into her eyes.

He was a huge young fellow, standing over six feet two, and broad in proportion; and Eva looked almost like a doll by his side. He was a good honest Englishman, with eyes as blue and opaque as a turquoise, golden hair in short tight rings about his small head, a massive throat and chest, and built after the model of the Hercules. He was the eldest son of a good old county family; honest as the day; handsome as Apollo; and as stupid as an owl. He had been "ploughed" for "smalls"[1] and everything else, and had finally only scraped through his various examinations by the skin of his teeth, as his friends said; but he was an admirable cricketer, and as admirable an oarsman; he was unrivalled in all games requiring physical strength and manual skill; he was the embodiment of good nature, moral weakness and obstinacy; and he had no more critical faculty or suspicion than his prototype in the ancient past, when he put on the shirt of Nessus[2] and died because he could not distinguish differences.

But the eldest son of a rich county family is above the need of brains; and Hubert Strangways found that his physical strength and good looks, his present well-being and prospective affluence, were quite sufficient to make life one long holiday to him, and to bring down from the skies as many roasted larks as he desired, without his taking any trouble in making the fire or spitting the birds.

---

[1] He had failed his examinations.

[2] Hercules died when his jealous wife Deianira gave him a tunic dipped in the blood of the centaur Nessus, whom Hercules himself had killed with a poisoned arrow.

Always in love with some one, at this moment be was enslaved by Eva Winstanley; though there were well-nigh insuperable difficulties in the way of a favourable settlement of this or any other contraband affair. To begin with, he was already engaged to Maud Disney; but even had he been free, he knew that this special charming little fairy would never have an authorized admittance into the family as his affianced wife. True, she was a lady by birth and as beautiful as a dream in person; but his people wanted more than that. They looked on their sons as goods to be sold high. They must have all things in exchange for a Strangways of Strangways—birth, dower, beauty, stainless repute and cultivated intelligence; and they had found all these in Maud Disney.

So they persuaded the young fellow that he was dying for Maud, when he was not, for all that she was very honestly in love with him; and they got up the betrothal almost as solemnly as the German *Verlobung*,[1] and thought that now they had done their best for the boy whom it was necessary to guide with discretion if he were to live with honour.

All this Hubert either knew as a fact or dimly felt as a motive. Nevertheless, he was rapidly drifting into an overpowering love for the beautiful little girl whose simplicity seemed to him the perfection of innocence and truth, and whose manners charmed him as no other girl's had ever charmed him before. If things went on like this much longer, he felt that he should one day say the irrevocable words and leave his people to fight it out with Maud Disney and her parents as they best could. Meantime he did not stint himself in lovemaking nor control his thoughts as either dangerous or dishonourable. He was the soul of honour in everything else; but a pretty woman overmastered, transformed and bewitched him.

While all these threads were weaving the substance of the Winstanley history, Perdita sat, sorrowful and alone, in a quiet part of Kensington Gardens. She cared little enough for ordinary pleasures, but she did care for flower-shows. She had a love for flowers that was, as were most feelings with her, intrinsically a passion; and she knew something of botany among other scrappy bits of learning which she had gathered up for herself. And it seemed to her an unjust dispensation of Providence that she should be sitting there, shut out, while her sisters were in the midst of things which she would have so lovingly appreciated and which they neither understood nor could rightly enjoy. Neither Thomasina nor Eva knew one flower from another, save as points of harmonious colour

---

[1] (German), engagement or betrothal.

when they were dressed for show; and they would not be able to tell her one single characteristic circumstance, she thought, with youthful contempt for ignorance that does not reach to the height of its own knowledge. They would not have noticed a new flower, nor would they have known its family or its special points if they had noticed it; while she—had she been there, she would have understood at the least half of what she saw and would have learnt as a new lesson the other half. What a shame it was that she had not been able to go! Mother might have made an effort for just this once, knowing how much she loved flowers!

Patient enough in general in the family ostracism wherein she lived, at this moment Perdita felt the isolation and injustice of her life bitterly, keenly. There was something in the jocund brightness of the day, in the atmosphere of abounding life and joy that surrounded her, in the freshness of the green, the clearness of the sky, the living perfume of the flowers, the stirring and disquieting influences of the spring, which made her strangely sorrowful;—and impatient as well as sad. Disinherited by nature, unlovely in person and with a blemish that counted for a deformity, disdained by her own and with no one in the wide world to love her—she who could love so well in return; who only asked for leave to love!—she yet was conscious in her humiliation of a life that could be lived to glory and good uses if her feet could but find the leading path— conscious of powers rusting now for want of use and of energies squandered abroad for want of fixity of purpose; but power and energies which could, if wisely employed, do more than write her name in water. Ashamed of the empty pretentiousness in that mean and showy life of theirs at home humiliated by the unpaid finery, the debt, the domestic insufficiency of her mother's management; longing to emancipate herself from these frayed and fettering rags and to be simple, honest and real; her brain thronged with inchoate images; her mind tormented with vague desires—she longed and lamented and beat the wide bounds of fancy and possibility without finding a resting-place or an issue.

While she was sitting there, lost in dreams which were half desire and half despair, her face turned slightly upward—the sunlight showing its passion and its thought as clearly as it showed the auburn tints of her heavy hair—a handsome but bold and confident-looking woman passed before her.

She was dressed with evident desire to be dressed well, and with as evident want of taste. Her artificially whitened hair floated about her face and down her back in a breezy, girlish, unconventional way, of itself sufficiently noticeable in a woman whose age was nearer fifty than forty;

and she wore a kaleidoscopic arrangement of colours that was simply barbarous. She had the look of a dummy in a third-rate shop-window: but her dress was expensive, and she was evidently a Somebody.

"Good morning, Miss Winstanley," she said in a caressing voice and with a sing-song intonation.

Perdita started.

"Oh! good morning," she answered confusedly.

"You do not know me, I see," said the walking rainbow with kindly indulgence.

"No; I am ashamed—I don't know your name—I have forgotten," stammered Perdita.

Like many short-sighted people, she never did know any one until familiarly acquainted with the general appearance.

"I am Mrs. Blount—Bell Blount," said the newcomer.

"Oh!" replied Perdita, the colour rushing in a flood over her face; "now I remember."

CHAPTER III.

THE CHAMPION OF HER SEX.

"I am glad you remember me," said Mrs. Blount, taking Perdita's hand and speaking with extraordinary tenderness. "I have thought of little else since I saw you."

"You are very good," replied Perdita with embarrassment.

Her yearning heart smote her for ingratitude in that she had not remembered even the name or face of one who had thought of little else but her since they had met.

"There is something in your face and manner that interests me so intensely," continued her new friend, pressing her hand. "I am sure that you are not happy, and I know now why—because you are not in your proper sphere. Your real place is with us."

Perdita opened her eyes. If too prominent for beauty they were singularly expressive, and showed her mind almost as clearly as words. Just now what they showed was simple amazement. Who were "us?" To what noble band of secret Illuminati did this kindly-mannered, odd-looking woman belong? What grand acreage of thought and endeavour was about to be thrown open to her, rusting as she was in idleness, starving for want of an object in her life, eating out her heart for want of something to do and some one to love?

"You do not understand me? You do not know who I am?" asked the lady.

"No," said Perdita. "I only know you as Mrs. Blount. I know nothing special about you."

"I am the Lady President of the West Hill Society for Women's Rights," said Mrs. Blount. "Did they not tell you that at the College?"

"No," said Perdita.

"But they told you something? You blushed so deeply when you said you remembered me, that I saw you had something in your mind. Was it pleasure at meeting me again or because you connected me with something?—and if so, what was it?"

Nothing could be softer nor more caressing than Mrs. Blount's voice, nothing more imperative and inquisitorial than her manner. Perdita felt obliged to reply.

It was the manner which compels candour, because delicacy would be misunderstood as weakness and reticence would read like deceit.

"They told me you had separated from your husband," she answered with simple directness.

"Who told you?"

"Miss Jones, the Principal of the College."

"Did she add anything to this? give any reason? make any commentary?"

"No," said Perdita. "She merely said that your husband was a reactionary, and that you were a gifted creature who could not find sustenance for your soul in his society."

Mrs. Blount smiled.

"That good Louisa!" she exclaimed with a curious air of patronage. "So you blushed because I am a separated wife? Was that it, little girl?"

"I blushed because I am an idiot!" returned Perdita with angry self-impatience; "because I cannot do anything like anybody else, and get hot and cold over the merest trifles. I wish some one would teach me how to cure myself of this absurd habit!" she added, her face as she spoke dyed crimson and her eyes moist with nervous tears.

Again Mrs. Blount smiled.

"Don't wish anything so suicidal," she answered. "Your blushes belong to you like your lovely auburn hair and creamy skin. They show the passion and vitality of your nature which are just the qualities that attracted me, and which will make your future life glorious and delightful."

"If it might be useful!" said Perdita in a low, intense kind of voice.

"Make me your friend, and it shall be both," returned the lady. "I can give you all you want—work, love, freedom and an object. I want nothing in return but your love and that you will let me guide you till you know your ground and can guide yourself."

Again that indistinct glimpse into the vast Unknown! Perdita's imagination burnt up into a sudden flame at the suggestive vagueness of her new friend's words. She felt as if about to be initiated into those hidden mysteries wherein the springs of human history are to be found—as if about to be admitted into a secret sect working beneath the surface of society, sapping the bases of wrong and preparing the ground for the glorious establishment of truth and justice. She raised her ardent eyes and turned them on the smooth, self-satisfied face looking at her with such a strange expression; but the fire died out as quickly as it had burned up. Something in Mrs. Blount's face chilled and repelled her, she did not know why; she only felt that this was not the ideal for which she was looking, and that the supreme good did not lie in the leading of that soft, milk-white, caressing hand. A little shiver passed over her like the quivering of the leaves above her head. Her colour faded, her eyes drooped and involuntarily she sighed.

"Don't look like that!" said Mrs. Blount, misreading her. "You may be fenced round with all sorts of natural barriers; a family that cares only for pleasure and frivolity; domestic tyranny that would hinder the free development of your nature and force you to think and act by line and rule; inherited conservatism and the fallals of gentility; but the cause which I represent is strong enough to break through them all! You can take your life in your own hands if you choose; and if you will be guided by me, you will. We are not in days when you could be forced into a convent to keep you quiet or sent to the Bastille by a *lettre de cachet*."[1]

"Thank you," said Perdita, having nothing else to say. Then she looked up again, and asked, simply: "But what do you wish me to do?"

"To work and be independent," said Mrs. Blount; "to dedicate your life to the cause of freedom for your own sex; and to resolve never to make one of those misguided victims who believe in the kindness and constancy of men! become one of us—a champion of Women's Rights, working for your own hand and practising the independence you preach—and you will soon see how the whole horizon of your interests will widen and what a beautiful thing you will make of life."

---

[1] (French), sealed letter.

"It would be a tremendous gain for me if I could do something to earn my own living," said Perdita, kindling again as this secret chord of her soul was so directly touched. "I long for nothing so much as to be able to earn money and be independent."

Mrs. Blount put her arms round the girl's slender, loose and stayless waist.

"I knew what was in you!" she said caressingly; and bending her face forward she kissed her. "That is my kiss of adoption," she added with fervour. "I claim you now as one of us!—the friend of woman and the enemy of man."

"Oh!" said Perdita ingenuously, "I do not think I am quite that, Mrs. Blount. Men seem to me so much larger and more generous than women, I cannot say I am their enemy. The best thing that we know," she added warmly, "is a man; and we owe all our ideas of magnanimity and justice to them."

"You speak as you have been taught, my poor child," returned Mrs. Blount compassionately. "So far from this, men have been and are the unredeemed tyrants of the world and the meanest creatures out, from Adam downwards! All that we have of good or true or pure we owe to women; and the struggle between us and man is just the struggle between light and darkness—the divine element in humanity and the diabolical."

"No! no!" cried Perdita, inexpressibly shocked.

"Too true, unfortunately!" continued Mrs. Blount, who had mounted her hobby-horse and was now in the full swing of its stride. "Men are the embodiments of greed and tyranny, of selfishness and animalism. History is made up of their iniquities and our sufferings; and were it not for us, society would be nothing but a horde of savages tearing each other to pieces. Look at those countries where women have no influence! Men there are worse than brute beasts, because more cruel. Who are torturers? Who are vivisectors? Who go out to kill and maim the poor innocent birds and beasts? Who put all their intellect into the discovery of the most perfect man-slaying machines, human and mechanical? Is it women? or is it men?—and it is men because women have not their rightful power and influence. No, believe me, my dear girl, the world will never be regenerated until women have the upper hand and men are relegated to their proper place as our slaves and the mere workers of the world. Let them use their great brutal muscles in the subjugation of nature. Let them be the hewers of wood and drawers of water—the miners and sailors and rough handicrafts-men as they were meant to be—while we take up our natural duties as law-makers, politicians, artists, leaders in all moral and intellectual questions whatsoever."

Perdita gasped. That dish of meat was terribly crude and strong! and her mental digestion was not trained to the assimilation of such upsetting food. She was at the age and in the mental phase when Liberty is a thing rather than a state—when poems like Campbell's "Song of the Greeks," Byron's opening song in "The Corsair," "The Isles of Greece," "The Irish Avatar," or such robust revolutionary hymns as "Ça Ira" and the "Marseillaise" could make her heart beat, her cheeks glow, and tears of passionate enthusiasm brighten her burning eyes. But all her aspirations were bound up with the central idea of men as the noble leaders, sacrificing their lives for this beloved Liberty, while women were the weaker aiders and devoted sympathizers—sacrificing their lives too, but with, and because of, men. A school of thought which divorced the sexes and placed them in such deadly hostility against each other was something entirely strange to her—and, at the first hearing, something inexpressibly revolting.

"I do not think that I should like to be in a world governed only by women," she said honestly. "They care so much about dress; and they are not straightforward."

"Men have made us what we are," said Mrs. Blount. "For their own abominable purposes they have demoralized us, denied us freedom and education that they might govern us more easily through our follies and weaknesses. They are responsible for all our vices. When we have shaken off masculine influence and dominion, we shall then improve, indefinitely. When we can develop according to the best law of our being, we shall cast off this slough of vanity and indirectness which now afflicts you and every honest soul among us. It is only the consequence of our dependence. Men make us deck ourselves out like slaves to please the master; and we are driven into deceit because they are tyrannous and strong and we are enslaved and weak."

"But we often dress as they do not like," said Perdita. "How often we hear of their opposition to a fashion, yet women still go on with it for years and years and will not change it whatever men may say."

"Another proof of their vileness," said Mrs. Blount tranquilly. "At the very moment when they spoke most against that hideous fashion of crinolines, say, would they have walked down Regent Street, think you, with a Japanese-looking creature of modern times? Not one of them! They get out of all responsibility in this way. They abuse an absurd fashion, but they would not stand by the woman who was not in it. They have no moral courage—not a grain! I do not know any woman who is as cowardly, morally, as all the men of my acquaintance—not excepting one!"

"Do all the Woman's Rights women think like this?" asked Perdita gravely. If she had to belong to the new school, she would like to know something of her schoolfellows.

"All who are sound; but unfortunately not all, so far as mere numbers go," returned Mrs. Blount. "I do; and so does my friend Connie—Miss Tracy—Connie Tracy, whom I hope to present to you. But some among us are weak sisters, I am sorry to say, and do not see the profound vileness of men as clearly as we do. They content themselves with seeking to share; we will be satisfied with nothing short of supremacy."

Perdita did not answer. She felt bewildered and shocked, while at the same time she was fascinated and attracted. Mrs. Blount, kind in manner, handsome if less than pleasant in face, soft in speech and uncompromising in views, was in a sense a revelation to a girl longing for some vital interest and suffocating in the stifling atmosphere to which she was condemned. Yet she had all the while an uneasy sensation rather than a definite feeling—a sensation analogous to that which we may imagine a saint might have when there appeared before him the Prince of Darkness clad as an Angel of Light—a clever disguise and the cloven hoof well covered by the shining garments, but only a disguise at the best—not the real thing!

"Now I want to strike while the iron is hot—that is my way," said Mrs. Blount, rising with a smile and drawing the girl by the hand which she had kept during the whole of the interview. "Come with me to my house. I live close by here, and close by you too. Connie is at home and she will give us some tea. I want you to know Connie. She is my little wife, as I call her, and you shall be our friend."

Perdita hesitated. Between vaguely longing for freedom and activity, and taking the independent action of making a friend of a woman whom her mother did not know, and who certainly was not after that mother's favourite pattern, was a wide step and she stood irresolute.

Mrs. Blount laughed aloud.

"You cannot have any objection to come and see two working women of good character and a social position equal to your own!" she said lightly. "We are not men in disguise, I promise you; and we have none of the odious creatures about us! Had we, then indeed you might hesitate; and ought! As it is, I want to introduce you into a very safe kind of sheepfold—warranted well defended against wolves. Come!"

"There can be no harm in it," thought Perdita; and laying her other hand frankly on her new friend's arm, she said, impulsively, "Thank you. Yes, I will go with you to see your home and your friend."

Mrs. Blount's face flushed vividly. She startled and nearly scared Perdita by suddenly taking her in her arms and kissing her with strange warmth.

"Now I have secured a convert!" she said, as if to excuse her familiarity; "secured a convert, and saved a noble-natured woman from the debasing influence of men!"

"But indeed, indeed I do not hate men," said Perdita, objecting to the classification with all her honesty and straightforwardness.

Mrs. Blount smiled in a superior kind of way.

"*Ça viendra!*"[1] she said airily, and turned to leave the garden.

A short walk brought them to the door of a house in Prince Christian's Road, one of those rows of "bijou residences" so often found at the back of stately squares and terraces. The door was opened by an odd-looking woman, neither servant nor lady, dressed in an alpaca gown much betrimmed, without a cap, but with her hair arranged in an ugly and elaborate manner.

"Well, Miss Long!" said Mrs. Blount, as she entered. "I have brought a young lady home to tea, you see."

"Yes, I see, Mrs. Blount," said the woman, in a manner as odd as her appearance—familiar, and at the same time as if on the defensive. "You'll find Constance in the sitting-room."

Mrs. Blount nodded, and opened the door of a small room on the right.

"Connie!" she called in a caressing voice.

"Bell!" responded a little woman, darting up from the sofa and flinging herself into her arms.

They kissed each other fondly; as friends who had been separated for as many months or years as they had been parted hours.

"This is my good little wife!" then said Mrs. Blount, turning to Perdita; "and"—to Constance Tracy—"I have brought you a new friend, dear. She is to become one of us."

Constance smiled, held out her hand, and said: "I am glad to see you," as was expected of her.

But her smile was more forced than spontaneous, and the quick, scrutinizing look with which she measured Perdita from head to foot had less of welcome in it than of suspicion and latent hostility. A rival or a friend?—that was the question which Connie Tracy asked herself

<hr />

[1] (French), that will come.

THE REBEL OF THE FAMILY 55

when this sad-looking newcomer was introduced: and she left to time the unrolling of the answer.

This Connie Tracy was a pale, light-haired, mousey-faced little woman, with delicate features and large, light-blue, floating eyes; and she lived with Mrs. Blount on those terms of dependence and subserviency which the champion of her sex found so infinitely degrading when they exist between men and women. It was Mrs. Blount who had the money while Miss Tracy had nothing but her industry and devotion. Yet these were not despicable quantities to add to the store. She was everything that one woman could be to another—lady's-maid, milliner, house-keeper, amanuensis, panegyrist in public, flatterer and slave in private; and Mrs. Blount thought the arrangement honourable to both as things were; when, had it been a husband to whom her friend had been devoted and on whom she had been dependent, it would have been a degrading institution and the sign of woman's shame and destitution.

Whether jealous for the possible future or no, Connie Tracy knew her place too well not to show Perdita all rightful attention. The bell was rung and Miss Long was asked to bring the tea in a certain apologetic manner that struck Perdita as both uncomfortable and peculiar. Her own mother was a martinet, in fact, but always well-bred to servants in manner. She never commanded, she always requested; but she did not speak as Connie Tracy did, as if half afraid and half ashamed to ask a favour of an equal. All the same, the tea was brought, and Mrs. Blount was served first by her "little wife;" then Perdita; and then Miss Long, who sat down and drank her tea in company.

Perdita was a democrat, impassioned for equality, furious against injustice; nevertheless, when this woman who was evidently the servant, for all that she was called "Miss," sat down to tea with her new friend and herself, she did experience something that might be called a moral douche. It was quite right, she thought—quite! but how odd and how unpleasant! The old Adam of conventionality asserted itself against her better reason; and practice and theory warred together, as they often do in the lives of men. The oddity of the incident, however, soon came to an end; and, the tea being ended, Miss Long took out the tray and left the three ladies to themselves.

When Perdita rose to leave, she found the time close on the dinner hour at home; but she did not confess the fear that she felt, nor tell Mrs. Blount of the displeasure which awaited her. She left, her head on fire and her heart throbbing with the arguments and the entreaties of "Bell Blount," as she preferred to be called, urging her to take her life in her own hands; to get some work to do that should make her independent of her mother; to leave home and go into lodgings by herself—unless, indeed, which would be better, she could arrange to make one of the household here.

"You would have friends then always at hand," said Bell; "and Connie and I would look after you. It is the only life worthy of a rational woman—a life of self-support, of independence, of friendship with her own sex; and men, who are our enemies, discarded and thrown overboard!"

"I will think of it," said Perdita, with the same confused feeling of repulsion and fascination as before.

"Do," returned Bell Blount. "And when you have made up your mind, let me know. I foresee you will be one of us, and an ornament to the cause."

"Anything would be better than my present purposeless life," Perdita said with a sigh.

"And nothing could be grander than that which you might have if you chose," returned Bell. "It is waiting for you—take it up while you can. Freedom and independence—what can be more glorious!"

Perdita did not answer. The programme was seductive and inspiriting, yet it lacked something, she did not know what. It seemed to offer all that she most desired; nevertheless, it was imperfect. It was heaven without the sun, a garden without flowers, a summer without warmth, and hope cut out of life. But she did not speak; she only looked sad and wistful, unconvinced and unsatisfied.

"And if you want love," said Bell, putting her arm tenderly round Connie Tracy; "you have it here—the best and truest that the world can give—the love between women without the degrading and disturbing interference of man."

"Yes, I know," said Perdita, a little blankly. "Good-bye; I must think. At all events, I want to work. That is clear enough!"

"And the rest will become so," said Bell. "Till then, goodbye, my dear girl; and God bless you!"

CHAPTER IV.

FREE TO CHOOSE.

WHEN Perdita reached home she found the place in confusion; and, fortunately for her, the dinner hour set at eight instead of seven; by which piece of good fortune she escaped the lecture properly due to her unpunctuality, and in ordinary circumstances sure to have been paid with full interest.

The cause of the general domestic skirmish going on when she entered was, that Mr. Brocklebank had invited himself to dine with the widow and her daughters; whereby the wits, like the resources, of the household were taxed to their utmost to get things in good order betimes. The cold mutton, which was to have formed the not too luxurious staple of the family dinner, had to be shunted that the regulation soup and fish, entrée and roast, sweets and fruits of a nineteenth-century impromptu meal, strictly "without ceremony" might be prepared; and though a friendly confectioner undertook the order, still, even confectioners want time, and Mrs. Winstanley's notice was short.

Thomasina heard her truant sister run swiftly up the stairs in the eager way of one conscious of lost minutes and vainly seeking to recover them. As she passed the door, the eldest sister called to her; and Perdita dashed into the room expecting to be scolded—as perhaps she deserved.

"How late you are, Perdita!" Thomasina began, her calm voice and graceful quietude very slightly tinged with what in any one else would have been called peevishness.

"Yes," said Perdita, denial being impossible.

"Fortunately for you, it does not signify. We dine an hour later to-day, as Mr. Brocklebank is coming. And now you really must make yourself look as respectable to-night as you can, Perdita! If you come in at all—as I suppose you must—you must indeed take pains with your appearance, and look nice."

"I would far rather not come in at all," said Perdita.

Never in harmony with her family, she felt less than usual in accord at this moment when the disturbing counsels of Bell Blount were echoing in her ears, and she seemed to herself to be standing on the threshold of a new life.

"That would be the best thing, certainly," said Thomasina in a matter-of-fact way, not meaning to be unkind, simply stating a self-evident proposition. "But I am afraid that Mr. Brocklebank would think it odd. He asked for you to-day at the flower-show, and I know that he wants to see you this evening, because he said so. No, you must come in, Perdita; but"—she repeated her phrase as if it had been a comprehensive and exhaustive table of directions—"you must make yourself look nice."

"That is just the difficulty," said Perdita with that painful manner of confessed ostracism traversed by pride natural to one living in a state of chronic humiliation, but one who is conscious all the while of powers which, if well used, would place her beyond shame. "Mother said only yesterday that I disgraced you all."

"Yes, I know," replied Thomasina, trying the effect of a new braid, and turning her head and face into a dozen different lights and at as many different angles. She spoke in the same matter-of-fact way as before, with no more idea of personal offence to Perdita than if she had said the day was cold or the sky cloudy. She merely spoke of things as they were. "In general you are awfully scrubby, I must confess, but this evening you must do the best you can; and above all, do not have inky fingers or untidy hair. Take anything you want of mine, if you have nothing good enough of your own. Look in that top drawer—don't make it untidy—and take what you like."

"Thank you," said Perdita, with more pride than gratitude; "you know I never borrow."

Had her sister offered her this large loan out of sisterly interest, and with any wish to make her more personable for her own sake, she would have been grateful enough. As it was only to make a show; in itself substantially false; and as a politic concealment of her normal condition—dressing her up as a family supernumerary, of no account in herself but bound to look well on the stage for the sake of general effect—she felt more indignant than grateful.

"I know that you are very silly," returned Thomasina, still occupied with her braid. "I do really believe that you have not a particle of common sense nor a spark of family feeling in you! You do not care how much you disgrace us by your eccentricities, so long as you indulge your own childish fancies. You really are very provoking, Perdita."

"I do not wish to be provoking," said Perdita, coming nearer to her sister and speaking earnestly; "I only want to be myself, and honest."

"That is just it; you think only of yourself and not of us; and what you call honesty is simply egotism and want of common sense. Here, take what you want and go and dress," she added impatiently. "You really are very tiresome, Perdita, and we are very good to have so much patience with you."

"Oh, Thomasina!" cried Perdita with a burst of passion; "if you only felt for one week what I have felt almost ever since I can remember— the pain of being always scolded, always in disgrace you don't know why, found fault with, laughed at whatever you do and though you try your best to do what is right—you would not say that! I cannot say what I do not think, and I do not think that you are good to me—not any of you—neither you nor mother; and you encourage Eva to be insolent and annoying more than I can bear at times! And why? Only because I am awkward and ugly. But how can I help myself? I was born what I am; I did not make myself!" she said, with pathetic patience, accepting her guerdon of unloveliness, her portion of one of the disgraced by nature, as if it were an undeniable and unchangeable certainty.

"Turn the thing the other way and try to realize what we must feel with such a hopeless girl as you are; and then what would you say?" replied Thomasina, speaking with that passionless directness which wounds so deeply but which is so difficult to resent—speaking as if Perdita were a thing of inferior condition, and had no feelings to hurt; or, if she had, then it did not signify whether they were hurt or not. When we snip off the tentacles of a sea-anemone, or fix down a frog's foot under the microscope, do we think of or care for what the creature feels? Neither did her family allow for Perdita's susceptibilities when they took it in hand to admonish her and tell her unwelcome truths. "Think for a moment how things stand with us," Thomasina continued. "We are poor, and we are ladies; we cannot work—"

"Why not?" interrupted Perdita; "that would be the best and most honourable thing to do."

"That is simple nonsense. Work! what could we do, in the name of fortune? Are we to be housemaids or dressmakers?" answered Thomasina. "Work! that is impossible; but what we have to do—what we must do—is to marry. Now hear what I have to say, Perdita, and do not interrupt. You are not such good style as I am, and not so pretty as Eva; and we are both more likely to get married than you; but you do what you can to spoil our chances, having none of your own, by what you call your honesty—that is, by professing the extraordinary opinions you have got hold of, no one knows how or where—by dressing unlike every one else, by making yourself ridiculous and unconventional in every direction. And of course you lower us to your own standard, because we are your sisters. I grant that in some things you are the best of us. You are the cleverest, and all that; but all the same you are our disaster. I want to make you see this clearly; and then perhaps you will do better—for you have a good heart. I have always said that; only you have a very flighty and inconsiderate head. And you are working against yourself too—for when Eva and I are married, things will be much better for you. You and mother will live comfortably together; and you will see she will be quite changed to you then. She will have no one else to care for and nothing to worry her; no debts; no daughters to get off her hands; and you will have quite enough to live on with what Eva and I will allow you. But we must marry well—we must have money even for your own sake and mother's; and you must not hinder us by your follies and absurdities, else you will have to go away from home till we are settled. Now I have done, and said what I wanted to say. Go and dress for dinner, like a good girl; it is getting time; and make yourself look like a Christian if you can, and less like a Zulu than you generally do. And behave like a rational creature and a lady, while Mr. Brocklebank is here. And remember that all I have said to you is for your own good as well as ours; and if I do not wrap it up in sugar, it is because I have not time and you prefer honesty."

"And you have been saying all this to me now, because Mr. Brocklebank is coming to dine here?" asked Perdita.

"Yes," said Thomasina with a languid drawl.

"Are you in love with him, Thomasina?" her sister asked again, standing breathless for an answer.

"That has nothing to do with the question," was the cool reply. "A girl who respects herself could not possibly confess herself in love with any man before he had made her an offer. Whether she would marry him if he did—whether she would think it a good thing to allow him to make the offer—that is another matter altogether."

"And I would rather break stones on the road than marry like that, just for a settlement and without caring whether I loved the man or not!" cried Perdita passionately. Then, in a soft tone and with a sudden yearning, earnest look in her eyes that transformed her face to almost beauty, she added: "And if I did love him, I would marry him whether he was rich or poor, and whoever he might be!"

"No doubt: a costermonger or a chimney-sweep. That would just suit your principles of equality, and all that. I hope, however, you will choose a good-looking costermonger when you are about it, and see that your chimney-sweep takes warm baths when he comes home."

Thomasina spoke with quiet disdain. She was as angry with her sister as she ever permitted herself to be with any one, and felt that she was indeed, as she had said, hopeless and ungrateful. She had spoken to her, as she thought, both rationally and kindly; and it piqued her that her good intentions had brought forth such indifferent fruit, and that Perdita had made such a bad return for her care.

"Costermonger or chimney-sweep, whatever he may be, I shall love him if I marry him, or I will not marry at all," said Perdita as her parting shot. "And a noble-hearted man of the people is a better thing than a low-minded fine gentleman."

"*Chacun à son goût,*"[1] returned Thomasina, tranquilly, putting the finishing touch to her head. "For my part I prefer the gentleman; and please, Perdita, will you go out of my room and dress for dinner? This is the third time I have told you."

Not refined to the point of accepting with the noble simplicity of sincerity the meagre conditions of her state, Mrs. Winstanley was yet essentially a lady, according to the conventional meaning of the word. She knew how things ought to be; and though she made the mistake of attempting more than she had means and appliances to execute to perfection, still she had the art of arranging her material so adroitly that, as has been said, she hid many of the lacunae and gave an air of old inheritance to the shabbiness which could not be denied. The well-worn furniture of the drawing-room was set so as to best conceal the stains and darns and threadbare patches; the ornaments were placed where the chips and cracks did not show; and what if that showy-looking table at the side was covered with trumpery little trifles, carried away from cotillons and Christmas-trees?—nothings as they were in point of money-worth, they were valuable as so many points of color, and did as well in some respects as Salviati glass or Oriental china.

The quick eyes of Mr. Brocklebank, so keen at appraisement, saw the whole thing at a glance—commercial worthlessness, but artistic cleverness and the praiseworthy desire to make a good impression. So far, his natural self-esteem was satisfied. For a man must be exceptionally suspicious and humble-minded in one, if he thinks that everything done for him is on account of his money and nothing for himself; if, while he detects the fine Roman hand of the Belgravian Mother[2] writing out a lien on his fortune, he does not believe to see also the delicate little lines of the tender-hearted maiden to whom his money is an accident while he himself is the essential substance.

With Mr. Brocklebank, personality was so large, self-content so strong, that it would have been impossible for him to have accepted the Winstanley attentions as due only to his fortune. He himself, the man, was greater than his money; and it was he they flattered, not his purse to which they laid siege, when they tried so heroically to make the *res angusta*[3] look generous and sufficing, so that his tastes might not be wounded nor his habits disturbed.

---

[1]   (French), each to his own taste.
[2]   Belgravia: a fashionable London neighborhood.
[3]   (Latin), meager affair.

The dinner passed off as well as such a dinner could possibly pass. The soup was heavy and cold and the fish just on the wrong side of freshness; but the entrée was well-seasoned and the joint was succulent. The wine was execrable; it always is in houses presided over by women who pride themselves on their ignorance and consider a keen discrimination between port and logwood unfeminine; and, knowing this feminine characteristic, it was not much worse than Mr. Brocklebank had anticipated. But the ladies were charming; and if the flowers which dressed the table were faded and dashed, those of breeding and manner were perfect.

Mrs. Winstanley, foolish in attempting too much, was wise enough not to apologize for mistakes. She did her best; then left things to justify themselves and did not call attention to dilapidations by excusing them. She trusted to her own powers of fascination to make all seem to go right, and to cover up the marks of that which would go wrong. And she seldom trusted in vain. Still, she felt secretly ashamed of her flowers, of her dinner, of her house, of her appointments—and of Perdita.

Poor Perdita! Whatever went wrong, she was always the culminating point—the coping-stone of the whole crooked tower. And yet to-day she might have been spared the usual creeping blight of maternal disapprobation. She had really taken pains with her appearance, and had made herself look nice, as Thomasina called it, in good earnest. She had repented of the temper with which she had received what in her heart she knew had been meant as good advice, however distasteful to her own nature; and, translating her penitence into action, she had honestly, as Thomasina suggested, done her best to look more like a Christian and less like a Zulu than in general. And though she was by no means beautiful, and was too shy and conscious and uncomfortable in address to be graceful, yet she had a good figure when she let it be seen, and did not make herself like a sack tied round the middle; and her face was full of intellect and power, of passion and sympathy, which counted with some for even more than beauty.

"Miss Perdita did not honour us at the gardens, to-day," said Mr. Brocklebank during the blank pause that ensued between the soup and the fish.

"No," she said simply; "I had no ticket."

"We are such a large party to go about!" explained Mrs. Winstanley blandly. "And Perdita is such a dear, good, unselfish girl, she always gives up to her sisters. Besides, her pleasures are of a higher class," she added with a smile that puzzled her daughter and charmed her guest.

Those higher pleasures of hers did not often come in for her mother's approval, thought Perdita with mingled astonishment and pain;

but Mr. Brocklebank considered the expression pretty and the smile the evidence of a fond and appreciative maternal love.

"Still, a little recreation every now and then does young ladies good," said Mr. Brocklebank; "and Miss Perdita would have enjoyed the flowers. She would not have learnt her lessons any the worse to-morrow for being a rose among the roses to-day."

Eva opened her eyes, and Perdita's uncomfortable habit of blushing nearly brought the tears into hers. Mrs. Winstanley looked sweet and smiled pleasantly, turning to Perdita with the most delightful air of loving endorsement of their guest's flattery.

"All work and no play makes Jack a dull boy, you know," continued Mr. Brocklebank; "and it makes Jill as dull a girl. Not that Miss Perdita is dull; far from it; still, it would have done her undoubted benefit, and I am sorry that she had not the opportunity of enjoying herself. If I had given it a thought, I would have procured another ticket from the commencement, and would have included her as one of us. But I confess I was only occupied at the moment with the consideration of Miss Winstanley," turning to Thomasina.

"Oh, thank you! but it would have been a pity to have spent so much money on me," said Perdita impulsively.

Mrs. Winstanley crisped her lips; Mr. Brocklebank looked benign and half-amused, but pleased. Though the speech showed the lines of the family poverty too plainly for good taste, yet its thoughtfulness for himself was amiable; and as amiably received.

"I think I could have afforded half a sovereign to give a charming young lady like Miss Perdita an afternoon's recreation," he said, ostentatiously jingling his heavy gold chain, but with kindly intention all the same. "Still, I like the nice feeling that considered the expense before the recreation. Young ladies in general reflect on nothing but their own amusements and let the money take care of itself. Mrs. Winstanley deserves infinite credit for the high principle she has manifested in the education of her daughters and evidently inculcated in them. I make her my best bow; and congratulate her."

"I have always been particular about two things with my children—good breeding and unselfishness," said Mrs. Winstanley.

"The last is the flower of the first," said Mr. Brocklebank.

On which Perdita raised her shining eyes full to the ironmaster's face, and something seemed to leap out from them into his.

"How can they call her plain?" he thought. "She is better than merely pretty. She has brains and a heart, and she shows it!"

"Ah, I see you hold the same principles as Perdita and myself," continued Mrs. Winstanley, catching the look that passed between the rich bachelor and the most unpromising of her daughters, and rapidly reflecting whether it might not be her better policy to turn her attention to Perdita rather than Thomasina. It would be a splendid thing to get Perdita married before her sisters. These latter were safe, if not to-day, then to-morrow; and if not with John, then with Thomas: but Perdita was not every man's choice, nor a paying investment in any way. If Mr. Brocklebank should prefer her, Thomasina was too wise and proud to object. She would simply cast her line afresh and perhaps make even a better catch; and the family would be relieved of its unconformable rebel, its indigestible sandwich, its clumsy and inharmonious ugly duckling.

"Perdita, you too believe that manners are founded on morals, do you not, my child? I always say," she continued, addressing Mr. Brocklebank, "that the truest Christian is the best-bred gentleman."

"I don't quite know about that," returned Mr. Brocklebank. "I have been acquainted with many good Christians who were extremely unpleasant in their ways and nasty-tempered into the bargain. But they attended church regularly, had their children baptized and considered me worse than a heathen Chinese because I patronized a Unitarian Chapel and took leave to question their orders!"

Mrs. Winstanley turned a shade paler than usual; Eva again opened her big blue eyes to their widest; Perdita, with her unlucky sympathy for revolt and iconoclasm all round, longed to shake hands with Mr. Brocklebank for no other reason than that he dissented from rule and recipe—but Thomasina, turning to him gracefully, said, in an interested voice of the nicest gradation:

"You must tell us where the difference lies between you and us, Mr. Brocklebank. We are not very good theologians in this house, though mother is the daughter of a bishop! Perhaps that is the reason."

Mr. Brocklebank looked pleased, Mrs. Winstanley relieved. It was no new thing for Thomasina's tact to release them from a difficulty; and her mother prized her for this inestimable social quality more than for any other that she possessed.

"I will inform you of these differences when you have arrived at Armour Court," said Mr. Brocklebank. "The subject is too long to enter into over a dinner-table. You will all honour my poor place, you understand? Miss Perdita with the rest. What says that young lady?"

Perdita looked at her mother for a lead. Her mother looked down on her plate and did not answer either Mr. Brocklebank's words or her daughter's eyes. It was a dreadful nuisance, unless it should prove a fertile tillage. She would have to spend more money than she could afford to fit out Perdita for the visit; and if no good were to be done by it?—if Mr. Brocklebank's interest were merely general and due rather to his admiration for Thomasina than to any direct charm that Perdita might have on her own account? And if, which was quite likely, a great deal of harm were to come of the unconquerable stupidity of this embryonic revolutionist? For who knew of what folly she might not be guilty?—what wicked nonsense she might not talk about liberty and the working man that would make a staid, sure business man like Mr. Brocklebank hesitate before allying himself with a family which held such an undesirable member? Mrs. Winstanley had thought all this before; but it was a thing so self-evident and serious, it would bear a second and a third consideration. Still, she could not refuse when Mr. Brocklebank so evidently wished the girl to go; and she could not, before his face, dictate the line to Perdita which she secretly wished her to take, and make her understand that she must refuse for herself.

"Thank you very much indeed," said Perdita with effusion; then, in a more hesitating way: "I do not often—"

"Visit Armour Court?" interrupted Mr. Brocklebank with a laugh. "Just so; but when you have once found your way there I hope you will find it again. Come! I am a positive man and never take 'No' when I mean a young lady to reply 'Yes.' I accept no refusals from young ladies, mind that!" laughing.

"You are very kind," said Mrs. Winstanley; the Belgravian Mother in her satisfied, the paymaster uneasy.

He bowed elaborately and again fingered his massive gold watch-chain.

"No one could be 'kind' to such a charming family as this," he said. "It is quite the reverse. It is Mrs. Winstanley and her young ladies who are kind to admit me as one of their friends."

Every one smiled but Perdita; and she felt more inclined to sigh than to smile. That Mr. Brocklebank should congratulate himself on the friendship of a family which was loaded with debt and worth absolutely nothing in the world—and which, if Thomasina's words upstairs were true, had by no means the most honourable designs on him—seemed to her one of the saddest things that had come into their life. She longed to open his eyes to the truth; but it was not her business after all, she thought. Mr. Brocklebank was older and more experienced than she was, and he ought to be able to see how matters were. If things went too far and he was going to be really entrapped, then she might speak;

but it would be indelicate and premature now. She must sit still and keep silence; but she bore her protest in that very silence, and her grave face made Mr. Brocklebank wonder.

Soon after this the ladies adjourned to the drawing-room, according to the silly stock phrase; and Mr. Brocklebank was left in the shabby dining-room alone, to enjoy his inferior fruit and abominable wine as he best might.

"Mother, what did you wish me to do about going?" asked Perdita, so soon as the door was shut and almost before they were out of hearing.

No waiting for convenient times and seasons for that uncomfortable whirlwind! What had to be done, must be done now at once, whether the times were fitting or not.

"Not to accept," answered Mrs. Winstanley when they had reached the safer stage of the drawing-room. She was quite bland and quiet as to manner, but her voice was as cold as if her words were icicles, though it was smooth and free from spiteful emphasis. "You know you have nothing new; you wear your things out so unmercifully that I am obliged to keep you less well supplied than your sisters; and it will be a great expense to fit you out."

"I looked at you to see what you wanted me to do, but you would not look at me," said Perdita in an aggrieved tone.

"You see, my dear, I sometimes forget how exceedingly inept you are and how you have to be guided like a child at all points," said Mrs. Winstanley. "Your sister Thomasina is so full of tact, so quick to understand and arrange, and the child is so sweet and complying, that I never have to think for them. It is difficult to remember that I cannot trust to your discretion as to theirs. At your age you should have sufficient wisdom and conduct for yourself."

"But when I do decide for myself I am always in the wrong," said Perdita, still aggrieved.

"That is not my fault," returned Mrs. Winstanley, with even more of that glacial smoothness which with her betokened boredom.

"Now, Perdita, do not worry mother any longer," said Thomasina, who understood her mother like an open book. "You always choose such inconvenient times for your discussions! Why could you not wait till to-morrow, when we should have had this evening off our minds? Who can attend to all these troublesome little details now?"

"We might as well have it over now at once. It would be just as tiresome to you to speak with me to-morrow," said Perdita with her sorrowful accent of hopeless discordance.

"Very likely," answered Thomasina, quietly.

"And if I have to go to Armour Court we must arrange something at once," continued the girl, a little irritated. "I do not care about going, and if you can get me out of it, I am sure you may; but if I do go, something must be done immediately."

"You are ungrateful, my child, to say you do not care to go," said Mrs. Winstanley; "ungrateful both to good Mr. Brocklebank who has asked you, and to me whom it will cost more than I can well afford to fit you out and make you able to be one of the party."

"I do not mean to be ungrateful, mother," said Perdita.

"But you see you are," said Thomasina; "and it is very tiresome all round. However, we cannot help ourselves and so must make the best of it. Do not trouble about the expense, mother," she added, speaking to her mother; "I have heaps of things, and can fit her out almost entirely."

"You are very good, Thomasina," said Mrs. Winstanley with a look of relief.

"Ina? Ina is the best young princess in the world!" cried Eva. "Give Ina a crown, and she would make us all little hoop rings out of the shavings!"

"What do you mean, my child?" asked Mrs. Winstanley innocently.

"Little Eva's meaning is not always either clear or important," said Thomasina, arranging a few toys in better array. "Her voice is fresh and her laugh pleasant, but we do not get much satisfaction if we dig for her meaning. Intellect is vulgar, is it not, Eva?"

"Ask Perdita," returned Eva gaily. "What do you say, Perdita? You are the Superior Person, you know."

"I think want of it more vulgar," Perdita answered with grave intensity; "and ridicule of it the most vulgar of all."

"You never understand fun, Perdita," said Thomasina. "You are always so distressingly in earnest!"

"I never know when you and Eva are in fun," answered the girl. "You seem to me to say such cruel things; but because you say them gently and Eva says them with a laugh, you get out of all blame by declaring you are in fun! If I said half that you do, I should be violently angry and wanting to vex some one."

"A confession not to the credit of your amiability, Perdita," said Mrs. Winstanley; and at this moment the door of the dining-room opened and Mr. Brocklebank was heard coming heavily up the stairs.

"Just in time!" said Mrs. Winstanley, ringing the bell as he entered. "We were this moment hoping you would come up for coffee instead of having it sent to you alone in the dining-room."

Mr. Brocklebank bowed, and looked critically from one to the other of the four women before him. What made Perdita's sensitive face flame as his eyes rested on her? He thought it was because he looked at her—the man's natural and pleasing delusion!—not suspecting that it was shame at her mother's glib hypocrisy which drove the blood through her veins with a bound that made her for the moment feel as if on fire. What an interesting-looking girl she was! and how pleasant to feel that he had but to throw the handkerchief to whom he would, to have it picked up and gratefully accepted. Eva, the beautiful little rosebud in the perfection of her dewy freshness; Perdita, with her poetry and passion, her fire and earnestness, her vigorous intellect, bold thoughts and ardent mind; Thomasina, who might be a young queen for grand style, for dignity and good breeding—any one of the three he might marry next week, he said to himself, if he chose to ask the question and press the date.

As for Mrs. Winstanley, she was of course; but also of course out of the running. Men think that the poor old dears of fifty and beyond are to be had for the beckoning—flattered as they must needs be by this frosty renewal of their springtime, this late and sickly shine of an Indian summer born out of due season!—only they are not beckoned; and fifty and beyond wears rue for roses.

However, there it was, so far as his own confident belief went. Here were four women, of any one of whom he had the fee simple whenever he made up his mind to choose which.

Which should it be? He did not know; had not decided; but he had almost made up his mind that it should be one. But before choosing irrevocably, he would study them all closely down at Armour Court. He could judge of them better there than as a mere outside visitor here. Even six days in the close companionship of domestic life would tell him more than he knew now, after six months' ordinary acquaintance; and when he felt decidedly more inclined to one rather than to the others, he would act according to his inclinations. Meantime, he devoted himself with public assiduity to Thomasina, while studying Perdita and watching Eva, to make it clear to himself which of the three would suit him best.

On her part Thomasina was debating within herself: "Can I marry him when he asks me? He is so little the kind of man I like! But then I do not love any one else; I do not think I ever shall love any one else. I never have yet; and I am twenty-three now. He is so deliciously rich; and we are so dreadfully poor! I think when it comes that I shall say yes. I suppose I must; I know I ought; but it will be a sacrifice, though we have not sixpence and he has thousands upon thousands!"

CHAPTER V.

FORCED TO YIELD.

Armour Court, built by Mr. Brocklebank senior—vulgarly called Old Brock and sometimes the Old Limb—was one of the lions of the county and an eloquent witness of the profits to be run out with the iron when furnaces were tapped and molten masses of potential gold flowed through their appointed channels. Its ornamental shrubberies and its sub-tropical garden, its flowers and its grass, its wall-fruit and its early vegetables, were matters of historic notoriety and local pride; and the name of John Jukes, Mr. Brocklebank's head gardener—or, as he preferred to be called, his Chief Cultivator—was a formidable one to the rank of exhibitors in the great horticultural shows of the county. Or rather it had been, but was so no longer. For he had swept away the prizes so persistently that at last he was disqualified for competition; like Aristides,[1] who wearied men by the monotony of his justice, the very excellence of his method of perpetuating sports and creating new varieties, proving at once his honour and his bane.

No man in England was prouder of the stone hut wherein he makes his bed, or more attached to that relatively insignificant plot which he fences round with walls and calls his own, than was Benjamin Brocklebank, the ironmaster, of Armour Court and all that it contained. It belonged to the man's nature to be satisfied with his own things; to envy no one else; to wish for no more than what he had already; to be triumphant in the present and stolidly sure of the future. When he said Armour Court, he said the microcosm; and when he invited his friends to partake of his hospitality, as his usual phrase went, he felt as if he had invested them with a visionary Order of the Garter or Collar of the Golden Fleece; and that, come what might, for once in their lives they had known domiciliary perfection.

He acted as showman to his place with a simplicity of contentment that disarmed criticism. His flowers were unapproachable; and there were no such grapes to be had in all England as those grown by John Jukes and paid for by himself. No house within the four seas had such

---

[1] Aristides "The Just" (530–468 BC) was so respected throughout Greece for his fairness that Athens assumed leadership of the alliance against the Persians.

a view; and where would you match those two marble pillars of the porch, with the broad white marble steps leading down from the hall to the gravel sweep? Look at the noble proportions of the elevation—was there ever such a grand bit of domestic architecture? He challenged Florence or Venice, about which folks bragged so loudly, to beat the real beauty of Armour Court—good, solid, substantial beauty, worth a city-full of your foreign gimcracks and veneer! Had any one objected that his house looked bare—that a few creepers about it would have given it a tender kind of grace and a few trees near at hand the sentiment of warmth and protection, he would have answered that ivy is for ruins and creepers are for cottages; that trees impede the circulation of the air and intercept the rays of the sun; and that Armour Court would be spoiled were the tiniest little leaf to be permitted against its stucco walls, or were even a good-sized shrub to throw its pleasant shade across a window. Change anywhere would be an injury and a disfigurement; and naturally his friends fell into his humour and adopted it for their own; so that the absolute perfection of this big, white, pompous house was a fact as undeniable in Mr. Brocklebank's mind as is the infallibility of the Pope to a good Catholic or the perfection of the Taj Mahal to a patriotic Hindu.

Apart from this not unamiable weakness, the ironmaster made a very pleasant host, and no one was found to complain of scantiness of courtesy, of hospitality, or of welcome. He was a little heavy; and his self-contentment was a little tiresome, perhaps; but when you eat a man's bread, if only for a day, you are bound to respect his whims and to call his barber's basin Mambrino's helmet[1] if he has a mind that way. Paying visits involves more than a dress-coat for dinner; and a guest may think himself let off easy who has no more *gène*[2] to undergo than to make himself an echo of his host's harmless vanities. Sometimes those vanities are not harmless; and then the yoke is heavy enough. But in general Mr. Brocklebank exacted nothing more than praise of the place all round; and the confession that no ancient Chase nor lordly Hall, no Queen Anne's mansion nor Elizabethan manor, came near to Armour Court for all that makes life lovely and a domain perfect.

The present party, gathered together on the platform for the journey down to this famous monument of industry and enterprise, was no more likely to break the flattering spell than any other had done. Even Perdita

---

[1]   Refers to an episode in *Don Quixote* (1605) by Miguel de Cervantes (1547–1616).
[2]   (French), trouble.

would scarcely say that the house was bare and ugly, and that the gardens were oppressive in their extent and magnificence. And what she would not do, be sure no one else in her family would venture on. Mr. Brocklebank, who would cheapen a Finnan haddock from eightpence to sixpence, and discharge a cabman just within the two miles' shilling fare, could do things royally when he chose; and he chose to be magnificent to-day. As six full-grown Christians in one compartment would be too close packing for his taste, he said, he took a saloon carriage for the occasion, and bore the brunt of the expense without contributions from anyone. Even his wealthy sister was franked like the rest; and, rich people having odd little turns of parsimony, she was as much pleased by this to her unimportant gratuity as was Mrs. Winstanley herself, to whom it was of vital benefit. Hence, the party set out in good spirits, all like instruments at concert pitch and in perfect tune; and Perdita herself, who seldom found society amusing, shared in the general lightness of the hour and made herself happy in her own way.

Mr. Brocklebank too, always under reserve of supreme devotion to Thomasina, was impartial in his attention to her, and even something more. He did not let her feel shunted nor out of place; and visibly raised her status with her mother and Mrs. Merton by the kindly interest with which he listened to her views, now on this and now on that, and the trouble which he took to draw her out on her own subjects. Mrs. Winstanley, who had husbands for her daughters on the brain, wondered again, more distinctly than before, if this was to be the right thing after all—if Perdita, so long despised, was to prove the Prudent Betsy of the rich man's choice; Thomasina thrown over for the sister who was not fit to be her lady's-maid, according to her estimate of things. And thinking this, her manner, usually of that *aigre-dolce*[1] kind which unites vinegar with sugar and steeps peppercorns in syrup, lost something of that inner bitterness by which Perdita was wont to feel more pained than she was soothed by their outer sweetness. She was almost natural and very nearly genial to the daughter who generally lived in the cold shade of her displeasure; and Perdita had the sensation of a condemned creature whose prison doors are thrown wide open, and who is suffered to stand once more in the sunlight and hear the skylark singing overhead.

"Miss Perdita will be interested to know that we are traversing the site of such and such a famous battle-field," Mr. Brocklebank would say at one place. "Tall chimneys and busy factories on the locality where

---

[1]   (Italian), bittersweet.

were arrayed armed hosts of billmen and archers—nineteenth-century triumphs of civilization over the effete barbarities and tyrannies of the past."—"If Miss Perdita will place herself here she will discern the tower of that celebrated church where such and such a monarch was crowned, and in whose precincts such and such a mighty noble lies interred."— "Miss Perdita will please remark the bridge we are about to traverse. It is considered a marvel of engineering skill, and from its commencement to its conclusion, cost no less a sum than so much."

His attention to Perdita continued at high pressure throughout the journey; but in return, Thomasina had the best place, corresponding to that of her mother, and the seat near Eva was piled up with illustrated papers, cakes, sweets, flowers, and one or two pretty trifles from Regent Street; Mr. Brocklebank saying to Thomasina, "The young princess must reign with the queen;" and to Eva, "Sweets to the sweet, and flowers to the rosebud just commencing to blow."

"So, who was it?" thought Mrs. Winstanley, more perplexed than pleased by this catholicity of gallantry. How much she wished the man would know his own mind, and, in knowing his, relieve hers!

The same kind of thing went on at Armour Court; and if this same catholicity of gallantry could have won canonization, really the hard-featured ironmaster would have been made a saint on the spot. He was all things, not to all men, but to each of the five women forming his little court, including Clarissa with the rest. He anticipated their fancied wants, and played a distinct and separate part to each, according to the ideal character laid down in his own mind for each. To Mrs. Winstanley he was devoted, respectful, companionable, with the finest mingling of the brother and the son that could be imagined. To his sister he was frank, easy, confidential, affectionate. With Thomasina he was as a courtier in the service of a princess, admiring and gallant, but more ceremonious than tender, and, while assuming her to be in a special sense his care, never transgressing the most rigid boundaries of polite loyalty and courteous championship. With Perdita he was intellectual, controversial, instructive; he complimented her on her understanding while proving her to be all wrong and he meant it for flattery that he never condescended to badinage or frivolity when talking to her, and that he supposed her incapable of laughter or fun. But to Eva he was the exact reverse. He never spoke to her save in quips and cranks, in metaphor and hyperbole, as to a creature made of sugar and spice, to be set apart from the dull prose of life as it is and kept in a kind of enchanted garden where nothing real and nothing serious might enter. And all these different characters he put on with the bewildering rapidity of a Proteus;[1] till Mrs. Winstanley grew almost faint with fatigue; not knowing where to have him and wanting the charm by which she might compel him to retain one form and become tangible and coherent.

His sister, who knew him and understood the whole meaning of this display, ministered to his humours and picked her way dexterously. She knew that he was thinking of marrying and that the Winstanley family had taken his fancy. She also believed that he would choose Thomasina—cut out for him as she was by the fitness of things, and formed by nature to make him an harmonious wife. But she knew that it amused him to play the great Mogul and make feints with that hand-kerchief of his, watching how each tantalized slave should behave; and that not the vainest woman who studies looks and gestures before her glass, delighted in "showing off" more than did this grave, stolid, heavy, middle-aged manufacturer of pigs and rails.

For her own part she actively wished him to marry Thomasina as a woman both sensible and ladylike, good to look at and tranquil to live with, ornamental for society and too well-bred to be anything but placid and peaceful at home. Eva, though so charming and bewildering now, would, she thought, prove but a thorny little rosebud if transplanted into the heavy earth of Armour Court; and Perdita would get her husband and herself into all manner of scrapes by her reprehensible opinions. It would not do for Benjamin's wife to say at the head of his table, that she hoped to see a republic established in England, and believed it would come before another generation was over; that she held Gambetta to be the future of France, and sympathized with the Communists, denying all that was said of their iniquities; that she abhorred a landed aristocracy and considered hereditary legislation a crime when it was not a sham; that she held the famous formula of Liberty, Equality, and Fraternity dearer than life, and meant always to act up to it. So she would; Clarissa felt sure of that. She would go among the puddlers and stokers full of her princi-ples of democracy and equality; and if trouble fell between them and the management, she would side with them and proclaim the management to blame. A democrat as the wife of a rich manufacturer—a woman who sympathized with the "hands," and thought that capital had its duties and labour its rights—a woman who felt rather their common womanhood with the poor slatternly wives than the isolation of her station—why, such an upsetting rebel as this would be the focus of a local revolution, and the

---

[1]   In Greek mythology, a god of the sea who could change shape at will.

neighbouring gentry would cut her and hers as deliberate traitors to their order! "No, not Perdita! certainly not Perdita," thought Mrs. Merton. "If a Winstanley at all—and a Winstanley was as good as any other; Benjamin did not want money with his wife, nor did he want blue blood of a specially deep tinge; the daughter of a major and the granddaughter of a bishop would be blue enough for him; if then, a Winstanley at all, surely it would be Thomasina! No chance of a good fit else!"

All this however was only thought, not said; and no one could have seen by Clarissa's eyes, voice or ways, that she had an idea beyond the mere pleasure of the day, or that she was taking stock of all that was about her, and thinking what she could do to put her invisible little spoke into the wheel, should it turn in the direction which she did not wish to see it take.

It was one of Mr. Brocklebank's "whimsies" that there should be no private pairings off at his house, and that his guests should keep in a compact little body together, clustered round himself as—in this present instance—the Apollo of the three Graces and two of the Muses, according to his own heavily facetious epigram. He did not like to see them strolling off two-by-two, talking no one knows of what; and as he knew how to make his will a pretty stringent law, even Eva, who never obeyed any one when she wanted to have her own way, found herself forced to obey him, and Perdita had to conform to the majority, which in general was pain and grief to her fiery, dissentient soul.

They were at this moment in the garden, sitting at the farther part of the lawn in the shade of a clump of ornamental trees which Mr. Brocklebank valued as if they had been unique in England. True to his system of impartiality, he was seated between Thomasina and Perdita. Forming half a circle, Mrs. Winstanley sat next to Perdita, and Clarissa separated Thomasina from Eva. The conversation, which had begun on "Bits and Bearing-reins," drifted into woman's rights and woman's work—Mr. Brocklebank ridiculing the idea of the franchise, but approving of the higher education and the extension of the sphere of female usefulness.

"What does Miss Perdita opine on this momentous question?" he asked, turning to the rebel sitting flushed and palpitating, longing to speak, but afraid of herself and more afraid of her audience.

"I think that women should work," she said, eagerly and shyly with passion and reserve all in one.

"So they do," said Mrs. Winstanley. "What do servants and milliners, governesses and shop-girls and charwomen do but work? A great deal is done by women."

"No, I mean a higher class than these—poor ladies," rejoined Perdita.

"My dear, how can ladies work?" asked Mrs. Winstanley with emphasis. "Physique, education and the opinion of the world are all against ladies doing anything menial."

"But there is so much that they might do which is not menial," said Perdita, looking at Mr. Brocklebank.

"Amiable dreams, my child, but impracticable," returned her mother quietly.

"Would you like to be a flower-girl, Per?" asked Eva, as if quite serious. "If I had to be anything, I would be that. I would not mind milk and eggs or Berlin wool, but I would prefer flowers."

"I should like to be something better than that," said Perdita. "I mean better," she added hastily, correcting herself as having spoken disloyally to her democratic flag; "only in the way of education. It does not take much learning to sell flowers, and I should like to do something that I would have to learn to do well, and to be well paid for when done."

"Oh, you horrid mercenary little monkey!" cried Eva. "I always thought you were fond of money, and now, you see, you say that you are!"

All this time Mr. Brocklebank had not spoken. Now he broke into the discussion in his elephantine way, laying down the law as if his words were so many planks and girders which settled the basis of the whole thing once and for ever.

"Miss Perdita is right," he said; "it is far better to work honourably than to live in shows and shams."

Perdita bent forward and looked up into his face, as she had done once before, her whole soul burning on her own.

"Thank you," she said. "That is what I want to do."

"And you want to do what is quite right, and confers honour on you for your desire," he answered.

"Oh, Mr. Brocklebank! do you encourage this new subversive and unfeminine movement?" cried Mrs. Winstanley.

"I encourage nothing subversive, dear lady," he answered; "but, you see, the great fact is this—women must live like the remainder of mankind; and to be independent of masculine aid in pecuniary matters is not necessarily unfeminine or subversive. Want of means of their own impels many a score to marry; and I assure you, we men do not like to feel that we are married only for a settlement. Mark, I say 'only.' As a man of the world I confess the important part played by money in one's life, and I do not advocate love in a cottage with bread and cheese, and perhaps not sufficient of that. Still we might compound for a little truer personal interest—a dash of something, which for want of a better name I will call affection."

"But how are mercenary marriages to be prevented because a few restless girls descend from their natural position and go out into the world to earn their own livelihood?" asked Mrs. Winstanley, with admirable self-control curbing her impatience with the whole subject.

"It would lessen the necessity by so many as succeeded," said Mr. Brocklebank; "and for my own part, I would give a helping hand to any young lady of my acquaintance who desired to learn self-support and independence."

Again Perdita raised her eyes to his, her face as eloquent as a poem, as expressive as a chant; and again something seemed to pass from her to him, as if the slack fires of his soul were kindled at the burning blaze of hers.

Mrs. Winstanley was in despair. Natural repugnance and inherited prejudice; the sanctity of caste, in which she, a lady born in the velvet, was so devout a believer; the rapid calculation of chances between Benjamin Brocklebank and such a man, say, as Hubert Strangways—compliance with the one meaning offence to the other, but opposition to the ironmaster probably leading to estrangement—and he was a valuable friend; Thomasina's likely "take" in the deep waters, and Eva's just as likely, but Perdita's present apparent chance not to be ignored—oh! if a kind Providence would but incline this man to take her!—all kept her silent and perplexed, wearied with her tiresome rebel's perpetual disturbance of the smooth surface of things, and worried and uncertain all round. She dared not refuse; and it was like draining her very life-blood to consent. How she wished there was such a malady as temporary dumbness, and that Perdita might be taken with a mild attack of it!

She turned for help to Mrs. Merton.

"What do you think?" she asked, heroically smiling. It would have been easier to her to have cried instead.

"My brother has such good judgment, his opinions ought to carry weight," said Clarissa suavely. "For myself, I have no views. I could not work if I tried; but it would be better if women were not quite so dependent as they are in money matters. Still, all the strong-minded that I know are so ugly and dress so badly!"

"There should be no intimate connection between bad millinery and useful work," said Mr. Brocklebank.

"No," answered his sister. "As you say, there should not be."

"But what does our spirited Miss Perdita desire to do?" asked the ironmaster, turning to Perdita and looking at her with a certain softness of feeling that, had he been any other man, would have made his eyes dark and tender; being what he was, it made them only dark and a little fierce.

"That is just what I do not know—perhaps get a place in the telegraph or post-office," she said.

"Perdita!" remonstrated her mother a little below her breath; but her revolutionary daughter had the whip-hand of things for the moment, and with Mr. Brocklebank to back her determined to have it out fairly and fully.

"Would you deliver our letters and wear a uniform? What fun!" cried Eva, clapping her hands.

"Light-hearted fairies like Miss Eva have no business to interpose in these grave discussions," said Mr. Brocklebank with a smile, playfully striking Eva's pretty little dimpled hands with a leaf. "But Miss Perdita is quite right—what I call nobly right; and I think I can arrange so as to get her an appointment—nomination rather, I ought to say—to the Post-office Savings Bank. The remainder will depend on herself."

"Thank you! thank you!" cried Perdita, with a very passion of grateful excitement. "My highest ambition would be fulfilled!" she added, speaking wide in her agitation.

"To be a telegraph girl? how funny!" said Eva gravely, as if considering the question on its merits. "It is like being a shop-girl, or that post-office girl at the grocer's shop in High Street—don't you know, Per? that fuzzy-headed girl who sits, in a little railed-off kind of cage and sells you stamps and clicks at those funny little handles? Don't you know?"

Mr. Brocklebank pursed up his lips and looked displeased. Eva was a very delightful little fairy, no doubt—a rosebud washed in dew—an *ingénue* as void of vice as of brains—anything you will most fresh and bewitching—but even Eva must not put her wilful little fingers into his pies, nor seek to prize up his joists and girders when he had once laid them down.

Mrs. Winstanley, taking it all in at a glance, hastened to restore the equilibrium so far destroyed.

"It is very praiseworthy of Perdita, certainly," she said, speaking smoothly; "but the proposition has naturally taken me by surprise. It is the first I have heard of it, and I am a bad person to endure sudden shocks and unexpected attacks. And then, though we are not rich, we are scarcely so poor that my husband's daughter should find it necessary to go out into the world to earn her daily bread like the daughter of a colour-sergeant or a canteen-keeper."

Those last words came with a certain irrepressible bitterness, nature asserting her right of expression in spite of the stern discipline to which she was subjected.

"Unless very wealthy, all assistance to the family income is good and valuable," said Mr. Brocklebank. "And should Miss Perdita accomplish no more than gain her own little pocket money, she will be so much the richer and have so much the more in hand."

"Mother, you know it would be a relief to you, if one of us was off your hands," said Perdita with her unlucky frankness.

She meant no harm; had no second intention whatsoever; slung no stone by her phrase; just said simply what she knew and felt; but she made her mother quiver from head to heel, and secretly cry out in her heart against Providence who had cursed her with such a disaster as this, punished her through this filial cross so unmercifully and unjustly.

During the talk that had gone on, Thomasina had turned paler than even her wont, and had stiffened out of her usual quiet grace and easy dignity into an odd, stony, glacial kind of rigidity.

"What line does Miss Winstanley take on this question?" asked Mr. Brocklebank, turning to her deferentially.

"I am not of the new school at all, in any way," she answered. "I think that women ought to stay at home and be taken care of."

"But if there is no one to take care of them?" said Perdita, taking her to mean, as indeed she had meant, the protection of men.

A very good imitation of tears came into Mrs. Winstanley's eyes.

"The allusion to your poor father was a little cruel, my dear Perdita," she said. "But if he is not with us in the body, we should yet make it a point of duty to live according to his wishes, and to do nothing that he would disapprove of if he were here in our midst."

"Would he have objected to my working for myself, mother?" asked Perdita excitedly. "He was a brave and upright man and always said that truth and honesty were the best qualities in life."

"I do not quite follow you," said Mrs. Winstanley. "I think you are a little wide of the mark. What have truth and honesty to do with a young lady's going out to a telegraph office, and perhaps catching mumps or small-pox?"

"There is always that danger, certainly," put in Clarissa. "And I don't think they can keep their hands clean!"

"And bring it home to us!" cried Eva almost in tears.

"Vain phantoms and false fears, ladies!" said Mr. Brocklebank pleasantly. "Miss Perdita will take no harm, rely on it. The proposition is agreeable to me; and if it were not too familiar, and the young lady were a young gentleman instead, I should call her a brick! It will be a noble example; and we never know where the influence of a noble example ends."

"If you approve so warmly, of course I should be very sorry to interpose any objection," said Mrs. Winstanley, yielding with the best grace she could command.

"I would not go without your express sanction and permission, mother," said Perdita, unconsciously forcing her mother's hand.

"You will give it now—formally—delivered with deliberation and duly attested by these witnesses," said the host jocularly. "Come! pronounce it in good round style, Mrs. Winstanley."

"If you are pleased with the proposal, I have nothing to say in its disfavour," answered Mrs. Winstanley, with the pride of concealed pain.

Mr. Brocklebank laughed aloud.

"Shake hands on it!" he said, and placed the girl's hot, nervous hand in the cold and flaccid grasp of her mother.

So the visit to Armour Court was made memorable forever by this sudden settlement of Perdita's future, and the promise extorted from her mother that she should be nominated at the Post-office Savings Bank, and thus be allowed to earn her own livelihood, if she succeeded in passing her examination.

Mrs. Winstanley wept bitter tears in Thomasina's room that night, and Thomasina's still face looked bored and severe.

"There is nothing to be done with her, mother," she said at last. "As Mr. Brocklebank has chosen to protect her, she must of course go her own way; but he owes us something for the trial to which he has subjected us. I only wish you had had the courage to oppose him. I would, had I been in your place."

"My dear, I dared not!" said Mrs. Winstanley. "He is too valuable to us to offend."

"Then he ought to be made to pay," said Thomasina quietly.

"He shall," replied Mrs. Winstanley. "I consider that he is deeply in my debt for this."

CHAPTER VI.

THE HOME AUTHORITIES.

WHILE they remained at Armour Court, Perdita escaped the domestic punishment which, had she been as far-seeing as she was single-hearted, as shrewd as she was intense, she would have known she had prepared for herself. But she was not a prophetic creature; and though her intelligence was clear and strong, her understanding in matters of daily life and policy was not acute. To gain her point and have leave to work—that was all she thought of. What might come after was not in the circle of her calculations at all.

For the immediate present, however, everything went well. She was under the especial protection of Mr. Brocklebank, who liked what stood with him for sound commercial views in this matter of feminine bread-winning; and her mother, compelled by her own ideas of policy to give in to the rich man's humour, did not dare to throw aside the mask of compliance and show her real face of dissent while under his roof. But when they came home and there was no longer a wealthy host and much desired son-in-law to throw the ægis of his approbation round that obnoxious rebel, then Perdita was made to understand the heinousness of her sin; and things went rather hard with her.

She was in disgrace all round. Even Thomasina, who never went out of her way to worry her—who indeed, being more charitable than malevolent, would rather have taken a little trouble to keep her straight and prevent her from falling into disgrace with the others: this being the least vexatious thing in the end—even she washed her hands of her now, and abandoned her to her fate. Too hopelessly wrong-headed to make good advice of any avail, she left her to the full force of the maternal displeasure, and did not attempt to knock up the frailest little ark for her shelter—did not throw up the most insignificant little break-water against the tide. She had sinned, and she must suffer; and Thomasina would have none of her—keeping towards her that frosty silence which is not peace so much as banishment and the confirmation of hopeless depravity.

"I told you the other day, Perdita, that you were selfish and inconsiderate, and now you have proved how right I was."

This was her last and final sentence, and from this she would not recede. Nor yet did she care to repeat or augment. Thomasina was not one to waste her strength in any direction whatever, and belabouring Perdita twice where once had no effect—using strong words where just ones failed—was emphatically a waste of strength.

Mrs. Winstanley, too well-bred for railing, took as the sword and spear wherewith to pierce her daughter's evil heart, the most pathetic resignation under this terrible affliction, the meekest spirit of patient martyrdom under the crushing blow that had been dealt her by the dear child of whom she had always been so proud, and in whose honour and affection she had so implicitly believed. She had prized Perdita's mind and character beyond expression, she said one day in her softest most heart-broken voice; and she had a considerable range of intonation. She was speaking to Thomasina, her faithful companion and friend; not to Perdita herself; though the girl was sitting there in her old place in the bay of the window, now, as whenever she was in the drawing-room at all, "cramming" for the examination which had to come. If she had not taken her out into society so much as the other two, she went on to say, it was because she had recognized her higher nature and allowed for it. All her children were equally dear to her, and her eldest and youngest made the joy and sunshine of her life; but while confessing their sweetness, their charm, she had always imagined that Perdita had something more in her than they. And it was because she had respected and recognized her studious, thoughtful nature, and had liked her to live her own life unhindered, that she had so often left her out of the little gaieties which bored rather than amused her. But she never expected this terrible insult as her reward! She never thought that Perdita, who had always seemed to be such a high-minded kind of girl, would have disgraced her dear father's memory and dishonoured his name by going out to work like a shopgirl or a milliner! She could not understand, she said, how Mr. Brocklebank could possibly have countenanced such self-will and folly. He knew the world and understood the exigencies of society; and it was a marvel to her at the time, and still more so when she thought of it, how he could have supported a wicked girl like this in her wrongdoing! It was the most painful thing she had ever suffered; the most distressing trial of all that she had undergone in her exceptionally sad life. And the end had not come yet. She shuddered to think what that end might be!

All this Mrs. Winstanley said for the purpose of smiting Perdita to the heart, truly, but all in perfect good faith of reprobation. She did really think that she had been good and considerate to her inharmonious daughter; that she had honestly provided for the peculiarities of her nature; and that she had been met in return by the most shameful and unpardonable ingratitude. No student of human nature has yet fathomed the depths of self-deception, nor measured the transforming power of displeasure.

"For myself, dear mother, had I been in your place I would have refused Mr. Brocklebank," said Thomasina with graceful and therefore non-irritating opposition. "I would have made him understand that gentlewomen like ourselves could not possibly allow of such a thing as 'bread-winning,' as the cant word is, in their family. And I would have made him feel that he had been underbred and vulgar in proposing it."

"It was impossible, as things were," said Mrs. Winstanley. "We were his guests and had just received great kindness at his hands. I could not, Thomasina! I was forced to yield!"

"You are always so sweet, dear mother, so considerate of others! but sometimes, however disagreeable it may be, we are bound for our own sakes to stand out against even influential friends," said Thomasina in the same quiet but decided voice.

"It was Perdita's fault; she made her account out of the difficulty in which I was placed," said Mrs. Winstanley, almost angrily. "She thrust me into a corner, so that I could not defend myself. I must confess," she added with that acid smile which means more than condemnatory words, "she had the merit of craft that was supremely clever. It was almost genius! No practised diplomatist could have chosen time or place more cleverly. For the future I shall know what to think of her 'honesty' when she puts it forward to excuse her blunders. I shall remember the way in which she managed things at Armour Court!"

Mrs. Winstanley's voice was thin and acrid; one might have believed that all her blood had turned to vinegar. Evidently, for this time at least, Perdita had better have been a dunce than a genius, and blundering would have been preferred to diplomacy.

"I blame Mr. Brocklebank quite as much as Perdita," said Thomasina, sticking to her point in a quiet, half indifferent way. "She was silly, but he was worse for upholding her. If he had not taken her part, she would have been forced to give up her foolish idea."

"She obliged him to take her part. I saw through it all," said Mrs. Winstanley with that liberal kind of vague accusation which relieves a person's mind at the expense of accuracy. "She knew the terrible position in which she put me, and of course built on it. And I, whose only fault towards my children has been too much indulgence, to be so bitterly punished by the one to whom I have been so specially indulgent—so anxious that she should live as she liked best—it was too bad! I feel as if I should never get over it—as if I had had a shock from which I shall never recover."

"Mother!" said Perdita, coming forward into the room, her eyes dilated and her mouth quivering with agitation; "I would attend to what you say, if there was any reason in it."

"Perdita! if you think mother unreasonable, it would be more polite and respectful not to say so," remonstrated Thomasina.

"I do not mean mother herself, but her objections; and they are unreasonable," repeated Perdita, she also sticking to her point, but not quietly and by no means indifferently. "Mother, dear, listen to me! What real disgrace can there be in what I am going to do? On the contrary, is it not far nobler to work honestly and get more money than we have, than to live as we do, in debt to every one about?—keeping up appearances, as you call it, with not enough to keep them up on! There is no degradation in work of any kind; and other ladies, as well-born as we are, have found themselves obliged to get their own living. It is not right to say that I am going to disgrace you!"

"Will you give me that silk, my dear?" said Mrs. Winstanley to Thomasina, ignoring Perdita as if she had not spoken and were not in existence.

"Oh, mother, you will not understand me! You will not see things in my light!" cried the girl, with that unconscious egotism of intense conviction which demands that the whole world shall accept the truth as framed by it. "You think me selfish and impertinent because I want to do what I feel to be my higher duty, and to use my life worthily instead of squandering it on frivolities and wasting it in idleness! There is no life for me here at home. I am nothing to you or the girls. You do not care for me; you never want to have me with you; and I only feel a nuisance to you all when I am with you. You all go into society, where, as you say, I do not care to go, but where, mother, you would not take me if I did, because I am ugly and you are ashamed of me; and I have nothing to occupy myself with but just a little desultory reading that leads nowhere and is not real study. The only time even when I can practise is when you all go out in the middle of the day; and then, if it is fine, I want to go too," said poor Perdita wistfully, she who loved the sunshine and the flowers, the blue skies and sweet nature so much more than they did! "I am a burden to you in every way! My presence gives you no pleasure, and I am just so much expense to you to keep; and it is not selfishness that I want to get out of all this and do something better both for you and myself."

Her words had come in a rapid flood which yet left each syllable clear and distinct. Her cheeks were on fire; her large eyes, glistening with half-formed tears, had that floating look of short-sighted eyes which makes them at once so dreamy and so intense, so soft and so pathetic; her lips were quivering; her body was thrown forward as if to give a kind of physical impulse to her pleading words; and her hands were clasped nervously together, the knuckles strained and whitened.

"My goodness, Per! what a splendid actress you could make! You ought to go on the stage and play Lady Macbeth!" said Eva with her melodious laugh.

"Have you answered Mrs. Disney's note, Thomasina? Her garden-party is for Thursday, is it not?" asked Mrs. Winstanley, still unconscious and imperturbable.

"Mother! you treat me as an outcast—you will end by making me one!" cried Perdita, her quick passions up in arms. "It is not right to treat me like this! I have done nothing to deserve it! It is not just—not fair!"

"For shame, Perdita!" said Eva, going up to her mother and putting her arms round her neck. "What a shame to speak like that to poor sweet, darling mumsey!"

"Now, Perdita, you had better leave the room before you make bad worse," said Thomasina, for her quite sternly.

Mrs. Winstanley put her handkerchief to her eyes and gave a little sob. Her tears were genuine in themselves, they were not make-believe; whether the real cause was the same as the apparent one was another matter.

"Mother! I am so sorry! I did not mean to make you unhappy! I am too unhappy myself to wish to see any one else so!" said Perdita, full of contrition. "Mother, dear, say that you forgive me and believe I did not mean to hurt you!"

"Never mind now, Perdita. It does not much signify what I say or think," returned Mrs. Winstanley in a slightly broken voice, wiping her eyes and taking up her work. "When you have ruined the family and broken my heart, you will then perhaps be sorry, and see things a little differently."

"But I am not going to ruin the family or break your heart, mother!" said Perdita, quite seriously. "I am not going to commit a crime because I want to make enough money to pay you for my keep."

"Well, let us say no more about it," said Mrs. Winstanley, with a weary air. "You are of age and must do as you like; but you make me sometimes wonder, whether you are my own child after all or whether you were not one day changed at nurse. I cannot see a daughter of mine in the extraordinary and unconventional young person that you have become."

"How funny it would be if Per were not our sister!" said Eva; "if we found our own in a gipsy's camp and Per turned out to be a gipsy's child!—what fun!"

For a moment Perdita looked at her mother with a white, scared face as if she had been suddenly frightened. The blood left her cheeks, her breath stopped and her large eyes, opened wide, were dilated till they became all pupil. She looked as if she were about to faint or burst into a torrent of tears. Then the tide turned and she blazed out into a fierce and uncontrollable fit of passionate despair.

"And if you do not believe that I am your child," she said, her voice quivering with wild emotion; "I can scarcely believe that you are my mother. You do not act like one towards me; and I might be nobody's child for all the home or mother I have! I wish I could find out that I belonged to the gipsies, or to any one else rather than to people who treat me as all of you do!"

"Leave the room, Perdita," said her mother, rising with dignity. "You shall, or I must."

"For shame, Perdita! you really are too horrid! You ought to blush for saying such disgraceful things!" said Thomasina, outraged for her mother's sake, yet in her secret heart as sorry for that wicked and ill-regulated girl and as angry with silly little Eva, who would play with fire, as it was possible for one of her unemotional nature to be. "And do be quiet, Eva!" she added, turning to the child, who was on the point of speaking. "Do not say any more to her. Why do you try to make bad worse by provoking her? Let her alone, for goodness' sake! Go out of the room, Perdita, and don't disgrace yourself by any more foolish wickedness."

"Why do you all torture me till you make me mad?" cried Perdita, clasping her hands over her head.

"Why are you such a spitfire and get so angry at every little thing that happens?" retorted Eva. "You are a perfect fury when you are angry; and you are always angry about something!"

"Are you going to leave the room, Perdita?" said her mother sternly.

"Mother, forgive me!" she cried.

"When you have come to your better self and can ask forgiveness calmly," her mother answered. "Till you are calm, leave us!"

"Oh, that I might die!" cried Perdita, as, torn by a dozen painful passions, angry with herself and despairing of her future, humiliated in her self-esteem and as much ashamed of her own intemperate language as her severest judge need wish, she uttered a passionate, wailing kind of cry and dashed furiously from the room.

"Oh, my sin! my sin!" she cried, when she had reached the safe fastness of her own bare, miserable little chamber. "Oh! when shall I be able to conquer this terrible sin and be meek and patient? Forgive me, Father, and give me patience!—soften my wicked heart and make me sweet and good and gentle! Oh! why will they stir me up as they do?" she said half aloud, her thoughts going back from heaven and grace to earth and shame—from future help to present pain. "They know what my besetting sin is and that, although I do strive against it, I cannot overcome it; and they are like cruel men who stir up a wild beast in its cage till they make it mad—and then they beat it for being furious! What a wicked wretch I am! Oh, this horrible heart of mine! this shameful passion! But how cruel they are to me! They make me commit myself; and then I put myself in the wrong and they are to be pitied for having such a shameful creature among them! What can I do? where can I go? This life of mine is too wretched to be borne; and all my youth is slipping away in misery and wrong-doing, without one ray of happiness, one day of love!"

So she sat and bemoaned herself; her heart heavy, her self-respect wounded, her sense of justice outraged; but ever the wild desire to do what was right—the fervent aspiration towards the better thing and the prayer that, though she had failed this time, she might stand fast when next tempted and turn the self-loathing of shame to the peace lying in a pure heart and a clean conscience—ever the willingness of the spirit to redeem that discordant weakness of the flesh!

While she was fighting thus painfully with wild beasts upstairs, her mother and sisters in their turn pitied themselves for the hard trial laid on them by her. They wondered where all this was to end; and asked each other what they could possibly do with her. She was unbearable as things were and there seemed to be no prospect of improvement.

"She is so detestably cross," said little Eva, pouting. "She never takes fun as it is meant; and the least thing makes her so awfully savage!"

"Still, Eva, it is not wise to tease her so much as you do," said Thomasina. "If she has an unfortunate temper, it is better not to rouse it. She cannot bear being teased; and you know you are too fond of trying her!"

"Then she is a horrid bad-tempered girl if she cannot bear a little fun!" said Eva, rather too warmly for the Winstanley tone of manners.

"That is not the question, child," her sister answered, sensibly enough. "We know that she has a bad temper when roused; when she is let alone, she is quiet enough; and the question is, whether it is wise to rouse her temper by teasing instead of letting her keep quiet by leaving her alone."

"One can't be always thinking whether what one says will make Perdita cross or not!" said Eva, herself more cross than need be.

"It will end, I fear, in our having to send her from home," said Mrs. Winstanley with a sigh. "These scenes will kill me; and the consciousness of her excitability is too fatiguing and wearing. It is like living over a powder-magazine where men are always striking lucifer-matches."

"Perhaps she will settle down when she has something to do," said Thomasina, her natural passionlessness and artificial suavity enabling her to be both just and reasonable. "Such a strong-natured, turbulent creature as she is, she may be better for having a fixed occupation after all! You see, she is no companion for us and of course we are none for her; and her life must be rather dreary, when you think of it. At all events, the experiment has to be tried; and if it fails, Mr. Brocklebank will be responsible."

"You always make the best of things, Thomasina," said her mother with as much fondness as she could feel for any one or as she considered it good breeding to show. "But even your sweet serenity will scarcely make a success of your poor unfortunate and misguided sister."

"I wish she would go away!" said Eva with uncompromising frankness; "we should all be much happier without her!"

This was the kind of thing that went on day by day, at this time, varying the outside form but ever in the same spirit; the mother and sisters were humiliated and annoyed at the whole being and circumstance of this uncongenial member of the family, while Perdita, now roused to semi-madness and now sunk into despair, was either way equally distressing to their nerves. But though she was so supremely miserable, she did not give way. She had tenacity as well as passion; and having made up her mind that this project of earning her own living was the wisest and best in all the circumstances of her life, she held on to her point, and let nothing beat her from it. She thought her mother and sisters cruel, so far as she herself was concerned, and superficial in their judgment of right and wrong while unable to rise to the higher levels of morality; and they thought her selfish and self-willed, low-minded in her aims, and criminally indifferent to the best interests of the family.

Even Thomasina's liberality did not go farther than making the best of things as they were. She did not dream of excusing her sister; she only said that, being what she was, it was wiser not to make her worse by needless irritation. It was a horrible thing that she was about to do; and she had a most unpleasant temper; but opposition was useless and teasing only made her worse.

Yet, as Mrs. Winstanley said one day, what but horrible things could be expected from a young lady of good family who was so lost to all sense of propriety as to call herself a democrat?—a young lady who wanted to see England made into a republic, when every one knows that a republic means communism and petroleum, vulgarity of manners and the scum of society taking the lead and at the top of everything! No one need be astonished, whatever she might do, with such principles as she had! A bishop's granddaughter talking such wicked nonsense indeed!—the daughter of a major and a gentleman turning into one of those abominable strong-minded women who dress like men, give public lectures, worry about things they have no business with, want to vote and go into Parliament, and who talk of improper things with men as boldly as if modesty were not a virtue! What a shocking thing it was! what a shameful anomaly! Perhaps she would go to America, and come back saying that she had had a "good time," and "guessing" and "calculating." She might even develop into an atheist. Her religious ideas were already anything but what they should be; and as for her manners, they were simply atrocious in a girl brought up as she had been and with such blood in her veins as she had. To see her shake hands as she did one day with that dirty old charwoman!—it was enough to make a mother's hair turn grey!—and the way in which she spoke to the men in the shops—just as if they were her equals! It was too terrible! She might be clever and all that, but, so far as Mrs. Winstanley was concerned, she would rather have seen a daughter of hers just one remove from an idiot than anything so dreadful as Perdita. Yes, a half idiot with nice soft manners, who knew how to make herself charming to young men of family and fortune, who could choose a bonnet with discretion, dance prettily, talk small-talk nicely and wear the fetters of society with grace, was worth all the clever women in the world; and the wisest people said so.

"Clever women are a mistake," said Mrs. Winstanley, laying down the law. "Men dislike them and women are afraid of them; and they are odious creatures, always. They are always horribly dressed and they have no manners to speak of; they do not know how to come into a room or how to sit down or get up; they can only talk politics or some dreadful 'ology which no one else understands; and they use such hard words!—horrid pedantic things! it is worse than toothache to listen to them! No, depend upon it, dears, a clever woman is a mistake. We are meant to be charming, not learned, ladylike, not strong-minded."

What wonder, then, that things worked inharmoniously in a family where one hostile party declared that the principles which were as vital as religion to the other were either socially blasphemous or intellectually impious?

In the midst of all this discomfort, Mr. Brocklebank suddenly returned to town and once more gave the poor ugly duckling the shelter of his friendship.

"I do believe Miss Perdita is glad to see me!" he said, smiling pleasantly when he shook hands with her and saw her soft eyes brighten and her sensitive face flush into almost beauty with the affectionate kind of joy that broke like sunshine through its habitual sadness.

"I am," she said fervently; "very, very glad!"

"Ah! I am rejoiced at that. You feel that I am your friend," he said more naturally than was his general manner.

"You must not spoil the dear child," said Mrs. Winstanley a little jealously.

"Not possible, madam! not possible!" he answered. "Miss Perdita is of stuff that does not easily spoil; and a little encouragement does young ladies good!"

"I wish that Mr. Brocklebank would take a fancy to Perdita and make her an offer," said Thomasina to her mother, when the ironmaster had gone and they were alone.

"It would be a splendid thing, certainly," answered Mrs. Winstanley; "but not the right position for her and not the right choice for him," with meaning.

"No; but that is his affair," she returned tranquilly. "At all events, it would be a magnificent settlement for Perdita; and he really seems to take great interest in her."

"She is so wrong-headed that in all probability she would refuse him if he did make her an offer," said Mrs. Winstanley almost fretfully.

"I don't know about that," answered Thomasina. "She looked excessively delighted when she saw him to-day; and though she has such an unpleasant temper she is very warmhearted. At all events, time will show."

"Yes, time will show," echoed her mother; "and I hope before very long," she added with her weary air—fretted by Perdita, frightened by her duns, and feeling that a crisis somehow was at hand.

CHAPTER VII.

AT FIVE-O'CLOCK TEA.

Before that memorable visit to Armour Court, Mrs. Merton had not known much of the Winstanleys. She had made their acquaintance at her brother's request, to be a chaperon always at hand when he wanted to have Thomasina without her belongings, so that he might study the young lady more at his ease and with less distraction than when a mother, who might be Belgravian, who knows? sat watching him from between her narrowed lids. But there had been no voluntary seeking, hitherto; and passive compliance does not make active desire.

Now however, Clarissa meant to cultivate them for her own sake as well as her brother's. For that brother's, certainly. Benjamin, though everything that was kind, was, without question, something of a bore. For want of some one else on whom to bestow himself, he hung round her neck with embarrassing pertinacity; and since the full enjoyment of her widowhood had set in she wished that he would marry, as the charter of her own completed freedom. And as Thomasina would do as well as any, and better than most, she was glad to help on the affair, as has been said; determined if she could to transfer this golden burr to one to whom his adhesion would be advantageous, and where his boredom would be only one of the inconveniences of wealth.

Also, for herself she thought she might do many more foolish things than draw as close to the widow and her pretty daughters as they or she thought desirable. Taking them all round, the bad with the good and the loss with the profit, they were on the whole useful people to know. Poor as they were in this world's goods, they had graduated in a higher social school than hers; and so far were her superiors. She recognized the thousand subtle hues of that nameless and delicate good-breeding which comes from inheritance and early education—hues which made those velvet rags of theirs infinitely more beautiful than her own glittering brand-new cloth of gold; and she had sense enough to be conscious that she herself, with all her nice soft ways and splendid comfort, wanted the last fine polish of perfected manner. Wherefore, she made up her mind to cultivate the widow and her daughters who had the cachet which she wanted, and were safe in these things wherein she was shaky, if only showy in others where she was solid.

For all this she was not tormented by that incurable disease, social ambition. In this complete satisfaction with themselves and their belongings she and her brother agreed; though they came to the same result by different methods. His content was from pride, hers from self-indulgence—his was mental, hers physical. Possession was the highest good of his existence, personal enjoyment of hers. If she had fine clothes and beautiful jewellery to wear, she was content with wearing them though no one saw them. Even when dining quite alone she dressed as for a grand dinner-party, and took as much delight in uncovering her fair shoulders and hanging her "white, warm neck" in golden chains and amber beads, as if she had been the chief guest at a state banquet. It was the same kind of thing with her house. She kept very little general society and she had no desire of rivalry in any of her appointments. There was no intention of outshining her neighbours in her display; and her sole thought was to have and enjoy what she herself liked and took pleasure in. Her Axminster carpets, as soft as beds of moss, were for her own walking on; her magnificent mirrors for her own looking in; it was she who drank those matchless wines which her husband had laid down with so much skill in the choice and so much indifference to the cost; it was she who slept in that luxurious bed; she who dozed away the rainy afternoons on that still more luxurious sofa. If that small portion of the world which wandered through her rooms liked to praise and admire, it was well; but their admiration was only an accident born of the nature of things, not in any degree part of her aim.

Yet she was not selfish, as we mean by selfishness. On the contrary, she was giving and kind when she had not to sacrifice her freedom or her comfort; but for all her amiability of temper, her indolence and self-indulgence might lead her to do cruel things if the occasion served, for simple want of that fibre which enables us to do strong ones.

When they were all settled again in London, Mrs. Merton asked the Winstanleys to a five-o'clock tea, where, among a few others, Sir James Kearney of course found himself, bringing with him his friend, Hubert Strangways. Eva, who did not know all, but who did know that Sir James was the common friend of Hubert and Mrs. Merton, spoke to her stalwart admirer—Maud Disney's fiancé—of the invitation; and said how funny it would be if he could go too and how nice to meet him in a new place! Wherefore, acting on the hint which was essentially a desire, Hubert begged Sir James to take him in his skirts and present him to the rich widow. And Sir James consented, with a certain undefined hope that he had introduced a relief-guard rather than a rival.

Mrs. Merton was an awfully nice woman, and he should be eternally obliged to her for all her kindness to him and they would be the best friends in the world to the end of time; but he could not be always devoted to her and her alone. He had been her very sincere friend and admirer and was so yet; but that little Winstanley girl was an angel! If his friend Clarissa—well! let that pass. A fair exchange is no robbery, thought Sir James; and Hubert should take him to the Winstanleys in return for his introduction here. He little knew that his acquaintance was to come about by that good soul, Clarissa herself, who had not chosen to make the thing of so much importance as to speak of the Winstanley girls in this little five-o'clock tea which she meant to give. She thought it best to let them come in with the rest as of no special importance.

Perhaps it was rather rash to bring them in contact with her own especial friend and favourite. She had a vague idea of robbers introduced into a treasure-house floating through her head; but she was a woman for whom the present has no future and who lived in a gilding, easy, extemporaneous way that had its dangers if its pleasures. But also she was clever enough to know that it is unwise in a woman of her age to be a young man's Cerberus[1] in the matter of pretty girls. Better be his minister and medium! Mature Sirens have no other chains. If knowledge of life and the nature of young men teaches them anything, it teaches them that the chains woven by the most charming woman in the world who is mature, how much soever also a siren, are full of weak places, and must be worn loose if they are not to break. And Clarissa Merton had learned this lesson, and took occasion now to act on it. Perhaps she had defined that dim uncertain feeling of the relief-guard, and had thought on her own side that a lure would not be bad policy. At all events, she asked the Winstanley girls to her five-o'clock tea and made a point of Sir James's coming as well.

Beautiful as she had looked, standing in the sunlight on that day of the flower-show, Eva Winstanley was still more lovely to-day seen under the soft light of a London drawing-room—one of those luxurious rooms whence the sun is excluded as the worst enemy that women and lovers can have, and where the salvation of waning beauty consists in discreet obscurity. Mrs. Merton was a past mistress in this kind of coquetry, as well as in all the arts by which the dial-hand of Time may seem to be kept at a standstill. Her windows were veiled with lace of the tenderest pink, like the heart of a blush-rose; her walls were of that pale neutral tint which enhances the brilliancy of showy women and makes the pallor of the white kind chaste and refined; rich stuffs disposed in artful places served as the backgrounds whereon gracious heads and pretty costumes were seen to perfection; and the very chairs were harmonious frameworks for the human figure. Her rooms were notorious for pleasantness and were of the kind which all agree to praise. Nothing jarred, either in form or tint; and the result was a universal sense of bien-être[2] and perfect taste. Beside all this she gave the most delicious cakes and sweetmeats; fruit that was a poem; tea that was perfection; chocolate that made you sigh; and "cups" which every one tried to imitate and none could come near.

It was a pity that she knew so few people, seeing to what perfection

---

[1] In Greek mythology, the three-headed dragon-tailed dog that guarded the entrance to Hades.

[2] (French), well-being.

all her appointments were carried and the pleasure that she could dispense, with a fortune that made numbers of no consequence.

"I hope you have been quite well since I had the pleasure of seeing you," said Sir James to Eva, as his not too intellectual manner of beginning a conversation.

Hubert, as the stranger, was told off on duty to the hostess.

"Yes, thank you, I am always well!" answered Eva laughing.

She knew the musical value of her roulade, and gave it on the smallest provocation.

"You look so. You look as if you have never had a day's illness or an hour's sorrow," said Sir James with admiration.

"Oh! I suppose I had all the horrid baby illnesses when I was a little tiny tot," said Eva; "but I have never had even a headache since I grew up. And as for sorrow—what use is there in being sorry about things? When things go wrong they don't come any better because one cries and makes one's eyes red."

"That is the best kind of philosophy! But would you not cry for some things?" he asked.

"I don't know; I never do cry; it's so missy and silly. I always laugh, and that is far more jolly."

"It is certainly far wiser, far better. But we cannot always laugh," persisted Sir James, who had his sentimentalities and who had even coquetted with the gloomy poetry of Pessimism and the weak-backed Worship of Sorrow. "We could not laugh at the funeral of the one we loved, for instance. Even you—an embodied joy as you are, Thalia and Euphrosyne[1] in one—even you could not laugh then!"

He looked at her tenderly. He wanted her to realize his funeral, the death of the young knight and bard, her lover, and to be touched and softened.

"What a horrid idea!" she said, making a pretty little grimace.

"Yes; you are right; and I ought to beg your pardon for it. We should not speak of such things to you. You are in the morning of life and have nothing to do with its storms or its darkness," he said apologetically.

"Now that is more like me!" cried Eva innocently. "I have a horror of night and the dark and always sleep with a night-light. Don't you hate the dark? I feel as if something was creeping on the floor and wanted to take hold of my feet if I have no light; don't you?"

Sir James laughed. It is not often that we see the flawless realization

---

[1]   In Greek mythology, two of the three graces: Thalia (Good Cheer) and Euphrosyne (Mirth).

of any ideal whatsoever, from a cabbage to a woman; but here was one for him. Dark and nervous, his fancy in woman naturally went to the vividly-coloured sugar-plum kind of thing of which Eva was so perfect an example. Fuzzy golden head, eyes the colour of the sky and skin like milk and roses, a round soft supple figure—if the mind and heart within corresponded to this delightful envelope, Sir James felt that, friend or no friend, whether it offended his mother to the heart or not, he would enter the lists with fate on the spot and do his best to win the favour of the little girl who was his ideal in the flesh.

"Now tell me what you have been doing since I saw you," he continued, in a slightly freer tone.

They were rapidly becoming good friends; and poor Hubert, making excuses to come with tea or chocolate, cakes or sweetmeats, felt a certain hot jealousy of his friend and more than once devoted him to the infernal gods, while thinking his handsome hostess a bore and his initiation into her good graces an unmitigated nuisance.

"We have been to Armour Court," Eva answered, looking at him with her wide-open innocent eyes.

"To Mr. Brocklebank's place? with Mrs. Merton?"

"Yes."

"I did not know that you had been there," he said in surprise.

"Oh yes; we were there from Wednesday to Monday; Mrs. Merton was with us all the time."

"It is a fine place, I hear," said Sir James jealously.

"Yes," said Eva, in a cool half-impertinent way. "That is, it is a great overgrown kind of thing. But it is too big and staring—it looks too new and as if it was built only yesterday. It is not like one of those beautiful old houses that look as if they had belonged to the same family for centuries, and that are so lovely!"

Sir James Kearney smiled. His place was old and looked as if it had belonged to his family for centuries; as indeed it had, in a way, if, like the famous Bucentaur,[1] it had been repaired so often that very little of the original fabric was left.

"And then," continued Eva, "those horrid works are so near; and the smoke from those dreadful furnaces is so disagreeable; and at night they make the place look like Pandemonium—flaring out at the top in that awful way. It all looks shoppy," laughing.

---

[1] The huge gilded gondola used to solemnize the symbolic marriage between the Venetian doges and the Adriatic Sea.

"It looks like what it is then," said Sir James, who disliked Mr. Brocklebank quite as much as Mr. Brocklebank disliked him. "Sometimes looks are true, you see."

"Oh! they always are!" said Eva, in her character of sweet innocence too ingenuous and unsuspicious to be critical. "I always trust to them."

"A dangerous doctrine, if a charming delusion," said Sir James in his character of poet probing the hollowness of the world and coming to the conviction of bran for blood.

"Oh, I am sure not!" she answered eagerly. "Pretty people are so much nicer than ugly ones! How pretty Mrs. Merton is and how good she is!"

"And so are some others I could name," said Sir James warmly.

"Yes; isn't Mr. Strangways handsome?" returned Eva, still keeping her eyes turned to Clarissa and her new acquaintance.

"Do you think so?" asked Sir James with sudden coolness.

"Yes; don't you? I think he is splendid—for a fair man. I like dark men best myself; but he is magnificent for a fair one!" all said with the most delicious, the most enchanting, audacity of innocence and unconsciousness.

Sir James felt as if he had taken a glass of wine for the pleasant tingling that came into his veins, the delightful warmth and brightness which mounted to his brain.

"And I like fair women," he said, his voice full of that rich intoxicating spiritual wine. "I like small women with golden fuzzy hair and blue eyes and rosy cheeks—women that remind you of flowers and the spring-time, sunshine and dancing and music and everything else joyous and beautiful in life!"

"Do you?" she cried, like a pleased child; "little things with fuzzy head and blue eyes? How nice! that's like me!"

"Yes, just like you," he said. "I have never seen any one more exactly my style than you are; and certainly never any one more beautiful."

Eva laughed and showed all those small white teeth of hers; her red lips and white teeth so curiously suggestive of the double action—kissing and eating.

"How nice of you—and how funny!" she said.

"Is it rare for you to hear that you are an ideal perfected?" asked Sir James.

"Oh, I dare say some people who like that kind of thing think I have a nice funny little face," she said. "But of course I know that I am not beautiful. Ina is—my sister Thomasina. She is like a queen; we call her our princess; but I am only a stupid little thing!"

"Yes, Miss Winstanley is very handsome," said Sir James, rapidly sinking into the depths. "But you must let me contradict you—you are more beautiful than she is."

"It is quite too nice of you to say so, and I cannot quarrel with you for it, but it is a great big story all the same," said Eva with a smile of childish incredulity and childish directness. "And I am sure," she went on to say in the same sweet unconscious way; "if I am nice-looking, you are too, so we ought to be very well satisfied with ourselves."

Certainly the young people were getting on apace, and the hay was being rapidly made in the sunshine. Just then, Hubert Strangways, released from duty, came up and sat down on the other side of Sir James, both facing the beautiful little fairy queen of the hour.

What a contrast the two young men made! Sir James tall and spare—nervous, olive-tinted, dark-haired, keen-featured—his strength that of nerve and sinew only—tenacious, combative, wilful; and Hubert Strangways like a young Norse god—simply direct, obtuse, powerful—Baldur the Sun-god in form, but as little able as he to recognize Loki, or any other evil spirit, when disguised as a beautiful woman who smiled on him and flattered him; while Eva, like a rosebud of any clime, sat at the point of the triangle, the soft luxurious beautiful little witch who had spells for each alike.

She was charming to both; showing all her loveliest points; laughing in her most musical cadence; saying in her most guileless manner all sorts of risky things and phrases full of double meaning if any one should choose to look below the surface; in fact, being herself without let or hindrance and weaving golden threads about these two poor victims, either of whom she would take if she were asked and one of whom she must therefore sorrow and disappoint. But that was in the future. For the present it was all sunshine and no cloud came, even when after a short time Mrs. Merton joined them and placed herself next to Eva. The widow thought she had given Sir James his head long enough; it was getting time now to draw him up.

It was strange that an astute woman like Clarissa Merton, and one who had studied so deeply the grammar of "looking nice," should not have seen that Eva was not a desirable replica of herself; though on the other hand she was in her way adverse to Eva. They were too much alike, too much of the same type, to do well together contrasted under the present conditions; for Mrs. Merton was Eva grown fatter and older, with a harder colour in her face and some of the dew taken out of her eyes; and thus their several charms rather damaged than enhanced each other.

Mrs. Merton showed what Eva would be when she had passed her first youth; Eva showed all the way that Mrs. Merton had gone; the one was in the exquisite freshness of the dawn before the day had fully risen—the perfect present, but with the mirror of the somewhat impaired future before her; the other was in the luscious ripeness of maturity before decay, but with the inventory of what had been and was no longer written in unmistakable lines on the beautiful image of her own past by her side. It was a mistake; but one often made. The hope which springs eternal in the human breast has for its undying partner the belief in her own unspoiled beauty, no matter what her age, which is part of the very life she breathes to the pretty woman accustomed to the admiration of men.

Soon after this the little party broke up; and two young men of means were now in love with penniless, fuzzy-headed Eva. And Thomasina was not jealous. It was not often that she was distanced, even by this fairy queen; but as a good sister she allowed her to have her innings—in moderation. Prosperity to any one of them would be prosperity to the family and a relief to the mother—the one person in the world whom Thomasina honestly loved. It was well to make hay while the sun shone; and Eva was perhaps wise to have two victims in her chains at once. For herself, she said, she wanted only one at a time; whoever he might be—only one at a time. Thomasina's ideal of happiness was safety, not excitement. She longed to have a fine house and a carriage and pair; an income which provided handsomely for all needs and left a practically inexhaustible margin for superfluities; she longed for the peace of sufficiency; for deliverance from the degrading debts and difficulties which she knew were eating out the very life of her mother; for freedom from the necessity of close calculation and the annoyance of self-denial; and she kept love and admiration out of the question, save for the use which they were in the great object of her life. With her, beauty was only a means to an end; with Eva admiration was the end itself; and with Perdita love only was the divine bond between man and woman, and all the rest served only to "feed the sacred flame."

When the mother and her two daughters reached home and while they were standing on the step waiting for the page-boy, so cook called him, to open the door, Perdita came hurriedly down the street. She was excited, flushed; and she looked a little wild. Her hat was not quite straight; one glove was unbuttoned, the other was in her hand; her whole appearance was somewhat disordered and wanting that nice touch of the woman who cares to make the best of herself. She scarcely looked the sister of those well-dressed girls, scarcely the daughter of that still handsome and aristocratic woman whose whole life was made up for society and who if Mormonism had been the creed of the "best people," would have undergone the ceremony of sealing[1] as a tribute to fashion. She might have sighed; all the same she would have sealed.

"My dear Perdita, you really look as if you were hunted by wild beasts and had come through a quick-set hedge," she said quietly, as her daughter dashed up at full speed with that odd manner of one pursued or pursuing which persons intent on some great object unconsciously have.

"Am I untidy, mother?" she returned in a breathless way, but smiling and evidently full of joyous excitement. "Never mind for once! I know I am a dreadfully careless girl; I don't think somehow of my appearance. But it is all right, mother. I have had my name put down, and now I have only to pass when the time comes!"

"Never mind for once? Your once is always," said Mrs. Winstanley, ignoring the fact of the nomination and passing into the hall as the door opened.

"Your name put down where, Per?" asked Eva, with apparent interest.

"At Burlington House; for a clerkship in the Post-office Savings Bank," she said, falling into the trap. She always did.

"How funny it will be!" cried Eva laughing. "Will you sit on a high stool with a pen behind your ear, Per? Won't it stick in your hair? What will you have to do? Count the money? Will you bring back any of it at night? A savings bank is like a pawnbroker's, isn't it? Don't you put pennies into a little box with a slit, and sell old clothes and things? How odd it all is!"

"No, Eva, a savings bank is not like that," Perdita answered quite seriously. "I shall not have to count up the pennies out of a box and I shall not bring home any money."

"And not sit at a high desk with a pen behind your ear?" asked Eva.

"I may do that. I don't know yet what the desks are like," resumed Perdita. "If the others do, I dare say I shall get into the way too."

"It is all heart-breaking and disgraceful, however one looks at it!" said Mrs. Winstanley; "and it will never bring a blessing to you, Perdita. You have begun this new life in express opposition to my wishes, and no child who disobeys its parents can succeed in life. However, if you come to harm, I am free of all responsibility."

"No evil can come from it, mother," said Perdita. "It can do only good to me and you and every one! I shall not want you to spend any

[1]   A temple ordinance according to which believing Mormons are "sealed" together forever as families through marriage.

more money on me for dress or anything else; and after I receive my first quarter's salary I will pay you for my board. I shall not be on your hands any more now that I am going to earn my own living; and surely that will be something to the good, mother."

"Earn your own living! the very phrase is a disgrace in the mouth of a young lady," said Mrs. Winstanley with a shudder. "You are not a servant-girl, Perdita, nor a shopwoman; yet you talk as if you were."

"Mother, do not be so vexed with me! I must have done something!" she pleaded. "I should have gone mad outright in the idleness and want of purpose in my life, unless I could have found something real to do."

"And why were you idle, pray?" asked her mother. "You could always have found occupation had you wished, and of a more refined and lady-like kind than that which you have chosen. I never encouraged any of you in idleness. Thomasina and I are always employed; you never see either of us with our hands before us doing nothing—why not have taken a lesson from your eldest sister?"

"I could not do what Thomasina does," answered Perdita. "Embroidering strips of silks for gowns and painting little frames for photographs are not real work nor real art to me. I could not have found my life in either of them, mother. I must have done something more serious."

"Is not this confessing yourself a distressingly undisciplined and unfeminine young lady?" asked her mother. "Why should not home, and all the quiet duties and pleasures of home, be sufficient for you as well as for your sisters?"

"We are not the same kind of girls, mother."

"No, my dear; and I am sorry for it," said Mrs. Winstanley significantly.

"You are an emancipated woman now, are you not, Per?" asked little Eva, opening her blue eyes.

"That depends on what you mean," said Perdita, with a flash in hers that betokened a certain stirring of the waters boding no good. "If you mean emancipated from prejudices that make us less than women, because we are ladies, I hope I am."

"Yes, that is just it," said Eva; "emancipated from being a lady any longer. You are not a lady now, Per, are you?"

"Perhaps not in your sense, Eva. I hope I am in my own," she answered.

"There can't be two ways," said Eva with curious gravity. "You are either a lady, or you are not. Mother and Ina and I are; if you are different, then you are not."

"Mother! say you do not condemn me," said unwise Perdita, turning abruptly from her sister and vainly struggling with fate.

"I cannot tell a falsehood, even to please a wayward child," her mother answered coldly.

"Now, Perdita, leave the thing alone," said Thomasina. "Be content to have your way unmolested, and do not ask mother to approve when you know how much she dislikes it all."

"I dare say you are right," said poor Perdita, the tears starting to her eyes; "but it is like living with people who are deaf and dumb to me and only talk among themselves. It is like a world of shadows or the dead!"

"You have made your life, Perdita," said her mother; "and you have only yourself and your exceeding wilfulness to thank for your isolation. Blame yourself, not us, and then we may hope for some improvement. Come, my dears," to the satisfactory two of her daughters, "it is time to dress for dinner. The dinner-bell has rung."

CHAPTER VIII.

HIS PROTÉGÉES.

ARE fairies and brownies still extant? Is Santa Claus a living personage no longer devoted only to the service of children but taking in grown people by the way? We know that once upon a time unseen beneficent beings helped on the lives of men without trouble and sometimes even without merit on the part of the recipients; and one day, not long after the visit to Armour Court, the old belief was pleasantly verified at No. 100, West Hill Gardens.

It was one of the best of our good English days. The sky was as blue as it is possible for a London sky ever to be, and the sun was shining with real living heat. If those who love nature and are doomed to cities regretted the turf and trees, the flowers and fields of the country, to the Londoner, *pur sang*,[1] such a day as this was worthy of all praise and sufficient for all pleasures, mutilated though its glory was by the thousand chimneys which represented hot milk and broiled bacon. It was a day which creates meetings abroad in the cooler hours and invites male friends to drop in during the warmer ones; which necessitates fresh gowns and dainty hats; which makes an improvised fête out of nothing

---

[1]   Pure-blooded.

more costly than a cup of tea at five, or a seat in a shady part of the Square garden. It was a day when even the prosaic feel that life is lovely and when the imaginative look for something to happen before nightfall; perhaps the prince, who is always on his way and never comes to hand, will really draw rein at the door to-day, or the golden shower which has been so long accumulating will fall at last! It was a day when young hearts palpitate with tremulous desires, young veins run quick with eager blood; and when even the old turn back to the scenes of their golden past and warm their chilly hands by the fires of memory.

And so, with brains astir and blood aglow, the great population of the metropolis began its daily doings.

Coming down to breakfast Mrs. Winstanley found on the table, side by side with the tea and toast, a neatly-arranged parcel bearing her name and address. Much to Eva's disgust she set it aside till prayers were over—and the chapter for the day was an extra long one. When she opened it she found it contained four smaller parcels, addressed to herself and her daughters—"each one, one." The girls had gathered round in excited surprise. What did it all mean? from whom had these little parcels come? and what was it that had come? they asked in a breath altogether. Mrs. Winstanley, smiling benignly, her graceful hands a trifle tardy, handed each parcel according to its superscription; and in a moment the room echoed with exclamations. Even discreet and self-controlled Thomasina broke out into interjections like the rest, and Perdita and Eva were like two showers of verbal fireworks. For to Thomasina had been sent the loveliest Etruscan patterned gold necklet; Eva had a charming little gold porte-bonheur; Mrs. Winstanley a cameo brooch. Perdita had no jewellery. Her present was a common washleather bag-purse, inside which was a crisp banknote for twenty pounds, and, "For expenses incurred," written in a clumsily feigned hand on the envelope.

Evidently elves and fairies were about, and the Winstanley family had set up its private brownie! Or—it was Mr. Brocklebank. His name came simultaneously to the lips of each; but Mrs. Winstanley, for once more politic than even Thomasina, put in her quiet demurrer and said:

"We are not sure, my dears. They may come from a great many other people. We have many friends to whom I am sure it would give much pleasure to make us their little offerings! Mr. Brocklebank is not our only friend."

"But I am sure it is Mr. Brocklebank!" said Eva. "It is just like his funny way of doing things."

"If I discover that it is really Mr. Brocklebank, I shall feel compelled to return the gift," said her mother, with warning gravity. "We could not possibly accept them, you understand, if we knew the donor."

"Oh, I dare say it was not him!" said Eva, ungrammatical and frightened. "He is too heavy and stupid to think of doing anything half so nice. We will not try to find out, mother. I am sure I would not part with my dear little porte-bonheur for all the world. Don't think it, mumsey; so don't try to find out."

She put her arms round her mother's neck and kissed her forehead. Mrs. Winstanley smiled and patted the blooming pretty little face that looked into hers with such coaxing irresistible sweetness, fresher and prettier than ever with the excitement of the moment.

"It is scarcely likely that we shall discover the donor," she said. "People who send presents anonymously do not wish to have it known, else they would have given them openly. Of course I cannot let such a thing as this pass without making some effort to find out who and why; but at the same time I cannot send round the bellman or advertise in the daily paper! I shall not make a silly fuss, in any way," she added smiling.

"But we may wear our things, mother, whether we know who sent them or not?" asked Eva, who had already clasped the bracelet round her wrist and was studying the engraved flowers and filigree volutes as diligently as if she could never be tired of such excellent lore.

"You may, because yours is a thing to wear every day; but Thomasina and I shall not," returned her mother, who found it hard at any time to refuse her youngest born.

"But, mother, I do not like to take this money," said Perdita, whose face was paler than usual with the excitement which had flushed Eva's face from brow to chin and made even quiet Thomasina almost sparkling and vivacious. "I wish you would have it, even if it is kept. It is far more than I shall ever want, and you would know how to use it."

"My dear Perdita, you have the right to your good fortune as well as we," said Mrs. Winstanley with unwonted kindness. "You will have to get a waterproof or an ulster[1] or some abomination of that kind if you go out in the morning; and you will want money for cabs on wet days; and then you must have luncheon; and your hat is disgraceful. Your absurd career is not to be all gain, you see, and the money will be extremely useful to you."

"But I would rather you had at least some of it, mother!" she insisted. "Give me five pounds and take the rest for yourself and the girls."

---

[1] A long loose overcoat.

"Keep it, my dear, and be thankful," answered Mrs. Winstanley. Her refusal was worthy of praise. In her chronic state of genteel indigence, any windfall was a godsend; and fifteen pounds would have done a good deal towards rubbing out a certain black line that rather troubled her rest and gave her bad dreams at night. But Mrs. Winstanley was not intentionally harsh to her unsatisfactory daughter. Perdita provoked and disappointed her, and so far justified her in her continual displeasure; but for all that she did not wish to be cruel or unjust and she was glad that the sun should shine on her as well as on the others, if it took nothing away from herself or those others. Perhaps, if sorely pressed, she might have to take a plum or two out of that unexpected cake; but for the moment she was magnanimous, and refused.

"What a worry you are, Per!" said Eva. "Why can't you be quiet over things?"

"It was kindly meant, my dear," said Mrs. Winstanley gently. "Perdita must not be blamed, poor child, when she means well."

Her democratic daughter was a nuisance, truly, in more ways than one; but gross injustice is bad breeding, and Mrs. Winstanley set her hopes of salvation on her good manners. Besides, *le plaisir fait le coeur si bon!*[1] and, elated as she was by what had happened, she could not find it in her heart to snub even objectionable Perdita for wanting to give her fifteen pounds out of a gift of twenty.

"Thank you, mother," said Perdita, penetrated by this unusual advocacy. To testify her gratitude she brusquely kissed the back of her mother's neck, whereby she startled her so that she nearly dropped Thomasina's necklet into the teapot, and gave her the "cold shivers" from head to foot.

"Don't do that, Perdita!" she said angrily. "You know I hate to be kissed like that!"

Poor clumsy Perdita! It was the old fable of the lap-dog and the donkey,[2] she thought bitterly. Eva's caress was returned and rewarded, hers was rejected and rebuked; yet hers was as true as her sister's, or perhaps worth more in the right estimate of values and would wear longer.

With this mistake however, the glory of the moment passed, and breakfast began—a little cloudily.

All that morning Eva was watchful and restless; running in and out the

---

[1]   (French), pleasure makes the heart so good.

[2]   Aesop's fable tells of a clumsy ass who, desiring to be loved by the master, breaks loose from his stable, enters the house, and causes much damage by trying to behave like the lapdog.

room, peering out of the window, excited if the door-bell rang and more than usually unable to settle down or do anything that was worth doing.

It was the heat, she said, when her mother mildly remonstrated with her. It was really so hot she could not sit still!

"Perpetual movement does not make people any cooler," said Mrs. Winstanley.

On which Eva laughed and said, "No, but it is less tiresome than sitting still."

At last a well-known lordly ring came to the bell, and a heavy step was heard in the hall. Eva rushed out of the dining-room, where she had taken up her last position, and met Mr. Brocklebank on the stairs.

"Don't say you gave us those things, you dear good Mr. Brocklebank!" she said in a caressing whisper, in her earnestness burying her soft little hand within the collar of his waist coat. It felt like a bird or a warm white mouse on the ironmaster's broad chest, and he held it imprisoned by his own as if it were something that would flutter or run away. "Mother will make us give them all back if she knows where they come from. I say it's you, because I know what a dear good generous darling you are; but you must not confess you know. It would break my heart to part with my porte-bonheur," kissing it.

"Very well, my dear. The fairy queen and I will have our little secret together," he answered, pleased, caressed, flattered. "I will not affirm that it was I, because perhaps it was not, you know," winking his small eyes waggishly.

"Have I to thank you for some most beautiful and unexpected presents which came to us all to-day?" asked Mrs. Winstanley, after the formal greetings were over and the ironmaster had settled himself comfortably in the one easy chair that he affected, prepared for a comfortable session of any imaginable length.

"Mrs. Winstanley has not to thank me at all for anything," he answered.

"Whoever sent these things," said Mrs. Winstanley, laying her hand on the open cases which she had placed near her on the table, "was wonderfully clear-sighted as well as kind. But of course I could not keep them if I knew to whom to return them! They are lovely presents—a splendid surprise altogether, giving each of us what is most useful and what we most desired. Still, it would not do to keep them, you know, if we found out where to return them."

"My advice to Mrs. Winstanley is not to inquire and not to discover," said Mr. Brocklebank. "A fairy was the culprit. He arrived before cock-crow this morning and brought these trifles with him—effected an entrance through the key-hole. Fairies are the most useful creatures in the world and save us poor mortals no end of trouble."

He laughed as he said this as at the best joke made for centuries.

"I fear our fairy was rather too substantial to pass through the key-hole with or without a parcel in his pocket," said Mrs. Winstanley pleasantly; and Thomasina, raising her fine eyes, smiled with the most consummate grace she had—the loveliest elegance of muscular movement at command.

"It would be pleasant to thank if not to return," she said, looking at him with a whole volume of thanks in her face.

"The gratification of the recipient is the reward of the donor," said Mr. Brocklebank. "Besides, no one merits thanks. When fairies convey little offerings anonymously, it is because they do not require acknowledgment, only acceptance. My advice to Mrs. Winstanley and her young ladies, is to take the goods the gods provide and say no more about it. And now what are these fairy gifts? May I be allowed to inspect them?"

"Willingly," said Mrs. Winstanley, placing the cases in his hand.

Eva crept up to him confidentially, and held out her arm saying: "Mine's here. I'm wearing mine, and will never part with it, night or day!"

Mr. Brocklebank looked enchanted.

"A most excellent selection," he said; "evidently a fairy who was well acquainted with this charming family! A necklet for our young Princess—they say like the necklet Nasiker wore when she washed the family linen in the running brook; a porte-bonheur, conducing to happiness, for the rosebud who is born for happiness; money in a useful purse for the practical worker of the family; and the head of Juno in a brooch for the mother of all. I think the selection admirable whoever may be accountable for it."

"It was most judiciously done—charmingly comprehensive reading," said Mrs. Winstanley. "And really as an act of gratitude I will take your advice, Mr. Brocklebank, and not try to find out to whom we are indebted for so much pleasure. We will waft our thanks through the air and perhaps they will reach the right quarter."

"Mrs. Winstanley is the soul of wisdom and discretion," he answered; and with this the discussion ended.

"And where is Miss Perdita, my good young protégée?" he presently asked. "I consider Miss Perdita quite my charge and shall always take a lively interest in her career."

"You are very kind," said Mrs. Winstanley; but the ring of cordiality was lost and her thanks were artificial and glacial.

Unquestionably he was very kind and it had been very nice in him to make them these handsome presents; but all the same it was excessively annoying that he should uphold Perdita as he did and force her mother's consent, like a conjuror's card thrust on her to be played out when required.

"And you are now reconciled to our decision?" continued Mr. Brocklebank, with the confident air of one who has just bought her answer.

"I have yielded to you with pleasure," answered Mrs. Winstanley.

Her visitor rubbed his hands and jingled his chain.

"Good! good!" he said.

Mrs. Winstanley looked annoyed.

"Naturally such a total change in our *manière d'être* cannot be accepted *tête baissée*," [1] she said, with a little drawl. "It is so different from anything that we have been used to, and of course it has been painful. You can understand that? My daughter must leave home early, I suppose, when she does begin, and come home late; she must go in all weathers; and the very fact of her thus going out early every day, no matter what the weather or the season, will make the neighbours talk and wonder. They will think she is a governess or something horrid like that!" said Mrs. Winstanley, caste irritation carrying it over gratitude and tact.

"They will think then, that she is wise and honourable enough to work for her living," returned Mr. Brocklebank with a certain masterful emphasis which was at once a warning and a rebuke.

He spoke as if the whole affair and the family too, belonged to him, and that he had the right to be annoyed if they dissented when he dictated.

"Yes; of course that is the best way of looking at it," said Mrs. Winstanley, covering her mistake. "I was speaking from the outside only. Among ourselves we judge differently."

"I am glad to hear such sentiments," said Mr. Brocklebank, dropping his stiffer manner for that more familiar which was becoming natural to him when with the Winstanleys. He was satisfied with his triumphs and her civility. The fish had put up its head and been knocked back into the frying-pan again; strength had conquered and weakness had yielded; and so far things were well. But Mrs. Winstanley did not relish the process. She did not like to feel the master's hand upon her. Her only consolation was in her secret resolve to make that master pay heavily for his privileges, and to take care that, if she had to simmer in the frying-pan it should be in one of gold and with a sufficiency of lubricating oil.

"And now, where is Miss Perdita?" the ironmaster asked again.

---

[1] (French), way of being, with lowered head.

"Call your sister, my dear," Mrs. Winstanley said for answer, turning to Eva. "Tell her that Mr. Brocklebank is here and wishes to see her."

"If convenient I should prefer to visit her in her own apartment," said Mr. Brocklebank, rising. "I should like to come upon her unawares, as I call it, and see what she is doing when she is at home. Miss Perdita's occupations must be interesting!"

"She is in the morning-room," said Mrs. Winstanley, doing her best to conceal her trouble, for that morning-room was woefully shabby, and the sun was so cruelly bright to-day. "Let me send for her!"

"With gracious permission of the authorities I would rather go to her unannounced," said Mr. Brocklebank, making a few steps towards the door. "I am fond of surprising young ladies in their studies; little birds in a nest found by chance."

He laughed. He was always the one appreciative listener to his own good things.

How to refuse a man who has just been spending sixty or seventy pounds on you? the thing is impossible! A man who would rather die than sell his conscience must of necessity take a bribe for innocent complaisance; and Mr. Brocklebank had bribed Mrs. Winstanley pretty heavily.

"Eva, my dear, take Mr. Brocklebank to your sister," she said, without changing a muscle.

And Mr. Brocklebank, with a kindly recollection of the soft warm little hand that had nestled under the collar of his waistcoat like a bird or a mouse, went down the stairs with the little rosebud, and thought as he went: "Am I too old? A child-wife like this—the prettiest little plaything in the world!"

But this other, this studious, thoughtful Perdita—she was no pretty plaything wherewith to amuse a man's idle hours—no child-wife to be dandled and caressed as not so long ago she dandled and caressed her own doll—no waxen-natured creature to be treated with all imaginable tenderness because too soft to bear the rasping of reality, too simple to understand the tragic complexity of life and how the sweetest songs of men are indeed those which tell of saddest thought! She had nothing in her of the eastern odalisque doubled with Manon Lescaut[1] which made the charm of little Eva—and the danger. Perdita was essentially a man's companion, friend, and lover: his companion by virtue of her intelligence; his friend because she understood the duties of his civic

---

[1] Lighthearted prostitute, heroine of the novel *Manon Lescaut* (1731) by l'Abbé Prévost (1697–1763).

life and the need of civic virtues; and his lover by that quality of passionate intensity, of whole-hearted self-surrender which makes the loving
woman's highest happiness and purest glory.

She started up when Mr. Brocklebank came in piloted by Eva, and
looked at him with genuine warmth. She was the most sincerely grateful of all; perhaps the only one who was sincerely grateful at all. Delight
in receiving pleasure is not gratitude; and her mother and sisters had
nothing deeper nor truer than personal delight from receiving personal
pleasure. But Perdita, whose nature was more sincere and her feelings
ever at fever-heat, was touched to her heart; and, if she had been asked,
would have said that she loved Mr. Brocklebank for his kindness. It was
not because she had been gratified, but because he was good that she
looked into his face so lovingly and grasped his hand so warmly; and it
was this because which made all the difference.

"Always studious!" said the ironmaster, still with the air of one to
whom the whole family belonged, and who was in his right to be
charmed at the well-doing of this and displeased at the failure of that.
"Miss Perdita sets us all an example! What says the rosebud of this establishment?" turning with heavy playfulness to pretty little Eva.

"Yes, she does," answered the rosebud demurely.

If it made part of the ironmaster's manner to patronize that funny old
Per, she would not run the risk of his disfavour by telling him her own
opinion. So far as she thought of things, if Perdita was an example, it was
one to avoid with all the care imaginable, certainly not one to follow.

"You are very kind," said Perdita, her soft, shortsighted eyes suffused
with tenderness. "You are one of the kindest men in the world, Mr.
Brocklebank!" she added warmly. "Every one must love and respect you."

The ironmaster's heavy face brightened like a girl's. Like most
honest-hearted men he was densely obtuse about respectable women
and no more difficult to deceive, when social conditions were safe, than
is a rustic by a conjuror. Well-born adventuresses were creatures of
whom he could not take stock and he always maintained that Becky
Sharp[1] was a libel. Had Perdita been even as artful as she was sincere,
her voice and eyes would have touched him; being what she was,
absolutely earnest and truthful, she sent a glow through his heart which
made him long to take her in his arms and let her feel how she had
made it beat.

---

[1] Adventuress heroine of the novel *Vanity Fair* (1847–48) by William Makepeace Thackeray
(1811–63).

"Whatever little kindness I may have been enabled to manifest to Miss Perdita, has been more than repaid by her own valuable use thereof," he said clumsily.

"I should be the most ungrateful girl in the world if I did not do all I could to please you," she answered.

"Oh, you two horrid spoons!" thought Eva, to whom these courtesies were somewhat mysterious. "I'll tell Ina what a snake this old Perdita is! What a shame of her trying to cut out poor Ina. Only it serves her right."

"And what are these formidable-looking tomes about?" asked Mr. Brocklebank, taking up one of the books on the table. "Preparatory to our examination?"

"Yes," she answered with a smile.

"No danger of our Miss Perdita losing her chance! Our Minerva will not have a feather plucked from her plume!" he said with a curious mingling of ideas and images.

"Oh, I should be sorry indeed to be plucked," said Perdita; "it would break my heart. I should kill myself for shame!"

"No, you would do nothing of the kind," said Mr. Brocklebank, laying his broad hand on her shoulder. "You should come to me and say, 'Forgive me!' and I would forgive you; and you would add, 'Help me,' and I would help you. That would be a wiser kind of thing to do than taking a header off Westminster Bridge and being fished out by a Humane Society's drag!"

She laughed to make believe that tears were not in her eyes.

"I do not think I shall fail; so I shall not have to be fished out of the Thames," she said lightly. "Only, if I did, I could not bear it!" she added in her more usual manner of grave intensity.

"Trust in your friend Benjamin Brocklebank," he said. "Whenever you commence to feel discouraged come to me and I will put things square for you. And now I must wish Miss Perdita good-morning. I must not intrude longer on these sacred studies; and our rosebud here is out of place among these learned lucubrations."

"What a pedantic old goose he is!" thought Eva, smiling in her sweetest way. "And what a horrid old flirt! He makes love to us all in turn, and pretends to like first one and then the other! I am sure I wish he would leave me alone!" she said as the final word of her soliloquy, while laying her dimpled hand on his arm as they went back up the stairs; saying aloud in her most caressing voice:

"You are too awfully good to us, Mr. Brocklebank; I don't know what we should do without you. And we are all so fond of you, you can't think!"

A minute after she repented of her enthusiasm. They had not fairly seated themselves again in the drawing-room, where Mr. Brocklebank devoted himself to Thomasina and Thomasina accepted his devotion with regal affability, and trotted out all her prettiest little battle-horses for his benefit, when the tramping feet of men came up the stairs, and the page-boy ushered in "Sir James Kearney and Mr. Strangways," the first visit which the former had paid at the house.

A thunder-cloud settled on Mr. Brocklebank's face; the dark eyes of Sir James flashed. The dislike between the two men was shown as plainly as is possible in a society which prides itself on its waxen surface and suffers neither the enthusiasm of love nor the bitterness of hate. Mrs. Winstanley, who had never yet met with the circumstance that was stronger than her own tact, received the young baronet with the cleverest ignoring of all kinds of cross purposes. Hubert Strangways was a neutral and did not count. It was known that he was engaged to Maud Disney, consequently he was harmless; but Sir James was a trespasser on ground which Mr. Brocklebank had began to think his own private preserve, and there were evidently old griefs between them which made matters yet more difficult to arrange. Still, Mrs. Winstanley was equal to the task; and by her consummate tact kept the two antagonistic elements apart, so that no explosion was possible, at least for the moment. She herself engaged Sir James, and let Hubert "spoon" little Eva; while Thomasina, always smiling, always trotting out her battle-horses, offered subtle incense to the wealthy ironmaster and kept him so far soothed and in good humour.

But the charm of the day had gone for him. Where he could not be all he did not care to be a part; and after he had wandered about the room a good deal more than was polite; examined things as if they belonged to him; asked questions with intentional familiarity; spoken with a certain abruptness and *sans façon*,[1] as if he had the right to do here as he liked—his elephantine courtesy laid aside as a man lays aside his orders when at home—he took up his hat and prepared to depart. But before he went he drew Mrs. Winstanley aside and said to her in a stage whisper, which Sir James was too much occupied with Eva to hear:

"I advise you not to cultivate the acquaintance of that young man, Mrs. Winstanley. I know something about him; and what I know I do not like."

"Something to his discredit?" asked Mrs. Winstanley quite simply.

---

[1] (French), without formality.

"Nothing, perhaps, that would bring him to the Old Bailey," he said coarsely; "but something that certainly does not redound to his credit."

"Have you cautioned your sister?" asked Mrs. Winstanley with admirable simplicity. "We met him first at Mrs. Merton's house, and naturally your sister," smiling in the most delightful way, "is a paragon among us and one whose lead may be followed without doubt or question."

"My sister is as good a soul as ever breathed," answered Mr. Brocklebank; "but infernally obstinate whenever she has commenced to take a thing into her head. I have warned her against this young coxcomb, but to no purpose. She will retain his acquaintance in spite of all I can say or do; and I am powerless. I am sure I shall not have to repeat my warning twice here," he added with meaning. "Mrs. Winstanley is too wise a mother not to be careful to whom she allows the privilege of her charming daughters' acquaintance; and one word from as staunch a friend as I am is as good as twenty."

"Thanks, very much, yes," said Mrs. Winstanley, giving his large hand a friendly pressure, and thinking his caution the most unpardonable liberty that had ever been taken with her.

As Mr. Brocklebank turned from the room, Sir James laughed.

"Where did you pick him up?" he asked contemptuously. "How on earth can you have such a confounded bore as that about you! You are Samaritans, I must say!"

"We know Mrs. Merton," said Mrs. Winstanley quietly; "and she is charming. She is a friend of yours, is she not, Sir James? Yes, I remember now—we met you at her reception last week."

"Yes, Mrs. Merton is a great friend of mine," he answered; "and she is really very nice; but she is a widow, and not compromised by any masculine impossibility. But this animal is so offensive with his formality on the one side and his impudence on the other!—and then his common sense is worse than all. I hate common sense!—don't you?" vaguely, but intended for Eva.

"It is prosaic; but we want a little of it surely as ballast," said Mrs. Winstanley.

"A little would go a long way with me!" answered Sir James. "Your fellows who count the vibrations of a musical note and can tell you how a sunset is made, they ought to be shot! I consider them blasphemous and the destroyers of poetry and beauty."

"I did not know that Mr. Brocklebank was scientific; I thought him only commercial," said Mrs. Winstanley; "and commercial men are bound to be prosaic, don't you see? else things would go badly with them."

"Commerce is an odious thing, and I agree with Lord John Manners,"[1] said Sir James. "These bagmen and fellows who dabble in business are of a different race from others. I wonder if they have souls? If they have, and go to heaven with the rest of us, I know I shall petition for a snug corner out of their way."

"Fie! fie!" said Mrs. Winstanley who, like all well-bred persons was religious and held the proper patronage of things spiritual part of the duty as well as one of the privileges of her order; "no jesting with sacred subjects here."

"Is Mr. Brocklebank a sacred subject with you?" asked the young baronet defiantly.

"No," she answered gravely; "but the future condition of your soul is."

"Thank you, Mrs. Winstanley; I deserved that rebuke," said Sir James. "And of course it was awfully rude of me to speak against a man met in your house; but the fact is I don't like him and he does not like me, and we are like oil and vinegar when we meet."

"And which is the oil?" asked little Eva prettily; "for I am sure you both looked like vinegar just now!"

At which they all laughed as at the very essence and last perfection of humour, and Hubert Strangways forgot that such a person as Maud Disney was in existence, while Sir James thought this pretty little girl the very flower of humanity as he repeated mentally: "Brains and Beauty—no versus this time! The whole thing perfect all round!"

CHAPTER IX.

BETWEEN TWO FIRES.

THERE are many unpleasantnesses in life; and the mutual coolness of common acquaintances is one of them. But when it comes to the declared animosity of two friends, from each of whom you hope to receive benefits but neither of whom can tolerate the presence of the other, the narrow pass is difficult; and how to steer clear between the

---

[1] "Let wealth and commerce, laws and learning die, / But leave us still our old nobility" from *England's Trust* by Lord John Manners (1814–77).

threatening rocks taxes the cleverness of even the most consummate mistress in the art of conciliation and tact.

Mrs. Winstanley was in the very heart of this narrow pass and scarcely knew which way to turn. Mr. Brocklebank was useful now and of illimitable prospective advantage; and it would be suicidal folly to offend him. She had proved her appreciation of this by the sacrifice which she had made of her most cherished prejudices in the matter of Perdita; but there were limits; and, still more, there were comparative values. Sir James Kearney had evidently taken to them all, and was especially attracted by Eva; Lady Kearney was a woman after Mrs. Winstanley's own heart—the perfected masterpiece of the type whereof she herself was only a smaller copy, and her social recognition carried a stamp that gave value to any person on whom it was bestowed. Hence the prospective advantages to be got out of this connection were as great as that hoped for from Mr. Brocklebank.

Yet how to keep these two discordant elements together while not allowing them to clash and explode? The one denounced the other for some mysterious evil that rendered him unfit to be received into the family of which it was hoped he himself would become a member; and the other seemed to think it debasing to his dignity to meet in the same room a man of whom it was in Mrs. Winstanley's secret designs that he should one day have to say: "My wife's brother-in-law!" Between the two what was to be done?

"What a nuisance all these social enmities are! Why cannot people take their dislikes as discreetly as their debts, and refrain as scrupulously from taking the world into their confidence on the one as on the other? All these strained situations and strong emotions are so horribly ill-bred;—and they are quite unnecessary! The world is large enough for us all to move in freely and without uncomfortable jostling. This kind of tyrannous objection to such and such individuals belongs to a bygone state of society," said Mrs. Winstanley, with admirable liberality.

"We must keep them apart as much as possible," said Thomasina, at all times her mother's confidante and adviser. "The Kearneys would be nice people to know and it seems a pity to give them up simply to please Mr. Brocklebank. If we knew what his objection to Sir James really was, that would be different; but these vague accusations tell us nothing."

"But if we find out, we must, I suppose, throw over one," said her mother anxiously. "Which would you recommend, Thomasina?"

"Mr. Brocklebank is the more solid friend; the Kearneys are the more brilliant acquaintances," she answered. "Mr. Brocklebank would do things for us and help us in a dozen practical ways; but of course if we could make anything like a friendship with Lady Kearney, I should recommend keeping to her. If we cannot, then Mr. Brocklebank."

"You have a great deal of good sense, my dear," said Mrs. Winstanley. "I do not know what I shall do, Thomasina, when you leave me."

"You will have one occasion the less for the exercise of wisdom, my poor mother," said her daughter kindly. "When Eva and I are off your hands, you will do very well with Perdita."

"She is the least congenial to me of all my children," Mrs. Winstanley answered, as if she were telling a piece of news.

"Yes; now; because she does nothing to help on the fortunes of the family, but on the contrary goes directly against our interests," said Thomasina. "But she has a good heart and a fine nature; only she has spoilt herself by encouraging those foolish opinions of hers and by her unlady-like indifference to appearances. With her brains, if she had chosen to go in for social wit and cleverness, she might have made her mark as distinctly as both Eva and I have made ours; and without interfering with us."

"And that is just why I do not get on with her," sighed Perdita's mother. "It is both so silly and so unladylike to think as she does! A child of mine a democrat!—disloyal to the queen and royal family!—talking of equality and the rights of man!—it is really enough to make one's hair turn grey, Thomasina!"

"Yes, dear mother, so it is. I feel with you and for you; but when you are left alone with her and do not care for society any more, none of these annoyances will tell; and her good heart and affectionateness will come to the front."

"You are very sweet to say all this in excuse of your unfortunate sister," said Mrs. Winstanley; "but even your kind advocacy cannot reconcile me to Perdita's vagaries or make me feel her anything but a disaster to the family."

"Poor mother!" said Thomasina sympathetically; and the conversation dropped.

It had done its work and just a little checked Mrs. Winstanley's rapidly increasing displeasure with the ugly duckling of her brood. That displeasure would be impolitic if suffered to become too visible; and Thomasina a little wondered that her mother did not see the mistake she was making. It was desirable above all things, in this matter of Perdita, to please Mr. Brocklebank, their most valuable friend. Their first step towards the coveted region of sufficiency would be to get him as a husband for any one of them, no matter which. Thomasina was prepared to marry him next week should he ask her; prepared also to hand him over to Perdita without a pang should he prefer her instead; or to urge on Eva the necessity of swallowing that heavy gilded pill should it be offered for her acceptance. She would be sorry for Eva, certainly, if this were her fate. Dainty, pretty, fairy-like Eva deserved something better; but Thomasina was not a gambler by nature and thought realization, when you can, better than holding on for better chances.

Her one passion ran parallel with her mother's—the rescue of the family from the slough of debt and impecuniosity into which it was plunged; and to this all personal considerations and affections were subordinate. As then Mr. Brocklebank so evidently favoured their democrat—and as he was the family trump-card for the present—it was not wise in mother to gird so continually at poor Perdita. And after all, though the girl was dreadfully tiresome, she was not intentionally bad, and, if judiciously handled, might be made something of.

The passionlessness of Thomasina's character had this good result—it left her reason absolutely free and unclouded; and a just mind sometimes supplements a cold heart.

Others, beside Mrs. Winstanley, stood between two fires in this matter of Sir James Kearney's sudden amity for the deceased major's family, and his desire to see whether the inside corresponded with the envelope or no—and specially whether pretty little Eva were a real bit of luscious fruitage or only a Dead Sea apple with a rosy skin and ashes for pulp. Lady Kearney was one; Mrs. Merton was another; but Sir James, who was still essentially a spoilt boy, had pretty much his own way with both. He generally ended by making his mother do as he wished, after a wrangle, and Mrs. Merton had long abandoned the habit of saying No to his Yes. His double object now was to get his mother to call on the Winstanleys and to induce Mrs. Merton to invite them to her house continually, so that he might meet them there as often as he liked. The former was a tough piece of work—a thing requiring all the resources of temper and diplomacy, will and cajolery possessed by the young fellow; but the latter was as easy as giving a command couched as a request.

"I wish you would, carina!" he said, after he had stated his desire; and in saying this he took Clarissa's plump white hand and kissed it.

"You are just a spoilt boy," answered Mrs. Merton, smiling and passing the tips of her fingers lightly over his hair. "If I were not the best-natured woman in the world, I should say No; and indeed, perhaps I ought. Lady Kearney dislikes me quite bitterly enough as it is—I who am so perfectly harmless!—what will she say when I am the medium between you and positive danger, and let you meet that silly little penniless beauty at my house only to fall deeper and deeper into her net!"

"What rubbish, Cara!" said Sir James petulantly. "As if a fellow cannot admire a pretty girl and like to be in her society without being in love! Don't you know I never intend to fall in love again? I gave my heart to you two years ago and you have it in possession still."

"My nine points?[1] Rather shaky ones, I fear," said Mrs. Merton with a sudden blush and an embarrassed laugh.

Sir James laughed too, and his fair friend's embarrassment found an echo in his own. But both agreed to ignore the little difficulty, whatever it might be, conjured up between them; and with a light "Firm as the foundations of the earth!" the young man glided off that slippery bit of ground and hurried away to something firmer than the widow's possession of his heart.

Before he left he had arranged a great many things; one was, that he would go to the opera to-morrow night, where he should find Mrs. Merton and the two Winstanley girls in one of the boxes on the pit tier; another, that Cara would go to the theatre to-night with him. He had a box, and he would not ask his mother but would take her instead, if she would go; and after the amicable settlement of this point, he went back on that totally unjust adjective of "shaky" and made her confess that her possession was absolute and would never be destroyed. For no man knew better than Sir James how to make a woman, whom he had once loved and who still loved him, assist in the establishment of her rival by assuring her that he was still her dutiful slave, while only the artistic admirer of the mere drawing and colouring of that other—by swearing that if strange shadows might have sometimes flitted across his mind they were only shadows, while she was the substance—phantoms while she was the reality. Who so credulous as a loving woman? who so complaisant as one who desires to keep and dares not inquire? Jealousy belongs only to a second-rate kind of passion; self-abnegation goes a step higher.

So Sir James thought when he said to himself: "Wonderful creatures, these women!" thinking how odd it all had been; how odd it all was—and what was to be the end?

Clarissa Merton might be soft-hearted and complying, but Lady Kearney was of tougher material. The one a Mature Siren, with a decided weakness for the young fellow, thirteen years her junior, who at one time had had as decided a weakness for her, made herself the

---

[1] Possession is nine points of the law (familiar saying).

good-natured Mentor to her reckless young Telemachus, and undertook to be his chaperon with the Calypso[1] whose fascinations were to obscure her own. But the mother was not so easily won.

When her son expressed his wish to her, as he had done to Clarissa, that she should call on Mrs. Winstanley and invite them to her house, she answered back in plain terms: No. She would not think of doing such a thing, she said. She did not want to know them, would not know them, positively refused their association; and then she asked, with all the scorn of her order discussing the demerits of social mud, "Who on earth are these Winstanleys that I should visit them! They are not in my set; and I neither know anything about them, nor wish to know."

"They are ladies, mother," said Sir James, keeping his irritation well in hand. "Mrs. Winstanley's father was the bishop of —, her husband a major in the Artillery. You cannot find any flaw here!"

"But I do not find it necessary to make the acquaintance of all the bishops' daughters and majors' widows whom I may meet in society," returned Lady Kearney. "Your Winstanley people must have better vouchers than this bald statement of pedigree and alliance before I should feel myself justified in visiting them."

"They have the vouchers of perfect breeding and flawless character," said Sir James warmly.

"Your informant?"

"Mrs. Merton knows them; so does her brother," he answered boldly.

Lady Kearney curled her disdainful lips into an exasperating expression of contempt and doubt.

"Your friends' social sponsors are not much in my way," she said coldly. "As I decline to know Mrs. Merton and look on Mr. Brocklebank as a horror, I am scarcely disposed to take these Winstanleys on their recommendation, or at their valuation. Doubtless the daughter of a bishop and the widow of a major are *de la haute volée*[2] to them. All things go by comparisons."

"You are not just, mother," said her son.

"And you are eminently unwise, my dear," she replied. "Your democratic tendencies are most regrettable. You seem to me to have no proper views of the obligations imposed on you by your station. You are ready

---

[1]   Telemachus was the son of Odysseus; Mentor was his tutor. Athena (goddess of wisdom) often took the form of Mentor to appear to Telemachus or Odysseus. Calypso was a nymph who lured Odysseus to her island.

[2]   (French), high flyers.

to make friends with any and every one who suits your fancy. It is lamentable: and, with your stake in the country, it is a social crime."

"You make too much of a very small matter, mother," said Sir James. "I do not see what democracy or my stake in the country has to do with our knowing three very charming women, who are ladies—who know friends of our own—and against whom no one has a word to say. If you do not think either Mrs. Merton or Mr. Brocklebank good enough for you as social sponsors, as you call it, there are the Disneys: and surely they ought to satisfy you! The Winstanleys visit them."

"Certainly the Disneys are rather more satisfactory than your tradesman's widow, or her brother the manufacturer," replied Lady Kearney. "Before committing myself, however, I should like to know how much they know of these people in whom you are so profoundly interested, and where they became acquainted with them. Even people as careful as the Disneys are sometimes led into indiscretions; and acquaintances formed at seaside places, or on the Continent, where you are thrown together more than in ordinary London life, may not be desirable though not easy to avoid and still harder to shake off. Doubtful people, who have an object in being patronized by the safer kind, stick like burrs; and not every one has tact or courage enough to get rid of them. Do you know where and how the Disneys know these Winstanleys?" she asked disagreeably.

"No," answered Sir James shortly.

He was getting angry. His mother was cruel and unjust, he thought; and, spoilt as he had been by over-indulgence—emphatically a mother's son from his earliest years—pampered and given way to and made to feel himself the centre of the whole domestic system, he was indignant at her refusing his request, which was essentially disobeying his command.

But Lady Kearney was in a singularly obdurate mood to-day. She would sacrifice herself for any whim whatever of her son's, she thought; but when it came to sacrificing his own best interests to his whims—then things were different and it was her duty to stand out.

"Tell me something about these strange people?" she went on to say, speaking of them as if they had been red ants or black beetles—curious creatures with whose habits she was unacquainted and whose existence was distasteful to her. "Mrs. Winstanley was the daughter of a bishop, you say?"

"Yes," said Sir James, carefully examining the carving of an ivory papercutter, which he remembered ever since he could remember anything.

"Bishops are sometimes men of very queer social antecedents," she returned. "A butcher's clever son may rise to be a bishop, if his father can afford to send him to college in the first instance. But the lawn[1] sleeves would not quite cover the blue apron in my estimation; and I should scarcely care to make his acquaintance. He would always betray the butcher's shop to me! And the major—this famous major, who was he? He might have risen from the ranks, you know! What is his family?"

"About as good as our own, I fancy!" said Sir James with insolent carelessness. "And he did not rise from the ranks."

"I dare say you know nothing about it, James, and speak as you wish, not as you know. At all events, I dislike a family of women without a father or brother or responsible man among them. They are scarcely respectable. Surely Mrs. Winstanley has some brother, or something, who would take his position as head of the family and give a certain solidity and respectability to them all!"

"Have you the recipe for conjuring up male relations in your pocket, mother? I never knew till now that it was disreputable for a woman to be a widow or for girls to be fatherless."

"You are impertinent, James."

"No, mother, it is you who are strangely unjust to a family of perfectly inoffensive people against whom you have set yourself without the shadow of a reason. I have never seen you so cruel, so unlike yourself! You refuse to know them simply because I wish it."

"Perhaps so," said Lady Kearney, lifting up her eyes with a sudden flash of indignation and suspicion. "If you were not so extraordinarily eager on your own account I might have yielded to your wish without a second thought. But I confess I do not like to see this odd heat and insistence from you. I know the world better than you do, and I know what widows with marriageable daughters hanging on hand are capable of."

"Have your own way," answered her son, rising from the sofa on which he had been sitting. "Of course I cannot force you to receive them, but I shall go my own course all the same."

He walked away to the door. His hand on the lock, he turned back.

"I shall not dine at home to-night," he said.

"No? where do you dine?" she asked, more authoritatively than was wise, considering the cross-lying of their present relations.

"With a friend," he answered; and again turned away.

"A rather meagre reply," said Lady Kearney, pulling down her lips.

"As my wishes have so little interest for you, I do not suppose my actions have more," he said; and with this he opened the door and

---

[1]   A fine sheer linen or cotton fabric.

passed through, more deeply offended with his mother than he had been since he came to manhood and the baronetcy.

It was the first serious contest between them; and according to the laws of human nature novelty had a double power—its own and that belonging to the circumstance. Also, her opposition only strengthened his resolve.

Here then was a curiously composite cauldron at boiling-point, of which the Winstanleys were the innocent thorns crackling beneath the pot! Sir James and Mr. Brocklebank—Sir James and Mrs. Merton—Sir James and his mother—to which might perhaps be added Hubert Strangways and Maud Disney—all these worthy people in a state of "molecular disturbance," because Thomasina had style and a perfect smile, and Eva's blush-rose face took the heart out of men and made the wise like unto fools! So it has been ever since the sons of God lost their heaven for woman's eyes; and so it will be till the end of time— or the beginning of the Emancipated Woman's supremacy.

In this contest with his mother, Sir James came off eventually the victor. He made life so hard and himself so disagreeable to her that she was forced to reconsider her position and ask herself whether it would not be the better policy to yield rather than stand out. He morally starved her into capitulation. He was rarely at home; and when he was, he shut himself up from her as entirely as if they had been mere strangers living on terms of politeness which excluded confidence. He dined out every night and would not tell her where he went; he received a great many notes—evidently from ladies—and he displayed them a little ostentatiously; but said only "a friend of mine" when she asked who was the writer? and "business" when she asked what were they about? He kept his thin lips compressed into a line which hid all the red as well as barred in all the words; and affected to consider their whole lives from hence- forth based on two parallel lines which ran side by side but never met. He made the poor woman profoundly miserable and himself perfectly odious; and in a quiet, silent, negative way he gave her to understand that unless she relented he would not change, and that without the introduc- tion of the Winstanleys there would be no peace at home.

Then came the inevitable result—the policy of ill-temper triumphed, and the mother gave way. His will was the more arbitrary of the two, his temper the more tenacious; and he was the younger and more easily amused. He could live without his mother more pleasantly than she could live without him; and their rupture cost him infinitely less than it cost her. He had his club, his friends, the Winstanleys themselves and Mrs.

Merton; while she had lost the very lamp of her life, the very idol of her temple in losing him; and she found it impossible either to endure or to replace. For twenty-six years now he had been the centre of her whole existence, the sun of her fondest worship; and this eclipse was unendurable. But though she gave way, it was not in her to do so gracefully. She had more temper than tact and more weakness than compliance. In this Mrs. Winstanley, whom she despised, might have given her a lesson; and the daughters, whom she dreaded, were her mistresses in wisdom.

"Things cannot go on like this, James," she said abruptly to her son, one morning after breakfast. "If you choose to make your duty and affection to me, your mother, dependent on my recognizing these undesirable friends of yours, I must give way; that is all! It is a hard necessity, but you impose it on me; and anything is better than the life we have been leading of late."

"So I think, mother," was his answer made with animation, his handsome face kindling and his dark eyes sparkling. "I have set my heart on your receiving the Winstanleys and nothing else will satisfy me."

"You are a very undutiful, ill-tempered boy," said Lady Kearney peevishly. "Extremely undutiful! You know how much I dislike what I am doing, and you simply force me, to keep peace between us."

"Never mind, mother! You are doing what you dislike now, but you will get to like them afterwards, as every one does. They are the most charming people I have ever seen. Even your fastidious taste will find nothing to condemn in them."

"I think you are bewitched!" said Lady Kearney, by no means letting her imagination take light at her son's enthusiastic fires; "and I am afraid I am doing very wrong to countenance the acquaintance."

"Which would go on without your countenance quite as much as with it," said Sir James hotly.

"Then I do not see the necessity for my going," said his mother.

"Please yourself, mother," was his ungracious reply.

"What an uncomfortable, unpleasant creature you are now, James!" she said crossly. "When I am sacrificing myself to please you, you have no better thanks for me than this cool impertinence."

"Now, mother, let us drop the subject," he returned with sudden sternness. "If you choose to call on the Winstanleys and ask them here, you will give me great pleasure and I shall take it as a personal kindness; if you do not, go your own way. But in that case things will never be different between us from what they are now; and I shall certainly not rank my mother as my best friend."

Tears came into her eyes.

"Oh, you men, you cruel, cold-hearted, selfish men!" she said passionately. "From our cradles to our graves we women have to be your slaves, and even our sons, whom we have only loved too much, will turn against us for the first pretty face they see! I wonder why God made you all such horrors—such monsters!"

"Are you better after this?" asked her son coolly.

Then he went up to her and kissed her.

"How can you be so foolish, mother, as to make such a mountain out of such a molehill!" he said. "One would think I had asked you to invite Jack Ketch or Old Nick."

"I would almost as soon!" said Lady Kearney hysterically.

CHAPTER X.

"OUR GENIUS."

YIELDING against her better judgment, Lady Kearney was yet not wise enough to make the best of her position and to accept frankly the acquaintance which she had not had strength to refuse. Though she had been morally starved into surrender, she would not haul down her flag as the conquered should, but kept it sullenly flying in defiance of all the rules of war and dictates of common sense. She would go to the Winstanleys, as this was the price which her son had set on the renewal of peace between them, but she plainly showed that she meant to go with undisguised reluctance and to make things as disagreeable as she well knew how.

She began by exaggerating the importance of this visit till she made the whole thing a nuisance and a bore. It might have been a grave diplomatic mission on which hung the fate of empires for the formality with which the terms of this simple morning call were arranged. The day and hour were discussed and appointed with punctilious nicety; and had it been possible, Lady Kearney would have stipulated for the exact number of steps to be taken by herself and Mrs. Winstanley before they came to the meeting-point by the door—for the precise depth of the courtesies with which the one was to enter and the other to receive. And even when all was ordered and the day had come, she speculated on the feasibility of a headache; and when finally yielding, shed a few genuine tears behind her handkerchief for rage at her defeat.

It was the daughters of Heth again;[1] and the chance of destruction for her beloved Jacob weighed heavily on her heart.

But Mrs. Winstanley, for all her pleasure at this recognition of my lady, was grandly equal to the occasion. Polite and amiable, as was demanded by good breeding, she was neither servile nor elated. Lady Kearney was a woman of birth and position; so was she herself; and the only difference between them was that of money, which is an accident that has nothing do with intrinsic quality. She was glad to be admitted into my lady's sacred enclosure; not because this was a grace beyond merit: on the contrary, it was eminently her due by the very nature of things: but because it was a recognition that would, she hoped, make certain social difficulties easy and bring Sir James so much the nearer. But for policy's sake she took care that no one should say she had descended from her own pedestal to kneel before Lady Kearney's shrine, or darkened her own light that this other might burn the brighter.

Lady Kearney, going to West Hill Gardens as an act of condescension, was forced to abandon her entrenchments and to recognize an equal. She was received by a woman with a manner as dignified as her own, and a great deal more graceful—by a woman with blood as blue, and clad in inherited velvet of as soft an original texture, as her own—by the presentation of personal refinement and artificial smoothness equal to that met with in the best society, and almost better than the best; and the contemptuous condescension which it had been her intention to show was foiled and changed to respect.

It was all as subtle and indefinite as the melting of the morning rime; but it was there; and the result was visible though the process was not. Before my lady had been five minutes in this shabbily furnished room, she was speaking to Mrs. Winstanley without effort and with quite natural politeness, as if she were really a woman and a sister,[2] and not a social acrobat shot up by some nefarious spring-board from a lower region.

Diplomatically, in view of an unmarried son with great destinies before him, it was disagreeable to know Mrs. Winstanley as an equal; but personally her acquaintance was pleasant, and she was forced to confess that those two horrible daughters of hers were charmingly well-mannered,

---

[1]   See Genesis 27:46, in which Rebekah, with high drama, warns her son Jacob away from an unsatisfactory marriage with a Hittite woman.

[2]   Refers to the antislavery slogan, "Am I not a man and a brother?"

and really beautiful. The whole group was not bad to know just up to this point; but, thank you, no!—no nearer acquaintance than this!

Sir James, more nervous than he showed or his mother suspected, saw the whole drama from the sofa where he had established himself by Thomasina, instinctively leaving Eva unnoticed. He understood every line of that keen, irritable, haughty face, and watched the gradual thaw, the gradual lightening of the cloud, and the change from war to peace, as narrowly as a man would who had so heavy a stake on the event. His own manner, too, was one of such admirable indifference to Thomasina that his mother, who was watching him as narrowly as he watched her, felt sure that here was no danger; and even she, suspicious as became a woman who thought herself responsible for her son's future, and that it came into her maternal functions to regulate his fancies, forbore to turn up the corner of the veil to look for what was not shown. As his manner was satisfactory to Thomasina, with whom he was talking, she did not think of Eva, to whom he did not speak. And when, soon after their own arrival, Hubert Strangways came in, and engrossed the whole attention of the "fairy rose-bud" because he gave her exclusively his own, the veil was made so much the more obscuring, and Lady Kearney was so much the farther from the truth. Perhaps there was no harm in these people, after all! she thought. It might be a quite innocuous fancy on the part of her son—a mere liking that had no dangerous tendency, and she had frightened herself in vain. Hubert Strangways seemed a thousand times more *épris*[1] than James; and Hubert was openly engaged to Maud Disney: she wished that she could say her boy was openly engaged to Agnes, the younger sister. Perhaps these Winstanley people were not of that difficult and detestable class—ladies by birth and adventuresses by life—people who had really jags and tags of purple velvet to show as family heirlooms come to them by righteous inheritance, but who were not straight in money matters, and who went perilously near the borders in other things—people who would not object to any stratagem that should secure a rich husband for one of the girls, and so give the family a firmer foothold and a higher point of departure for the pursuit of other matrimonial quarry. Mrs. Winstanley, handsome, lady-like, knowing her conventional grammar to perfection, and meeting Lady Kearney as an equal on her own ground, had not the air of an adventuress. Thomasina, as well-bred as her mother and even handsomer, was too unaffectedly indifferent to Sir

[1] (French), infatuated.

James to allow of any suspicion in her direction; and in this Lady Kearney's perspicacity was not at fault. The little one was a mere child yet, prospectively dangerous enough, but for the immediate present harmless. So at least judged the mother of Sir James, according to arrogant wisdom of half a century, which despises youth as immature, and thinks that a rose-bud not wholly free from the green of the sheath is not worth the trouble of guarding, because not in danger of plucking.

These rapid thoughts wrought so far for good that Lady Kearney, one of the most exclusive women in London—a very dragon of drawing-room virtue, whose social endorsement carried with it as much weight as that of the Bank of England across a bill, and whose patronage could have floated any one on whom it was bestowed—Lady Kearney, who made it her boast that no one could deceive her and no one get round her, lowered her guard, forgot her fence, and accepted what she saw with the frank faith of a tyro newly initiated and not familiar with the passwords. It was a triumph for Mrs. Winstanley; and, all things considered—honor being due to cleverness wherever found—a triumph well deserved.

Things were floating with the current in the smoothest way imaginable. Shakespeare and the musical-glasses were being discussed with the blandest conviction of their intrinsic importance. Lines of relation were established and common friends made out, chiefly through the Disneys who were eminently of Lady Kearney's set, yet of whom Mrs. Winstanley was careful not to say too much nor to put them forward too ostensibly, as if they were the wooden horse which held her whole effective army. Halcyon days reigned all around; and no painted ship upon a painted ocean was ever less in danger of wreck by storm or loss by fire than, to all appearance, these present amiable conditions were in danger of abrupt disturbance; when suddenly the door opened and Perdita's unlucky head made its appearance.

In discreet twilight as the room was, she was half-way in before she saw that visitors were there. Had she known of their presence she would have avoided them as carefully as her mother or sisters could have desired; but she had been absorbed in her books and had not heard the door-bell ring; and, shortsighted as she was, she never saw things at a glance, rapidly.

When she made out the fact of three strange forms scattered about the room, she stopped in an awkward and embarrassed way, and looked uncertain what to do. It was the attitude and manner of a person on the point of running away and while gathering courage for the flight.

Lady Kearney looked at her curiously; Sir James and Hubert with the indifference of young men of fashion brought face to face with a girl who is not pretty and not in the mode. All three thought her Eva's governess, and wondered at her familiarity in daring to come into the drawing-room as if she had the right to be there.

Mrs. Winstanley did not change a muscle of her face. If the nobility of her nature had been as great as her tact in moments of social difficulty, she would have been fit to take her place by the side of heroines and saints. What a pity it was that her spiritual splendour was so superficial!—that her moral gold was only lacquer when put to the test!

"My daughter Perdita, Lady Kearney," she said quietly, but in her heart she wished that she could have said: "A mere nobody, whom I have brought up for charity. Indifferent as she is now, think how much worse she would have been but for me!"

"Indeed!" said Lady Kearney with surprise. "I did not know that you had three daughters, Mrs. Winstanley."

"This one seldom goes out. She dislikes society and abjures all gaiety. She is our Genius," said Mrs. Winstanley with a smile.

"She has the air of one," returned Lady Kearney enigmatically. "In what direction?—art?—music? Are you fond of music?" she asked, speaking to Perdita.

"Yes, very, but I play very badly," answered the genius, blushing and looking dreadfully unaccustomed to well-dressed ladies of rank and polite society generally.

"Ah! I suppose then you paint? In what genre?—landscapes or figures?" continued my lady.

"No, I do not paint; what I do is merely daubing," said Perdita with even more bashfulness and increased awkwardness.

Lady Kearney looked perplexed. Here was a genius and no outward or visible sign of her power—no intelligible ticketing of what she was worth and what she could do!

"Does she write?" the lady asked, turning to Mrs. Winstanley, and speaking as people do when they are dealing with that strange monster, a genius, as if it were a harmless kind of Caliban that had no nerves and only rudimentary senses, and might be discussed before its presence without regard to its susceptibilities.

"Not yet," answered Mrs. Winstanley, who felt keenly her failure in the establishment of Perdita's pretensions.

"Oh, I shall never write, mother; I have so few words!" said Perdita, modesty and truth warring against this assumption of finer feathers than were hers by right.

Lady Kearney smiled a little disagreeably. This genius of the family was too much of a paradox for her taste. Neither in music which was respectable, nor in painting which was allowable, nor yet in literature which might pass under protest and according to style and subject—where, then, did her talents lie?—for what good gifts of intellect was she entitled to be ugly, ill-dressed, and dowdy-looking?—to have awkward manners and an embarrassed blush?—to wear spectacles and not to know how to hold herself? As things looked she was an impostor; and, as a hempen strand in a silken rope debases the whole length, so one bit of pretentiousness that was not to be verified by facts, vitiated all these fine appearances and made my lady go back on her first impression and ask herself once again: "Are they merely well-born adventuresses climbing up the ladder anyhow?"

"Where, then, does your genius lie?" she asked frostily.

"I have none at all," replied Perdita; "unless you call the desire to work genius. I do not."

"Work? at what? Do you do point-lace or 'crash'?" she said, her manner thawing. These were pet employments of her own; and she thought a good art-needlewoman a few degrees nearer to heaven and a great many degrees more valuable as a woman than one who could neither design nor stitch.

"No, I cannot do lace-work or this new embroidery," answered honest Perdita. "My sister and mother do a great deal; but I mean a different kind of work. I should like to do something real—something serious; teach if I could—only I cannot, I have not been sufficiently well taught myself; but I should like to have a clerkship, or be a hospital nurse, or study medicine—anything that was real work."

Lady Kearney looked at Mrs. Winstanley; Mrs. Winstanley looked at Lady Kearney and then at her daughter, a quiet, half-amused, and wholly affectionate smile on her face.

"You see what an enthusiast she is, Lady Kearney!" she said blandly. "I call this the fermenting period of her life; but she will come right in time."

"I see," said Lady Kearney. "One of those awful creatures, a strong-minded woman!" she added below her breath with a little shudder; while Sir James asked Thomasina in an audible whisper, "Is she really your sister? Not your half-sister?"

"No, really our sister," Thomasina answered with her lovely smile. "And the best child in the world!—but, as mother says, in the fermenting stage, and so full of thoughts and energies she does not know how to work them all off. She is odd; but, when you know her, really grand!"

"Rather uncomfortable in a house, I should say," drawled Sir James; "but then I have no sympathy with any kind of turbulence in women." To him women were lovely creatures to be painted in pictures and celebrated in poetry—houris in boudoirs and drawing-rooms always beautifully dressed and exquisitely got up, with paint and antimony and dye if these would make them any the lovelier—gracefully reclining on shining silken couches, and drinking scented tea out of egg-shell china cups; while he, the adorer, sat on a low chair by their side, and poured out nineteenth-century dithyrambics to their honour, all in prose and with due regard to decent drapery. But when it came to a woman of his own class who went out of this region of idle loveliness, did useful work, dressed without taste, lived less than luxuriously, talked politics that were elemental principles and not the mere social actions of prominent men, and did not make "conquest" the aim of her existence, then the poet and the gentleman alike were revolted in him, and he thought such a woman as this as infamous as an infidel—as abominable as a red republican—and as much a traitor to her order as one who vilifies the Three Estates of the realm is a traitor to the English Constitution.

Perdita Winstanley ranked with him as a family disgrace. It was one of the egg-shell china cups cracked and defaced—a houri with the odour of onions on her hands and a soiled patch on her dainty tea-gown.

"There is a great deal of real work, and good, useful work too, that a lady can do quite well," said Lady Kearney. "She can make flannel petticoats for the poor; and a friend of my own, Lady Cammell, attended those cooking classes at Kensington. She is slightly eccentric, I must confess, but she did really learn how to make an omelette, and I know that she could boil potatoes. Why do you not do something of that kind? You meet excellent company at the classes."

"It would not be much use my learning to cook," said Perdita, who had the foolish habit of believing that people were always in earnest and meant what they said to be taken seriously; "I could not go out to work and mother would not let me be the cook at home. I do not see that this would do any good. No, I should like to have some profession, some real work. It would be so far better for everybody if I had."

"Now, my dear, suppose you leave off declaiming your theories," said Mrs. Winstanley quite smoothly. "Lady Kearney has been very kind to listen to you so far, but patience has its limits; and you are absorbing the whole conversation."

"I am interested in hearing your daughter speak," said Lady Kearney.

"This is the first time I have met with a strong-minded woman, and it amuses me."

"But what is there amusing in what I say?" asked Perdita.

Samson making sport for the Philistines was not in her way.

"My dear young lady!" said Lady Kearney in a tone of banter mingled with remonstrance; "who would not be amused by hearing a young gentlewoman of family and position talk of going out to work, as if she were a farmer's daughter or a shopkeeper's 'young lady'? What lady works? The thing is in itself a contradiction. If you work you are not a lady—*voilà tout*. You cannot combine the two. And I should be sorry to think that I had made the acquaintance of people who were not *pur sang*. That is why I am amused. The *näivete* of your ideas—the childishness, I may say—would amuse any one of my age who knows the world and society. Does not your mother laugh at you? I should say so," she added, looking at Mrs. Winstanley, who was sitting there with a perfectly serene face, quietly stirred by an amiably compassionate smile.

"That is just the point," said Perdita eagerly. "That is just what we are wanting to prove, that women may be ladies and yet honest workers—that bread-winning does not necessarily include vulgarity."

Lady Kearney put up her eyeglass and looked at Perdita as if she had been some foreign moth or caterpillar impaled for her to study.

"Who are 'we,' my dear child?" asked Mrs. Winstanley, always with that waxen smoothness. "Not your mother and sisters, surely?"

"No; the school to which I belong," said Perdita; "the people who think as I do."

"And what is the school to which you belong, may I ask?" inquired Lady Kearney.

"Those who care for human nature more than for society," said Perdita, now at the flood— "who believe that women are women first and ladies afterwards; that work is honourable and idleness disgraceful, and poverty that might be removed by industry more disgraceful still; that we are all one great family and ought to share one another's burdens; that the poor are our brothers; and, still more, that it is not right for the rich to have everything and the poor nothing. This is the school to which I belong."

"My child, what a tirade!" said Mrs. Winstanley with a gentle laugh.

"Oh!" said Lady Kearney; "you are a demagogue, I see. You uphold those dreadful *pétroleuses*."[1]

---

[1] Anti-monarchist women during the Second Empire supposed to set fires with gasoline.

"I do not uphold them, because I do not believe in them," said Perdita hardily. "There were no such things as *pétroleuses*. It was all a fabrication of the Versaillists—of the enemies of freedom."

Mrs. Winstanley and Thomasina exchanged looks.

"If you let Perdita loose on politics, there will be no end to it," said Thomasina, in the sweetest way imaginable. "You dear enthusiastic old thing!" she added, going up to her sister and taking her arm; "I want you to do me a kindness, will you?"

"Yes," said Perdita, looking pleased.

She liked to be made use of; and when Thomasina was human and not frost-bitten, she had a certain amount of influence over the girl.

"Go upstairs to my room, will you?" said Thomasina, with her favourite smile; "and look for that cushion I am embroidering. I want to show it to Lady Kearney. Do not come down without it! Be sure not to come down till you have found it."

"No," said Perdita, carrying herself and her uncongenial democracy out of the room, and embarking on a sleeveless errand, as her sister knew.

"Your daughter seems to hold some very extraordinary opinions!" said Lady Kearney with a displeased air. "One seldom hears such sentiments from young ladies of her position."

"She had a friend much older than herself, who had had her head turned," said Mrs. Winstanley. "She had great influence over my poor child, and did her incalculable harm; but she will grow out of it in time. It is just one of the diseases of youth."

"It is to be hoped she will," said Lady Kearney. "For myself, I do not believe in young people growing out of diseases of this kind. And at the best," she continued, with a glance at her son, "some thoughts and frames of mind are like small-pox and leave their mark for life."

"Yes, they do," assented Mrs. Winstanley, and then turned the conversation adroitly on to the war and the latest telegrams.

Soon after this my lady and her son took their leave, and Hubert Strangways remained sole possessor of the field. He improved the occasion as much as if Maud Disney were not wearing that diamond ring which he had given her, and as if he were not bound by honour and his promise to marry her next autumn. The young fellow was not much troubled with introspection or conscientious scruples when his desires were strong. If he liked little Eva Winstanley, he did; and the fact was as final as a fiat. Had he been remonstrated with, he would have said: "What can a fellow do?" and to his own mind his question would have been unanswerable. If a fellow falls in love, why, he does fall in love and there is nothing more to be said on the matter, Hubert would have reasoned; and if a fellow is in love with one girl, how the deuce can he marry another? No man can help falling in love, but no man need marry where he doesn't love; and by the look of things he would be one of those who could not in the one case and would not in the other.

To Mrs. Winstanley, however, being engaged, this handsome eldest son of the Strangways of Strangways was as safe as an old church clock. She would as soon have been afraid of little Eva's flirting with a fountain or a sundial, according to the odd proclivities of Mr. Gilbert's maiden man-haters,[1] as of cherishing undue interest in a man already affianced; so she left them together with a clear conscience and an untroubled mind, while she and Thomasina went into the dining-room on some domestic consultation of present importance. While they were leisurely descending, Perdita came flying down the upper flight of stairs.

"I cannot find your work anywhere, Thomasina!" she said in her breathless way.

"I did not expect you would," said her sister coldly.

"But I looked everywhere I could think of," Perdita returned. "I am sure it is not in your room."

"No," said Thomasina: "it is in the drawing-room."

"Shall I fetch it?" asked that incarnation of obtuse simplicity and blind earnestness.

Mrs. Winstanley took her arm, not roughly, but coldly and somewhat harshly.

"Do not go into the drawing-room, Perdita," she said in a slow displeased way. "You have done enough mischief for one day."

"What mischief, mother?" the girl asked.

"You are either the most finished hypocrite or the most obtuse clod that could possibly exist," said her mother angrily. "I do not like to believe you the one; and I can scarcely think you the other."

Perdita burst into a sudden passionate fit of crying.

"Mother! mother! why are you always so angry with me?" she said. "I do not know what I do to vex you, but you are always so hard to me—always so angry. If only you would tell me quietly what I do to offend you—but I never know where I fail, and I never know what it is to be treated fairly or kindly by you!"

---

[1]   Apparently referring to Gilbert and Sullivan's operetta *The Pirates of Penzance*, first produced on 3 April 1880. Linton may also be referring to her own article "Modern Man-Haters" (*Saturday Review*, 29 January 1871, 528–29).

"What can I do with her, Thomasina?" said Mrs. Winstanley in despair. "Things are really becoming intolerable!"

"Mother! why are you so vexed?" cried the poor girl, lifting up her disordered face full of tear-stained and pathetic entreaty.

She tried to take her mother's hand, but Mrs. Winstanley shook her off irritably, saying: "Don't touch me, Perdita!" Then, as if to give a reason for her impulse of repugnance, she added coldly: "Your hands are all wet."

"If only I knew what to do!" exclaimed Perdita with a burst of despair that was only another form of her "besetting sin." "Oh that I might die and have done with it all," she cried, clasping her hands against her forehead.

"You are a very wicked and undutiful girl to talk so," said Mrs. Winstanley severely.

"Now go, Perdita," put in Thomasina. "Don't you see that mother is tired? You always will talk when you had so far better be silent! Go away and don't worry any more; and if you want to know what you said and did that was wrong, I will tell you afterwards. I do not think she means to be so tiresome as she is," Thomasina said to her mother when Perdita had dashed away like a whirlwind. "She is horribly provoking, but I think it is ignorance more than wilfulness. She has no tact, that is it."

"Then she ought to have it," returned Mrs. Winstanley. "She has seen nothing but tact and good breeding ever since she was born; and her stupidity is really sinful. I do not know what Lady Kearney could have thought of her! I should not be surprised if it costs us her friendship. I saw that she was disgusted."

"I will try to make matters right the next time I see her," said Thomasina soothingly. "Poor Perdita has some good points and one can always make the best of them."

"You can if any one can," replied her mother. "But your poor sister is a hopeless subject to make anything of with such a woman as Lady Kearney."

Just then Perdita came downstairs again, dressed this time for walking. It was in her habits to go out alone. No one ever wished her to make one of a party or to be her solitary companion; and Mrs. Winstanley could not condemn her to perpetual seclusion and inaction. Hence it was nothing strange to see her with her hat and gloves prepared to dive into the streets and Gardens alone. She passed the dining-room, the door of which stood open showing her mother and sister sitting within, consulting on the feasibility of asking "the boy upstairs," as Mrs. Winstanley called him, "to stay to dinner." She did not speak to them nor they to her. She looked at them as she hurried by in rather a wild heart-broken way, wishing vaguely that this might be for the last time. She was weary of this perpetual strife where she was always worsted, and where she never knew her cause of offence. A half-insane desire for flight into some far-off country, where she would be utterly unknown and where she might begin life afresh as if born only to-day, and born capable and mature, mingled with the no less insane desire for eternal rest—to have done with all this turmoil—young as she was to turn aside from active life and all its hopes, all its possibilities—to dash the glorious cup to the ground before she had fully tasted the wine it held. Heart and brain and blood—all were seething and fermenting alike; and, scarcely knowing what she did, only conscious of her dumb desire and sharp distress, she passed out from the house and away into the peopled solitude of the streets.

She went at a swift pace through the Gardens and to the banks of the river. How peaceful it all looked! How good it would be to bury herself and her sorrows in that calm, gentle stream! The love of individual life had gone out of her—as a light might be extinguished—and she had a strange vague feeling of longing to return to the great source whence she had come. What was there in her own existence to make it worth all the pain and trouble which an unfriendly fate had given her? No one loved her; she was of no use in the world; she, whose whole soul was one great chord of passion—who wanted to love some one beyond herself and to live for some great aim that should help forward the human race—she, who yearned to be loved by one and to be of value to many—she was of no more good to her generation than that green leaf floating on the waters on its way to the sea. How peacefully that leaf floated onward! What was she but just such a leaf in the great forest of humanity? Who missed that from the tree whence it had fallen? who would miss her? How pleasant it would be to shut her eyes and go to sleep, only to open them in the great garden of heaven, in eternal sunshine and repose! How she would like to float onward there with that leaf, free forever from rebuke, from self-reproach, from sorrow!

An hour passed and she was still standing there looking at the water. Her hands, clasped loosely in each other, hung mournfully before her; her figure was drooping and tears were unconsciously falling quietly and silently from her eyes. The longing for rest was growing in her heart; the strange fascination of those calm waters was increasing. To make one step only, and to be borne away to eternity and peace!—to hold out her arms and fling herself on to that quiet breast and there to fall asleep as a tired child, never to wake up to sorrow, to despair, to passion or wrong-doing! All that was about her faded from her sight—she knew only the quiet waters flowing there, whispering to her to come with them to her home, to find in their depths her own eternal rest.

"I am ready!" she half sighed; when suddenly some one took her hand and drew her forcibly away from the water's edge.

"Are you ill?" asked a strange voice kindly, the hand which held hers tightening its grasp.

She woke up from her dreams and looked up; confused as if she had been suddenly startled from real sleep.

A tall, handsome, brown-haired man stood by her, holding her hand in one of his; the other he had placed on her shoulder. His grey eyes, as full of honesty as her own, looked into hers with compassionate inquiry; his grave face, composed, steady, full of thought and sadness, seemed the reflex of her own sorrow, but with more control and with more of the peace of endurance. His voice was gentle but firm; his manner protecting but commanding. He seemed to have read the secret writing of her poor wayward, passionate soul, and to be standing there, guarding her from herself.

Perdita cleared her eyes of their tears, and came back to life and herself with the quick consciousness of her sensitive nature.

"I am not very well—I was dreaming," she stammered, her pale face suddenly aglow.

"A bad place to dream in," he answered quietly. "Let me see you safe through the Gardens. It is getting late to be here alone."

CHAPTER XI.

THE ALLUREMENTS OF EMANCIPATION.

STARVATION makes men grateful for any kind of nourishment, and the moral nature follows the law of the physical. The starved soul is like the famished body—glad of any food wherewith to appease its hunger; and just as dry bread seems the ambrosia of the gods to the man who is dying for want of sustenance, so are questionable attachments and doubtful excitements golden gifts of fortune to the soul that is wasting for want of sympathy and love.

So little pleasure came into Perdita's forsaken kind of life, and so little affection fed that heart-hunger of hers—that passionate craving for love and loving which, as things were, brought her but the desolation of despair—that chance kindness met with more gratitude from her than is usual with girls who hold themselves in the proud reserve belonging to untried hopes and virgin possibilities. In fact, girls as a rule are not grateful. They receive tribute in the love that is given them; but they receive only, they do not repay.

Perdita was not like her age or sex in this. Her thoughts wandered back again and again to the man who had taken her hand in his and drawn her from the water's edge. She knew that he had saved her from possible suicide, which to herself excused and accounted for her overpowering desire to see him again. She had not gone into the Gardens with fixed intention, but she knew that but for him she should probably have flung herself into the river from pure weariness of the strife—from pure desire of rest and despair of life—and she wanted to thank him.

How kindly he had talked to her as they walked through the Gardens, and how strong and full of protection he had been! She was calm now; alive to the reality of things; no longer blinded by sorrow or misled by the phantoms which haunt those who are dying of hunger and destitution. She wanted to see him again for this, too—first to thank him and then to show him that her hallucination had passed.

Day by day she wandered about the place where she had met him, scanning the passers-by with those earnest half-seeing eyes which made more than one man look at her curiously and smile when he passed. One young fellow indeed, swaggering along with his hat on one side, cutting the air with his cane, stopped as he met her walking onward searching the faces of all she saw; and with a fatuous laugh said jauntily: "Will I do as well, my dear?"

She gave a frightened bound as he spoke, and dashed on, blushing and ashamed; but soon she began again that fruitless scanning, searching—searching—and never meeting!

This went on for more than a week; and for all this time how bright the radiant summer was in the morning, how dull all life in the evening! When the day came she sprang up with the feeling that she must go out now at once to meet—what? She did not know what she expected; but she felt as if the day would not end without her having found her desire. It was hidden there among the golden hours like a pearl lying in the heart of a rose. She would come upon it unawares, when she least expected, and without pain. The sun would shine, the flower would open, and the treasure would fall into her hand. But her dreams must not interrupt her duties; and above all things she must study for her examination. She must work before she might enjoy, and let no hope, no fantasy draw her aside. All day long, she sat in the morning-room absorbed in her books, and after dinner, when the shadows began to lengthen—just at the same hour every day and that hour the same as when she had rushed into the Gardens half-crazed with trouble—she went back to the place where her unknown friend had met her, and looked for him, longed for him, prayed for him to come, as if her speechless thoughts had the force of deeds and her desire could draw him as with a living magnet irresistibly.

But she looked and longed in vain. She seemed to meet the whole human race, one after the other in endless procession; but the one who at this moment gave her life its meaning, and whom she most desired to see—he alone was not to be found.

So she passed her days, though ever disappointed not so unhappily as in olden times, because feeling that she had a friend somewhere in the vague distance, a friend who, separated from her for the moment, was yet ever journeying to meet her.

At home things went somewhat less harshly for her; and if she had no more love than heretofore, she had less blame. For her own part she was more dreamy, more abstracted, more silent and consequently less aggressive in her principles and less annoying in their utterance than was usual with her. She seldom spoke, and yet she was not sullen; and her mother and Thomasina were too glad of a respite from their duty of perpetual rebuke to disturb a peace which might be death, but all the same was rest. Even Eva forbore to tease her; and as Perdita was never cross without provocation—though furious enough with it!—to be left alone meant to be left tranquil and amiable. And then, gradually, gradually, constant disappointment did its accustomed work, and the girl left off looking for the unknown saviour who never came. Perhaps he would some day come again into her life—some day when not thought of or expected, as he had in the beginning. He had flashed like a god out of the darkness and brought light into her night; and so he would again. How glad she would be to see him!—how warmly she would thank him for the good that he did her in that dark day of her passionate despair, and how she would bring to him as tribute the happiness that she would then have conquered!

For through all this troublous time, Perdita ever looked forward to the future when she should have prevailed over fortune, and when her life should be set full and fair in the sunshine. She must be happy—she would be happy!—if not in one way then in another; if not now then hereafter. Life was too strong in her to let her be content with sorrow. Pain so sharp as to make death a relief—that she knew; but of that melancholy pessimism which sees in life nothing but confusion and deception—of that discontent with joy, of that indifference to love which makes both of no avail against despair—she had happily not a trace. While there was a new truth to learn, a glorious sunset to watch, a human joy to share or a sorrow to console, life would have its charms and its duties, and she could bear the worse for the sake of the better—endure reality for the sake of hope.

Still, the days were dreary; and her path was not ornamented with many flowers if tolerably free from thorns. She worked hard for her examination; as if the mild ordeal to be passed before she could be appointed a clerk in the Post Office Savings Bank had been for a Senior Wrangler's place—but then intensity was in her way—and she learnt a great deal more than was at all necessary. Mr. Brocklebank often paid her a little visit in her den and his interest and friendliness certainly increased. His pronounced patronage did her good with the mother and in some degree consoled her for the disappointment of this filial disaster. If after all Perdita should draw the first prize? what a gain that would be!—what a piece of good luck! The possibility made Mrs. Winstanley sometimes almost tender to her provoking democrat, almost disposed to find her good-looking, well-mannered and not too hopelessly foolish in her views. As for Perdita herself, her affectionate nature went out in floods of gratitude to the ironmaster, whom she loved and reverenced as her protector and best friend. Had he struck then when the glow of that loving heart was at its height he might have done with her what he would. But the situation interested him; and the fable of the dog and the shadow[1] had no meaning for him.

He was in his own mind the potential owner of each of these three girls in turn; and when he would he could translate that potentiality into fact. It pleased him to play with each according to his humour—to pay court to Thomasina, to befriend Perdita, to caress little Eva. He kept the various threads clear and distinct, and by his strict impartiality never gave the mother cause to ask:"Who is it?" or:"When will it be?"

He played his part to perfection, and went in and out the house as if the whole thing belonged to him. He was of good service to them

---

[1]   Aesop's fable in which a dog, carrying meat over a bridge, sees his reflection in the water below; thinking it to be another dog with a larger piece of meat, he lets go his own to attack the other dog, thus losing what he had.

in many ways; but his enmity to Sir James Kearney was embarrassing; and between the two stools Mrs. Winstanley thought ruefully of the ground. She wanted to sit on both; and the feat was difficult.

One day Perdita bethought herself of Mrs. Blount. Mr. Brocklebank was very good to her and took her part at all times with zeal; but she was getting tired of waiting for her examination, and she had a girl's natural desire for a woman's praise. She knew that Bell Blount would stimulate her courage; sometimes, as was but to be expected, Perdita asked herself whether filial obedience was not nobler, after all, than living one's own life and educating one's faculties to their highest point—in disobedience. When her mother was friendly to her these doubts tormented her sorely. Yet for all her sincerity she did not wish to be convinced that she had been wrong; and she did want to be assured that work was the highest life and following where one's principles led the truest holiness. Wherefore she set out to pay a visit to the Champion of her Sex—the woman who believed that all iniquity comes from men and all righteousness is lodged with women, and that the reign of justice will never be established until Omphale,[I] in the lion's skin, sits supreme on the throne while Hercules offers his broad back for her footstool.

She found the two ladies at home; Miss Long opening the door and throwing into her action that air of acid condescension, of patronage which meant standing on the defensive, belonging to a person who holds herself superior to her work. It was manner inexpressibly distasteful to Perdita, democrat as she was. She was not condescending nor patronizing to servants, and she did not see why this woman should be so to her. She always treated both men and maids as equals by virtue of a common humanity; and she resented that she should be treated by one of them as an inferior. Nevertheless she took her allotted portion quietly, and went unannounced into the room where Bell Blount and her friend led their odd lives in concert.

Never had the unlikeness between her own home and this struck her more forcibly than it did to-day. At West Hill Gardens every thing was laid out for show and kept in perfect order. Litter of any kind was a crime in Mrs. Winstanley's eyes, and work did not excuse snippets. Here in Prince Christian's Road beauty, arrangement, order, were conspicuous by their absence, and the room had a queer hybrid look, as if tenanted by

---

[I] Legendary queen of Lydia. Hercules served as her slave for a while, in penance for the murder of Iphitus. During that time he wore women's clothes and did women's labor, while Omphale wore his lion's skin and carried his club.

men who owned some of the furniture of women and not all of their own. The table was littered with pamphlets and reviews, old envelopes and letters, bills, journals and general waste; on the chimney-piece, among some common vases filled with half-decayed and neglected flowers, stood a box of Spanish cigarettes; one slipper, much worn and down at heel, had been flung into one corner of the room—its fellow was under the table and a pair of boots stood against the wall. The white shavings in the fireplace were strewed all ever with half-burnt vestas and torn scraps of paper; and the bar of the fender was scratched and bent by the incessant wearing of feet. Bottles of beer, soda-water and brandy were on an ill-kept kind of chiffonier; a plate of water biscuits stood near; the carpet was covered with crumbs. The whole place was bare, mean, unlovely, disordered; and yet neither Mrs. Blount nor her friend looked poor. They were hideously dressed in expensive clothes, and they wore a good deal of jewellery; and though Miss Tracy was a thin, half-vitalized, vaporous little creature—one of those lean kine[1] not to be fattened up by any amount or quality of food—Mrs. Blount's whole person bore evidence of good living—of flesh made firm by meat and blood rich by stimulant.

Perdita was received with acclamation—welcomed as the provident virgin[2] intent on trimming her lamp betimes and knowing where to go for oil.

"I knew you would come back to us! I knew I had marked you!" said Mrs. Blount, putting her arm round her for welcome; "and now tell us what you have done since we last saw you."

"I am reading for my examination as a clerk—a Post-office Savings Bank clerk," said Perdita. "I have got a nomination, and now it depends on myself whether I shall be accepted or not."

"Excellent!" said Bell Blount warmly. "There is no fear of your making one of the melancholy army of failures. You will always do what you have set your mind on!"

"I hope I shall in this, at all events," said Perdita. "It would be worse than death to me to be plucked now after I have had to fight so hard for leave to try."

"People opposed, of course?"

"Yes, mother does not like it. I am so sorry to vex her, but I cannot go on living in idleness as I have been doing. I must have something to do; and then we are poor."

---

[1] See Genesis 41:18–21.

[2] See Matthew 25:1–13.

"Always the way with women of a certain class," said Bell Blount; "better rags and semi-starvation with white hands and an empty head, than a good income got by using the faculties God has given them. I am sick and tired of all this affectation!"

"It is education," said Perdita sensibly enough. "We are taught to believe that idleness is ladylike; and I do not wonder at my mother not liking the new school and the new ideas," she added with frank loyalty to the absent.

"And you, poor dear, have been led a life all this time, I dare say?" said Bell, taking Perdita's hand between both her own.

Connie Tracy's pale face flushed, and she looked askance through her white lashes.

"They do not like it," answered Perdita with a certain reluctance. She wanted sympathy for herself but not reproach for her family; and she shrank from the domestic treachery of carrying tales out of her home even to the most sympathizing friend in the world.

"Oh, I know it all! Have I not gone through it myself and has not Connie there? When I made up my mind to leave my husband, and Connie her father and mother, do you think we had not troubles and difficulties enough? We have been every step of the way, my dear, and could tell you just what you have had to go through—and will have, so long as you stay at home. But the next thing to do is to come and chum with us. When you have once known the pleasure of independence in work you will want it in your life all through; and with us you will be entirely independent. You shall have a latch-key—we each have a latch-key; no one will interfere with you—no one will ask where you have been or what you have done. You can go out or stay at home as you like—invite your friends when you like, and any one and as many as you please; and when you do not want to be disturbed you can receive them up in your own room. In fact, you will live as free a life as a man; and there will be no one to question or spy after you."

Perdita's face had flushed and paled alternately while Mrs. Blount had spoken. Freedom had been the ideal of her life, the goddess of her worship, ever since she had had a conscious mental existence at all; but the details, when applied to her own every-day doings, frightened her.

"I should scarcely like to be so independent as that," she said. "I should feel lost, and not right in some way, if I lived like a man."

"Just as a Chinese woman with her cramped feet cannot walk without support, and as wasp-waisted women, who have paralyzed their intercostal muscles by tight-lacing, 'break in two,' as they call it, without their stays.

These poor creatures have been physically mutilated for the false ideas of fashion and of what is 'becoming' in women; and so it has been with your free-will. You have been so long accustomed to the coercion of home, the bondage of society—so used to be tyrannized over, checked, thought for, to be debarred the rights of your own nature—that I can understand how, in the beginning, you would feel like a Chinese woman set to walk alone, or a poor, weak, hysterical thing—waist eighteen inches and all her organs displaced—when her stays are taken off. But that does not make feet the natural size and ribs which leave the heart and liver to act as they ought, immoral or unfeminine; and your emancipation from the tyranny of home, and given the free use of your own nature, are just the same things."

"Not quite," said Perdita. "This extreme independence does not seem natural for any woman; but for an unmarried girl—oh, I don't think it would be nice!"

"And why should a woman, married or single, lead a different life from a man? Tell me that if you can! When society is in that barbarous state where men take most delight in hacking their neighbours to pieces, stealing their cattle and setting fire to their houses, then I grant you, women, who are weaker in the arm, have to be protected by one set of brutes of whom they are the cattle and the slaves, from another set of brutes who want to lift them with the cows and make them their own slaves instead. But in times when you can call a policeman if you are molested, there ought to be no difference between the sexes, either in life or morals. Women in England should be as free as men; and what is wrong for a woman to do is equally wrong for a man. There is no sex, I tell you, in morals."

"I cannot agree with you!" said Perdita, earnestly and apologetically. It was a dreadful thing to differ from an adept in the mystery of life, as Mrs. Blount was; but she must. "Surely it is not all the same thing, and men may do what we must not! There is a difference between us!"

"I should be glad to see it," said Bell Blount coolly. "Come let us argue it out fairly. But first I must have my cigarette. I talk better when I smoke. Do you smoke?" she asked in a matter-of-fact way, as if she had said: Do you take sugar in your tea? or milk with your coffee? She took a cigarette-case and match-box out of a pocket in the breast of her jacket, and chose one with a practised air, then offered the case to Perdita.

"I? Good gracious, no!" cried Perdita, startled into the impoliteness of a disclaimer that meant disapprobation.

"Ah! I see you are very far yet from being as emancipated as you ought to be!" said Mrs. Blount compassionately. "Connie and I are what our more whole-souled cousins call clear grit all through. We don't go in for half measures in any way; and we know the value of nicotine, don't we, Con?"

"I should miss my weed dreadfully, I confess," answered Connie; and Perdita thought how odd it sounded to hear that slang word from this pale, delicate, refined-looking little woman, with her innocent white eyelashes and sharp peaked mouse-shaped face. It was far more incongruous than with Mrs. Blount, who had a certain flourish of masculinity about her that made a cigarette between her full hard lips infinitely more natural than a knitting-needle in her hand. Her present attitude, too—lounging in her easy-chair, her head thrown far back, and her right foot crossed over her left knee—was more in accordance with her being than the angular attitude of Constance Tracy, who only made herself an ungraceful woman by all that she did and could never transform herself into the handsome hybrid which her friend strove so hard to appear and to be.

"And so you don't smoke?" continued Mrs. Blount, making rings in the air.

"No, no!" said Perdita. "Even my father did not; and he was an officer."

"Ah! he didn't know what was good nor realize what he lost," said Mrs. Blount quietly. "A man who does not smoke is only half a man; and life would not be worth having to me without my cigarette and B. and S.[1] Come! try this pretty little thing," she said, again choosing a cigarette and offering it to Perdita. "It is as mild as milk and will not hurt you. I will initiate you; and this day month you will thank me."

"No, no, indeed not!" said Perdita, turning away her head. "I do not want to learn."

"You ought to want to learn everything," Bell Blount replied. "That is cowardice, my dear."

"There are some things I would rather not know how to do; and I do not want to learn to smoke," Perdita persisted, looking half frightened, as if Bell Blount would take her by main force and initiate her against her will.

The elder woman laughed. Her laugh was loud and strained; rasping artificial unmelodious volley of gutturals, as far removed from Eva's silvery little trill as if it did not belong to the same family of human expressions. It made Perdita shrink back within herself. There was an incongruity between the woman's handsome face, which fifty years of life and passion had hardened but not disfigured, and her unsexed mind—her costly if

---

[1] Brandy and Soda.

ungraceful clothing and her mannish attitude—that seemed to Perdita more monstrous than piquant; and the discordant laugh with which she received the instinctive repugnance of a modest girl for aught that savoured of coarseness or fastness completed the unpleasantness of the impression. Nevertheless, she had a strong fascination for Perdita—a fascination which the girl was half afraid and half ashamed to confess to herself; wondering in her heart whether it were a thing to yield to as a beneficent impulse or to resist as an unholy spell—whether this emancipated woman had found a truer life by the adoption of manly freedom than other women have who cling to their feminine fetters and make their sex of more account than their individuality.

"Afraid of freedom and disdaining nicotine—and you call yourself a lover of liberty!" laughed Mrs. Blount again. "No, my dear girl, you only think you are! You have no knowledge yet of the real thing! What you desire is only that ideal vapoury phantom which is lodged in odes and nourished by legends. Confess now, your notions of freedom are centred in an heroic hand-to-hand fight on some rampart, with a handsome youth holding a banner in one hand and flourishing a sword in the other. By the way, he could not do much in the cutting and hacking line if he did! A beautiful girl—yourself—is by his side, half patriot, half lover, with all her back hair down and doing nothing in particular; for we can scarcely believe that she would have nerve or strength to chop off an invader's head if it appeared above the battlement. Fal-la! I know the whole thing so well! I have been through it all, as every girl has who has any imagination. But this is not the liberty that works or washes. This is just moonshine; and what we want today is something real. Now confess—is not this your dream?"

"How can it be when we have no wars or invasion?" asked Perdita blushing, for she had been correctly read, at least in one period of her mental career. "If we had, we should be glad of this kind of personal bravery, which would be as valuable now as ever it was."

"Nothing of the kind. Even war has entered on a new phase, and arms of precision and guns laid at a plaguey long range"—Mrs. Blount affected technicalities—"have taken the place of heroic individualism. The best marksman is now the best soldier and scientific engineering has put a stopper on personal gallantry. Rubbish, my dear girl! All that kind of thing has gone by. It did for the Keepsake and Annual time of day; but our aims are much more prosaic and practical. What we want now are equal rights for women—rights in work, in bread-winning, in education and in professional possibilities, in worldly advancement, in liberty of action. We want to abolish the tyranny of sex and to be what God meant each of us to be—free to live our own lives, and, provided we do not hurt our neighbours, to do what we best like ourselves."

"But this kind of equality, this personal freedom, would scarcely do if we married," said Perdita, honest instinct supplying the want of dialectic training. "And married life is the happiest for women and the most suitable."

"The most suitable!" repeated Mrs. Blount with disdain; "you mean the most unsuitable, the most miserable! Married! I would rather a friend of mine throw herself into the river than that she should marry one of those vile creatures called men! Why do we marry? In nine cases out of ten to be kept. What infamy to be forced to sell ourselves for an existence, as we do now, because we are not allowed to adopt those professions which would keep us! to be the slave of some odious tyrant and the mother of a lot of squalling children, that we may have clothes to wear and food to eat—what a degradation! If this is all you have to oppose to us you have not much to say for yourself. But you speak by the book, my dear. You say what you have been taught to say, like any other pretty little girl parrot; and evidently you have not thought out the subject for yourself. That has to come. You come and see me. I will clear your mind of all these spider nets and rubbish; and Connie there will show you that a woman can be emancipated and yet not be a monster sprouting horns or wearing a beard!"

"Oh, but being married to a good man and having children of your own is better than all this," said Perdita, with strange passion. "After all, work is only a substitute!"

Mrs. Blount did not answer. She only lifted up her eyebrows and smiled with compassion and reprobation combined. Then she flung away the end of her cigarette, and stretched out her limbs like a man rousing after repose.

"Come and see me very often, my dear," she said. "I will soon knock all that rubbish out of your head. When will you come again? to-morrow? I must send you away now, because Con and I are going to our committee; but say when you will come again—to-morrow?"

"The day after to-morrow," answered Perdita, always stumbling between the two questions—was she yielding to unwise temptation or honestly following the light sent to her for holy guidance?

CHAPTER XII.

LEFT TO HERSELF.

THE time came for Perdita's conclusive trial. Suddenly called up for examination at Burlington House, she had to prove that she could spell properly and add up rows of figures correctly, that she knew a little geography, could write a letter in fair grammar, find the common denominator and unravel the intricacies of the rule of three;—and thus was in all things calculated to be a satisfactory clerk in the Post-office Savings Bank.

She passed, as of course, triumphantly; and came back to her uncongenial home treading on air, her veins filled with ichor[1] not blood, her life more glorious to her than the sunrise, more fragrant than the pine forests or the flower beds, the moorland heather or the fresh sea breeze. No similitudes could have fitly expressed the state of divine delight in which she was on this sultry sullen summer's day. Whatever desire might blossom out of the present for the future, in this present, as it was, she was fully satisfied. She had reached that definite point which she had placed before her as the one to gain; and for the moment there was no more to ask. The appointment was sure to come in good time; and she was too much elated with the fact of firm rooting to trouble herself with the day of fruition. That day of fruition was certain, and she had not had time yet to become impatient.

She had forgotten everything that had ever been distasteful, painful or even pleasantly disturbing in her life. Mrs. Blount and her pale friend— that strange man of whom she had dreamt so often, whose strong hand had led her back from darkness into light, and from unwise despair to her truer and braver self—her turbulent ideas of liberty and her upsetting theories of republicanism—her mother's chilled affections—her sisters' unsympathetic companionship—even Mr. Brocklebank, whom she had learned to love as her guardian, extra the Court of Chancery—all were alike forgotten; and the one burden of her song was: "Success! Success! I have succeeded!"

How beautiful everything was to-day! The streets were like long-drawn aisles up which marched triumphal processions of noble men and radiant women. She could not believe that any of these creatures,

---

[1]   In Greek mythology, an ethereal fluid taking the place of blood in the veins of the gods.

met on her way home, had heartache for sorrow or minds racked for anxiety. All the race was blessed as she was blessed; all conquerors as she had conquered. No matter that the sun did not shine and that the blue haze lying in the distance was thicker and greyer than usual; the whole city was as if illumined with heavenly fire; and had she been asked she would have said that the sun shone from a sky of Egyptian blue tempered to the loving tenderness of an English early spring. The Green Park and the leafy Gardens were like Paradise to her; and for very joy in her life she felt reluctant to leave the place where, not so long ago, she had been willing to abandon hope and life together because she had given herself up to despair. But the hours passed and she was obliged to go home—to leave the tropical glory of enthusiasm for the cold north-light of adverse criticism and moral discipline.

"I have passed, mother," she said half shyly when she entered the room.

It was strange how timid she felt now that she had won and had no longer need to fight.

"Passed what?" asked her mother coldly.

"My examination," said Perdita.

Mrs. Winstanley made no reply; Eva laughed.

"How funny to hear a girl talk of passing an examination!" she said. "Men do that when they go to college and take their degrees and all that; but how odd that a girl should!"

"Because you think everything that a girl does beyond dancing and needlework odd and unnatural," said Perdita.

"Was it difficult, Perdita?" asked Thomasina smoothly. What a heedless little goose this Eva was! What was the good of these perpetual frays and skirmishes? And Eva certainly did begin them by useless provocation. Perdita was far too passionate and furious in her temper certainly, and very silly for her own part to take any notice of what such a foolish child as Eva might say; still, she never began a quarrel, and if not annoyed was never aggressive.

Perdita turned her face to her elder sister lovingly.

"No," she answered; "there was only a little writing, geography, arithmetic and grammar."

"What a fuss you made about nothing then!" cried Eva. "If all those awful books that you used to read with the tip of your nose were not necessary, you need not have made yourself like a bear in a cage, as you have done."

"I did not know I had made myself like a bear in a cage," answered Perdita.

"Oh yes, you have! Hasn't she, mumsey," said Eva.

"Perdita is never very sociable, my dear," answered Mrs. Winstanley. "But I was not aware that she had been less so than usual of late. To me she seems to have been just the same as she always is."

"Ten times worse," said Eva with the authority of conviction.

"And when will you begin your work?" asked Thomasina, always intent on keeping peace. She was the bit of moral camphor in the family, and kept the dangerous elements apart as well as she could.

"I am waiting for my appointment now," said Perdita gratefully. "Everything is done but to receive my actual appointment."

"And then you will be very busy?" said Thomasina graciously—very graciously indeed, but with such a curious air of condescension and patronage!

"Yes," answered Perdita, her colour rising with the pleasure of the thought. "I will make myself known as the most reliable and industrious of them all."

"Leave others to say that, my dear," said Mrs. Winstanley coldly. "It is not good breeding to vaunt oneself."

"But is resolving to do well vaunting oneself, mother?" Perdita asked, prepared to argue the point on its merits.

"Boasting that you will surpass every one else is," she answered; "and pray do not begin a discussion," she continued with a weary air. "You are so dreadfully fond of arguing, Perdita!"

Tears started into the girl's eyes as she thought to herself, "Surely mother does not know how cruelly she misunderstands me! She cannot mean to hurt me as she does, but—how little she knows of me! And she will not learn!"

She did not speak however, for she had taken the habit of silence of late. But she felt crushed and humiliated, as if flung roughly out of heaven down to the thorny wastes of earth again. She turned from the room and went slowly up the stairs.

"I wonder if it would do to live with Mrs. Blount," she thought. "Anything would be better than home!"

As she left, her mother sighed: a patient, but intensely weary kind of sigh.

"I think Perdita would be much happier, and so should we, if she could find some nice people to live with," she said. "She does not do well with us, she is so dreadfully combative and difficult."

"She will be better when she has something to do," said Thomasina.

"Oh, no, she will not! She will never be better," said little Eva, putting on a gravely magisterial air.

The appointment so ardently desired did not come just yet, and Perdita's buoyant hopes began to grow faint and sick. Meanwhile, the early summer passed into its maturity and the Winstanleys, like all well-principled people, prepared to leave town for the regulation six or eight weeks at the seaside. Perdita was not to go with them; she did not wish to go and they did not desire her company. If she was oppressed by them, they were irritated by her, and both were happier apart. Also, it would have been unwise in her to have left town just now. At any moment she might be summoned to her work; and with the consciousness of this she would have been too anxious and restless to have enjoyed even the grandeur of the sea or the strength of the mountains. Wherefore Mrs. Winstanley put her diminished establishment on board wages, narrowly calculated; and with an injunction to Perdita to behave herself with as little eccentricity as was possible, she got an old governess to come in as ostensible chaperon, and left London for a possible two months' sojourn at Trouville. Here she counted on seeing the gay world at small cost, making pleasant acquaintances which might fructify, and carrying on some already made free from certain risks and difficulties hemming them round at home.

Sir James Kearney was one of those whom she found it desirable to cultivate free from risk and far from home. He was going to Deauville for the races, and Lady Kearney was not. Also, Hubert Strangways was going with him, and Maud Disney would be at their own place in Gloucestershire; and Mrs. Winstanley believed in the policy of heating two irons at the same time and stringing her bow with a double string.

Not that she would have confessed that Hubert Strangways was in any sense an iron in her fire or a string to her bow. He was engaged to Maud Disney, as all the world knew, and was therefore a barren investment and fallow ground; all the same, engagements are not finalities, are they? and if young men of family and fortune do change their minds before that irrevocable "I will"—and, from partners cut out for them by the fitness of things branch off to others who have only beauty and the charm of natural magic—are those others to blame because they enchant? and is a wise mother to forbid an innocent acquaintance because there is just a possibility of the charm working? We have high authority for the doctrine that a man must first care for his own house-hold; and Mrs. Winstanley was a firm believer in the doctrine.

Wherefore Deauville races, with Sir James Kearney and handsome Hubert Strangways as the probable attendants on the ladies to the course, made a pretty picture which she was not disinclined to contemplate.

At the first her freedom was delightful to Perdita. She felt so peaceful and so at large! Miss Cluff, the ancient governess, had an attack of rheumatism immediately on her arrival and was glad to be left undisturbed. She understood the metaphor of her chaperonage as Perdita wished that she should, and did not interfere with the arrangement of the drapery beneath the cloak. A bed to sleep in, an easy-chair to sit in, a roof to cover her and food to eat, all free of cost, were luxuries beyond words to the poor soul who scraped her meagre existence with pain and trouble; and to sit there in a half doze, lazily calculating her savings, was the *summum bonum* of her colourless existence. The house was shut up, save the back room which was Perdita's own by right of use and want of beauty; and she and Miss Cluff, and the old woman who was left in charge, were put on an allowance which scarcely covered the absolute necessities of life and certainly did no more. But nothing of this troubled the girl. She was at peace; she was free; and she was daily expecting to be employed by the Imperial Government—to be made one of the servants of the State, helping in the machinery of the executive, as well as a breadwinner on her own account. It was the happiest time she had ever known. Never had her soft eyes been so bright, her step so elastic, her heart so light, her imagination so thickly peopled with brilliant images as now;—and never had her mother taken so dangerous a step with regard to her uncomfortable and unmanageable daughter! She had given her the dream of her life—honourable, permitted, innocuous freedom; and the question for the future would be—would she ever go back to the old coercion?—would she voluntarily place herself again under the harrow?—patiently offer herself to be bitted, with the knowledge that this included to be scourged at pleasure?

Certainly not, if Mrs. Blount could prevent her!—and Mrs. Blount did her best that way, and tried all she knew to induce her to make a third with herself and Connie Tracy.

Perdita often went to see these two Emancipated Women, of whom only one loved her while the other feared her as a future rival; listening to Bell Blount's endless harangues on the subject of woman's wrongs and man's iniquities, woman's rights and man's duties, till her brain almost reeled and the earth seemed unsteady beneath her feet. Had she been living in a delusion all her life?—and was it indeed true that men, whom she reverenced as her superiors and the chivalrous protectors of the weaker sex, were really the worst enemies women could have?—tyrants and executioners who used them as prey and sacrificed them as victims? She had the natural woman's instinctive admiration for masculine strength—the loving woman's instinctive glory in acknowledging her own comparative inferiority—and she had the modest maiden's vague desire to love and be beloved. Her nascent maternal instinct was beginning to manifest itself in a greater love for children than heretofore; and a strange feeling of divine possession, as if she cradled the universe in her arms came over her when she held a baby against her breast. She thought that the happiness or unhappiness of married life depended chiefly on the woman, and that wifely submission was essentially womanly grace; but when she listened to Bell Blount all her instincts were derided and her theories turned out of doors as false words inspired by the Father of Lies; while their place was filled by ideas of a much more vigorous kind.

Bell Blount laughed at the very name of Love, and called it something else that was less refined, but, according to her, more to the purpose. She vilified the maternal instinct as the most animal and degrading of all emotions; and maintained that only the lowest type of women cared for either men or children, while the choicest spirits repudiated marriage and maternity alike and made their happiness out of friendship with their own sex. She pooh-poohed too, all Perdita's democratic theories as beside the mark. Work and wages, a peaceful foreign policy except where liberty had to be encouraged, republican forms of government, Home Rule, the land question—nothing of all these equalled in importance the grave necessity of giving women the franchise—of making the wife pecuniarily independent of the husband, and, while legally entitled to his support, freed from all obligation to contribute to his—of giving mothers the sole care of the children, so that right or wrong as wives their power over their offspring should be absolute:—in short, the grave necessity of relegating men to their rightful position as henchmen and placing women in that of liege. No other objects were worthy of a woman who loved liberty and desired the salvation of society!

But Perdita, convinced while she listened to the flood of words and arguments which Bell Blount poured forth so rapidly and smoothly, went back on her old feeling and took up again the mental attitude which was more natural to her so soon as she got alone and could think without disturbance. Love seemed so much better than all this hard antagonism!—womanly submission so much sweeter than all this egotistical independence!—reverence for the sex which gave the world Socrates and Plato, Homer and Shakespeare, the prophets and the lawgivers, the patriots and the martyrs of history, so much more certain than contempt for what has been proved best in favour of what might lie in the unknown! And then surely motherhood fulfilled the law of life more nobly than that arid childlessness which Bell Blount seemed to consider the crown of womanhood! But these talks perplexed her all the same, and both fevered and bewildered her.

Besides this, the bills which Mrs.Winstanley had not been able to settle before she left came in with painful rapidity and humiliating demands; and Perdita was more than once obliged to meet the angry tradesmen, who swore they would cut off the supplies unless something was paid on account.These scenes made such an impression on Perdita, sensitive and Quixotically honourable as she was, that she curtailed even her shabby allowance and lived with more than her usual stoical simplicity, as the only right thing to do in the circumstances. Her chief fare was suet-pudding and oatmeal porridge; which she did her best to find both appetizing and sufficient by thinking of the poor creatures who had neither. It was trying to cool a fever by thinking of a glacier, or to warm her frozen limbs by imagining a fire.

And it had much the same result. Suet-pudding and oatmeal porridge, rich as they might be in nitrogen and phosphates and all the rest of it, were not exactly an ideal dietary for a young lady not brought up to either; and the end was easy to foresee.

When her appointment came, as it did at last, and she attempted to work through her fatigue and excitement on such insufficient nourishment as this, she failed, as she needs must; and one day on coming home she was seized with a sudden faintness just as she was passing a chemist's shop.

She knew the place by sight, but she had never been in before.The doubtful honour of the Winstanley custom was given elsewhere.

It was rather a severe-looking place—more like a dispensary than a chemist's shop. The lower panes of the window were darkened and there were none of the ordinary frivolities on sale here. "Leslie Crawford" was in small black letters over the window.

Perdita turned at the open doorway and went in staggering and faint. She sat down on a chair pale and speechless, and her head sank forward on her breast. A man came from behind the desk where he had been writing, and laid his hand on her shoulder.

"Are you ill?" he said; and then he exclaimed:"Good Heavens! it is you!"

Perdita opened her eyes, roused by the voice, the touch, the words.

She saw again the clear, honest, grey eyes and the handsome kindly face with its sadness and its strength; she heard again the voice, rich in tone and tender while full of command, which she had heard in the twilight in the Gardens; and she felt once more the hand which now as then brought her back from darkness to the light.

"You want rest, Miss Winstanley," he said gently. "Let me take you upstairs to the mother."

"Thank you," said Perdita, to whom obedience to his wish came with fatal facility.

But when she rose her weakness overpowered her again; the world grew dark before her eyes, and she fell forward fainting in the arms of Leslie Crawford, the chemist of High Street.

CHAPTER XIII.

ABOVE THE SHOP.

WHEN Perdita recovered her senses she found herself lying on a sofa in a strange room, with a middle-aged woman bending over her doing something to her—she did not exactly know what—but something disagreeable that made her throat smart and her nose tingle; while the man of the shop was standing a little way off, with a couple of medicine bottles in his hands, as if giving directions—as, in fact, he was.

For a few moments she was dazed and uncertain, not knowing where she was nor what had happened; but by degrees her brain regained its ordinary power and she understood how things were. She had fainted in the shop, and had been carried up here to their private room, where she was being cared for by the chemist and, she supposed, his mother.

How long had her fainting-fit lasted? It seemed to her as if it might have been for days or years—everything was so confused and displaced. What a nuisance she was! she thought, tears stealing from between her closed lids. She was always doing something that gave others trouble and brought herself into difficulties!

She raised herself with a spasmodic effort, and, weak as she was, broke out into the tumultuous regrets and excuses characteristic of her.

"I am so sorry, so ashamed!" she began, her pallid face and failing voice contrasting strangely with her eager words. "I cannot imagine what made me so stupid. I am so sorry, so much ashamed! But I am quite well now," she said, making a vigorous attempt to get up and walk in proof of her assertion, but ignominiously ending by falling again on the sofa, weaker and more helpless than she could have believed possible from so simple a mishap as a fainting-fit.

"Pray do not think of moving yet, Miss Winstanley; and do not distress yourself about us," said the chemist, gently pressing her back against the cushions. "You have given us no trouble, I assure you! On the contrary, the mother is so fond of nursing, that I am certain she is more obliged to you than not for giving her this opportunity of doctoring you. Is it not so, mother?" he added, with a smile, wishing to re-assure the poor girl and cut short those hysterical self-reproaches.

"Yes," said Mrs. Crawford pleasantly. "I am glad to be of use to any one, and especially to a neighbour as you are."

"Do you know me?" asked Perdita, opening her soft, short-sighted eyes with almost a start.

They had taken off her spectacles so that she could not see clearly; and the floating, vague, unfocussed look of those large loving orbs gave her face a certain helpless expression unspeakably touching. It softened Mrs. Crawford, whose whole nature was compassionate; and the chemist felt as strong men do feel when a woman who is sympathetic to them seems to need help and protection.

"My son Leslie knows you," said Mrs. Crawford very kindly.

"I see you pass every day," put in Leslie.

"But a great many people pass every day. Do you know them all?" asked Perdita.

The chemist smiled carelessly; but a certain slight embarrassment of manner did not fit in quite well with that airy assumption of indifference.

"You remember when I met you in the Gardens?" he asked with that bold kind of honesty which implies effort. Simplicity of intention never squares its elbows nor stiffens its back, still less does unconsciousness of hidden motives.

Perdita looked confused, Mrs. Crawford attentive.

"Yes, I remember," said the impetuous rebel in a low voice, not liking the reminder.

"One day after that evening I saw you go up the street just as I was leaving the house. I had the curiosity to watch where you went, and followed you to No. 100, West Hill Gardens. The Directory told me the rest. Since then I have noticed you pass twice a day, regularly; and I am not surprised at your fainting-fit. You have been doing too much, and I have seen it."

"Oh!" said Perdita.

She felt the triviality and baldness of her exclamation, but it was all that she could say. She was pleasantly surprised that this man, who had once done her such a good turn—was it so good after all?—had cared enough about her to find out who she was and where she lived. All the same she was keenly alive to the terrible fact that her ideal—because her rescuer—had resolved itself into the undeniable prose of a pharmaceutical chemist, standing behind a counter, and himself, on a pinch, serving the public with rhubarb draughts and aloes pills. She was disgusted with herself for allowing a feeling, which she would have been the first to stigmatize as base, to break through the nobler recognition of human worth independent of conventional conditions. But education and inheritance are powerful influences even over minds strong enough to break new ground for themselves; and for all Perdita's natural democracy, the teaching of her youth and the disdain with which her family would hold a man who was not a gentleman by Act of Parliament, made her wince.

During this little passage of explanation, Mrs. Crawford had watched both Leslie and Perdita with a covertly uneasy feeling that bordered on but did not quite touch suspicion. Though the one had spoken openly—and openness presupposes innocence—and the other had evidently not known of this mild pursuit and objectless discovery, still, there was a vague something, a film of consciousness over both, that a little disturbed her.

"I thought Miss Winstanley was perhaps a customer of yours, Leslie," she said rather gravely.

"No," he answered; "some one else has that honour."

"I do not know much about the honour," said over-candid Perdita, remembering the bill that was brought in the other day and the man who brought it—the angry threats which he had used and the hard things which he had said and of which she had had to bear the brunt—because of the dainty toilette requisites considered indispensable by her mother and sisters, though there was no possibility of present and but small chance of future payment.

"I am glad you all enjoy such good health; but I should consider your custom an honour, however small it might be," said Leslie, with such obvious shop mannerism as made him a tradesman on the spot and his speech only a professional compliment of no personal value.

Even Perdita, for all her absurd habit of believing in the sincerity of others because herself sincere, even she could not accept the phrase as if it had been meant for literal acceptance.

She wished he had not said such a silly thing! To her savage abhorrence of shams, it seemed to take something from him—to lessen by so much the supreme nobility of his nature as she had constructed that nature out of the depths of her inner consciousness.

"Your way of business is too grand for us," she said quite seriously. "We get only stupid little things, like toothpowder and hair-pomade. We never have prescriptions made up. Mother is a homœopathist, and doctors us herself when we are ill. It is so much cheaper; and the medicines are not nasty."

Leslie smiled, this time naturally.

"So much the better for you," he said. "At all events, no harm can be done; and very often nature is the best physician. And, as you say, the medicines are not bad to take, which ours are. But now I must go back to business. Mother, keep Miss Winstanley for a while, till she has quite recovered her strength and may be trusted out alone. And give her some tea; it will refresh her."

"Will you not stay for some yourself, Leslie?" asked his mother somewhat anxiously.

"Not now, thank you, mother; I must go back to business. I will not say good-bye," he said, turning to Perdita. "Perhaps you will pass through the shop on your way out, so that I may see how you look?"

"Yes," said Perdita, "I will; thank you. But I think I will go now. I do not like to trouble your mother any longer. I do not want any tea."

"No trouble, Miss Winstanley, a pleasure instead," said the kindly woman, laying her hand on the girl's shoulder. "I should be quite glad if you would stay a little longer with me."

"And it is now tea-time," put in Leslie.

And as Perdita felt it was only right to do as they wished and stay for their pleasure after she had been here for her own benefit, and as she felt strangely—her mother would have called it sinfully, happy in this pleasant, airy, well-furnished room above the shop, she smiled in acquiescence and obediently sat down again, saying: "Thank you very much," and wondering why Leslie did not stay too; surely his business could wait for a few minutes. He could not be wanted all day long in the shop!

Perdita was only a woman; and there never yet was a woman who did not deny the exigencies of a man's professional duty, nor one who did not hold that the time taken from her and given to that duty was time filched as well as lost.

Suddenly a child was heard coming up the stairs, protesting shrilly against some baby indignity offensive to its feelings. Mrs. Crawford laughed softly. She looked as if she had heard the loveliest passage of the sweetest song.

"There is my Lily come home. Little darling! what ails her?" she said, getting up and going towards the door. She looked a little longingly at

Leslie, who did not look at her. "Are you fond of children, Miss Winstanley?" she then asked, turning to Perdita.

"Very," answered Perdita, also rising, and full of eagerness.

No doubt she was very fond of children, but she was not always stirred by them to her present pitch of excitement.

Mrs. Crawford laughed again. It was such a soft pleasant kind of coo! such a musical little expression of that maternal instinct which is the best quality of womanhood and the most potent antiseptic of society!

"All nice girls like babies," she said, pleasantly.

Opening the door, she called out, "Susan, bring baby here. Do not take off her things, but bring her just as she is."

And on her words a young woman brought in a pretty little dark-eyed, dark-haired, olive-skinned child of about two years old, and, as she phrased it, "stood her down upon the floor."

"Gramma!" cried the little one, running into Mrs. Crawford's skirts. "Dadda!" she then said, making a dash at Leslie, and lifting up her bright little face to be kissed.

"My Lily! my little darling!" said Mrs. Crawford, taking her up in her arms and kissing her fondly. "Kiss her, Leslie! see how prettily she asks you!" she added.

With strange want of spontaneousness, Leslie bent down and kissed the child's soft cheek. He was quite gentle and courteous, but he was neither loving nor playful, as a man generally is when he caresses his child; and he seemed troubled, almost annoyed, as if ill at ease.

His mother looked at him with an earnest face that was half beseeching and half reproving.

"She grows more like you every day, my boy," she said, as if putting forth a plea.

Perdita opened her eyes and wondered. Leslie was a calm, quiet, blue-eyed, fair-haired, thoroughly English-looking man, and the little child was dark and vivacious, petulant and nervous, with black, beady eyes, and a singularly foreign look all through. Where was the likeness? Surely not in features, nor yet in coloring, nor, by the look of things, in temperament. Where then? and how could Mrs. Crawford be so blind?

The chemist turned away abruptly. His mother's plea had not touched him to tenderness.

"I really must go," he said; with a certain impatience that struck Perdita with a sense of discord in this quiet little home scene; and adding, "I shall see you on your way out, Miss Winstanley," he turned and left the room.

"Evidently," thought Perdita, "he is a most unaffectionate father. But how can he be indifferent to such a beautiful little angel as this?" And then she thought, "I wonder what the wife is like, and why she does not come in!"

She felt a certain odd sensation about her throat, she scarcely knew why. If not the remains of her faintness, it was presumably because Leslie Crawford, the chemist, was less than loving to his child. It could not be for wounded pride, because his wife did not think it necessary to pay her the attention of coming into the room to see her. That there was a wife at all had come upon her with a feeling of surprise that was not all pleasure. Though the most natural thing in the world, somehow her imagination had not blocked out the figure of a "sacti," or female energy of the god to whom she had given the form and features of Leslie Crawford. Of course; it could make no kind of difference to her whether the man was married or single; but the mind is so odd! When you have believed things to be one way, it creates such a feeling of confusion, almost of disappointment, to find them set in another. And it does not do, somehow, for unmarried women to make their ideals out of other women's husbands. Wives do not like to see too much admiration bestowed on their legal possessors; and such a mother as Mrs. Crawford would be the last person in the world to encourage superfluous affection, even for her son.

Without question, the discovery of the wife was an unwelcome matter to poor Perdita, head-long, impulsive, idealizing, affectionate as she was; and it took all her power of self-control to choke down that rising lump in her throat, and accept the idea of this intrusive "sacti" as that of a beneficiary deity on her own account and the worthy pendant of the original divinity.

But now that she was here, and Leslie had gone down-stairs, this rebel of ours thought she might as well make the best of it, and do what she could with things as they were. Perhaps the wife could come before she left. Meanwhile she devoted herself to the pleasant task of making love to the baby—thereby winning not only a gracious acceptance of her devotion from the small tyrant herself, but also a warm place in Mrs. Crawford's heart.

All things, however, came to an end at last, and Perdita was obliged to go home. But she did not pass through the shop.

"Please tell Mr. Crawford that I am quite well, and did not like to disturb him," she said, as she shook hands with her hostess.

And Mrs. Crawford said, "Yes, my dear, I will," and liked the girl all the better for her consideration and reticence.

It was odd that tears should stand in Perdita's eyes—those soft, short-sighted hazel eyes—as she hurried along the streets; that she should feel lonely and disappointed, she did not know why, and disposed to take a gloomy view of all things in life when she reached that home which poets tell us is the dearest place on earth. To her, home had never been specially sweet; and this evening she thought it more than ever melancholy, less than ever satisfying.

She found poor old Cluff waiting for her with that pathetic patience of the powerless and needy; while the charwoman was maundering over stories of young maidens decoyed and made away with in the heart of that terrible city, as she dropped her snuff over the plates and visited the gin-bottle at intervals.

The home-coming of the truant then was hailed with the acclamation of relief from anxiety; and so far was a welcome. But though usually so quick and sensitive to kindness, this evening she felt as if her heart was that typical stony ground whereon it is useless to scatter good seeds of any kind.

She apologized with extraordinary earnestness for her illbreeding in keeping her ancient governess waiting so long for the miserable meal called by courtesy their dinner-tea; but she did not say what had detained her; and Cluff did not ask. Poor old Cluff had delicate fingers and dreaded hot coals with the fear that comes from experience. She thought it best that Perdita should fight out her own life without implicating others who would only have to suffer let what would happen. Wherefore she asked no questions, but accepted the girl's apologies as eminently satisfactory—quite as satisfactory as the fullest explanation would have been.

So the evening passed rather more silently than usual; and Cluff pondered, while Perdita tried to reason down her nameless sadness and to account for it to herself by the strange sensation of fainting, and the lassitude left on her in consequence.

And she made herself believe too, that she did not tell Cluff where she had been, nor what had happened to her, simply not to make her uneasy for the one part and to save herself from unnecessary watching for the other. Poor old Cluff was such a good creature—she might think it right to send a letter to mother at Trouville; and then mother would worry about her (Perdita's) going to the office and perhaps make her throw up her appointment. So that, on the whole, keeping a calm sough was the best wisdom, said Perdita to herself; and she was not deceitful because she did not tell. It was such a trifling matter indeed, there was scarcely anything to tell. How many people faint! What was the use of making a fuss about such an ordinary accident? it would be silly and missy, said Perdita; and she hated being silly and missy.

A train of reasoning which answered all purposes required and satisfied everybody.

CHAPTER XIV.

HER NEW FRIENDS.

FEVERISH and excited, Perdita had but little sleep that night. In spite of her republicanism she was sorry that the man who had once saved her life and who seemed so specially delightful to her should turn out to be only a chemist. Of course it made no difference to her; but it did with her family. She could not bring the Crawfords home to mother and the girls as else she would have been so glad to have done. What a pity it was! and what a wonderful man he seemed to be—for a chemist! and how sweet Mrs. Crawford was; but where was the wife? And in thinking of the wife she grew somehow less feverish than before, cooling down into the showers which succeed the heats; till at last, weeping for no reason whatsoever, she fell asleep.

But only to dream of Leslie Crawford with his handsome face and quiet ways; of his mother, so still and gentle and Quaker-like; of the dark-eyed child; and of that shadowy wife whose features she could not make out, but who was somehow mixed up with the idea of the angel with the flaming sword barring the way to the Garden of Eden. And then she woke with a start and found that it was broad daylight and time to get up.

"Chemist or not, he is a very good, clever man; and his mother is delightful—how kind and sweet she is! I dare say the wife is just as nice too; and the little one is exactly like a lady's child, with its dear little French-looking face and head and its pretty quaint costume. And I shall go and see them very often; and I don't mind if they are tradespeople and live over a shop!"

These were Perdita's waking thoughts when she had done with dreams and had come back to realities. Then she went on thinking to herself as clearly as if a voice were speaking to her.

"As he is married there can be no forwardness in my going, and my motives cannot be mistaken. For though he is a chemist, and of course any silliness on my part would be out of the question, still, people are so apt to say ill-natured things of girls; and they might, even of me! I hope I shall like his wife as well as I like his mother. Though they are tradespeople they are better than half the gentlefolks we know; and then a chemist is not like a tailor or a shoemaker. A chemist must be a man of education and is next thing to a doctor. And a doctor, of course, is any one's equal. Mother would not like it, I daresay; but I shall go again, because I ought. And I hope I have made real friends. I am sure they are good people. They are both so kind and quiet and without any finery or nonsense about them!"

As a further argument, inciting and persuading her to do that which she had already determined on doing, it was only good manners, she said, to call on Mrs. Crawford and thank her for her kindness. Even mother would allow that! she thought, as she sat brushing her magnificent hair with more than ordinary vigour. For though she was what Eva had once called, with more force than elegance, "an untidy toad," she was delicately clean; and though her hair was put up anyhow, her careful combings and brushings kept it as soft and fresh as newly spun silk.

"If I do not go very soon—next Sunday say—it will seem as if I were too proud because I am what is called a lady and they are shopkeepers. And I should be so sorry if they thought that of me! It would not be true; and how shameful if it were true! I could not bear that they should think so meanly of me as this. So I will go next Sunday; and how glad I shall be to see that dear woman and that sweet little thing again!"

All of which unspoken reasoning proved simply this—that honest Perdita was a daughter of Eve like any one else, and could, on occasions, deceive herself.

When Sunday came, Perdita, almost for the first time in her life, was anxious to look nice, and to have everything in order. Fresh trimmings everywhere and the addition of sundry little ornaments, hitherto looked on as superfluous naughtiness and the signs of a feeble intellect, made her really pretty enough to be her mother's daughter. And even she herself knew that she looked well; and took pleasure in that knowledge; as she prepared to set out for her visit to the chemist and his mother. Without vanity as she was, she could not but be conscious of something more agreeable than was usual in her appearance as she stood before Thomasina's pier-glass. It was a wholly new thing that she should look at herself full-length at all; and she felt secretly ashamed, as if it were more than half wrong and something that brushed the skirts of modesty.

But she wanted to make a good impression on Mrs. Crawford, she said to herself by way of excuse. She saw how perfectly well-ordered everything was in her house and how deliciously fresh she and the child were; and she should be so sorry if she herself, a lady by birth, should fall below the standard set by a shopkeeper's mother! It was only that kind of honourable pride, part personal and part generic, which belonged to her by place and inheritance. And Mrs. Crawford herself, with all her simplicity, would be the first to understand it. It was not that silly vanity which makes women prank themselves out like so many dolls for show. It was not a trap for admiration; it was only a mark of courtesy to others and of respect for herself and for her mother; she being in her absence that mother's representative.

And this last argument, coming into her mind as it did like a flash of light, pleased her more than all the rest because more conclusive than all the rest—giving the sanction of filial duty to her desire to stand well with Mrs. Crawford, the mother of the chemist in High Street.

Her visit was so far successful in that she found Mrs. Crawford at home; but there was no sign of Leslie and none of his wife. She sat with her new friend for some time, and the two talked of the few things common to women of such different ages and disconnected spheres. One of these things was Perdita herself, her parentage and family, and how it came about that she was alone in London during the summer—that migratory season when every one with a soul to be saved is among the mountains or at the seaside; and who was with her as companion and caretaker?

For to be born in the velvet and the purple is all very well, but velvet may be stained and smirched like common calico; and for her own part Mrs. Crawford did not care to encourage the visits of a young lady of unquestionable genealogy and doubtful conduct—nor yet of any one whose personal propriety was unassailable but one whose family inheritance was one of dishonour.

But Perdita's biography showed no weak places. Herself and her family were equally respectable; and if there were skeletons in the home cupboard she was evidently ignorant of them. She said in her candid foolish way that they were not rich and that mother was often hard put to it for money and she showed these dry bones of comparative impecuniosity so openly that it was plain she would have dangled the cord had there been an ancestral murderer, and would have confessed the keys of the genealogical burglar.

And being thus straitened, she went on to say, she, the middle girl, thought she ought to do some something to lighten the home burden and help the general income. This was her manifest duty; and yet her sisters were not to blame in that they did not follow her example. She said this with a generous kind of haste that struck Mrs. Crawford as an evidence of more than it showed. Her eldest sister, she said, was her mother's right hand and companion and could not be spared; the youngest was too child-like to be put to serious work; and both were too beautiful to go out by themselves.

"Mother never allows them to go anywhere alone, except in the common garden," she said. "Indeed it would be impossible for them to go about as I do. They are very beautiful and every one notices them so much! It could not be!"

"Then your mother does not object to your going about the streets by yourself?" asked Mrs. Crawford with frank surprise.

She was not a lady, and did not understand that kind of maternal love which is apportioned by the measure of good looks.

"No, I am different," answered Perdita simply. "Mother knows that no one would look at me twice; and we make such a large party when we are all together. But," she added ingenuously, honesty forcing her to confess the exact truth, "I must tell you that she does not like my working. It was only through the influence of Mr. Brocklebank, a rich friend of ours who likes Thomasina and for whom mother has a great respect, that I got leave at all. He backed me up; and then mother gave way."

"I think you are right to do something for yourself if money is scarce, seeing that you have your mother's consent," said Mrs. Crawford, after a short pause. "It would have been wrong else."

"Would it?" asked Perdita eagerly, the colour coming into her face. "Do you think filial obedience the highest virtue of all, and that one's own conscience goes for nothing? Should children give up what seems to them absolutely right and necessary—the best things in life—if their parents hold different opinions?"

"In most cases, yes," answered Mrs. Crawford. "There are very few instances indeed in which filial disobedience is justified."

"But what do you make of conscience?" asked Perdita. "How many of the early saints and martyrs who helped to plant the Church of Christ were what would now be called disobedient children and undutiful wives!"

"That is quite another thing," said Mrs. Crawford with true feminine reasoning. "You cannot compare those holy women, upheld by the power of the Holy Spirit as they were, with your pert little creatures of modern times, whose only ambition is to escape from all control and to lead the lives of young men rather than of young women. I am not of the new school, my dear young lady! I do not hold with the emancipation of woman, anyhow. I do not believe in her rights, and I respect only her duties."

"But the right to work is also a duty if we look at things properly," said Perdita. "We would think a labourer's daughter very wrong who refused to go out as a servant or a mill-hand; and it is only extending the principle to include poor ladies like myself, for instance."

"I do not say they should not work, but it should be work done at home—either their natural home or within the four walls of another person's. I do not approve of office life or clerkships or any thing of that kind. I like nothing which takes women into the streets; and I am too old-fashioned to change. All this wandering to and fro—all this unrest and excitement tends to no good, depend upon it. It is a false state of things from first to last, and one of the worst signs of a dangerous time."

"Oh," said Perdita with a distressed face, but lifting up her eyes and looking into Mrs. Crawford's honestly. "I am so sorry! Then you will not like me; for I am in the Post-office Savings Bank, and go to the City—to St. Paul's Churchyard every day."

"I would rather you dusted the drawing-room at home and helped the cook to make the dinner," said Mrs. Crawford quietly but firmly.

"But being even a real servant and saving mother the cost of a housemaid, would not give me forty pounds a year; and I am to have forty and in time seventy," said Perdita simply.

"No; but it might save something more precious than even seventy pounds will buy," returned Mrs. Crawford.

"What?" the girl asked earnestly.

"The love of home and the habit of home-staying," answered the chemist's mother.

"Yes, I know; but after all, dear Mrs. Crawford, it is not quite what one goes to school for and educates oneself for at home, to make the beds and clean the knives, is it now?" said Perdita, sticking to her point faithfully enough, but all the while in secret dread lest she should offend the woman whose favour she especially wished to gain.

But how strange it was, she thought, that she should always be thus at odds with those whose love and sympathy were so essential to her happiness! Her mother against her on the one side because of Mrs. Grundy and society—Mrs. Crawford against her on the other because of certain mythical proprieties and impracticable conditions—and she so passionately convinced in her own strong heart that she was right and they were wrong; and that Bell Blount in the van of all went too far!

"Ah, my dear, things are going ill with the women of England!" said Mrs. Crawford. "The abandonment of domestic duties, the relaxation of parental authority, the want of all home discipline and personal restriction, are the crying sins of modern society. I should like to go back to the time of our grandmothers, when women kept at home and minded their families instead of spending all their strength in gadding about seeking after pleasure or in copying the lives and actions of men. Present ideas seem to make housekeeping the one degrading employment of women and marriage and maternity a cross and oppression rather than a glory and a duty."

"I do not think so; believe me I do not!" said Perdita with earnestness. "But what are we to do when we are poor and cannot marry? After all, the kind of work that we want to do is only a substitute," she added naively.

"And a bad one," said Mrs. Crawford.

"How differently you see things!" cried Perdita, thinking of Bell Blount and all her contempt for the domestic life of woman.

"Differently from whom?—yourself or your mother?" asked Mrs. Crawford, not relishing the comparison.

"No, not from us, but from a friend of mine—the most advanced of all the Woman's Rights women, the most Emancipated of any one I know."

"Then no fit friend for you, I should say," returned Mrs. Crawford.

"I think she is good and I am sure she is sincere; and she has been very kind to me," said Perdita.

She was too true and brave to abandon a friend even under pressure; and the pressure of desire to win Mrs. Crawford's regard was very great.

"Who is she, may I ask?" said Mrs. Crawford.

"Mrs. Blount—Bell Blount she is generally called," answered the girl.

"Mrs. Blount? I know Mrs. Blount!" cried Mrs, Crawford, with as much disdain as one whose Quaker blood commands self-suppression all through could allow herself to show. "She lived down in the place where I was born and brought up. She is younger than I; but I remember her for years."

"Do you know her? Tell me something about her, Mrs. Crawford!" said Perdita. "I only know her from having met her here in London. I know nothing of her history."

"There is not much good to be said of her, my dear. She is the daughter of a country lawyer; and she married a clergyman—the vicar of the parish where we lived. He is a very decent, worthy kind of man;

but she left him and her four daughters, about three years ago, to take up the questionable position of Champion of her Sex. She spends all her strength in proselytizing, and is only happy when making speeches on public platforms and bringing herself before the world. She is no fit friend for you, Miss Winstanley! I would not have allowed my own daughter to have known her."

"I am so sorry!" said Perdita vaguely.

"Does your mother visit her?" asked Mrs. Crawford.

"Mother? Oh no!" said Perdita, as if she had denied that her mother had two heads—or, perhaps a juster parallel, that she had ever consorted with Satan. "She is not in mother's way at all," she added.

"And are you right to make friends with any one whom she does not know and would not approve of?" asked the chemist's mother gravely.

As she spoke a sudden rush of consciousness sent the blood with strange force into her delicate face. Was it not more than likely that Mrs. Winstanley would disapprove of herself and her son as friends for this wild, visionary, erratic daughter of hers? Proud as she evidently was, by Perdita's own showing, would tradespeople, however well educated and intrinsically refined, come within the category of the socially permitted?

As rapidly as this doubt flashed into her mind was the resolve to breach the question now to-day before Perdita left the house and to tell her that she must not come here again. For though Mrs. Crawford was mild and quiet to a surpassing degree, she had an immense deal of that sturdy, honest, middle-class pride which resents patronage and super-ciliousness in equal measure, and neither envies superior rank nor brooks contempt for its own condition. She did not wish to have one of the "connecting links" at her house for any personal pride there might be in the association; and assuredly she did not want to put herself in the way of a rebuff from any lady mother extant, and to be told that she, honourable and blameless as she was in her own sphere, was not fit to be the friend of that lady mother's daughter. Like to like was best, she thought; and false notes were to be avoided in association as well as in music.

Thought is so much quicker than speech that Mrs. Crawford had made out all this in her brain while Perdita was saying the first words of her answer.

"Mother does not much care what I do," she said. "If I do not worry and get in her way she is quite satisfied. And after all, I must have some one to speak to," she added, with a spice of her old tremulous passion. "I cannot go on living so entirely alone as I have done!"

"My dear! how can you be alone? You have your family and your family friends," said Mrs. Crawford with gentle rebuke.

"No; that is just what I have not," answered Perdita, who was getting excited.

"No? Why 'no,' my child?"

"I cannot tell you. They do not like me and I do not like them. That is all I can say, dear Mrs. Crawford. Mr. Brocklebank is the only one of all who come to the house who has ever been good to me; and he likes me only because he is in love with Thomasina."

"At least you have one friend among them. Perhaps more, if you will think calmly," said Mrs. Crawford kindly.

"No, no more! I never see any one indeed, for I hate what is called society and never go out when I am not obliged. I do not dance so well as my sisters and I cannot talk to young men. They are so silly and say such absurd things; and I am so stupid, I cannot answer them back in the same strain! And then they laugh at me; and I hear afterwards that I have been talking politics, or history, or something that was considered dreadful. And then I am so ugly and awkward that mother does not care to take me out; and I know that it makes everything worse for me when I have to go. The fact is, Mrs. Crawford dear, I do not get on well at home; and neither mother nor the girls care for me!"

Here poor Perdita's lips began to quiver. Yearning for love as she did, the picture of her home isolation always broke her down when she contemplated it.

"I thought so," said Mrs. Crawford. "I was sure of it! But whose is the fault, my dear?"

"Perhaps mine!" said Perdita hopelessly. "But if it is I do not know it, and cannot help it. I try to make them like me, but I cannot. I would love both of them so much if they would let me! Thomasina is so gentle and wise, and little Eva is such a darling when she is nice. But Thomasina repels me when I want to be good friends with her; and when Eva is cross, or has nothing else to do, she teases me till I get wild and say and do all manner of violent, wicked things. And then mother is angry with me, Thomasina despises me, Eva is more impertinent than ever, and I am broken-hearted! It is a miserable life for me, Mrs. Crawford; and before I had this work to do at the Post Office I was as much alone in my own home as if I had been an orphan!"

On which, self-pity conquering both pride and her desire to stand well with Leslie Crawford's mother, to whom she instinctively felt that all passionate display of feeling, all want of reticence, would be abhorrent, she gave way to her hysterical passion according to her wont and burst into an agonizing flood of tears.

Poor Perdita! she, like some others of us, had to pull her pound on that uphill way of moral discipline; and the task was both painful and difficult.

Her tears, her evident loneliness and want of guidance, the spiritual peril in which she was from her association with Bell Blount without counteraction from wholesome home influences, did what nothing else would have done—conquered Mrs. Crawford's bourgeois pride; overcame her natural repugnance to the undisciplined temperament only too evident in Perdita; overcame too, her cherished principle of filial obedience, and determined her to do what she could to save the poor child who had come like a lost lamb to the door of her fold. She felt as if the girl had been given into her hand by the Lord Himself to direct and guide aright. Providence works by mysterious ways, she thought, and no law is absolute. The whole thing looked so like an overruling will—so like divine direction! Would she not be doing unfaithfully were she to refuse the charge that seemed to have been so intentionally given her?

"Poor child! my poor misguided, uncared-for girl!" she said pityingly. "You shall not be left. God will care for you if you pray to Him aright; and this may be only a trial to bring you nearer to Him. Come and see me, my dear, as often as you like. You will be always welcome to me and I will be as much of a mother to you as I can. You shall be my daughter till I meet my own again," she added, the tears starting to her eyes as she raised them, with patient and pathetic sorrow, and cried out to God in her heart.

"Thank you! thank you!" said Perdita, lifting up her disordered face, but smiling through her tears with that passionate quickness to feel, that strange mobile power of receptivity which made both her danger and her charm. "Oh, Mrs. Crawford!" she cried, flinging herself on her knees by the elder woman's side and holding both her delicate hands, which she kissed with almost southern fervour; "if you knew what it is to me to hear a woman speak to me like this!—if I might feel that I had something like a real mother, something like a true, sympathetic friend in the world!"

"You shall, my child. I will be your friend so far as I can—your mother, if you like to call me so. And I will pray to the Lord that I may be of good service to you, and that the charge which He has delivered into my hands I may fulfil worthily and as He would have me."

On which the sweet pale face bent down till it met that flushed and eager one held up to it in such tumultuous passion of grief and hope and joy; and then the two women kissed each other, and the one felt that she had found a mother, the other that she had recovered a daughter. For the moment both had forgotten Leslie and his wife, and what he would think of this new adoption into the house where, if his mother was mistress, he at least was master.

What Mrs. Blount would have called the "disturbing element," if she had not given it a harsher name, was brought back to their consciousness however, by the opening of the front door and the sound of a man's feet coming up the stairs two steps at a time, according to the manner of the energetic.

Perdita had just time to get up from her knees, brush away the tears from her eyes and the hair from her face, and stand up like any other rational creature preparing to take leave, when Leslie came in. Whether or not he had expected to see only his mother he did not say, but he glanced eagerly round the room as he entered, as if looking for more than the well-known face; and when his eyes fell on Perdita he smiled, coloured and tossed back his hair with an action expressive of both pleasure and relief. But she turned deadly pale, by very force, as it were, of contrast.

It is so delightful to see one's ideal realized in the flesh—though that realization be only a chemist and druggist selling nasty compounds over the counter and with a wife somewhere about the world! Why should we moderns be denied the joy that Pygmalion knew? He created his supreme delight in marble and we make ours out of living man. What the hammer and chisel were to him, gratitude and imagination were to Perdita; and to each the ideal was perfected.

"Oh, Mr. Crawford! I was just going," she said awkwardly, but with a happy laugh for all her nervousness.

Undoubtedly that poor dear sandwich had no manners to speak of! There was never any one so easily put out of countenance as she; no one whose wits were less difficult to be sent wool-gathering.

"I am glad that I have come in time to see you," he answered smiling. "Are you better? All right again? No return of the attack?"

"No, none; I am quite well again now, thank you," she answered. "I came to show myself to your mother and thank her for her kindness. I could not come before, because I have to go to the office every day."

She said all this hurriedly. Had she stopped to think, she might have asked herself what need was there for this explanation to Leslie Crawford?—who asked for it or expected it?—and why should she give any reason at all for being found with his mother? Was it not something in the spirit of *qui s'excuse s'accuse?*[1] There was no special reason for telling Mr. Leslie Crawford why she was here, unless she had something to hide or was afraid he might believe something that was not.

"It was very good and thoughtful of you," said Leslie quietly. "Somehow I thought you would come to-day."

"Did you?" answered Perdita in an odd tone and with the faintest little shadow of reproach in her honest eyes.

"I was obliged to go out, else I should have waited at home for the sake of seeing how you were," said Leslie in the most natural manner possible.

Perdita turned to him with a flush on her face that was like light.

"You are very kind," she said with a burst of feeling and an exuberance of gratitude somewhat unnecessary, all things considered.

She certainly was terribly excitable! She could not take anything in life with the quiet dignity, the self-contained composure of her class, but boiled over on the smallest provocation and spent as much moral energy over a mere trifle as others took for the support of a catastrophe or the warding off a danger.

"But," thought Mrs. Crawford, "this is just where I shall be useful to her. She is too hysterical, too excitable as she is. I must do what I can to quiet and control her; and when she has got the grace of self-restraint she will be a fine creature. She is lost now by very excess; but she will be all right when she is toned down. And I trust I may be permitted to be made the instrument of her salvation."

Soon after this Perdita went away and Leslie said that he would walk home with her. If only Mrs. Winstanley, sitting on the sands at Trouville, could have seen the iniquity at this moment being transacted at West Hill Gardens! But a merciful fate has limited human vision; and youth makes its account out of the restriction.

They had a very pleasant talk as they went slowly along the streets, and one which seemed to bring them closer together than would have seemed possible in so short a time, because one which revealed a great deal of each to the other. Leslie asked Perdita who were her favourite authors; and she asked him who were his. They did not quite agree in their choice. Hers were of a more florid, romantic, impassioned style than his; his quieter, more thoughtful, less excited than hers. To her, Byron was the great god of the English Parnassus, such bits of Swinburne as she might read seemed to her like a revelation, and

[1]   (French), she who makes excuses accuses herself.

Longfellow made her weep when her mood was gentle and her state sentimental; to him Wordsworth ranked before any of the three, and one page of Pope was better than all that has been produced by the best modern lyrists and romanticists. She had not studied Shakespeare with the zeal that he had given, and she did not know Homer as well as he. He had had the solid groundwork which her education wanted; and she felt the difference keenly—for, after all, she was a lady and he was only a chemist, and she should have been his superior all through. He felt it too, but pleasantly. She was so gentle and receptive, so thoroughly vitalized and so evidently desirous to improve, that he foresaw an endless line of pleasure in helping her course of reading and, better still, in helping the arrangement of her thoughts. He could be of use to her; and, with such a nature as his, this was the strongest tie between them that could be established.

"I hope we shall often see you at our house," then said Leslie, when the time of parting came. "The mother will be glad to see you at any time, that I can assure you of; and you know that I shall be so too," he added with a smile.

"Thanks, you are very kind; I shall like to go," said Perdita.

"You will always find us the same," he went on to say. "We are constant folks and do not change."

"Nor do I," she said.

"No; you have faithful eyes," he answered.

And on this Perdita raised them to his, and more than had ever leapt out from them when she had looked at Mr. Brocklebank flashed like a line of light from her to him, and back again.

What did they say to each other? Who knows! Had each been asked neither could have told; but whatever it was it was something that made Perdita blush and quiver, while Leslie grew suddenly cold and constrained, as, without even shaking hands with her, he lifted his soft felt hat and turned abruptly away, as his manner was.

"He might have shaken hands with me. He need not have gone off in that sudden way," thought Perdita, a little aggrieved. Then a flush came into her face and her sensitive mouth smiled. "He said my eyes were honest," she said, half aloud. "If he thinks that, he must like me more than he dislikes me. I am so glad, for his mother's sake—and for his wife's," was her last thought.

Whereat she ceased to smile, and began instead to wonder what that wife was like, and whether it were probable they would be good friends or not. She rather fancied not.

CHAPTER XV.

THE MOUSE AT PLAY.

FROM dead monotony Perdita's life had now suddenly become full of variety, and from absolute isolation she found herself in the midst of associates whom perhaps it would be premature to call her friends.

First in importance among the latter came the two who represented the opposite poles of the feminine magnet—Mrs. Blount and Mrs. Crawford. The one stimulated her intellect and ministered to that spirit of revolt against established usage which was Perdita's chief mental danger, though it sprang from her best quality—her love of truth; the other appealed to all those home affections, that depth of love and sense of duty, those shy sweet instincts lying at the root of womanly tenderness which were the ruling characteristics of her moral nature and the direct antitheses of Bell Blount's unsexed doctrines. Both together kept her in a state of moral counterpoise and mental activity which prevented excess in any one direction, as well as unwholesome brooding over the shortcomings of her life.

Then there were her fellow-clerks of whom to take present stock for future choice; and there was Mr. Brocklebank who every now and then wrote to his protégée from Armour Court, desiring to be informed of her present health and condition; or who came upon her suddenly, without a word of warning, to see for himself how she was progressing in that task of bread-winning whereof he always claimed the merit of having set the oven.

And last of all there was Leslie Crawford to idealize as the embodiment of all manly virtue and to listen to as the mouthpiece of all manly wisdom; and it must be confessed, to wonder at more and more that a man so cultivated, so refined, so thoughtful, should be only a chemist and not a gentleman.

It was a new existence altogether; and the girl showed by her looks and bearing how much better she throve in the richer ordering of human interests than she had done under her former pinched and starved conditions. Her sensitive face was fast losing that half-sullen sadness which had clouded the natural sunshine of its youth. Rounder in outline, fairer in colour, smoother in texture, it was readier now to break into smiles than to flame into wrath or quiver down into tears. Her manners were less awkward because she had no fear of rebuke; and she was becoming graceful in proportion to her sense of ease and absence of dread. She, who had been such a Puritan too in the way of ribbons and bibbons—so simple in fashion, so quakerish in colour—she was now actually touching the fringes of coquetry in adventitious decorations, and paid almost as much attention to her appearance as would have satisfied her mother. In consequence of all which, the girl, who had been the family cross because of her comparative plainness and ungainliness, was "commencing to become quite a pretty creature," as Mr. Brocklebank said to his sister Clarissa—straightening his back and stroking his chin with the self-complacency of a man who has turned out a satisfactory job from poor materials, and scored a success where others had marked a failure.

Every one saw the change, and all rejoiced in it, save Bell Blount; and she feared that it might prove to be the sign of future unsoundness, which, if not checked, would spoil all. On the other hand, Connie Tracy was glad, and sowed artful seeds of encouragement by whispered flatteries and short hymns of praise when Bell Blount was out of hearing. This potential coquetry, this dawning vanity was the little cloud which she trusted would soon obscure the whole sky, and blot out that bit of dangerous blue in her "husband's" affection for the new comer. For the one standing fear of the mousey-faced little woman, whom the Champion of her Sex called her "wife," sprang from that kind of jealousy which belongs to those whose status rests on the caprice or fidelity of another—not bound. Connie Tracy was as much Bell Blount's creature as if she had been a man's mistress to be discarded, without a pension, at pleasure and for sake of a new face. Bound to serve and to obey—to take no other "friend" from among her own sex, and to abjure the love of man as an unspeakable crime against herself, her vows, the Cause and her woman-"husband"—giving body and soul for maintenance in the present, and the hope of a permanent provision in the future—in what was her position different from that of any other woman whose temporary wifehood rests on nothing more solid than fancy, to be dissolved for nothing more serious than satiety?

She knew this well enough—for she was no fool if less than wise; and writhed under the chains which she had made believe to hug; wherefore, while appearing to welcome Perdita as a sweet friend common to herself and her owner, she secretly dreaded her as a rival and possible supplanter, and hailed the first indications of a personal coquetry which meant the admiration of men rather than the approbation of women; thinking that herein she might find the lover which would enable her to lift this dangerous third out of her path.

Her jealous fear however, had a respite; for Mrs. Blount was suddenly called to a certain provincial capital, where she was wanted to aid in stirring up the local womanhood to a right sense of their position. The fuglemen of that ungazetted Society of Shrieking Sisterhood,[1] of which the vicar's wife was such an important member, bade her do her best to convince those down-trodden creatures, who had not yet been brought to a knowledge of their misery, that they were the slaves and victims of that hard-handed tyrant Man, and that their first duty lay in revolt—their only hope of salvation in emancipating themselves without delay from the duties, the modesties and the restrictions of their sex. But though absent in body, Bell was ever present in spirit, and no day passed without a long letter to Perdita, wherein it would have been hard to say which was the more extraordinary—the warmth of her expressions of affection for the girl herself, or the fierceness of her ceaseless denunciations against men, marriage and maternity.

They were letters which made Perdita's cheeks burn, she scarcely knew why; but certainly with more pain than pleasure. Yet, affectionate and craving for love as she was, it might have seemed as if Bell Blount's ardent protestations would have satisfied her heart and given her new life. Because they did not, she reproached herself with ingratitude, and wondered at her own want of responsiveness. Why could she not frankly return the friendship so frankly offered? She could not answer her own question. All that she could make out about herself was that she was in a strange halting state of feeling altogether. Half attracted and half repelled—fascinated by the woman's mental power and revolted by something too vague to name yet too real to ignore—Bell Blount was to her one of those living enigmas the true value of which we cannot determine—one of those sphinxes which are beast and human in one, divine for the one part and satanic for the other.

The same odd restriction of interest followed her to the office; and among the crowd of fellow-clerks working in the big room, where she too had her place, not one attracted her magnetically at first sight and only one drew her with the silver cord of liking on further acquaintance. She was evidently in an abnormal state of mind altogether—standing in that cautious, hesitating, unsatisfied way of one who is waiting for the right thing to turn up and is afraid of patchwork and previous possession. For few young people are eclectic to the extent of making friends

---

[1]   Refers to Linton's article "The Shrieking Sisterhood" (*Saturday Review*, 12 March 1870, 341–42).

and finding good in differences; and the more loyal the nature the less catholic, in those years which come before experience and its growth, tolerance. As the tap-root of Perdita's character was loyalty to her convictions, it was scarcely to be expected that she could find their own value in things which went contrary to her sense of right.

And the girls at the office went contrary to her sense of right and disappointed her all through.

She had expected to find in them the same political principle and high-strung earnestness which she herself carried into her work—the same proud consciousness of participating in the conduct of the Imperial Government which made her routine business letters and dry rows of figures essentially poems; and she found instead the dullest indifference to the whole thing, save as the bank whence they might draw so much per annum. Neither heroines nor martyrs were they, but just a congregation of commonplace young women whose family finances were scanty, and who preferred employment that took them away from home and into society, to that which would have kept them within four walls and in the bosom of their family.

They were of all kinds; but no kind after the pattern of Perdita. There were quick girls who worked with the due amount of conscientiousness, but placidly and without a trace of political enthusiasm—fast girls who looked on the serious part of the business as a horrid bore and the rest as a good joke, valuable for the street flirtations and risky adventures which it included—noisy girls who chattered—silly girls who giggled—rude ones who stared and made remarks in audible whispers which reached the ears of those discussed and satirized—and sensible girls who did none of those things; there were minxes whose pertness was irrepressible—dolts whose stupidity was impenetrable and whose appointment was the standing marvel of the corps—beauties whose pretty faces were as camels laden with sins, and who were suspected and girded at, watched and vilified—and there were bright, intelligent womanly creatures, fit for something far better than this dull office-work, and whose career as clerks under Government was the world's loss, inasmuch as, had they been wives and mothers, it would have been the world's gain.

But among them all, good and bad alike, Perdita found the one same prosaic unconcern to the Imperial importance of their doings. Not the faintest trace of sentiment, enthusiasm, or patriotism illumined their path with ambition or fortified it by principle. Their work was undertaken simply because of the pressure of poverty and for the sake of a salary; and Perdita's magnificent way of looking on hers as a political function seemed to them one of the funniest things imaginable and exposed her to unending ridicule. It was gravely debated among some whether she were to be dreaded as insane or pitied for imbecility, laughed at for folly or despised for affectation. Any way she was to be held as outside the circle and not to be brought near to that esoteric body which always exists in a community. She might be "drawn" for sport, but by no means sheltered against assault cunningly perpetrated; and she was never to be treated as other than the jester of the office, good to create laughter when other jokes and jokers failed.

This want of high-mindedness among her fellow clerks and the ridicule poured on her own ideas were Perdita's first disappointments in her new career; and only those fatally sincere souls who believe in the absolute purity of motives, and that actions are founded on principles not expediency, know the pain of the fall when their waxen wings of faith melt under the cruel fire of proof.

There was one girl however, a certain Mary Chesterton, who was better than all this and who, if not quite up to Perdita's romantic height, was far beyond the average. They were so far on the same plane as enabled them to understand each other's thoughts if those thoughts did not always run parallel; for though Mary did not carry into her writing and ciphering at the Post-office Savings Bank the same exaltation as did poor Perdita, yet she did her duty with the sense that it was duty, and she was faithful and exact, modest, pure-minded and sincere.

She was the daughter of a barrister with fewer briefs than olive branches, and more liabilities than assets. Consequently the girls of the family had to turn out into the world all the same as the boys, to do what they could to bring grist to the family mill. Mary had chosen the Post-office Savings Bank; one sister was a governess; another a hospital nurse; a third worked at art-embroidery and a fourth kept at home and helped the mother with the housekeeping and the younger children. Each did something; but the unity of the family was not broken for all this divergence of employments, and the girls were in no wise tainted with masculinity or strong-mindedness. They were just a family of women who worked quietly and well without blare of trumpets or cackle of publicity. And they found that good work had its reward, whether it be done by a man or by a woman; and that when women's work fails or is underpaid it is because it is inferior and not because the sex is oppressed.

Her friendship with Mary Chesterton was one of the pleasant passages in Perdita's present life; but it went no deeper than pleasantness. It was refreshing and unexciting, and nothing more; for it would have been folly, even in an enthusiast, to have made a poetic ideal out of one who was only a very nice dear good girl incapable of either the heights or the hollows of morality, and whose greatest merit would have been in her docility as a wife, her devotion as a mother and the faithful care that she would have taken of her husband's property, his children and his name. And of what use to spend that wealth of passionate love, which had been one of Perdita's two-edged cradle gifts, on a girl all of whose affection went to her own family and who had nothing but a very mild measure of interest to give to a friend? The 'waste' would have been too great and too evident even for Perdita, who yet was not clever at calculating moral interest; wherefore, instead of her alter ego, furiously beloved and idealized out of all likeness to her real self, as might well have been, Mary remained only a very charming acquaintance, bringing no dreams and causing no heartaches; and things were all the more wholesome because of this absence of excess.

Mrs. Crawford was Perdita's dearest friend at this time; and her weekly visit to the rooms above the shop was as the flower of her days. Theories of life might not square and temperaments might not match, but all the same the two, so dissimilar in age and character, loved each other tenderly. The mild well-disciplined woman pitied the aberrations of this rich and vigorous nature so profoundly as to touch the proverbial kinship—yielding to love because yearning to save; and Perdita had an almost filial reverence for one whose views might be cramped but whose heart was so good—whose nature was so sweet!

Perhaps the two loved each other because of the very differences which at first sight seemed so disturbing. Perdita's passionate eagerness stirred the Quaker blood with a sense of growth and life and exuberance and power; while Mrs. Crawford's modesty and reserve, her quiet home-staying and essentially feminine life, her moral refinement and gentle piety, came like the touch of a cool hand to one burning with fever.

If only she were not quite so narrow! Perdita used to think with regret; if she would but allow that women had some kind of rights in life, some claim to their own individuality and were not so entirely the subject class, so completely cut off from all the power and privileges granted to men! But though she thought this often enough, she seldom uttered even so much as a mild regret that her mother-friend was not more as she was herself.

Yet kind and sweet as Mrs. Crawford was to her—how much kinder and more sympathetic than her own mother!—there was always the same object before her as before the real mother, namely, that she,

Perdita, being all wrong as she was, must be pulled and patted into something quite different from what she was before she could be pronounced on favourably or held to be satisfactory. Really something ought to be made of her before she was done with! If she had to be lost it would not be for want of hands trying to save her! Here stood her well-mannered mother preaching ladylike texts out of the Institutes of Fashion, doing her best to impress this unconvinceable rebel with the need of conformity to the laws of drawing-room religion;—there was Bell Blount flourishing the new charter of Woman's Liberties before her dazzled eyes, while urging her to forget the restrictions of her sex and the modesties of her age;—and here again was gentle Mrs. Crawford counselling reticence, restraint, the suppression of all personal freedom, the abnegation of all the fervid instincts of her youth, the excision of all the activities which her temperament demanded—the three agreeing only in one thing, that she was fearfully in need of guidance and improvement, and that *this* was the path she must be made to take, *this* the code she must be induced to accept. And all the while that wilful rebel accepted none of the three methods, but reasoned out the laws of life for herself, as every strong soul must.

Though Perdita saw a good deal of the chemist and his mother, she knew no more of the absent wife than she did at first. Being absent and not talked about, the natural conclusion was that she was dead. Leslie never alluded to her in even the most distant way, and Mrs. Crawford only rarely spoke of her as "My poor dear daughter"—"my poor precious darling"—plaintively. Once she showed Perdita the photograph of a very pretty silly-looking made-up young person, with large painted-looking eyes, hands clasped after the manner of the 'intense,' far more hair piled up on her head and floating about her shoulders than ever grew on one scalp, and a general appearance of gewgaw, affectation and bedizenment which was neither graceful nor ladylike.[1]

This picture made Perdita grow hot and cold in rapid alternation. This the portrait of Leslie Crawford's wife?—this the girl whom his delicate mother called so lovingly her "poor dear child," her "precious" and her "darling"? It was as unlike the natural wife of Leslie Crawford as if the pretty creature had been a Circassian odalisque or a Zanzibar negress!

"This was after she became artistic," said Mrs. Crawford with quaint regret. "She had her year in France; and when she came home she fell

---

[1]   This description of Florence Crawford resembles Linton's "Girl of the Period" (*Saturday Review*, 14 March 1868, 339–40).

in with some South Kensington girls who persuaded her to adopt their style. It is not after my taste, but I did not interfere. I left that to Leslie. Poor darling!—poor sweet Jessie!"

The photograph and this little explanation, if indeed it might be called so—these rarely-made plaintive allusions of Mrs. Crawford and her unmistakable tone of sadness when she spoke of anything whatever connected with this absent wife and daughter—were all the indications given of her lost existence. Where she died, or how, or when, or if she were dead at all, or where she was if alive was never mentioned. She had been and was not; and Perdita was too sensitive to inquire into family histories not spontaneously offered. A mystery evidently hung about this made-up, artificial-looking young person—a mystery and a sorrow—but of the nature of either not the smallest hint was given by husband or mother. That the latter regretted the girl's absence and lamented some misfortune was plain; but the former showed no more of what he suffered than the closed coffin shows the features of the dead within. Only one thing was plain—he had suffered.

If he never spoke of his wife, he took but little notice of his child. It might have been a foundling and not his at all for the strange indifference with which he treated it. Perhaps he was not fond of children— all men are not, thought Perdita, unconsciously excusing him for what in any one else she would have considered a grave blot on his character. But then Leslie was "so good," and when one person thinks another good, blots somehow disappear and faults are not allowed to count.

Again, his manner to Mrs. Crawford was scarcely that of a very loving son. It was more courteous than tender, more respectful than affectionate. He seemed as if anxious to do what was right rather than acting from spontaneous impulse—as if he wished to make up to her for some loss rather than offering himself and his care by the force of filial tenderness. The difference was very faint and subtle, but there it was; and though Perdita had not the key, she could not deny the enigma.

As to herself, she and the chemist were on pleasant but not what might be called familiar terms. A great deal of literary and ethical discussion took place between them, wherein she was always ardent, direct, narrow because intense, and with that wonderful conviction of absolutes so characteristic of sincere faith; while he was wider, calmer, as sure of certain principles but able to perceive difficulties even in the way of that divine justitia which ought to be done—and sometimes must not! They had many a friendly war together, wherein the girl held her own with what, considering all things, was strange pertinacity—a pertinacity which made Leslie himself wonder. But that was just the difficulty of her character—the contradiction over which so many stumbled. So plastic, so sensitive and loving and easily moved as she was by temperament, who would have expected such an unconvinceable kind of mental core—such an absolute necessity of working out all the problems of life by herself—such an inability to learn other than by self-taught experience? However, there it was; and she and Leslie fought over political questions and the comparative claims of authors, and whether truth was at all times the one absolute virtue or might be deposed in favour of some other more paramount at the moment after the manner of their kind; and the only conclusion to which they mutually came was that he thought her the finest-hearted, noblest-minded girl he had ever met, but terribly in want of firm, judicious, manly guidance; and she thought him the finest-hearted, noblest-minded man she had ever met, but how much grander he would have been if he had been happier, and what a pity it was that he had that trouble, whatever it might be, about his wife! He would have been so much better if he had been happily married!

And then, as so often before, she wondered what the mystery was and whether the wife were alive or dead. At first she thought for certain that she was dead; but now—no, she did not think she was dead. She would have been hard put to it to give a reason for this thought—if he had been a widower he would have been different somehow from what he was; and yet once or twice lately she had begun to waver back to her first belief.

Certainly not because Leslie was any kinder, any more familiar, to her than before; rather the contrary. A certain artificial reserve was creeping into his naturally quiet manners; and when he talked to her he was sometimes almost cruel in his sharpness and more than once he made the tears come into her eyes. But when he saw that he had pained her he made up for his hardness by so much sudden sweetness—by some word or look so full of tenderness and admiration—that Perdita was more than consoled, and felt as if she would willingly have borne the pain twice over for the sake of the healing that came after.

"I do not think he dislikes me," she said to herself more than once. "I am not sure, but I do not think he does. I hope he does not."

Leslie Crawford certainly did not dislike Perdita. No man who dislikes a woman remembers what she had said and done on such and such an occasion with such faithful accuracy; no man who dislikes a woman gives himself so much trouble to convince her that she is on the wrong tack and that he is a better moral pilot for her than she is for herself—looks at her as Leslie looked at Perdita, as though she were the incarnation of all beauty—upholds her moderately good points as absolute perfection of their kind—maintains her undeniable blemishes as so perfectly harmonious with the rest of her character, she would not be half so charming without them; but for the most part refuses to admit that they are blemishes at all—watches her so closely without knowing it—is so keen in the anticipation of her wishes, the quick reading of her desires—listens to her voice as if he hears more in it than the mere words—greets her with such irrepressible welcome—gives her good-bye with such ostentatious indifference: no, Leslie Crawford did not dislike Perdita, if the signs which stand as signals with others might serve as indications with him.

But what of that? It was perfectly immaterial, so far as the history of events went, whether he liked her or not. They were as far apart as if mountains and seas were between them. Free or bound as he might be, the great spectre of conventional status stood like an afreet between them; and though they might be the consecrated "halves" one of the other, the chemist's shop was stronger than nature and caste more powerful than sympathy or love.

But why talk of love? Of course there was no question of love. Leslie Crawford was a chemist; Perdita was a lady; and if this were not barrier enough between them, how about the wife?

All this, however, made the girl's portion at that banquet of life where hitherto she had been such an unfortunate guest, richer and more delicious than she had ever anticipated. Yet in her heart she felt that she was but the mouse at play in the absence of that sleek-skinned creature, with the sharp claws and the velvet pads, taking her pleasure abroad; and that for every happy hour now she would have to pay back two of misery in the future.

But how delightful it was to be free from blame and in full liberty of person! How bright this waning summer was! how good was God, how noble humanity at large! She went to sleep with a smile; she woke in the morning with a song. Never had her youth been so full of sunshine, of music, of poetry, of delight—never had life been so dear or the world so beautiful! It seemed almost strange to her when a child cried in the streets, or a miserable-looking woman begged for charity and pity for the love of God. How was it that they were not all as blessed as she? If they were free and knew good sweet people and were not tormented by social laws which had no meaning or use in them, why were they not happy and content?

Poor little mouse frisking in the loft while the cat is watching the birds on the lawn! Enjoy while you can. It will be time enough to go back to fear and distress when your day of liberty is over.

One evening, after she had returned from the office and while she was sitting at "high tea" with poor old Cluff, a tremendous knock came to the door, and a resounding ring followed after, in double emphasis of summons. The charwoman tumbled up from the depths below in the fumbling way of her tribe. She had an indistinct idea of burglars, mixed up with that of the family suddenly come home and nothing ready for them. But perhaps that of the burglars was uppermost, for she opened the door on the chain and cautiously stood behind the crack.

"Is Miss Winstanley at home?" asked a woman's voice, its loud tones softened by its caressing accent.

"I can't say, I'm sure, but I'll go and see," said the old woman, hastily shutting the door in the inquirer's face.

"Oh, that stupid old Mrs. Gally!" cried Perdita, who had heard and understood. "Why, that is Mrs. Blount!"

On which she ran out into the hall, nearly upsetting Cluff, who also rose to look; but she did not wait to apologize, and in another moment she herself had opened the door.

And positively at that moment, Mrs. Winstanley, sitting in the lengthening shadows on the terrace of the Trouville casino, had a sudden shiver, and said in a slightly peevish voice, "I wonder what that poor child at home is doing now!"

"You are barricaded as if you were in a beleaguered city," said Mrs. Blount with a light laugh. "Perhaps you are right. You are so much safer from the arch-enemy, Man. But you might be more hospitable to your female friends."

"Mrs. Gally is such a stupid, blundering old creature," answered Perdita with good-humoured impatience. "She never knows when to let in people and when not. She turned away Mr. Brocklebank the other day because, she said, she thought he was a tax-gatherer; and she let in a man who nearly frightened poor Cluff out of her senses, for he would not go and insisted on her subscribing to something, I do not know exactly what. I am so sorry you have been kept standing there. Do come in. We are just at tea; come and have some."

"I have no business here at all, you know," said Mrs. Blount with a queer smile. "It is the house of Baal to me; and what would your lady mother say if she were to see me here? But I don't mind going over unholy thresholds if I can rescue a sweet little deluded votary like you." Here she kissed the girl fondly, and said, "My darling!" softly below her breath.

"You are so good to me," said Perdita, involuntarily shrinking from her embrace; but her heart was full of gratitude for Bell's kindness all the same. "But do come in and have some tea," she repeated.

"I will go in, but I will not have your tea," said Mrs. Blount, a little stiffly. "You cold, inflexible, unimpressionable creature!" she added, lightly tapping the girl's burning cheeks.

"No, no, I am not cold, and you will not be able to resist a cup of tea when you see it," said Perdita rather incoherently, as she led the way to the shabby back-room where she and poor old Cluff were in the midst of their not too luxurious "dinnertea."

Mrs. Blount looked at the table critically. She had a man's full-flavoured appreciation of good living; and weak tea, stale bread, with a hard-roed herring as food and relish both, did not smile on her.

"No, nothing to eat or drink, I am obliged to you," she said dryly; "unless you have a bottle of Bass[1] or a B. and S. And I don't think you have, judging by what I see," she added, laughing with a certain spice of affectation.

"No, we have neither," said Perdita simply. "Shall I get you some?"

"By no means. Heavens! the house would explode! No; go on with your tea, and do not let me disturb you. I only came to ask you to go to a lecture to-morrow night at the West Hill Hall. It will be small, but important; mainly composed of the most advanced among us; the speeches will be strong and the speakers good—that I can promise; and I am to take the chair."

"On what subject?" asked Perdita.

"The Degradation of Married Women," said Mrs. Blount.

A little quiver passed over Perdita's face. It was the flutter of her soul throwing a shadow as it stirred.

"The evening will be devoted to a consideration of how best to force the legislature to grant us our rights," continued Mrs. Blount. "We want enactments which shall insure us absolute possession of our own property, free from the control of our husbands and from all obligation to contribute towards the support of the family. That is the man's affair, not the woman's. Also we want enactments which shall recognize the mother's absolute and unshared right over the children, free from the father's interference—and this even in those cases where the man's brutality has driven the wife into such a line of action as gives him the right of divorce according to the present infamous laws. I shall speak, of course; and you must come and hear me."

---

[1] A brewery in Burton-upon-Trent, England.

"Thank you," said Perdita with hesitation.

She was grateful to her friend Bell for thinking of her but she had no desire to make one of her extreme section. Mrs. Crawford's quiet theory of home duties and womanly suppression might go too far on one side, but surely this rampant revolt went too far on the other! Still, Mrs. Blount was no fool; and every one who thinks has a claim to be heard. Besides, she was kind, though imperative; and after a little hanging back by the one and determination from the other, Perdita promised to go to the West Hill Hall to-morrow evening to hear what could be said in favour of the moral extinction of man and the universal supremacy of woman. And after this she had to submit to a great deal of hugging on the part of Bell Blount, who seemed to think she had achieved a victory and got even more than the traditional hair.

But with a strange feeling of needing a moral counterpoise, Perdita wrote a little note to Mrs. Crawford, telling her where she was going and begging her to go too. She knew that it was not much in the dear woman's way to attend public meetings of any kind, and that her presence at one of this extreme sort was scarcely to be looked for. Yet if she would not go, was there not Leslie? and would not he do as well? He was as right-minded as his mother and less impatient of discussion or contradiction; and he would be better able to point out the fallacies and more just to the verities of the lecture. Yes, Leslie would do quite as well as Mrs. Crawford, if only he would take the hint and go.

And with this hope Perdita went through the next day's duties briskly, waiting for the evening and Bell Blount's chairwomanship, the lecture and that one possible and hoped-for unit in the audience.

CHAPTER XVI.

AT THE HALL.

THOUGH London was still empty, and no one with any social pretensions had returned from the moors, the seaside or the Continent, yet West Hill Hall was fairly full; and by eight o'clock, the advertised hour of the lecture, an audience had gathered sufficiently numerous to satisfy even the demands of the chairwoman. Curiosity to hear what the notorious Bell Blount and her bodyguard of Shriekers had to say in favour of principles which would make woman the essence and man the accident, as well as the general idleness and need of amusement proper to the summer season, led the unconverted Philistines to the place. But the bulk of the listeners was, it must be confessed, composed of sincere sympathizers, who looked on the cause as the pivot of national morality and the touchstone of political righteousness.

For the most part the men of this extreme section were a feeble weedy-looking set—men who had given themselves up to the worship of women and who evidently went in fear of their wives; and the women were odd and unlikely. Yet they were very much in earnest and taught their gospel without misgiving or qualification; proving the right of woman to reign over, and her capacity to legislate for, the whole community, by the utter absence of all that practical wisdom which goes by the general term of statesmanship.

Perdita, as some would have said already too much emancipated, and by no means wanting encouragement that way, took her place as one of the public in the body of the hall. She had no companion with her and saw no one whom she knew; but she was accustomed to loneliness and did not feel the awkwardness of going about without an escort.

She had that kind of shyness which is self-effacement when unnoticed and is timidity only when brought to the front and made conspicuous; and sitting there in that middle row, one among many, she seemed to herself to be as much obscured as if she had put on the cap of darkness which allowed her to see and hear all—while seen and heard of none.

As soon as Bell Blount swept on to the platform at the head of her cohort, her quick eye spied out her latest "fancy" sitting there among the general audience. She leaned backward and spoke to Connie Tracy, telling her to go down and bring up Perdita to the platform to take her place with the pledged; and at the same time she made a smiling but imperative sign to the girl herself, which made the people turn round and look asking each other in loud whispers: What is it? Who is she? Thus, from the most complete and comfortable obscuration, Perdita found herself the centre of all observers; and, her quietude and unconcern gone, she sat there with crimson cheeks and profound embarrassment, half resisting and half yielding to the command sent to her from above.

She dreaded going on to the platform and she dreaded still more remaining here as a target for the curiosity of the room. She was half rising saying, "Indeed, I would rather not," when Leslie Crawford came up to her quite quietly, took the seat immediately behind her, and said in a matter-of-fact way:

"I see you are here alone; allow me to consider myself your caretaker for the evening, Miss Winstanley. I presume you are not going on the platform?"

"No," said Perdita with a quick sigh of relief; "I would rather not go, though Mrs. Blount has been kind enough to send for me. Thank you very much, Connie, but please give her my love, and say I would rather stay where I am."

"As you like, dear, of course, but Bell will be put out," said Connie Tracy with a little smile, not malicious so much as gratified.

She was not naturally bad-hearted—she was only in a false as well as a dangerous position, and forced to think how best to make it real and keep it safe.

When Mrs. Blount received Perdita's refusal her handsome artificially serene face took on itself that kind of satirical smile which is more expressive of displeasure than a frown. She nodded her head in token of acceptance, always smiling in the same made-up way; but all through the meeting she ostentatiously forbore to look at Perdita and her manner expressed repudiation as plainly as words would have done.

"Now I have offended her," thought Perdita to herself with some dismay; but common sense whispered, "You did right."

The business of the meeting began by Bell Blount as chairwoman giving a sketch of the past proceedings, the present aims and future hopes of the Cause. She spoke in a round flowing style, wherein was nothing feminine save verbal redundancy and the ignoring of practical impossibilities. The working part of her principles, however, was not Bell Blount's affair. She was simply the mouthpiece of Truth, and left it to others to be the hands—to draw out plans which should square with reason and find methods of execution which should come within the limits of possibility.

"Fiat justitia!" she said, pointing her white-gloved fore finger to the ceiling of the hall. "Ruat coelum!"[1] she added her final peroration, spreading out both her hands somewhat as if she were swimming.

Then, amid great applause, she introduced as the first speaker a lady from America, with three Christian names before a doubled surname, making five in all, and a toilette from Paris that would have made the typical duchess envious.

The lady from America was a practised public speaker, and did her business in a workmanlike way, with no more agitation, shyness or

---

[1]   (Latin), Let there be justice [though] the sky fall! Linton translates this in Ch. XXII, "Let the universe crack if it will, but let Eternal Justice rule."

embarrassment than if she had been a man to whom being "put up" was an everyday experience. She did not say anything that was new nor what had not been repeated ad infinitum; but what she did say was well said, and she had a certain dry humour that took immensely with her audience. She told a few pithy anecdotes and made a few smart jokes which pleasantly enlivened the staple of her discourse. And she was not sparing of her epithets nor fastidious in her choice of similes when she wanted to be incisive and to show her oratorical power. She spoke of the opponents of the Cause with contemptuous pity—called them ascidians and acephala, earthworms and invertebrates, crabs and retrograde, tadpoles and undeveloped; and her hits were allowed to be hard and telling. To be sure she had a thin dry metallic voice and her intonation was not euphonious; but she never lost her thread; never stopped for a word nor entangled herself in a phrase; never stuttered nor stammered nor went back over the ground already quartered, but spoke and spoke and spoke with the limpidity and fluidity of a torrent. She was the most finished specimen of a female public orator to be found; yet the general effect was not pleasing. There was nothing coarse nor masculine nor slangy about her; she was supremely well-dressed; yet she was not what we mean by womanly and her case-hardened self-sufficiency was as ugly as a physical deformity.

She was followed by a pretty, graceful, affected little person, who came to the front with a sheaf of papers, a note-book and a pencil in her small well-gloved hands, as if prepared to make an oration at some length. She had a sweet face, a weak voice and a strong lisp; and she stood there as if she had really something to say and brains to say it with. But she did not go very deep into the bowels of the land; and, though she incessantly referred to her notes, to all appearance she found little help therefrom. Women paid taxes; therefore women should have the vote. This was the one nucleus of her discourse and she kept tight hold of it; meandering round and round about in words of all hues and sizes, but going no farther afield in the world of ideas; always returning to the one solitary peg in her possession—women pay taxes, therefore they should have the vote.

But her speech was violently applauded and she herself was made much of. She was the Venus of the Emancipated Olympus; and the leaders knew the value of her wavy golden hair and large blue eyes, her lovely curved mouth and slender figure. They knew also the value of her pathetic history as a suffering angel evilly dealt with by an impious husband, with dark suggestions of a frightful kind to give tragic force and intensity to her story. What, however, was certain was, that she had left her home and now supported herself by giving lessons in elocution to young clergymen and barristers. All the same she said "wuz" for "was," she pronounced "poor" and "pore" in identically the same manner, and she carefully padded each "s" with a protecting "h" between it and the following vowel, which was scarcely the elocution that an English Talma[1] would have endorsed.

Others beside these came forward and spoke more or less closely to the point. One was a woman with close-cropped hair, a Tyrolese hat with a cock's feather at the side, a shirtcollar and a shirt-front, a waist-coat and a short jacket. In everything outward she was like a man, save for whiskers—which, however, she simulated in a short kind of cheek-curl; and for moustaches—which were more than indicated.

Another was a breezy, asthetic-looking creature in a pre-Raphaelite costume of green, long and lean as a lizard. She made a rambling speech on woman's wrongs, wherein, mother of children as she was, she let fall the words, "The degradation of maternity." The words woke up a murmur of dissent from the body of the hall where the Philistines were mainly congregated. The fathers and mothers seated there took the slight to heart and carried the epithet home to their own beloved nurs-eries. One sturdy fishmonger called out an energetic 'Shame!' but he was hushed down by the majority and recommended to shut up; and soon after this the mother who had blasphemed maternity sat down under the rebuke of a dead silence.

Then came one who offered herself emphatically as a woman—woman, pure womanly. She said of herself that by nature she was the most opposed to publicity that any creature could be. Her ideal of life was to live in close retirement with her books, her art, her music, her embroi-dery, her flowers and her birds, as her best companions. She shrank from all noise and notoriety and would like to glide through the world unnoted and unseen; but she was impelled to take public part in these public proceedings, because of the righteousness of the Cause and the dictates of her own conscience. It was against her inclination; but she must obey her heart—she must listen to the voice of her conscience. She spoke no nearer to the point than this. For the delicate, sensitive, claustral crea-ture that she gave herself out to be, she talked a good deal of herself and took the public into her confidence with greater freedom than might have been expected; and she spoke—with remarkable fluency.

---

[1] Francesco Giuseppe Talma (1763–1826), Napoleon's favorite Parisian tragedian; known as a reformer of the antiquated tragic alexandrine cadence, he strove for a more natural diction.

After her came a good, heavy, plain-featured person who pretended to nothing beyond the ordinary run of womanhood, but was just a warm-hearted, illogical, uncultivated enthusiast, sincerely believing that women were horribly ill-treated by men and the laws, and that giving them the vote would put everything to rights. She was a woman of large sympathies and boundless credulity; singularly happy in her own marriage and by reason of that very happiness wanting to see every one as blessed as herself. She was ready to lend a hand to any scheme that, as she thought, would promote the welfare of the race; and this was one of them. She was the best of the whole set, because the most sincere, the most unselfish and the most unpretending.

Save the lady from America who was trained, and the pretty creature who had but one idea and could not beat up a second, the most notable thing about these fair speakers was their discursiveness. They gambolled over whole prairies and launched their toy-boats on the biggest seas. Wife-beating and bad calico; garotting and the restrictions of trustees; woman's inability to add up her account books—somehow the fault of man, as that she should have to add them up at all was but another instance of his tyranny; the familiar laundress with her seven small children and drunken husband; the evil of billiard-tables and club life; the exclusion of women from the bar and the bench; the comparatively high wages earned by man and the strike of the Coventry watchmakers against the employment of women; the degrading character of all the work which they had to do and the ennobling power of all that from which they were excluded; the shameful partiality of public schools and the right of Girton girls to university scholarships, professorships, tutorships, masterships; the shamefulness of a standing army and the sin of tobacco—but here the chairwoman crossed her legs, shook her head and smiled with a deprecating air as she leaned aslant in her chair and spoke to her neighbour behind her hand—these were the chief topics touched on. And these topics were for the most part illustrated by the most amazing stories of man's tyranny and woman's suffering that could be devised—stories which beat the Smithfield wife-selling all to nothing and made one wonder whether it were of England or of Dahomey that they were told. But the speakers evidently believed in what they said, and the audience in what they heard; and at each successive romance the hall echoed with cries of 'Shame!' from the excited and 'Hear! Hear!' from the more parliamentary. And as each speaker sat down the applause of the sympathizers was deafening, while the dissent of the opponents good-naturedly expressed itself by silence.

"Do you really believe all this astounding rubbish?" asked Leslie Crawford of Perdita, who had been taking it all in like gospel, without stopping to sift or dreaming of doubt.

This contemptuous question came like a cold douche on the red-hot fervour of her faith; and cold douches of reason on the fervid belief of youth are either blasphemy or torture.

She raised her large eyes glittering with excitement, dark with emotion, and gave a little start of mingled surprise and indignation.

"Of course!" she said. "Surely they would not dare to say what was not true!"

Leslie laughed; and an hour ago Perdita would not have believed that Leslie Crawford's laugh could have ever sounded to her so unpleasant, or that she could have considered him cold, cynical and wilfully blind to truth.

"I thought you had more discrimination," he said a little hardly. "Quick sympathies and generous enthusiasm are all very well in their way, but they are perilously apt to lead one into a very quagmire of absurdity unless kept in check by the critical faculty. Everything that we hear is not true."

"But unless we know that they are false we cannot say that the things we have heard to-night are not true," said Perdita. "How can we possibly deny what we do not know?"

"By general knowledge," said Leslie smiling. "If you were told that a man had flown in the air from Islington to Kensington, would you believe it?"

"No, not quite," she said hesitatingly.

"Not quite! not at all, I trust, Miss Winstanley. With your power of intellect this unquestioning kind of faith is the last thing one would look for. You owe it to yourself to cultivate your judgment and starve your inclination to believe, superstitiously, without proof and against reason."

Here then was another person who praised her intellect and condemned its use—who thought that she had been meant by nature to be all right, but that somehow she had got pulled out of shape and was all wrong, as things were!

"It makes everything very difficult," said Perdita wearily. "I like to believe that what I hear is true."

"Old women riding on broomsticks and magicians who call up the dead among the number? You might as well believe these as the stories we have heard to-night. How could society hang together if men were, as these emancipated women say, the declared and implacable enemies of the sex? Do you think that husbands, fathers, and brothers, care nothing for the happiness of their woman-kind and are only solicitous to ill-treat and oppress them, out of sheer fiendish brutality?"

"Not all; certainly not all," she answered; "but some men are very very bad to women and the poor things do want protection."

"Women are pretty much the same as men," said Leslie with sudden bitterness. "We have our vices and they have theirs, just as we have our virtues and they have theirs. And if their vices are less than ours, their virtues are weaker."

"Oh no!" said Perdita, a distinct undertone of displeasure in her voice.

Though she admired the strength and greatness of man, she was so far a child of the generation as to think it a little monstrous that one of them should dare to criticise the weaker, but still the more worthy sex, as if he were criticising a man or a picture. If not prostrate, he ought at least to stand bareheaded in the presence of women; not seeing too clearly nor scanning too closely.

"You do not agree with me? Do you not think that a woman's devotion, however admirable, is somehow smaller than a man's heroism? Which strikes you as the grander, a woman's patience or a man's magnanimity? But on the other hand a man's virtue is not equal in degree to a woman's purity."

"If people were as good as they ought to be, everything would be right," said Perdita with true feminine vagueness, slipping from the point and launching into space.

Leslie smiled.

"At all events you will not help to make things more right by joining this noisy section of Emancipationists," he said. "They carry things too far. To say that some men are cruel and some women have wrongs which should be redressed, and are not, is to say that humanity is imperfect, society experimental and the reign of justice not absolute. But there are graver questions which press for settlement before this—the land question, the labour question, perfect freedom of conscience so that no kind of speculative opinion should carry with it any disabilities whatever—these are more important matters than giving women the vote or granting them the liberty to plead and the power to judge."

"Not more important than protecting their lives and granting them the means of self-support," said Perdita loyally.

He looked at her with undisguised admiration.

"You are terribly hard to move!" he said. But though his words taken by themselves might almost seem as if he had taxed her with a fault, there was no blame—far from it—in his voice and manner.

"I wish I could be more easily moved," said Perdita; "but I cannot. When things seem to me right or wrong, I cannot change. And I could not pretend to believe or disbelieve, when I do not, to save my life or keep the friendship of the person I loved best in the world."

"I see that," said Leslie. "It is a grand quality, but one that you must expect to suffer from. Yet how much better it would be if all persons were as sincere as you—all as faithful to the truth as they see it. There is no quality that I admire so much as truth—no moral necessity so great with me as to be able to trust. Slipperiness, deceit, unfaithfulness, these are the true cankerworms of humanity. Ruffians do less harm than thieves."

His face changed as he spoke. A sudden passionate scorn came over it that startled Perdita, used as she was only to the gentle kind of sadness, the quiet melancholy of repose, which was Leslie Crawford's dominant expression. He turned away with a contemptuous angry gesture; then checked himself with a sudden effort like a horse pulled up in mid-career.

"Let the crowd go first," he said quite quietly. "I will take you home."

"Thank you," said Perdita, pleased but also frightened.

It was one thing to call at the house and see her friends—within the safe four walls of their own home, and another to walk through the streets with Leslie, in the sight of all men and with the chance of being seen and reported to the authorities when they came home. Neither was it pleasant to her to know that she was doing something which she was willing to hide and afraid to have known; something of which, despite all her democracy, she was slightly ashamed. But liking and desire conquered her scruples; and she smiled and blushed and looked pretty and content as she stood with Leslie Crawford waiting for the last of the crowd to pass out. And when they had all gone, she took his arm, which he offered, and the two set off through the streets to West Hill Gardens.

It was one of those sweet and balmy nights which, even in this wilderness of bricks and mortar, touch the soul and stir the senses— one of those dark, clear, starry nights which suggest the song of nightingales and the faint sweet perfume of clematis and wild roses—a night made for lovers and poets, for youth and that divine madness which gives to youth the sovereignty of life. It was a night, not for rapid speech but for long spells of tender silence, when lips were closed and only hearts were open—when longing thoughts flowed into each other— when love mutually cherished was mutually revealed, even if still unconfessed in word. And it was a night when home was no haven, no place of rest, but a place of imprisonment and a barrier of separation.

Without speaking, Leslie crossed the street that led into West Hill Gardens and took that which carried them by the side of the Gardens and the Park. It was past the hour when they might walk within the enclosure, but they kept close to the railings and caught the delicate scents and the faint flutter of the leaves as if these had been words passing between them both.

"When do you expect your people home?" asked Leslie suddenly, after a long silence.

He spoke so abruptly that Perdita started. His question hurt her too, she could scarcely have said why. But it came as the skeleton in the feast, the death's head among the roses.

"I do not know exactly," she answered, as if waking out of a dream. "I have not heard very lately from mother, and she said nothing about it in her last letter."

"You will be glad when they come back?" said Leslie interrogatively.

"For some things, yes," answered Perdita.

"Not all?"

"Scarcely all," she answered.

"I should not have thought you would have been happier alone than with your family," he said rather slowly.

"We do not always agree in our opinions or ways," was her reply, made a little reluctantly.

"So I suppose, from what the mother has told me. I fancy you are a little too democratic for them—probably too extreme altogether."

"Yes, I dare say it is all my fault," said poor Perdita with her old manner of pained humility. "But I cannot help myself. I cannot say what I do not think nor deny what I believe. It is very unfortunate, both for them and for myself," she said with a sigh.

"But you are not to lose heart nor to waste your time in grieving," he returned, stopping in his walk and looking down on her kindly. He held the hand on his arm a little more closely pressed, and laid his own over it. "Trust in the good guidance of Providence," he said with grave tenderness. "When things look at their worst they are often at the point of mending. 'The darkest hour is the hour before dawn,' and there is no reason why a misunderstood girlhood should not have a happy womanhood."

"I do not think I shall ever be happy," said Perdita sadly.

"No? why not? You are not weak enough to think yourself specially marked out by fate for misery, are you? Why should not you be happy like any one else—well married and well cared for?"

She turned her eyes to the ground and shook her head.

"Trust!" he said in a low voice; "it will come some day. Remain as you are; be your true brave self whatever happens. Trust in God; believe in man; and the morning will break at last. Now we must turn back. It is getting late for you. But you will remember this night, will you not?—and do as I tell you. Be patient in the present and hopeful for the future."

"Yes," said Perdita, with the feeling of having taken a vow and bound herself by an oath—to what?

CHAPTER XVII.

THE SHINING SANDS.

TROUVILLE WAS crowded. The season this year was one of the most brilliant in its by no means sombre annals; and never since the little fishing village first became a fashionable watering-place, had the stream of life poured in so powerfully. The lucky possessors of commodious houses and well-furnished apartments to let, suddenly found themselves affluent; and even the veriest little dog-kennel, convertible into a sleeping room, commanded a princely rent, with much self-gratulation on the part of the lucky renter.

Every one was there. Republican ministers and old St. Germain nobility; reigning beauties of good repute and queens of the demi-monde without a rag of character wherewith to line their silks and satins; pressmen and artists; "petits crevés"[1] and men of science; Russians and their roubles; Americans and their dollars; English people, reserved, suspicious, shy; swaggering Berliners and lively Viennese—it was a real social microcosm that gathered on these smooth and shining sands and kicked the ball of pleasure heaven high.

Never had M. Pasdeloup's concerts been so well attended; never had the balls been so brilliant nor the administration of the casino so radiant, so content with fate and business. The card-room and the reading-room, the verandah and that odd little offset where the adventurous play at "little horses" for fifty centimes, the bathing-machines and the tents, the rocks and the sands, the streets and the shops—every available nook where

---

[1] (French), referring to anti-revolutionary rabble-rousers during the Second Empire.

human beings could bestow themselves was crowded, and the fun of the fair went on from dawn to dawn with very little intermission.

Among them all, notable as so many were, handsome Mrs. Winstanley and her two beautiful daughters were well-marked individualities; but not coarsely conspicuous. They were universally admired—but the French could not be made to believe that Thomasina was unmarried, and always called her Madame—and they were known as "les belles Anglaises." Credited with as much fortune as "chic," many attempts to get on familiar terms with them were made by Frenchmen on the look-out for wives with fat jointures. But Mrs. Winstanley was wary. No one knew better than she the need of caution if she would make a good thing of life; no one veiled more skilfully the keenest desire to sell with the nicest appraisement of potential buyers—the sharpest watch for chances with the most innocent appearance of looking the other way when a likely purchaser came in view. She posed with consummate skill and did not let an inch of the supporting framework appear. The men whom she most coveted as sons-in-law were only "friends of the family" common to all and assigned to none, like good Mr. Brocklebank—or "dear boys" whose intimacy was safe because of their own previous engagement, like Hubert Strangways—or pleasant acquaintances of a superior flavour, like Sir James Kearney, whose title was a barrier against the designs of the portionless; rank being rightfully, as she said, the consort of wealth.

This was the position that she took up in the market-place—these the leaves and feathers which she laid across her traps, believing that now they were securely hidden and that she might stand there in stately quietude free from all suspicion. But who, save herself, could tell the terrible anxiety with which she watched her snares and the golden plumaged fowl which hovered near?—who, save herself, could measure the alternations of hope and despair as one possible purchaser after another sauntered up to her pitch in the market-place, examined her dainty wares, seemed well disposed to buy, yet never came to a definite offer? Poor woman! Her life was one long chapter of effort and frustration, of that hope deferred which makes the heart sick, of perpetual skating on breaking ice, of endless realization of mirages and floating bubbles. And how could she be blamed? With only rags and tatters left of her inherited velvet, it was but human nature that she should cast about for wealthy sons-in-law and rack her brains for the best method of securing them. She was a match-making mother, granted; but after all what sin is there in a mother trying to get a suitable husband for her good-looking and well-principled daughter? She does not cheat the man in any way. She does not palm off on him damaged goods for fresh, but offers him a full equivalent for value received. Is this more dishonourable than when a man makes secret interest to hoist his own son into a snug berth for which, maybe, his neighbour's is more fitted? Yet this is held to be a father's absolute duty, but the mother who schemes for her daughters is vilified and condemned—surely unfairly, thought Mrs. Winstanley to herself, reviewing her own conduct and its motives.

The ladies had been for some weeks at Trouville, but as yet it had been all mere pleasure for the girls and corresponding loss of time for the mother. No fresh business of any importance had been done; and things already in train had not advanced an inch. No one had come over from England as had been agreed on; and it was hard work to keep up heart and hope on starvation diet. They had made a few new acquaintances who shifted every week; and latterly they had been taken hold of by a certain Vicomte de Bois-Duval and his friend the Baron de Laperrière, both of whom seemed all right enough; but, good heavens! who knows what these foreigners really are! thought Mrs. Winstanley, more perturbed than gratified and not daring to play this new game boldly.

These gentlemen had in a manner forced their acquaintance on the Winstanleys; and, for all the mother's discretion and reserve, had compelled her to accept their attentions. They had begun by some insignificant little gallantries which went on into more substantial kindnesses—such as preventing the overreaching of tradespeople, placing rather exclusive tickets at the disposition of Madame, managing a capitally got-up bit of sham heroism and mock salvation, and so worming their way with the persistency of a couple of moles and in almost as much obscurity. And in some degree Mrs. Winstanley found them useful. Without committing herself too much to their protection she allowed them to ward off others who would be undesirable; and as both spoke English fluently—the Vicomte indeed almost like an Englishman—she did not feel that they were quite so dangerous as the mass of their countrymen. They had so much saving grace accorded them! And then they really were what they gave themselves out to be. M. le Vicomte de Bois-Duval was really M. le Vicomte de Bois-Duval, and his friend was as indubitably M. le Baron de Laperrière. Mrs. Winstanley had been wise enough to make sure of this. What she had not discovered was, that they were both roués and gamblers—among men what "les filles de marbre" are among women.

Since her acquaintance with these young men Mrs. Winstanley's position had been a trifle less difficult, her duties of chaperonage undeniably less onerous. She had no need to guard herself or her daughters against them, for they were the masters of discretion and high-priests of etiquette; also Eva had become quieter on her own account and was less persecuted by attentions from strange men than before; and even Thomasina, always wise and satisfactory, seemed to have found a kind of bodyguard that was of value.

Dear little Eva was a difficult treasure to carry about. Mrs. Winstanley and Thomasina agreed on this between themselves. She was too pretty and too ingenuous to be safe at such a place as Trouville, where no one knows his neighbour and all are massed together in such a closely packed mosaic, that "Thou shalt not make friends of strangers" is the eleventh commandment and discretion the mother of all the virtues. And dear little Eva was not discreet. Creatures as innocent as she never are. She had such pretty eyes and such a dreadfully fascinating way of looking at men—like a tame fawn or a newly-awakened child; she was so sweetly unconscious of her own beauty that she went about attracting every one's attention by the charmingly inconsiderate things which she did with as much gay carelessness as if her wild-flower face had been as expression-less as a cod's; she gave in so readily to unauthorized advances; she confessed, within hearing, her admiration for handsome Alcibiade or fascinating Narcisse just as frankly as she might have said that she liked dancing or swimming, big dogs or eating ices; she was so lovely—such an ideal but distracting ingenue—that, seeing the perfect propriety of her mother and sister, she bewildered the Frenchmen with whom she opened her frank relations and gave that mother and sister themselves more trou-ble than even Perdita would have done. And it was impossible to go beyond this. She captivated more than one susceptible Gaul whose fancy entangled itself in the golden meshes of her gracious head; but no one had been suffered to knit up anything like friendly relations save Bois-Duval and Laperrière; and since their time somehow no one had tried.

For so much then Mrs. Winstanley was grateful to her new friends; and for the rest she had no fear. Why should she fear? They knew their business too well to make difficulties for themselves by rousing suspicions in a mother; and what ulterior designs either had, were buried as deep beneath the waxen surface of grave politeness and devoted cares bestowed on Mrs. Winstanley, as the run of the animal of which they were the human ethical representatives is buried beneath the smooth turf. They openly admired the young ladies; Bois-Duval made his preference for Eva felt rather than seen and Laperrière meandered mildly about Thomasina; but neither showed his cards nor forced the game and both kept a calm sough[1] and paid court to Mrs. Winstanley. Of the two girls, however, it is only fair to say that Thomasina was the typical iceberg round which the lively Baron meandered to no small loss of time; but what Eva was the future only would show and the Vicomte only could judge.

It was a fine starlight night, and all Trouville was sitting on the sands. The moon was too young to give much light or to cast a definite shadow, but the stars were bright and the sea was phosphorescent. The pleasure-boats rowing close in shore made long tracks of light and each little wave as it broke on the sand or ran along the jetty shook off showers of drops that shone like silver as they rose and fell. A diver was plunging from the head of the pier, making himself like a mass of white fire as he swam about in the water and splashed up sparkling cascades with his hands. But the shining stars and the phosphorescent sea, the beauty of the scene and the sense of power and majesty that pervaded all nature, were in striking contrast with the human beings assembled there, for the most part with the sole object of drowning Time in the enchanted waters of pleasure. It seemed almost a desecration that hetairæ[2] should be the queens of such an hour, and roués the kings—scarcely fitting to the time and place that Adèle should be cutting Marie's flimsy reputation into airy shreds and that Marie should be telling Adèle's most important and cherished secrets—that Narcisse should be boasting of his conquest over "la petite Julie" and Alcibiade should be scheming how he could deprive him for his own installation—that Jules should be deep in calculation of how to make his debts pay for his pleasures and Antoine deeper still on the chance reduced to certainty of his new martingale[3]—that M. le Vicomte de Bois-Duval should be planning how best to slip that little cocked-hat note now in his waistcoat pocket into Eva's pink round moist little hand and that M. le Baron de Laperrière should be fuming at his wasted endeavours to thaw that impenetrable iceberg Thomasina—that Eva should be coaxing her mother for a new dress which she did not want and coaxing her in a voice that Bois-Duval might hear—that Thomasina should be weigh-ing Mr. Brocklebank and Laperrière in the scales of chance and value—and that Mrs. Winstanley should be scheming, like Jules yonder, how to squeeze superfluities out of an income not large enough for necessaries. But so the world goes; and the stars shine in vain overhead, blotted out by the enchanted waters below.

---

[1] Whistle or sigh.
[2] Prostitutes.
[3] A system of betting in which a player increases the stake by doubling each time a bet is lost.

The Winstanleys were sitting in a charming triad, their chairs firmly planted in the sand. They were becomingly swathed in the most delightful wraps; and each looked a perfect picture with her lace scarf or pointed kerchief round her face and head. Such as they were, they sat there playing gracefully at maternal satisfaction and maidenly content.

M. le Vicomte de Bois-Duval and M. le Baron de Laperrière were sitting at a short distance near enough to make their admiration felt and to serve as a bodyguard in case of need, but not so near as to be intrusive or to suggest to maternal prudence the value of retreat. They were smoking their cigarettes and talking together in low tones; and were altogether humble, inoffensive and pleasant. Eva was laughing with extra lightness in her bird-like trill; talking fast and loud, so that her clear-carrying childish voice could be heard a long way off. If she could not be seen she thought she would at least be heard. She would stir up the imagination if she could not appeal to the senses; and she knew that the one was as powerful as the other. This little blind drama was going on in full swing—Eva talking for Bois-Duval to hear and Bois-Duval making her conscious that he understood as he was meant to do—when suddenly a loud, cheery, well-known voice, followed by one thinner but more refined, struck on the Winstanley ears; two familiar forms loomed out of the darkness into the broad strip of light that fell on the ladies from the lamps of the casino; and down the steps came hurrying Sir James Kearney and Hubert Strangways.

"We thought we should find you somewhere about here when we could not see you in the casino; and then we heard Miss Eva's voice. How jolly!" said Hubert impulsively, shaking hands with Eva first of all.

Sir James minded his manners better and greeted Mrs. Winstanley as the principal person of the group—also the one whose good-will it was important to cultivate.

"How nice! It is just like a game at blindman's-buff!" said little Eva in a shrill voice. She fell to laughing again, but in an odd, strained, spasmodic way, as if she had not hit the right key somehow.

Then she turned to Sir James.

"How nice!" she said again, clapping her hands as if with delight. "But," looking round; "where is Mrs. Merton?"

"Where is Mrs. Merton?" repeated Sir James, also laughing in a key as false as the child's. "Am I my sister's keeper? Mrs. Merton is doubtless at Armour Court, chaperoning another bevy of fair ladies. Mr. Brocklebank has a craze for making up parties of young ladies."

"Not a bad craze with such a place as that in which to receive them," said Mrs. Winstanley smoothly; "though it does certainly want all that mellowness and refinement which comes from long inheritance and generations of possession."

"Yes, I hear it is an enormous place," he returned. "But I fancy with no more taste or beauty in it than a factory or barracks."

"When did you come?" asked Thomasina of Sir James. She turned to Hubert. "Look! there are some chairs," she said. "Are you not going to sit down with us?"

"Yes; of course," said both the young men in a breath; as they "collared" a couple of chairs, according to Hubert's vernacular, and planted them close to their fair friends, making a merry, laughing, intimate little party together. And all save Eva felt as if a stretch of arid desert had been passed and a fresh green corner of meadow-land reached at last.

Though by what right did Hubert Strangways feel as if he had been in the desert when at home and that this special strip of foreign sand was the corner of a flowery meadow? He had come from Strangways, where he had seen Maud Disney every day and had been as often congratulated by his parents on his good fortune in having secured such a charming creature for his future wife—one as entirely devoted to him as he was to her. By the law of lovers he should have felt desolate and in exile at this moment; the farthest possible removed from meadow-land or sunshine. He should have been thinking of Maud and wearying for her presence, not pleasuring himself here, hundreds of miles away and with that tumbling sea between. He should have been picturing to himself the smooth dark hair which made that compact tight little head like a ball of shining satin, not looking at a fuzzy fringe of gold which the gaslight brightened into a kind of enchanted web spread like a veil over the clear cuplike brow. He should have been thinking of the calm grey eyes which seldom wept and as rarely smiled, which never grew dark with passion nor wild with fear nor yet dim with shame—not of these bright blue orbs which were like magic lakes wherein men lost themselves if only they looked down into them; of the quiet voice that fell in such measured accents, so unexcited in its tones, so gentle in its speech— not of these shrill clear bird-like notes which rang out in the still evening air like sweetest music on his ear. He should have been bathing his memory in that sense of superiority which hung like a perfume about Maud and made him ever feel the inferior, as a man should, not revelling in his own consciousness of strength and power and manhood as the supplement to this beautiful little angel's weakness. He should have been worshipping his own Maud, not Mrs. Winstanley's Eva; and this place should have been the desert, not Strangways nor Beechover, where the eldest daughter of the Disneys made believe to return the love which the eldest son of the Strangways made believe to give. To be sure he admired and respected his Maud as much as any man could. He said this to himself and others freely; but he knew that he did not love her and that something much less excellent, in fact something decidedly inferior, would have suited him better.

And he knew where that thing was; and rushed off to Trouville, to find it on the sands.

Sir James went on the same errand too; but neither confessed his secret weakness to the other. Each said he wanted to see the Deauville races; each said carelessly, "perhaps he would come across the Winstanleys"; and both believed that the fiction was accepted and the pretence not seen through—as indeed was the case. For neither Sir James read Hubert Strangways aright, nor Hubert Sir James. Was not the one engaged to Maud Disney, and the other—well, ask Mrs. Merton about that other! Perhaps she could say something. Thus, they joined forces together in perfect good faith and mutual blindness; and the veil so far was not lifted.

How pleasant it was to be all together again, just as if they were in England—only England with a clear sky and balmy air. The two young men showed their delight without reserve; Mrs. Winstanley was warm and quite maternal; Thomasina was the most delightful elder sister possible; while Eva was—what could Eva be but herself if she would be perfect? And then, as the ladies were at home, as it were, while these dear fellows were strangers, it was only right that they should be taken in tow, like boys home for the holiday—only in accordance with the duties of hospitality that Mrs. Winstanley should ask where they had lodged themselves? and how they were served? and whether they were being fleeced beyond reason or not? It was all very domestic and intimate and refreshing; but Eva, glancing to where M. le Vicomte de Bois-Duval was sitting smoking his scented cigarette, wished in her heart that the Englishmen had not come just yet, or else that every one had not been so nice and that she could make up her mind which was nicest.

The two Frenchmen, watching the whole play, put on a sudden air of indifference so soon as the young Englishmen came up. "Les belles Anglaises," hitherto their pleasure and delight, ceased to be on the sands at all for them. From a watchful and respectful bodyguard they became independent, detached and slightly insolent. Their voices were a little louder, their laugh a little harder and more pronounced, their conversation more risky, their asides and stage whispers more suggestive than was quite "good form." Sir James and Hubert looked round at them with the Englishman's disdain of all men not of the Anglo-Saxon race, and thought it presumptuous that they should dare to sit there and talk French and enjoy themselves after their own fashion in the presence of English ladies. But the men whom Hubert would have called foreigners, had he spoken of them here in their own country, saw the milords no more than the miladis, and for all recognition of any humanity than their own, might have been blind or deaf. They kept their places, smoked their cigarettes, talked both at the same time and were exceedingly merry—as they had a right to be if they chose. But somehow their manners and their propinquity grated on both Hubert and Sir James; and if they could, with decency, they would have given both M. le Vicomte de Bois-Duval and M. le Baron de Laperrière an impromptu bath in a pond.

When the ladies rose to house themselves for the night in the cupboards for which they paid as bedrooms, the Frenchmen rose too and stood against their chairs like military men on parade.

"Bon soir, mesdames," they said in their sonorous French style, hats off and with elaborate reverences in acknowledgment of the stately, graceful and fluttered salutations respectively bestowed on them by the Winstanleys.

"Dormez bien, ma belle!" added M. le Vicomte, in a low voice to Eva, who passed close enough to receive the note which under cover of the darkness he passed into her hand.

The two Parisians followed the group at a short distance, laughing at the whole masculine part of the British nation; as if those sturdy sons of Albion, who think themselves more than a match for the world in arms, were nothing better than machines or gorillas.

"Do you know those two fellows?" asked Hubert, hastily.

He was as good-tempered as strong men usually are, but a Frenchman was beyond his philosophy. Had he been a thinker and bold enough to question the ways of Providence with men, it would have been on the point that Frenchmen were permitted to exist. This fact was one of the severest stumbling-blocks to his faith in the parental guidance of the world that he could have had—the only one indeed; and he often found himself wondering why it was allowed.

"Do you know them?" he repeated, his fair-skinned face flushing even in the dark.

"Slightly," said Mrs. Winstanley in an indifferent way.

"One cannot help knowing a little of people here; but it commits one to nothing," said Thomasina quietly.

"And Frenchmen are so fascinating!" said Sir James with polite sarcasm.

"Do you think so?" asked Thomasina. "They are very well-bred certainly, especially to women; but they seem to me to want stability; not to be so reliable as our own men."

"Reliable! I should think not!" said Hubert in a rather loud voice. "No Frenchman knows what truth or honour means; and his good-breeding is only skin deep—bows and fine speeches, and there it stops."

He did not consider this outbreak against the nation, by whose hospitality he was at this moment profiting, a breach in his own good manners. He was English; consequently he need not trouble himself about the susceptibilities of foreigners.

The two Frenchmen were quite near enough to hear something of what was said. They understood English, as we know; and Hubert's voice was loud and clear and carried well on such a night as this.

They looked at each other; and each understood the other's eyes.

"So be it," said M. le Vicomte. "I will undertake the office. These English canaille[1] want to be taught manners."

"We shall not be clumsy tutors," returned the Baron; and both men involuntarily assumed a more martial bearing and dangerous air.

Then Eva's bird-like notes rang out sweet and distinct:

"I think you Englishmen are the most jealous creatures in the world!" she said gaily. "What is the great difference between you and Frenchmen, I wonder! There are good and bad everywhere, and some Frenchmen are better than some English, and some are worse."

It was a marvellous bit of reasoning for the child, but she was impelled by motives which brightened her wits just as fear lends strength to the muscles. She wanted to conciliate one of those following and to make matters pleasant all round.

"The little one has the most sense of all," said Bois-Duval; "I will rid her of these puppies."

"And profit by the clearance?" returned Laperrière, laughing.

"I will do my best—all that is possible to a brave man," returned his friend; and then the two turned into the casino and tempted Fortune at the tables.

And when Hubert and Sir James sauntered in a short time after, they made it slightly unpleasant for the English newcomers, and relieved them of a few hundred francs—just by way of initiation.

---

[1] Scoundrels.

CHAPTER XVIII.

PLAYING WITH FIRE.

LITTLE Eva was an ingénue by profession, but an ingénue to whom coquetry was as the breath of her nostrils and stratagem her daily bread. She had a child's inconsequence, as well as a child's rash courage, and never looked farther ahead than the pleasure of the hour, nor planned for more than the successful ruse of the day. Her intrigue with M. le Vicomte de Bois-Duval, begun out of pure idleness and native naughtiness, was just one of those dangerous things which it was in her nature to begin and in her power to carry through. That odd mixture of shrewdness and folly characteristic of the class of woman to which she belonged, kept her undiscovered and unsuspected—and undiscovered because unsuspected. Even Thomasina, who saw through her more clearly than did their mother and who never allowed herself to be misled by pretty pretence nor by false sentiment, even she thought her little sister too much of a child to go really wrong. Had she spoken broadly, she would have said too much of a fool to deceive any one who had eyes. She had to be watched and guarded, kept from the free exercise of her own silliness and what seemed absolute mental incapacity to learn prudence; but for planned and fruitful fraud—for an intrigue undertaken and carried on before their very eyes—no one who knew foolish light-headed babbling little Eva could suppose her capable of anything so serious!

This was Thomasina's deliberate conviction; and she did not want for perspicacity. That her young sister should have been able to blind her so completely told more for the child's cleverness than against the woman's penetration.

Eva was so far innocent in that she did not understand the extent of her danger in this underhand intercourse with Bois-Duval. She was like a child playing with fire—breaking cherrystones on a block of dynamite—cooking a doll's dinner in a powder magazine. She neither foresaw consequences nor feared them; and not foreseeing, not fearing, she had no caution in her plots, only sleight-of-hand in their management. She liked the excitement of encouraging that handsome young Frenchman beyond the limits allowed by her mother and so rigidly defined by Thomasina; and she did not calculate the chance of not being able to stop the ball which she had set rolling, when she wanted to give up the game. The danger of letting loose forces which might be beyond her control when set free, troubled her no more than it troubled the wizard's servant when he pronounced the magic words which called up the demon, without being certain of those which were to banish him when done with.[1] It pleased her to feel that she was of secret importance; and that she could hoodwink her mother and that strict rather cross elder sister who thought she knew everything. It gratified her pride to feel that she was queen of the day, and that out of the five men most immediately connected with them at this time, three were in love with her; while that graceful, excellent Thomasina had but two strings to her extremely elegant bow. And one of these strings was a very tough bit of piano-wire; while the other was only a poor thin squeaking fiddle-string, not nearly so rich or good as hers. As for poor old Per, sister though she was, she was out of the present running altogether. She had no string of any kind; unless indeed she had half of Thomasina's coiled away there at Armour Court. To distance her in the number and value of conquests was no more honour in Eva's estimate of things than it was an honour to the hare to distance the tortoise in the race. But it was a feather in her cap to leave Thomasina in the rear, and to throw dust in her eyes into the bargain.

Still, the honour and the dust-throwing were alike difficult and dangerous; and how to manage three lovers abreast, of whom the first was engaged to another girl, the second was jealous and undecided, while the third was forbidden and in secret, was a feat that might have taxed the powers of a more finished diplomatist than herself.

But there was no use in worrying, she thought, when things got hot. Luck and her own wit would help her over the stiles when she came to them; and to luck and her own wit she trusted. A true human ephemeris, she lived for the hour and the sunshine, incapable of reflection, careless of the morrow, shutting her eyes to the night. She wanted only the day's pleasure and the gewgaws scattered by Folly on her path; and whether her coquetries should break a strong man's heart, or ruin a good woman's life, would touch her conscience no more than it touches the conscience of a tiger-cub when it mumbles the bones of an antelope—of a sparrow-hawk when it strikes down a nightingale. Such things come by the laws of nature; and Eva acted after the law of hers, like the tiger-cub and the sparrow-hawk.

---

[1]   Refers to "Der Zauberlehrling" (The Sorcerer's Apprentice), 1799 ballad by Johann Wolfgang von Goethe (1749–1832).

The note which Bois-Duval slipped into her hand was only a preliminary kind of declaration. It went over the ordinary ground of sleepless nights and anxious days, of dreams and thoughts, vague sorrows, vague wishes and the image of a gracious and adorable presence ever before his eyes. It was cautious and respectful, ardent and suggestive, all in one. It planned nothing, asked for nothing and implied all; it was simply, by word, so much homage laid at the loveliest little feet in the world, and, by spirit, the first call to surrender. It was the soothing fanning of the vampire-bat; but it meant the life's blood.

Bois-Duval had no scruples in thus laying siege to the happiness and repute of a young unmarried English girl. Had she been one of his own nation, he would have held himself as dishonoured as dishonourable, had he tried to tempt her to indiscretion. At all events he would have waited till she was married. Being an English miss made all the difference in his code; just as it would make all the difference to certain thieves whether they found the door open or had to break this bar and pick that lock. A French mother bars her doors and double-locks them as well; and her precautions are respected; but it is those fools of English mothers who do not look after their daughters who are to blame when things go wrong, not the men who take advantage of the lax guard. If the law cannot punish this neglect, circumstances ought; and Bois-Duval did not think himself consecrated to prevent the swing of the hammer. It is not in the nature of man to refuse the good things thrown in his way; and if this pretty little girl liked to play the fool under the shadow of her mother's skirts, it would be a pity to balk her humour.

There was evidently not money enough among these pretty Englishwomen to make marriage wise or possible. They were not up to his price. But plucking wayside flowers is one thing and buying land for profitable tillage is another. The former is every man's individual right—the latter is a family affair to be undertaken only for the general good by acknowledged consent and after grave consideration.

How fluttered and flattered, yet how frightened, little Eva was as she read the note by the light of her miserable bedroom candle! It was the first time things had gone so far with her as this; and she wished now that she had been more discreet and less ambitious as to her score. She knew that either Sir James or Hubert Strangways would be a far better match for her than even a French nobleman; and she was afraid lest she might be made to realize the old fable of the dog and the shadow, and by grasping at too much end in losing all. Nevertheless she was in for it now and she must go on if she would get out of it. And worrying and losing her rest would only make her eyes dull and her complexion cloudy; wherefore, the best thing that she could do was to go to sleep with all despatch—the note crushed under her pillow and the next twelve hours at the least safe.

"Running over to Deauville races" meant, in point of fact, going to see Eva Winstanley, to the two young men who had been so suddenly taken with a desire to see how the French stud was getting on; and they had come with the natural intention of having a good time and making things pleasant both for themselves and their friends. There was a curious strain of reticence between them, and a still more curious condition of mutual blindness. According to Sir James, Hubert, engaged to Maud Disney, was safe as a matter of course. Being an honest and honourable gentleman, he could not possibly be in love with Eva Winstanley; and his evident affection for the family was without question nothing but the purest fraternal kind of friendliness. And, according to Hubert, Sir James could not be in love because he was his, Hubert's, friend; and friends do not enter into the lists against each other, just as hawks do not peck out other hawks' eyes. Hence they pulled together in perfect amity and complete unsuspicion; and that great, good, stupid trust of Englishmen, through which they do not see what is straight before them, kept both blind and both silent.

This was by no means the first visit of either to a French watering-place; and before this they had always amused themselves "to the n'th," and had found the whole thing awfully jolly. The fun of the sands had been unending; and they had laughed at the odd spectacles afforded by unconscious bathers as if it had all been one huge farce acted day by day for the benefit of the joking public. But then they had been alone or with other young men of their own set and kind. They had not had the ladies of their own families with them; nor been as now, associated with others as dear as their own. It would have annoyed Sir James beyond his rather scanty stock of patience had his mother seen anything doubtful; and Hubert would have blazed had his sisters turned away their disgusted little faces from disagreeable dissolving views. But when it came to Eva, to Thomasina—Eva's sister, to Mrs. Winstanley—Eva's mother—then the young Englishmen felt inclined to challenge the whole manhood of the place *en maillot*[1] who did not respect the division of the cord, and who came up from the depths, dripping like Tritons, and apparently as oblivious of propriety as if they had been so many mermen born into the habit of skin-dresses. It seemed an insult to these modest, prudish English ladies

---

[1] (French), in armor.

of whom they had assumed the natural protection, that portly mothers and obese fathers should exhibit themselves with such terrible fidelity; that young men, known as equals in ordinary dress, should show themselves as so many acrobats minus the spangles; that little children should dance about with only heaven between the sun and their brown, freckled skin; and that one girl should suggest another by the generous provocation of her attire. Above all, it seemed an insult too direct to be endured, that M. le Vicomte de Bois-Duval and M. le Baron de Laperrière should disport themselves in striped tricot under the very eyes of the Winstanleys, and evidently "play" to them by their ridiculous gambols in the water as actors play to their friends in the stage-box. The whole thing offended British feeling from first to last; but the annoyance caused by these two was of a more personal character than the rest, and touched on more dangerous ground. The bathing-hour passed, however, without untoward event of any kind, save that Bois-Duval, in his haste on leaving the water all dripping as he was, ran against Hubert Strangways and nearly knocked him down by the suddenness of the shock. As he said "Pardon, monsieur!" and made a bow, the young fellow was obliged to accept his excuse and keep his very English objurgation inside his teeth. But he made a mental note of the accident and said to himself that he owed the French puppy one for that! And Hubert Strangways generally paid his debts—especially of this kind. Something was in the air between him and Bois-Duval; and what is in the air comes to the earth before very long. The Englishman was nettled by the impudence of the Frenchman in hovering about the Winstanleys now that he and his friend had come; and the Frenchman was more than nettled at the arrival of the Englishmen, both such "beaux garçons"[1] as they were, and Hubert so evidently on such good terms with little Eva. It was all subtle and vague and undefined; but it was there. It was thunder in the atmosphere, but no storm as yet. That would come when the clouds met.

After the bathing was over the Winstanleys took refuge in their own special tent on the sands, where the two young men came to share the shade and discuss the humours of the scene. It must be confessed that both Hubert and Sir James expressed themselves with more asperity than belongs to young men bent on amusing themselves. They might have been old maids for the severity of their strictures. But as their ill-humour was due to that vague virtue "nice feeling," Mrs. Winstanley passed it by with indulgence, on the plea that it was better for boys to be too strict

---

[1]   (French), good fellows.

than too lax, and that mothers need not object even to puritanism in the young men with whom their daughters are associated.

"After all, England for the English," said Hubert; "this going abroad so much as we do is a mistake. We find nothing equal to what we leave and many things a great deal worse."

"The climate?" asked Mrs. Winstanley courteously.

"Ours is the best in the world!" said Hubert. "We have no extremes as they have in these blessed old places where the wolves come into the villages in the winter, and you get sunstroke if you put your head out of doors in the summer."

"Oh, what an awful story!" said Eva with an enchanting smile. "We have been out all day long ever since we came; and I don't believe the wolves come here in the winter. What a dreadful story to tell!"

"No; Hubert is right, Miss Eva," said Sir James. "There is no question that such a climate as ours is the best, all things considered, and makes the best men and women. The summer is not too hot and the winter is never too cold for exercise and hard work; and I believe there are more days in England when we can be out of doors all day long than in any other country in the world."

"You do not allow for the discomfort?" asked Mrs. Winstanley pleasantly. "Those London fogs, the spring east winds, those chilly wet Julys—do not these count?"

"They do not exist," said Hubert quite gravely.

On which there broke out a chorus of protest, negation, remonstrance and laughter; and while the laugh was at its loudest the dark, handsome, well-trimmed heads of the two Frenchmen appeared at the entrance of the tent—the first time they had ventured on this familiarity. And they ventured on it now only because their rivals were there, and they wished to claim as many privileges as these had and display as much friendly intimacy.

"Good morning, mesdames; may we enter?" said Bois-Duval, making that quasi-military salute, doubled with a dancing-master's grace, characteristic of the nation where every man is born a soldier and is taught to waltz.

Though Mrs. Winstanley would have been glad if one of those strong currents which sweep round the Trouville shore had carried her two French friends safe away to Havre, yet she proved herself now, as always, equal to the occasion, and invited the young men to enter, like a graceful and well-dressed Astræa dispensing equal justice to all alike. She presented the two pairs of rivals to each other, and made room for the

Frenchmen to sit beside her own chair; but Bois-Duval, with rather an affected air, cast himself on the sand at the feet of Eva, saying, "The footstool of woman is the throne of man."

Hubert and Sir James looked at each other. The former flushed angrily, the latter smiled disagreeably. One would have said he had toothache and was trying to hide it.

"Confound the brute's impudence!" muttered Hubert, flushed and heated.

"He has to learn his place," thought Sir James, pale and constrained.

Eva blushed and looked pretty and confused. Her compatriots thought she was distressed and making almost an appeal to them for protection; and Bois-Duval thought she was elated by his homage if fluttered by its publicity.

"If our footstool is your throne, you manage to kick it over very easily," said Mrs. Winstanley with as much seriousness as if she had been Perdita herself. "The phrase is pretty—I question if the fact be true."

"On the honour of a Frenchman, madame!" said Bois-Duval, laying his hand on his heart.

"One assertion does not prove another," said Sir James, a thin film of insolence over his conventional manner. "'Quis custodiet custodes?'[1] Bail must be tested before it can be taken."

"The test is capable of proof at any time desired," returned Bois-Duval with perfect urbanity.

"No proof is needed beyond that already given by history," put in Mrs. Winstanley in her sweetest way. "The honour of the French nation is too firmly established to be questioned."

"Bayard was a Frenchman," said Thomasina, as her contribution of oil.

"And Philip Sidney was an Englishman," said Sir James.

"But it was a Frenchman who said: 'Gentlemen of the guard, fire first!'" little Eva cried in her simple childish manner.

"And it was our noble compatriot Cambronne who said: 'The guard dies, but does not surrender!'"[2] said Bois-Duval, with a smile to Eva which made both Hubert and Sir James feel as if he had struck them.

"Pshaw!" said Sir James with supreme contempt. "Can you quote such a myth as this for history, M. le Vicomte!—a pure invention, a bit of audacious *blague*,[3] due to Duruy's[4] own imagination only! That a

---

[1] (Latin), who will guard the guards?
[2] Refers to Ch. XIV of *Les Misérables* (1862) by Victor Hugo (1802–85).
[3] (French), sly joke.
[4] Victor Duruy (1811–94), author of *Histoire de France* (1864).

test! You might as well claim the excesses of the Revolution as proofs of your national self-constraint and humanity!"

"As monsieur may claim his burnings at Smithfield[1] as proofs of his national liberty of conscience," said Bois-Duval with a sneer. "But pardon! in this matter of Cambronne's you are mistaken. The fact is an historical truth—as sublime as true."

"Just as true as the sinking of the *Vengeur* with all hands on board!" said Sir James. "You claim this too among your heroic actions, when, in point of fact, captain and crew were brought ashore to England and kept as prisoners till the war was over."

"It is a bad cause which takes to denial and perversion," said Bois-Duval loftily. "But in truth it is no new thing for the conquered to claim the victory; it hides the national blush."

"When did the French conquer us?—at Waterloo?" exclaimed Hubert.

"At Waterloo, monsieur, the Prussians had the honour of defeating us and turning your overthrow into success," said Bois-Duval with the same imperturbable urbanity as before.

Both Englishmen started to their feet with a forcible exclamation.

"Gentlemen, surely you are not going to have a political quarrel here before us!" said Mrs. Winstanley in her most dignified manner. "Pray calm yourselves, and let us change the conversation. It is never wise to discuss politics with strangers; and it is especially unwise among men of different nationalities who were once enemies and now are friends. Let history settle itself. You four young men cannot make doubtful matters clear, nor put crooked questions straight. Sit down again, I beg, and let us talk of something else. When do the races begin, Vicomte?—the day after to-morrow?"

A little ashamed of their unseemly heat, the Englishmen, with an awkward laugh from Hubert and a sudden resumption of cold dignity from Sir James, sat down again as Mrs. Winstanley had desired; while Bois-Duval, raising himself on his elbow, answered Mrs. Winstanley as smoothly as if no brush had taken place.

Yes, the day after to-morrow, and he and Laperrière had secured the best places at command for 'les belles Anglaises'—places whence they could see everything and where they would be the flowers of the fête themselves, he added gallantly, with a veiled look to Eva at the end of his open and prolonged regard to Mrs. Winstanley and Thomasina.

"Thank you, Vicomte," said Mrs. Winstanley. "You are really very kind."

---

[1]   Traditional place of execution outside London, especially known for the burning of heretics.

But she wished that he had been slightly less kind, and that she and her daughters might have been spared this somewhat embarrassing obligation.

"We will call for you at the right hour, and hope that we may have the pleasure of driving you over," said Bois-Duval.

"I thought we were to have had that pleasure, Mrs. Winstanley?" said Sir James.

"We came for the very thing," said Hubert.

"Pardon, messieurs! the old saying of 'first come first served' holds good here," said the Vicomte airily. "You are a little late in the field."

He said this with the gayest kind of good humour, and at the same moment managed to take Eva's hand under cover of her embroidery which had fallen to the ground, and which he picked up before Sir James or Hubert could reach it—returning it with a courtly bow for public acceptance and this audacious bit of practice for private use. But the child, though she blushed, did not resent; and Bois-Duval even fancied that her soft pink fingers returned the pressure of his.

"Perhaps we can arrange so that we can all go together," said Mrs. Winstanley. "A good break will hold seven."

"My carriage, madame, holds only five," said the Vicomte somewhat stiffly. "As I did not know of the arrival of these gentlemen I could not possibly arrange for their accommodation," he added with an undeniable dash of superciliousness.

"We came for this!" cried Hubert again, with more agitation than the occasion seemed to warrant.

"I am so sorry!" said Mrs. Winstanley. "But if you had only given us notice that you were coming! We could have managed then—"

"And thrown me over," laughed Bois-Duval. "Never mind, Laperrière! If madame does accept our escort only as a *pis aller*,[1] we have the benefit of the fact and can afford to let the motive go!"

He said this with the most delightful good temper and good breeding. But he nearly maddened Hubert; and Sir James felt as if he had suddenly swallowed poison.

"I should never have been other than obliged to M. le Vicomte for his kindness, but I am not one to throw over old friends for new," said Mrs. Winstanley with a delightful smile to each in turn; "nor," she added with extreme grace, "am I one to throw over new friends for caprice or self-interest."

"Can nothing be arranged, Mrs. Winstanley?" asked Hubert hastily.

---

[1] (French), second best.

She looked at Bois-Duval.

"I think not," he answered smiling. "I can speak to my man and tell him to see if he can get some kind of ark on wheels that will hold us all, but I fear it will not be possible. Every public vehicle in the town is engaged. I fear these gentlemen must get over in their own way. If we had but known in time—"

The rest of the sentence was lost in a murmur of sounds which might mean regret or something else.

Mrs. Winstanley looked grave. The faces of Sir James and Hubert were not reassuring.

"I appreciate your kindness," she began to the Vicomte in a hesitating way, thinking whether it would not be the best policy to abandon these new satellites for the old on the spot, and throw all her chances into the national scale.

"Pray do not mention it!" said Bois-Duval, interrupting her airily. "I knew the difficulties, which you did not; and I was aware that if I was not prompt in securing the comfort and convenience of mesdames betimes, they would come badly off in the press. I assure you if you do not allow me to carry out my programme you will have no possibility of getting over save by walking—which I fancy you will scarcely care to do. In your own interests, madame, let me beseech you to leave the arrangement as it stands. I will say nothing of myself, or of my disappointment if all that I have so carefully planned should be upset; but in your own interest only, let things go on as they are now!"

It all seemed frank and reasonable enough; and it would have been decidedly ungracious had Mrs. Winstanley refused thus at the eleventh hour the arrangements already made and accepted; or if those hot-blooded friends of hers had objected.

"You see—what am I to do!" she said with a helpless smile that meant capitulation.

"What a pity we did not know you were coming!" said Thomasina. "We could all have gone together then. It would have been such a pleasant party!"

"Yes," said Bois-Duval tranquilly. "But in these matters the forelock is everything!"

"At all events, we can go and see about the break," said Hubert, jumping up in an excited way, as if there was not a moment to lose.

"Do so," answered the Vicomte. "You will then satisfy yourself that what I have said is correct, and will understand the necessity of submission to the inevitable."

"I prefer to use my own judgment and find out the truth of things for myself," said Hubert with very unnecessary firmness of tone.

"Quite right. Nevertheless, here on my own ground I may be allowed to be the best judge of the circumstances attending Deauville races. In the miseries of a London fog I should yield the pas to monsieur!"

"Pshaw! that fog! A Frenchman can do nothing but talk of our fogs!" cried Sir James irritably.

"Pardon! there are other things too," laughed the Vicomte. "There are your wife-beaters, your garotters, your burglars, your lordly shop-keepers, your rich eldest sons while the younger grovel in the mire. There are many other things in your great nation of which we speak in ours. But the fogs are the least distracting. And at all events they are undeniable and frequent."

"We have sunshine sometimes!" said Mrs. Winstanley smiling.

"And a morality that will bear favourable contrast with that of France," said Sir James.

"But the sunshine is not so bright as this, is it, Mr. Strangways?—is it, Sir James?" asked little Eva appealingly.

"It is much pleasanter," answered Hubert for his part.

"If you say this is brighter it is so, Miss Eva. But some faces in England make one forget the comparative want of sunshine," said Sir James for his.

At which Eva laughed and said, "How nice! what a pretty speech!" while M. le Vicomte de Bois-Duval turned a shade paler than usual, as he raised his eyes with an odd impertinent look to Sir James, and said in an affected voice:

"Well said. Ma foi! Monsieur is almost gallant enough to be a Frenchman!"

"Do you mean that for a compliment, M. le Vicomte?" asked Sir James.

"Surely! the highest I could pay," answered the Frenchman.

"And I regard it as a piece of decided impudence," said Sir James angrily

"My dear friend!" remonstrated Mrs. Winstanley.

"Do not insult us by having a quarrel in our presence," said Thomasina in a low voice.

Little Eva sighed like a troubled child.

"Oh dear, how cross you all are!" she said with a pretty pout. "You are spoiling all our fun by your ill-temper."

"Allons! Miss Eva is right. It is bad form!" said the Vicomte gaily. "Vive la gaieté! vive la bonne humeur! à bas le spleen![1] and let the best man win!"

---

[1] (French), Here's to gaiety! Here's to good humor! Away with anger!

"Win what?" asked Eva innocently.

"Paradise!" answered Bois-Duval.

CHAPTER XIX.

THE TRAIN LAID.

THERE was a dance at the casino to-night, and the Winstanleys were going. As they were here they might as well profit by such amusements as were to be had; and though these balls at the casino were certainly quite un-English, still they amused the child, and that was everything. It was so natural that she should like to be amused, and that they, the staid elder sister and the indulgent mother, should like to see her pleased!

So said Mrs. Winstanley to her compatriots when half-explaining, half-excusing an action which really wanted neither explanation nor excuse. Had she been quite clear in her conscience—had she not been guilty of coquetting with chances in the person of Bois-Duval—she would not have made that little speech. It was a defence and a shield, a blind and a mask, and she thought herself well-concealed behind it. And when the young men said "Of course," things looked smooth and pleasant enough, and the circumstances of the evening were accepted as simply as if public dances at a foreign casino were part of the ordinary experience of well-born English ladies.

Hubert and Sir James went up together to ask Eva for the first waltz. It was a friendly kind of rivalry, in which neither was jealous of the other, though each desired to win. But little Eva shook her head.

"I am awfully sorry," she said, making up a distractingly pretty and penitent face. "I cannot help it, you know, but I am engaged to the Vicomte. He asked me first, so what could I do?"

"What a shame!" cried Hubert hotly.

"That fascinating gentleman certainly understands the value of the 'forelock,' as he calls it," said Sir James with a sneer.

"Yes, doesn't he?" returned Eva innocently. "He is so awfully quick! He is not like you Englishmen, who are so nice and deliberate, but he takes one's breath away like a whirlwind!"

"It is vilely bad form to be like a whirlwind, as you say," said Hubert angrily.

"Yes, isn't it?" returned Eva; "but if one gets into one, what can one do? I feel just like a stick or a straw or a feather, when I am with those kind of people," she added in her peculiar grammar, making another distracting face.

"But, my dear child, you should not make engagements so long beforehand with such comparative strangers," said Mrs. Winstanley.

Now that her two great hopes had turned up, she would have been glad to have shunted the French Viscount, or at most to have made use of him as a spur to the resolution of these others.

"What could I say, mumsey, when he asked me?" pleaded Eva. "I could not tell a story, you know, and say that I was engaged when I wasn't, could I?"

"You should have made him feel that his request was inconvenient," said Mrs. Winstanley. "It is not as if we knew either him or the Baron intimately—as if we knew them like Sir James and Mr. Strangways. It was very thoughtless of him, and you were not quite up to the mark, my child."

"I am too young for that kind of thing, mumsey," said Eva, lifting up her blue eyes sweetly. "I don't think I shall ever learn to be diplomatic. At all events, I am too young yet."

"Yes, yes, so you are. You are too young and fresh for anything but your own sweet candid innocence," said Sir James.

"And you will always be too frank for diplomacy, I hope," echoed Hubert with a flush.

"Too frank to repress undesirable attentions?" said Mrs. Winstanley pleasantly. "My dear boy, we poor women would come off but ill in life if we could not use our only power of protection—the art of freezing and repelling."

"Yes, I know; but Miss Eva is so perfect as she is, one wants no change in her—at least not yet," said poor Hubert, full of his stupid admiration.

"How nice!" said Eva gaily.

"But when did the Vicomte ask you? and when did you engage yourself, dear?" asked Thomasina in a rather low voice.

Eva did not hear.

"I only wish I could cut myself into three Evas!" she said prettily, looking first at Sir James and then at Hubert. "But I can't, can I?"

"But when did you promise the Vicomte?" repeated Thomasina; and this time Eva was obliged to hear.

"This morning in the tent," she answered quite frankly.

"Indeed! I did not hear you," said her sister, arching her eyebrows.

"No, you were all talking about the races," answered Eva; "but M. le Vicomte was not so rude," with a fresh bird-like cadenza that enchanted and distracted Hubert, while it excited and did not quite satisfy Sir James.

Thomasina said no more. She had not asked for spite, only to make sure; and now she was sure that something more than she knew was going on between the Vicomte and her sister. She did not suppose it was much; but it was something.

All this took place as they were strolling towards the casino; and the discussion ended as they reached the door. Sir James was obliged to be content with only the third dance, Eva having voluntarily offered herself to Hubert for the second, as he had been the first to ask her.

"I think you might have left that to me," said Sir James in an aggrieved tone to his friend.

Though they were brothers in their joint resistance to these foreigners, and standing shoulder to shoulder in close alliance of abhorrence, and though there was no suspicion as yet one of the other, and no perception of the truth, still there were possibilities of enmity if things became too evident; and Sir James was as jealous as Hubert was rash and impassioned.

"First come first served!" said Hubert in a good-humoured way, as Bois-Duval had said before him. "Besides, I could scarcely be expected to give up that dance, even to you, old man!"

He had got the prize and could afford to be gay-tempered.

"Why the devil did you put yourself forward at all?" cried Sir James irritably. "In your circumstances, Hubert, you should be more careful than you are. You lay yourself open to nasty remarks, and have cut me out most unpleasantly where it can be nothing to you."

Hubert turned first red and then pale. He bit his cheek, as his manner was when annoyed: but presently his honest face cleared as he looked into his friend's and held out his hand.

"Come, old fellow, no misunderstandings between us," he said pleasantly. "We have been friends too long for that."

"Friends or not, I suffer no man to cross my path," answered Sir James stiffly; and with this the two followed the ladies into the dancing-room, and the business of the evening began. So far the preface had not been very harmonious; it remained now to see what the end would be.

The music struck up, and M. le Vicomte de Bois-Duval came to demand the honour of Miss Eva's hand for the waltz about to begin; and Eva, with the prettiest, most bashful, most fawnlike kind of look to her mother, rose and took his arm, and was soon whirling about the room like a pretty pale-blue teetotum,[1] with a golden head and a wooden heart.

Hubert took Thomasina, to have at least a pretext for hovering about his unconfessed divinity; while Sir James sat by Mrs. Winstanley, eating out his heart with moody jealousy, and more than half inclined to throw the whole thing up now at once and go back to England and Mrs. Merton, as at least safe and worthy if not wholly satisfactory.

The waltz ended without any contretemps, and Eva had no cause to complain that Bois-Duval was either a cold wooer or a prosaic interpreter. She had never been deluged with so much delicious flattery—never ever been swept away in such a fervid whirlwind of love-making. Frightened while intoxicated, she listened with lowered lids and crimson cheeks, and wished it was not wrong nor dangerous. She knew that she was playing with fire—that this was not the kind of thing her mother would sanction, nor was it the kind of thing that Bois-Duval ought to do, or would have done, had all been really right; yet she could not resist, still less rebuke. It was very naughty, it was very dangerous—but it was very delightful; and Bois-Duval had at least the merit of rousing in her something that was more real than anything she had hitherto felt or made believe to show. Even Hubert Strangways who, up to now, had been her chief personal favourite, was distanced without mercy by this clever and audacious diplomatist; while Sir James, whose title and fortune had been her principal magnets outside her irrepressible desire for "conquest" sank far far into the background—his high-strung, nervous, melancholy temperament and poetic pessimism seeming to her just unmitigated boredom when contrasted with the gay insouciance, the delicious daring and that absence of all inconvenient restraint by principle which characterized her French "flame." But it was all very naughty and very dangerous; and she knew that she was running grave risks, and that the day of reckoning would be heavy when it came.

Then the dance ended and she was brought back with all due decorum to her mother. M. le Vicomte de Bois-Duval knew his social grammar too well to commit unnecessary solecisms. When he offended against the syntax endorsed by Mrs. Grundy it was for some good purpose; but as at the present moment nothing was to be gained by keeping the little girl beyond the time formally allowed by conventional propriety, he delivered her up as he was bound to do—but he delivered her up engaged for at least five out of the twelve dances on the card.

---

[1] A small top.

And when she danced with Hubert, she found him heavy to talk to and clumsy to dance with; while Sir James was decidedly stiff and uncongenial and did not amuse her anyhow.

Then came another turn with Bois-Duval; more ill-humour from the Englishmen; more perplexity from Mrs. Winstanley; and more surety of conviction from Thomasina that something was going on between these two more than was prudent, and that she would set herself to the discovery, and make it.

At the end of the second waltz with Bois-Duval, Eva disappeared from the ball-room. No one had seen her go and no one knew where she had gone; for the two young men were dancing—one with Thomasina, and the other with a pretty little French girl of fifteen by looks and twenty-two by dates; and Mrs. Winstanley was occupied with a friendly neighbour placed there by Bois-Duval purposely to call off her attention. Thus, when the last chord sounded from the orchestra and the moving kaleidoscope on the floor dissolved, Eva and her partner were not forthcoming, and were not to be seen anywhere.

Much indignation and even terror broke out among the friends waiting there to receive her.

"Where is she?" "Have you seen her?" passed from lip to lip. Mrs. Winstanley half rose.

"Naughty child! I must go and look for her," she said, her handsome face a trifle stern and blanched.

"No, do you sit here, Mrs. Winstanley. I will go," said Sir James.

"We will go," echoed Hubert; and the two went off quickly, even before Mrs. Winstanley had given her consent.

Nothing of vital consequence had happened to the child. Bois-Duval had only taken her into the corridor which was filled with people, and where, though he might say what he liked, he could not even take her hand, for the number of eyes about. To our way of thinking it was a perfectly harmless and legitimate thing to do; according to the French standard of morality it was an offence, and highly improper. You may sit with your young partner on the topmost step of the dark stairs, or be alone with her in the conservatory where you are concealed by the camellias and the palms, if you are in an English house and yet not irretrievably damage her character. If you parade your ingenue in a well-lighted corridor crammed with people in a French casino, it is death and destruction to her repute, and her friends would have the right to demand an explanation. But Bois-Duval was a man of nerve, and held to the doctrine that it is no part of a man's duty to take care of a woman's character. That belongs to herself if she be married, to her mother if she be a maiden. If the one chooses to go to the devil, why prevent her? if the other is not guarded by the mother's vigilance, peste! was he to be the nursemaid? This pretty little English girl liked being made love to as much as he liked to make that love; and it was not for him to be ungrateful to opportunity.

To do him justice, no man was more grateful; and at this moment he was vigorously improving the occasion when suddenly the stalwart figure of Hubert and the pale, keen face of Sir James Kearney were seen in the distance as the two young men made their way straight to the place where Eva was sitting with Bois-Duval in the shadow of a friendly column.

"Your mother has desired us to take you back to her without a moment's delay, Miss Winstanley," said Sir James.

He spoke with extreme stiffness, severity and authority; like an angry brother who was justly offended and who expected to be obeyed. As he spoke he offered the little sinner his arm.

The Vicomte took the girl's hand and drew it within his own arm. They were all standing.

"Pardon!" he said gravely. "This young lady belongs to me. I will deliver her into the hands of her mother."

"Miss Winstanley, your mother wished us to take you back," reiterated Sir James, not answering the Frenchman and emphasizing the pronoun.

"Is this your pleasure, mademoiselle?" asked Bois-Duval with a look that made her tremble, partly for dread of losing him as a lover should she offend him by going with her compatriots, and partly for dread of being punished by his betrayal of her folly should she rasp his self-love.

"No!" she said with a really heroic assumption of childish ingenuousness to hide her very real trouble; "I am not going to be handed about like a great ball of silk. We will all go back to mother together. That will be quite a royal escort!" she added with her merry laugh.

"Thank you," said the Vicomte, still grave and intense, holding her hand closely pressed against his side and leading the way in triumph.

"Monsieur," said Sir James, livid with rage; "in England we respect authority."

"And in France, monsieur, we respect innocence," returned Bois-Duval, the "beau phraseur,"[1] again pressing Eva's hand against his side as the practical exemplification of his epigram.

---

[1] (French), maker of clever phrases.

"We shall hear next that they have found out how to make gold in France," said Hubert with a snort of defiance. "The one is about as true as the other!"

"In France, monsieur, we make gentlemen," said Bois-Duval coldly; "do you consider this in England as rare a creation as the making of gold?"

"According to the country, yes," said Hubert. "In some countries it is very rare."

"I agree with you," said Bois-Duval, looking at the young men by turns. "As you say, monsieur, it is in some countries very rare. But that country is not la belle France!"

At that moment a rather large and noisy group came surging up from the dance-room and separated the two Englishmen from Eva and the Vicomte.

"I should like to knock that puppy down," said Hubert in a voice that disdained caution. "His insolence shall be checked—that I swear!"

"Leave him to me," said Sir James irritably. "Why the deuce should you interfere, Hubert? He is more my affair than yours."

"And he is as much mine as yours," returned Hubert with undeniable warmth.

By which it was evident that the annoyance of the moment was serious enough to endanger friendship as well as to create enmity.

"I am glad to have humiliated your compatriots, ma belle," said Bois-Duval in a low voice to Eva.

"How naughty of you!" said Eva, with a laugh.

"How nice, you mean to say! If you have any compassion for me, any love for me, ma chérie, as I think you have, you will be pleased at my victory—as you are; is it not so?"

"I am pleased if you are," said Eva, fluttered.

"Any proof of the superiority of a French gentleman counts for my good," said the Vicomte superbly.

"Oh, I think Frenchmen delightful!" cried Eva.

"One—not all; only one," he returned.

She looked up at him, doing her best to be simple; but nature was too strong; and she dropped her eyes, blushing with a delicious kind of tremor at the dangers and delights of the enchanted wood into which she had voluntarily wandered.

By this time they had got back to the dancing-room, where the Vicomte took her to her place and deposited her on the seat next her mother; leaving her to fight the battle in her own way, and thinking that he himself would be best out of it.

"Where have you been, Eva?" asked Mrs. Winstanley, for her quite sharply. "You know you are not allowed to go out of the room."

"It was so hot, mumsey! I only went into the corridor for a little fresh air," replied Eva, with cheerful innocence.

"How can you be so imprudent, Eva?" said Thomasina. "You know this kind of thing is not considered proper in France. We are not in England; why will you be so silly?"

"Oh, she meant no harm!" said good-hearted Hubert, who winced under those rebukes far more than did Eva herself; "but that coxcomb knew that he was landing her in a hole. It is he who deserves rowing, not poor Miss Eva."

"You are always so good and kind!" said Mrs. Winstanley, who had her own reasons for being strict on this matter, before them. "But Eva has been very imprudent indeed. She must really learn to be more considerate. Nothing but her extreme youth and ignorance of the world can possibly justify her."

"And these do," said Sir James, a slight dash of pedantry in his tone.

"Yes; so please, Mrs. Winstanley, let poor Miss Eva off for this once. She will know better another time," Hubert said, again making himself the pretty little sinner's advocate.

They all spoke as if Eva had been just a naughty child who had stolen a bon-bon or broken her doll; and no one seemed conscious of the absurdity and pretence of the whole matter, when treating of a girl, round whom three men were fluttering, each of whom was jealous of the others.

"How cross you all are to me!—poor little me, what have I done! What harm was there in going into the corridor for a little fresh air?" cried Eva with a pretty pout. "One would think I had done something really wrong!"

"Nothing absolutely wrong perhaps, but something very imprudent, my dear child," said Mrs. Winstanley, still grave if forgiving. "It would have been wrong had you been older and known better. As it is, you are to be pardoned on consideration of your ignorance."

"Now you are a dear darling mumsey again," said Eva, kissing her mother in the face of the multitude. "And now you shall have some sweeties! Only if you promise to be good though, and won't scold me any more?" she added, holding back the box and looking round from each to each with a grave inquiring air.

Mrs. Winstanley smiled.

"What a child it is!" she said pleasantly. "My dear Eva, will you ever become a woman?"

"Now for the sweeties, Miss Eva!" cried Hubert joyously.

He looked on the bon-bons as the ratification of the pardon just granted; and perhaps no one was so relieved as he at the happy ending of this difficulty.

"Here they are!" said Eva, bringing out of her satchel pocket a small box of chocolate creams. "That nice dear M. le Vicomte whom you all abuse so much, and who is such a dear kind old thing, gave them to me; which is what neither of you have done."

Mrs. Winstanley shrugged her shoulders as if she had been a Frenchwoman born.

"So! he treats you as a spoilt child, like every one else!" she said, glancing with a smile first at Sir James, then at the rest, as if this explained everything. There could be nothing serious in an affair wherein the girl was given chocolate creams and treated like a spoilt child all through!

But Thomasina, looking curiously at the little box in Eva's hand, recognized it as one which she herself had bought this very afternoon at the confectioner's and given to her sister who had begged for it.

The whole incident, imprudent as it had been, passed without further remark for the moment; but there were black looks without disguise and emphatic ejaculations not given in whispers when M. le Vicomte de Bois-Duval came again to claim the promise given by Mademoiselle Eva for another waltz. Nothing was to be done however; and unless Mrs. Winstanley was prepared to break with her French friend she must give her consent as of course and let her daughter dance with him as with any other person in the room. The home authorities were forced to content themselves with watching the two as they whirled about, now fast, now slow, now with breathless vehemence and now with tender languor. They watched in vain. Despite those eight eyes so sharply fixed on them the Vicomte managed to slip into Eva's hand a note which he had written in the interval between the maternal lecture and this delicious waltz; and Eva managed to secure it in the bosom of her gown without one of the four watchers having the faintest idea of the transaction. Love laughs not only at locksmiths but at Argus himself; and there has never yet been found the spell which he could not break when he would.

The evening passed without more disturbance. M. le Vicomte, conscious of his misdemeanour and properly penitent, took care not to transgress again. He danced frequently with Eva; but then this is the fashion of the place. It is not an offence against decorum, as in England, but a mark of politeness and the expression of care and protection. He danced also with Thomasina as often as he found her disengaged; and sometimes he sat out and talked to Mrs. Winstanley when both her daughters were dancing with the Englishmen. He managed all the little threads with consummate skill, and got the mother so far on his side as to make her feel that coldness on her part would be boorish and displeasure ill-breeding, and that really this handsome versatile English-speaking young Frenchman was a delightful creature all round, and those foolish boys must accept him.

Thus the little hitch created in the beginning of the evening by his impropriety and Eva's imprudence seemed to be quite got over; and by the time the last dance came to an end the whole thing was apparently laid as straight and smooth as if that embarrassing kink had never been.

But appearances are rarely faithful exponents of things, as the words which passed between the two pairs of friends plainly proved.

"I shall insult that fellow," said Hubert passionately. "I am only waiting for the opportunity."

"Keep your hands to yourself," said Sir James dryly. "I will do that business."

"No—it is my affair," persisted Hubert.

"My dear fellow, don't talk rubbish," returned Sir James hastily. "You are an engaged man. I am not. If we are to have a row, it is better for me to be in it, not you."

"Engaged or not, the Winstanleys are my friends as well as yours, Jamie; and mine before they were yours," said Hubert.

"Your friends, yes; but perhaps something more to me," Sir James replied, speaking slowly and keeping his eyes fixed on his friend.

"Good God, Jamie! do you mean to say you love her?" cried Hubert in extreme agitation.

"Yes; I do love her," the other answered, still speaking slowly.

"Her? but which? tell me, James—which of them?"

"You must be blind to ask that, old man! Which? Well—not Thomasina! What is the matter, Hubert? Are you ill?"

"No, nothing—nothing—there is nothing the matter with me," stammered the young fellow. "That cursed waltzing has made me feel a little sick, that is all. It is nothing, Jamie; don't look like that, old man. I am all right, I assure you."

"Take a B. and S. and turn in. A night's rest will put you square," said Sir James.

"Yes, that is all I want. I want just that," returned Hubert, as quietly as he could speak. "Good-night, old fellow."

"Good-night, old man. You'll be all right to-morrow morning," said Sir James; and then the two parted—the one enlightened but the other as dark as before.

The Frenchmen were more discerning.

"Which is it?" asked Laperrière. "The big blond or the dark milord?"

"Both," answered Bois-Duval.

His friend gave an expressive whistle.

"Ma foi!" he said laughing; "the Britannic pot boils!"

"Boils? do you call that tepid simmer boiling? I do not," said Bois-Duval. "Those flabby sons of Albion never boil. They have swallowed too much frost and fog."

"And my friend, M. le Vicomte de Bois-Duval does boil, in faith," laughed Laperrière.

"I hope so. Life would not be worth the trouble of boots and gloves if I had not more fire than those stiff-backed English marionettes," he returned. "Poor wretches, they are to be pitied! However, each does his best in this world; and for the present these two feel what it pleases them to call love for the pretty little demoiselle."

"And she?"

"Bah! our ingenue is a finished coquette and takes all who come with grand impartiality. I flatter myself that since she has had the benefit of my lessons she has no great weakness for either of her compatriots. But she makes believe, and so holds the stage; and they, the louts, see nothing, but have gone head downwards into her traps. They are destined to receive their lesson. I have it all in train."

"For which? the big blond?"

"Without question. I will make the best mark," answered the Vicomte with masterly coolness. "Though I intend to fight, I do not intend to die. I prefer laurel to cypress and the little one's kisses to her tears."

"There is always risk in these affairs; and the big blond looks dangerous," said Laperrière.

"As a buffalo, who makes an ugly rush with his eyes shut and his head down. You spring aside, phew! the great big stumbling brute is caught in the toils or dashes himself down a precipice. No; I don't fear that big blond, my friend. The milord is more dangerous."

"If it were my own affair I should rejoice, but for you, my friend—" said Laperrière, with a tremulous kind of hesitation.

"It must be done. It is for the honour of France, as well as to punish poaching and presumption," returned Bois-Duval, lightly striking his breast. "These miserable creatures permitted themselves to ridicule the sublime heroism of our history and dared to talk of Waterloo. What would you have me do? The honour of France and the dignity of my manhood both demand this duel."

"You are right, my friend," said Laperrière, catching his tone. "As you say, when the honour of France is in question, there can be no doubt or hesitation."

Then the two shook hands; took a grog apiece; and went to bed, saying with a significant look and tone as they parted, "To-morrow!"

CHAPTER XX.

THE MATCH APPLIED.

THERE was no question about the probable fineness of the day. The weather was settled to fair with a constancy of which our capricious old climate knows nothing; and prophecy or discussion on that which was fixed as fate was mere waste of time. It was hot, certainly; and the road from Trouville to Deauville, short as it was, was a very desert for dust; but there are worse things than heat borne in pleasant company with pretty faces under rose-pink umbrellas; and the dust was only an excuse for the daintiest and most coquettish wrappers imaginable— wrappers which made the ladies as they rolled past look like so many flowers in great grey calices—which would presently unfold and display the full gorgeousness of the petals beneath.

All the beauty and fashion of Trouville and Havre, of Étretat and Honfleur, a sprinkling of grandees from London following in the wake of an Exalted Personage, and a contingent of the "fine fleur" from Paris assembled on the Deauville race-course to-day. The Trouville sands were deserted, save by a few nurses with their children, and here and there a sober bourgeois family which took its pleasure cheaply and preferred to watch the waves and the sea-gulls rather than to bet on the hoofs of a string of horses galloping past a shouting mob: or it might be a pair of young lovers newly wed, who in their turn preferred solitude and unrestricted love-making to the gaiety, distraction, and enforced propriety of a crowd; while at Deauville there was scarcely standing-place on the course, and no one gave his neighbour courteous elbow-room.

It was a bright and animated show. The pretty toilettes worn as only

Frenchwomen can wear them; the smart, well-got-up look of the young men; the grave severity of the police, dark, silent, mysterious—the executive skeletons of the feast, the more cheerful swagger of the gendarmes, those generals in calico; the fraternal mingling of uniforms and blouses; the peasant women in their white caps and showy colours; the total absence of squalor, dirt, second-hand finery, miserable pretence, together with the bright sun, the glittering sea, the wooded hills and the lovely country everywhere—all make a race-day and a race-course of exceptional charm.

It might have been thought that even the most spiteful Gallophobist would have confessed the brilliant influences of the moment; but both Hubert and Sir James voted the whole thing slow and in no wise equal to Ascot or the Derby. They wondered how people could say so much about these humbugging Deauville races when we did things so much better at home. But some people were determined to find everything better ordered in France, whatever it might be. To be French was to be all right; to be English all wrong. Frenchmen were better bred and Frenchwomen were prettier than Englishmen and women; French manners were more polite, French customs more delightful, even French races were more enjoyable—though every one knows that the English have gone ahead of all the world in the matter of horseflesh, and that no Frenchman can ride or drive better than the average English tailor or bluejacket! It was revolting to see such folly, all because the sky was hard, monotonous and blue, and the sun glared down with such force it seemed to shrivel up your very marrow! And when you had said that you had said everything.

Which settled the question so far comfortably between them, and gave their ill-humour the look of reasonableness, at least to themselves.

For they were at this moment decidedly ill-tempered, else they would not have plumed themselves on talking nonsense.

Of course no break large enough for the whole party had been found in Trouville; and the Vicomte's carriage did not hold more than four inside, with the coachman and Laperrière on the box. Thus the two young men had been forced to drive over in a wretched little shandradan in such patience as they could command, knowing that they were in the wash of the big boat—in the dust of the triumphal car. It was an ignominious position for two young men of fortune and family—proud of themselves and their nation, their developed muscles and their inherited acres, and with the true British contempt for all foreigners whatsoever—but perhaps most of all for Mounseer, that ancient foe across the water. They felt it keenly; but of the two Sir James was perhaps the more disdainful and Hubert the more angry.

Poor Hubert indeed was in an abnormal state altogether today. He was still reeling under the blow of his friend's confession, but trying to pluck up courage to leave temptation, Eva and Trouville by the first train to-morrow morning, and go back to duty and Maud Disney. The knowledge that his friend loved this beautiful little idol of his dreams, roused him to a full consciousness of his own position, its dishonour and what should be its hopelessness; and he was working hard and loyally to clear his eyes and strengthen his heart. But he could not get things settled; and he was knocked about between love and duty till he felt sore and bruised all over. No sooner had he taken firm hold of the one than the other dragged him away—no sooner had conscience commanded than desire pleaded—and when desire determined, then conscience forbade.

The state of turmoil and uncertainty in which he stood showed itself on his face; and his temper and bearing to-day had a totally different expression from that which was natural to him.

Sir James saw that something was wrong, but he left that something alone. It was not his duty to dry-nurse his friend; and the less said the better when there was nothing pleasant to say and there might be a great deal that was disagreeable to hear. He was sorry to see Hubert look so "down," but he supposed he was seedy from last night and would soon pull himself together. And as he himself hated to be worried and made a fuss with when he was seedy, he did by Hubert as he would be done by, and forebore to bother him with questions or commentary. But they were not a very lively couple on this brilliant sunshiny day of amusement; and their appearance somewhat justified old Froissart's famous saying about the English and the melancholy manner in which they take their pleasure.

The race-course was as disappointing as the way thither had been. There was no getting near the Winstanleys save in a sense by permission—when they were allowed to pick up the crumbs left by the rich men of the feast. Only in the intervals between the races, when the Frenchmen went to make their bets with the book-makers behind the stand—only then could the two poor distanced Englishmen take brief possession of the vacated places and sun themselves in the treacherous light of those bright-blue flattering eyes.

How bright they were! how treacherous their light and what flattering falsities they said! And how they looked to each in turn as if with special love and liking! love and liking, be it understood, such as a maiden and an ingenue might give. They threw poor Hubert deeper and deeper into the fog of doubt, of distraction, of uncertain balance, of secret dishonour, of acted untruth; and they touched the keen and passionate sensibilities of the young baronet, till he lost that clear possession of his own dignity which was his by nature, and even abased his pride so far as to let himself be made a kind of almsman subsisting by the bounty of a Frenchman.

Then, when the money business was over—when the old bills were settled and new ones made and the two Amphitryons[1] returned to take possession—those large blue eyes spoke volumes to Bois-Duval by the very care with which they avoided looking at him at all. And this conscious bashfulness was more eloquent than the bolder coquetry played off on the others. His notes were in the bosom of her dress; his hand met hers under cover of friendly folds and flirting fans, and his expressive touch was returned with a fainter but all the same an undeniable pressure. He could afford then not to meet those bewildering eyes in prolonged straight looks, such as were given to the others, and even to feel specially distinguished by her shyness. But the whole position was tantalizing; and Bois-Duval was resolved to make the little girl commit herself more boldly. Playing with fire might be a pastime for her, but what about that fire itself?—and the risk? Houses once lighted cannot be extinguished at pleasure; and if the tepid sons of Albion are manageable by coquettes, the warmer lovers of la belle France are not. But all this was in abeyance for the moment, and only the caressing flatteries of that little hand, the shy confession of those big blue eyes, stood as the language between them.

Meanwhile, Hubert Strangways and Sir James Kearney picked up the crumbs with craven gratitude to her—hot and fiery indignation against him. It was almost more than they could bear when the course was cleared and the stand began to fill with its appointed occupants, as the jockeys rode out, to have to yield to the force of circumstances and retire to their own remote places. They felt like hedge-sparrows whom the cuckoo had shouldered out of their rightful nests, and longed to have it out with that cuckoo; as indeed they would. They were only waiting their opportunity; and opportunity comes to all who know how to wait.

There was no "good time" for them anyhow. Even when the Winstanleys descended from the stand and paraded the enclosure with the

---

[1]   Hero of Greek legend (and of plays by Plautus and Molière), supposed father of Hercules. Zeus took Amphitryon's form to make love to his beautiful wife Alcmene.

other beauties of the day and place, even then the Frenchmen took the lead and left the Englishmen in the wash. The mother was between the two daughters, and the line was flanked by Bois-Duval on the one side near Eva, and by Laperrière on the other near Thomasina. Where then was room or place for Hubert and Sir James? They could not break the line. French custom demands that a mother should keep her daughters by her side in public; and English good-breeding prevented a public scrimmage and a fight with fisticuffs for forcible possession. Unless the two unlucky hedge-sparrows chose to walk behind and talk to their fair friends through the backs of their heads, they were no better off in the promenade than on the stand. It was all very humiliating—very disappointing—and both wished they had never come to Trouville at all, or that, being here, they had some kind of chance given them for cutting out those cursed Frenchmen:—as they could, of course, if they had but that chance!

It was embarrassing for Mrs. Winstanley too, and she heartily wished that things had been different; but she was in a cleft stick and could not help herself. It had seemed to her better policy at the time to accept the offer made by these men to be taken comfortably and free of expense to the races, than to wait on the chance of Sir James and Hubert Strangways turning up in time. If any hitch had occurred and they had not come, then she would have had to spend four or five pounds on the diversion into which it was part of her present duty and social existence to enter. And four or five pounds spent, where it could be saved, was a loss not to be lightly undertaken.

As things had turned out it was a pity—a thousand pities! as she said to Thomasina; and she was as much disgusted with fortune and as cross with fortune's manikins as a well-bred lady ever permits herself to be. It was the realization of those detestable old adages about too many irons in the fire and sitting on two stools at once—and yet no one was to be blamed, though she and her plans had in a certain sense come to the ground. Certainly she herself was not to be blamed!

She did her best to make square things round, and to rub off spiky corners, by being specially sweet and maternal to the hedge-sparrows when they fluttered down for a moment to pick up their crumbs. But it was hard work. Naturally she was in polite slavery to the men who had franked her and given her and hers this pleasure for the payment of pleasant looks and exclusive devotion; but she had her chances in England to consider as well as those which were offered here; and it was her duty to keep her eggs well divided among her various baskets.

Thomasina understood the position as well as her mother, and she made better play because she was less bound by responsibility. She had never favoured the Gallic coalition and had always voted for constancy to the British chances. Unfortunately, Eva's persistence and restless need of excitement carried the day over her calmer counsel; and Mrs. Winstanley, who had brought herself to believe that it was her wisest policy to satisfy the child at all risks—she being her best investment—let herself be persuaded by the one who was least able to reason aright or to see beyond the mist of the moment, and was thus bound in the chain of her own actions. Thomasina, freer, did the best she could by being more glacial to the Frenchmen than she would have been had not Sir James been there to fume and Hubert to rage. She was so cold, so still, so unresponsive, that to those lively, hot-blooded Parisians she was just a wet blanket of fine and silky texture, very lovely to look at, but decidedly uncomfortable to sensitive skins. On the other hand she was quite sisterly to the poor dear fellows who had been so unmercifully fully shouldered out of their expected places. She was really a comfort to them; a kind of angelic godmamma who gave them secret manna and spiritual balm, and somehow trimmed up the ugly edges of the truth so that it looked less ragged and distasteful than it was in real earnest.

She played her part of silent peace-maker to perfection; and Mrs. Winstanley felt again, as so often before, that her good Thomasina was the staff and stay of her steps, and that without her she should simply collapse. But her very usefulness made the mother feel more and more strongly the necessity of getting Eva married the first of her brood. Perdita did not count; indeed she was almost forgotten in these latter days. But Eva must be married before her eldest sister. She, the mother, would be so entirely at sea without that far-seeing Mentor, that wise young Ulysses in a tied-back skirt and long straight folds! She could not face the restless require-ments, the unwise demands of the child if she had not her eldest to turn to for counsel, for support and for aid. And this determination to endow Eva because she was naughty, before Thomasina who was good, was only another instance of that melancholy truth which pervades all life—that unwritten law which ordains that the better you behave the more you knock down your own fortunes, and the more selfish and unfeeling you are the more you advance them. If virtue were not its own reward, the poor hungry empty-handed saint would have none at all!

The races went on in their course, and now one and now the other of the owners and the backers lost, according to the merit of the animals and the skill of the jockeys. Hubert and Sir James betted behind the stand like the rest—a little more freely than the average Frenchman, and with persistent ill-luck. And this again did not tend to make things pleasanter. Though the money dropped over the purple and orange, with more sent to keep it company over the red and blue, represented no personal sacrifice to the young fellows—no more than if they had lost a box of cigars which they could replace at the next tobacconist's—yet, naturally enough, it annoyed them to lose; and especially to lose to Frenchmen over French horses.

"These humbugging animals!" they said with pettish contempt; "who on earth can tell how they will run or what they will do! And how do we know that they run straight at all!"

Had they plunged over an English race they would have taken their punishment like lambs; and had they lost even heavily to-day, yet been the sworn and recognized cavaliers of the Winstanleys, they would have come up smiling from the douche and thought no more about it. As things were, it was too irritating—too disgusting; and they fell foul of French stables and stablemen as if the whole concern were a den of thieves, because two Parisians had cut them out with three Englishwomen and reduced them to the condition of eclipsed satellites.

They had managed however, to slip in a few bets of gloves and bouquets, of bon-bons and chocolates, which they took care should be "morals" against themselves. The girls had by now a formidable amount of pretty trifles to receive; and Mrs. Winstanley felt that Providence was kind and watchful when she reckoned up the number of dozens secured to her daughters and written off the bills of the future. But at the last race of all, Hubert, to have the charm of a gift from the little witch who was misleading them all so impartially, induced Eva to back a hopeless screw for a pair of gloves and the second place. The beast had not the ghost of a chance, so Sir James said "he ran only on three legs" and the "moral" was certain. Hubert knew that he should win and that Eva would lose; but he wanted those gloves. He intended to keep them as a sacred possession for all his life. Perhaps he would have them worked in seed-pearls; framed in gold; put under a glass case as if they were holy relics; labelled mysteriously so that no one should suspect and no one have reason to ask why they were so honoured; perhaps he would have them buried with him—these dear gloves, which in truth he was "going for," perhaps more entirely than he himself knew. It was to be the one little bit of brightness in this disappointing day; and he watched the race with as much interest as if the screw had had a chance, with more than a pair of white kid gloves, No. eight and a half, depending on the issue. A trail of colour, a deafening roar, the winner his own length ahead and the screw nowhere—this was the race; and to Hubert the culminating point of the day. He had gone for the gloves—and he had won them.

"Oh, no, what a story!" said Eva, when Hubert went up to her with a flushed face, almost too much in earnest for tact, and said in a moved voice, "Now then, Miss Eva, you will give me the gloves!"

"No, I don't owe you the gloves, Mr. Strangways, it is you who owe them to me," she said. "I backed that one in pink and white, not that horror in black and yellow!"

"Oh, Miss Eva!" he remonstrated; "and you marked Rococo on your list!"

"It was a mistake," said Eva with a shrill laugh.

Had she followed her inclination she would have pouted and perhaps cried, for she had lost the gold chain which Hubert had wagered against her gloves and which he intended to give her under the name and style of "Rococo's apology." She did not know this and was consequently inconsolable in her own way.

"But look! see here!" said the young fellow, clumsily insisting on his rights and the truth. "Here is your own mark against Rococo."

He showed her his list with her big broken-backed E. set against the name of the beaten horse.

"You wrote it yourself," she said. "I am not going to pay you those gloves. I won the bet!"

"Well! you shall win the bet; but pay me the gloves all the same!" said Hubert.

"That would be only fair," put in Sir James, who had been listening to the conversation with a kind of joint-stock feeling in the affair.

If not himself, it was his friend and compatriot who was engrossing the attention of this little queen of many hearts; and that was the next thing to his own personal innings.

"No, that would say that I was in the wrong," replied Eva with mock gravity. "If I am right, as I am, I ought not to pay."

"That is cruel," cried Herbert with strange warmth, seeing that it was a mere joke which was being carried on. "I had counted on those gloves!"

At this moment Bois-Duval came back from his final settling behind the stand; and as the balance of the day had been against him, he too came back by no means in a good humour, but irritably ready to catch at straws and make lakes out of puddles. The whole quartet was in decidedly "bad form," and it was evident that a very little would bring about an explosion unless some kind of diversion were effected.

"What is it?" he asked in a politely disagreeable way, as he came up to the group and saw how Eva's wild-flower face was flushed and, for all her bird-like laugh, how dark and angry were her eyes, how ardent and eager was Hubert Strangways, and how earnest and animated Sir James. "What is it?" he asked again, scanning them all as at once an inquisitor and a judge.

"Oh, nothing! only a little private business of our own with Miss Eva," said Sir James haughtily.

"Mademoiselle with secrets? with private business of her own?" said Bois-Duval, lifting his eyebrows and speaking in a strange rasping kind of voice.

Eva looked suddenly frightened. She turned her face to him, but she did not look at him. She only turned to him as if complaining and appealing.

"Mr. Strangways said I backed Rococo and I did not—I betted against him," she said. "He lost and I did not."

Hubert was not eager now. The boyish glow that had come into his face during his discussion with Eva had deepened into an angry man's flaming wrath. It stung him as much as a direct insult would have done, that this man should be taken into confidence at all—made free of the little comedy that had been played by them. What business was it of his to interfere? and where did he get the right to ask what was on hand between him and Eva Winstanley? Surely her own fellow-countrymen stood nearer to her than did this foreigner! "It was cursed cheek," he said to himself in modern parlance, cheek that had to be stopped and punished.

"Do not be disturbed, mademoiselle," then said Bois-Duval in the most insufferable manner of insolent protection. Turning to Hubert he added, "Monsieur need not be alarmed. I pay all mademoiselle's losses to-day. What is it? a pipe? a pair of gloves? how much?"

He took out his betting-book to inscribe the debt among his graver transactions, looking up as he paused for details before writing. Hubert laid his large hand a little roughly on the book.

"Shut up," he said angrily. "Do you want me to pitch you and your book off the stand?"

"I would rather that monsieur remembered he was in the presence of ladies, and that he himself is a gentleman—that is if he can—at all events, that he is dealing with a gentleman," said Bois-Duval slowly.

"We will discuss this matter by ourselves, M. le Vicomte," said Sir James, whose face was as white as Hubert's was inflamed.

"At your own time and pleasure," replied the Vicomte.

Without speaking, Hubert laid his hand on the Frenchman's arm. Grasping it like a vice he almost lifted him from the stand and led, or rather dragged, him to the space behind. It was done so quickly that the two were gone before the others had quite seen what was happening.

"What is it? what does he want?" cried Mrs. Winstanley in some agitation.

She had seen that something was amiss, but she had not understood it all.

"It is nothing," said Sir James. "They have their accounts to settle, that is all."

"There is more than that," said Thomasina rising; but before she had finished the last words Sir James too had disappeared. "Now see what you have done, Eva, with your abominable coquetry and disgraceful flirting," said Thomasina in a low voice to her frightened sister. "Those men will have a duel; one of them will be killed; and you will be the cause of it!"

She said this just as Hubert, standing face to face with Bois-Duval, was saying in the low voice of concentrated anger: "Monsieur le Vicomte de Bois-Duval, you are an insolent cad!" at the same time striking him full in the face. "Name your time and place," he added; "I am ready to give you satisfaction."

Bois-Duval smiled as he recovered himself from the blow. It was a smile that was more ghastly than a frown.

"Monsieur has insulted me," he said; "and a Frenchman never forgives an insult. I shall be happy to meet monsieur—and to kill him."

"You should have left that to me, Hubert," said Sir James who came up a moment too late. "This was my affair, not yours."

"No, it was mine more than yours," said Hubert excitedly. "You love her and may marry her. My life is worthless!"

CHAPTER XXI.

LAUREL OR CYPRESS.

It was like a dissolving-view. The frame and the uprights remained, but the picture had disappeared and a dead grey wash was in place of the former brilliancy and colour. The sands and the sea, the "fine fleur" of the aristocracy and the staid backbone of the bourgeoisie, the rampant queens of the demi-monde, the casino, the baths and the "little horses"—all were the same as before; but Trouville was now as sterile as the shores of the Dead Sea to the Winstanleys; and the mother had but one desire—to escape as soon as possible from its expensive disappointment and go home to economy and the mending of her nets.

It was on the day after the races that this sudden dissolution of the picture took place, when the two Frenchmen and the two Englishmen— the former of whom had been the especial friends, and the latter the strongest hopes, of "les belles Anglaises," departed together, leaving no addresses on their cards of adieu.

"I am sure something is wrong, Thomasina," said Mrs. Winstanley again and again. "What can it be?—what do you think?"

Thomasina's thoughts were clear enough, but of what good to give them? If it would have been of real use to tell her mother that something undesirable was going on between Eva and Bois-Duval, she would have done so; but it was just that use which was problematical. She had no solid proof to offer; only conviction built up on airy nothings and suggestive trifles. And however strong such unsubstantial conviction may be to the one who entertains it, it is impossible to be passed on to another. She knew her mother too, both in her strength and in her weakness—how the one quality was shown in her determination not to be overcome in this hard battle of life waged with such insufficient weapons—how the other came out in her habit of prophesying smooth things when rough ones were about, and shutting her eyes to disagreeable truths unless absolutely compelled to open them. How would she take the news that Eva was doing her best to ruin both her own chances and the careful calculations of maternal prudence? Would she believe her, Thomasina, without more proof than there was to offer?—and, heavily handicapped as she was, half-strangled by that Black Care ever sitting behind her, was it well to add to her burdens?—to give an extra grip to the demon already in such cruel possession? Thomasina thought not. It was her bounden duty to spare her mother and, if she could, to manage Eva unassisted. At all events she would try. She would keep her knowledge to herself and do her best to make her mother's path smoother, not more thorny.

"What can I say, dear mother?" she asked after a pause. "It's odd, their all going away together; but who can account for young men's fancies?"

"Do you think there has been any quarrel?" asked Mrs. Winstanley. She might as well let the murder out! Her fear was too great to keep.

"I hope not," said her daughter quietly. "But, as I said, who can tell what young men will do? They are no more reasonable than so many monkeys."

"They all seemed very angry and uncomfortable yesterday," said Mrs. Winstanley. "I did not quite understand it all—it had something to do with Eva's bet with Hubert, but the Baron was talking to me and my attention was distracted. Still, I saw they were all disagreeable together, and I should not be surprised at anything. It would be awful if they were to fight; but I cannot say I should be astonished to hear of it," she repeated with the weak reiteration of perplexity.

Eva looked up with a white scared little face.

"Mumsey, don't say such dreadful things!" she said almost in tears. "Why should they fight? What an awful idea! it is too dreadfully awful, really!"

Her round red under-lip quivered, and tears gathered into her blue eyes as she stooped and pretended to work down an imaginary discomfort in her dainty little shoe.

"My dear Eva, do not look like that!" said Mrs. Winstanley, whose main endeavour was, as we know, to preserve the serenity of her little Benjamin and the bloom of the prize rosebud intact. "There is nothing to go into hysterics for! I was perhaps rash to speak as I did; but really you need not take my words to heart as if you were Perdita, poor child!"

"A little fear is good for girls, mother," drawled Thomasina; "it teaches them prudence."

Eva's face lost its look of scare and dread and became what the French call mutinous.

"I don't see why you should say that to me, Ina!" she said, putting up her head like a white mouse or a tomtit showing fight.

Thomasina looked at her over the top of a Japanese handscreen with which she was playing; and Eva caught her eyes. She crimsoned to her temples and trembled all over. This look told her that her sister had seen through her and that she knew what was going on. How much did she know? and would she betray her?

"My dear Eva, do not take things in that brusque way," put in Mrs. Winstanley gently; "your sister Thomasina had no personal motive in what she said; and her principle was eminently correct. Girls cannot be too careful of their conduct, more especially girls like yourselves, without a father or brother to protect you, in a strange country, and by no means ordinary looking. Foreigners are too ready as it is to speak against English girls because of the greater liberty allowed them; and I must say I do not think that as a nation we are careful enough not to shock the prejudices of the country where we may be. We only get misjudged for our own parts."

"That is what I am always saying, mother, but Eva is really too heed-less!" said Thomasina. "She will act as if she were a child, when she is out now and no more a child than any other girl who is introduced; and if she does not mind she will be getting herself and all of us into some awful scrape some day."

"My dear Thomasina, is not your judgment a little too severe?" said the mother with a deprecating manner, not liking to hear her youngest blamed but not willing to contravene anything that her eldest might think it well to say.

"Ina!" began Eva angrily.

"Now don't speak, Eva," interposed her sister. "You know quite well that you are very heedless, very giddy, and that I am always giving you advice and warning you to be more steady; and that you do not attend as you ought to what I say to you. You never take my advice, and always pretend that I am old-maidish and ridiculous and making a fuss about nothing."

"You cannot do better than follow your sister's counsel implicitly, my dear Eva," said Mrs. Winstanley. "She has excellent judgment. If I, who am so much older and more experienced, find her such a valuable assistance, what must she not be to you, my child?"

"Oh, yes, I know that Ina is ever so much older than I am," said Eva saucily. "She was a full-grown woman when I was a little tiny tot, and of course she has had years and years more experience; but that is no reason why she should be always scolding me as she does."

"Eva! when do I scold you? Good advice is not scolding," remonstrated Thomasina.

"My dear! Thomasina is incapable of scolding, as you call it," said her mother. "As she says, advice is not scolding; the one is admissible from the best-bred person in the world, the other is a rude and vulgar habit fit only for the second class and servants."

"Mumsey, you do not see," said Eva; "and you do not hear."

"Now, Eva, do not talk any more nonsense. Come with me; I want to alter your fichu,"[1] said Thomasina, suddenly rising and taking her sister's arm.

"I don't want to," said Eva childishly.

"My dear Eva! go with your sister like a good girl," said Mrs. Winstanley, who saw in Thomasina's manœuvre a desire to cut short a discussion which threatened to become a little more bitter than was

---

[1] A woman's light triangular scarf that is draped over the shoulders and fastened in front or worn to fill in a low neckline.

allowed by the Winstanley code of manners; and who thanked her in her heart for the tact and determination which always knew when a dangerous moment was reached and how it should be dealt with. "When you have finished your little arrangements put on your things and we will go for our last bathe. I propose to leave to-morrow for home. I have had enough of this place, and I suppose you have, too. So go, my love, and get your fichu arranged."

And Eva, yielding to the pressure put on her, went, ignorant of what she was going to hear but fully conscious that she was to hear something disagreeable, to say the least of it.

"Now, Eva," said Thomasina, when they were alone; "I know all about you, so do not begin to deny and tell stories. You are a very naughty, deceitful, inconsiderate little thing—and worse; and you have got yourself into a dreadful mess by your horrible flirting and deceit. You have been flirting with these three men at once—with the Vicomte, of whom we know absolutely nothing, and who may be a vicomte or may be a hairdresser for what we can tell; with Hubert Strangways, though he is engaged to a girl we know and whom you pretend to like; and with Sir James Kearney, who is sensitive and jealous, and would not touch you with his little finger if he knew what you had been doing. If you had had a particle of common sense in you you would have cooled off to Hubert, and never have begun your silly practices with the Vicomte at all, but would have just kept yourself for Sir James, who evidently admires you. But you have no common sense. You are just a great baby, fond of flattery and sugar-plums; and I despair of your ever doing well in life."

"You had better despair of yourself," said Eva, with a naughty toss of her pretty fuzzy head. "You are very wise, Miss Ina, and as correct and stiff as a ramrod; but you are twenty-three years old and are not married yet; and I don't think you need talk to me. If I am not married before I am twenty-three, then you may; but you had better look at home, and see what your wisdom has done for you before you lecture me on my folly!"

"You are a naughty girl—a bad, wilful, shocking little thing," said Thomasina angrily; "far worse than Perdita, because you are deceitful, and she is not. And if these men have gone to fight a duel, as I believe they have, all about your silly little face, and one of them is killed, it will be your fault. And if you like that idea I make you a present of it: I should not like to think that I had been the cause of any man's death by my own wicked vanity and silly love of admiration!"

"And you are a horrid, cross, jealous, selfish old wretch!" cried Eva, bursting into those tears which mean fear and anger, not grief; then suddenly slapping her sister's face.

It was an action that proved the strength of human nature over conventional restraint, and showed how others, besides Perdita, had undisciplined passions when the fitting moment came for their expression.

"You are very silly and very impertinent," said Thomasina, recovering her dignity and calmness with an effort. It would never do for the two Misses Winstanley to have a slapping match together; and Eva was in a state of hysterical over-excitation that made her as capable of plunging into a battle royal as if she had been Perdita herself. "I have a great mind to tell mother and have you punished," Thomasina continued quietly. "If I do not, it is only because I do not want to pain her, not because I care to spare you. Come here, you tiresome little thing, and let me fix this for you! You are a greater plague than even Perdita!" she added, taking up a length of muslin, which she put over her sister's shoulders, while Eva wiped her eyes and pouted and twisted her shoulders into unfittable positions—Thomasina remonstrating between whiles.

During this process of fitting and fixing, Thomasina had naturally to press her hand against the bosom of Eva's dress. Something that was not cotton nor yet flesh gave under her hand and crackled.

"What is that paper inside your gown?" asked the elder sister, stopping suddenly in her work.

"Nothing," said Eva, putting up her hand.

"They are letters," cried Thomasina. "Give them to me."

"They are not; and I shan't," returned Eva.

The elder was the stronger of the two, and indignation, coupled with a certain horrible fear, gave her even greater strength than her own. She held both the soft little hands in one of hers, and with the other tore open the front of the bodice, to the damage of half-a-dozen buttons and in spite of the writhings and twistings with which Eva sought to defend herself—in spite even of that last desperate effort at self-protection when the child bent her pretty head and fastened her small, sharp, white teeth in her sister's arm.

It was all in vain. Strength prevailed and authority conquered. Thomasina drew out from their hiding-place a packet of letters, addressed in a neat small foreign hand to "La belle Anglaise; La reine des fées; La trop chère ange de mes rêves; Ma bien aimée,[1] Eva," in progressive warmth and familiarity.

---

[1] (French), beautiful Englishwoman, queen of the fairies, dearest angel of my dreams, my beloved.

She opened them, and rapidly read four love-letters from Bois-Duval, beginning with formal and respectful flattery and culminating in the free audacity of confessed passion.

"I knew that something of this kind was going on, but I did not expect to find anything so bad as this!" cried Thomasina indignantly. "How could you be so wicked, Eva? How could you be so bold and forward? Now I must tell mother all about it, and she must talk to you."

"No, Ina, no; you must not! You must not, dear, good, sweet Ina!" cried Eva, taking her sister's hand, and kissing it just below where she had made her cruel little teeth nearly meet in the fair flesh. "I will be good if you will not tell mother. I will, indeed! I will put the letters in the fire; and if he sends any more I will return them. Besides, we are going home, and he does not know where we live," she said, hurriedly.

Did she forget that she had given him their London address?

"I cannot trust you," said her sister, sternly. "You are so incurably false, Eva. I do not think you can help being deceitful."

"I will be good; I will, Ina!" pleaded the child, caught in the trap as she was, and writhing under the pain of her position.

"If I see you burn these letters, and if I see you write and post the letter that I will dictate, then I will believe you; but only then," said Thomasina.

"I will, Ina; indeed, I will! And you may dictate what you like," sobbed Eva, who was ready to promise the Italian "mountains and seas" so long as she might escape the dreaded exposure and be free of immediate punishment.

And on her word, and always with the feeling of sparing her mother, Thomasina let her off for this once, and undertook to keep her secret. But she undertook also to keep her in view, and to make it almost physically impossible that there should be another such escapade as this which had brought their whole summer into disrepute, and changed its pleasures into perils of a grave and disastrous kind. She was shocked at the whole thing, and revolted by her sister's conduct on every side. A proud, pure-minded girl by nature—with a frozen temperament and the dignity characteristic of those women who claim homage because of their sex, and who think that they honor men when they permit their worship—she was outraged by this ready capitulation of her young sister, this grisette-like acceptance of familiarity, this self-debasement of a vulgar intrigue. That they had to marry, and marry money because of their birth and poverty, that she knew only too well; and she accepted the necessity as a cross laid on them by an unfriendly fortune. But an honourable marriage, made because of the fitness of things, even without the pretence of romantic love, is a very different thing, she argued, from a secret and dishonourable flirtation of this kind. A bargain struck openly in the face of the world, where so much poundage of living flesh, so much grace and beauty and suavity of temper are set against a fine house to live in and a fat banker's book to live on—that is a bargain which no wise mother disdains for her daughter, no girl of sense thinks a degrading sale of herself. Eva's was a very different affair, and must be checked at once; and with this determination Thomasina bade her wipe her eyes and bathe them in cold water so that her mother should not see she had been crying, reminding her again that she was under strict surveillance from this day onward, and, in a sense, on her trial like a suspected person.

"And I will do as I like for all that; and you shall not see, though it is under your very eyes, you great, horrid thing!" said little Eva to herself; while aloud she assured her dear Ina that she would be the very pink and pattern of propriety from henceforth, and that she was sincerely penitent and ashamed of herself.

Meanwhile, the four young men had ridden off to Étretat, where they had their duel according to the strictest laws of honour and humanity. The result was a foregone conclusion from the first. Bois-Duval was a practised duellist, with a nerve of iron and a heart of steel; Hubert had never been 'out' in his life, nor had he ever contemplated the possibility of such a chance in his own sober-blooded country. To the one it was, and would be, no more a matter of sorrow if he killed his man than it is to the sportsman when he knocks over a hare and hears it cry; to the other, now that his blood was a little cooled, it was a horror that he might kill, and not a very comfortable prospect, if not a very terrible one, that he might be killed. He had the natural reluctance of strength and youth to die, though he said to himself that after all it did not much signify. He had got himself and his affairs into a frightful tangle, and he had not wit to see where he could untie the knots so as to lay the confused threads smooth. Better, then, cut it right through, and so have done with it all; and yet the sun was bright and life was very good!

He stood before his adversary in the early light of this sweet summer morning; mechanically obeyed the directions given to him by his second; placed himself in position, and waited for the signal; and when it was given, he fired with an unsteady aim, missed his man, and fell to the ground dangerously, but just not mortally wounded.

This was where a pair of blue eyes and an engagement thrust on him by his parents like a conjurer's forced card, had led him—this was the result of a flirtation that had been half levity and half craft; half for mischief and half for gain, on the one side; if on the other, pure, passionate, great-hearted, and thick-headed devotion.

More than the mere wound made this duel an awkward episode in Hubert's life. When a young fellow has a father and mother and sisters and a fiancée, and is moreover heir to a fine estate, his actions become public property by just so many as are interested in his career, and a family is apt to think that it has certain rights over its several members, and that each of those members has a duty to the family. So that Hubert's present state and action entailed a decided difficulty, inasmuch as both must be confessed, and yet the true cause of the latter must be concealed.

It would not do to make it public that he had fought about a woman, Eva Winstanley or any other. It would not do to let it be thought that he had got into a racecourse brawl—a shady gambling transaction; but outside these, what likely casus belli was there? Politics? No man in his senses would quarrel with a stranger on moot points of international history; and yet this was the only groundwork that could be given. A hot dispute on Waterloo and the Vengeur—yes, that was it! There was just so much colour in the fact as to redeem it from pure invention and blunt the points of those avenging prongs, which prick for falsehood; and silly though it might be to fight a duel on such a matter, there was a dash and spirit and true British manliness and patriotism about it—a fine hardihood in chastising that insufferable Gallic insolence—which touched old Mr. Strangways to the heart. So that he said to his wife with tears in his eyes, as he read Sir James Kearney's letter:

"The lad is true blue, Ellen! English to the backbone, I am glad to say! I am proud of him."

But his mother wept and saw nothing to be proud of at all—only a great deal to be very sorry for, to be agonized by, and to live in daily dread and discomfort on account of, until she had nursed her darling back to life and strength in the hotel where Sir James had carried him after he had been struck.

"I told you what you were doing," said Thomasina to her sister as severely as if she had been Minos judging for eternity. "If Hubert Strangways dies you have been his murderer."

"I don't see that," said Eva defiantly. "It was not my fault if he chose to quarrel with M. le Vicomte. I did not tell him to!"

"I will take care that nothing of the kind happens again," said Thomasina; and Eva looked into her trunk demurely and said nothing in reply.

They were packing for their journey back to the land of fogs and Sabbatarianism, where at least the elder sister believed they should be safe from such complications as arise from secret letters addressed to "ma bien aimée," by a handsome young man of unknown antecedents and unverified conduct. But she did not know that Eva had already given Bois-Duval their London address, and that he had promised to call when he went over in the autumn.

And all this time Hubert was lying between life and death in that brisk hotel on the Belgian frontier, with the question still undecided— was he to wear the laurel as the brave champion of his country's honour, or must his family plant the cypress which should mark where his young life lay quenched for ever in the grave?

It would not be for want of care if he fell through the meshes into that yawning gulf below; for his mother and Sir James, his sister and Maud Disney, were all so many hands and feet for the two sisters of charity who were the recognized nurses at his bedside; and if six people, foreby a doctor, could not save the life of one, of what good was human care or skill?

CHAPTER XXII.

ON THE OLD WAY.

HOME again and nothing done! On the contrary, a great deal had been undone and certain carefully potted blooms, so far from having advanced, had been put back and were perhaps altogether nipped and blighted.

When she reckoned up the losses and gains of that Trouville campaign, poor Mrs. Winstanley found herself forced to confess that the former outweighed the latter. They had spent a great deal of money— and all to what purpose? to attract a French nobleman who had not declared himself and who had spoilt the game for every one else! For there seemed to be no chance now of Hubert breaking off his engagement with Maud Disney for the sake of Eva and her wild-flower face. A man who is nursed through an illness by his mother and his fiancée is scarcely likely to escape from their hands into other keeping; Sir James would probably be too jealous of Bois-Duval to care to enter the lists with him on his own account; and Mr. Brocklebank would be sure to be disgusted with the whole affair. Perhaps he would be disgusted to the extent of grave displeasure; so that he would withdraw that large, hard and heavy but on the whole beneficent hand of his which gave good gifts and useful advantages, even if it did a little abrade the tender flesh while giving. The dead and wounded of her hopes came to a formidable number when fairly calculated; and Mrs. Winstanley knew what it was to lament her slain, though she could not yet give them final burial.

The great thing that she kept to herself was, how much she knew. Not Thomasina herself guessed this riddle; and what was not revealed to her we may be very sure was dark as night to every one else. Even Eva, who had the penetration of guilty fear to help her, could not see through the mask of unruffled placidity which it was in the mother's role to wear; and the outside world was completely baffled.

The duel, which had got into the papers, was naturally the main topic of conversation and conjecture among all the friends common to the Winstanleys, the Strangways and the Kearneys; and letters innumerable were written to Mrs. Winstanley inquiring how? why? and what? As the one of the group who had last seen the young men—and the only one who was acquainted with the Frenchman who had fought the duel—she was the well into which each dipped his or her sieve hoping to find Truth among the trickling waters. But Mrs. Winstanley was the soul of discretion and the angel of ignorance. She knew nothing. Voltaire's Huron[1] could not have presented a blanker sheet than was the unsullied page of her unconsciousness. Certainly there had been a slight discussion in her presence among the young men on one or two historical facts; and she remembered in a vague way that Waterloo had been spoken of; but for her own part she had attached no kind of importance to the conversation, and they had all parted on quite amiable terms. It was a very ordinary little discussion. Perhaps the Englishmen did get just the least in the world in earnest—by no means angry—only a little heated; as young men will do when discussing politics. But it was no more than this; and she had thought nothing of it at the time or after. What serious disputation there had been, to lead to this most melancholy result, must have been after; and when she was not present.

This was all she had to say; and this was what she did say to each inquirer in turn. And by her candour, her want of suspicion and her

---

[1]   Naïve Indian hero of Voltaire's novel *L'Ingénu* (1767).

charming womanly ignorance of evil, she convinced all who questioned her that the thing must have been as Sir James had given out—a sudden quarrel between two hotheaded young braves of different nationalities, each anxious for the honour of his country and each trying which should crow the loudest.

So the conventional nine days passed and the wonder diminished as the time increased. The two girls followed their mother's lead and took her cue; and not the most skilful dredging brought up anything to reward investigation or to pay for the trouble of casting.

Perdita of course was out of the whole affair; and it was very certain that no one would seek to bring her into it. She was told nothing about it; not given even the trimmings and parings of the story; and thus could make no mischief as else she would have surely done, had she been trusted with a delicate little subterfuge to negotiate or a bolder lie to pass off as truth. Her eyes alone would have betrayed everything and her silence would have been as eloquent as speech. No, certainly Perdita was not to be let behind the scenes, where even the mother stood veiled and Thomasina respected her disguise.

Moreover, Mrs. Winstanley had returned even less than before in sympathy with her rebel. Those two months' sojourn at Trouville had added the savour of French *convenance*[1] to the older form of English Grundyism; and Perdita's independent passage to and from the office seemed to her mother something more shocking and disgraceful than she had realized prior to that page of French experience. After having had to be so careful in her conduct at Trouville, she said to her eldest daughter—so vigilant, so watchful, on account of what the French might think—it was almost more than she could bear to have Perdita wandering about the streets as independently as if she were a man; and if she consulted her own inclination and sense of right she would put a stop to it without delay.

To which Thomasina answered: Yes; it was extremely unpleasant and annoying; but perhaps Perdita was less embarrassing now when out of the way and with something to do, than she had been when more in the house and always turning up at wrong moments—as on that dreadful afternoon when she had shocked Lady Kearney so fearfully. And then her money would come in usefully; would it not? and she had been very good and careful in their absence, and had lived on far less than one would have thought possible; had she not? and did not mother

---

[1]   (French), conventionality.

think her wonderfully improved? She herself, Thomasina, saw a great change for the better in her; and really she had grown almost pretty and very nearly ladylike!

"She owes you a great deal of gratitude for your persistent advocacy," said Mrs. Winstanley with her gracious smile. "You inherit one of the beatitudes, Thomasina—that of peacemaker."

Though she still went on with her work in the Post-office Savings Bank, Perdita's essential freedom was, if not quite at an end, yet undeniably curtailed by the return of her family. She had no longer the key of the fields at her girdle; and Bell Blount and Mrs. Crawford were removed from the foreground to the middle distance in her social landscape. Her hours were marked, and she had to be at home more punctually than when she and poor old Cluff had eaten their herrings at all odd times together, and made believe to find them as toothsome as nutritious. Hence there were only rapid rests of two or three minutes—no more peaceful anchorages of one or maybe two hours' length—in those quiet rooms above the shop where she always heard words of good counsel, and which she left with the feeling of having been spiritually washed and cleansed—perhaps a little too much toned down, a little overwatered, but undoubtedly washed and cleansed! There were no more doubtful evenings spent in the untidy bosom of that uncomfortable little household in Prince Christian's Road; where Bell Blount, with Connie Tracy as her "wife," Miss Long as her lady help, the Emancipation of Women as her occupation, and the conversion of Perdita Winstanley from a hero-worshipper into a man-hater as her hope, found the world good and life sweet. She had found it bitter enough at her married home down there in the quiet country, with her good-hearted but not brilliant husband and her two pretty but not intellectual daughters—her companions and her treasures as some would have said—the millstones round her neck and the fetters on her feet as she herself held them to be! Doing her unexciting little duties to the poor of her husband's parish was sorry work for one whose special glory and delight lay on the platform, and who would open all careers, without exception, to women as to men; but smoking cigarettes, drinking bitter beer for breakfast and B and S at all hours of the day, acting like a man and forgetting that she was a woman—that was an existence worth having, and to make others like herself an object worth pursuing!

What danger lay for Perdita however, in the bold mind and anarchical ideas of this petticoated bachelor, was lessened now by a large amount, so far as frequency of association went; and her intercourse with Bell became, like that with Mrs. Crawford, a fearful kind of joy to be snatched only at peril and in hot haste. She saw both at intervals truly, and her mind was still their shuttlecock, ever tossed between the two alternatives—the freedom which was so seductive and the duty which was so ennobling; the emancipation which appealed to her ambition, her pride, her energy, her democratic desires, and the home which fulfilled the devotion, the power of self-sacrifice and all the best instincts of her womanhood. As a further element of indecision and mental vacillation, she loved Mrs. Crawford personally, although her teaching, intellectually cold and dogmatically cramped as it was, often chafed her; and personally Bell Blount was antipathetic, though the main current of her social philosophy attracted her as the sense of space and freedom ever does attract the young, the ardent and the generous. But unlike as they were, either was more sympathetic to her than her mother and sisters; and both households were more pleasing, each in its own way, than that odd jumble of insufficiency and show, of prettiness and penury, which made her own home; for both were real in all that they appeared to be, and this last was a sham.

Between herself and her people the battle had begun again for poor Perdita, and on just the old grounds. Though improved in appearance and less of a Zulu than before, she was still not up to the mark according to the Winstanley standard; and the smoother manner which had come chiefly from the absence of reproach and consequent self-consciousness, lost itself again in the abrupt, ungainly, uncomfortable shyness which was at once the cause and result of perpetual rebuke and ridicule. Moreover, she was no wiser than she had been before. The wisdom of reticence and toleration comes but very slowly to a nature which errs by excess of conscientiousness and moral courage; and Perdita was, if anything, even more democratic, more sincere, more convinced of the sacred value of elemental principles and the wickedness of compromise for the sake of existing interests than she had been before. Fiat justitia!—that was her motto as it was Bell Blount's. Let the universe crack if it will, but let Eternal Justice rule without the loss of a thread in her garment, no matter who may go bare! Thus the old battle broke out again between her and hers, as has been said, on exactly the same lines as before; and the old unhappiness, the old sad feeling of domestic ostracism, began to creep over her like a blight and to manifest itself in her looks and manner.

Naturally her new friends had their nostrums.

"Leave your people and come with us. You are base and cowardly to submit."

This was Bell Blount's advice, urged with all the strength of her will and the power of her words.

"Submit patiently to your mother's will; whether you like it or not, submit," said Mrs. Crawford. "Never forget that she is your mother, and that obedience to parents is a commandment given by God."

Leslie, in whom the Quaker blood was not so strong and the Quaker quietism a good deal modified, demurred to this extreme doctrine of filial submission almost as much as he demurred to Bell Blount's masculine independence. He said:

"No; you have your own life to lead, your own nature to perfect, and you may carry submission and self-repression too far. Atrophy is not health and paralysis is not repose. Keep clear of the unsexed exaggerations of your woman's rights friends, but remember also that you are an accountable being, and that no one virtue is the whole duty of man. More goes to form the catalogue of perfection than even submission to parents."

And this form of the golden mean seemed to Perdita the wisest and best of all the doctrines propounded. She was not much of a temporizer certainly; but if Leslie Crawford thought half measures the best, she was sure he must be right. At all events, she did what she could to follow his advice, and once or twice did actually hold her tongue when the "common people" were spoken of disdainfully; when Eva asked her if they had a uniform like soldiers, or wore blue things like butchers in her office? when her mother and Thomasina, rising out of the ordinary region of fashion and social engagements, said they hoped that all the Russian Nihilists would be killed and that the French Republic would be overthrown by either an Orleanist, an Imperialist, or a Legitimist: it did not signify which of the three, so long as Gambetta was humiliated and the Republic was overthrown. She knew that these were red rags flourished in her face; and if at times she gave in to the lure and raved as she was wont to do, at other times, and not infrequently, she quietly left the room on some pretext, or buried her head in her book and persistently would not hear. This latter plan however, was not very successful, for she could not make herself deaf for very long; and when she pricked up her ears to open her mouth, then there was a skirmish wherein she was sure to go wrong and to be severely punished.

One day, when she went to Mrs. Crawford's house for one of those rapid little visits which were her brief stages of refreshment in her dreary life, she found the child slightly indisposed. There was no cause for grave alarm, yet Mrs. Crawford was in a state of nervous depression such as Perdita had never seen her in before. Her manner to her "Young friend," as she was wont to call Perdita, was shaded with something that looked almost like embarrassment, unless it were displeasure. And that it could scarcely be! She spoke, for Mrs. Crawford, a little abruptly, and did not look into the good, honest, freckled face with the same steady, half-mournful, half-observing gaze which was so essentially "her way." She wandered in an aimless kind of manner about the room and looked restless and disquieted; almost as if the girl's visit were unwelcome; and yet how often she had said: "Come whenever you will; you are always welcome and I shall rejoice to be of good to you."

Altogether the trifling ailment of a little child worrying over its teeth seemed scarcely cause enough to account for the decided discomfort of a woman generally so quiet and still, so much herself and so unruffled as Mrs. Crawford.

Leslie was not upstairs when Perdita came in, so that she was alone with Mrs. Crawford, when she heard the news of little Lily's indisposition and marked the disquiet of the grandmother.

"I hope she will soon get better, poor darling!" said Perdita, full of hearty sympathy.

Going up to Mrs. Crawford and kneeling down by her as she was wont to do, she took the soft cool hand in her nervous feverish fingers and held it warmly clasped.

"Yes, I hope so," said Mrs. Crawford, but not speaking as if little Lily's health were really the pivot and centre of her thoughts, as she had given Perdita cause to think.

"You must not fret; you will make yourself ill if you do," continued Perdita. "Children are so soon ill and well again!" she added sagely.

"It is the Lord's will," said Mrs. Crawford with a sudden rush of tears. "I never fret, my dear; but some things are hard to bear," she said, her thin lips quivering.

"Yes," said the girl.

She know—who better?—that some things are hard to bear; but these were not the burdens in her friend's present wallet of woe; and again it struck her that things were a little confused here to-day, and that Lily's slight attack did not explain everything; or else, it was no slight attack at all, but on the contrary a dangerous malady the true nature of which was concealed.

Presently Leslie came into the room. Something had evidently also passed over him. He was wonderfully sweet and courteous to his mother; and Perdita thought him also kinder and more expansive to herself than he was in general. For the most part he made her feel that he liked her, but he said nothing that carried an echo, did nothing that left an impress. It was more a sentiment, an atmosphere, than a fact; but to-day that sentiment was more visible, that atmosphere less subtle. There was something in the whole interview that interested her beyond herself, so that she stayed a longer time than usual and stayed far into the dusk. She could not tear herself away. It was in her nature to try and brighten up Mrs. Crawford, if indeed she might; and to help in the quiet comfort given by Leslie's kindness. He was so good, so noble! she said to herself in self-explanation and excuse. She liked him so much! and she felt that he did her good when he talked to her so kindly, discussed such and such questions with her as no one else did, and took so much interest in her mental life, in her thoughts and views. And not even Mr. Brocklebank did that really; though sometimes, to please her, he would pretend that he did. However, staying into the dusk as she did, Leslie said that he would walk home with her. He did not like her walking alone when the daylight had gone; and Perdita was not disposed to quarrel with his championship. She was glad that it was dark. It not only gave her the pleasure of his companionship but it hid her from the possible observation of her own people. She would not like her mother or Thomasina to meet her walking through High Street with Leslie Crawford the chemist. There was no harm in it; no kind of reason why she should be ashamed to accept and thus be induced to refuse her friend's escort. He was her friend and a high-minded well-read gentleman. He was a chemist certainly; but what of that? Are we not all brothers and sisters by the great law of human fraternity? What was there to which to object in her action?

Nevertheless she felt that she was doing something wrong insomuch as it was secret. She knew that she would not go in open-mouthed to her mother and say: "Mother, my friend Leslie Crawford, the chemist, walked home with me."

She ought to do so if she would act up to her own principles; she knew that very well; but she knew also that she would not. For if she did she would be forbidden to go to the house again; and she did not feel as if she could give up the companionship of that sweet dear woman who was more like a mother to her than her own.

As they were walking along, somehow—Perdita did not know how—the conversation drifted on to the subject of mésalliances.[1]

---

[1]   (French), mismatched marriages; also refers to Linton's article "Mésalliances" (*Saturday Review*, 26 September 1868, 419–20).

"The only real mésalliance is that where there is want of moral and intellectual equality," said Leslie. "When two people are on the same platform in refinement and education, and when their ideas as to what are the best things in life agree, there is no mésalliance. A duchess counting money as her chief good, and a chimney-sweep millionaire counting aristocratic recognition of his wealth as his, are fitly matched, though she had thirty-two quarterings and he once climbed the flues. And on the other hand, a lady of good birth who looks' for higher things than mere conventionalities, makes no mésalliance if she marries—what shall I say?—a shopkeeper let us suppose, equal to herself in all but the arbitrary rulings of society. The worst mésalliance of all is to mate frivolity with earnestness; love with indifference. All the rest is child's play compared to this."

"Yes," said Perdita in a low voice.

"Are you ambitious in your views of life?" asked Leslie with odd abruptness.

"In some things perhaps; not in mere station," she answered.

"Would you marry what is called beneath yourself, for instance, if the man personally was all right and it was only the conventional station that was askew?"

Leslie spoke in a studiously careless voice, looking up at the electric light as he passed it.

"Yes," answered Perdita tremulously.

"You would care for the man and not for his grandfather? But the family cares so much for the grandfather! If Milton himself had kept a shop, I question if the Marchioness of Carabas would have shaken hands with him over the counter. Do you think she would?"

"I do not know. I am not the Marchioness of Carabas," said Perdita simply.

"There are always the colonies if things get too uncomfortable at home," continued Leslie. "Would you go to the colonies with the man you loved?"

He looked at her from under the brim of his soft felt hat, and she saw his eyes glisten even in the darkness.

"I would go into the desert!" she answered in her passionate whole-sale way. The colonies made but a tame simile! Nothing short of the desert with its drought and solitude, its perils and wild beasts, to express the possible devotion of that devoted enthusiastic heart!

"Take my arm," said Leslie suddenly. "This crossing is bad and you are short-sighted."

He took her hand, and himself laid it on his arm where he held it for just a moment before he took his hand away.

"You are a brave beautiful girl!" he said warmly. "God bless you!" Then after a pause he added with strange coldness and restraint, "You deserve a good husband, Miss Winstanley. I hope when you do marry, it will be one worthy of your love."

"I never shall marry," said Perdita, tears choking her voice, she scarcely knew why. Really life was a very dreary affair and Heraclitus[1] was a true prophet! It was so much easier to weep than to laugh; yet a moment ago she would have said the contrary.

"Yes, yes, you will," he answered with forced cheerfulness. "And you will make me chemist in ordinary to your household."

"Don't, Mr. Crawford!" cried Perdita in a pained voice.

They were close now at her own door. The lamplight fell on her face but left her in the shadow.

"But you must not shut your eyes to the fact that I am only a chemist, a shopkeeper selling my goods over the counter," he said. "One whom your own people would say was no fit friend for you, a lady by birth and family association as you are all through."

"You are a better man than I am a woman; you are too good for me—for the friendship of such a foolish ungoverned thing as I am!" said Perdita hastily. "Your friendship honours me, not mine you; and I do not care if you were twenty times a chemist, I should still always respect and like you!"

A light came into his eyes, a smile broke round his lips, as suddenly he took both her hands in his and drew them up to his breast.

"Married or single," he said with tenderness so intense as to be pathos, reverence so deep as to be love; "you may always count on me as your faithful, firm, unchanging friend. I understand something of your heart and nature, and the more I understand the more I love and respect you. God bless you—dear!"

Out in the street as it was—before the very door of her own house—the lamplight from that aristocratic if impecunious dwelling falling full on her flushed face—the man before her neither of her own station nor yet a declared lover—Perdita bent her head and kissed the ungloved hand that held her own.

"And God bless you!" she said, lifting her large eyes to his.

Then she ran up the steps with haste, her blood on fire with shame

---

[1] Heraclitus of Ephesus (535?–475? BC), known as "The Weeping Philosopher."

and confusion at what she had done. And yet she could not feel sorry nor wish it undone. He was only a chemist, truly; but he had once saved her life; he had tried to make it noble; and now he had made it blessed!

But poor Mrs. Winstanley! How she was to be pitied! Here was she scheming schemes and weaving spells; out of her three daughters— Thomasina was out in the cold, no man's confessed choice; Perdita was looking into the face of a chemist and druggist with eyes which over-flowed with love; and Eva was watching for the post, in fear lest the letter daily expected from her French Vicomte should fall into other hands than her own, and the whole intrigue be blown into space before its time!

CHAPTER XXIII.

THE GREAT MOGUL.

BENJAMIN BROCKLEBANK did not, as a rule, implicitly believe women; still less did he trust in men. He thought that mankind in general found falsehood a vast deal easier than truth; and that the one came by nature while the other had to be learned by grace. But he would have scorned to doubt the word of a lady of a certain social standing, and he made trust part of the law of courtesy. If Mrs. Winstanley, for instance, said that such a thing was or was not, he would take her word for it though the whole weight of evidence went against her; he would even have been inclined to make it a personal question had any one thought differently and main-tained that smoke meant fire and that when linen was wet it had been in the water, if that handsome Juno of No. 100 declared the contrary.

Of course he, like the rest of the world, heard of the duel between Hubert Strangways and a French nobleman; and he, like the rest, applied to Mrs. Winstanley for her version. And when he had it, he accepted it as incontrovertible, and said so to his sister to whom he showed the letter.

"A very satisfactory explanation, my dear Clarissa," he said triumphantly. "I am glad our fair friends were out of it. I feared they might have been implicated, seeing that this young gentleman is a friend of theirs."

Mrs. Merton, who, unknown to her brother, kept up an active corre-spondence with his bugbear, Sir James, echoed his sentiments, his triumph and his convictions; accepted Mrs. Winstanley's version as the truth; ran up a pretty little symphonic scale as an accompaniment to his condemnation of the young fellow's rashness for quarrelling with a Frenchman at all, intermingled with commendation of his patriotism in taking up the cudgels for his own country; and made herself all through the soothing, flattering, sisterly echo which was both her pleasure and her role. But she had an odd trick of looking straight down her small blunt nose when she did thus echo her brother; and in the faintest way possible would pinch up her nice round mouth, and be very earnest about the proper adjustment of her sleeves and cuffs. For Sir James, who had made her his confidante from the first days of their friendship, had shown her just so much of the cat so snugly fastened in the bag as could be seen in this one phrase: "And the brute had forced himself most insolently on the Winstanleys, and had taken quite an insufferable tone of familiarity with them."

This was not showing much, but it was enough for an acute social osteologist, as Mrs. Merton was in her own way. Out of this one bone the fair soft-voiced widow made out the complete anatomy of the creature—from this one brick constructed the whole temple; and neither creature nor temple was much out of the straight line when she had done. But as she was far from wishing to make mischief between her brother and the Winstanleys—as she rejoiced in the fact that it had been Hubert and not Sir James—and as she could not very well say whence or how she had got her better information—she carefully hid her bone, locked away her brick in the secret recesses of her heart, stopped up the chink through which the light had come; and in the sweetest way possible looked down her short blunt nose, pinched up her nice round mouth, and agreed with her brother to accept the theory of political impersonality contained in Mrs. Winstanley's natural and innocent version.

And now all things went spinning in the old way down the old grooves just as if there had been no break at all: no Trouville sands with Bois-Duval here; no chemist's shop with Leslie Crawford there; no wounded lad lying in that inn on the Belgian frontier; no grave and sorrowful friend learning at last the truth through the ravings of fever, and pondering over the knowledge. The dropped threads were taken up with the most delicate precision, wherever it was possible; and the game began again just where it had left off.

When the Winstanley family came back from their disappointing campaign and took up their residence again at 100 West Hill Gardens, Mrs. Merton came back to her luxurious home, and her brother Benjamin ran up to town from Armour Court to resume that place of family guardian and moral investigator which late events had interrupted.

He himself would have gone over to Trouville during the time of his fair friends' stay there—how thankful they all were that he had not!—if he had not been compelled to make what he called an industrial excursion through Sweden and Denmark, part of Holland and a bit of Germany. He had to inspect some iron foundries of which he had heard alarmingly favourable reports; and he had to open new as well as retain old markets for his own pigs. For, rich as he was, his soul was in his business as a hunter's is in his game; and he enjoyed cutting out a rival and extending his own lines over foreign territory, just as much as if the pounds accruing were of consequence to his pocket and his funded property wanted feeding. Now however, with the passing of the summer came the re-establishment of old home relations; and the Winstanleys were the first of the knots which he tied in his social quipos.[1]

The three ladies were sitting in the drawing-room in the dark, waiting for the servant to light the gas before dinner. This was an operation which Mrs. Winstanley never hurried. So long as she could keep the girls quiet and amused, she saved so much in the quarter; and she was wise enough not to despise fractions in housekeeping. Perdita had not yet come home. At this moment indeed, she was walking up High Street on Leslie Crawford's arm. By only a minute did the rich ironmaster pass the chemist's shop before she came out of the private door. It was one of those providential interpositions which help the imprudent young; but as Perdita did not know the danger from which she had been preserved, she could neither tremble at her peril nor thank the Great Power which had influenced the goings and comings of about half a hundred persons and carriages that she might be saved from a scolding which perhaps, all things considered, she deserved. And just as she and her friend were discussing that suggestive question of mésalliances and her own willingness to marry below herself in social status, Benjamin Brocklebank thundered at her mother's door.

"I hope I see Mrs. Winstanley and her charming family well! Glad to welcome them back to their native land," he said, his sonorous voice vibrating through the room and echoing from the walls in such strength and volume as almost to hurt the ears of those who heard it.

It was really sweet, and almost touching, to see the pleasure—one might even call it well-disciplined emotion—with which graceful Mrs. Winstanley received her loud-voiced, broad-shouldered, hard-featured

---

1 Strands of cord or thin wool strings used by Inca Indians as an accounting or mnemonic device.

guest. There was something inexpressibly maternal in the smile that beamed on her well-preserved face as he entered with his noisy stamp and heavy tread, as if he had had four feet instead of two. Her delicately graduated accent, passing from the self-betraying caress of surprise to the conscious restraint of conventional propriety, was as eloquent as an embrace. Indeed her first impulse of welcome—both hands held out as if to take him to her handsome bosom—was essentially an embrace in spirit, and was the finest expression of womanly tenderness that Benjamin Brocklebank had ever received. She bore herself in these first sweet moments of pleasure and surprise as if some dear son had returned from foreign parts where there had been danger from wild beasts and the presence of savages and pirates—as if some wept-for Jonah had been unexpectedly cast up on the sands at her feet, when she had been thinking of nothing more exciting than star-fish and sea-anemones. And if she was thus sympathetic, Thomasina and little Eva were equally charming; and the welcome from all three accorded to the master of Armour Court made him feel as if every stubby hair of his close-cropped grizzled head had been smoothed the right way, and as if that mysterious organ, the cockles of his heart, had been well warmed with "'thirty-seven port."

"How good of you to look us up so soon!" said Mrs. Winstanley with her best air of refined gratitude.

"How nice to see you again!" laughed little Eva, clapping her pink, plump hands together, as if that ponderous Benjamin had been a wax doll or a pantomime, a new trinket or a box of sugar-plums.

He turned to Thomasina for her contribution. Mrs. Winstanley's eldest daughter said nothing; but she raised her large clear eyes with a sweetly glorifying look and smiled her best smile as she turned them on him—two inarticulate poems setting forth his praise, wherein that smile was the dumb music.

Her silence touched the ironmaster quite as much as Mrs. Winstanley's matronly caress, the little rosebud's childish delight. It was like Miss Winstanley to be quiet and undemonstrative even where she felt most deeply; and silence is sometimes more eloquent than speech. The voice has the foolish trick of trembling when the heart beats fast; and emotion somehow damps down the smoother notes and only allows to escape those queer, rough, deepened sounds which betray so much more than is desirable! Yes, Thomasina was right not to speak. Poor young lady! was she then so hard hit as this? She was a beautiful creature; but was she not looking a little thin after her Trouville trip? Her eyes were as lovely as ever; but surely, surely, the faintest little network of lines was beginning to engrave itself about the corners? Without question these two months had not improved her—and where was Miss Perdita?

Where, indeed?

When he asked this question of Mrs. Winstanley he instantly saw that his protégée was, as he said, on the wrong side of the account.

"She is dreadfully late to-night," the mother answered tartly, in spite of her desire to be as sweet as honey all through. "I hope no accident has happened," she added, shaking off her acidity into anxiety.

"Public officials are not always able to be punctual to the moment," said Mr. Brocklebank largely. "I imagine there has been press of work in the office, and Miss Perdita has had more than her usual allowance."

"It may be so," said Mrs. Winstanley with a restless glance round the room; "I hope it is only that."

"And I hope, too, that she will soon return," continued the ironmaster; "for I have come to make Mrs. Winstanley and her charming daughters a proposition. I wish to inaugurate this happy reunion of friends with a fête appropriate to the occasion. I have already ordered a dinner at the Continental that I trust my fair friends will do me the honour to partake of; and after that I think we shall find a box at the —— Theatre awaiting our occupancy. It is a large box; said to be capable of holding six. We are only five; so there is a place to spare for General Manners!"

On which the ironmaster laughed and the ladies dutifully joined in the chorus.

"It is most good of you, most kind! What can I say to such a delightful proposal?" said Mrs. Winstanley, looking at her daughters with a pleased air.

"How nice!" cried Eva, always the first to welcome pleasure.

"How very thoughtful and kind!" said Thomasina gently, her smile giving life to her words.

"I am glad that I have gratified Mrs. Winstanley and her charming young ladies," returned the ironmaster with a friendly chuckle; "it affords me so much pleasure to procure them enjoyment! And they accept my little friendship's offerings, my humble tributes so graciously, it is quite inspiriting! Now we only want Miss Perdita to make the whole thing complete. Ah! I do verily believe here she comes!" he added, as the sound of feet running up the steps and a nervous ring at the bell seemed to speak of haste and a bad conscience.

And sure enough they heard Perdita's voice in the hall saying to the servant, "Is dinner ready? Have I kept anyone waiting?"

Why they heard so distinctly was due to Mr. Brocklebank's lordly impatience and masterful assumption of domestic rights. For as soon as he heard the bell he strode to the drawing-room door and opened it, standing there to catch that naughty rebel on her way upstairs and, as he fondly hoped, make her as happy as he had just made the mother and sisters.

"Ah! come at last!" he said a little eagerly, as she ran hurriedly by. "And we fancying all sorts of uncomfortable disasters! Welcome home, Miss Perdita—we are all waiting for you! Come in! come in and hear the news!"

Her face pale with an emotion that was not pain and yet was scarcely pleasure—her large, soft, prominent eyes vague, humid, dreamy—her generous mouth a little parted as if to give the fast-coming breath a freer passage—her whole being touched with the living light of passion—Perdita came face to face with Mr. Brocklebank and with a little exclamation of honest joy laid her hand in his.

His heavy face brightened like a schoolboy's at a generous "tip." He took it all in—and took it all to himself. Not graceful like Thomasina; not beautiful like Eva; but how much more interesting than either! Greatly fascinated as he was pleased to be with each of the other two, this shy-mannered, short-sighted, freckle-faced girl had somehow struck a deeper chord and called forth a richer harmony than any one had ever done before. The passion that was in her gave fire and heat to the dull slag of his heart; and though by the law of fitness he knew her to be nowhere in comparison with Thomasina, yet by that of personal sympathy, which makes the unlike the supplement not the contrast, she was foremost of the three.

It was all for him! All the tenderness in her eyes, all the emotion on her face, the breath that came so heavily, the heart that throbbed so fast—it was all his own! He was master of her affections, as he was of Thomasina's; and it was in his own will only which he would choose, and when. But he thought he knew now which it would be.

"Miss Perdita has always a kind word for her friends," he said, holding her hand in his as he led her into the room and looking at her with an odd kind of affectionate mastership. "She makes them so agreeably welcome."

"I hope we all do that," said Mrs. Winstanley gracefully. Her face was very sweet, but her voice was slightly acrid. She would not oppose Perdita's chance; of course not; and she would consider it the most beneficent act of an overruling Providence should Mr. Brocklebank relieve her of this troublesome rebel of hers; but all the same she would feel disappointed and aggrieved for her dear Thomasina; and while handing over the one, would have difficulty in refraining from injurious comparisons with the other and reproaches for the bad taste shown and the unworthy choice made.

"Yes," said Perdita heartily, but shyly too. "We are all glad to see you again, Mr. Brocklebank."

"Upon my soul, I think so!" he answered. Then he laughed. "I think you know who are your friends!" he said, and looked at Mrs. Winstanley. "But now we have no time to lose," he continued. "I am going to take you all to dine with me at the Continental, Miss Perdita; and afterwards we go to the theatre to see—let me see, what is it?" He pulled a programme out of his pocket. "Oh! 'Love Laughs at Locksmiths:' and 'When a Woman Wills she Wills,' and 'Between Two Fires.' A pleasant programme enough. I trust we shall find the acting in accordance with its promise. What do you say to that, Miss Perdita?"

With clumsy familiarity he took both her hands and swung them to and fro.

Perdita looked at her mother. Was it intended that she should go with them? or was it wished that she should refuse?

Mrs. Winstanley, still sweet and acid in one, looked at her uncomfortable daughter with eyes as cold and hard as crystal and lips which graciously smiled.

"You especially delight in the theatre, do you not, Perdita, my child?" she said as a lead; and poor Perdita's sensitive face was on the instant one grateful palpitating blush.

"Yes, indeed, indeed I do!" she said warmly. "I like nothing so much!"

"Not even me?" asked the ironmaster with another swing of her hands. She looked up at him affectionately.

"I don't think I would give you up for the theatre!" she said with a happy little laugh; and Mr. Brocklebank pressed her hand for this answer with such a vice-like grip that she slightly winced, for all her hardihood to pain.

"Now I must be peremptory," he said, releasing her and looking at his watch. "I can give my fair friends ten minutes for adornment. Not a second more! Who will be ready first, I wonder? Miss Perdita, I will wager my head!"

"Of course she will!" laughed Eva, as she slipped past the ironmaster balancing her arms with her favourite half-flying movement. "And I shall be last; you will see that I am!"

She really meant that, as Perdita made less account of her appearance than either she herself or Thomasina, she naturally took less time in her dressing: but Mr. Brocklebank, on the wrong scent throughout, thought that she had divined her sister's secret and meant that impatience for his society, and desire to win his approbation for the minimum amount of feminine vanity, would hasten her movements and bring that sensitive impassioned delightful rebel first to the room—and alone.

In this belief he sat and hugged himself while the ladies tumbled over their wardrobes and quarrelled with their clothes, after the manner of women to whom good dressing is more important than all the Ten Commandments in a bunch, when they have to make themselves look nice without due preparation.

Watch in hand the ironmaster sat waiting for the return of the ladies to whom he was playing the Great Mogul; hoping and believing that his protégée would redeem his word and justify his prophecy. But something that she could not explain—a bashfulness more instinctive than confessed—kept Perdita upstairs even after she had dressed. Of course she was ready before her sisters, or even her mother. Her style was simpler; she had fewer addenda to put on after the main structure was complete; and she wasted no moments in critical examination of all four sides by means of a hand-glass and a couple of candles. Still, she did not go down to the drawing-room. On the contrary, she knocked a little timidly at Thomasina's door and went into her sister's chamber, partly to go down with her and partly for her verdict.

"Am I all right, Thomasina?" she asked, standing awkwardly at the door.

"Come nearer and then I can see you better," answered Thomasina with genuine kindness.

She saw how things were going, but she was neither jealous nor disappointed. For herself it was only poverty and her mother's debts which made her desire to be married at all, which made it possible that she should marry a man like Mr. Brocklebank whom personally she loathed and intellectually despised. Marriage was her sole possible profession; a husband her sole source of income; and in securing these where she could, though she might outrage her womanhood, she only yielded to necessity. But if Mr. Brocklebank liked Perdita, and Perdita liked Mr. Brocklebank—à la bonheur![1] The game was safe, and she was spared the distasteful part of scoring it. She would not be so sorry for Perdita as she would be for herself, or for poor little Eva, should the choice fall on her. Perdita would not marry if she did not love; and that, Thomasina supposed with a tranquil kind of speculative wonder, made all the differ-

---

[1]   (French), Here's to their happiness!

ence. Thus, she was neither jealous nor disappointed because the iron-master with his millions in his pocket seemed to prefer Perdita to herself. Quite the contrary. For indeed outside the degradation of morals insep-arable from the self-confessed intention of selling herself to the highest bidder, Thomasina was a girl without vices, free from petty faults, and capable of a reasonable stretch of virtue. Had she not been for sale she would have been as charming in character as she was beautiful in person; but that terrible standing in the market-place spoilt all!

"Yes, you look very nice, Perdita," she then said after she had exam-ined her sister with those grave critical eyes. "But you want something in your hair; you look too plain, too little *en grande tenue*[1] for the occasion. Here! you shall have this," she added, unfastening a flower which she had just pinned into her own magnificent, bought and unpaid braid. "I will wear a piece of gold ribbon, and this white rose will just suit your colour."

"No, no, I will not take this from you! If I want anything in my hair—but I don't think I do, Thomasina!—I will wear a piece of ribbon. I have some upstairs, and it is quite fresh. You shall not give me your pretty flower, dear!"

Perdita said this with warmth, effusion, gratitude, surprise, affection, reverence, all tumbled in a heap in her rash heart and eager voice.

"Don't be silly," said Thomasina in a cold voice; "I have my reasons for wishing you to look specially well to-night. I insist on it, Perdita; so please make no fuss."

"No, no, Thomasina, I cannot take it from you!" she said again.

"Sit down. I have no time to spare, and you must do as I tell you. What a trouble you make about everything! How silly you are, Perdita! Sit down, I say, and let me put it in."

"I do not like to take it from you, Thomasina! You look so lovely with it yourself, and I am not used to things like this. I shall only look a fright, as I always do; and then the beauty of the flower will be lost. Do wear it yourself, Thomasina!" said the unlucky one, rebellious through unselfishness and tiresome because she was good.

Thomasina laid the flower on her dressing-table. "Then please go out of my room and let me finish my dressing," she said with glacial dignity. "You really are too tiresome to be borne with."

"Don't be angry with me, Thomasina!" pleaded Perdita. "We have been such good friends since you came home, and you are the only one I can speak to!"

---

[1] (French), grandly made up.

"It is impossible to keep good friends with you, Perdita," answered her sister, still glacial. "You are just maddening from first to last and I wash my hands of you. I wish you would go out of my room!" she added sharply.

"What a dreadfully unlucky girl I am!" said Perdita to herself as she turned away, the quick tears in her big eyes and her eager heart heavy and damp. "I should love Thomasina so much if only she would let me—if she understood me a little better and did not so soon shut up against me! I never mean to offend her and she is often so kind to me; and then it all goes off in some unlucky fume like this! She and mother both want such tremendous obedience, and I cannot always bend to them—not at the first moment in little things like this—and never in the greater ones! But I won't vex Thomasina to-night. She is very sweet and good to want to make me look nice. I hate taking her things, but perhaps I ought. It is very detestable to me—but if she wishes it?"

These thoughts passed like lightning through her head in the brief moment of her passage to the door. Then she turned back, the big drops trembling on her long lashes.

"Dear Thomasina, it was only because I did not wish to deprive you of your pretty flower," she said humbly. "I did not want to vex you; and you shall put it in if you like."

"If you would only understand that obedience is far more proof of love than what you please to call unselfishness—but which is only self-ishness in disguise—you would get on much better than you do," said Thomasina as tranquilly as if there had been no dispute between them. "You give more trouble than any one else, simply because you will not fall into the ordinary ways of other girls; and then you wonder that we do not like it. There! you look far better with that rose in your hair; but now you want a necklet and bracelets. Here, take these of mine; and mind you don't lose them."

And Perdita, subdued to the proper pitch, meekly hung herself about with borrowed ornaments of mock jewellery—things which her soul abhorred—because Thomasina wished it, and the wish had touched her heart.

Then they both went down together; and because this little altercation and addition had taken up one or two of the precious minutes allowed, they were behind their time and the last of the group—of whom little Eva had been first.

Mr. Brocklebank's face was like a thunder-cloud. The watch was still in his hand, and he was standing like the impersonation of masculine punctuality with loins girded, ready to depart and hindered by unpardonable feminine frivolity.

"Miss Winstanley is late," he said, ignoring Perdita, with whom he was too displeased even to care to chastise. Excommunication is sometimes a more severe sentence than punishment.

"Yes, I am so sorry! It was all my fault," answered Thomasina with graceful heroism.

"My goodness, Per, how smart you have made yourself!" cried Eva laughing. "Why you have all Ina's things on! I never saw you so grand before!"

Mr. Brocklebank turned his eyes on the rebel with no sunshine in them, none of that glittering brightness which stood with him for tenderness. They were dull and pale and hard and fishy, almost as if a film were over them; as was the way with him when annoyed.

"Miss Perdita's unwonted magnificence is flattering to my poor escort," he said slowly; "but I own I like her best in her native simplicity; and I like best of all willingness to please and readiness to obey a well-meant suggestion."

"I am so sorry!" said Perdita, overwhelmed with confusion and feeling horribly ill-treated by fate and appearances. Really, it was too bad! Whatever she did she got blame and rebuke. Her life was a perpetual steerage between Scylla and Charybdis,[1] and she had the most extraordinary faculty, not only of never steering clear, but of falling upon both at once. In acting according to her own ideas of right she had offended Thomasina—in pleasing Thomasina she had offended Mr. Brocklebank; and she had been blameless in fact throughout. It was very unfortunate, and "I am so sorry!" she said with mournful truth.

"Let us lose no more time," said Mr. Brocklebank, still ruffled. "My carriage is at the door and dinner is already waiting. Allow me, madam," to Mrs. Winstanley, to whom he offered his arm—the girls following after.

"What a nuisance you are, Per!" said little Eva in an audible whisper. "Now, you have made that dear, good, kind Mr. Brocklebank angry and spoilt the whole evening!"

But when they were in the carriage—the ironmaster following in a hansom—Thomasina told her mother how the whole thing had happened; recommended Eva to hold her tongue and not tease Perdita any more; and to Perdita herself, whose tears were dimming her spectacles and

---

[1] In Greek mythology, two sea monsters who lived in caves on opposite sides of the Straits of Messina, separating Italy and Sicily, and who devoured sailors from passing ships.

dropping on to her gloves and gown, she administered the tonic of a cold rebuke, saying,

"Please, Perdita, don't make a goose of yourself like this. Do you want Mr. Brocklebank to think you care for him so much that his very natural annoyance makes you cry?"

"No!" said Perdita, with an indignant sob.

"Then dry your eyes and don't be silly. We do not cry when we dine at a restaurant and go to the theatre!" said Thomasina, with frosty disdain and undeniable good sense.

CHAPTER XXIV.

AT THE PLAY.

How much soever he might have been annoyed, it was not in the nature of man to remain sulky in the circumstances which Mr. Brocklebank had gathered round him. A well-washed, heavily-scented, modern Sardanapalus,[1] standing treat to four nicely got-up women of varying degrees of beauty and fascination—a Great Mogul with his handkerchief in his hand, looking round and pondering before throwing, and the potential possessor of any of the four—a beneficent kind of muscular fairy, a hirsute elf, giving three nice little fat natives as a ladylike whet to fastidious appetites; slacking youthful thirst with sweet bright sparkling champagne such as the feminine palate loveth; and "topping up," as he himself called it, with a gorgeous box at the theatre—an autocratic Pasha fêting his harem and rewarded for so much outlay of thought and gold by eight handsome eyes looking at him tenderly, eight pleasant lips smiling on him gratefully—how could he wrap himself so closely in the mantle of sullenness that the dew of those softer influences, the sunshine of that delicious and quickening gratitude, should not penetrate beneath the gloomy folds and reach the living heart beneath?

Mr. Brocklebank was by no means famous for geniality or plasticity of temper—not in the least the kind of man of whom people would say approvingly: "He is so easy to get on with!" But he was human like any one else and capable of being mollified if taken the right way. And

---

[1]   King of the Assyrians, and according to Clearchus, the most prosperous man in the world.

by the time the oysters had been eaten, the Chablis had been sipped and the first glass of champagne had been what he called "turned over," he had forgiven Perdita whose evident contrition touched him; thought Thomasina the perfection of good-breeding and graceful bearing; told kittenish Eva that she was the sweetest little mouse and prettiest little rosebud in the world, and had even given tender glances and said gallant speeches to the well-preserved mother of the triad. In fact, as Eva said afterwards, "the horrid old bear was spoons all round," and the whole thing began to go as merrily as marriage bells.

Every one was gratified and all were at their best. Mrs. Winstanley gave up guessing which, as a hopeless puzzle to be decided only by time, and let herself enjoy the good things of the present without worrying herself about that thick blanket of futurity. Thomasina warmed up under the influence of stimulating food and delicate wine into a very fair representation of a red-blooded vertebrate; and Thomasina warmed, was Thomasina entrancing. Eva forbore to say disagreeable things under the guise of childish innocence, and left off for the time her favourite amusement of picking holes in Perdita's sensitive skin; and Perdita herself, when the cloud of her patron's displeasure had lifted, was as bright as a summer's sky and full of frank pleasure and girlish excitement. She was so glad to be taken into favour again by the man whom she regarded as her benefactor, and therefore loved as a passionate and grateful creature does naturally love one who has been friendly. And then beyond these more evident causes of mild felicity she was bearing about with her the secret sense of having received some great gift of beauty, some sweet, strange influence of joy—of having met with an angel by the way that evening—of having had some spiritual grace bestowed, the glorious joy of which she had never known till now.

She was so happy, so much at ease, so free from that nervous shyness which was at once the bane of her peace and the blemish of her personality—she was so unlike Perdita the testifying democrat, Perdita the rebel against home law and fashionable command, Perdita the Stoic—that her mother looked at her more than once and wondered in her own mind to what cause this change was owing. Then she looked at Benjamin Brocklebank, and thought her undesirable daughter mad or blind. Could she love that man? If she encouraged him, she loved him. She was not one to marry for social duty like that wise Thomasina, and let love go by the board. But what detestable taste she must have! what a rough, coarse, unrefined mind to love that man!

"However, that is her affair not mine," thought Mrs. Winstanley with a little sigh. "I could have understood and respected my good Thomasina, who would have sacrificed herself to him from a sense of duty, who would have made the best of him, but would never have affected to love him; but that Perdita should have a real honest inclination for him—it is revolting! But I wish those debts were paid!" she mentally added, and gave another little sigh. "The last time I added them all up they were above two thousand pounds; and I have not two thousand pence to pay them with!"

After which she toyed with some grapes and resolutely ignored that Black Care sitting like Sinbad's Old Man of the Sea[1] across her neck, and laughed and talked with as much abandon as a ladylike mother might allow herself to show.

Then they all went off to the theatre, the ironmaster preceding his convoy in a hansom, as before.

"We will put the three young ladies in front, and Mrs. Winstanley and her humble servant will sit behind," said Mr. Brocklebank gallantly. "Three pretty maidens all of a row: and upon my soul they make my box the flower-bed of the theatre!"

"Then what are you? a flower too?" asked little Eva prettily. "What flower are you, Mr. Brocklebank? a sunflower?"

"I, Miss Eva? I am no flower at all, else I would be a sunflower as you say, and you should be my luminary; no, I am your gardener, which is the more proper thing perhaps."

"I think you are a very nice gardener," said Eva, with the sweetest, quaintest gravity that could be imagined. "And your flower-bed is delicious; I should like to be planted in it every night."

In return for which pretty speech, Mr. Brocklebank, who was rapidly becoming as familiar in action as he was oddly formal in speech, put his arm boldly round Eva's fairy waist and gave her an unmistakable hug. And Mrs. Winstanley looking on, prudent, ladylike, well-bred and the most careful mother in the world as she was, neither felt nor expressed dissatisfaction.

There are moments of mild Saturnalia[2] even for ladylike mothers; and this was one of them.

Naturally Eva was placed in the middle. It was the most prominent place, and for a show-girl the child was undeniably the most effective of the three. Thomasina's charm was one more of manner and nearer

---

[1] In the *Arabian Nights*, a man encountered by Sinbad on his fifth voyage, who compels strangers to carry him until they drop.

[2] Ancient Roman winter holiday whose traditions include role reversal and general merriment.

observation; but Eva's colouring told as a picture, and Mr. Brocklebank was anxious that his box should make a good appearance. Thomasina had the place of honour fronting the stage, and Perdita that which faces the house and necessitates a screwed spine for the boards. But it was a large box and all saw well, as also all were well seen.

They took their places just as the orchestra assembled and the lights were turned up. For Mr. Brocklebank, knowing what young ladies were in the matter of pleasure, as he said, had taken care to be in time for the very beginning of all things, and took credit to himself that they had not lost even the introductory tuning of the fiddles.

Nothing happened to disturb the serenity of the party. Perdita, like all people of her temperament, was passionately fond of the theatre. She gave the whole strength of her mind and attention to the stage; was indifferent to the glare of the gaslights; knew nothing of that twist in her spine, that contortion of her neck; saw no one in the place; lived only in the drama; and said but little even during the fall of the curtain. She was in a dream and she did not wish to be awakened.

Thomasina, looking to the stage, saw nothing of the house, and employed her time in taking mental notes of the leading dresses. With very few alterations they might be made the models of her own; and she was sure that they would become her superbly. She did not know much of what was going on before her, but she could have given an accurate description of the sleeves and skirts which made the importance of the play to her. Where others seized points she dissected shapes; where others watched faces, voices, gestures, she threaded the millinery maze with a quickness that was genius in its own way—knew whether that breadth was on the straight or the cross; where that end of sash was fastened; how those folds were looped and made. Eva's bright eyes roved far and wide among the audience and made no pretence of exclusive devotion to the piece; and while she was looking here and there she spied out, in the stalls, a well-known glossy, sleek black head, with the hair out into a fringelike festoon on the forehead, well-waxed moustache elaborately twisted, and that pronounced expression of kid gloves, a buttonhole bouquet and spotless linen, characteristic of gilded youth in general and the Parisian in particular.

One rapid glance betrayed the presence of the man whom, now in England, she most dreaded to see again.

Her fair face flushed to the roots of the hair; but she dropped her fan and the act of stooping to pick it up accounted for that sudden rush of blood which else might have attracted some attention. Bois-Duval made a rapid, half imperceptible little movement with his hand. The fingers, joined in a bunch on the lips, sent the airiest little kiss through space to the pretty creature overhead, and Eva, frightened though she was, and feeling trapped and caught, could not resist the temptation of a little bit of secret coquetry, and answered back the signal with an expressive flirt of her fan. Then Bois-Duval stood up boldly and looked at the group through his opera-glasses.

"Oh, mumsey!" said Eva leaning across Thomasina's back to her mother. "Who do you think I see in the stalls? that Frenchman you knew at Trouville, le Vicomte de Bois-Duval! How funny that he should be in London, and here to-night!"

"Indeed! Is he here? Does he recognize us?" asked Mrs. Winstanley, looking down while she arranged her tuckers.

"Yes, I think so, don't you, Ina?" replied Eva. "Oh, yes, he does!" here she smiled and waved her hand. "He is bowing to us, mother. Lean forward and bow to him, darling—I don't like to be the only one—bow, Ina!"

Thomasina's handsome face, which had been rounder and softer and more smoothed out than usual, during that study of stage millinery made with so much zeal, became white and rigid. She knew her little sister's possibilities and suspected underhand play; but this time wrongfully. Bois-Duval had come to London without preconcertion as to time, though Eva had told him where she lived and had expressed a hope that he would come and see them; and his presence at the theatre to-night was a mere coincidence, as sometimes happens for good or ill in life.

"Bow, Ina," repeated Eva impatiently.

"I do not see him," said Thomasina coldly, looking the other way.

"He is not there, Ina; he is in the stalls!" said Eva still impatient. "How odd that you cannot see him! You are not short-sighted."

"Who is Miss Eva dispensing her smiles to in that lavish way?" asked Mr. Brocklebank with more uneasiness than grammatical accuracy.

In his character as Great Mogul and potential possessor, he resented intruders and co-partners in equal measure; and it was something of a personal offence to himself that his ladies should have found another male acquaintance at the theatre where he desired to reign supreme.

"Who is it?" he asked again, craning forward and seeing nothing.

"A gentleman we knew in Trouville," returned Eva with the prettiest and most innocent animation. "It seems so funny to see him here! It reminds one of the sea—that delicious sea-breeze!—and of those funny bathing-dresses. Don't you remember, mumsey, those queer little children, just like monkeys? those two little things in striped blue and white that tumbled about all legs and arms and looked just like frogs? How funny it all was!" laughing.

"It does one good to hear little Miss Eva's merry voice," said Mr. Brocklebank appeased. "Without flattery I may say that I think that laugh of hers the merriest and most musical thing in the world. It warms one's heart to hear it!"

"You are very kind to say so," said Mrs. Winstanley with a gracious smile which hid the trouble into which the presence of Bois-Duval had cast her as effectually as a bandage hides a sore. "I sometimes fear I spoil her, just a little," she continued with a fond reflective maternal air. "But she is so sweet and charming—she is so full of fun and innocence—that I confess I have not the heart to check or sadden her. She is my little ray of sunshine, as her eldest sister is my prop and support."

"And my young friend, Miss Perdita?" he asked, looking from one to the other of the three girls with a benign smile, but looking last and longest at Perdita.

"She? She is my Genius, as you know," said Mrs. Winstanley, smiling in her sweetest way. "I love all my children, but I reverence my daughter Perdita as much as I respect Thomasina and delight in little Eva."

Mr. Brocklebank looked pleased.

"You are right, madam," he said fervently. "She is a young lady to be reverenced!"

At that moment a knock came to the door of the box and Mr. Brocklebank rose to open it.

A woman of decidedly remarkable appearance presented herself. She was dressed in a satin gown of flaming scarlet; round her throat was a broad, heavy, silver dog-collar, and on her neck rows on rows of those green iridescent shells which are the apotheosis of the street whelk. Her white hair, combed straight up from her face, fell down her back in youthful waves; and she had rings and brooches and bracelets and artificial flowers wherever they could be placed. It was our old friend Bell Blount, in what she herself would have called her war paint—at all events in the dress by which she hoped to convince an unbelieving generation that manly principles do not necessarily exclude feminine graces, and that it is possible to fight for woman's rights and yet retain her charms.

"Is Perdita Winstanley to be spoken to?" asked Bell in her most caressing voice and with republican simplicity of address.

Up jumped Perdita, glad, hurried, awkward, embarrassed.

"Oh, is that you?" she said, in the foolish way of people when they are taken aback and have lost their self-possession.

"Yes," said Bell, taking her hand in both of hers and kissing her affectionately. "Yes, I am here; and seeing you I could not resist the temptation of paying you a visit in your box. When are you coming to see me again? I have to talk to you about a great many things, and I want you to come to our next meeting. It is to be on Wednesday. Will you come, dearie?"

"If mother will let me," said Perdita with extreme confusion.

Turning to her mother she said hurriedly: "This is my friend, Mrs. Blount, mother." Looking at Bell she added, "My sisters—Mr. Brocklebank," and then wished that she could have dissolved into pure spirit or have fainted on the floor.

Perdita had no lack of moral courage; but moral courage is not obtuseness of perception nor want of the power to feel pain and dread strife. On the contrary, with all sensitive people and those who are not upheld by crazy vanity, the courage of their opinions includes infinite suffering, only second to that which would come to them through the self-abasement of disloyalty; and it is sometimes even a harder trial to have to stand by an inharmonious and unconventional friend than by an unpopular belief.

But Perdita was loyal to her finger-tips, and could no more have 'cold-shouldered' Bell because her presence here was unwelcome, than she could have committed a theft or told a lie.

"I do not understand your request, my dear," said Mrs. Winstanley suavely. "To what meeting does this person—this friend of yours—refer?"

"The second of our bi-monthly meetings, madam," said Bell in her clearest and most oratorical voice. "I am permanent chairwoman of the West Hill Female Suffrage Association, and I want my young friend Perdita to hear one of our most famous speakers, Mrs. ——."

"You must excuse me if, taken so completely by surprise, I decline to give my consent to my daughter mixing herself up in this very questionable movement—at least until further consideration. The whole thing has come on me like—like—a thunderbolt," said Mrs. Winstanley.

Bell Blount laughed, and at her laugh, so clear and resonant, many turned their opera-glasses to the box, and among them Bois-Duval, with a smile that said as plainly as words: "Qu'elles sont drôles, ces Anglaises!" [1]

"We will soon indoctrinate you, my dear lady," she said, with audacious good humour. "My little friend here was very hard at first to inoculate. But I think she has got it by now—hey, what do you say, honey?" putting her broad hand under Perdita's chin and turning up her face with ostentatious familiarity.

---

[1]   (French), They are so "droll," these Englishwomen!

Perdita did not speak. Mrs. Winstanley rose and looked Junonic and severe.

"I devoutly hope not," she said with emphasis. "Should you like to see your protégée one of those dreadful women's rights women, Mr. Brocklebank?" she added, turning to the ironmaster who stood at the back of the box indignant and revolted.

"Certainly not, Mrs. Winstanley! I would rather see her the honest wife of an honest man, submissive to her duties and casting up her weekly accounts with accuracy. I set my face against the whole movement, madam; and until she confesses it with her own lips I shall not believe Miss Perdita guilty of this folly, this extravagance. To go to the Post-office Savings Bank, and to be a John Jenny, wanting to cut off men's legs and sit in the House of Commons, is a very wide step; and I take leave to doubt that Miss Perdita has taken it."

"I think she has," said Bell Blount, still audacious and good-humoured. "We'll put her into the witness-box for herself. Speak, my pretty! Don't you think that, between fine ladyism and subjection, the condition of women is very deplorable, and that they ought to be more independent on the one hand and more industrious on the other? Do you think they were meant to be mere dressed-up dolls here, or poor, ignorant, down-trodden drudges there? Do you think they should be able to manage for themselves—live their own lives—be themselves—do their own busi-ness—or just wait like so many slaves in the marketplace till some man graciously consents to buy them for his married servant? Say what you think, honey! Tell truth and shame the old gentleman!"

"Yes, I think they ought to be both more independent and more industrious," said Perdita, she too speaking in a clear voice.

Bell Blount smiled, clapped her hard on the back and cried: "Bravo! I knew you were 'clear grit,' as the Americans say!"

Mrs. Winstanley shrugged her shoulders and sighed as at a new mani-festation of insanity; but Benjamin Brocklebank, as his last testimony to friendship—his last gun fired in defence of his protégée—said in a heavy, dictatorial, clinching kind of way:

"Miss Perdita is too good to be led astray. She must not be made a fool of; and Mrs. Winstanley, madam, I will undertake to cure her of this disease. It is like the pip in chickens and can be got rid of by proper measures."

Bell Blount's fine face became nearly as red as her dress.

"The conceit of that wretched creature man!" she said with a forced laugh. "We know our truest friends better than that, don't we, honey?" to Perdita.

"Mr. Brocklebank is my good friend too," said Perdita, looking at him affectionately. "The good friend of all the family," she added warmly.

"A heart of gold! A heart of gold!" said Mr. Brocklebank with pompous patronage, but enthusiastically as well. "Mrs. Winstanley need give herself no sort of uneasiness—none whatsoever, in any shape or form! Miss Perdita is true-blue throughout—a thorough woman, whatever little twist may have been communicated to her ideas; but no one need be afraid of her forgetting the proprieties due to her age and sex. And now, madam," to Bell Blount, "by your leave—the play has recommenced."

The play may have recommenced, as the ironmaster phrased it, but the glory of it had departed for Mrs. Winstanley. Between the embarrassing advent of Bois-Duval and the intrusion of this bold, odd-looking person who claimed Perdita as her friend and advocated independence in woman and disregard of men and marriage, she felt as if she were performing penance, not receiving pleasure; and caught herself wondering how people could be so silly and light-minded as to find amusement in the rubbish set before them on the stage. But she smiled at the right moments and said it was a lovely *mise-en-scène*, an excellent situation and charmingly acted; and when it was all over and they were putting on their cloaks and clouds, she thanked Mr. Brocklebank with graceful effusion for the delightful evening that he had given them—the most delightful she ever remembered, she said, drawing her lengthy bow without apparent effort.

Thomasina echoed her mother's words with more gracefulness if less effusiveness; while little Eva added a whole string of caressing epithets which fell like shining pearls or scented petals from her rosebud mouth lined with those small, sharp, white little teeth. Perdita looked at their Amphitryon, her honest eyes dark and warm, and said in a moved voice:

"It was delicious! How good you are!"

And somehow her thanks seemed to the ironmaster the sweetest, the most vitalized, the most musical of all.

Then they filed out by the narrow passage and down the stairs to the vestibule; and there at the foot of the stairs stood Bois-Duval, looking for them with a sharpened face and eager eyes; and there stood also the tall form of Bell Blount, with her flowing hair of silver falling against the scarlet satin of her showy gown, and her bold self-satisfied face scanning the crowd for her favourite Perdita—that rebel whom she was giving her strength to make more rebellious still.

There was nothing very noteworthy in the greetings mutually given and received by Bois-Duval and the Winstanleys. He was polite, courteous, interested in their health, delighted to see them again and finding them all looking charming; they were polite and courteous too, interested in his health, thinking him courageous to come to England in spite of its fogs and frosts, and hoping that he would not find the change from his own delightful climate too severe. He expressed himself as enthusiastic for England—English liberty, English religion, English manners; and they smiled, looked as if they believed him and returned the compliment on French politeness and French skies. Then he asked permission to pay his respects to them at their own house; and Mrs. Winstanley gave him their address and presented him to Mr. Brocklebank.

And when be had accomplished his main purpose, then M. le Vicomte made an elaborate bow and withdrew; and Eva crushed into her pocket a little note, written in the theatre, and passed with the skill of a prestidigitateur.

Meanwhile Bell Blount had talked fast to Perdita, and Perdita had promised to go and see her the first hour that she had to give away.

CHAPTER XXV.

THE ALTERNATIVE.

THE next day was Sunday. Mrs. Winstanley, like all well-conducted people, was decorously Sabbatarian. It was part of her code of good manners; the respect due to the established order of things, like making a court curtsy when presented or giving people of rank their proper titles. Thus, besides church once in the day, an early dinner and only sacred music allowed in the evening, there were special observances for Sunday mornings. The prayers were longer and an extra chapter was read after breakfast—prayers always were after breakfast at 100, West Hill Gardens. Things get so spoiled by being kept warm on the top of the kitchen oven; yet it is so tiresome to have to wait till they can be got ready! Besides, cook does not like it. For which reasons Mrs. Winstanley compromised between devotion and convenience, and ate her breakfast in comfort before she said her prayers for consecration.

Backing up these special observances, a certain set, we might almost say solemn, demeanour marked the early part of the day. By the afternoon this solemnity had considerably relaxed. The breakfast too, was touched with the characteristics of a minor fast, inasmuch as it was shorn of all superfluous adjuncts and reduced to its primitive elements; and altogether the outward and visible signs of Sunday morning were as well marked in the Winstanley household as if the faded crimson curtains were changed for a Sabbatical drapery of black or the dingy claret-coloured walls had an hebdomadal wash of grey.

And till prayers were over and the chapter finished, peace reigned between the ruler and the ruled whatever delinquency might be waiting for castigation; and it was only after the last good word of glad tidings had been said that the rod was taken out of the pickle.

On this special Sunday the breakfast was more than usually grave and silent. Respect for the day and the exercises that had to come kept the smouldering fires well under control; though in truth, smouldering everywhere beneath the surface, was fire enough for a general domestic conflagration. Thomasina, who always followed her mother's lead, kept a face as still as marble, a manner as smooth as ice, though conscious that Perdita had offended and would be chastised, and that Eva's secret sin threatened to be troublesome. Eva, all flutter and excitement, was elated yet terrified that Bois-Duval had kept his promise of following her to England, and specially terrified lest Thomasina should betray what she already knew and find out still more that was hidden; while Perdita, haunted by Leslie's voice as one is haunted by music, stirred by the unreal pathos of the play to which her own sincerity had given substance and truth, uneasy at her mother's evident displeasure and knowing that she had to suffer, was in one of those complex moods wherein glory and gloom traverse each other—rose-colour for love and sable for mourning crossing and interlacing in the great web of life. And Mrs. Winstanley herself—disturbed by the advent of Bois-Duval, but, unwilling to plough with that heifer, turning her wrath against her rebel whose misdeeds were as a waste-pipe always at hand for carrying off the overflowings of displeasure—sat at the head of the table like Nemesis in a becoming cap and well-fitting gown, waiting for the moment when she might come up with her victim and grip the offender's shoulder with her well-washed perfumed hand.

It was the dead calm that presages the storm; when the song-birds are silent and only the sensitive aspen-leaves are stirring. And in the Winstanley household when storms were threatened they always came. They might be storms which broke without much noise; all the same they did their work as effectually as those which made more clatter and were more uproarious.

When, therefore, the morning religious exercises were ended, the breakfast things removed, the books returned to their allotted places on the sideboard, the chairs set back against the wall, and the servant had shut the door, then Mrs. Winstanley came up with her culprit, laid her hand on her shoulder and took out the avenging rod.

Perdita was leaving the room as usual. Her intercourse with her family was little more than 'commons' eaten in company and digested apart; and no one resented her withdrawal or wished that she should stay. But to-day, as she was making good her accustomed retreat to her own especial den, her mother stopped her.

"Stay, Perdita," she said; "I wish to speak to you."

Perdita's heart stood still with her feet. Though of late she had gained a little self-control—or fondly fancied that she had—she was perhaps more sensitive to pain, and shrank from her mother's rebukes even more than she used before she had known the peace of respite and the joy of freedom.

"Yes, mother," she said nervously.

Her self-possession vanished. Old habits are strong; and the habit of opposition to, and expectation of rebuke from, her mother was almost as strong with Perdita as that of blushing when she was spoken to and of believing what she was told.

"Who was that creature who came into our box last night?" asked Mrs. Winstanley quietly.

She spoke with perfect calmness of voice and mien, as if she were asking an unimportant question free from all connection or result, while arranging a few lighters in the spillbox on the chimney-piece.

"She is Mrs. Blount," said Perdita.

"And where did you meet this Mrs. Blount, may I ask?" She pronounced the objectionable name as if it stuck to her lips and she had to throw it off by a jerk.

"At the Working Women's Self-Helping Institution," answered Perdita simply.

"My dear Perdita; what have you to do with working women or their institutions? And who in the name of fortune took you to such a place?"

"I went before you left town, mother—quite in the spring—before the flower-show even. You knew that I went, for Miss Cluff asked you to let me go with her. You knew all about it, mother."

What a grand thing to be able to say this! If mother had not objected at the time, then the burden of blame was shifted from those sore, over-loaded little shoulders to the handsome back that was broad enough to bear any amount of wrongdoing.

"I remember—yes; I remember I was foolish enough to allow you to go to some unearthly place one evening when your sisters and I were engaged to the Disneys; but I do not remember your telling me of any acquaintance formed there, still less of an intimacy so unpleasantly familiar as that which was displayed last night. Why did you not tell me of your—imprudence is too mild a term for your foolish conduct, Perdita! You said nothing about this creature in your letters. I can well understand why. You were ashamed."

"I did tell you, mother! I spoke of Mrs. Blount when I wrote to you," remonstrated Perdita.

"As if I could have supposed that a respectable Mrs. Anybody would be such a horror as that!" returned Mrs. Winstanley. "She looks out of her mind, or worse; if there can be anything worse. I do not know when I felt such painful humiliation!—and I hope I may never be exposed to the same thing again. She is unfit for the society of ladies, and it is degrading to be seen with her."

"She dresses oddly, I know, but she is thoroughly good and sterling, and as honest—oh, as honest as the day!" said Perdita with faithful advocacy.

"No sentimentality or heroics, Perdita!" said her mother in a warning voice. "Your phoenix is simply a vulgar oddity, and I forbid your continuing your acquaintance with her. I cannot have a child of mine claimed as an intimate personal friend by such a horror."

"Oh, mother, I cannot give her up! I have no reason! She is very, very good, though she has such queer taste in dress; and she was so kind to me in the summer while you were away! It was then I got to know her so well. It would be too ungrateful in me to give her up only because she dresses badly and looks odd."

Perdita said this with the well-known passionate ring in her deepened voice and the ready tears glistening in her eyes. Those tears betokened no weakening of the joints of her resolution. They sprang rather from the very force of her feeling—which with her was strength.

"You dislike to appear ungrateful, but you have no disinclination to be disobedient and undutiful?" said her mother with smooth severity.

"Mother, you ask so much of me! You want me to give up all that I hold to be true and right—you ask me for my conscience!" said Perdita in the strained and nervous way she had when deeply moved. "You allow me no freedom either of thought or action," she went on to say in increasing agitation. "You want me to be a mere machine. And I cannot give up my soul, even to a mother! What I feel to be right that I must cling to—I must, mother! I must!"

She put her clasped hands before her mouth as if to keep back more than it were well to say, her dilated eyes fixed on her mother, her supple body quivering.

"My dear Perdita, let me beg of you to remember that this is Sunday morning, and that I can have no hysterics before church," said Mrs. Winstanley quite quietly. "And I assure you I want no such awful sacrifice as you speak of. I do not want you to give me up your soul, my poor child, nor your conscience. I should be rather embarrassed with the possession of either. I merely want you to be a young lady like the rest of the world; like your sisters, for instance. Surely no such terrible condemnation!"

"They are your companions and you love them. I am the one shut out," said Perdita passionately. "I have no friends, no companions at home, and yet you object to my making them for myself out of doors. Mother, it is not fair, it is not just, it is not human!"

The flood-gates were lifting in good earnest, and the pent-up torrent was beginning to flow. A very little more and there would be one of those scenes of violence which Perdita had vowed to herself should never occur again, and which she was as powerless to prevent when the occasion arose as she would have been powerless to stop a runaway unbitted horse.

"If you would choose proper and fitting friends no one would be so glad to see you surrounded by good influences as I," said Mrs. Winstanley. "But your foolish ideas lead you into worse than foolish action, and I cannot trust your judgment. This person—this Mrs. Blount, as you call her—is no fit friend for me or my daughters."

"She will not trouble you, mother. She does not ask to come here. She only wants to see me every now and then at her own house," pleaded Perdita.

"You are my daughter and your actions implicate me as your mother," returned Mrs. Winstanley. "You cannot make acquaintances on your own responsibility as if you did not belong to us. A family must hang together; and what you do touches us all."

And in this she spoke sensibly enough.

"Am I to have no friends then!" cried Perdita in the accent of one wrecked and desperate.

"It is your own fault if you do not find your friends in your mother and sisters, and your companions in those whom they make their own," said Mrs. Winstanley. "Besides, you have one already—a very true and sincere friend—Mr. Brocklebank."

As she said this she turned her eyes suddenly on her daughter and looked at her with a keen, sharp, penetrating glance.

"Yes, he is very very good to me," said Perdita with exasperating affectionateness not betraying the faintest special agitation; "but he is not my friend as a woman would be. I could not talk to him as to Mrs. Blount or—" She was on the point of adding, "Mrs. Crawford" but checked herself in time.

"Still, he is your special friend and is sincerely interested in you," repeated Mrs. Winstanley. "He has helped you in this Savings-bank business against my wishes as you know; and therefore you owe him some gratitude. And evidently he does not approve of your Mrs. Blount."

"He would if he knew her; that is, if he is as good as I believe him to be," said Perdita hardily. "He might not agree with all her opinions, but he would respect her; and he would soon get over her appearance. Mr. Brocklebank is just the kind of person to like her, because he cares more for things as they are than as they seem to be."

"You are hopeless!" said Mrs. Winstanley, turning away. "It is simple waste of time to reason with you! But understand me clearly, Perdita," she added, turning back and facing her rebel; "I positively forbid your further acquaintance with this woman, and if you disobey me I will write to her myself and tell her so."

"Mother! No! Surely you will never do anything so cruel!" cried Perdita. "Poor Bell Blount, who has done nothing to offend you—who is so good and true—and who has been so kind to me! You could not be so unjust. Oh, mother, how can you say such a thing!"

"You hear me, Perdita?" repeated the mother slowly, as if it were a lesson to be learnt by heart. "If you continue your acquaintance with this person, against my command, I will write to her forbidding it;— and I will write such a letter as she will not soon forget. If you wish to spare your friend this humiliation," sarcastically, "drop her on your own account. It will be safest. Now silence! say no more. This is Sunday morning."

Whereon, to make sure of that Dominical calmness which was part of her good-breeding, and which, by the look of Perdita's face and attitude, was more than problematical if this interview were continued, Mrs. Winstanley beat her own retreat, and left the rebel standing about two feet from the hearth-rug, her flushed face bent downward, her eyes full of indignant tears, her lips quivering with grief and passion together, and her soul driven about in a very whirlwind of despair.

Thomasina had been sitting by the little side-table writing a letter during the whole of this painful interview. She had taken no part in it, thinking it better to let the two concerned have it out between them without interference from without. But she was sorry. She knew of course that Perdita was very rebellious, very tiresome, very irritating, yet she was anxious to spare her more sorrow if she could. Knowing what she did of Eva, whose colours were always fresh and flying, and suspecting she scarcely dared to say what, Perdita's chronic misbehaviour from silly Quixotism rather than intentional naughtiness, somehow seemed less reprehensible than in general; and she thought there had been enough 'discipline' on account of Bell Blount—with M. le Vicomte de Bois-Duval spoken to humanely and even invited to the house! Also she thought that probably Perdita was softened to the point when good counsel would prevail, and that if spoken to now, reasonably and kindly, she might yield and be led aright.

She got up from her writing and came to where her sister was standing, her poor wild soul tossed and driven in the tumultuous maelstrom of passion and despair.

"Now take my advice, Perdita," she said, speaking more tenderly than that ostracized rebel ever remembered to have been spoken to by her; "do not make a trouble between yourself and mother because of this woman, whoever she may be. Give her up without any more fuss, like a dear, good girl. It is your best wisdom, believe me!"

"But not my best morality!" said Perdita, with a sob for the one part, and a loving look at her queenly sister for the other.

Thomasina looked at her as compassionately as if she had been a suicidal lunatic. Penetrated through and through with the doctrine of social expediency, she was of the class which holds conscience as a luxury lawful only to the prosperous who want nothing from the world. For those in the fight it is an impediment, a folly, and a sin.

"I do not see what morality has to do with it," she said. "If anything, I should say it was in doing as mother wishes. This new woman cannot be so near to you surely as your own mother!"

"No, she is not so near to me, but she likes me far better than my own mother does," said Perdita, imprudent and sincere as usual.

Thomasina let the foolish words pass unheeded. She was not in the mood to embitter or entangle; she only wanted to make things smoother and softer.

"Besides," continued Perdita, "if mother had any real reason for her dislike, I should not say a word. But I do not think it a reason for hurting the feelings of a good woman who likes me and has been very kind to me, that she dresses showily and looks queer."

"It is not your place to ask or argue on mother's reasons," said Thomasina, mildly but firmly; "all that you have to do is to obey her."

"I cannot, Thomasina! I cannot do what I think to be wrong, even for mother. God is highest!" said Perdita with solemn warmth.

"You take things so tremendously in earnest, Perdita!" said her sister, a slight smile crossing her face. "There is no such high and mighty principle involved in this matter as you make out. You know a woman whom mother does not like and whose acquaintance she wants you to give up—and you talk of God and your conscience! Why, there would be no living if we all went on like this! It is breaking a butterfly on the wheel, child!—nothing less. How can you be so silly, Perdita!"

She spoke with temperate and patient sarcasm; not acid, but smiling, half-playful, remonstrating rather than contemptuous.

"Thomasina, dear, I cannot be different from what I am!" said poor Perdita, turning to her sister with sudden meekness but always in such terrible earnest! "I cannot see things as you do or think that it is of no importance whether we do right or wrong. I think it right to stick to friends who have been kind to me, and wrong to desert them without good cause and only because of some stupid little worldly reason, which is none at all! How can I help myself? how can I do what I feel to be base and cowardly?"

"Well! I am sorry. You are all wrong, and will not let yourself be put right," said Thomasina with a quiet little sigh. "It seems to me just insanity to make a principle of everything, and to see a crime in giving up the acquaintance of an odd-looking woman whom mother does not like. But you must do as you like, of course. I only thought it right to speak to you and do what I could to help you with mother. But no one has any influence over you, Perdita;—you are so awfully self-willed!"

"It is not self-will, Thomasina. It is not because I like to do so and so, but because I think it right or wrong," she reiterated.

"Well, let it drop now. I am sorry; for I dislike all these family quarrels so much, and I know that mother means to be firm about this woman. And if you were only a little tractable and more like other people, there would never be a disagreeable word among us. Eva and I never have a moment's unpleasantness with mother from one end of the year to the other; and not a week goes by without some horrible jar between you and her."

"But is it always my fault?" pleaded her sister.

"Always," said Thomasina steadily; "always your fault, Perdita. You do not consider other people enough—you think only of yourself. For instance, there is Mr. Brocklebank who is so good to you—when do you think of him?"

Thomasina spoke with quiet deliberation and, as her mother before her, watched her sister's face narrowly. But that face, usually so sensitive, told nothing. No blush came on it at the mention of the ironmaster's name, for no chord was struck in her heart to vibrate into consciousness.

"I do very often think of him," she said, astonished at the accusation. "I like Mr. Brocklebank very much indeed. I am sure I ought, for he has been very good to me; but what has that to do with Mrs. Blount?"

"What? Everything; because he would tell you to do as mother says—to give her up if mother wishes it."

"But if I do not think it right to do this for mother, how should I for him?" asked Perdita gravely.

"Yet he likes you the best of us all," replied Thomasina, throwing her fly.

"No, he likes you," answered her sister, rejecting it in all simplicity and good faith.

"Not at all—he likes you by far the best, Perdita! I dare say he will tell you so himself some day. Is that the church bell? We have no time to spare," she added hurriedly, as her sister was about to speak. "We must make haste, else we shall be late."

On which they both went upstairs to dress; and soon after the Winstanley family set out for church with the discreetest and quietest air in the world, as if halcyon days were as real at No. 100 as they seemed to be, and the moral sunshine there knew no break. And when they were in church, the prayers and hymns went to poor Perdita's heart as they had never done before; and though the sermon was nothing but dry bones, she lent it the pathos of her own suffering, and wept over platitudes which left the bulk of the congregation untouched, save that the phlegmatic yawned and the nervous fidgeted. But both prayers and sermon only strengthened her in her feeling of doing what was right, irrespective of consequences or conditions.

As they were coming out, a little check in the earlier-moving part of the congregation brought them all in a closely-packed mass at the door; and there, touching shoulders with Mrs. Winstanley, stood Leslie Crawford and his mother.

A quick flush crossed Leslie's face, and Mrs. Crawford smiled a pale watery kind of smile as she looked at Perdita; but they would have passed on without other recognition than that plaintive smile from her, and from him the raising of his hat, had not Perdita herself spoken to him. In truth, she would have been glad under present conditions to have let them pass without a closer greeting, but that troublesome conscience of hers said that this would be cowardly, mean, base, ungrateful; and if it were against her principles to be less than true to her intellectual convictions, so much the more was it to be less than loyal to her friends.

"How do you do?" she said, and held out her hand to each.

Her face was crimson and she really suffered. She felt as if he carried "Chemist in High Street" printed in one huge label from his hat to his boots; and that every one could read in her face what they had been talking of together last night. Still, she was nothing if not sincere to her faith and true to her friends; and right or wrong, she must do what she felt to be the best thing.

"Is little Lily better, Mrs. Crawford?" she asked with interest; and on the elder woman answering: "Yes, thank you, the feverish attack has passed," Perdita looked bright and said: "I am glad!" with real feeling in her voice.

"Perdita, who are those people to whom you spoke at the church-door?" asked Mrs. Winstanley with disdainful emphasis when they had got clear of the crowd.

Her quick eyes had discovered that they were not inheritors of the purple, ragged or otherwise—that Mrs. Crawford, sweet and gentle as she was, well-dressed too in her own quiet quakerish way, was without that untranslatable chic which is like a masonic sign to the initiated, and that, although Leslie was a handsome well-grown man with a fine face and a good address, he too failed in his shibboleth and could not spell his abracadabra as he ought.

"Who are they?" she repeated with an indescribable accent of superior curiosity.

"Mrs. Crawford and her son," answered Perdita.

"Yes? and then? Who are Mrs. Crawford and her son?"

"He is the chemist in High Street, where I was taken ill. I wrote and told you about it," said Perdita, trying to look indifferent, and failing.

"And you have become on intimate terms with them?"

"I go to see them sometimes," she answered.

"You visit them in private? shake hands with them in public?" said Mrs. Winstanley, speaking very slowly and distinctly, every word set clear from its neighbour.

"Yes; why not, mother?" answered Perdita. "Mrs. Crawford is delightful in every way, and so is he," she added with an effort that was really heroic. But as she spoke her face was overspread with that treacherous blood which forever betrayed her so cruelly, and her voice was a trifle husky.

"You have sunk yourself so low as this? You make a personal friend of a man who sells drugs and stands behind a counter?—of a man who keeps a shop? Perdita! are you really my own daughter?"

"Why not, mother?" she answered, rising to the necessities of her position. "I have put myself on the same level with good, generous, well-conducted people who know far more than I do and who are far better than I am—people who are as refined as we are, and who are as good as anything in the world can be. I do not call it sinking, mother. In reality it is honouring and raising myself."

By this time they had reached their own door. Mrs. Winstanley rang the bell, standing on the top step. She turned round and looked at Perdita who was on the pavement. The extra vantage of those three steps seemed to give her a corresponding increase of moral power; but Perdita by this time had brought out her flag and was in the full swing of faithful adherence even unto martyrdom and death. Of what good all her prayers and tears in church just now, if she could not remain firm under trial?

"Understand me, my dear," said Mrs. Winstanley, calm, scornful, inflexible. "You make your choice—your mother, your sisters, your home, or these new people whom you have taken up in our absence. You cannot have both. If you continue to live with me you must conform to my manner of life and content yourself with my friends. That creature of last night and these persons of to-day are inadmissible. I am sure I need not recur to the subject again."

As she said this the door was opened and they all went into the house, Mrs. Winstanley rather proud of the firmness with which she had put down the latest of her daughter's objectionable follies, and Perdita flung again as so often before into a passionate tumult of alternatives—forbidden to lead her own life and unable to accept that allowed her, and in the agonies of choice between obedience to her mother or adherence to the dictates of her own conscience.

Mrs. Winstanley was spared all trouble of this kind. With her there was no doubt as to the right thing to do. Her duty was clear, her line single. Perdita was wrong from first to last; morally, conventionally, as a daughter and a lady alike; and it was her own bounden duty, as the mother of the family, to crush this foolish rebellion from the outset and to protect her other children by preventing the wicked vagaries of this troublesome and unsatisfactory mutineer. It was not a pleasant task—but then duty is seldom pleasant; and this was duty.

As for poor Perdita, all that afternoon she sat upstairs in her own bleak room and wept and prayed—but came no nearer to a conclusion than if she had dismissed the subject from her mind and let things drift of themselves. She could not make up her mind to disobey her mother's express command, yet she could not do what she felt to be wrong and give up those dear friends who had been so good to her. Her heart failed her when she thought that she must never see Leslie again—he who represented to her all moral nobleness and manly worth! never have the joy of feeling that she had a friend in him, a mother in his mother, nor know again the calm and refreshment of a visit to those quiet rooms above the shop. And yet again, was she prepared to give up her own home for the sake of theirs? to cut herself off from the family that she might continue to know Bell Blount and the Crawfords?

She could not understand why she should be marked out for this perpetual rack of heart and torment of mind. She was conscious only of a desire to do the right thing—to live by principle and her own conscience. She did not wish to hurt any human being or to be other than faithful and true, loving and loyal. She was wicked, she knew, because she was passionate and violent and without self-command, but was she quite so wicked as mother said? Her life was one long day of trouble, confusion, unrest, perplexity. She was the pariah of the family, and, save for these dear friends whom now she had to give up, utterly unloved and alone. What was she to do? How could she go to them and say to the one: "Mother will not let me know you because you are tradespeople and keep a shop;"—to the other: "Because you dress in scarlet satin and wear your white hair in a cascade of girlish ringlets down your back?" How could she confess to them that nothing scored honours in the Winstanley game of life but dead forms and flimsy conventionalities? and that she, Perdita, the democrat, the seeker after truth, the believer in realities, was weak enough to follow the same bad lead? It was impossible! And yet—could she leave home and cast herself adrift on the world like a mere adventuress? What a dreadful alternative! what a terrible position!

So the day passed; and when evening came she was no nearer to the solution of her difficulties than she had been at noon. All that she had gained was a face so swollen by tears as to be horribly disfigured, and a head that ached as if it would ache itself into a dozen different pieces.

CHAPTER XXVI.

UNCERTAIN AND PERPLEXED.

WITH the moral strength of her convictions Perdita had also the emotional weakness of her affections, and the two were forever in collision. Hers was one of those composite and iridescent characters wherein each person affirms a different substance and sees an opposing colour. To some she was simply a fierce, ill-regulated, unfeminine kind of creature, whose misdeeds went beyond the limits of eccentricity and who needed a sound application of the chastising rod if she were to be made into a decent Christian like the rest of us; to others she was soft to want of self-respect, sensitive to an infirmity, her pity exaggerated to a vice, her sympathy to folly, her imagination to insanity, her conscientiousness to absurdity. Some saw her as hard, stiff-necked, unyielding; others as plastic, affectionate and eminently manageable. But her qualities were so strangely intermixed that no one was right and no one was wrong. It was as if this tract of fruitful mould suddenly ended in a barrier of granite, that marble quarry tailed off into a field of sand—as if here the fierce lines of red flowed into a wash of lucent gold, there the blue of heaven deepened into flaming orange. No one could hold her entirely nor bend her to the point beyond her own limit of right. When her love and her conscience came into collision, as they did so often, her conscience won but her love did not diminish; and when pity and truth were at cross-corners, she would tell the truth but break her heart over the pain she felt herself bound to inflict. Yet the one whom she loved would have counted on the victory as a foregone conclusion based on the strength of her affections; and the creature whom she wounded would wonder how it was that she had not strained a point for pity's sake, as any other tender-hearted woman would have done.

Still, with all this moral firmness, having as was said the weakness of her affections, she suffered as only those suffer whose hearts are torn by conflicting loves and discordant principles of action.

In this moment of trial there was no one to give her comfort. Bell Blount ignored the inherent modesties of her sex and blasphemed both the natural ties of home and all the sweet instincts of her womanhood. Mrs. Crawford ignored all need of mental freedom and condemned a woman's desire for any kind of life outside the narrow limits of domestic duties. And Benjamin Brocklebank, her special friend and patron, could no more sympathize with her present trouble than he could with her mother's when she objected to work as unladylike and to bread-winning as degrading.

Where could she go for advice and counsel? for confidential talk and wise monition? Scarcely, in this case, to the one to whom she would naturally have turned! She could not go to Leslie Crawford and ask him what she was to do. Her mother had forbidden her to go to his house, for no nobler reason than because he kept a shop and lived over it; and which then was her duty—obedience to that mother, or fidelity to him?

Yet, pressed by the need of human sympathy, she opened so much of her heart to Mary Chesterton as could be seen in a hypothetical case, put cautiously and without details, wherein a mother's commands clashed with a daughter's conscience; and she ended by asking what Miss Chesterton thought of such a position, and what would she do were she placed in it?

To which Mary looked with her clear, untroubled eyes full into Perdita's tortured face and said quietly:

"I can hardly understand the difficulty, Miss Winstanley. There can be no two questions about it. Of course a daughter ought to obey her mother. Why! how preposterous! Surely no girl could hesitate for a moment about that!"

So Perdita got no satisfaction here, and the composite nature was so far checkmated by the more simple.

As she was walking home from the office, her heart sad and her head heavy, she met Bell Blount streaming like a flamingo down the sunny side of Oxford Street, up which she was passing in such deep melancholy.

"The Philistines have been upon you!" cried Bell, taking the girl's hot hands in hers. "What have they been doing to you, my honey?"

Perdita tried to smile, but tears came instead.

"Oh! I say, this will never do!" cried Bell, turning back with her favourite and drawing her hand within her arm. "I am not going to stand your being bullied; that I can tell them! So just you open your heart, for I can see that something has gone wrong."

"It is only my own silly temper," said Perdita, with a little sobbing breath that seemed more eloquent of pain than perversity.

"Tut! Don't talk rubbish to me, my dear. You have been worried and trampled on and ill-treated. I can see that plainly enough; and before we part you shall have made a clean breast of it." She hailed a passing hansom. "Jump in!" she said to Perdita; "Prince Christian's Road," she shouted to the cabman. "Now we will have a quiet talk," she went on to say to the girl when they were settled in the cab. "My little wife is not at home, and we shall have an hour to ourselves."

So here was Perdita, forbidden by her mother to continue her acquaintance with Bell Blount, flourishing up Oxford Street in a hansom with her in the light of day, on her way to the house which she had been commanded never to enter again!

When they reached that queer, untidy, hybrid kind of place, Bell repeated her question.

"What is it, honey?" she asked, placing Perdita in an easy-chair, while she sat on the arm and lighted a cigarette. "Come! a clean breast and no reservations!"

Perdita looked down sorely troubled. Sensitive and softhearted, it was a dreadful punishment to her to have to say anything that might offend any one; but to hurt the feelings of a friend who had been ever good and kind to her, for no other reason than the most stupid conventional objection, was simply anguish. Still, she must be frank. It was the thing laid on her to do; but the trial was hard, the cup very bitter.

"I will tell you, Bell," she said, looking up and speaking with that earnest, half-caressing accent of self-abandonment which was one of her characteristics. "My mother forbids me to know you and the Crawfords."

"The Crawfords? That chemist fellow?" said Bell disdainfully. "There, my dear, your mother is right. Those Crawfords are no fit companions for you. You are a little lady and they are only tradespeople. I longed to tell you so when you threw me over at the meeting for that pretentious pedant, that long-backed Leslie, whom I remember as a gangrel gawky with his sleeves half-way up his arms. But I reflected in time. I thought it was no business of mine, and I was not called on to interfere. If you had bad taste enough to like them, you must go through with it, I said to myself. I could afford to wait," she added with an odd look. "Still, your mother is right, honey," she went on to say after a little pause which Perdita had not broken. "You ought not to make friends out of your class. We must respect social degrees as we find them. It is such a mistake when people push a wholesome principle into an absurdity; and the Emancipation of Woman does not include democratic equality or communistic mismash in any form. I have always steadily set my face against such wild ideas; and so must you."

"No," answered Perdita; "that is just what I cannot do, Bell! Men and women are men and women to me, not gentlemen and ladies on the one side and the common people on the other. And it is just as great a pain to me to have to give up the Crawfords, though they are tradespeople, as it would be if they were a duke and duchess. And greater," she added simply, "for I should never feel at home with a duke and duchess, and I do with them."

"I am sorry for it," said Bell gravely. "If you knew all about them perhaps you would not. No, my honey, you are wrong here and your mother is right. You must give them up."

"And you too, Bell?" asked Perdita, without a trace of sarcasm.

"No, that is another matter altogether," answered the Champion of her Sex with perfect good faith. "You are not to give me up—because your mother's objections to me are founded only on ignorance and prejudice. I represent a principle; and you must stick to your principles, my dear, whatever it costs you."

"That is just what I feel about the Crawfords," said Perdita.

"Then that is just what you should not feel about the Crawfords," returned her friend with calm decision. "That is all nonsense, Perdita! Sticking to me as your best friend and the Leader of your Cause—yes, yours; so don't look at me like that!—is a very different thing from keeping up an acquaintance you ought never to have made, with people not in your own sphere of life and who do not even belong to the good Cause."

"I do not think mother will see the difference," said Perdita, still unconscious of irony.

"Then she must be made," returned Bell Blount. "I will come and talk to her. If she has any reasoning faculty at all I shall probably be able to touch it. If she has not—" she shrugged her shoulders with a contemptuous, half-pitying air.

"I do not think you will stir her," said Perdita.

"Never say die, honey," returned Bell. "This dear little soul of yours is worth a few cold looks and even hard knocks to try and save," she added, putting her hand under the girl's chin and turning up her face which then she kissed.

"You are very very good, Bell, but indeed I think you had better not come to our house! Mother is not to be moved by any reasoning whatever. You do not know her, and she will only be so angry!"

"With me or you?"

"With both."

"For myself I do not care a button whether she is angry or not," said Bell; "and if she is too hard on you—you know your remedy. Leave home and come to us."

"That is just what mother herself says," answered Perdita. "She has given me my choice to give up you and the Crawfords or to leave home."

"Say you so?" cried Bell. "Bravo! That is all I want. Your course is clear, your duty as plain as those railings before us. You just take and pack up your things, honey, and come off to us. Connie will be as good as gold to you. I will be better than gold. Miss Long will do all she can for you; and you will be as happy as the day is long. It is just the thing I have been wanting and waiting for—just the occasion. So now Providence has smoothed the way for you and shown you the path. Glory! what a chance!"

But her jubilant enthusiasm fell flat on Perdita. This path, whether smoothed by Providence or not, was one which her feet refused to tread—the choice between her home and her friends that which she had no desire to make.

"I do not suppose you can hesitate," said Bell with a surprised little air and speaking slowly.

"Oh, Bell! not hesitate! Think what an awful thing it is for a girl to break with her own family! I know that mother is wrong in wanting me to make this sacrifice; but to disobey her so completely?—to leave them all and cut myself adrift? no! no! that is not a thing to be done lightly!"

"Not lightly, but firmly," said Bell in a deep voice. "The alternative is forced on you; you did not seek it. All you have to do is to choose and then hold fast. You cannot blow hot and cold together. You must be one thing or the other. To go so far and then turn back—to shilly-shally and let 'I dare not' wait upon 'I would'![1]—neither doing nor refraining—that is a weakness unworthy of you! Take your line and stick to it; but if you give up me and the cause of woman's freedom—the holiest cause in the world—you are not the girl I took you for, and I shall be sorry I wasted a moment's thought or care on you!"

"You do not know what it is to have to make such a choice," said Perdita, despairing of ever being understood.

"I do not? I? I not know what it is to have to make such a choice?" echoed Bell Blount with a raised voice. "I, who gave up husband and home and station and children for the good cause? I, who destroyed my household gods and went out into the wilderness that I might free my sex from their persecutors and bring them into the light of day? What

---

[1] Refers to Lady Macbeth's speech (*Macbeth* I:7) in which she urges her husband to murder Duncan, rather than "Letting 'I dare not' wait upon 'I would,' / Like the poor cat i' the adage." The adage is: "The cat would eat fish, but would not wet her feet."

nonsense you are talking, Perdita! If ever woman sacrificed herself for humanity and principle it is I, Arabella Blount!"

"But was it a sacrifice?" asked honest Perdita. "You are happier as you are. You love Connie Tracy better than any one in the world. You have often told me so, and how you bless the day when you had the courage to leave your home."

Bell Blount's eyes flamed with sudden wrath.

"I did not expect this scoff from you!" she said vehemently. "I who have taken you to my heart and who have hoped great things for you—I scarcely expected that you would have turned against me like this!"

"I did not turn against you!" cried Perdita, aghast. "I did not mean to be rude or scoffing, Bell; I only meant that your trial was not so hard as mine because you did not care so much. I meant that—no more, dear."

"You are unjust," said Bell, rising from her seat. "You always are unjust to women. You care too much for men to see things as they are. I foresee your destruction through these dangerous, disloyal, unwomanly tendencies," she added with a peculiar kind of snort, the sign with her of extreme displeasure. "Some day you will go to the dogs and I shall find you there."

"I do not think this is quite fair; and what has it to do with the matter whether I like men or women the best? In point of fact I like women," said Perdita, feeling as if another stone had been cast against her and another wound inflicted.

"Pshaw!" said Bell. "You don't know what you are saying. You like men ever so much better than your own holy sex. And if you did not you would not hesitate now."

"Why? What do you mean?" cried Perdita, trembling she scarcely know why. There was something in the very inconsequence and vagueness of the accusation that half frightened her.

Bell Blount turned and caught her to her breast.

"Oh, Perdita!" she cried with strange emotion. "Throw off this degrading instinct, this shameful soul-destroying inclination! See things as they are—see and acknowledge that men are our tyrants, maternity our curse, love our destruction—and devote yourself body and soul and life to the holiest Cause now on earth, the cause before which all the rest sink into insignificance. Leave that prison which you call your home, and come to me, your truest friend and safest love![1] With me your life will be happy and honourable, with any one else it will be ruined!"

---

[1]   "Love" only in first Chatto & Windus edition; "lover" in all subsequent editions.

Her passionate emotion gained on the girl so far that she returned her caress with gratitude and affection.

"If I do leave home at all, Bell, I will come to you," she said.

"Strike hands on it!" cried Bell, holding her still tightly clasped. But she started back and withdrew herself as suddenly as if Perdita had been a burning coal when the door softly opened and sharp-faced, mouse-like Connie stole noiselessly into the room.

"Congratulate me, congratulate yourself and her, my Con!" said Bell after a moment's quick breath and something more like an abashed silence and the look of having been "caught," than one would have expected from the Champion of her Sex. "Her people have put on the screw a little too tight this time, and the dear creature will break through it all and will come to us!"

"Grand news!" said Constance with a sickly smile and a nervous quiver of her eyelids. "And when will she come?"

"Ay! when?" repeated Bell, who by this time had regained her usual smooth self-possession.

"I do not know. I must see what they mean to do at home," answered Perdita, shrinking back, feeling as if she were being forcibly thrust into deep waters which gave no foothold, and which she could not breast if once in them.

"Whatever they may do, your way is clear and your promise given," repeated Bell, her face all aflame. "Liberty—you want liberty, sympathy, your rights—here you shall have them all. I cannot believe you will be so mad as to refuse the chance."

"No, not if I am pushed to it," said Perdita; but there was no ring of pleasure in her voice and her big eyes grew dark and humid as she spoke. "And now I must go," she said nervously. "I have been here too long, and I shall get scolded if am late."

"It is before you to have a life where you never will be scolded," said Bell.

Perdita smiled faintly and without any heart or vitality in her smile; but Bell kissed her fondly, and led her to the door with extreme consideration; saying "À bientôt!" as she left, and kissing her hand to her from the door-step.

"You are throwing yourself away on her, Bell!" said Connie as soon as Perdita had gone. "She will never be one of us. She is in love!"

"God bless my heart and soul, Con!" cried Bell with a start. "In love, you little owl!—how can she be in love? And with whom, pray, Mrs. Wisdom?" contemptuously.

"Leslie Crawford," said Connie tranquilly.

"Oh, I say, this is too strong!—Leslie Crawford? a married man? Oh, come! drop that, Con! That is slander."

"She is," said Constance. "I saw it at the Hall that night as plainly as I ever saw anything in my life; and that explains why she does not jump at such an offer as yours."

"Yes," said Bell, as if suddenly enlightened, tapping her front teeth with her thumb-nail; "that would, as you say, explain everything. I'll see to the bottom of this, Con, and if I find that it is so, I'll denounce her to her mother. May I never see to-morrow if I do not. But for the present, little woman, excuse me if I hesitate and take the liberty to doubt."

"You will find I am right," said Constance with a certain prim tenacity for which she was famous. "I can see through things of this kind at a glance."

It was quite dusk when Perdita reached home. Her meeting with Bell Blount had cost her an hour's valuable time, exposed her to suspicion, to the certainty of cross-examination and the consequent certainty of rebuke; and had done no real good. For she had by no means resolved on leaving home without making another effort to induce her mother to let her live her own life and keep her own friends; and, certainly, if she had to leave for the one part on account of Bell, she would not give up the Crawfords. It was all a dreadful confusion, and she was miserably sorry. But then she always was sorry about something, and it seemed as if she would never be anything else. Life to her was a cleft stick; and she knew no power by which to free herself.

Thinking of her difficulties and seeing no issue, she walked rapidly homewards, coming to the house at the same moment as the postman. He had a letter in his hand.

"I will take it for you," said Perdita good-naturedly, to save him the trouble of the delivery.

"Thank you, miss," he answered, giving it to her and passing on.

It was for Eva; and as Perdita went up the steps, conning the address as was natural, the dining-room blind moved and Eva's face which had been pressed against the window was withdrawn. Immediately after the door was opened by Eva herself—the first time in her life that the child had ever shown so much grace to "funny old Per."

"Oh, Eva, here is a letter for you," said the unconscious blunderer as she came into the hall. "I took it from the postman. What an odd mincing little handwriting!"

"Give it to me, and don't scream so!" said Eva impatiently as to spirit, softly as to volume and tone. "What a voice you have, Perdita! It is like a bellman's!" she added, as she took the letter from her sister and ran up-stairs with her hand in the pocket of her dress and the paper crushed between her fingers. "What a nuisance that Perdita is!" she thought to herself, grinding her pretty little teeth with rage. "She is always getting in the way. Fancy her coming up just as the postman came and taking this letter! I dare not tell her to hold her tongue; and she is such a great stupid thing, she is as likely as not to say something about it to mother or Thomasina. How I wish she would go away! It would be far jollier without her."

By the time she had formed all these thoughts in her head, her feet had carried her to her own room, where, locking herself in, she lighted the gas and sat down to her perilous pleasure—the letter which Bois-Duval had told her in his little note of Saturday night to look out for by the six o'clock post on Monday. It was a rash thing to do; and she was half angry that he had exposed her to such a danger! but as no harm had come of it, she could afford to forgive him and revel undisturbed in the delight of his delicious flatteries.

If Thomasina could have divined that at this moment her little sister was reading an impassioned prayer from Bois-Duval to meet him to-morrow afternoon in Kensington Gardens, by the sixth tree on the left-hand side of the Broad Walk! But as stone walls have no tongues and the sharpest eyes cannot look through deal doors, there was no chance of discovery if only that stupid old Per would hold her tongue.

In the hope that Perdita would be too dull and silent to chatter—and if Eva could prevent untimely words by her own abounding flow she would—the little one put in a few extra touches, which made her look supremely lovely, and which she knew would predispose Mumsey to any extent in her favour. All through dinner she was as sweet as any nightingale singing among the roses; delightfully caressing to her mother; prettily submissive to Ina; even humane and forbearing to that funny old Per who was as downcast as she was excited—downcast, so that she was like a death's head at the table, as Mrs. Winstanley said to Thomasina fretfully.

The direct consequence however, of Eva's extraordinary animation was, so far as Thomasina was concerned, to make her watch her little sister quietly from under those finely-drawn level brows of hers, asking herself: "What does it mean? and what naughtiness has she been doing or is she going to do?"

By which she proved that elder sisters are clear-sighted when mothers are sometimes blind; and that extreme amiability may be an indiscretion where concealment is more necessary than admiration.

Still, the evening passed away without any mishap; and Eva with her gaiety, Perdita with her sadness, worked through the hours that lay between dinner and bedtime without anything said that should betray the secret thoughts of either. As they were taking their candles and wishing each other good-night, Mrs. Winstanley hesitated for a moment whether she should speak to Perdita and ask if she had obeyed her commands or no; but, finally, she determined to leave things alone till something should happen to which she could not shut her eyes; and with Perdita's uncomfortable nature the mother felt very sure that she would not have to wait long. Meanwhile her debts were pressing and she had grave reasons for dreading the near future.

CHAPTER XXVII.

IN THE DAY OF TROUBLE.

THEY were all in it; the butcher, the baker, the candlestick-maker; every tradesman of every denomination; they were on her like so many hounds slipped from the leash, and no one held aloof from pity because she was a widow with three daughters to marry, or for respect because she was a lady and had inherited the purple. On the contrary, these vulgar persons held the interests of their own families before those of their handsome, well-dressed, soft-spoken debtor; and they said, in their rude way, that if she could not pay she ought not to buy; that, cutting a coat according to the cloth being one of the elemental moralities of a commercial society, if she had not enough for a cloak she could content herself with a jacket; and that if she could not be fine and honest too, she ought to be simple and let finery go to the deuce. They had to pay for what they had, they said; and by—a great many strange gods; but then they were only vulgar tradespeople—she should be made to pay too.

It was the day of reckoning, and she was without means to meet the score. Her debts had closed round her like a net; and she looked in vain for the mouse which should gnaw the cord and deliver her from its toils.

As a rule she kept her troubles to herself; but to-day she did not feel able to bear unassisted such a heavy burden as she was dragging on her well-dressed back; so she took Thomasina into her confidence and laid the whole state of things before her.

If any one could help her, it was this wise eldest daughter who never seemed to be overcome nor frightened nor to lose her presence of mind nor to be swept away by passion of any kind; but who was always serviceable and quiet and strong in one.

"It is but right that you should know the truth, my dear," said Mrs. Winstanley, when she had finished her uncomfortable story. "You are no longer a child: and I pay your good sense a compliment in taking you into my confidence."

"Yes, mother," answered Thomasina. "It is very good of you to associate me with your troubles. I would rather know the exact state of things than not. We can then talk more freely together and discuss the best plan for getting out of our difficulties."

"If any one can hit upon a good way, it will be you, Thomasina," said her mother. After a pause she asked, as if it were a thought that had just occurred to her: "How would it do to ask Mr. Brocklebank for a loan? He owes me something on account of Perdita," bitterly.

"I will manage Mr. Brocklebank," answered Thomasina, also after a pause. "He will come here to-day, and I will see him alone; unless you object, dear mother?"

Mrs. Winstanley held out her hand, tears were in her eyes.

"God bless you, my dear girl!" she said. "You are the best daughter that ever mother had!"

"Thank you, dear mother," said Thomasina, flinging her arms round her mother's neck with what was for her a strange outburst of feeling. "I love no one in the world as I love you; and I would give up everything, do anything that I possibly could, to give you pleasure or spare you anxiety. I care more for your happiness than for anything else in life!"

Mrs. Winstanley sighed.

"If only your poor sister Perdita were as wise and satisfactory!" she said with genuine regret. "If she, like you, had put her intellect into learning life as it is, instead of letting herself go headlong into all her wicked follies, what a comfort to us she might have been! As things are I cannot trust her. If she had the most brilliant opening made for her, the most glorious position offered to her, I doubt her acceptance of it—she is so wrong-headed, so intensely obstinate and wrong-headed!" she added with impatience, thinking of Mr. Brocklebank, of his strange hesitation among the three, and of Perdita's chances, quite as good as Thomasina's, but so impossible to be calculated on because of that stubborn and reprehensible eccentricity.

"Yes," said Thomasina; "if she had chosen the line of social cleverness she would have made a grand success. It was a thousand pities that she did not see this. She is very good, very much in earnest; but of course by her opinions and all that, she has cut the ground from under her own feet and hindered herself from being of any use to the rest of us."

And she too sighed in concert with her mother; but as neither sighing nor regrets could make a better job of the rebel than she had chosen to make of herself, they let the uncongenial subject drop, and Thomasina went upstairs to think out her plan of action alone.

Things looked black enough. All the well-laid schemes had gone agley;[1] and of the compact-looking web of future possibilities only one disastrous and one uncertain strand remained. The marriage of Hubert Strangways was now publicly announced for the first week in November; Sir James Kearney was in Paris—so was Mrs. Merton; Benjamin Brocklebank was always the huge, heavy humming-bird, ever poising and never settling; and that dreadful Bois-Duval was in London for no good! For whatever cause he had come, Thomasina knew it was for no good! Mother had not included him in the list of her worries, but she, Thomasina, had thought about him ever since Saturday night when they had met him at the theatre; and Eva's prettiness and gayety last evening had set her thinking still more. And then those dreadful debts! What an awful position for poor darling mother, who did all she could for them! It was only for them, and to get them well married, that she had got into her present difficulties; and of course it was their duty to do all they could for her in return. What they ought to do was to reward her by marrying well; and for her own part the Winstanley eldest was quite prepared to do her duty in that way. But the chance seemed rather remote at the present moment; and thinking of husbands in the clouds would not help mother out of her difficulties, with her angry creditors at the door. How these were to be staved off or satisfied was the question of the hour, and one which had to be solved at any cost.

Thomasina matured her plans. She prepared the statement that she intended to make to Mr. Brocklebank, and the discourse that she would hold with him as well as she could without the interlocutor to take up her cues. Then she dressed herself afresh, with extra care and supreme refinement, and did not even disdain artful little touches of pink and white and black where she thought they would tell and would not be revealed; after which she placed herself in the most favorable spot

---

[1] Refers to "To A Mouse" by Robert Burns (1759–96): "The best laid schemes o' mice and men / Gang aft a-gley."

of the pleasantly subdued drawing-room—waiting until the ironmaster should call.

Meanwhile Mrs. Winstanley went out with Eva; and Eva, taken with a sudden desire for autumn tints and falling leaves, besought her mother to go into the Gardens and feed the ducks on the Serpentine.

As Thomasina expected, the ironmaster did call; and she had the field to herself.

Nothing in the Winstanley eldest was ever caricatured or exaggerated. The highest charm of her manner was its sameness of tranquillity; and in all circumstances and under all conditions she was ever quiet, well-bred, and decorously amiable. To-day her manner was just as exquisitely delicate in tone as ever; and yet there was a certain difference—a certain increase of gentleness that touched upon melancholy—a certain sweet, sad note that ran through the harmonies of her voice like the faintest echo of pain. And faint though it all was, Benjamin Brocklebank, the unæsthetic ironmaster, caught it—as it was meant he should.

"Miss Winstanley does not seem in her usual buoyant spirits to-day," he said after awhile, looking at her critically.

Now buoyancy of spirits was certainly not Thomasina's characteristic; but it did as well as anything else for the moment.

"No," she answered; and then she paused, looked down, and seemed to reflect.

Mr. Brocklebank's deep-set eyes were still fixed on her. He saw that something was wrong; that some stone had stirred the quiet waters of that still not yet transparent lake; but his was not the vision that could penetrate the depths and see what went on beneath the surface.

"I may as well open my heart to you," then said Thomasina, looking up into the ironmaster's face. "You are so good to us all, so true a friend to the family; and women are so helpless by themselves! I want you to help me, Mr. Brocklebank, as you helped Perdita. Get me something to do by which I may earn money! Mother has received very bad news. She has lost a large sum of money by some investment; I do not know what; and I want to help her if I can."

"Miss Winstanley feels and thinks as I should have expected she would—with perfect propriety," said the ironmaster admiringly; "but the difficulty will be to find any employment that one so delicate can undertake to perform. Miss Perdita is of a robuster make; but what can a lily-lady like Miss Winstanley accomplish?"

"Every one has his or her proper sphere of usefulness," said

Thomasina, with the sweetest air of pious philosophy. "There must be something for me to do, if I only knew what!"

"We must get you well married, my dear," said Mr. Brocklebank, with startling familiarity. "That is Miss Winstanley's rôle," he added, going back on his old manner of cautious formality.

Thomasina raised her lovely eyes and looked at the window as if interrogating the skies behind the blind. She sighed gently.

"I could not marry merely for a settlement," she said, slowly leaving the heavens and fixing her calm, limpid eyes on the hard face before her. "I would do anything in the whole world for mother, but this; and—"

"And there is no one then at this moment for whom you have conceived any regard?" he interrupted, speaking brusquely and naturally.

The faintest colour came into the pure pale cheeks—the faintest quiver of embarrassment round the thin quiet lips. Then the girl smiled and bent her swan-like throat into a graceful curve and made a slight movement with her hand as though to ward off an inadmissible subject; and again turned her eyes to the skies behind the blind.

"This is quite beside the matter," she said gently. "What I want now, dear Mr. Brocklebank, is to help my mother in her difficulty, and to make some money as soon as I can. Indeed, if I cannot, I do not know what will become of her and us!" she added, her beautiful eyes filling with genuine tears.

"Tut! Tut! never say die!" said Mr. Brocklebank with that kind of jocose sympathy which grates on the nerves of people in trouble more than either grave opposition or serious rebuke. "We will find some stile, no doubt, for the little pig to get over—some turning in the long lane! I own I should not like to see my amiable friends incommoded; and if Mrs. Winstanley will allow me I will go into her affairs conscientiously and carefully and see what salvage can be gathered out of the wreck. As a man of business I may be of use."

"Thank you a thousand times," said Thomasina, with a smile that masked a gasp; "but I do not think that mother will tell you anything, Mr. Brocklebank! The fact is," she said, as if making a sudden surrender of confidence; "we have been ruined by one who seemed to be our best friend—by a man to whom our father confided us and in whom we have always trusted implicitly. He invested our money badly and we have lost it all! But mother will not betray him even to you, dear Mr. Brocklebank—and I know that she will take no proceedings against him. No! we are in an awfully bad pass; but we must get out of it by ourselves. I can say so much, confidentially."

"Fine feeling but bad business!" said Mr. Brocklebank, shaking his head. "I admire, Miss Winstanley; I admire; but I deprecate!"

"Ah, you do not know mother yet!" said Thomasina. "She is the soul of honour and high-mindedness. She is the essence of all that we mean by the word Lady."

"So I quite believe; and Miss Winstanley's advocacy of her mother commends itself to my heart; but there is justice as well as mercy—self-protection as well as refinement; and the scoundrel ought to be made to refund the moneys scattered and lost—the property of the widow and the orphans!"

"You must not speak to mother of this," said Thomasina earnestly. "You will only distress her more than she is distressed already. No! that way is barred, Mr. Brocklebank. Ah! what can I do for mother! my poor sweet patient ill-used mother!" she said, clasping her hands with something of Perdita's favourite gesture, and then throwing herself into an attitude of graceful despair.

Mr. Brocklebank did not speak. He sat with his eyes on the ground, tracing out the pattern of the carpet with his stick. Minutes that seemed like hours to Thomasina passed in this absolute stillness which nothing broke but the ticking of the ormolu[1] clock on the chimney-piece, the sudden laughter of a passing child, or the yelp of a frightened dog. And still the ironmaster traced with his stick the outlines of the roses and tulips, the poppies and forget-me-nots which formed the pattern of the worn and faded carpet; and still thought and hesitated, pondered and reflected, and weighed moral merit against social fitness, passion against admiration, as he had so often done before, without coming to any clear decision.

At last he looked up. He took Thomasina's hand and carried it to his lips.

"Miss Winstanley may rely on me," he said, his voice a trifle husky. "I will stand the friend of the family now and ever." Then he added abruptly: "Where is Miss Perdita? It is almost time she was at home."

"Yes," said Thomasina, drawing a deep breath of intense relief.

Then she was not to be sacrificed! She had done her duty, but she was not to be made to suffer according to the usual reward of those who stand in the breach and make themselves the Providence of the afflicted. Mother would be saved and she would not be lost. How good and true this hard-featured man of gold and iron was! He was not lovely—most certainly not lovely—but he was useful, he was solid, he was trustwor-

---

[1]   Golden or gilded brass or bronze.

thy, and to be relied on when reliance was the one thing necessary for salvation. And Perdita would draw the big prize after all. Thomasina thought vaguely something about jewels and snouts;[1] but that was not her affair. If Benjamin Brocklebank chose to put a shy, awkward red-republican at the head of his table, instead of one who would have made Armour Court the local St. James's, the minor Versailles, that was his affair, no other person's. Hers was the joy of having brought matters to a head so that her beloved mother should be delivered from the cruel fangs of her creditors—with a silent Te Deum on her own account.

"I think I will go and meet Miss Perdita," then said Mr. Brocklebank, rising. "She must come up High Street, I imagine?"

"Yes," answered Thomasina; "she generally comes through the Gardens, then by Long Lane and so into High Street. You will probably meet mother and Eva too. They said they would come home to five o'clock tea, and it is past five now."

"I will go in search of my family," returned Mr. Brocklebank with profound gravity; and after again kissing Thomasina's hand, he took up his hat and carried himself and his projects out of the house in search of the flint on which to strike the steel.

He walked slowly through High Street and Long Lane, and so to the great gate of the Gardens opposite the Broad Walk; but he saw nothing of Perdita, nor of Mrs. Winstanley, nor yet of little Eva under the maternal wing. It was vexing and chilling. The ironmaster had made up his mind; and he did not like his resolutions to get cool. It was a word and a blow with him; and as soon as he had heated his iron he liked to make his horse-shoe. For the second time within three days Perdita had made him wait; and had he been as clear-sighted in affairs of the heart as he was in those of the market, he would have known how far he had gone by the irritation which his disappointment caused him.

While he was hesitating at the Great Gate, asking himself whether he should go in and walk on till he met her, or bear back to No. 100, a clear bird-like voice struck on his ear, and Eva, gay as a lark, bright as a sunbeam, fresh as a rose, came through a side avenue, every now and then turning back to speak to her mother walking immediately behind her, accompanied by the dark-haired foreigner who had spoken to them at the theatre—M. le Vicomte de Bois-Duval.

---

[1]   Possibly a reference to Matthew 7:6: "Give not that which is holy unto the dogs, neither cast ye your pearls before swine, lest they trample them under their feet, and turn again and rend you."

He had met them by the purest accident in the Gardens and he had joined them as of course, said Mrs. Winstanley to her substantial friend in an aside; and she, feeling that it was only her duty to repay some of the hospitality of attention which he had shown them in his own country, had allowed him to join them in their walk. From all that she had heard, he was a most exemplary young man, she added, taking Mr. Brocklebank into her confidence—a man of good old family, with a fine estate on the borders of Spain; and altogether one whose acquaintance was more desirable than not. She was a most careful mother, she went on to say in the quiet undisturbed way of a sister consulting with a brother—but she could not deny her daughters all the acquaintances which were never meant to include marriage. And on this she smiled and looked up into Mr. Brocklebank's face as if a joke had passed between them of which this was the echo.

Then said Mr. Brocklebank, his mind suddenly illumined as if by a flash of lightning,

"Is this the gentleman who crossed swords with Mr. Hubert Strangways not so long ago?"

"Yes," replied Mrs. Winstanley with a simplicity that would have done credit to Eva. "Two hot-headed boys as they were! But I am happy to say that no harm has come of it. Mr. Strangways is fast recovering, and the Vicomte is so sorry, so penitent! Do you know I think it will be a lesson to him, Mr. Brocklebank. I devoutly hope it may. This horrid habit of duelling—it ought to be abolished by the law; and from what the Vicomte has said, and judging by his contrition, this will be his last duel as I believe it has been his first."

"Madam," said Mr. Brocklebank severely, "our great lexicographer[1] propounded that a man who makes a pun would pick a pocket, and I affirm that a man who fights a duel would commit a murder. He is a murderer in heart and is not to be admitted inside a thoughtful Christian's house. These are my sentiments; and Mrs. Winstanley must forgive me if I express strongly what I feel deeply. This gentleman has done his best to extinguish the vital spark in one of your friends, and in my humble opinion, madam, you ought to turn a cold shoulder on him and never let him within the sacred precincts of your home. My advice may not be worth much, but such as it is, there it is!"

"Your advice is worth everything to me," said Mrs. Winstanley. "I look on you as our best friend."

---

[1] Samuel Johnson (1709–84), whose *Dictionary of the English Language* (1755) is generally considered to be the most important English dictionary before the OED.

"You are right, madam," answered the ironmaster; "I am your best friend, and will prove it. Where is Miss Perdita?"

Ah, where indeed!

"Is she not at home? You have come from my house, you say?" asked the mother.

"Mrs. Winstanley has divined rightly. I have come from her house, but I did not say so," answered Benjamin Brocklebank. "I have had a charming conversation with Miss Winstanley—a most interesting, and what I may call intimate conversation; but Miss Perdita had not returned when I left, and I came here in the hopes of meeting her on her way home."

"I, too, expect her every moment," said Mrs. Winstanley, who had not thought of her until now—looking vaguely round comers where Perdita could not by any chance appear. "It is time she was at home."

"Time you were all at home," said Mr. Brocklebank irritably. "These evening damps and chills play Old Harry with one's bronchial tubes."

"Yes, let us go," said Mrs. Winstanley. "Eva, my child, we must go home now at once."

Eva started from a whispered talk with Bois-Duval. They had been standing behind the backs of the mother and the family friend—he beseeching, she neither refusing nor granting; playing with fire, tempting the deluge, excited by his passion, spurred on by her own coquetry and that pleasant form of vanity which stood with her for love. The mother's voice broke in on this talk just as she was pressed into a corner whence she could not retreat.

"I think I will return with my friends," then said Mr. Brocklebank uneasily. "Miss Perdita may have returned home by another way. We may find her safely ensconced beneath the parental roof."

"Yes," said Mrs. Winstanley; "in all probability we shall."

She turned to Bois-Duval with a bow of dismissal. He caught the hint, took off his hat, made an elaborate reverence and said "Adieu, Mesdames" as tranquilly as if he had not just now been beseeching Eva to grant him the happiness of his life—to dispense with forms and witnesses and conventional rubbish of all kinds, and to run off with him to Paris, to be made his lovely and beloved little bride. Then the three went home where they found Thomasina in her usual graceful quietude, but no Perdita. Where was she? Where could she be? It was long past the hour of her rightful return; and even if her mother had not been uneasy on her own account, Mr. Brocklebank's irritation would have made her so on his.

Where could the girl be? What on earth was she about? It was disgraceful!—unbearable!—and just on this afternoon of all the afternoons in the week, when something was evidently in the air, and it was of such vital importance to have everything smooth and straight.

Mrs. Winstanley had to use all her self-command not to say to Mr. Brocklebank crudely: "See to what your horrible office life and independent running about the streets leads girls!" but she refrained. She looked at Thomasina—Thomasina looked at her; but neither could say where this tiresome and upsetting rebel was.

The minutes dragged on, surely never so leaden-footed—never so slowly! The quarters chimed; the half-hours struck—dinnertime was at hand; and still Mr. Brocklebank stayed and still no Perdita appeared. The thing was becoming serious. Where was she? What could have become of her?

"Oh this horrible work, this dangerous liberty of English girls!" at last said Mrs. Winstanley, unable to bear the strain of the situation longer.

Mr. Brocklebank looked grave.

"Miss Perdita must be admonished," he said severely; while Thomasina felt as if the marble palace which she had built with so much care had melted into thin air, and the solid globe of gold which she thought she had tossed into her mother's lap had proved to be nothing but an iridescent bubble thrown on by the foam of the sea—and now burst and broken for ever.

CHAPTER XXVIII.

THE CRAWFORD SKELETON.

THE private door stood open and the maid was on the threshold looking anxiously down the street, as if watching for some one to appear. As soon as Perdita came in sight she ran to meet her, saying:

"Please, miss, will you come in? Missis is very bad and wants to see you."

Perdita needed no second invitation. With a little exclamation she went into the house and ran upstairs as one to whom the place was free. In the drawing-room she found Mrs. Crawford sitting on the sofa, her face turned inward to the cushions, weeping piteously. Leslie sat by her, holding one of her hands in his; but though his face was sad no tears were in his eyes, nor in his manner was there evidence of more acute distress, more profound melancholy than that which always clung to him. There was no more than the ordinary cloud, whatever that might be, which had evidently darkened the sunshine of his life and given him the chilled and reticent air of one who has something to hide and all to bear; but he seemed to pity his mother and to feel for her, if not for himself.

"Here she is!" he said, as Perdita came into the room; his words showing that they had been talking of and expecting her. "Now I shall leave you together. She will comfort you best alone, mother."

He rose from his seat; bending over the poor weeping woman he whispered a few kindly words and kissed that part of her cheek which was not hidden in the pillow; then going up to Perdita he held out both his hands, looking into her face almost as if he were asking her some question.

But he did not speak; and she was too much moved by Mrs. Crawford's anguish to have much consciousness left for herself.

"What is the matter?" she asked in a low voice, aghast at this strange breakdown, this passionate despair from one usually so calm and self-controlled as her Quaker-like friend.

"She will tell you herself," said Leslie; "it is best that you hear it from her. I shall see you before you leave?" he added. "When the mother has told you what she wishes you to know, I will take you home. But now I will leave you."

Perdita visibly trembled. To one of her keen imagination, mysteries, secrets, revelations, were terribly exciting. They overpowered her better judgment and made her fear she did not know what. That some mystery was in this quiet middle-class tradesman's family she had dimly seen from the first. She forgot it as time went on and she became better acquainted with the mother and son and more at her ease in the house; but when she cared to reflect she always knew there was something. And now she was to hear the truth and learn the name of the family skeleton whose presence she had discerned though she had not traced out its form. That wife, who was neither living nor dead, never seen yet not disowned nor in her grave; Leslie's undeclared sadness; his tenderness to his mother showing so much feeling in his nature, and his indifference to his child showing as much unnatural coldness; Mrs. Crawford's reserve on all facts relating to her daughter-in-law, mingled with the exaggerated intensity of her affection for one who after all was but her son's wife—yes!—there was evidently something to be told! Bell Blount had said: "If you knew all about them you would not care for them so much," and now the moment had come when she was to know all about them, and be taken behind the scenes and shown things as they were.

No wonder that she trembled, sensitive and imaginative as she was!—no wonder that, with her strange power of living in the lives of others and her dangerous tendency to enlarge the borders of fact by fancy, she felt as if the crisis of her own fate had come! She looked up into Leslie's face, her own scared and white.

"I am sorry you are in trouble," she said simply and earnestly; to which he answered: "Yes, I know you are," as simply and earnestly for his own part.

"Dearest Mrs. Crawford! how sorry I am!" the girl began, taking Leslie's chair as he left the room. She kissed the delicate hand that hung so nervelessly across the bent knees and held it to her soft warm cheek as if that would comfort the grieving soul. "What is it? what can I do to help you?" she continued, her voice as tender as a caress.

"Nothing! Nothing!" said Mrs. Crawford despairingly; and Perdita echoing the word, thought to herself: Why then was she wanted? If she could do no good, why had they wanted her, looked out for her, and told her to come in?

"Yes, dear, I can do something, for I love you," she said gently. "We can always help those whom we love."

"I have not helped the one whom I loved!" said Mrs. Crawford, with a fresh burst of weeping. Then she raised her face and took Perdita to her bosom. "I have lost her!" she said; "my dear, dear child is dead!"

"Dead!" echoed Perdita, with a cry as if stunned; "little Lily dead!"

"No, no!" said Mrs. Crawford; "not my Lily—her mother—my poor, sweet, unhappy girl!"

"Leslie's wife?" asked Perdita, in a low voice.

She was pale and frightened, and seemed somehow as if standing among quicksands where she was sure of nothing.

"Yes, his wife and my dear, dear daughter," said Mrs. Crawford with fresh tears.

The girl shivered as if a rude wind had passed over her. She was strangled, suffocated, though she could not have said why, save for sympathy with Mrs. Crawford's distress. For indeed she was essentially sympathetic and easily moved by the sight of sorrow. And this was a terribly painful moment. The motherless child, the bereaved mother, the desolate husband; and yet he was not desolate! Only the woman grieved and the child was motherless; the man possessed his soul in calmness.

"She did not know me!" cried Mrs. Crawford, wringing her hands. "She did not know me!" she repeated. "All yesterday and last night up to two o'clock to-day, when she died, I held her in my arms. She died in my arms—her sweet, pretty head on my bosom where she had lain when a little child—and she never once called me 'Mother'—never once recognized me! She called for me while I was there, but refused to believe that it was her own true loving mother who held her! My daughter! my dear, dear daughter! Oh, Perdita, my child, God keep you from such suffering as I have gone through for her!"

"My poor darling!—oh, how I pity you!" said Perdita in a low voice. "But what was it? was it fever? why did she not know you?" she asked, with the natural curiosity of sympathy. One must know what one has to pity and be sorry for!

"She had lost her reason for the last two years," said Mrs. Crawford. "And she died without recovering it."

This, then, was the mystery; this the shape of the skeleton! Leslie's wife, little Lily's mother, a maniac—dying in some place away from home and mad to the last! And Leslie was not broken-hearted; though the mother was.

"How dreadful!" said Perdita with a sob half of terror, half of pity. "Poor, poor mother!"

There was something in the girl's tender voice, her loving touch, her genuine warmth and sympathy which touched and soothed the poor mother's heart. Mrs. Crawford was before all things a mother; and her instincts had followed the natural course of her age. What she most desired and most felt the want of in her present life was the companionship of a grown-up daughter. She longed to have about her a girl, still young but no longer a child, whom she might gently sermonize and lovingly admonish, yet whose advice she could ask and whose help she could claim at every turn, relying on her in reality while assuming her to be still in leading-strings. Her little grandchild was her pleasure, her delight, her darling; but she wanted that grandchild's mother as the link between the generations. She wanted her daughter—or, if that were now impossible, then a daughter, no matter what might be the name of the mother who had borne her!

"Dear girl! my dear Perdita! you must be my daughter now!" she said, drawing the girl to her lips and kissing her forehead.

"I will!" said Perdita, kneeling down by her and putting her arms round her waist, while she looked up into the poor pained face with her soft eyes full of tears and her whole honest soul shining through them.

"God bless you!" said Mrs. Crawford, pressing her to her heart.

After this a soothing kind of silence fell between them. The elder woman got back by silent prayer some of her usual self-control, and Perdita felt as if she could have dedicated her life to the task of making

Mrs. Crawford forget that she had lost one daughter in the possession of another.

Presently Mrs. Crawford spoke.

"I have told you so much, my dear, I will tell you all," she began. "Half confidences are both useless and unfriendly. Better tell all or nothing. To begin with, did you know that Leslie is my nephew, not my son?"

"No," said Perdita, startled; "I always thought he was your own son."

"No," she sighed; "he is my brother's son but I brought him up from his babyhood and he married my daughter. Something went wrong—I cannot tell what it was—but some terrible split came between them. I cannot blame Leslie, for I know nothing in which he is to blame; and I cannot blame her." Here she wept again. "She was goodness and sweetness in person—a little giddy, perhaps; but then she was so young—and youth will be heedless! But there it was—a something which was like death between them, and which came on a little before the birth of Lily. From that time Leslie was never the same to her nor she to him. He was not unkind, but he suddenly seemed to have grown ten years older, and stern and shut up; and she was frightened of him. Once she came to me and said, 'Oh, mamma, what a fool I was to tell him!' But she would never say what it was that she had told him. I asked Leslie, but he commanded me so sternly never to allude to the subject again that I saw he was not to be trifled with; and I never did. Three days after the birth of Lily she had fever and lost her head. Nothing could be done with her. We kept her as long as we could, but we were at last obliged to put her into an asylum—where she died to-day. She had been ill only four days. When you called here on Saturday, and I was so unhappy, that was the first I had heard of her illness. I had seen her that day; but my presence excited and made her worse, and the doctors would not let me stay. Only yesterday, when all hope was over and she had sunk into a kind of torpor, only then did they let me keep with her. But she died without knowing me! If only she had recognized me once! She never did. Just at the last she opened her eyes and said, 'Leslie, forgive me!' She knew him, but she did not know her mother!"

And again the poor woman broke down into weeping as if she would weep her very life away.

"Was Leslie there?" asked Perdita, after the burst had a little subsided.

"Yes; he came early in the morning and stayed with her. When she said those last words he bent over her and kissed her, and said, 'I do forgive you, Florence. God in His mercy forgive you too!' But what was there to forgive? It is that which breaks my heart! What had my child done that was wrong? It could not have been anything bad; and yet Leslie is so gentle and patient and liberal—he would not have made a grave matter of a mere indiscretion, and at such a moment formally and solemnly have forgiven her. What was it? what could it be?"

But what she did not know Perdita could not divine; and the two beat the air in vain.

"And now you shall be my child," said Mrs. Crawford. "I will be to you as a mother, guiding, correcting, encouraging you in the right way; and you shall be to me as a daughter."

"Yes," said Perdita, with the solemnity of a vow.

"You must come and see me as often as you can—that is, if your own natural mother does not object," said Mrs. Crawford, with sudden remembrance of this possible obstacle.

"Yes, I will," answered Perdita again, ignoring the reservation. Whether mother objected or not she would continue to see the Crawfords; and without the internal combat, the moral doubts, which made loyalty to Bell Blount so difficult. It was a living, human, urgent duty that bound her to this desolate mother; and to desert her in her hour of need for no better reason than because Leslie kept a shop—no! that she would not do! She would despise herself too much were she to give in to such a contemptible snobbishness of caste. Humanity was before these wretched conventionalisms! Truth and love and goodness and carrying comfort to the afflicted—all stood higher than that miserable little barrier—the profession of a retail trader! Had Leslie been "wholesale" he might have had the friends and connexions of royalty in his counting-house; being "retail," he was beyond the pale of social salvation; and his personal gifts were not suffered to count. But with Perdita they should count; and mother must give way. She had made up her mind not to give them up, and mother need not ask her. So determined this wicked rebel in her own mind; daring to draw out a moral programme for herself and to put her individual love and conscience in place of the world's law and filial obedience. Which is not saying that she did right, but only that it was a difficult moral position in which she found herself—between her mother's commands on the one side and her own belief in what was right on the other.

It was now quite dark and the hour was late; but Perdita woke to the knowledge of how time was passing only when Leslie came upstairs to warn her that she must be going home.

"I will take you," he said quietly; and she assented without resistance. It seemed quite right and natural that he should walk with her through the streets and speak to her as if he had something to say. And yet—and yet—there was a strange confusion in her own heart which she could not disentangle. His marriage—his misunderstanding with his wife—her ghastly fate and tragic end—his mother no longer his mother but merely his aunt and his wife's mother—his freedom from all bonds and his evident want of natural sorrow in their painful breaking—his manner to herself only so late ago as Saturday—what did it all mean? The whole thing was an entanglement and a puzzle; she understood neither herself nor him, neither what was nor what had been.

But she knew that she loved Mrs. Crawford; and for the present that was enough.

"The mother has told you our sad history, I suppose," he asked as soon as they were alone.

"Yes," she answered; and she added impulsively: "I did not believe you could have been so cruel and unfeeling, Mr. Crawford!"

He looked into the flushed face which she had turned to him with candid reprobation.

"No," he said quietly. "I have not been cruel, Miss Winstanley. To save the mother, who has been like my own and whose heart it would have broken had she known the truth, I have endured in silence the greatest wrong that a wife can do to her husband; and I have accepted the consequences without taking the world into my confidence or appealing for relief to the law. Never mind the story. You do not understand me, I know. All I want is that you should believe in me. I have not been cruel. Say that you believe this!" he repeated with emotion.

"When you speak to me, I believe you—every word you say," said Perdita; "but the story as it stands seems so much against you, Mr. Crawford."

"No, not as it stands—as it appears to stand," he answered. "I cannot say more; and I will never say more than this. I wish to cast no stones against the erring dead, but for myself, for my honour, my happiness, my future, for you—yes, for you, Perdita—I must have your blind belief, your absolute faith!"

They were walking in the shadow of the street. Suddenly he stopped and faced her.

"I must have you trust in me!" he repeated in a low voice. "It is the last great good left me."

He took both her hands as he had done before, and drew them up to his breast, looking at her as if he would read her soul. His eyes, his voice, were as a revelation to Perdita. The thing was clear if the circumstances were obscure. Whoever might have sinned he had not; and wherever the fault might lie, it was not on his head.

"I do believe you," she said, turning to him in her old way of self-surrender. "I am sure you have done no wrong."

He gave a deep sigh and held her hands still closer to him, bending his face nearer and nearer to hers. Suddenly he seemed to check himself in some impulse. He let her hands fall, straightened himself as if on parade and in a cold constrained voice said only: "Thank you."

Then they walked on again—he saying softly to himself something which she was half afraid to hear.

As they turned up West Hill Gardens, they met, carelessly saunter-ing along as any other indifferent person might have sauntered through the street, M. le Vicomte de Bois-Duval, examining the bearings and taking stock of local possibilities. His sharp eyes made out Perdita at a glance, and he lifted his hat with an odd smile. Those sharp eyes made out her companion too; and the smile changed in character, but still continued a smile, as he repeated the salute, and this time took in Leslie Crawford.

"Good God! do you know that infamous scoundrel?" cried Leslie in a voice that made Perdita start.

"He is a friend of mother's—she made his acquaintance at Trouville, and we saw him at the theatre on Saturday night," she answered.

"You must not know him, Perdita! You must not! Give me your sacred word that you will not!" cried Leslie, moved to strange passion. "He is the most hateful scoundrel, the most unredeemed blackguard under heaven, and my worst enemy. It was he who ruined my home, and destroyed my happiness."

"Parbleu!" said Bois-Duval to himself, shrugging his shoulders as he passed, "the combination is droll! The excellent grocer and the little one's sister *bras dessus, bras dessous*;[1] and the wife—where? For a virtuous young man, *ce cher* Leslie knows how to construe opportunity. But it is evident these Winstanleys with all their airs of grand ladies are no such great things. If one of them can come home after dark leaning familiarly on the arm of a shopkeeper, I need not afflict myself with scruples!"

And with this he passed on humming gaily;—that wicked rebel little knowing the mischief which she had helped to work by her abominable democracy, in allowing a tradesman of the district to take the footing of an equal and to excite the interest of a friend.

---

[1] (French), arm in arm.

She knew nothing save that she was shocked and bewildered by what Leslie had said; that she longed to tell her mother to shut the doors against this shameful foreigner who had hurt her friend; that she felt this friend to be more mysterious, more inscrutable than ever, but that she believed in him, respected him, admired him more than ever; that she was pained and pleased, elated and depressed all in one; and that she felt as if she had a talisman hidden somewhere about her heart which would bear her up against the wrath that had to come, when her determination to maintain her relations with Mrs. Crawford was made known to mother and the girls.

CHAPTER XXIX.

THE GOLDEN BALL.

"At last!" said Mr. Brocklebank, as the door-bell rang and Perdita was heard coming up the stairs.

He drew a deep breath and wiped his upper lip, like a man relieved from some great tension; but he squared his shoulders as one who also knew that he had to go through a moment of embarrassment and to perform some kind of heroic feat.

No one spoke; no one called Perdita into the drawing-room on her way upstairs. They let her go in peace, waiting her own time of entrance. She was soon ready for dinner and came hurriedly into the room in the midst of an ominous silence. She herself was pale almost to ghastliness; but she did not look so nervous us usual, and her manner was more assured, her bearing less fluttered, less conscious than in general. It seemed as if the great trouble which she had just witnessed and the words which had been said to her had in some sense steadied and absorbed her, so that she neither saw the cloud impending nor heeded the signs of the outburst.

"My dear Perdita, you are late!" said her mother, when she had come fairly into the room, shutting the door behind her, and standing for a moment a little startled at the sight of Mr. Brocklebank.

He was her own special friend and protector and she was sincerely attached to him; but somehow the sight of him was not so pleasant to her to-day as it had hitherto been, and she felt ill at ease in his presence and wished that he had not been there.

"Yes, I am," she answered, going up to the ironmaster and holding out her hand.

He took it flabbily and without rising from his chair. Though so punctilious and heavily polite in his everyday life, at this moment he wished to show that he was displeased, and that he was the master. It was not necessary that he should pay the girl who had offended him the respect due to an ordinary gentlewoman. As his protégée, who had failed in her duty, she must be made to suffer that she might be taught to repent.

"Miss Perdita *is* strangely late," he said in a dry hard tone; and Perdita replied as before: "Yes, I am," in a frank one.

There was something in Perdita's odd mixture of frankness and shyness, of hardihood and timidity, which always touched Mr. Brocklebank. He had a little difficulty in keeping up the dignity due to himself when he heard her clear voice and looked into her sensitive face; but he thought it best to frighten her by playing out the character of Offended Master fully. Though he intended to forgive her before the evening was over and to make her happy by all that his forgiveness should include, still, she must be reduced now to sorrow and submission that she might rejoice more completely in her exaltation. Also it was a good opportunity to exert his own authority and to prove to her that he was indeed her master.

"My dear Perdita, what has kept you so long?" asked her mother.

"I will tell you all about it afterwards, mother," she answered, with a little hesitation.

"Am I in Miss Perdita's way? Shall I retire to afford her an opportunity for filial confidence?" interposed Mr. Brocklebank disagreeably.

"Oh, no! no! mother does not mind waiting for what I have to say," answered Perdita, full of belief in the meaning of speech according to its form.

"It is a pity that Miss Perdita should make mysteries out of nothing—what I call mountains out of molehills," said Mr. Brocklebank. "The confidence between mother and daughters is of course sacred—we all know that!—but friendship has also its claims, and a virtuous young lady like Miss Perdita cannot have anything to say, even to her mother, which her friend may not hear."

Perdita looked distressed. The old frightened hunted look came back into her face, and she turned her eyes appealingly to her mother. She turned them to a blank wall. Mrs. Winstanley was arranging the ruffle on her sleeve, and had no responsive glance to give to her rebellious daughter; so that she was forced to stand her ground unsupported. But she did stand it. It would have seemed a kind of sacrilege to have spoken of the Crawfords to the master of Armour Court. She know so well beforehand that he would not understand them or herself; that he would condemn her intimacy, ridicule her interest in them, disbelieve what she believed and doubt what she trusted. No! she could not speak of Leslie or his mother to Mr. Brocklebank. It would be hard to have to battle with mother, but impossible to confide in him.

"It is no great secret any way," she said, with an odd kind of shrinking; "but I would rather tell mother alone."

Thomasina moved some of the trumpery bric-a-brac on the table near her, and bent her head to study more closely the aesthetic beauty of a small shell-basket. What an unlucky creature that sister of hers was! Just when the ground had been prepared for her and the way made smooth, she in must needs knock everything to pieces—first, by her folly in being late again to-night as on Saturday night; and then by her obstinacy in not telling Mr. Brocklebank what he wanted to know! Thomasina herself would have let any one die of desire to know that which she chose to keep hidden, but then she would have found a substitute, a semblance of the truth, which would have done as well; and this knowledge of her own immovable reticence and facile tact combined made her find her sister's silence misplaced and this opposition to their friend a mistake, if not something worse.

"It is dinner time, so we have no time for Perdita's weighty confession," said Mrs. Winstanley, forcing a smile while she effected a diversion. "I scarcely like to ask you to share our very simple meal," she continued, with extreme graciousness of manner but with a heart that seemed to have turned into a lump of ice. "A family of ladies as we are, we live so simply! We are on almost nursery diet!" with a well-acted half-playful laugh. "But if you can dine off this nursery fare, I shall be very glad if you will stay."

"I thank Mrs. Winstanley most profoundly," said Mr. Brocklebank with an involuntary shudder, remembering his past experience, the cold entrées and the poisonous wine; "I will not derange her by my unexpected presence at her hospitable board. I will retire now that I have seen the stray lamb restored to the fold, and I will return when we have all ministered to the cravings of the inner man. Mrs. Winstanley and her amiable young ladies will have refreshed themselves by their simple— shall I call it ethereal?—food; I, as a more muscular animal, will have fortified myself with something grosser. And then, with permission, we will have a pleasant little evening together, when I shall say two or three words to my protégée here in private which will win her mother's approbation:—of that I am confident!—and which will not be unpleasant to my young friend herself. Till then, ladies, your humble servant."

He bowed to each separately, but to Perdita the last and with what he meant to be a tender smile qualified by a reproving shake of the head.

The matter of the dinner was poor, cold, overcooked and insufficient; the manner was silent, preoccupied, agitated. Mrs. Winstanley forbore to either chide or admonish; Thomasina was in an agony of doubt as to Perdita's acceptance when the offer should be made; Eva was too much absorbed by her own affairs to heed those of another; and Perdita was in her turn too much absorbed by Leslie to heed Mr. Brocklebank. No one spoke and only Eva ate with spirit. As yet no emotion had ever blunted those sharp little white teeth of hers, or made the richest corner of the pudding less than welcome and delicious. For the rest thunder was in the air; and even those who were not concerned were conscious.

Perdita was not questioned and, not being questioned, she did not tell the story which was the acorn that would break the jar wherein it should be set. She would have begun, *more suo*,[1] the moment Mr. Brocklebank had left the room, and had got as far as, "Mother, I stayed at the—" when Mrs. Winstanley stopped her.

"Not now, Perdita," she said coldly; "I would rather not hear what you have to say now. We will wait till to-morrow."

Thus things stood in their old places and nothing was moved; and in this odd thundery heavy way the dinner passed till grace was said and the ceremony came to an end. And in due time after Mr. Brocklebank returned and was ushered up into the drawing-room, where, what it pleased him to call 'this amiable family,' had reassembled—waiting on events and judgment.

After a little desultory talk, one by one those who were on this occasion supernumeraries left the room with delicacy without parade. Thomasina was the first to go. She slid away, no one knew how or when. It was as if she had vanished, so quiet and noiseless was her departure. Mrs. Winstanley, unable to efface herself in this vaporous manner, begged for permission to write a letter down in the dining-room below; and as soon as she had got to the door Eva called out: "Mumsey, darling! I want to speak to you!" She skipped across the room, balancing her arms as if trying to fly according to her favourite gesture, and was on her mother's neck before the door was closed. Thus the three supernumeraries disappeared

---

[1] (Latin), in her characteristic way.

before Perdita well knew what had happened, or that they had gone at all, and she was left alone with the ironmaster.

And when they were alone, Mr. Brocklebank got up from the chair where he had been sitting and came over to the sofa where she was, placing himself by her with a grave face and a ponderous air, as if he had the world's salvation to propose and insure.

"Miss Perdita distressed her friend," he began, clearing his throat. "She has distressed him twice of late, deeply."

"I am so sorry!" said Perdita, raising her contrite eyes to his face.

He took her hand. She did not withdraw it. Mr. Brocklebank was her friend, her guardian, almost her temporary father. It could not signify whether he took her hand or no.

"I am sure that Miss Perdita would not wish to distress her friend," he said, and gave her hand a fervent squeeze.

"Certainly I would not," replied that obtuse person, returning the pressure with affectionate instinctiveness and mole-like blindness.

The heavy face brightened. That long warm nervous hand, with the slender fingers clasped so frankly round his own, so rough and hard and hairy, seemed to touch his heart, to fire his blood, to spur his fancy, to make life a boon and the future a glory.

"Then confess and be absolved," he returned with elephantine playfulness. "Where was this charming truant, this naughty delinquent when she ought to have been safe at home under the maternal wing? hey? Say where, before pardon can be pronounced."

"I was at a friend's," returned Perdita with a tremor in her voice and love in her eyes.

"So? And what friends has this protégée of mine that I do not know of, and whose existence her mother seems equally unable to divine?"

Perdita hesitated for a moment. She shrank from taking Mr. Brocklebank into her confidence. It hurt her pride in those dear sorrowing friends of hers, to expose their griefs, to explain their condition—that condition so certain to be despised. Yet she was forced by the law of her nature to be candid and sincere; and after all—what was there to conceal?

"They are the Crawfords," she said quite steadily. "He is the chemist in High Street."

Mr. Brocklebank let her hand fall from his.

"No! that is an impossibility—that cannot be endured!" he said warmly. "A young lady like Miss Perdita delaying the family repast—setting all heads aching for fear of what had become of her—for a chemist in High Street. Gregory and St. James!" he cried, and when he used this adjuration he was in good truth roused, "that I should live to receive such a confession! It cannot be—it must not be! Miss Perdita, you must give up these people. You degrade yourself—a young lady like you! You lower yourself more than I can stand. It is unseemly, it is ugly, it is monstrous!"

"No, I cannot give them up, indeed I cannot!" said Perdita.

"No? what's this I hear? Miss Perdita says No when her friend says Yes? I think my ears have played me a trick!" said Mr. Brocklebank, with angry misgiving.

"They are fond of me and I of them," pleaded Perdita. "And I am of use to them."

Mr. Brocklebank rose and walked about the room. He was more agitated than he could quite understand. Perdita's simplicity of reasoning, so all-sufficient to herself, was without weight with him. She might be of use to them a thousand times, but that created no bond in his mind. If social things were out of gear, the human aspect of a friendship did not count with him any more than with Mrs. Winstanley.

"And I say Yes," he said after a while, coming back to her and again seating himself on the sofa. "I say Yes, Miss Perdita; and I have a right to judge and to ordain."

"You have always been very, very good to me; and I owe you gratitude and affection for all that you have done for me," returned Perdita, beginning quietly and ending warmly; "but these are dear friends too, and they have been very good too, and I owe them gratitude and affection as well."

"Not the same as to me," said Benjamin Brocklebank; "not the same as to the man who is to be your husband."

Perdita started up, but he took hold of her hand to prevent her running away as she seemed inclined. He raised his face to hers, with a look as if he had done something magnanimous, unanswerable—a look that said: "There now! see to what glory I have destined you—I great Ahasuerus, and you meek, loving Esther!"[1]

"Your husband," he repeated.

But Perdita, snatching away her hands, covered her face and cried out in a terrified voice:

"No! no! Mr. Brocklebank! never! never!"

The man's self-confidence was so great, his sense of superiority and mastership so supreme, that he mistook the girl's renunciation for the

---

[1] Esther 2:5–18. King Ahasuerus elevated the orphan girl Esther to the throne, because she was less demanding than others seeking to win his favor.

expression of joy so deep as to be almost unendurable, so great as to be wholly incredible.

"Yes, yes, my dear," he said, reassuring her. "It is true indeed! I have selected you from among the hundreds who will envy you; and you are to be my own, my very own. From the first you pleased me and stirred my mind. Your sisters are delectable, I grant. Miss Winstanley is like a young queen and the little one is sweetness and freshness in person; and I own that at one time I hesitated. But my fancy at last settled itself and Miss Perdita is my final choice. So now let us have no more escapades— no more consorting with chemists and such-like trash—no more making friends of demented-looking females who gyrate in scarlet and call you by familiar epithets of endearment. I must have my Perdita all that the mistress of Armour Court should be, as well as all that she is in herself: and we will begin the new page from this evening—from now when we stand pledged to each other as man and wife!"

"But we are not pledged!" cried Perdita, shrinking back with a scared face. "I cannot say Yes to you, Mr. Brocklebank. It cannot be!"

"You are not, and you are not, and you cannot be? Are you sincere, Perdita, or is this a bad joke—an exaggeration of coyness and maidenly modesty?" asked Mr. Brocklebank, a look of surprise gradually deepening into fierceness on his face. "You reject me?—and may I ask why?— you reject me as your husband?—you fly from Armour Court?—and may I know the reason why?" he repeated. "When have I offended Miss Perdita Winstanley? She has always been to me as my own ewe lamb; why this sudden tergiversation and repugnance? I thought I was liked in this quarter—have always flattered myself so:—how have the mighty fallen[1] and the secure been deceived!"

"So I do; I like you very much indeed, Mr. Brocklebank," said poor Perdita, with fatal earnestness.

She bent towards him to assure him more completely of her liking. Had it been anyone but Perdita, honest, sincere, obtuse, impulsive, the action would have been both a challenge and a caress: "Very much," she repeated; "but—"

"But what? But me no buts, Miss Perdita; say frankly what there is in your heart."

"I do not love you as a husband! You are my dear friend, but no more than my friend."

His heavy face lightened up into a broad laugh.

---

[1] 2 Samuel 1:19, 1:25, 1:27.

"That is all?" he said taking her hands, and swinging them to and fro. "Tut! Tut! a mouse's squeak!—not enough to frighten a baby! You will soon learn to love me as a husband, my dear, when I am one. We cannot feel what we do not know, and you are all abroad in your calculations! You will come to it, my dear, you will come to it! I should have expected this—this pretty coyness, from you, my dear Perdita. It is indeed what I should have preferred had I been asked to make my choice; just what I should have selected as the proper frame of mind in the young lady whom I aspired to make my wife; but coyness is not blockishness, and your want of certain feelings is not absolute refusal to allow them leave to grow. Come! let us get over this little hitch as of no manner of consequence. It is only a straw."

"It is not a straw!" said Perdita with energy. She felt as if she were to be taken possession of on the spot and married out of hand; and that she must be candid and firm, else woe would befall her. "I cannot marry you, Mr. Brocklebank. Do not be angry with me! do not be offended! but indeed I cannot!" she repeated.

"And my rival's name?" he asked, sternly.

"You have none," she said; but her eager face paled as she spoke. "You have no rival; but I love you only as a father," she added with frightful candour.

He laughed disagreeably and pulled up his shirt-collar.

"A rather young father, even for Miss Perdita," he said. "I am proud of the flattering distinction, but I cannot say I think the cap fits!"

"No, no, not in age," said the poor honest blunderer. "I only mean that I have the same kind of feeling for you—the same kind of respect and reliance on you, and all that—I don't mean that you are old!"

"Let that pass," he said angrily and majestically; for now he was really wounded. "I do not desire to be made acquainted with silly reasons for an insulting comparison. A lady's reasons indeed are seldom worth the trouble of being made acquainted with! I take my answer. It is 'No.' As a man of honour I have only to retire. I am sorry for this amiable family. I had hoped to have been of service to them. From all I hear, Mrs. Winstanley is in a bad way for want of funds; and as Miss Perdita's husband, the purse of the master of Armour Court would have been open to her necessities. That dream of benevolence and help is at an end. Dreams do come to an end in general; and I am a wiser man than I was half an hour ago; but Mrs. Winstanley is a sadder woman, and the Misses Winstanley are all poorer young ladies than they might have been! Miss Perdita had it in her power to redeem her family. She elects to say No; so No be it!"

"I am very very sorry for poor mother," groaned Perdita, clasping her hands; "but what can I do?"

"Do?—what you have done!" he answered brutally. "Say No to your would-be deliverer—reject the proffer of salvation. That is what you have to do, of course! That is the rational action of a well-conducted young lady and an affectionate daughter! There can be no two opinions on that!"

"Do not be angry with me, Mr. Brocklebank," she pleaded. "You would not have me accept you when I did not love you—would you?" she asked simply.

"I would have had your acceptance and your belief that you would have learned to love me," he answered. "As you would have done. How could you have helped it if you are really heart-whole and fancy-free? The thing would have come of itself—such a husband as I could have been to you—such settlements as I could have made—and with Armour Court as your place of residence. Am I a hunchback, or old or ugly in any way, that I should disgust you? You must have loved me! Gregory and St. James, and the deuce and all! why not?" he said in violent wrath.

"I am so sorry to have vexed you," said Perdita, tears filling her eyes.

"Then cease to be sorry and cease to vex me," he answered with sudden tenderness. It was his last throw. "Say Yes, and that you will be my obedient and faithful wife, and this little cloud will have passed as if it had never been. Redeem the fortunes of your family, gratify my wish, and make yourself happy with what I offer!"

"I cannot!" said Perdita, turning away. And her voice, though full of distress, was decisive in its pronounced repugnance.

Mr. Brocklebank stood manfully battling with the humiliation and surprise of this denial. He thought his young friend very mad and very bad, and wondered where she had got it from; but the day of force is over, and when women will not they cannot be made—so there the matter must rest.

Suddenly he turned his eyes on the poor culprit standing there in mute misery, but in resolute denial all the same. Her downcast face was sad and overshadowed, but showed no sign of yielding—her drooping figure was crushed and overweighted, but it still looked as if it could bear and not go down before the burden of his displeasure. Sensitive and strong, suffering and resolute—there she was, that complex and bewildering Perdita whom no one understood and whom so many afflicted.

"May I ask one favour of Miss Perdita?" then said the ironmaster stiffly.

She lifted her eyes.

"Surely!" she answered. "You know that I will do all I can to please you!" she added, with a burst of her old impulsive affectionateness.

He shrugged his shoulders.

"Words! idle words!" he muttered. "I have no respect for words; what I like is deeds! But that is beside the question. I have now to make one last request. Keep to yourself what I have said to you. I do not wish the whole of the family to be made acquainted with my humiliation!"

"Mr. Brocklebank! As if I should tell!" cried Perdita with energy. "Why, of course not! I shall not say a syllable to any one. Oh, I am so sorry! so sorry!" she added.

"I will take your word for it," he answered; and without wishing her good-bye or even shaking hands with her, he turned away abruptly and tramped heavily down the stairs.

Mrs. Winstanley came out of the dining-room to meet him as he passed the door.

"Miss Perdita is obdurate, madam," he said when he saw her. "I have spoken to her from my heart and done my best to bring her to a proper frame of mind, but I have been unsuccessful. She is as hard as the nether millstone, obdurate all through."

"I am sorry," said Mrs. Winstanley, her handsome face turning suddenly white. "I had hoped that you would have had some effect on her if I had none."

"I shared that hope, madam, but I have experienced its futility. Miss Perdita goes her own way, and I don't know the human being who could prevail on her against her will. I have failed!"

"Which says everything," said Mrs. Winstanley.

And the ironmaster answered back: "Everything, madam! Everything!"

"Perdita!" said her mother, coming into the room where the rebel was still standing dazed and discomfited, "what is this I hear from Mr. Brocklebank? You have treated him with insolence? Been obstinate, undutiful, ungrateful? He who has been your best friend! Are you really insane? Your conduct would seem to show that you are!"

"I did not know, mother, that I had been all that to Mr. Brocklebank," said Perdita, aghast at this roll-call.

"What has he been saying to you that has given him such a shocking impression of you? What has he asked that you have refused?" asked Mrs. Winstanley.

"I said I would not speak of his conversation," said Perdita softly. "I can only tell you one thing—he wanted me to give up my friends."

"Your friends? In Heaven's name, Perdita, what and whom do you mean?"

"The Crawfords," she answered.

"Those chemist people? Those whom I demand of you to give up?"

"Yes, mother."

"And what did you say?"

"I could not."

Mrs. Winstanley kept a dead silence for a moment. Then she turned round and faced her daughter, to whom hitherto she had been speaking over her shoulder and askew.

"Now, Perdita," she said, as sternly as if her words had been iron rods with which she belaboured this wicked soul; "let us understand each other. This is my final word:—you choose between your family and these new friends—you cannot keep both; and if you hold with them, you give up us."

"Mother—" she began.

"Not another word! You have your choice and my decision. If for the sake of these shopkeepers you choose to throw off your own family—to disgrace your mother and sisters—to be false to all the traditions of your order and your education—to dishonour your father's name and memory—you must. You are of age, and no one can prevent it if you wish to ruin yourself. But you shall not drag us down into your own shameful disgrace; and if you are obstinate, you know the penalty. Now go to bed and think over what I have said. No, do not kiss me; wait until you are good before you pretend to be loving. Go; and when you say your prayers to-night ask for a new heart and a contrite spirit."

CHAPTER XXX.

ET TU, BRUTE?

HAD he? Neither Mrs. Winstanley nor Thomasina liked to believe it possible that Perdita could have been so wicked—liked to acknowledge to themselves that the great chance had gone from them and the golden prize had slipped through their fingers. But he had—he surely had!— for though Benjamin Brocklebank was just the kind of man to spend a whole evening in sermonizing a delinquent on the sin of unpunctuality and the evil of undesirable associates, still, he looked more fierce and angry when he left than would have been justified by even a quarrel about that abominable woman in scarlet satin tartan; and Perdita had a curiously overwhelmed manner, as if she had heard something that was more than unexpected and worse than unpleasant.

Though devoured by curiosity and distracted by doubt, Mrs. Winstanley did not dare to ask the question point-blank. A strictly proper English mother may practically put up her daughters to auction, to be knocked down to the highest bidders, but theoretically she keeps them under a glass case. And to ask her daughter if a gentleman has proposed to her simply because he has been left alone with her for a couple of hours was too much against the recognized code to be thought of for a moment. Hence, neither mother nor sister could get at the true state of the case; and the doubt which was moral certainty remained unconfirmed.

But, if she had refused him, then ought she to be banished from home without loss of time. She was not only of no good to the family commonwealth but she stood in the way of the others and intercepted golden chances which she despised and those others would have utilized. Even Eva would have behaved with more common sense and right principle, more family feeling and filial piety, had this glorious chance fallen to her share; and as for Thomasina, it had been hers in the beginning and would have been hers to the end had not this tiresome rebel come in between. It was Perdita who had done all the mischief—Perdita who had turned the ironmaster from his appointed path and then shut against him that one of her own making which she had induced him to take—Perdita who had warped his better judgment and left him with the crook still unstraightened—Perdita who had warmed his frozen fancy to the point of melting and determined his halting choice to that of decision, and who, after all the mischief that she had so wilfully done, had now said coolly: "No! I have snatched the golden ball from them and I will not keep it for myself! They shall not profit and I will not enjoy!"

What wonder then that Mrs. Winstanley and Thomasina, thinking all this of the rebel, resolved on her banishment as a measure of general protection as well as of her own individual punishment righteously accorded. What a coil it all was! What a dreadful moment of disappointment and difficulty! What an indignity it was to have to submit to those insolent tradesmen with their threats of legal proceedings and getting by the law what they could not obtain by grace!—and what a heartbreak to think of the relief that had been possible and now was lost! Every one might have been paid off, and fresh scores begun—which would have lasted for another five years' run. The name of Benjamin Brocklebank as her son-in-law would have been as good to Mrs. Winstanley as so much in the Consols.[1] And here she was on the bare boards and her nose rasped at the grindstone, all because of that wicked girl, that shamefully disobedient rebel! Think too, what the position of the family would have been had this shocking person done her duty, or kept out of the way and let others do theirs! Thomasina would have been Mrs. Benjamin Brocklebank well endowed for life—or would have been left free for a fresh start;—Eva would have had a better foothold and a stronger springboard for her matrimonial vault;—Perdita herself would have been either provided for and translated from the place of family disaster to that of family benefactress, or she would have been rendered harmless by the safety of her sisters. And she herself, the mother, the schemer, the debtor, the harassed tiller of fields which would not yield, the sad sower of grain that would not ripen, she would have been like a second Juno on her throne with the world at her proud feet. And now the whole thing had gone by the board; and instead of Olympus it was shipwreck!

Altogether it was really an awful moment; and poor Mrs. Winstanley might be excused if, rendered desperate by her difficulties, she struck about her wildly—and struck cruelly though not quite unjustly. But she must not cry aloud nor call the world to witness her defeat. If she had to fall and there was no help for it, she must fall proudly, like great Caesar, and bide her wounds beneath her velvet decorously and nobly. On the brink of destruction as she was, she determined to keep a brave front and not give her enemies cause to rejoice over her ruin before the moment when concealment would be impossible. And one visit which she would make, with fife and drum and colours flying—that is, in a hired carriage and in her best attire; taking her two pretty daughters with her as witnesses of her worth—was to Lady Kearney, the blue riband of her visiting list. She wanted to see how things were in this quarter; and whether the duel had or had not awakened distrust in the mother and jealousy in the son. If it had, then she would encourage Bois-Duval, in secret and without the knowledge of Benjamin Brocklebank; if it had not and she found the lines where she had left them, then she would discourage him, and make him understand that he was *de trop*. This was a duty belonging to the hour and the circumstance.

They found Lady Kearney at home, and were ushered into the formal

---

[1]   Perpetual British government bonds.

drawing-room, where nothing spoke of ease or cosy carelessness, and where all was eloquent of wealth, propriety, exactness and the right thing. My lady's reception of her handsome visitors was, to say the least of it, frigid. She was polite, as a matter of course; but it was on the outside edge; and she took no pains to assume the grace of kindness beyond the obligations of ceremony. She had always been as much against this undesirable acquaintance of her son with the Winstanleys as was Mrs. Winstanley herself against that of Perdita with Bell Blount and the Crawfords; and in the absence of that son, it was easy to make the women feel how low she, Lady Kearney, held them and how inimical to them she was.

Well seasoned to social rebuffs as the major's widow was, the crushing coldness of her hostess was almost too much for her; and the difficulties of conversation were well nigh insurmountable. The only two topics on which Lady Kearney would open out, were that unlucky duel and Perdita's still more unlucky opinions. On the former she was almost eloquent in her scorn and disdain and showed clearly enough that she believed no word of that famous historical basis. She did not know which of the two girls to suspect, but she did suspect one and foul play all round: though Hubert, who had been in the fray, was as good as married to Maud Disney, and her own son, who was free, had been out of it. Yet for all this odd entanglement and appearance of general misfit, she felt sure that underneath this affair was something which Mrs. Winstanley did not wish to have known, and which would compromise her and hers were it known.

"It was a very odd affair from first to last," she said, looking at Mrs. Winstanley with her most unpleasant expression. "I never heard of such a thing in our peaceful days as a duel about a few feats in history! Can you say positively, Mrs. Winstanley, that no more personal motive influenced the young men?"

She turned her formidable pince-nez on the two girls when she said this. Thomasina, looking at a book of photographs, was simply passive and uninterested; Eva was playing with the Kearney Skye, which was tearing the fringe on her dress. Like many selfish people, and like many cruel people, she was fond of pets.

"No other motive was known to me," answered Mrs. Winstanley blandly. "There might have been a gambling debt; of that I cannot be sure. It was during the races that this most disastrous quarrel broke out; but I can give no more than a mere guess, and I would not care to be cited as an authority."

"The young ladies know no more than their mother, I presume?" said Lady Kearney with a sneer.

Thomasina looked up from her book of photographs.

"I know only what mother knows," she said with maiden serenity.

"And I know nothing at all," said Eva, wiping the dog's eyes with its ears and lifting up her own blue limpid orbs with the sweetest expression of innocence to be found on a human face.

"Your very outspoken daughter, who proclaims herself a red republican and an atheist and who is not with you to-day, has no different view, I dare say?" said Lady Kearney with a satirical smile. "I should like to have had a little talk with her. She would probably have had an original theory of her own. It might not have been correct, but it would be sure to have been bold and amusing."

"My daugher Perdita? she was not with us at Trouville. She knows less than little Eva," said Mrs. Winstanley, quite calmly and suavely. "I left her in town under the care of an old governess of hers; as, for certain reasons with which I need not trouble you, it was not desirable to take her so far from home."

"Ah!" said Lady Kearney; "She would be an inconvenient witness I would say, where things had to be concealed."

"Very," answered Mrs. Winstanley, with the most charming and delightful frankness. "She is the soul of truth and candour, and could neither tell a falsehood nor keep a secret to save her life. She would be sure to make the world free of what she knew. But as in this matter she knows no more than we do, and indeed not so much, she has nothing to conceal, because she has nothing to tell."

Lady Kearney looked at her visitor from head to foot; looked at her insolently, keenly, distrustfully. She was like a terrier sniffing round a closed box with a rat inside. She was conscious that the creature was there, but she could not get at it. She had no actual evidence that the Winstanley hand was in the duel, but her "flair" was unerring, and she trusted to it.

"It was a most extraordinary affair, look at it how one will," she said again; "and I confess I should like to get to the bottom of it."

"So should I, very much indeed," said Mrs. Winstanley, "if indeed there be anything to get at more than we know already. If there be, it is as much a mystery to me as to any one. By-the-way, when does my good friend Sir James return?" she added, suddenly.

"My son's movements are independent of me, and I do not regulate them. I cannot tell when he will return," answered Lady Kearney, with extreme stiffness.

She thought the question a liberty that warranted more than the reproof of coldness, and she would have liked to have marked her sense of disgust in other ways than by that of mere coldness.

"I am meditating a small party, just to amuse the girls; but I do not care to give it without Sir James," said Mrs. Winstanley genially, as if taking Lady Kearney into her confidence. "I hope every day to hear of dear Hubert's complete recovery, when his marriage with our dear Maud will come off immediately. And I want to give my little party as a kind of avant-propos of congratulation; but"—with even more of that quasi-sisterly friendliness with which she had begun her speech—"not without our dear Sir James! He is a host in himself—and so kind to my girls—so nice in every way, that I should be lost without him. And really young men in general are such unaccountable creatures—so difficult and odd—that it is delightful to get hold of one like your son, who is so amiable and friendly."

In general, Mrs. Winstanley was reasonable—for a woman remarkably so; but in her present mood she dropped the silken cord of her ordinary good-sense, and took up instead a goad, with the prod well sharpened.

"My son is much flattered by your appreciation, Mrs. Winstanley," drawled Lady Kearney. "When he has to work for his daily bread, as your daughter Perdita was so anxious to do, I shall feel justified in asking you for a character as lackey. You describe the functions admirably!"

"I shall be most happy to take him into my service," said Mrs. Winstanley, smiling.

Lady Kearney curled her thin lips.

"Precisely," she answered; "that is the whole thing."

"Then you do not know when he returns?" asked Mrs. Winstanley. "I must write to him. He is so amiable that I am sure he will even derange his plans that he may come to me for my little gathering. He knows what a favourite he is with us all. My girls look on him as a kind of brother. If a double maternity were possible, Lady Kearney, I should dispute him with you as my son."

The very bravado of her insolence silenced Lady Kearney. She could scarcely believe her own ears; and astonishment at this woman's impudence kept her tongue-tied.

Thomasina looked at her mother in surprise. Why had she cast policy to the winds in this odd manner? It was not like her to go out of her way to irritate one who could be so formidable an enemy as Lady Kearney and who might, if she would, be such a valuable friend. But Mrs. Winstanley was only human, like the rest of us; and for all her natural suavity and acquired self-control, she sometimes broke the cords and became natural, free and unwise, like more stupid and less conventional people.

"Unfortunately, my son chooses his own friends," said Lady Kearney, speaking slowly and with meaning. "He does not consult me, nor follow my counsels when I give them. It would be better if he did; but there are certain people whom he would not know, if he did."

"I quite agree with you, dear Lady Kearney," said Mrs. Winstanley, her acting admirable. "You may count on me as an earnest coadjutor who will use all her influence to maintain your prestige of maternal advice. The young of the present day are really too independent; but I will help you with your son, rely on it."

"I do not suppose, Mrs. Winstanley, that you mean to insult me?" said Lady Kearney, rising in her wrath.

"I insult? My dear Lady Kearney! quite the contrary! I meant to help you," said the bland visitor sweetly.

"Yet you must know that you have said the most cutting thing that one woman could say to another! the most insolent! the most insulting!" cried the mother of Sir James, with strong agitation.

"Regard it then as not having been said—accept my apologies for an unfortunate appearance of things!" cried Mrs. Winstanley. "I love your dear son and admire his mother too much to wish to offend. It has been a mistake—a mishap, voilà tout! You cannot refuse this apology?"

All this was said in the most caressing, the most velvety manner imaginable. Mrs. Winstanley was more than herself, she was Mrs. Winstanley *in excelsis*.

Lady Kearney stiffened as the other sweetened.

"I hate such misunderstandings!" she said sternly.

"And I also, dear Lady Kearney; but this was no misunderstanding. It was merely one friend speaking to another—a sister, I might almost say, to a sister."

"Mrs. Winstanley, when did I permit you to take this tone of intimacy?" cried Lady Kearney.

"My love for your son and your own sweetness and grace have emboldened me! Blame your own virtues, dear Lady Kearney, if you are loved better than you care to be!" said Mrs. Winstanley with a delightful smile. "Come, my dears," to her daughters, "we must really tear ourselves away. Your house is too delightful, dear Lady Kearney; but we must go."

"Never to be admitted again," said Lady Kearney even before they had gone. "If I quarrel seriously with that ungrateful boy—never again!"

"What an awful old toad that Lady Kearney is!" said Eva, when they had left the house. "What a humour she was in! Old horror! I should like to have beaten her! I longed to give her a good pinch, she was so cross and detestable. Poor sweet Mums; it was quite too awful of her!"

"She is not very suave," said Mrs. Winstanley quietly; "but we have to meet with odd people in life; and after all, does not our own superiority come out in such encounters? If we can show ourselves to be all right in manner, and these others all wrong—"

"So much to our score!" laughed Eva.

But Thomasina thought to herself that her mother had not acted quite up to her principles in this last encounter; and that she had played Lady Kearney's game because she had not been true to her own.

"She was frightfully trying, certainly!" said Our Eldest, as a kind of mental apology for her beloved mother.

And Mrs. Winstanley smiled benignly and answered, "Yes, frightfully; but I think she will not attempt to put me down again;" as if she had done a meritorious and not a socially reprehensible action, and had been wise in her generation instead of foolish.

The events of the day were not yet at an end, for soon after they reached home a resounding knock and peremptory ring which would have been eloquent enough to Perdita, announced the demand of Bell Blount for a conference with Mrs. Winstanley. One of those stormy petrels[1] of life who always accompany social convulsions, it was in the natural order of things that the Champion of her Sex should make her visit, which was to bring increased confusion, on a day already full of annoyance. It would not have been in harmony with her being had she gone to No. 100 when the family was in smooth water, as sometimes if so rarely happened; she must needs make her appearance to-day, when Perdita was already in such dire disgrace, and add to the punishment of the sinner on whose head it was scarcely worth while to heap more trouble.

It is to be supposed however, that Bell Blount was satisfied with herself, and in her own mind believed that she was doing what was best for the girl's future life, if the worst for her present peace.

"I owe you an apology for this intrusion, Mrs. Winstanley," she began in the oddly caressing and yet unsympathetic voice which made her so strangely out of harmony with herself.

Mrs. Winstanley, standing as she had just risen from her easy-chair,

---

[1]   An Atlantic seabird. The term "stormy petrel" has come to refer to a harbinger of trouble, perhaps because the bird was seen just before a storm.

received her unwelcome guest as glacially as Lady Kearney had just received her and her daughters. It was passing it on; and it pleased the major's widow to play off on another the uncomfortable airs which had just been played off on herself.

She did not disclaim the apology of the intrusion; she simply bent her head as stiffly as if her spine had but one joint, and that worked a little rustily, saying in a cold voice:

"To what am I indebted for the unexpected honour of this visit?" the accent on "honour" making it read "impertinence," just as a coloured light changes the hue of a landscape.

"I want to speak to you about your daughter Perdita," said Mrs. Blount, coming to the point. She was afraid that her patience would not hold out should she have to submit for any length of time to Mrs. Winstanley's fine airs; besides, she was too full of the subject of her visit to care for circumlocution.

"I do not know what you can have to say to me about my daughter Perdita," returned Mrs. Winstanley haughtily, still holding her head high and her neck stiff.

"If you will have the kindness to listen, you will find out," said Bell Blount coolly; "and if you will have the patience and propriety, madam, to hear me to the end, you will thank me for what I am going to say. Perdita is a good girl, a very fine, noble kind of creature in some directions; but she is on the wrong tack. She is too democratic, too unwilling to submit to the established rules of society; and she must be kept by force in the right way, else she will get terribly far on the wrong. I am, as you know, a Woman's Rights woman, heart and soul; and I have devoted myself to our emancipation from the tyranny of man and the restrictions of our sex; but that is not being a Red Republican, not a wild harebrained democrat and Nihilist as your daughter is. I would keep to the usages and the classes of society, as I would keep to anything else that was wholesome and beautiful; and the more strenuous my efforts to get great principles established in the teeth of popular prejudice, the more earnest I would be to preserve certain forms and fashions untouched. Your daughter Perdita would let everything go to destruction; and if asked to loosen the bearing-rein would end by taking off the head-stall and pulling out the linchpin."

"Will you kindly tell me the meaning and point of all this?" asked Mrs. Winstanley coldly, as Bell stopped to take breath.

"Willingly—I am coming to it. The meaning and the point are one thing, and that is—Leslie Crawford. Your daughter Perdita is bewitched with these chemist people, and I have come to you to tell you what I know, that you may stop the intercourse which should never have been begun. They are people belonging to my old home and I know all about them. This young man married his cousin—of itself a crime—and his conduct to her was so infamous that he sent her mad. She has been in an asylum for the last two years; and there she is still and is likely to continue. When he had shut her up tight and fast, he left our village and came up to London; established himself in High Street; scraped acquaintance, the mischief knows how, with that inconsiderate girl of yours; and now she is for ever running in and out their house like a tame cat, and takes the opinion of that ignorant and underbred shopkeeper and his half-idiotic old aunt or mother, whatever she may be, rather than she will take mine or yours. It is an infamy—an infamy!" repeated Bell Blount warmly; "and it must be put a stop to at once!"

By this time she had talked herself into a state of excitement. All her worst passions were roused through her jealousy, her anger, at this intrusion of the masculine element in a friendship where she desired to be sole and supreme. If, to punish her for her infidelity to the Cause and herself, Bell Blount could have done poor Perdita some mortal injury in body or spirit, she would have done so, she who so short a time ago had loaded the girl with caresses and desired nothing so much as the possession of her life, her conscience and her love! But the jealousy which such women as she feel against men as their rivals with other women is greater than jealousy of the more ordinary kind; and Bell would have forgiven her husband, had he loved another woman, sooner than she would have forgiven Connie Tracy had she found another "chum," or than she could suffer Perdita's natural inclination for Leslie Crawford. All her love for the girl had now turned to hate, and Mrs. Winstanley herself was not more resolute to enforce conformity with custom, more furious against these eccentric divergencies, than was Bell Blount, now that it had come to one of the oppressed taking a line of her own which did not run parallel with that of the man-hating Champion of her Sex.

"I have already spoken to my daughter about these people," said Mrs. Winstanley with less acidity than before. "I thank you for the hint."

"It is just this kind of thing which does the Cause so much harm," said Bell. "Because we fight for justice and equality—for protection and the right of self-support—that does not include such vagaries as these! We are not Red Republicans or anarchists because we want the schools to be opened to women equally with men—because we want the professions to be in common—because we think that University endowments should be shared with us—that all careers should be as free to the one sex as to the other. We do not want our lady-girls to marry tradespeople because we advocate independence. It is a loss to the Cause that such things should be done or thought!"

"I confess I always classed you all together," said Mrs. Winstanley. "I have been much afflicted by the strange ideas and democratic tendencies of my second daughter; and I do not deny that, when I heard she had added the Emancipation of Women to her repertoire, I gave you credit for aiding and abetting her in all her unwisdom."

"See there!" cried Bell with energy. "See what harm such silly exaggeration does! I am a conservative, Mrs. Winstanley, a strong conservative; and democracy is abhorrent to me. I honour the throne and respect the nobility; I love the Church and reverence the hierarchy; and my only difference with received opinion is that I hold women as sacred creatures and all men as their inferiors—only some more so than others."

"I cannot understand then your friendship with my daughter, she whose democracy is so pronounced, so dreadful!" said Mrs. Winstanley.

"No? It was her strength that attracted me," answered Bell. "But now that I see how mistaken she is, and how she clings to her old-world ideas and persuasions and fal-lal feminine instincts and all the rest of it, I have done with her; and I put you, her mother, on your guard, simply that she may not be irredeemably ruined."

At that moment Perdita came home.

"Come here Perdita," her mother said as the girl entered the room, amazed and dismayed when she saw Bell Blount sitting there as one at home. "You think me hard and harsh to you," she went on to say; "you dispute my commands because you imagine yourself more enlightened than I, your mother—more *au courant* of the greatest principles of life; and now I want to show you to yourself. Here is one of your prized leaders, Mrs. Blount, of whose friendship you have spoken to me with pride, who has come to denounce you and your folly to me; and to engage me to take measures by which your further extravagances may be prevented."

"I do not understand it all," said Perdita, holding up her head and meeting Bell Blount's eyes straightly, clearly, fearlessly.

"It means, Miss Winstanley, that I have been telling your mother of your infatuation—for I can call it nothing else—for that chemist fellow and his mother—those Crawfords of High Street—a man who sent his wife mad by his evil conduct and who presumes to go about with a young lady like yourself as his equal. A married man casting sheep's eyes at a virtuous girl!—a tradesman speaking and acting as if he were your equal!"

Bell's handsome face became livid as she spoke. Her enmity to this presumptuous shopkeeper was surely strangely strong to warrant such a display of passion, of hatred, of revenge.

"He is my equal; and more—he is my superior," said Perdita's clear voice. "It was not his evil conduct that sent his wife mad, but her own. He acted nobly, grandly, like a hero. And he is not a married man—she is dead."

"Then, Mrs. Winstanley, look out!" cried Bell, rising in extreme agitation. "That fool of yours is in love with him, and, by the Lord, she will run off with him!"

"Bell!" cried Perdita; "is this what you mean by friendship?"

"Friendship! I have no friendship with a girl who forsakes the Cause and forgets what is due to herself as a lady!" answered Bell. "If you had kept with me I would have protected you with my life; but, renegade as you are, you must not count on my support."

"Now you see where your folly has led you, Perdita!" said her mother. "Every one abandons you, even your own friends."

"Every one but God and my own conscience," said Perdita with solemn passion. "And while these stand by me, I will let the rest go!"

"God and your conscience!" cried Bell Blount. "You mean your perverted instincts and your worse than silly fancy! If Leslie Crawford had been five foot nothing, and pitted with the small-pox, you would not have found God or your conscience either in sticking to him. Call things by their right names, Miss Winstanley!"

"But this is intolerable—it is insupportable!" said Mrs. Winstanley. "Mrs. Blount! I cannot submit to this! Do me the favour not even to imagine such a horror as possible. My daughter with any personal feeling for a tradesman! That she should like the woman as her friend was bad enough—this is unendurable!"

"It is the truth," said Bell. "She cannot deny it."

"I do not know what it is that I have to deny," said Perdita.

"That you love Leslie Crawford," said Bell.

The girl turned deathly pale, but she stood her ground.

"If you mean that I respect him and believe in him—I do," she said firmly. "And I love his mother."

"Trash!" said Bell coarsely. "It is the son, not the mother, I tell you! If you deceive others you cannot deceive me. Mark my words, madam," to Mrs. Winstanley; "before the year is out you will have a shopkeeper for your son-in-law."

"I would rather see her dead at my feet!" cried Mrs. Winstanley passionately.

"Mother!" cried Perdita, shocked and revolted; "this is blasphemy against humanity! The man ranks before the station—Christ came as a carpenter!"

"Leave the room, Perdita! be thankful that I do not say leave the house—that I do not disown you!" cried Mrs. Winstanley, pointing to the door.

"You have already disowned me, mother, in heart and substance," returned Perdita; "you might as well finish with it. It wants only the form. But I did not think that this would have come to me through you," she added, turning to Bell Blount.

"Blame yourself, not me," answered Bell; "and blame that vile man most of all."

"Go, Perdita—not another word!" said Mrs. Winstanley. "I thank this friend of yours, this Mrs. Blount, for her proper feeling—her womanly information."

"Mother!" cried Perdita.

"Go!" repeated her mother; and Perdita walked somewhat proudly out of the room, feeling that surely now her cup was full. But such a cup as hers holds a fearful amount before it runs over.

CHAPTER XXXI.

WITHIN THE SHEEPFOLD.

HUBERT STRANGWAYS lost to her and secured by his own—Sir James a laggard threatening to become a deserter—Benjamin Brocklebank probably rejected and certainly affronted—Thomasina not sought by any, though a jewel fit for a prince to wear—Perdita consorting with tradespeople as their friend and fit companion—her debts heavy and her creditors troublesome, where could poor Mrs. Winstanley look for help?

When the door-bell rang and the servant ushered in M. le Vicomte de Bois-Duval, it was to the harassed widow as if the empty lucky-bag had had another shake and she had been allowed the chance of another prize—a meagre one if you will, but as the last of the series, better than none at all.

A titled son-in-law, though only a "fusionless" foreigner, would stop the gaping months of her creditors with the whipped cream of expectation and a big word; and as Madame la Vicomtesse de Bois-Duval, little Eva would be socially well placed enough. Not so well certainly as if she had been either Lady Kearney or Mrs. Strangways; still, not badly for one whose face was all her fortune—not so badly as to lessen Thomasina's chances or to cause contempt for her own choice. Mrs. Winstanley, rapidly reviewing all the points of her position, received the young Frenchman gracefully; and no one would have thought by her manner that she was greeting the all-but-murderer of the man whom she had so cleverly played and so ardently desired to land as her son-in-law. Poor soul! There was more gratitude in her grace than she would have cared for him to know—more desperation in her hospitality to a potential son-in-law than she would have confessed even under torture.

This visit was in more senses than one a reconnaissance made by the Vicomte. He had an idea that things were rather shaky in this solid-looking, respectable English home, and that these pretty creatures standing in the marriage market-place were waiting rather too eagerly for their purchasers. He saw that it would not be difficult for any man with twopence-halfpenny of which he could make threepence to become Mrs. Winstanley's son-in-law and the husband of one of Mrs. Winstanley's daughters; and by this he made out that their own portions would be slender. He did not think that they had none at all and were to be given away gratis; still less that the man existed who would take them on these terms—bearing them on his shoulders as a lifelong burden unpaid for. So far as he himself was concerned, he had no desire to take them on his, *dot* or no *dot*.[1] He had no intention of marrying and ranging himself just yet. The free field of bachelorhood was more to his mind. Notwithstanding the large crop already raised, he had sackfuls of wild oats yet to sow; and Eva was a pretty little thing, just cut out for the part which he had decided that she should play.

It was her mother's fault and her own folly, he said to himself, twisting his moustaches. The one ought to be more careful of such brittle wares as youth and beauty, and the other ought to be more prudent. When shepherds wish to keep their lambs safe they shut them up in the sheepfold and let the watch-dogs loose. But if one imprudent little ewe lamb will creep through the fence and deceive the dog, is the wolf to forswear his nature and forego the dainty morsel that comes of its own free will between his paws? Not if that wolf were M. le Vicomte de Bois-Duval, and the dainty morsel an English girl without father or

---

[1] (French), point or no point.

brother to avenge her, and only a mother casting about for husbands to watch over her!

Besides this reconnaissance for Eva's sake and his own future, Bois-Duval wanted to understand how it came about that familiar relations existed between a Winstanley and Leslie Crawford. Wherefore he called at No. 100 boldly—for all that project in his pocket which dealt with the invasion of the sheepfold and the ewe lamb struggling through the fence; a project which, it might have been thought, would have made the mother of little Eva just the one person in all the world whom he would have least cared to see.

He found Mrs. Winstanley alone. Thomasina and Eva had gone to a friendly five o'clock tea with no other companionship than their own. To do her justice they did not often "beat the fields" on their own account and unaccompanied by her; but to-day she was too much preoccupied to feel up to the task of smiles and small-talk. The duns who crowded round her, the sons-in-law whom she could not catch, and the great prize of all which she had felt sure had been rejected, together with Perdita's shameful sin of practical democracy, according to the accusations of Bell Blount, had overwhelmed her. She must have an hour or so of absolute quiet, else her health and her nerves would break down—and then where would they all be?

But it was unlucky that Bois-Duval should have called today of all the days in the week, and thus should have caught her out in maternal negligence which to him would seem more reprehensible than it was. It could not be helped now; and an improvised chaperon would be a white lie, good at a pinch and hurting no one.

After the usual introductory phrases had been exchanged, Bois-Duval asked after the young ladies with scrupulous formality as to terms, but suggestive warmth as to manner. That manner was so warm and yet so delicate, it would not have surprised the mother had he opened negotiations on the spot. It made her heart flutter as if she had been a girl herself waiting on the humour of her lover and yearning for the moment when he should have done with indecision and come finally to the point of declaration.

"They are quite well, thank God!" she said with that kind of maternal love tinged with piety which is so effective and edifying; "always well and always good!"

"I trust I may have the pleasure of seeing them;" said M. le Vicomte with graceful desire, looking round the room as if he expected to find them hidden behind the chairs or between the folds of the curtains.

"Oh yes; they will soon return," she answered. "They have only gone to a friend's, close at hand."

"Without you?" he asked brusquely.

"Actually!" she answered with smiling sweetness. "I put them in charge of a trustworthy chaperon; and doubtless they are wearying themselves as young girls do in formal reunions where all the gentlemen are on one side of the room and all the ladies on the other, like antagonistic forces!"

"I do not know this style of reunion in England," he said dryly. "All that I know belong to a freer style, where the gentlemen and the ladies mingle together without constraint, and the chaperon is for the most part conspicuous by her absence from her charge."

"Yes? That is, I know, one of the forms of English society; but not in the class to which we belong," said Mrs. Winstanley with the unostentatious pride of secure caste. "My lady friends and myself—we seldom, if ever, lose sight of our daughters or delegate our duty to any one else. Sometimes, of course, it is unavoidable, as to-day; but we hold to the duty of strict surveillance and the value of maternal companionship."

"Yet your English young ladies have a great deal more liberty than we Frenchmen can understand," said Bois-Duval, as he had said twenty times before.

"Some have greatly too much," she answered. "I have never gone into the new system myself, and I deplore it in others. I keep my daughters as close as a French mother would keep hers and reap my reward in their perfect innocence and sincerity. They know nothing of evil and they could not deceive me."

"Ciel! such a thing would be impossible!" said Bois-Duval with perfect gravity: it was almost too perfect. "And yet," shaking his forefinger slowly before his face, "not quite like French girls, believe me, madame."

"No?" She lifted up her eyes and raised her eyebrows in surprise. "In what do they differ?"

"The two whom I have the honour to know are probably in accord with my ideas," said Bois-Duval; "but that one of madame's daughters whom I have not the honour to know and who walks arm-in-arm with a stupid grocer or chemist or some such canaille[1]—that, madame, is an anomaly impossible with us. Such a thing could not exist in France. It would be as monstrous as if a well-born young lady were to go about the streets in a blouse and casquette."

---

[1] (French), scoundrel.

Mrs. Winstanley turned pale; but she kept her voice steady if her blood proved a traitor to her self-command.

"A daughter of mine on the arm of a chemist?" she repeated with a forced smile. "Are you sure of your eyesight, Vicomte? You must have made a mistake. These false likenesses are so bewildering and misleading."

"It was the young lady whom I saw in your box at the theatre the other night, and who is, I presume, the sister of those two charming demoiselles who are confessedly your daughters?" said Bois-Duval airily. "If she is their sister then it was your daughter, madame, whom I met the other evening at dusk walking under the escort of Leslie Crawford, a chemist. I mention the fact merely as an illustration of the difference existing between the English code of manners and our own. It has no other significance for me!"

"That young lady is my daughter," said Mrs. Winstanley; "but let me assure you, M. le Vicomte, this is not an ordinary occurrence in our society; and it is too extraordinary to be believed."

"Truly?" He spoke as if asking for information. "I am glad to hear this for the sake of the nation, but sorry that I spoke. Perhaps I ought to say sorry that I saw, for the sake of the young lady herself."

"No, it is best, if it be really true and is not an error," said Mrs. Winstanley, her parched lips moving with difficulty.

"At the worst it was only an act of caste imprudence, a piece of too openly defiant democracy for good taste and good sense," said the Vicomte soothingly. "There can be no personal danger in it, for my brave grocer is already married; or was, when I knew of his miserable little existence some two or three years ago."

"It is odd that you yourself, Vicomte, should have known anything about such a man!" cried Mrs. Winstanley, turning against her visitor with as much ferocity as it was in her nature to feel.

"I?" he laughed. "I know my brave grocer like my glove! I was slightly acquainted with his little wife. She was at the same school in Paris as a certain young protégée of my aunt's, and I used to see her at my aunt's house en petit comité on the jours des vacances. She was a pretty little person, but polissonne—ma foi![1] she was all that and more! When I was last in England chance threw her in my way; and I thus became acquainted with my chemist, her respectable husband, with whom, I confess, she was not always enraptured. That is the little history, madame. You see it is neither odd nor mysterious."

---

[1] (French), I used to see her at my aunt's house "for a little chat" on the "vacation days." She was a pretty little person, but "low-class—my goodness!"

"Mysterious, no; but always a little odd that a man of M. le Vicomte's position should have cared to become personally acquainted with people so far beneath him in the social scale!"

It was quite a relief to Mrs. Winstanley to be able to say this. It shifted the burden by half an inch or so, and slackened the strain of her own discomfort by passing it on to him.

He shrugged his shoulders.

"A man may condescend and not be hurt, where, to a woman, a lower scale of association is destruction," he said carelessly. "What harm can it possibly do me to know a pretty little bourgeoise more or less familiarly? But when it comes to an unmarried girl knitting up strict relations with a shopkeeper—that, madame, I think you will allow to be another matter altogether. But, faith! I am sorry I spoke. I used the fact merely as an illustration of manners, not in any sense as an accusation. Now let us speak of something else. Our grocer is getting as tedious to us as he was to the little Florence."

He turned the conversation abruptly into another channel, and talked of Trouville and the company which had assembled there; of the races and the bathing; the things which had happened last season and which he trusted would happen next; but—was it fancy? Mrs. Winstanley thought she saw a certain subtle something in his manner, a film of mockery that just suggested disrespect; as if the discovery that one of the daughters of the house was on familiar terms with a tradesman lowered the status of the whole family, and put them that one step below himself which rendered the last polish of courtesy unnecessary.

That unlucky Perdita! By what terrible decree of fate was it that she had been told off to be their scourge! Her comparative plainness, her awkward shyness, her reprehensible opinions, her almost criminal conduct, her unfeminine democracy, her unladylike love of liberty—everywhere she stood between them and the sunlight and brought shadows and annoyances upon them! Had Mrs. Winstanley been superstitious she would have believed in some great family crime, committed in the ages long ago, of which this ill-starred rebel was the family retribution. As things were, she was an anomaly in good sooth!—a cuckoo in the hedge-sparrow's nest, a crab-apple among the golden pippins, a field-daisy on the same stalk with a triad of highly-cultivated garden asters. How she came among them at all was a mystery to the distracted mother—a mystery and a scourge in one!

Presently the girls came home. All three were together, Perdita having overtaken her sisters at the end of the street; and naturally all three came into the room together. For though the rebel was under sentence of capital punishment, reprieved only for a few days to give her the chance of repentance, she was not completely shut off from the family, and her presence among them, if not desired, was not resented.

Bois-Duval rose and greeted the two whom he knew—Thomasina with respectful admiration, Eva with flattering warmth. Then he bowed with formal politeness to Perdita and looked round at Mrs. Winstanley.

It was odd to see the difference in the manners of the girls. Thomasina was suavely cold and smoothly haughty; little Eva was fluttered, frightened, excited, shy; while Perdita, recognizing the man against whom Leslie Crawford had warned her, flushed from brow to chin, and turned away with the rude brusquerie of a sincere girl who thinks it incumbent on her to make a scamp understand that she knows he is a scamp and therefore holds him to be out of the pale of charitable association altogether.

Her mother, who was watching her, saw both her flush and her abrupt movement. She read these as the signs of embarrassment in being thus brought face to face with the witness of her misdemeanour. Bois-Duval, knowing what Leslie could say if he would, perhaps had a different interpretation for his own private use. What he might think, however, was nothing to the purpose. Thoughts are not words;—may we not be thankful for the power of putting on the armour of hypocrisy as a protection against discovery? And as part of that protection, Bois-Duval emphasized this little scene by turning to Mrs. Winstanley, with a half comical, half appealing look, slightly raising his eyebrows, as if he had said:

"These the manners of a Winstanley? This the breeding of a sister to the potential Vicomtesse de Bois-Duval?"

"Perdita, Monsieur le Vicomte de Bois-Duval," said Mrs. Winstanley, somewhat unwisely. It is always well to let sleeping dogs lie; and Perdita's uncomfortable sincerity was a dog which had all his teeth.

Perdita, thus admonished, made the slightest inclination of her head possible to be construed into a bow. She was just not savage enough to the point of refusing this act of recognition; her truth would bear no greater strain than this; but she was angry with herself for not having the courage to refuse even this.

"I had the honour of meeting mademoiselle the other night," said Bois-Duval, breaking the first lance.

"Yes," said Perdita hardily; "I saw you."

"I was saying to madame how much I admire your English democratic feeling," said Bois-Duval with a pleasant philosophizing kind of air. "This *is* the young lady, madame, of whom I have just spoken to you," he continued, turning to Mrs. Winstanley—"the young lady whom I met in the dark leaning on the arm of the grocer Crawford—one of the class which we, in our benighted aristocratic pride, would call the canaille."

The word made Perdita wince. It was false as applied to Leslie; all the same it made her wince. Mrs. Winstanley did not speak. She could not; her tongue was too dry, her lips too parched for words. Thomasina drew herself up like a young queen, indignant with both delinquents alike; and from Eva's pretty blue eyes came a flash of anger which, had it had veritable "dynamic" force, would have crushed the unlucky rebel on the spot.

"The courage with which young ladies like mademoiselle act out their principles of democratic equality, here in your brave England, is beyond all praise," continued Bois-Duval, still sweetly philosophic. "We are now a republic"—in politics M. le Vicomte was an Imperialist, and only regretted that he was in the age of his milk-teeth during the glorious era of Compiègne[1]—"you can understand then how, as a Frenchman of the present day, I admire this courageous testimony!"

"There is no courage in taking the arm of a good and honourable man like Mr. Crawford," said Perdita, making a tremendous effort over herself to conquer her shyness for the sake of her truth.

"A grocer quand même? Admirable!" cried Bois-Duval.

"If Mr. Crawford were bad or dishonourable, then it would require courage to be seen with him, even if he were a prince!" said Perdita, warming to her work. "As it is, I am proud of his acquaintance."

"My dear Perdita!" said her mother, forcing a smile that was a spasm, a laugh that was a groan. "Your extraordinary ecstatics again!"

"Do you feel this exaltation for his wife as well?" asked Bois-Duval quite simply, as if sincerely anxious to know. "And how is that pretty little polissonne? She had good eyes if I remember right; but for all the rest—body and mind, heart and brain—pouf!"

He flicked his fingers. This was the measure of her value to the man for whom she had sacrificed her life and all that made that life honourable or worth having.

"I did not know the wife; but from what I do know you ought not to speak of her like this!" said Perdita hotly.

This time Bois-Duval's surprised look was genuine. He had expected that Leslie Crawford would have denounced him, but not that he would have given the reason why. Had he then made this young unmarried

---

[1] The "Imperial Town" 50 miles north of Paris, originally established as a residence for the kings of France, later associated with Napoleon III (1808–73) and the Second Empire.

girl his confidante and told her the infamous truth? If so, the information which had been meant for bale would prove in reality for blessing, and Mrs. Winstanley ought to have been warned. And he need have no scruples about Eva. It was in the family; and at all events he was better than Leslie Crawford.

"I am at a loss to understand what mademoiselle means," said the Frenchman slowly. "I knew Miss Crawford when a little school-girl in Paris, and before she had married her Puritan cousin; and afterwards I did her the honour of calling on her. A gentleman may patronize a bourgeoise without loss of caste or dignity, where, if a lady condescends to a grocer, she is simply destroyed for life. But I do not know why mademoiselle should speak of my good word as specially deserved by la belle pharmacienne! I have no reason to idealize this little polissonne!"

"You are talking in riddles, Perdita. What can you possibly know of this young person, or of M. le Vicomte's acquaintance with her?" said Mrs. Winstanley, again forcing a laugh that was in substance a groan.

"You funny old Per! You always know such a lot about everything!" said Eva in an undertone.

Thomasina said nothing. She had her own ideas; and though she thought Perdita horribly unhandy, detestably gauche in all her works and ways, still she did not feel disposed to question her accuracy in this matter, or to champion Bois-Duval.

"I know quite as much as I care to know," said Perdita, with the feeling of protecting her virtuous own from contaminating contact with a scoundrel. It was a trial having to do this thing; but is not all life a trial? and are we not sent into the world to testify and suffer? "Mr. Crawford told me, mother, that M. Bois-Duval was a man whom you ought not to know, and that I was to warn you against him. So I do."

Bois-Duval's olive-coloured face became livid; but he laughed with a nonchalant air, slightly tapping his forehead as he said compassionately: "Poor young lady—toquée!"

"Perdita, I command you to apologize to M. le Vicomte," said Mrs. Winstanley slowly. "Are you mad to insult a guest in my house in this unheard-of way, for no better reason than what a vulgar insolent shop-keeper may have said to you? Forgive her, Vicomte!—she is incorrigible! we can do nothing with her! she is hopeless!"

"So I thought," he said; "but madness is a dangerous inheritance," he added thoughtfully, as if brought face to face with an unexpected danger.

Between madness and insolence, Mrs. Winstanley was almost sorry that she had put the alternative! The one seemed as bad as the other—each indeed was the worse the nearer it was looked at.

"You never believe me, mother!" said Perdita passionately. "If I were told anything by an angel from heaven you would not believe it, simply because I said it to you!"

"Is this grocer your angel from heaven, mademoiselle?" asked Bois-Duval quietly.

That was a charming blot to hit!

"Apologize to M. le Vicomte, Perdita," repeated her mother.

"No, mother, I cannot," answered the rebel. "He is a bad man, and I will not pretend that he is a good one."

"Let me beg of you, madame, to let the matter drop!" pleaded Bois-Duval, with exceeding grace and courtly magnanimity. "Do not let the calumnies of a wretched scoundrel like this Crawford be the occasion of a moment's uneasiness! Suffer the young lady to calm herself. I am sure of my ground with you," smiling sweetly; "and her heated brain will only become more excited if the question is pressed. Let it drop, I beseech you!"

"At the Vicomte's request I will pass over your extraordinary conduct, Perdita," said Mrs. Winstanley after a pause. She was really uncertain how to bear herself in this, one of the worst of the many difficulties in which her daughter had so often placed her. "I think you have lost your senses," she continued; "but these things are not pleasant to discuss before strangers. Leave the room now and come and speak to me afterwards; but leave us now."

"Is she safe to be left alone?" asked Bois-Duval in an audible whisper.

"I am not mad," said Perdita quite gravely.

"Of course not! of course not!" he answered with forced eagerness. It was the right tone to take in speaking to a lunatic whom he must soothe by compliance, not excite by contradiction. "Mad! whoever thought you were?" he added.

"If you are not you ought to be," was Eva's logical rejoinder.

"I have done my duty," said Perdita, flaming on the instant. "This is a bad man, and he has no business in your house, mother."

When she had shot this last bolt she turned and left the room; feeling as if she had been walking among red-hot ploughshares and had not wholly escaped burning.

Soon after this Bois-Duval too left; and even Thomasina did not catch the moment when that little note passed from his hand to Eva's, as he stroked "poor pussie," curled up in a round white ball in her arms, and said: "Jolie petite chatte! belle Minette!" with an emphasis and a look which she alone understood.

When he had gone and Eva had scampered upstairs to her own room to read that fatal note, Mrs. Winstanley turned for comfort and counsel to her eldest daughter, whose silence and quiescence during all this disagreeable scene had struck her as somewhat extraordinary.

"What are we to do with her, Thomasina?" cried the poor mother in tears. "She grows intolerable! worse and worse every day! I cannot bear it much longer—and I feel that in duty to you and Eva I ought not."

"She is very uncouth, very tiresome, and does everything in the wrong way. One could shake her even when she does right," said Thomasina, throwing her rebellious sister's manner to the wolves; "but I think there is something in what she said; and she thought she was doing her duty, poor little thing," she added, guarding the matter.

"Something in what she said? do you think him bad, my dear?" asked the mother anxiously.

"More bad than good," Thomasina answered. "I watched his face and it was dreadfully conscious, though he tried to laugh it all off like a bad joke. I do not like him, dear mother," she continued earnestly; "I never have—and I have never trusted him. He is a frightful flirt, and means nothing all the while. He pays little Eva too much attention, for I am sure he does not intend to make her an offer."

"My dear!" remonstrated Mrs. Winstanley. "I have never seen anything to object to in his manner to the child! Surely you are exaggerating, and frightening yourself needlessly."

Thomasina looked at her mother, and an expression of the tenderest pity came over her face. That poor harassed mother! she would not add to her troubles! What there was to be done in this matter she would take on herself to do. She would keep it all as quiet as she had done hitherto, and make herself her sister's guardian—to save poor mother who had enough to worry her already!

"Well, perhaps I am too anxious about Eva," she answered. "She is such a pretty little thing, and so innocent, that one cannot be too careful of her. By-the-by," she added as if carelessly, "Sir James has returned; I saw him in Mrs. Merton's carriage. I suppose we shall see him here soon."

"Returned? I am glad of that," said Mrs. Winstanley as carelessly. "But what are we to do with Perdita, Thomasina? This horrible intimacy with this man—this tradesman—this dreadful chemist creature, must be put a stop to, or really and truly she must leave the house. It is not fair to you girls to keep her, and this thing going on. What can she be thinking of? This disgraceful affair! I feel my very head turn when I think of it!"

"She must be put a stop to—or she must go; for a time at least," said Thomasina quietly. "It would spoil everything to have it known."

"Sir James for one would not care to continue his acquaintance with us; and I am sure that Mr. Brocklebank would not," said Mrs. Winstanley, looking at Thomasina.

"They must not know," the wise elder daughter answered. "She must not stay at home," she repeated, "unless she will promise to give up this dreadful association. And that I do not think she will do."

"Why does she cling to it so tenaciously?" said Mrs. Winstanley. "I cannot believe that she is so lost, so abandoned, as to really care for the man. I believe it is nothing but a bit of her crazy democracy and wicked opposition. If it is more than this, Thomasina, it would break my heart for shame to think that a daughter of mine should so disgrace herself!"

"Oh, I can scarcely think this, dear mother!" answered Thomasina soothingly.

"If it is so, there will be no use in arguing with her. She will go her own way whatever may be said," Mrs. Winstanley returned. "But if it is so, she must be disowned. I could not own her, Thomasina. I could not have the children of a chemist and druggist calling me grandmother! It would curdle my blood—I could not bear it! And so important as it is that you should all marry well—with these dreadful debts preying on me!"

"We will, dear mother; at least Eva and I will," said Thomasina, going over to her mother and kissing her. "Never fear—do not lose heart—all shall come right!"

And at the moment she felt strong enough to affront fate and fortune, and conquer both, in the service of that beloved mother whose self-command and high diplomacy—which a base world would have called manœuvring and deceit—had always roused her admiration and seemed to her the ultimate of womanly perfection.

CHAPTER XXXII.

THE SCAPEGOAT.

PERDITA was a light sleeper. She was too intensely alive to sleep in the heavy way common to young people, and was easily awakened. Consequently, a slight noise on the night of Bois-Duval's visit roused her to full activity, where no one else would have been troubled even by a dream; and she was up and about in less time than it takes to tell.

The noise that aroused her was as of some one stealing softly about the stairs and passages. The flooring of No. 100, West Hill Gardens was of that loquacious kind which betrays the steps even of unshod feet, the ill-laid boards creaking if only so much as a mouse ran over them; and this was undoubtedly something heavier than a mouse, though there was no sound of footfall or click of shoe-sole. Perdita made sure of burglars—men in masks with crowbars, jimmies, skeleton keys and pitch plasters, and as ready to take human life as to lift gear. But brave as some nervous women are, imagining everything and afraid of nothing, burglars or not, of course it was her imperative duty to protect the sleeping household, and give the alarm to the police before the robbers should have time to frighten mother or the girls. She was always ready for duties which demanded courage and exertion—duties which are best carried out by unselfishness and energy and where clumsiness and want of savoir faire do not count. She lighted her candle, opened her door, and with beating heart and straining eyes followed the footsteps down the stairs; forgetting that she offered herself as a target to any Bill Sykes[1] who might be roaming about with a revolver in one hand and a life-preserver in the other. Indeed, she seldom thought of her own risk at any time—never when her blood was up and she had something to do or more to say.

Always following the creak of the tread she went downstairs and came into the hall; and there she found Eva in the dark, in her hat and waterproof, a small carpet-bag on the floor beside her, with the chain in her hand on the point of opening the street-door.

---

[1] Bill Sikes (Linton's misspelling) is a thief in Dickens' *Oliver Twist* (1837–38). Sikes kept a life-preserver hung by the chimney to aid in his housebreaking schemes; he used a revolver to threaten Oliver into participating in his plans.

On the other side stood some one gently tapping with the tips of the nails against the panel.

Eva gave a smothered cry as Perdita suddenly seized her arm.

"Eva! what are you about?" said the rebel with natural indignation and surprise. "What on earth are you doing here at this time of night, dressed for going out, and opening the door? Are you mad?"

"It is no business of yours," said Eva defiantly.

"It is my business; it is every one's business!" answered Perdita warmly. "Who ever heard of such an extraordinary thing! Why, what are you doing? Where are you going?" she repeated.

"It is nothing. I was only going into the Square garden for fun," said Eva sullenly.

"The Square garden at twelve o'clock at night? That is not true, Eva," was her sister's reply. "There is something more in it than this. Hark! what is that at the door? Stand back and let me see what there is."

"You shall not. You horrid interfering, meddlesome thing, what right have you to speak to me like this, or interfere with me in any way?" cried the girl, but always in a whisper; "and you shall not open the door!" she repeated.

Made desperate by fear and strong by anger, she set her soft little back against the door and stood there fronting her sister and defying fate.

"I will know," said Perdita, excited to the last point and fearing she did not know what.

With one vigorous wrench, she displaced her sister, turned the key, flung open the door and stood face to face with Bois-Duval, standing there like a conspirator, in a slouched hat, with a Spanish cloak flung over one shoulder and hiding the lower part of his face.

"Wretch! how dare you!" was all that she could say, appalled and terrified as she was at this mystery of iniquity meeting her there on the threshold of their own home.

"I did not know that she would hear!" cried Eva, wringing her hands and unconsciously betraying herself and her lover.

"Peste!" said Bois-Duval brutally; "these maniacs are inconvenient! Do not cry, chère petite," to Eva; "I shall see you again, and without inconvenient intruders. Better chances next time. Do not be afraid. No harm will come to you. Au revoir; dormez bien—and keep the maniac in good order!"

And with this he made an ironical bow to Perdita, kissed Eva's hand and darted down the street just as the policeman, slow, majestic, innocent, thinking no evil and only yawning at the slow progress of time, came round the other corner.

Perdita shut the street door with a slam that made the public protector start and put an end to all idea of silent secrecy at home; and then Eva turned against her in fury—Euphrosyne doubled with Alecto.[1] But in her rage she did not forget prudence, nor the fact that although stone walls have no ears, sleeping mothers and vigilant elder sisters have; and that pelting an obnoxious busybody with invectives had better be done below the breath, with sobs well kept under, rather than in the clear excited tones in which that busybody herself spoke—she having nothing to conceal and being constitutionally indifferent to prudence.

In these few moments of anger, shame, and disappointment, Perdita heard more than she had ever heard before about herself and her qualities—what they thought of her among themselves—in what special abhorrence Eva herself held her—how ugly and horrid she was in person, how stupid and unlovable in mind—how they all hated to be with her and how much ashamed of her they were;—heard more than she had ever dreamed of; and yet she thought she had known her standing pretty well by now.

She bore it all with praiseworthy philosophy for a while. She understood that Eva must be dreadfully angry to have been caught as she had been; and that of course she would say bitter things in revenge—things which must be borne with patience. Those who have put others in the wrong can afford to be magnanimous—the victor can smile at the futile despair of the vanquished. But even the patience of the victor has its limits; and little Eva was not one to trouble herself about the exact line which it would be unwise to pass beyond. When it came to "And we all hate you, Perdita—Thomasina and mother and I—we all hate you; we hate you; and we wish you anywhere but at home; we wish you were dead!"—then Perdita's strength gave way, and she broke out into that strange mixture of grief and rage which was at once her sin and its chastisement.

"You cannot wish me away more than I want to go. If you wish I was dead I wish so too. I would rather be dead than live here with you all!" she cried, clasping her hands and holding them up to her face.

Eva was frightened by the wild loud tone, the scared heartbroken look. The shaft had struck deeper than the foolish little archer had intended that it should. Nevertheless it was true; they did dislike that inharmonious and obstructive rebel—and if they did not wish her absolutely dead, they did wish her away from home and off their hands

---

[1]   In Greek mythology, Euphrosyne was one of the three graces, daughters of Zeus, associated with Mirth. Alecto was a fury from Hell.

for life. She need not have said so, but having said so she would not retract; for even Eva had her shadowy sense of truth which she was bound in conscience to obey.

"Hush, Perdita! don't make such a noise! Do hold your tongue and don't cry like this! You will wake mother and Thomasina, and then there will be a far worse row than even this is! And don't be such a goose as to take everything literally that one says in a passion," said Eva in a softened voice. "We don't wish you were dead—you great baby, crying like this over a hasty little word! For goodness sake, Perdita, don't go on like this!" she added, pulling at her sister's dress. "Ina and mother will hear you if you do; and then what will become of us?"

"I don't care! I don't care what becomes of me!" sobbed Perdita.

Her heart was really broken this time, and she was indifferent to all but the anguish of that terrible fracture.

"But I do," said Eva; "and I am sure if any one has cause to be unhappy I have," she added whimpering. "I have been very silly, and you think me a great deal worse than silly; and everything has gone wrong all round; but I don't want to make bad worse, so I shall go to bed."

With which she clutched her little bag, took off her hat and crept up the stairs like a soft little white cat turned back from mousing; Perdita following, her candle in her hand, her brain on fire, and her poor, big, soft heart crushed, as she thought, for ever.

She had no sooner shut herself into her own room than Thomasina opened the door and came to where she was sitting, thrown forward on the bed, her face buried in the pillows and her whole body one great palpitating throb of misery.

"Perdita, what is all this about?" said Thomasina, not quite so coldly as usual.

She did not know what had caused the quarrel between the sisters at this time of night downstairs, but she knew that Perdita would tell her the truth.

"I am glad you have come, Thomasina," said Perdita, speaking as well as she was able. "You ought to know all; and you are just and will not take sides."

Poor Perdita! how she, and such as she, cling to straws of loving faith against their sadder knowledge!

"Tell me what it all means," repeated Thomasina.

And Perdita gave her the little history: how that she had been awakened by a noise; had thought it was burglars and had gone downstairs to see; had found Eva in hat and cloak dressed for a walk, with a small carpet-bag on the floor, on the point of opening the door to some one tapping on the outside; had herself opened it and come face to face with that abominable Frenchman standing there muffled up like a man on the stage; how then Eva was furious with her, and after saying a great many horrid things against her, had finally wound up by telling her that they all hated and detested her and wished that she was dead. And then poor Perdita wept again; horror at her sister's sin lost in the egotism of her own suffering.

Thomasina turned paler than even Perdita herself when she had confronted Bois-Duval. Had it then come to this? Was the family indeed doomed? Not only Perdita to destroy for the others those good chances which she would not utilize for herself—to lower the whole tone of their social position by her personal oddities and democratic associates—but Eva also; Eva, one of the best investments, the most solid-looking hope—Eva also turned traitor, ruining her family, breaking her mother's heart and flinging herself into destruction.

As she sat thinking out the position and its remedy, Perdita's tears touched her no more than the pattering of the rain against the skylight. The peril in which they all stood, and the mother's anguish were she ever to know the truth, were the deadly serpents which swallowed up the little cankerworms.

"Promise me, Perdita," she said after a pause; "whatever happens do not tell mother about Eva. Bear or conceal anything, but do not tell her."

"If she asks me, how can I tell a falsehood?" said Perdita, much as if she had been asked to commit a murder or to build the pyramids.

"Tell a thousand rather than the truth!" her sister answered. "Promise me this, Perdita?"

"I cannot promise to tell a lie. I cannot tell lies," the rebel answered with solemnity.

Was there ever such an inconvenient conscience?—such a troublesome code of morality?

"Selfish and egotistical as usual!" said Thomasina with disdain. "I would not have your morality, Perdita, for the whole world! You would not stir a finger to save mother from an annoyance that might perhaps kill her, if you had any silly superstitious idea that it was wrong to stir it! You care only for yourself and for what you choose to think right; and you do not care for what you make others suffer. I am sick of such selfishness! I know I would tell a thousand falsehoods to save either Eva's character or mother's pain."

"What does it matter what I do?" cried Perdita, flinging up her hands. "Whatever it is I am always wrong. Let me go away from you all, Thomasina. You will all be happier without me and I cannot be more miserable than I am! Let me go and never be heard of again."

"I have told you twenty times before, you owe everything to yourself," said Thomasina. "You do everything that you ought not to do, and then you wonder that we do not like it. You make disgraceful friendships with people below us in station; you flirt and bring on a man like Mr. Brocklebank, who is not accustomed to such conduct, and when he makes you an offer you refuse him: no, you need not look like that, Perdita; I know very well what has happened!—you are selfish and disobedient to mother; and when I want you to do as you ought and save her from a tremendous sorrow by concealing a thing that might kill her if she knew it, you fly into a rage and want to leave home! However, it is too late to argue now. All I beg you to understand is, that you are not to tell mother about Eva; and that if need be, you must bear the blame yourself rather than betray her."

Whereupon Thomasina left the room; and poor Perdita was once more free to eat out her heart in solitude and anguish.

What was told the mother Perdita never knew, and she dared not ask. So long as she was not brought face to face with any accusation, nor called on to tell a direct falsehood, she would bear blame where she had been innocent to save her sister who had been guilty. Her savage love of truth would go no farther than this. She would let judgment go by default and not plead her innocence, but she would not say that she was guilty—no! not even to save her mother pain.

That something had been said which made her the scapegoat was evident enough when, after dinner the next day, Mrs. Winstanley said to her in a solemn judicial kind of way:

"Come here, Perdita. I have something of importance to say to you. After the disgrace of last night you cannot be surprised at what I am about to say," she began, speaking with severity but also with the difficulty of strong emotion.

Between chronic displeasure with an unruly daughter and active banishment from the family is a wide step, and one that no mother can take without reluctance and sorrow. And though Mrs. Winstanley thought herself bound to banish Perdita for the sake of Thomasina and Eva, still, it was an awful thing to do when the moment came; and she felt it.

Perdita looked at Thomasina—Thomasina looked at her. The soft humid tender eyes with their mingled pathos, terror, and appeal, met the elder sister's cold, steely, handsome orbs which dominated and silenced her. They seemed to defy her to remonstrate; to command her to submit; and Perdita's sank confused and overcome beneath their pitiless gaze.

"Things cannot go on like this," continued Mrs. Winstanley. "The very reputation of my family—of your sisters—is at stake. You are not only ruining yourself but us; and though you are my daughter, your sisters are also my daughters, and I must think of them as well as of you. Once more I put it to you, as your last chance:—Will you give up these friends of yours—these common tradespeople, with whom you have made such a degrading and compromising intimacy? If you will, I will overlook all that has passed, disgraceful as it is; if you will not—for the sake of your sisters and to maintain my own dignity and position, you must leave home."

"Mother, it would be giving up my life!" said Perdita.

The Crawfords were her only friends. In abandoning them would she not be giving up all that made life other than so much physical mechanism?

"Then you renounce your family?" said her mother with a slight tremor in her voice.

"Why need I do either? What does it signify to any of you what I do or who it is that I may know outside the house?" cried Perdita, beating the air for reasons.

"We have discussed all that before," said Mrs. Winstanley. "You talk wilful nonsense, Perdita, when you speak like this. It is your family or your friends. You cannot have both."

"Mother! Mother!" cried Perdita, sitting down and hiding her face in her hands.

"Think well before you decide," said Mrs. Winstanley very mildly. "Think what you give up—what you choose instead of your mother, your sisters, your natural friends, your father's family, my love, your own social position. Once done, you can never retract—never!"

There was silence. Perdita was touched by her mother's unwonted gentleness of tone, gentle even while so firm. Her heart softened as it ever did when she was treated with humanity and tenderness. She hesitated, wept, lamented. It was all so shadowy, so intangible! Why might she not hold on by these new friends whom she loved, yet not be discarded by her own people? Why was she to be shut out like a pariah, disinherited, dishonoured, because Mrs. Crawford had a nephew who sold drugs by the ounce instead of by the pound?

Then said Mrs. Winstanley as a further indictment—she was not always wise:

"I am generous in allowing you this alternative, Perdita, after all that happened last night; but I promised your sister Thomasina that I would not speak of it to you, nor punish you as you deserve."

"What does Thomasina say did happen last night?" cried Perdita, flinging off the brooding doubt, the oppression of despair, the subjugation of her sister's looks and reasserting herself according to her wont. Here at last she came face to face with a fact. "What did she say I had done?"

"Leave that to me," said Mrs. Winstanley. "She told me quite enough to warrant all that I am saying."

"Mother!" cried Perdita excitedly; when Thomasina's clear calm voice broke in.

"Now, Perdita, keep silence," said the elder sister slowly.

"Why should I? I am to be turned out of the house because—" began Perdita, her colour rising and her voice deepening.

"Because you are a wilful wrong-headed girl," again interrupted her sister; "because you will not do as you ought, nor obey mother when she commands you. It has all been your own doing."

"No, Perdita, you are not turned out of the house, you turn yourself out," said Mrs. Winstanley. "At the eleventh hour I would forgive everything if you would come back to reason and propriety and give up those undesirable, those disastrous friends of yours."

"No, there is more than this," said Perdita. "You condemn me for what I have not done—it is not only the Crawfords."

"It is only the Crawfords—nothing but them," said Thomasina a little hurriedly. "Mother only asks you to give them up; and it is shameful in you that she should have to ask you at all—that you ever made the acquaintance in the first instance and that you have held to it for a moment after she desired you not."

Perdita put her face into her hands and thought. It was asking her for her life—for all that made the hope, the charm, the consolation of her existence—for her confessed delight, her secret love. And to have in return—what?—unfriendliness and isolation, a dwelling-place but not a home, relations and not a family. She could not! She would rather accept the banishment which was but the seal of her lifelong loneliness. Away from them all and made dead, she would be no longer either a hindrance or an irritation; her absence would be their gain; and she— she could not be more miserable and she might easily be less so. And then, Leslie's adjuration that she would not give him up—come what might, that she would be faithful to her friends! No, it was impossible. She must stand by the true and forsake that which was only seeming— she must not give up the Crawfords.

She turned her face to her mother, not defiantly, but set and stern with her pain, and strong with the power of her love.

"No," she said in a low voice; "I cannot give them up. They are dearer to me than life itself!"

"Then you abandon your mother and sisters," said Mrs. Winstanley, with the accent of one who has finished the business on hand and pronounced the final word. "I knew that harm would come of this horrid office life—this disgraceful rambling about the streets by yourself; and I was right. Now go upstairs and pack your things. I will put you into lodgings to-morrow, with Miss Cluff as your chaperon. Insolent and disobedient as you are, you are my daughter, and I will do my duty to the last!"

"Go, Perdita," said Thomasina, who saw that her mother was breaking down, and who dreaded nothing so much as her distress.

"Poor darling Mumsey, but we love you!" said Eva, putting her arms round her mother's neck and kissing her.

And for the moment her caress was perfectly sincere. She forgot all that had been done whereof she herself was the starting-point, and remembered only that she loved her mother and wanted to make up to her by her own sweetness for the sorrow which that horrid Perdita had caused her. Feeling is a fact truly, but it is a fact like coloured glass. The landscape is not quite the same when looked at through a yellow pane as when looked at through a blue one; and just now Eva's feelings were in the highest degree transforming.

Here then was an end of all things and Perdita's fate finally fixed. She was to be banished from home not only for what she had done but for what she had not done—not only because she was yoked to her own misdeeds but also in some mysterious way saddled with Eva's. And she had to keep silence and bear with the dignity of a martyr condemnation which she had not earned, save in that general way by which her ill-luck had laid her open to perpetual condemnation ever since she had become an individuality at all.

The root of it all was want of money. Had Mrs. Winstanley not been so much in debt and so poor, the efficient settlement of her daughters would not have been a matter of such vital interest. Perdita's comparative plainness would not have been such a loss, as the beauty of the other two would not have been so important an investment; hence she would not have been left so much to herself to think without guidance, to act without control; perhaps she would have been less democratic—and yet, her democracy was in her very blood! it was bone of her bone and flesh of her flesh—and she would certainly not have been thrown on the sympathy and friendship of people in a lower social sphere like the Crawfords, or of those in a different phase of thought like Bell Blount. Yes, it was all due to those velvet rags and Mrs. Winstanley's natural desire to retain the velvet and hide the rags.

Thomasina confessed the whole thing in her self-communings when making up her mind how to act. She was very sorry for Perdita; but there was no other way to save all than by sacrificing her. It would never do to let mother know the truth about that foolish little Eva. She was the biggest prize and she must be well married. She was a fool—there was no doubt of that—and a naughty fool too; but Thomasina knew that she did not mean all the harm into which her folly would have led her, and that even this last and most dangerous escapade meant silliness and what she chose to think was love, not vice or anything horrible. Perdita was a family disaster, if a good girl in herself; and she was sure to bring them into disgrace. It was no use saving her for the common weal; she was useless; and it was better to let her be sacrificed even if unjustly than that Eva should bear the penalty of her own misdeeds, whereby they would all be ruined outright. We all have to suffer one for the other, thought Thomasina—down to lambs and those poor little singing birds! A few pet beasts are sacred; but only a few; and for the rest the whole scheme of life is sacrifice, the whole law suffering. It was very sad and she was really sorry.

Tears were in her eyes as she thought of poor Perdita and all that she would suffer. But it must be. It was better that she should be unhappy than that mother should be broken-hearted and the family ruined; and if she would keep up with those chemist people she had better keep up with them out of the house and where the family were not implicated, than while living at home and tainting them all with the same low-bred strain.

With which reasoning Thomasina, the incarnation of common sense, justified herself. No kinder than fate, no softer than law, she followed as her reason led, and acted on the axiom of the greatest happiness for the greatest number[1] as steadily as the most enlightened political economist could desire. It was by no fault of hers if that axiom included the victimization of the innocent. When was it otherwise? What had the poor scapegoat done to be laden with the sins of a people? and why should Andromeda be chained to a rock, that the mass of the multitude might be saved? So with Perdita. She was the ballast flung out to lighten the sinking ship—Andromeda devoted to sacrifice that her mother and sisters

---

[1]   Refers to "Utilitarianism" (1861) by John Stuart Mill (1806–73).

might be saved—the scapegoat driven off into the desert laden with sins not her own—all that judgment might be averted and destruction staved off where, though it was due, it would fall so much more heavily!

Yes, Thomasina had done well, according to her lights; now to finish this tough piece of work, and bring Bois-Duval to a sense of his guilt and to the relinquishment of his prey.

CHAPTER XXXIII.

TO THE RESCUE.

WHAT a miserable breakfast it was! Eva was in bed, half offended, half frightened by the severe scolding that Thomasina had given her yesterday; Mrs. Winstanley had a headache, and might be marked dangerous; Thomasina was pale, glacial, inscrutable; and Perdita had the swollen eyes and parti-coloured complexion of one who has not slept and who has cried all through the night. It was a very nexus of distress for every one alike, and to Mrs. Winstanley it was as if she had touched the ground.

The breakfast passed in silence; only when she was leaving to go to her office did Perdita break through the uncomfortable stillness of the hour.

"What am I to do, mother?" she said with a sob in her voice. "Am I to find lodgings for myself, or come back here, or what am I to do?"

"Come back here. I will have found a place for you," answered Mrs. Winstanley, not looking at her daughter.

Her maternal instinct had never been strongly excited for this uncomfortable rebel; still it was there—if in a very minor degree, all the same it was there.

"Good-bye, mother," then said Perdita, beginning to tremble.

"I shall see you again. You need not take leave in this formal manner," said Mrs. Winstanley brusquely.

She did not mean this as unkindness. On the contrary, her very brusqueness was a kind of self-defence against breaking down on her own side. But Perdita read it as a snub, and left for her work with a heart more sore and sad than need have been.

"That poor misguided child!" said Mrs. Winstanley with a curious mixture of anger and distress.

"She is terribly annoying," answered Thomasina, quietly. "But you must not fret, dearest mother. When Eva and I are married things will be quite different then. She will have had a lesson; we shall not be here to make you feel the difference between us and her; and then she can do the family no mischief."

"You forget this dreadful chemist," cried Mrs. Winstanley. "The disgraceful mystery of the night before last—where could she have been going at that hour of the night, Thomasina?—the terrible chance there is of her marrying him. No; things will not be put entirely to rights even when you and Eva are married! And when will that be?" she sighed to herself with the sickness of deferred hope.

"If she does marry him of course we must discard her," said Thomasina. "That will be a necessity for our self-respect. But perhaps she will not go so far as that. And at all events she cannot marry him just yet, so that we have time before us."

Mrs. Winstanley smiled. It was but a pale and watery kind of smile truly, still it was better than the former look of grim despair. She sighed as well as smiled.

"You always cheer me, Thomasina," she said. "You have a wonderful knack of putting things in the best light. I only hope that this time you may prove a true prophet."

"Believe, mother; that is better than hoping," her daughter said, answering back her smile, but not her sigh.

And now something else had to be done, and Thomasina was the one who must do it. It was a bold step to take; but when matters are desperate boldness is the best policy; and matters were desperate enough now! This foolish wickedness between Eva and Bois-Duval was of even more consequence than the rebel's craze for the chemist. It must be put a stop to at once, and Thomasina was the only one to do it. Mother must know nothing about it; Eva could not be trusted to break off the affair; she would promise "mountains and seas," but she would break her word while the breath was warm on her lips; and Perdita was of course out of the question. In any family matter whatever, where nice handling and delicate diplomacy was needed, that tactless savage was worse than useless. No, Thomasina herself was the only one who could undertake the business of the moment; and she made up her mind what to do, bold, hazardous, extreme as her action might be.

"Mother," she said, soon after the last word on Perdita had been spoken; "I am going to Mrs. Merton, if you have no objection. I will be back before luncheon. We can look for Perdita's lodgings in the afternoon if you do not mind my going to Mrs. Merton now."

"Certainly, my dear, go if you like," answered Mrs. Winstanley, not expressing any kind of surprise.

She believed in her daughter's good sense, and felt sure she had a wise reason for all that she did, even though things might look odd. Therefore when she said that she would go and see Mrs. Merton in uncanonical hours, Mrs. Winstanley assented without opposition, merely saying:

"Go if you like; and give her my kind regards."

Thomasina kissed her mother as she left the room; dressed herself with care; put a thick black Shetland veil into her pocket; and drove off in a close cab—not to Mrs. Merton's house but to M. le Vicomte de Bois-Duval's hotel. It was a tremendous thing to do; but Thomasina had calculated closely. It was just the kind of thing that would touch the imaginative chivalry of a Frenchman; and Bois-Duval, though unscrupulous and dishonourable, had his high lights like the rest of us. And more than this—it flattered his vanity that this frosty Venus, this impenetrable and excellent Thomasina, should thus put herself in his power, should abase herself so far before him, should trust so grandly to his generosity, to his honour as a Frenchman, to his dignity of man. When the lady closely veiled, who had been ushered into the room where he sat in gorgeous dressing-gown and slippers flirting with his coffee and toying with his roll, took off that Shetland mask from before her face, and showed the clear-cut handsome frozen features of Thomasina Winstanley, he knew what was before him as clearly as if the scene had been already rehearsed. And he admired her courage. Pardi! it was un-French, but it was sublime! As he stood with all his Gallic grace and gallantry, bowing low and asking to what was he indebted for the honour of this visit? and would she not do him the honour of sitting down? he half wondered for a moment whether this excellent young lady had gone down before him like so many others, and if she had come for herself among other things. But he did not wonder long. Thomasina was not the person to allow false impressions to remain when they were not part of her plan.

"Thank you," she said, deliberately choosing the most comfortable chair in the apartment, and the one where she could dispose herself and her train with most grace.

Had it been Perdita, she would have thought it carrying meat to idols—confessing Satan—had she sat down and made herself comfortable in the room of the abhorred—had she prepared for a quiet argument on social expediency, or done anything but stand like a sentinel in defence of outraged virtue, while denouncing the sinner like a Pythoness.[1]

"M. le Vicomte," said Thomasina when she had comfortably seated and gracefully adjusted herself. "I have come to speak to you about my sister Eva."

Her voice was as quiet, her manner as composed as usual; two burning spots on her checks alone showing that she was not quite so cold as that famous "carved lady on a monument."

Bois-Duval smiled and bowed.

"The charming child!" he said almost paternally.

"You know, M. le Vicomte, you do not intend to marry her," continued Thomasina, just in the same cold quiet unimpressionable way. She would have shown more interest had she been speaking of a new gown or a day's pleasure. But what was the use of hysterics? She wanted the thing settled, and it was far better to take it up on a common-sense basis and in a business-like manner than to dash off into Pindarics either of crimination or entreaty.

"I could scarcely aspire to the honour of Mademoiselle Eva's charming hand," said Bois-Duval with profound self-abasement.

A look of scorn shot from Thomasina's eyes.

"Just so. But as things are you stand in the way of her marrying any one else," she said.

He spread out his hands in graceful deprecation.

"Mademoiselle," he said; "you afflict me; and you surprise as much as you afflict. The little Eva is but a child to me—charming, gracious, adorable, but only on the threshold—an ingenue in the freshness and charm of her innocence, but for anything deeper or nearer, the idea until now has never presented itself to my mind."

"Granted; I accept your version, M. le Vicomte. But having now received another from me—having heard from me the deliberate statement that your attentions are disastrous to the future well-being and your presence here is hindering the fit establishment of my little sister, will you not act with the proverbial chivalry of your nation and efface yourself? Will you not leave England at once—this very day? I appeal to you as a man of society. You know the vital necessity of a good marriage for a young girl like Eva, without fortune, and fatherless." Here

---

[1] In Greek mythology, Python was a great serpent, the son of Gaea, Mother Earth, produced from the slime left on the earth after the great flood. The monster lived in a cave near Delphi on Mount Parnassus and guarded the oracle there.

Thomasina raised her eyes with a sudden flash that seemed almost to scorch the man's heart by its intensity of scorn. "An excellent chance is lying at her feet and nothing but the disturbing influence of your presence stands in the way of her immediate acceptance."

"Your demand is somewhat sudden, mademoiselle," said Bois-Duval, as gravely as if all this was true—as indeed it was in substance if not in form. "I have business in London which demands my attention. To leave so à l'improviste—"[1]

He looked from the ceiling to the floor and back again, as if between the two lay the obstacle to his going.

"Your business surely may wait for a short time," she urged. "As soon as Eva is married there can be no objection to your coming back. It is only until then—to remove the charm and fascination which unfortunately you exercise over her, and which you yourself, as a man of honour, a true Frenchman, know is unutterably disastrous, seeing that you do not intend to marry her yourself."

Bois-Duval was touched. This kind of reasoning—the only kind that would have moved him—took him at the right place.

"Mademoiselle, you are fit to be the leader of a political salon!" he said with admiration, almost with enthusiasm. "I yield to your reasoning. It is sublime. I will not be an obstacle to the marriage of the little Eva. A Frenchman knows how to retire—to suffer, if need be, for the good of another, and that other an adorable child like the little Eva! Pray assure yourself of my fidelity to my promise. I leave London to-night. Perhaps fate will permit me to renew my friendship with your charming family, when, if the little one is married, our intercourse will be freer."

His eyes flashed when he said this. He thought it a masterstroke. The secret threat which underlaid it indemnified him somewhat for the substantial checkmate that he had received.

"When she is married she will then be her husband's care, and we shall not have the responsibility," said Thomasina. "Till then our mother, and I, as her eldest sister, are her guardians; and our first duty is to marry her according to her beauty and social standing."

"Just so," said Bois-Duval. "And believe me, mademoiselle, it would be better for English society in general if more eldest sisters thought as you do and acted with the decision and good sense that you have shown."

"Thank you," she said coldly. "Fortunately however, it is not often needed in society," she added somewhat enigmatically. Hazy grammar

---

[1] (French), suddenly.

makes a safe kind of veil when it is not desirable to show a thought too clearly. "Then I have accomplished my mission, M. le Vicomte?" she said, after a short pause. "You leave London to-night; and you swear not to write to Eva"—she stopped herself at the "again" which very nearly tumbled over the heels of her sister's name—"nor to make any attempt to see her?"

"On the honour of a Frenchman!" was his answer, putting his hand on his heart.

"I have no more to say," said Thomasina rising from her chair. "Adieu, M. le Vicomte. I trust to your promise. Bon voyage."

"Adieu, mademoiselle," he answered; "mademoiselle the peerless."

He made a profound bow; his face was full of genuine admiration. Had she wept or raved, reproached him with his conduct or threatened him with its consequences, had she declared what she knew or defied him to excuse himself, had she done any of the wildly sincere and generously passionate things which Perdita would have done, she would not have had the smallest influence over him. He might have promised anything and everything to gain time and end strife; but he would not have stirred an inch from his design. But this quiet immorality, this cynical good sense, this apotheosis of worldly wisdom, penetrated him through and through with respect; and he yielded to her as to a mistress in the art where he too aspired to be a master.

He half forcibly took her hand and kissed it.

"Mademoiselle, you are divine!" he said with ardour.

Thomasina shuddered and instinctively wiped her hand. Proud, pure, cold as she was, it was contamination to have been touched by his lips even through the protecting glove. If to him she was a divinely beautiful and gifted woman, mistress of his most sacred art, of the highest grade in his highest school of social philosophy, to her he was only a human reptile to be cajoled out of her path merely because she was not strong enough to crush him beneath her heel. Cajoled or crushed he was nothing but a reptile, and his touch made her shudder. She turned away; and at the door which he held open for her made him a stately courtesy— as stately as the courtesy of a queen acknowledging the service of a vassal; then slowly descended the stairs, feeling as if she had come out of some terrible conflict where the stakes had been for life or death;—and had come out victorious. She had discomfited the most deadly enemy of their family fortunes, saved her mother from heart-break and her sister from shame; packed up the sin that could not be denied in a neat little parcel which she had strapped on to innocent but befitting shoulders;

and had cleared the way for Sir James Kearney to take when it should please him to walk down the Via Sacra of matrimony.

Thomasina knew but little of the pain that follows on bad actions and an uneasy conscience; she knew almost as little of that inner glow which accompanies meritorious effort and sacrifice of the finer sort. But to-day she did feel that inner glow. She had done her duty bravely and heroically and she deserved well of fame and fate.

She drove off to Mrs. Merton's, jubilant in heart if just as calm in bearing as was her wont; with the feeling of a gambler in luck, as if all that she did must succeed and she had only to go in and sweep the board.

Mrs. Merton was at home. She was rather surprised to see this incarnation of social propriety at such an unconventional hour; but when Thomasina explained to her that they wanted to secure her for an afternoon which they were about to give, with music and recitations to amuse the unspoiled and bore the blasés, then she accepted the innovation as a personal compliment, and was quite prettily touched by the friendliness and grace of the girl's action.

"What does she mean by it? What does she expect to make by me?" thought Mrs. Merton to herself, while smiling and purring, thanking Miss Winstanley with such nice soft comfortable warmth and saying how glad she should be to go.

"And you will be sure to bring Sir James Kearney as your body-guard?" said Thomasina with a flattering insinuation of Mrs. Merton's superior power in that direction. "There is to be a young debutante in whose success my mother has taken great interest, and we want Sir James to hear her. She has a magnificent voice; and we know how fond Sir James is of music. Mother prefers her voice to Nilsson's."[1]

"Is she pretty?" asked Mrs. Merton carelessly.

"Not very," answered Thomasina. "She would have too much if, with her voice and genius, she had beauty too. She would leave nothing for others."

"No, it is a wise dispensation of Providence that geniuses are so seldom pretty," said Mrs. Merton. "Homeliness has the brains and beauty goes without."

"But sometimes pretty people are clever enough," said Thomasina a little dryly.

She knew that she herself was pretty; and she thought that she had just been very clever.

---

[1] Christine Nilsson (1843–1921), Swedish soprano, possibly the source for the character Christine Daaé in Gaston Leroux's *The Phantom of the Opera*.

"Not often," insisted Mrs. Merton lazily. "Look at your two sisters for instance—a case in point. See what a beautiful little creature Eva is, but no one would call her clever; just as no one would call your sister Perdita, who is so clever, pretty."

"That is not quite a case in point," drawled Thomasina. "For Eva is no fool; and Perdita would be really quite charming if she would but take pains with herself and make the most of her points."

"My dear, she has no points to make the best of," said Mrs. Merton. "How she came to be the sister of you and Eva is always a mystery to me. What could your mother have been thinking of!" she added naïvely.

"She has the kind of face which those who like her think handsome, and those who do not like her call plain," said Thomasina. "As I like her very much in spite of all her oddities I think her handsome, my poor Perdita! but very unformed and not set off."

Mrs. Merton raised her eyebrows and made no answer. And as just at this moment the little indicator, which clicked in the drawing-room when the visitor's bell rang downstairs, gave its warning sound, there was something else beside Perdita's comparative beauty or plainness to discuss.

"That must be my brother," she said quietly, raising her sleepy eyes to Thomasina's face.

"We have not seen him very lately," answered the girl quite as quietly. Again she felt as the gambler in luck when he stakes and knows beforehand that he shall win. "And really," she added with the finest and nicest shade of tenderness that was ever thrown into a face and voice; "I can hardly understand life without Mr. Brocklebank taking some part in it. He has been such a good friend to us."

"He is very staunch when he once takes up people," answered Mrs. Merton as the door opened and Benjamin appeared.

Clarissa rose to meet her brother; after a moment's hesitation Thomasina rose too. It was against the rules of conventional propriety, but the ironmaster was a man whom it was wiser to soften rather than to pique. Those fared best with him who expected least from, and did the most for, him; and Thomasina understood this clearly.

"We have not seen you for such a long time!" she said, lifting up her beautiful brown eyes and smiling with that lovely smile of hers which was like a subtle perfume interpenetrating the whole atmosphere.

"Miss Winstanley is very good," said Benjamin stiffly; "but sometimes absence is more desirable than association; and perhaps I have imposed myself once too often on the family at No. 100."

"No; that would be impossible," said Thomasina with divine sweetness.

"We are constant people at our house and never weary of our friends."

"You may disappoint them," answered Mr. Brocklebank with a certain gloomy irritation the meaning of which Thomasina understood only too well.

She smiled again with increased sweetness.

"Not intentionally," she said. "Believe me, none of us, from mother to Eva and down to our very servants, would annoy you intentionally. I hope no one has done so by inadvertence. Oh! I remember now, you were displeased with Perdita the other night? She was obstinate and tiresome and would not do as you wished her about these new friends of hers? But then, you see that is just Perdita! If she has made up her mind that such and such a thing is right, no power on earth can move her. But you must not visit her eccentricities on us!" she added in a pleading voice and almost caressing manner—decidedly caressing for such a frosty Venus as she was.

"Miss Perdita is a very wrong-headed young lady," said Benjamin severely.

"Yes," sighed Thomasina; "very; but true-hearted," she added. "She has fallen under bad influences of late, and the very strength and loyalty of her character give these people power over her. It is a great pity. We are all so much grieved!"

"I know nothing about all that," said the ironmaster disdainfully. "I only know that she does not recognize her friends or understand her duties, and that I have done with her—washed my hands of her. She may sink or swim as she can, for me; I will not trouble myself about her again."

"But I hope that we shall not all share in your displeasure?" said Thomasina with a suspicion of pathos in her voice.

"My dear, will you excuse me for a moment? I have some household business to attend to," said Mrs. Merton, lounging up from her comfortable chair. "Benjamin, as Thomasina is here"—she did not often call the young queen so familiarly by her name—"she can entertain you till I come back. You won't mind?"

"No," said Thomasina gently; and "No," said Benjamin decidedly.

"And how are things progressing at West Hill Gardens?" asked the iron merchant in a confidential way, when his sister had left the room. He brought his chair a few feet nearer to Thomasina's.

"I cannot say very well," answered Thomasina: "and as I feel you ought to know everything about us, dear Mr. Brocklebank, I am so glad that I have met you this morning. I should like to tell you all."

"I hope Miss Winstanley has nothing very unpleasant to narrate," was the grave response.

"Indeed, not much else," she said. "Mother has decided to send Perdita away from home for a little time. She will be better for a change, and perhaps the strange influence that is now over her will be broken. At all events, she is going with our old governess, Miss Cluff—and that is the first thing to tell you."

Mr. Brocklebank gave a sigh of relief.

"It is well," he said. "I am glad of it."

"And then the old pecuniary strain continues," said Thomasina, still quiet and gentle. "Mother is so brave and good about everything, it almost breaks my heart to see her, knowing as I do what she is suffering. Poor Perdita having turned out so unsatisfactorily—having misused her freedom so terribly—tries her very much; and then this dreadful loss of money! Oh, Mr. Brocklebank—you who know everything and can do everything—put me in the way of earning money so that I can help my mother!"

How lovely her eyes looked with that clever artificial tenderness, that histrionic pathos thrown into them! Benjamin felt his veins tingle as he gazed into the superb face that looked into his, all its pride softened, all its coldness melted. Had he made a mistake? Had he chosen the less and left the greater and the better? Was it too late to repair that mistake? He had never been quite sure, he said to himself; and perhaps Thomasina had been the magnet all along, even when he had suffered himself to be deflected by her sister.

"If Miss Winstanley chooses she can save all," he said in a low voice.

"How?" asked Thomasina with sweet unconsciousness; but a little tremor passed over her and she turned deadly pale.

"I will write to her this evening and tell her," said Benjamin Brocklebank.

"And not now?" she said, still playing at unconsciousness.

"I will write," he repeated huskily.

She looked at him again with eyes as innocent as Eva's. Then something seemed to come into them that made her drop them as if struck with secret shyness and the sweet shame of maidenly love. Yet the quivering of her lips and the shiver that ran through her were in flat contradiction to this shy sweet shame. The one spoke of bliss—the other betokened agony. Between the two, which was true?

That evening a letter came to Thomasina in Benjamin Brocklebank's well-known handwriting. When she had read it she went up to her mother and put her arms round her neck.

"Mother, you are saved!" she said in a low voice, but firm as the voice of a strong heart braced to sacrifice. "Mr. Brocklebank has asked me to marry him."

"Thank God!" said Mrs. Winstanley, letting her work drop from her hands. "Thank God, who has protected me!" she repeated piously, believing what she said and that the Eternal had mingled in her affairs so that she might not have to suffer for her own misdeeds of extravagance and folly. "My own good child! my own dear girl! Ah, what a blessing you have always been to me, my Thomasina! What should I have done without you! What do I not owe you?"

"You owe me nothing, mother," her daughter answered quietly. "I have only done my duty."

"But how unlike your poor sister Perdita! She might have saved me too, and she would not. Oh, Thomasina, if I could once feel safe and free! If I could but have you and Eva well married and all my debts paid off!"

"You shall, mother," said Thomasina. "We will get you straight and well provided for; and Eva shall marry Sir James. The beginning of the end has come."

"And you do not dislike him?—say you are not making too great a sacrifice!" said Mrs. Winstanley, holding her daughter's hand in hers.

Thomasina turned away abruptly.

"Do not let us speak of that," she said hastily and with a shudder she could not hide. Then she turned back to her mother fondly. "Do not trouble yourself about me, mother," she said with a brave smile. "I like him quite well enough to marry him and make him a good wife. And you will be happy!"

She said this just as Mrs. Merton, discussing the Winstanley family with her brother, and repeating to him what she had said to Thomasina about the apportionment of beauty and brains between Eva and Perdita, wound up by saying with a smile:

"I should have excepted Thomasina herself, for she is both beautiful and clever—the cleverest woman I know, out and out."

"And the most fortunate," replied Benjamin enigmatically.

CHAPTER XXXIV.

LOOKING UP.

MATERNAL instinct—the divine Storge[1] by which the world is saved—was not strong enough with Mrs. Winstanley to overcome her personal distaste to the habits and principles of her democratic daughter; still, though entirely unsympathetic she wished to be pre-eminently just, and if less than maternal to be in nowise wanting in consideration. Indeed she prided herself on her justice as the moral equivalent of personal politeness; and she would have been as ashamed to have done any one a wrong as to have committed a breach of good manners. Passion and wilful prejudice were to her essentially the ill-breeding of morality; though righteous chastisement smoothly administered was the rebuff which a self-respecting dignity both allows and enjoins. She would have herself to blame had she suffered to pass unrebuked conduct that fell short of her standard of propriety. All the same there are ways of doing things; and Mrs. Winstanley was a stickler for ways.

She really was a good woman according to her lights. The whole contention lay in the quality of those lights, and whether they were such as man may walk by to the profit of his soul, or to be avoided as only marsh-lights flickering over morasses and the graves of the dead.

Perdita was to be banished; but she should be banished with all due regard to decorum and the safe keeping of the family linen. She should be put into lodgings, with poor old Cluff to throw the gauze of respectable appearances about her; and she should not be entirely cut off from her friends. She was to be removed as one would remove a barrel of gunpowder from the hearth before the fire; but they would sometimes go to see her, and she should come and see them when no one else was here or likely to come. So long as she kept herself from irremediable disgrace she should receive such moral support from her family as she could find in this kind of intercourse. If she did worse than she had done already, she should be cut off without reprieve, and buried out of sight without even an *In Memoriam* to mark that she had once lived in their affections.

---

[1] One of the three Greek words for Love used in the New Testament; it refers to affection, or mother-love.

This was how things were to be ordered; and when Perdita came home in the evening she found that all had been prepared for her exodus, and that she had nothing left but to accept the portion assigned to her. Old Cluff had been retained for the cost of her board and lodging; dingy but supremely respectable rooms had been found for a moderate rent in the ancient district of Lamb's Conduit Street—far enough removed from West Hill Gardens to make the crossing of the several orbits exceedingly improbable; and Perdita was told that this was to be her home till the family history had somewhat settled itself and her eccentric fireworks of talk and action were not so full of peril as now. This was doing the best for every one, according to Mrs. Winstanley's ideas, and padding the burden laid on the poor scapegoat with the softest wool at command.

It was a trial when it came. That was only natural. Mothers are mothers even if the maternal instinct is stunted; and daughters are daughters though the lines of thought do run at right angles to each other and the sons of God to the one are the sons of Belial to the other. Perdita, for all her love of freedom and hatred of shams, wept at leaving home; and Mrs. Winstanley, for all her sense of relief from danger, wept at banishing one who was part of herself—lopping off a limb, though by no means a handsome one.

But it had to be done; and it was done. After the due amount of tears and assurances of frequent intercourse—with a sudden afflux of softness all round, and some difficulty in holding to a resolution as against ruth—the sacrifice was accomplished; and Perdita drove away with her boxes like a discarded servant, setting out for a new place. Even little Eva whimpered and Thomasina's perfect self-possession was shaken for a moment; but nothing came of the tears which glistened in the blue eyes of the one, nor of the quiver which disturbed the pale lips of the other; and the cab rolled off carrying the banished rebel to poor old Cluff and those dingy rooms in Lamb's Conduit Street.

Discarded like a dishonest servant; banished from her home and her family; thrust out as a moral leper; removed as a danger and a nuisance:—and why? Because she believed that certain principles of life were righteous and holy, and said what she thought—because she feared God rather than man—honoured truth before expediency—obeyed her conscience sooner than social observances. It was not for her faults that she was punished, but for her faithfulness to the higher law as taught her by her conscience. And when she realized this she felt that despair which overtakes us all when we are dealt with unjustly—that despair which makes us lose our faith in man's goodness and God's providence alike.

Days passed and Perdita made no sign, put in no appearance, save at the office, where she went to her work as usual. She was not sulking, though it looked as if she were; she was only ashamed and grieving. She shrank even from the Crawfords. To have to tell them that she had been turned out of her house was a trial to her pride which she was cowardly enough to delay the longest possible. And something beside cowardice held her back. Too much and too little had been said to make it easy for her to seek them of her own accord. Yearn as she might to see Leslie Crawford again—faithful to their friendship as she had proved herself already and meant to be to the end—it was not for her, she thought, to put herself in his way unsought. She was too sore all over not to be proud and almost distrustful; wherefore, at this time of trial when they might have been of the sweetest consolation to her, she herself deserted these dear friends and added to her pain by unnecessary self-torture. On her side Bell Blount had abandoned this poor rebel who had been as recalcitrant in the vanguard as in the rear ranks. The Champion of her Sex could have nothing to do with a spiritless creature who coquetted with the other side and honoured the enemy. So that neither was Prince Christian's Road a place of refuge for Perdita in her banishment; and she was cut off from the stirring sophistries of Bell Blount as completely as from the more cramped logic of Mrs. Crawford.

Thus her first days in her new home were melancholy enough; and she more than once wondered where the charm of freedom was to be found. How unlike the time when she and poor old Cluff had kept house together in the summer—with little to spend and less to save— but where Hope had been the protagonist holding the stage while Love was waiting for his time to appear! Then, insufficiency had been heroic, because voluntary and undertaken for a good purpose; now, it was enforced, and degrading because enforced. Then, though the room in which they lived had been shabby and bare, still there had been books about, the house was fresh and spacious and had both the aroma of refinement and the sentiment of home. And though London in August and September is dusty, parched and stifling all through, yet the atmosphere was clearer in a new district like West Hill than farther down towards the City and the East End; the common garden was a resource, and Kensington Gardens—the Gardens *par excellence*—were always delicious and a very lovely substitute for nature.

Now all was on a lower level—infinitely lower. Squalid children played about the door and made their Tom Tiddler's ground of the steps and street; the landlady was a pinched and parched old maid who could scarcely get a living for herself out of her poor venture, because of all that she had to do for a wretched sister left a widow with six children and never a penny to buy them bread; the maid-of-all-work was grimy, unkempt, inapt; and the lodgers above and below were people who said "kyows" when they spoke of cows; and one had even perpetrated the iniquity of "which you was." The whole thing was mean and wretched to an excess; but it was of the highest order of respectability in its own poor grade, and Perdita's acquaintances were not likely to be scandalized by her surroundings, seeing that she had none to scandalize. It was all unspeakably doleful from first to last; but the days had to be lived through whatever their complexion, and strength is only of value according to the strain that it can bear.

But if she were miserable, how clear and wide her going had made the old home to those left within it! It was as if the place had grown suddenly larger, not to speak of safer—as if a huge obstructive log lying across the threshold had been flung clear away out of the door—as if a packet of explosives had been taken from before the drawing-room fire. Such a feeling of security from anxiety suddenly sprang up in the place of annoyance and danger! It was the lifting of the fog, the clearing of the clouds, the dying away of the tempest; and those who had formerly been darkened and oppressed were now proportionately enlivened and relieved.

Meanwhile the poor cause of the oppressive fog, the miserable source of the disturbing tempest, gloomed and sorrowed and smarted and wept in her shabby little rooms in Lamb's Conduit Street; and poor old Cluff said: "My dear, do eat a little more," twenty times in vain; and: "My dear, it breaks my heart to see you so sad," about as often and to no better purpose.

No one openly confessed the relief that had come upon them all save Eva, who when it suited her had Perdita's directness if not her truth; and she gave utterance to the voiceless sentiment common to them all by throwing up her arms as one who has just laid down a heavy weight and saying with a short laugh:

"How comfortable it is without that funny old Per! What a temper she has; and how cross she gets about nothing!"

"Leave Perdita alone, Eva; she is not here to annoy you or to defend herself," said Thomasina with quiet sternness.

Eva flushed at her eldest sister's rebuke, reading in it more than was patent to the mother who merely wondered at her good daughter's severity. She pouted just a little to give herself countenance and take off the appearance of embarrassment, but she held her tongue as commanded. Yet if Ina did not mind what she was about she would get to dislike her as much as she disliked that disagreeable old Per, thought the rosebud to herself; and then where would she be?

The afternoon tea which Thomasina had arranged so cleverly came off in due course; and really, as Mrs. Winstanley confessed, she felt as if she could breathe freely to-day. There was no danger of that poor dear misguided child coming in and disgracing them all as she did in that dreadful way when Lady Kearney had called. It was quite a relief to feel safe.

Over and above this feeling of safety because of the rebel's absence, the gathering itself was eminently successful. Mrs. Merton and Sir James Kearney came—together; but Benjamin Brocklebank was not there. He had gone down to Armour Court; as Lady Kearney had gone to Hibberton, though not for the same reason, which on her side was simply to avoid the Winstanleys and this party. Many others, however, filled up the gaps created by these two, and made a crowd such as Londoners love. And among them came Agnes Disney and her mother, to confirm the final destruction of the meshes woven about Hubert and his broad acres by announcing his approaching marriage fixed for next week. They also came to evidence the magnanimity of the victors who can afford to be generous to the slain.

At the first Sir James was cold and stiff. He was jealous by nature and spoilt by admiration; and he thought himself a precious vase moulded out of finer clay than that which makes the ordinary human pipkin. Hence, he thought that all things which he desired should be kept sacred for his use, and that no one should long for aught which he had marked with the broad arrow of his fancy. He had been shocked by the discovery of Hubert's love for Eva. It offended his sense of honour in relation to Maud; wherein he was right; and gave him the impression of poaching on his own estate. When transacted in fur and feathers he held poaching to be one of the seven deadly sins, deserving a punishment not far short of hanging; when brought into homes, with pretty girls for partridges, he thought it an offence demanding expulsion from the club and warning off the racecourse. Moreover, he held the rational theory that no smoke can rise without some fire underneath; and his pride was revolted to think that both Bois-Duval and Hubert Strangways should have been laying sticks under the cauldron which he had decided to boil for his own pleasure.

Altogether things were undeniably disagreeable for the young baronet, and he kept even step with those things. He was so gloomy and grumpy and horrid, that even Mrs. Winstanley's patience got strained, and her well-oiled hinges began to creak. He had come with Mrs. Merton; and he devoted himself to her alone; sitting by her as persistently as if they had been Siamese twins; when forced to make conversational excursions, returning to his former attitude of exclusive devotion and the unseen apron-string, as if that had been a *corvée*[1] and this was his delight.

But human resolution is a very frail kind of thing when sandwiched between a pretty woman and a young man's fancy. Eva was too lovely to be shunted, too coaxing and bewitching to be laid aside when it was her whim to be taken up. She had the power of a veritable witch to make things seem different from what they were, and as she chose they should appear.

Her wildflower face was so guileless, her blue eyes so ingenuous, her manner so simple, her affectionateness so transparent! She was such a bewitching combination of cleverness and simplicity, of childish grace and womanly charm, of harmless little sensualities—how the red ripe lips closed over bonbons, and the white sharp little teeth buried themselves in the fleshy pulp of fruit!—and of naïve innocence of evil, that no man with a man's heart in him could fail to be touched when she chose to stir him. And if there had been such a one, it was not Sir James Kearney. Then too, Mrs. Winstanley was so charming and Thomasina was so delightful! The little witch—no, the little goddess—was to be forgiven something for the sake of her people as well as for her own sweet self; and when Mrs. Winstanley, changing her tone, laid aside a little of her extreme suavity and let her well-oiled hinges creak, Sir James, who was always more or less in opposition, suddenly became amiable, smoothed down his bristles and unrolled himself from his hedgehog-like mental attitude as if a miracle had been worked free of charge.

He soon came to the point of touching the secret core of his displeasure; which was a concession and the first step to reconciliation; and so Mrs. Winstanley understood it.

"You have had that scoundrel Bois-Duval here, I find!" he said, holding his head high, and curling his long thin upper lip.

"He has been in England, and he came here once," said Mrs. Winstanley, who had the wisdom of never telling unnecessary untruths.

"Why did you receive him?" exclaimed Sir James irritably. "He should have been kicked out of the house."

---

[1] The tradition of the *corvée* entitled a feudal lord to several days of work a year from each of his habitants.

"Well, you see, my servant did not know him!" answered Mrs. Winstanley with a pleasant smile. "It was only after he had made good his entrance that I was able to tell him my doors were closed against him."

"And you did say that?—you did then turn him out of your house?" he asked excitedly.

"M. le Vicomte de Bois-Duval will not enter my house again!" was her dignified reply.

Why did the moisture start so suddenly on Eva's smooth forehead and short curved upper lip? This dull November day was cold and chill, but she took a fan from the table and fanned herself as if she had been under a tropical sun.

"I fell in with some people who knew him well," said Sir James looking round disdainfully. "He is a bad lot all round—a man of utterly worthless character, loaded with debt, suspected of dishonesty at cards and cheating at races, a Viscount by birth and a blackleg by life. His acquaintance is a disgrace and an insult to any nice girl!"

He almost shouted when he said this, looking out of the corner of his eye at Eva whose flushed face kept its muscles as tranquil as if it had been a wall covered with roses. The betrayal of colour was in it—no more.

"What a pity it is that so many foreigners are so disreputable!" said Mrs. Winstanley, gliding off into safe generalities and British virtues.

"And what a pity it is that Englishwomen are so easily taken in by them!" said Sir James with uncontrollable irritation. "Any scoundrel with his foreign false veneer goes down before an English gentleman of worth and substance, who would scorn to flatter as he does, but who would perhaps do more in the long run!"

"Yes, indeed, that is quite true with a certain kind of Englishwomen—not with the best kind, but with a very large class," said Mrs. Winstanley with sublime tranquillity.

She was an excellent discourser on social ethics—always ready for a hand at that safe rubber! Sir James looked at Eva. She was playing with the kitten—that eternal resource! Fanning herself and the creature alternately, and making it shrink and blink its eyes at the unwelcome puff. Then she laid down the fan and tied her handkerchief round its head and neck.

"Oh, you dear funny little old woman!" she said laughing, as she held it straight up and made it mew. Then suddenly she cried out to her mother: "Look, Mumsey! isn't kitty like the Vicomte! It has just his face, and kitty's whiskers are his moustaches with their queer waxed ends!"

For one of the rare times in her life human feeling got the better of Thomasina's suavity.

"How can you be so atrociously childish, Eva?" she said with strange passion snatching the kitten out of her sister's arms and tearing off the handkerchief. "For shame!"

Her anger, which was perfectly natural, spontaneous, unconsidered, was the best thing that could have happened. Had she acted for a purpose she could have devised no better play for the exigencies of the moment. Sir James was delighted. Had that excellent Thomasina been the victim, and the beautiful little rosebud only the object? Had the frosty Venus thawed, while the childish Euphrosyne had only sported and laughed and run among the flowers, and made believe to be in earnest, while all the time she was only in play? But that other had been serious; and the merchandise marked with his own broad arrow had been kept sacred.

This thought put him into a good humour, cleared off the mists and broke the invisible apron-string. He deliberately got up and went over to the sofa where Eva was sitting with half a dozen other young girls, and there before the whole assembly paid her that kind of attention which people call 'marked,' and which makes a clatter like the wind among dry branches; attentions which every one sees, of which every one makes his own interpretations and the significance of which is by no means diminished by transmission from lip to lip. Mrs. Merton looked on at the scene from between her narrowed lids and wondered what was the matter. Her future sister-in-law was strangely moved; little Eva the comedian had acted to perfection; still it was acting. Mrs. Winstanley also had acted to perfection, but here again the rouge and stage lights were evident; there was a manifest undercurrent which vitiated the worth of appearances; and the widow for one brief moment thought:

"Shall I find it all out and put a stop to everything?—break it off with my brother, detach James, and expose their deeds to the world at large?" And then she sighed, her ample figure seemed to shrink a little together, as reason whispered to her: No! It was better that Benjamin should marry, and Thomasina Winstanley was just the wife for him; and if Sir James had grown tired of her he would find some one else, even if she forced him to give up Eva. And why should not little Eva have what she herself, poor mistress of the art of soothing, could not continue to hold? She had to yield the place which had been hers— why not to this little fool as well as to another? Yes; she had to yield her place. It was the law governing the relations of Mature Sirens, and neither she nor any other of the class could help the fate allotted. Stop-gaps—that is all! But the day comes when the church consecrates the

374 ELIZA LYNN LINTON

peace of love; and then the stop-gap of friendship is flung aside, no longer needed. No; she need not disturb herself or any one else by unnecessary discoveries and virtuous denunciations. The moment of abdication is always bitter; but she had known all along that it had to come; and she was too good-natured, too indolent and too rational to encourage unreasonable jealousy.

This was what her reason whispered to her; and she heeded the still small voice that so seldom leads us wrong, and never into folly!

Before the afternoon was over the chains which had been temporarily loosened were riveted afresh, and in the ardor of the reaction Sir James Kearney all but committed himself. He saved himself from the irrevocable words only just in time.

When Agnes Disney and her mother left, the conversation naturally fell on Hubert's marriage. Sir James was to be his best man, in spite of that unwelcome revelation, but the Winstanleys were not asked either to the church or the breakfast. They were invited for the evening ball, and that was all.

"What a nice wife Maud will make!" said little Eva with delightful enthusiasm. "She and Mr. Strangways are just suited. She is the very wife for him."

"Just," echoed Mrs. Winstanley. "I do not know any girl that I like better or respect more than Maud Disney; and Hubert is the best young man in the world! He is the very ideal of a fine young English gentleman, but not 'all of the modern time!'" laughing.

To which Sir James said gravely:

"I agree with you. It is quite an ideal marriage; the very thing that should be; a precious combination of harmonious and mutually helpful elements!"

And again Eva's wildflower face became crimson and the ungenial afternoon like a tropical summer's day. These frequent changes of colour and strange sensitiveness showed Thomasina, more than anything else would have done, how deep that matter with Bois-Duval had struck into the superficial nature of her little sister, and how it had gone through the froth into such substance as she had. But, taken with her bearing to Sir James, they showed her also that neither she nor her mother need fear. Eva knew her duty to her family and herself; and she would do it when the time came. If only that poor misguided fervid and unconvinceable rebel could have been made as malleable—would have let herself be taught with as much docility!—if only she had seen the things which were best for herself and for others, and had taken that heavy-handed ironmaster with his millions in his pocket! In doing her duty she would have obviated the necessity of another's sacrifice; whereas now—Thomasina put her face into her hands as she sat in her own room thinking, and in spite of herself tears forced themselves through the long lashes and the slender fingers, and fell like rain on the frilling of her dressing-gown. Poor Thomasina! There was no help for it. She had vowed herself to the service of a master who demands the living sacrifice of love and maidenhood in return for wealth and worldly position; and there was no question with her of drawing back or of refusing to obey.

CHAPTER XXXV.

CONFESSED.

"Leslie, what can have become of that poor girl? Is she ill, think you? We have not seen her for days and days! She has never been so long as this without coming in; and it is odd that she should keep away after I had asked her so specially to come and see me! I am getting quite uneasy. What is the matter, think you?"

Mrs. Crawford asked this of her nephew-son as they were sitting together in the evening, she at needlework making a frock for the child, he with his microscope, intent on certain studies which were to land him in the Royal Society when they were complete. "F.R.S."[1]—this was one of the points to which his ambition reached. Not that he would ever be anything but a chemist. His theories went to the elevation of work by the thoroughness of the worker, not to the degradation of his profession through what is called the social advancement of the man. He was a chemist, a scientific explorer in his own way, an experimentalist and a discoverer. He would be recognized some day and receive his magic initials; but he would always keep the shop.

"I do not think that she is ill," he answered quietly. "She goes to St. Paul's Churchyard as usual; but she does not live now at home."

"No? where does she live?" asked the mother, surprised, a little shocked indeed, and with a vague idea of wrong-doing somewhere that perplexed and distressed her.

---

[1] Fellow of the Royal Society.

"Somewhere in the Russell Square district, but I do not know the street. At all events she is no longer at West Hill Gardens with her family."

He was adjusting his microscope as he spoke; and he had never found it so hard to focus the object. That little bit of epithelium in the field was as if alive and seemed to fairly dance under his hand.

"But why has she gone?—what a dreadful position for her! Whose fault is it, I wonder?" asked the mother, womanlike.

"Not hers!" said Leslie.

A slight shade of displeasure traversed by suspicion crossed her face.

"How do you know all this about her, my boy?" she asked, trying to speak with indifference.

"By inquiry. I missed her and found out what had become of her," he answered quietly.

She looked up and watched his face. She saw nothing but the sad self-contained and yet perfectly honest expression familiar to her— nothing but the broad clear brow, the calm eyes, the handsome well-cut features where nothing seemed to be concealed and nothing was revealed.

"Why have you made all these inquiries about Perdita Winstanley?" she then asked, an idea of danger dawning over her mind like the presage of a storm in the sky.

"For the same reason which made you speak to me of her," he answered. "From interest in her."

Mrs. Crawford was silent. She loved Leslie like her own son—was he not her son through those long years of maternal care, and then through his marriage with her daughter? To suspect him of a warmer feeling for Perdita than he would have had for his own sister would be to take from him some of that love, because it would lower him in her esteem and take from him some of her respect. Her own heart was half broken by the death of her daughter, whose virtues she imagined and whose vices she had not known; and she would have thought him wicked beyond words had his been whole. If he were as good as she believed him to be, he would be as unhappy as she was; and he would be as incapable of forming a new attachment so soon after his loss as he would be incapable of any other crime or dishonour.

"She is a good girl, but she has her faults," said Mrs. Crawford in a hesitating way.

"You mean that she is human?" he answered. "Of course she has her faults, but they are faults of temperament not of character—faults to be explained by the state of her nerves and the relative size of her heart and brain and lungs. They are faults for which she is scarcely responsible, as we mean by responsibility."

"Hush, Leslie! I cannot bear this materialism! It is sinful and atheistic to speak of an immortal soul as if it were nothing but a bit of matter, as if the spirit were subject to the conditions of the nerves and the blood! It is awful!" said Mrs. Crawford with a solemn kind of irritation. "Where will it all end if you begin like this?"

"Where will all what end?" he asked. "My judgment on Miss Perdita Winstanley's temper as influenced by her physical condition? Not in what you mean by materialism or atheism, dear!"

"Better men than you have gone astray," she said, still irritated and solemn.

"The truth cannot lead any one astray, dear mother. And one need not be a materialist—that is, a disbeliever in God and the immortality of the soul—because one acknowledges the power of the body over the mind."

"The mind should be superior to the body and should control it," she said gravely.

"Up to what point?—the delirium of fever? the depression of jaundice? the suicide due to a loaded liver? or the homicide of sudden mania? We have power over ourselves only up to a certain point and under certain healthy conditions; beyond these we are no more free agents than so many stones set rolling down the hill or so many leaves blown about in the wind. But to go back to our starting-place. Miss Perdita Winstanley has no power over those quick blushes and ready tears, that passion against injustice, that necessity for truth at any cost which rule her physical and underlie her moral nature. She cannot help herself; and only time will be of any use to her. When she is sixty she will have toned down into just ordinary excitability; but it will take all that time before she does!"

"Rather a bad prospect for those with whom she may be connected," said Mrs. Crawford as dryly as if a lappet of Mrs. Winstanley's mantle had fallen on her.

"Her best help will be in her friends," returned Leslie very steadily. "Those who love and understand her best will help her most. Believe me, she is not one to grow well in the atmosphere of rebuke and suppression. She needs the sun; and tenderness will do more for her than condemnation."

"You seem to understand her with extraordinary insight!" said Mrs. Crawford, still less like herself than Mrs. Winstanley.

"Perhaps I do," he answered. "I have studied her closely. She has interested me."

"She must take her chance like the rest of us," returned the mother. "Neither she nor any one else can have the way of life made smooth. We all have to suffer, and man is born to sorrow."

"Some have more sorrow than others if we all have our share; but I hope that Perdita Winstanley will be spared as much as is possible, if only for the sake of the general sum of good in the world. She will be such a much better woman if she is happy than if she is unhappy! She does not want pruning and she will thrive so well where cherished!"

"Those whom the Lord loveth He chasteneth," said Mrs. Crawford. And then the conversation dropped; but enough had been said to make the mother uneasy, remembering that Leslie was now a widower, made free by her own irreparable loss, and that if he chose to bring Perdita home as his wife there was nothing on earth to hinder him—save the afreet of caste and the chance of the girl's own refusal. And this latter chance was worth—how much?

The next day Leslie went to St. Paul's Churchyard and calmly waited outside the office of the Post-office Savings Bank till the girls streamed forth. Then, with the most natural manner in the world, he went up to Perdita and held out his hand.

"What has become of you this long, long time?" he said. "My mother has been asking for you."

"Oh, it is you!" said Perdita, with a deep sigh of sudden relief. Her pale cheeks flushed, then suddenly the colour faded till they were whiter than before. She smiled as if the sunlight had flashed over her face, and then her eyes filled with tears. "I am so glad to see you!" she said simply. "It seemed to myself as if I had lost you."

"Never!" he answered, taking her hand and drawing it within his arm, where he kept it clasped for a few seconds.

"You will lose us when you wish it, and not before. Do you want to lose us?—to lose me?" he asked. "I do not want to let you go out of my life—do you want me to go out of yours?"

Imprudent, unreflecting, impulsive, Perdita forgot all the proprieties at a blow. She knew only the passionate emotion of the moment, which demanded some kind of expression, else she should surely die of the pleasure that had become pain, the ecstasy that had passed into agony. Her heart swelled, her throat contracted, her eyes grew dark.

"No," she said in a low voice. Then almost unconsciously, with no trace of boldness, of coquetry, of forwardness, only impelled by the overpowering instinct of Love, she pressed his arm against her beating bosom and clung to him with a fervent touch that betrayed her forever—if indeed such betrayal had not been already made.

"My darling! my own darling!" he whispered, taking her hand and holding it as he had done before.

It was a horribly prosaic time and place, with cabs and carriages, drags and omnibuses grinding along the roadway, and passengers by the score jostling them as they walked. But Love annihilates time and transforms all places to the likeness of her own enchanted land; and to the two walking arm in arm along the crowded streets, Cornhill was as peaceful as Arcadia, this murky, sunless London as bright and glorious as Eden. To be there by his side, to feel that she had found him again, to know that he loved her, to say to him in her own way that she loved him—that was enough for Perdita. She had slipped off her mourning garment and had put on her royal robes—she had turned her back on the gloomy night of sorrow, and her face full to the sun and to joy. And what she felt Leslie felt too—with as much intensity if with more self-control.

He looked at her with divine tenderness. Gratitude for her love, admiration for her sincerity, respect for her purity, that yearning to protect her, such as men feel for the women whom they love and who are alone, all contrasted with the reticence demanded by the newness of his freedom. Yet he could not let the moment pass without some binding word. It must be respectful to the dead who had not respected him, but it must be binding on the living. He would not spread his marriage feast on his wife's new-made grave, but he must know the future and be sure of it.

"Can you trust me and wait?" he asked, pressing her hand tenderly. "Do you understand me, Perdita?"

"Do I?" she answered, not looking at him. "I can trust you in all things," she added.

"You will trust my love?—you will wait until the mother can bear to hear that I am going to bring a new wife home? And you will be that wife?"

He spoke so quietly that the man who elbowed him as he went by did not catch the echo of his love—that the flower-girl sitting on the steps scanning the faces of the passers by did not read the secret that was on his; but Perdita, poor Perdita! by the unstinted eloquence of hers made a policeman look at her twice and follow them for the whole length of his beat.

"Will you?" he said again, waiting for the answer which her very emotion strangled before it could reach her lips.

He felt her hang a little heavily on his arm, as if she had suddenly become tired and found walking difficult. And then through all the tumult of the thronged street he heard the faint soft "Yes," which was the rivet in the golden chain that henceforth was to bind them in a lifelong love.

But the strain was too much for her. He saw her face grow pale and felt her sway as she walked, and he had just time to place her in a cab, when, with a look of such supreme and ineffable delight as haunted him for days after—a look as if the divine burden of her soul for the moment crushed down her body—she suddenly turned to him as a child might turn to its mother, flung her arms round his neck and saved herself from fainting for a second time in his arms, only by a passionate flood of tears and the rendering up, as it were, of her whole being in that one self-abandoning caress.

He knew how to soothe her. His very voice could do that! and when they reached his home in High Street she was not much more stirred than was usual with her, and only pleasantly excited when he took her upstairs to the mother.

"Here is our truant," he said, holding her hand as he led her into the room. "She has come to give an account of herself. I have not got the whole story yet."

No! only the essential part, the core round which all the rest clustered, the keystone on which the whole arch depended!

"My dear, I am glad to see you. I have been wearying for you," said Mrs. Crawford, with a maternal affectionate kind of remonstrance in her greeting. "Where have you been all this time? what is amiss with you? I can see that something has gone wrong; you are so pale; and how thin you have grown!"

Perdita's chameleon-like face became instantly the colour of a crimson rose.

"I have been very unhappy," she said in her soft shy way. "But I am so no longer," she added, looking into Mrs. Crawford's face with eyes that shone like stars; and yet they were veiled and humid as well as bright!

"Come! tell me all about it. How long can you stay?" the elder woman returned.

"I can stay—as long as you like to keep me," answered Perdita. "I am not now at home."

It cost her something to make this confession; but she had to say out all that told against herself as bravely as the rest.

"So Leslie said. He said to me only yesterday that he was sure you were not at home. But where are you, my child? and why did you leave home?"

"Mother told me to go," she answered; and then she stopped.

"Why? what had you done to make her take such a terrible step? Tell me frankly, Perdita."

Mrs. Crawford spoke with a certain gravity, a certain suspicion which in another moment might become condemnation.

The girl hesitated. How could she tell the truth? Though she did not know how, yet she did know the fact well enough—she had been sacrificed for Eva; she had been made the scapegoat laden with vicarious sins and sent out into the wilderness to expiate offences which were not her own, yet which it was incumbent on her by the laws of honour and kindness to conceal.

Mrs. Crawford turned on her an uncertain kind of look. Her eyes were half full of tears, while her lips were hard, compressed and bloodless. She was sorry, yet she was not satisfied. She sympathized but she suspected. Perdita's poor tortured face became white and scared. When should she be at rest? Was there no security for her on earth? She whose whole nature was sincere, whose whole life was honest, never knew what it was to live believed in and not blamed. What was this curse of condemnation and distrust that followed her wherever she turned? Even now it had come like the serpent into Eden; and she thought that her decree of banishment was to be pronounced here as it had been at home—that Mrs. Crawford was to repeat the miserable mistake made by her mother, and to augment it.

"I cannot, must not, tell you why," she said in a low voice.

"Do not pain her by asking, mother," said Leslie. "Let us respect her secret."

A smile flashed over her face that gave the impression of her having laughed aloud.

"Thank you; you understand me," she said with a glad blithe accent; and she held out her hand as to a comrade.

"Girls cannot have secrets which they may not tell yet which are not to their discredit," said Mrs. Crawford, speaking from the ordinary point of morality and common sense, and not over-well pleased at this little incident of *camaraderie* between these two.

"In this case it seems that they can," said Leslie, holding Perdita's hand in his with as much respect as tenderness. "Mother, have faith! Do not let us prolong this discussion. Whatever it may be that has happened, it is all right so far as she is concerned—my life on it!"

"Yes indeed, indeed it is!" said Perdita earnestly.

Going over to where Mrs. Crawford was sitting by the table—her head leaning on her hand and her spirit full of doubt and distress, Perdita put her arms round the dear waist, while she knelt by the side of the chair and looked up into the pale pure face as she had done on the first day of her self-revelation.

"Believe me, dearest Mrs. Crawford, I have done nothing wrong—nothing even imprudent so far as I know," she said. "Yet mother has sent me away in anger, and I am in disgrace with all at home. I would not speak like this in silly riddles if I might tell you even what I know—and I don't know everything; but odd as it all sounds, there is nothing against me; and if mother has been made to believe that I have done wrong she has been deceived."

Mrs. Crawford looked into the pleading upturned face, sensitive, excitable, uncontrolled, passionate—but how honest! how sincere! No lie lurked behind those candid eyes—no wrongdoing turned to rust the silver of that pleading voice. Wherever the evil lay it was not here—and yet things looked so bad for her!

"Must I believe her, Leslie?" then said the mother, speaking slowly.

"Yes," he answered with emphasis; "believe her implicitly, mother."

Mrs. Crawford sighed.

"It is against all my education," she said almost plaintively; "but I suppose Leslie is right. He generally is. I do trust you, my dear," to Perdita. "I am sorry for you and for all that must have happened to distress you, but I trust your word that you have not been to blame."

"My darling—my own dear dear—my second mother!" cried Perdita, laying her face on the elder woman's bosom, and kissing it fondly, fervently. It was only a black stuff dress that she kissed, but it was better than nothing. At this moment she must have kissed something—had it been only the back of a chair.

After this she took off her bonnet and stayed for the whole evening, happier than she had ever been in her life before; and pleasanter, more delightful than the Crawfords had ever seen her. Though shy and tender she was not awkward nor embarrassed; when she was silent her face was eloquent of happiness, and when she spoke she had neither fear nor restraint. Her whole being seemed to have undergone some subtle strange transformation—as much so as if she had suddenly become clothed in light and crowned with an aureole like the goddesses and saints of old. She filled the room with radiance; her voice echoed like music and lingered on their ears like a song; she was the incarnation of all womanly peace, of all girlish blessedness, of all human joy; and Mrs. Crawford was no more able or willing to resist the charm than Leslie himself who had wrought it and for whom it was wrought in return. And when the evening passed and Leslie took her home, once more the great secret of life was translated for her benefit, and the earth on which we poor mortals live became heaven inhabited only by angels and the Divine—a place of glory beyond what it had been even in the summer when she had first tasted freedom and had lived with Hope expecting Love.

When Perdita got home she found poor old Cluff in a state of trepidation. Queenly Thomasina had been there, and had sat for some time waiting for her sister to return. She had left, dreadfully annoyed, but with a message to Perdita, saying that she would call to-morrow at the same time, and her sister was to be sure to be in. "She was greatly put out," said poor old Cluff; and then she added gingerly: "And where have you been, my dear?"

"At the Crawfords'," said Perdita, her face in the shadow; and her ancient governess asked no more. What with one thing and the other she found the Winstanleys difficult to deal with, and dreaded those burnt fingers with which she was ever threatened.

But Perdita's curt reply was not from spikiness—quite the reverse: and so she made poor old Cluff feel by the kindness of her manner and the pretty affectionate little embrace that she gave her, as each took her chipped white candlestick and went to the bed which Cluff always said to herself was stuffed with chicken bones for feathers and knots and ends of rope, not honest wool, as was averred. And when the next evening came, Thomasina came too; according to her regal announcement of the day before.

The young queen came meaning to be kind, with intentional condescension. Of course it was humiliating that one sister should be in the position to receive condescension from another; but we must take what we can get in this life; and it is the best wisdom to receive things as they are meant. And though Perdita resented the indignity of brow-beating, she endured meekly enough that of patronage from those whom she loved.

Wherefore when Thomasina drove up in a four-wheeler, with a twopenny bunch of chrysanthemums and six finger biscuits as her donation, Perdita received her with effusion, and very nearly spoilt all by the warmth of her welcome. For nothing was so unpalatable to Thomasina as excitement, whether of anger or of love. Wherefore she employed the first moments in snubbing that unlucky volcano into a more fitting and peaceful attitude of mind; and then she opened on her errand.

"You will not be long here now," she began. "Mother will soon take you home again, unless you are sillier and more wicked than even I give you credit for. Do you remember my telling you a long time since how it would be when Eva and I were married? Mother and you would live together then, and you would have no more quarrels. She is quite prepared to forgive you and take you back when we have gone. I thought you would like to know this, so I came over to tell you."

"What has mother to forgive?" asked Perdita a little hotly. To her unsophisticated mind, wounded and sore as she was, it was she, not mother, who had to forgive.

"Well, we will not go into that now," said Thomasina coolly. "That is not the question. What I want you to understand is that Eva and I are going to be married—she to Sir James Kearney, and I to Mr. Brocklebank—and that when we have gone you are to come home."

"Oh, Thomasina, how dreadful!" cried Perdita. "Eva engaged to Sir James when only such a short time since she was on the point of running away with that Frenchman, and you going to marry Mr. Brocklebank when—"

She stopped. Was it right to speak of his offer even for the sake of reminding her sister, who had, however, said that she had known all about it? It seemed to her something dreadful that this thing should be; but was she her sister's keeper? This proud, wise, far-seeing Thomasina, was she not fit to manage her own affairs?

"Never mind about Mr. Brocklebank, what he has done or what he has not done," said Thomasina. "All that concerns you, Perdita, is the fact. Now, mind!" she added, raising her hand as her sister was about to speak. "You need not say anything; the less you say the better. We are to be married on the same day, Eva and I," she went on quietly. "Since his engagement with her, Mr. Brocklebank has become quite reconciled to Sir James. If you remember, he used to dislike him so very much at one time. He will not tell me why; but that has all quite passed and they are now very good friends. So in about two months from now mother and you will go into the country to live. She has given up the lease of West Hill Gardens, and she has seen a place down at Horsham that she likes. It has a nice little garden; and though it is rather lonely, I think it will do. Mother says she is tired of society; and you never cared for it."

"I never cared for society, but I do not think I should like to live in a lonely country place with mother only," said Perdita bluntly. "It would not be a very happy life for either of us."

Her heart sank with dread at the bare idea of such a thing. Alone with her mother—the most unsympathetic of all companions in the world—and Leslie? and her work? her opinions? her freedom? What anguish in the thought!—and yet—her duty?

"You surely would not let mother live down there in that dull place alone while you knocked about in disgraceful London lodgings?" cried Thomasina with indignation.

"My being with her would not make it any better for her," said Perdita.

"Perdita! are you mad? or entirely bad?" cried her sister. "Have you no spark of family feeling, of filial duty left in you?"

"It is not fair to say this," answered Perdita. "You send me out of the house and banish me from home in punishment for something, I do not know what, of which I have not been guilty, and then you expect me to go back the instant you want me, as a criminal who has received a pardon—some one disgraced taken into favour again. You expect me, Thomasina, to be a mere doll—a log of wood—a bit of wax that you can do with as you like; and you get angry because I object to be treated like this and say that I do not deserve it and do not like it."

"I get angry because you are so intensely selfish," said Thomasina; "because you can never forget yourself and your absurd ideas for the good of the family. If you had, there would not have been all this disturbance, and mother would have got on as well with you as she does with us. But I did not come here to quarrel with you. I have proved my interest in you so far as to give myself all this trouble, first to tell you what is going on, and then to make your present discomfort more bearable by letting you know that it will soon be at an end; but you are ungrateful, as you always are—you are just hopeless, Perdita, and that is the truth!"

She sighed in confirmation of her words; and she believed in them while she sighed.

"Let that pass," said Perdita. "I despair of ever being understood by any one of my own family"—her voice gave way when she said this, but she continued bravely enough—"If you like to think so ill of me as you do I cannot help it, but you can at least tell me the truth. Tell me, Thomasina, what it was you said to mother which made her send me away? You said something; what was it?"

"I screened Eva," answered Thomasina. "It was better for every one that she should be screened. It would have half broken mother's heart if she had known—it would have prevented her marrying Sir James—and Bois-Duval would not have married her. It was better in every way that mother should think that you had been imprudent rather than that Eva had."

"And what did you tell her?" asked Perdita, breathless.

The pillory for the truth—that she would have borne with a brave heart and unflinching courage; but the pillory of banishment from home, the pillory of her mother's displeasure, of condemnatory prate—and she standing there bound to keep silence—that was hard!

"I told her that you were going out of the house at twelve o'clock at night," said Thomasina quietly. "And I trust to your honour not to undeceive her."

"And after this you expect me to sacrifice my whole life that you and Eva may flourish in your wickedness—never, never!" cried Perdita.

"Yes, you will," answered Thomasina. "You will keep the secret for my sake and Eva's, though you bear the blame to the end of your life; you will live with mother at Horsham, and you will be as happy as such a turbulent creature as you are can ever hope to be; and you will have the satisfaction of knowing that you have done your duty and sacrificed yourself for your family. I know you better than you do yourself, Perdita, and I know what you are capable of if you are taken the right way."

"Not of this," said Perdita passionately, thinking of Leslie.

"It will be this or nothing," answered her sister, fixing her calm eyes on her with that cold, still, penetrating gaze for which she was famous. "It will be this—or you will be disowned forever by mother and us all."

Perdita put her face into her hands and sobbed. What a dreadful life hers was! What a succession of heartrending alternatives! Her sister went up to her and forcibly drew down her hands from her face.

"Tell me the truth," she said sternly. "What is the meaning of all this? are you in love, Perdita? Consider, and answer candidly."

"Yes," said Perdita, brought to bay, but shrinking back.

"With whom?" her sister asked again, still stern and cold.

The rebel hesitated. It was partly the sense of desecration, partly the pain of his humiliation that kept her silent; but the trial had to be met. Then the sense of his nobleness, of his mother's saintly purity, came about her like a golden cloud—fell on her soul with great peace and sustaining honour. She cleared her eyes and raised her head, looked her sister in the face, all shame, all hesitation, all shyness and bewilderment gone; her nervous agitation was stilled and she was only conscious of his worth and her own love.

"With whom?" she answered. "The noblest man on earth—Leslie Crawford, the chemist in High Street."

CHAPTER XXXVI.

THE TOILS UNLOOSED.

THE murder was out and the *dies irae*[1] had come. Henceforth Perdita was struck off the roll-call of the Winstanley clan—lopped like a useless branch from the genealogical tree—plucked up like a weed from the family flower-garden. Sorry as Thomasina was to distress her mother by telling her that one of her daughters had confessed herself so degraded as to love a shopkeeper, the fatal secret was too important to be kept from her; and thus the poor young princess herself was compelled to pain that one beloved being whose sorrows, had it been possible, she would have borne on her own back or have piled on the shoulders of any vicarious Atlas who might have passed that way.

Yet when she knew of it, what could Mrs. Winstanley do? That fearful disgrace must go on if Perdita so willed. She was of age; and the English law recognizes no sin of rebellion against parental authority so soon as the magic age of twenty-one is reached. There is no *conseil de famille*[2] with us to restrain the hotter-headed members; no necessity for *sommations*, respectful or otherwise, to obtain parental consent to an undesirable marriage; no Bastille to prevent the irremediable mistakes and punish the follies of the young; and Perdita was not quite mad enough to lock up in a lunatic asylum. Hence this terrible affair must go on, and the rebel must do as she would. All the same she should suffer for her misdeeds; and ostracism complete and crushing was the least that she could expect.

She dropped out of existence almost as if she had never been. Her mother and sisters kept her name as sacred as if it had been a spell wherewith to conjure up demons which could not then be laid; Sir James honestly forgot her existence; and Mr. Brocklebank had his own reasons for "preferring her room to her company," as he said to Clarissa.

To Mrs. Winstanley it was as if she had lost a child by something that was as final and not so consoling as death; to Thomasina there was always the sentiment of disgrace lurking in the background and a shaky place in the foundations; but to Eva it was the pleasant carting away of

---

[1]   (Latin), day of judgment.
[2]   (French), family council.

something inharmonious and ugly, something that used to make her both cross and ashamed.

Meanwhile the two engagements went merrily forward, and in the absence of Perdita no rocks loomed ahead save one—that dreadful mass of debt which Mrs. Winstanley could not pay, and which as yet Mr. Brocklebank had not paid.

The ironmaster was far too shrewd a man of business to part with his money on statements made in the air. Let him go into the whole matter; have it in black or white, as he said; discover for himself the defalcations of that fraudulent friend; and then he would come down handsomely to balance the deficit. He would make all square when he knew the measure; but nothing short of absolute knowledge should wring a five-pound note out of him. He commenced as he intended to proceed; and he would be Mrs. Winstanley's good friend in proportion to the trust she reposed in him. No diagnosis, no cure; no statement of difficulties, no relief by cheque. This was logic: and he stood four-square on his position.

Mother and daughter were in despair. But it was flint and feathers. Not a spark was struck; not a cheque was conjured out of the ironmaster on the faith of mere representation; and Thomasina sat and pondered, and thought again and again, what could she do to help that poor mother whose difficulties were increasing daily—with the wedding breakfast and the double trousseau to provide! She had but one resource—to go to the moneylenders on her own account, and trust to Providence and her allowance after she was married. It would never do to let Mr. Brocklebank know that she had made up a plausible story which had no truth in it save the truth of impecuniosity. She instinctively knew that her plea of filial piety would not stand her in good stead in the analysis of motives, and that her falsehood would be taken raw, unmodified by cooking or condiment. Like all who have to do with masses of men—rulers of things and hands—Mr. Brocklebank laid great store by truth. It was the moral police without which nothing was safe; and he forgave anything sooner than crookedness of statement or directer falsehood. When safely married, Thomasina thought she could brave all; meanwhile she must be careful to secure the price of her self-immolation, and to have handsome settlements through which might filter golden rivulets for her mother's benefit.

In appearance everything went on velvet. Sir James was desperately in love, and only as jealous as was necessary to give body to the cream and redeem the sweet from insipidity. Benjamin Brocklebank was in love too; but he could not divest himself of the feeling of having bought a fine work of art for which he was paying handsomely—a work of art that witnessed to his own good taste and solidity of capital. Lady Kearney, violently opposed to her son's marriage as she was, had nevertheless to give way and offer the tips of her lean fingers by way of congratulation: James was a foolish undutiful boy, but he was her all, and it was better to accept his undesirable little wife than to lose him as her son. So she argued, and with pain and difficulty brought herself to act on her argument—accepting Eva as her daughter-in-law elect, but in the most niggardly manner that was possible, merely cutting the ground of complaint from under her son's feet, but giving no foothold of satisfaction. Mrs. Merton, however, had the grace to congratulate both Eva and Sir James as if she meant it. She accepted Thomasina with as much pleasant sisterliness as if she believed her really fond of Benjamin and honestly glad to be his wife; and she half closed her sleepy eyes, purred softly and spoke sweetly to all around, and was, as she had always been, the incarnate ball of swansdown with no angles to rasp even the most sensitive, and with soft pillowing for all the world. Mrs. Winstanley was the soul of maternal pride and ladylike satisfaction—not rudely exultant as a servant-maid who had won the police sergeant, but serenely gratified, like a queen who has concluded an equal alliance. The girls were all that they should have been. In Eva's wild-flower face not a trace could be seen of the escapade, which it would be profanation to call by the noble name of Love; and her manner to Sir James was of the most bewitching and delicious kind—coaxing, childlike, artless, innocently suggestive of hidden feelings not yet revealed to herself, and loving more than she knew; while Thomasina was the impersonation of gentle dignity and well-bred content. It was peace and fitness all round; and the absence of that inharmonious rebel helped in the general charm.

If it had not been for those odious debts the Winstanley heaven would have been cloudless, and the family sea without a rock, as has been said—but those debts! those maddening bills! and the insolent tradesmen who presented them!

Naturally Thomasina knew very little of business forms—still less of how money could be raised by young ladies of quality with only their pensions as the orphan daughters of a major to call their own. But she had heard of joining in cutting off the entail, of post-obits and IOU's, of bills at sight, of rent-charges and of mortgages; and she had a vague idea that she and Perdita together, both being of age, could mortgage, give post-obits, cut off the entail and draw bills and IOU's at pleasure— at all events, that they could raise a sum of money for that poor darling mother of theirs which should set her straight for the moment. And after the moment—what good to look ahead? Armour Court was one fact, and her settlements should be another, thought Thomasina. Meanwhile something must be done, and that at once.

Wherefore, ignoring the decree of banishment, Thomasina came again to her unsatisfactory sister and proposed her plan of relief. She knew beforehand that Perdita would make no kind of objection, and would neither stand on her dignity as the Discarded who refused to be let down and taken up again at pleasure, nor show any petty feeling of malice or revenge. Selfish, as it had pleased Thomasina more than once to call this recalcitrant rebel, she knew that no one could be counted on with more certainty to do a generous action—no one was a safer moral investment than this poor social mole who groped her way according to the law of right rather than that of expediency, and preferred the ridicule of men to the condemnation of her own conscience. And the result proved her correct.

After her first outburst of wonder, pleasure, amazement, fear, all following each other in rapid succession, Perdita accepted her sister's plan as quite sane and businesslike. They would go to the old family lawyer; cut off the entail; give post-obits and IOU's; borrow money on rent-charges and mortgages to any amount; and then mother would have a sum of money to go on with, the rocks would somehow sink into the sea, the clouds would vanish from the sky, and the velvet would be softer than ever.

And of course when they did go they broke their basket of eggs, and found their rosy-cheeked apples mere skinfuls of dust. The old lawyer called them his pretty dears; explained to them their ignorance and his impossibility; laughed at their misplaced technicalities; and carefully buttoned up his pockets. So nothing was done here, and the pressure remained as great as ever.

The day after this notable excursion into Lincoln's Inn Fields, because she looked sad and he asked her why, Perdita told the whole story to Leslie; and how her mother, apparently in the full tide of prosperity, was in reality on the very brink of ruin; when, if the rapids were reached, there would be a general shipwreck of everything—the home broken up, the seams and rents in the velvet displayed before the eyes of the mocking world, and the marriages of the two sisters without question broken off.

She said it all to him one bright, brisk, frosty Sunday when they were in the Zoological Gardens, together with the privileged hundreds who liked to see the lions fed and to feel the crisp gravel scrunch under their feet and the fresh air blow on their cheeks. They were walking up the broad walk, she leaning on his arm, happy in spite of the tears which stood in her soft eyes—he more than happy in spite of the length of way which had to be gone before he could call her his wife and come to his inheritance of joy—when they came full on the family taking its pleasure too in the Gardens, all the same as the meaner sort. The two lovers were behind, each with his assorted love; and Mrs. Winstanley and Mrs. Merton walked in front as the vanguard of the little body.

"Mother!" said Perdita impulsively.

A spasm crossed her mother's face, but at that moment her conversation with Mrs. Merton touched such an interesting point that she neither saw nor heard anything beyond her companion. Certainly she did not see Perdita; nor did Mrs. Merton; nor did the two lovers; nor did Eva; but Thomasina looked at her neither kindly nor unkindly—just calmly and genteelly—and gave her a little nod that lifted her out of oblivion but scarcely into real recognition.

It was very dreadful to Mrs. Winstanley to have this thing to do. She was horribly angry with Perdita; nevertheless it went against her mother's heart to "cut" her thus in public. But it was impossible to do otherwise. How could she introduce Leslie Crawford, the chemist, to Sir James or Mr. Brocklebank as their future brother-in-law? how present to them the chemist's affianced wife as their future sister-in-law? The thing was impossible! The great god Caste is a divinity not to be lightly disobeyed, and the necessities forced on us by our social position are imperative. She was but a unit—one part of the great system; it was not for her to flout the unwritten law or break down the shadowy fence; and if poor Perdita's bread was bitter to the taste, who but herself had brewed the yeast for the baking?

Yet her mother cut her just as her eyes were full of tears for sympathy with those heavy maternal troubles—just as she had opened her heart to Leslie, and said with a sigh: "If only I could do something to help her!"

"Are you made unhappy by their passing you by?" Leslie asked after a short silence. He saw by her poor sensitive face how deeply the blow had struck—that face which never masked her feelings—and a thought passed through his mind born of as much disdain for them as of love for her.

"Yes," she answered; "I am very unhappy. Though I do not agree with them, I have always loved them. It is they who do not love me, not I who do not love them."

"Never mind, my darling," he said. "I will be all to you that they have not been; and perhaps I may do you some good even with them. They are to be bought!" he added bitterly below his breath.

But Perdita, looking up into his face, shook her head.

"If they knew you, you could do everything," she said simply. "But they will never let themselves know you; they will not give themselves the chance of finding out how good and true and noble you are."

"At least they shall find out how much I love you," he returned, pressing her hand against his arm, overjoyed by her praises which were true to him as exponents of her love if not of his own merits.

That evening, Sunday as it was, Leslie Crawford went to No. 100, West Hill Gardens, and sent up his card, asking to see Mrs. Winstanley. She wondered at his insolence, she said to Thomasina, and refused to go down. What could he want with her but some horrible annoyance? perhaps to announce his approaching marriage with that degraded girl, and go through the farce of asking her maternal sanction; perhaps to remonstrate because of that public ignoring of his and Perdita's existence in the Zoological Gardens to-day; no, she would not go down to see him. She would send him away by the servant; she would not debase herself so far as to receive him.

Then said Thomasina in her quiet voice:

"I think I should go and see him, dear mother. No harm will be done and you will hear what he has to say. See him in the dining-room. He does not look an impudent kind of man; and if he is insolent you can always ring the bell and turn him out of the house."

"It is impudent enough his daring to call here at all!" said Mrs. Winstanley pettishly.

"Yes; but we had better hear his motive," answered Thomasina.

"If he has come to ask my consent to marry Perdita, I shall not give it," said Mrs. Winstanley.

"Certainly not. That would make you a party to the affair; but there may be some other reason," said Thomasina.

And Mrs. Winstanley, who was by now completely under the influence of her eldest daughter, sent a message to Leslie Crawford, whom she had kept standing in the hall all this time, to the effect that she would be with him presently, and that he was to be shown into the dining-room.

After a sufficient time had elapsed for the assertion of her dignity, Mrs. Winstanley went downstairs to confront this insolent chemist and druggist who dared to love that member of the family whom her own people did not think worth the trouble of keeping to themselves. He was standing with his hat in his hand, examining the prints hanging against the walls—standing and examining just as unconcernedly as if he had been in the house of an equal, and not of one so immeasurably superior as was Mrs. Winstanley, the daughter of a dead bishop and prospective mother-in-law of a live baronet.

She made him the stiffest, the haughtiest of courtesies in acknowledgment of his quiet, "Good evening, Mrs. Winstanley," said as any other gentleman would have said it—with no washing of his hands with invisible soap like a draper across the counter; no staccato "Madam;" no tradesman's sign or manner anyhow; just— "Good evening, Mrs. Winstanley;" and then a slight pause.

"I dare say you are surprised at my calling," he said after a moment's silence.

"I am!" briefly replied Mrs. Winstanley. Her manner added; "and displeased."

"Perhaps you are aware of the attachment between your daughter Perdita and myself?" he then went on to say, as coolly as if he had been Mr. Brocklebank himself, or a gentleman of high degree offering bags of gold for the pleasure of relieving Mrs. Winstanley of an onerous charge. Her grand airs evidently did not impress him the least in the world. He thought them silly, artificial, contemptible; and he was by no means overcome by them, as it was intended he should be.

"I consider your allusion to this an insult," replied Mrs. Winstanley.

"No, Mrs. Winstanley, no insult!" he said. "We have to look facts in the face; and this is a fact which must be accepted."

"No, I will never accept it! It is an insult," she repeated.

"Let that pass," he said. "I did not come to proclaim what you already know, nor to press a point that is already settled. I came to put your own affairs on a better footing if I can, and to do what will make Perdita happier."

"The happiness of an undutiful and self-willed girl cannot interest me, her mother though I am," said Mrs. Winstanley. "Her happiness is her sisters' disgrace and my shame."

"Come, Mrs. Winstanley, not quite so bad as that!" said Leslie Crawford with a smile. "I am only a tradesman, I know; but I do not think you will find anything very far wrong in me outside that damaging fact of the shop! I do not degrade you or your daughters by taking Perdita as my wife. Degradation does not come from the name of a man's business if the man himself be just and honourable. But I did not come to assert my integrity any more than to proclaim my attachment to your daughter."

"Then why did you come, pray?" interrupted Mrs. Winstanley glacially.

"I came to see if I could be of use to you," he answered. "Perdita tells me that you are in money difficulties of a rather pressing kind; and for *her* sake," emphasizing the pronoun, "to prove to you how cruelly you have misunderstood her, I, as her representative, come to offer you such help as I can give you. I have saved money, and I am ready to hand you over a certain portion for Perdita's dear sake, that I may buy your respect and better understanding for *her*."

Mrs. Winstanley was silent. She felt as we do when we have braced ourselves up to deliver a tremendous blow—and strike in the air. She was prepared to anathematize her enemy—and lo! here stood her deliverer; she was sure that the pivot of this visit was insult and wrong, and instead she found only help and consolation. It was a cup of healing that he offered to her lips; but it was gall and wormwood all the same. It went against her pride to owe her salvation to this man; but pride must give way to necessity, and indeed her necessity at this moment was terribly great!

"You are very good," she faltered, her handsome face set and white; "but I am deeply involved, and perhaps you do not know what you offer."

"I cannot quite pay the National Debt," he answered with a smile; after all, it was for Perdita! "but I dare say I can manage enough to release you from your present anxieties. It is worth your consideration."

"Your terms of course are my recognition of your engagement to my daughter?" she said with all her former frostiness.

"No; but recognition of your daughter's self," he answered as haughtily as if he had been of her own blood. "For myself, Mrs. Winstanley, I desire nothing—I ask for no recognition—but I do demand for Perdita, whom I love better than my life, restoration to her rightful place in the family. Cut me to your heart's content, but let me know that I have bought her readmission."

"You are not selfish," said Mrs. Winstanley, scarcely knowing whether to like or dislike, praise or ridicule this strange man who did such a generous action with such an odd mixture of cynicism and tenderness, buying for the girl he loved what he so cordially despised for himself. "You have saved me from a dreadful embarrassment," she went on to say half hesitatingly. "I am pushed into a corner, and, frankly, I do not know where to turn. What a pity that you should be a chemist!" she added for the coda, sighing as she spoke.

"Rather, what a pity you should think a man's merit to be determined by his profession, and that a shopkeeper cannot have the instincts of a gentleman!" flashed out Leslie Crawford. "What a pity that you should make artificial classification of more account than natural worth, and hold a titled scoundrel as superior to an honest commoner. It is this false god of Caste which is the ruin of English society—this absurd belief in rank *per se* which is taking the true manhood out of our country."

"We must have dignities and distinction," said Mrs. Winstanley stiffly.

"It is more important that we should have men," said Leslie hardily. "But let us drop this discussion. It will lead to nothing useful. Tell me instead what I can do for you in your present difficulties; how much will release you? and when will you ask Perdita to your house as a sister with her sisters? your daughter as they also are your daughters?"

"Dear child!" said Mrs. Winstanley, her displeasure melting as her pride succumbed to necessity and she prepared herself to accept this tradesman's money; "it was never my wish to banish her!"

Fortunately for the peace of all concerned, Perdita herself shrank from going to the house when the lovers were about, and refused the offer to be her sisters' bridesmaid, which Mrs. Winstanley honourably made her by way of keeping her agreement with Leslie. The story of her engagement to the chemist had leaked out by now, and both the sons-in-law elect were furious—each in his own way.

"It is an unheard-of indignity—a crushing disgrace!" said Sir James after he heard this damning fact from his mother. "His brother-in-law the chemist and druggist," was a knife which she did not disdain to use, and which she turned in the wound with cruel persistency. "If your sister comes to the wedding," he said to Eva, "none of my people shall. If she cannot be prevented marrying that fellow, at least she shall not be countenanced; and I for one discard her without mercy."

"Tut!" said Mr. Brocklebank, jingling his heavy chain. "We will not be too hard on them. We will buy our drugs at their place—that will put a little money in their pockets; and I dare say I shall sometimes have a few old coats and waistcoats that will save the tailor's bill. We need not receive them, but we can be compassionate and perform our part in alleviating their wants."

And when Mr. Benjamin Brocklebank, the master of Armour Court, took this tone, those who knew him understood the depth of disdain, the unfathomable contempt, from which it sprang.

"Mother has been saved, that is all I care for," said Perdita; "and by you, my best, my darling!—by the noblest man on earth, the wisest and the most generous!"

"Whose highest title to honour is that he is loved by the best girl on earth!" said Leslie, with a lover's foolish pride; "one who has known how to appraise the things of life at their true value; who has thought love a better dowry than rank; a woman's duties higher than her rights; the quiet restrictions of home more precious than the excitement of liberty, the blare of publicity."

"Poor Bell Blount! I wonder what has become of her?" said Perdita. "How angry she was with me, and how she flung me off and turned against me!"

"Well for you that she did," said Leslie. "At one time you were in danger, but you were happily saved."

"By you," answered Perdita with infinite tenderness. "If I had not loved you I should have gone into the Movement out of mere despair at the aimlessness of my life."

"You do not repent your choice?"

"No! I never knew true happiness before; and I did not know that life held so much peace and joy for me as I find it does now when I am with you and I feel that you love me," she answered, looking into his face.

"And will to my life's end," said Leslie fervently.

All the same he was only a chemist and druggist, serving the public with rhubarb and colocynth[1] across a counter; and she was the daughter of a major and the granddaughter of a bishop—a rebel and a democrat, not honouring, as she should, the purple lappet which fell across her soft smooth shoulders—the blueness of the blood which ran in her wicked veins—not honouring anything so much as human worth and the truth of things, and that Love which alone makes our life divine.

THE END.

---

[1] The spongy fruit of a Mediterranean and African herbaceous vine (*Citrullus colocynthis*) related to the watermelon, from which a powerful cathartic is prepared.

Appendix A: Contemporary Reviews of The Rebel of the Family

1. *The Saturday Review*, vol. 50 no. 1308, 20 November 1880, pp. 650-51.

The materials of Mrs. Lynn Linton's latest story are in their essence familiar enough to novel-readers. A mother who makes a hard struggle to keep up appearances; her daughters, only one of whom—the Rebel—is a disappointment to her pride in her careful education; two or three men with whom the daughters flirt with varying results, and a hero to marry the heroine, are the chief characters in a story which has, it need hardly be said, a great deal of cleverness and also a great deal of oddity. It may be said that some of its oddities give the book an additional interest, in that the reader's attention is roused, apart from the intrinsic merit of the story, by an ardent desire to find out whether what seems at moments the author's advocacy of strange views is serious or not, whether she means to sympathize with or to laugh at her heroine's convictions and inconvenient theories, and whether or not she thinks Perdita's example a desirable one, on the whole, to follow. On none of these points is the reader likely to get much satisfaction; for at one moment he will think that Mrs. Linton is disposed to applaud, at another to condemn, the unattractive, if conscientious, ways of the Rebel of the Family; and he may even cherish a secret doubt whether there is not a considerable touch of sarcasm in the author's eloquent approval of her heroine's marriage with a chemist and druggist, whom she exalts into a hero because he has pulled her back from the brink of the pond in Kensington. Such a marriage may no doubt be a fitting one for a well-brought-up and well-educated young woman who prefers the intimate friendship of questionable people to association with her own mother and sisters, whom she is for ever offending by her gross want of tact and even of manners. But in the matter of manners Perdita is not the only eccentric character in the book. On one point, that of the woman's rights agitation, Mrs. Linton's opinions seem to be clear enough. Her portrait of Mrs. Blount, or Bell Blount, as she preferred to be called, is as forcible as it is unsparing. In executing it with complete fidelity, the author has once or twice had to deal with somewhat risky matters, and has dealt with them with marked skill. The scenes in which Bell Blount figures cannot possibly be pleasant, in the sense in which a pretty landscape is pleasant, and some of their features are markedly unpleasing; but Mrs. Linton knows where to insist and where to touch lightly, and the whole result is what no doubt she aimed at—to exhibit in a strong light some of the absurdities, and worse than absurdities, connected with a movement which she seems to dislike. The character is, as we have said, drawn with remarkable strength, and in many of its touches there is a strong, if grim, sense of humour. [...]

It is Mrs. Linton's merit that, except in the case of the heroic chemist and druggist, she does not take a one-sided view of any of her characters. There is good even in Bois-Duval, scoundrel as he is, and there is much good in the worldly-minded and mercenary Thomasina, who has the cleverness and the courage to put herself into Bois-Duval's power in order to save her sister, the flirt who affects the *ingénue*, and whose flirting has for once gone too far. [...]

We have said as yet comparatively little of Perdita herself. Her character is drawn with great care and truth, but, we confess, interests us less than it was perhaps meant to do. We trust that she was as happy as may be with her chemist and druggist, but we do not think it unlikely that he got considerably bored with her.

2. *The Athenaeum*, no. 2771, 4 December 1880, p. 741.

In "The Rebel of the Family" Mrs. Lynn Linton appears to much greater advantage than in that tract in three volumes which she styled "Under which Lord?" The public are now pretty well acquainted with the author's merits and defects. Her novels are exceedingly well written, the dialogue is full—perhaps too full—of point, the descriptions are carefully worked up, and every effort is made to develop an interesting plot. On the other hand, she possesses little of the novelist's most precious gift—the power of creating characters. Most of her *dramatis personæ* are carefully constructed lay figures, who speak and act consistently, but fail to impress the reader with a sense of their reality. In this respect, however, "The Rebel of the Family" is more successful than most of Mrs. Linton's books. Perdita, the heroine, is really a charming character, and her worldly mother is excellently drawn. On the other hand, Leslie Crawford is dreadfully wooden; and a most conventional French viscount, who has figured in scores of English novels, mars a work that might otherwise be pronounced a brilliant success. As it is, "The Rebel of the Family" cannot rank above the second class of novels, but among them it merits a high place. So good, however, is it that Mrs. Linton would do well to eliminate her villain and recast the work, confining it to two volumes.

3. *The British Quarterly Review*, January 1881, p. 116.

Though this novel does not show the sustained strength of Mrs. Lynn Linton's first novel, or the "Atonement of Leam Dundas,"[1] it is in several respects an advance on her last one, "Under which Lord [?]." This story is well constructed; and if it does not aim high, it realizes pretty well that at which it aims; and it goes without saying that it is full of Mrs. Lynn Linton's satiric reference and reflection, which sometimes imparts piquancy and is sometimes wearisome and a little harsh. In this respect she does not always observe the French rule of not too much. [...]

Mrs. or rather Bell Blount, the women's rights heroine, with whom Perdita comes into contact, is admirably done; and the various personages whose society Mrs. Winstanley seeks, lead us sufficiently into "high life" to allow Mrs. Lynn Linton room for the play of her cynical turn. On the whole, the story is clever, readable, and reveals some tendency to study pressing present-day social questions, and to play with them rather than to treat them seriously.

4. *The Academy*, 19 February 1881, p. 131.

What Mrs. Linton means us to infer from her last novel we know no more than she does herself. Perdita, the "Rebel of the Family," is a truthful, energetic, passionate—not to say violent—girl, living at open war with a matchmaking lady-mother and genteel lady-sisters. Disobedience is as the breath of her nostrils, whether against her parent's wishes she engages herself as clerk in the Post office, joins the Women's Rights Movement, or takes stolen walks with a neighbouring chemist. For the Movement vagaries she is snubbed and reformed by the authoress, who yet winks at the walkings-out and other like matters. In fact, the writer, beginning without any fixed moral basis, flounders into a network of dilemmas, and then leaves poor Perdita to put herself right with the reader how she can. On the whole, we gather that she is meant for a martyred *femme incomprise*,[2] more especially from her instinct for forming undesirable acquaintances. Nothing can be more grandly ferocious than her rampant love of truth—she scorns the bridle upon her lips whenever, by uncalled-for revelations, she can expose the poverty and frailties of her family, or harry her mother by an effective scene—she cannot possibly tell a fib to save her sister from infamy and her

---

[1] Linton's first novel was *Azeth the Egyptian* (1847). *The Atonement of Leam Dundas* appeared in 1876.
[2] (French), misunderstood woman.

mother from ruin; but somehow, after this supreme sacrifice to Truth, she can slip out on the sly to the chemist's to revel in a purer moral atmosphere than that of her despised home. This chemist, by-the-by, has a guilty wife somewhere in an asylum, but, of course, she dies off when required. That Perdita should never have learnt or even enquired about her existence, or have resolved the mystery (which, grotesque as it is, we prefer not to explain) of the dark, bullet-headed baby nursed by old Mrs. Crawford, is simply incredible. But, after all, Perdita is a good, well-meaning girl, and quite worth reading about. Her mother is a hackneyed character, but well finished; and the elder sister is still better. Here Mrs. Linton has succeeded in the portrait of a placid, narrow-minded beauty, heroic in her daily sacrifice to Mammon, true as steel to a false ideal of social and home duties, almost pathetic in her devotion to her mother—the only sentiment she permits herself to indulge. The perfect sympathy and friendship of these two frivolous fellow-souls is an admirable touch. The younger sister is, like most of the other characters, a mere burlesque. Mr. Brocklebank, indeed, is simply a caricature of a caricature—Josiah Bounderby,[1] without the common-sense. We cannot pretend to accept English baronets who, on being introduced by ladies to French gentlemen, begin by insolently rallying them upon Waterloo and then challenging them. But if the gentlemen are rude throughout the book, the ladies are abusive. One scene, in which the ineffable Mrs. Winstanley calls upon the exclusive Lady Kearney expressly to insult and be insulted, or, in other words, to have it out with the woman, is enough to appall any male reader. In a long and clever description of a Women's Suffrage meeting the authoress, we suppose, has taken off the peculiarities of the leaders of the sisterhood in no kindly spirit. Bell Blount, however, the masculine lady who inveigles Perdita into her friendship, is a character too odious, and the scenes in which she appears too repulsive, even for comment. The style of the book is as bright as usual, but terribly monotonous after a few pages, the padding being compounded of cynical sentiment, seasoned with myriad metaphors. It is, in short, a bad book by a practiced writer.

---

[1] The "hard facts" industrialist in Charles Dickens' novel *Hard Times* (1854).

Appendix B: Essays by Eliza Lynn Linton

1. "Mary Wollstonecraft," *The English Republic* vol. 4 (1854), pp. 418–24.

Out of the dead level of our modern fine-ladyism every now and then a woman rises like a goddess standing above the rest: a woman of fair proportions and unmutilated nature, a woman of strength, will, intellect, and courage, practically asserting by her own life the truth of her equality with man, and boldly claiming as her right also an equal share in the privileges hitherto reserved for himself alone. None stronger, more independent, or more noble, than Mary Wollstonecraft, one of the first, as she was one of the ablest, defenders of the Rights of Woman.

MARY WOLLSTONECRAFT was born in 1759, on the 27th of April, the second child of her parents, respectable common-place people of the middle-class, who never comprehended and still less cared for the wonderful genius of their child. Her early life seems to have been very painful. Her father was a man of violent and unequal temper,—now kind and indulgent, now harsh and tyrannical; the mother was devoted to the eldest son, and treated her daughters with much more severity than tenderness. To Mary she was peculiarly harsh, thinking probably that a character so independent and a will so strong required "breaking" and "keeping down," as is the case with most common-place parents who have original characters to form. Mary alludes to her home-life in these words, taken from the *Wrongs of Woman*: "The petty cares which obscured the morning of my heroine's life; continual restraint in the most trivial matters; unconditional submission to orders, which as a mere child she soon discovered to be unreasonable, because inconsistent and contradictory; and the being often obliged to sit in the presence of her parents, for three or four hours together, without daring to utter a word."[1] A sufficiently intelligible description of what her own young days had seen and suffered. Violence, cruelty, blows, and even more than blows threatened: all these made the young girl's life one prolonged series of tortures, which saddened her whole character. Perhaps, though, strengthening her mind by forcing on her so early the necessity of self-sustainment, and obliging her to think and act and judge for herself.

One of Mary's earliest friends was a clergyman, a Mr. Clare,—a delicate, sensitive, deformed recluse, whose cultivated mind, however, was of great use

---

[1] *Maria, or The Wrongs of Woman* was Wollstonecraft's last work, published posthumously with an introduction by Godwin in 1798.

to Mary, brought up as she had been almost entirely without instruction, a mere wild, beautiful child of nature, whose intellect was left to chance and to herself. Mr. Clare was very kind to the young girl, and kept her in his house for days and weeks together, giving her instruction and forming her tastes, supplying in fact the workman's skill to that glorious unknown marble. But indeed every one out of her own family was conscious of her power of intellect, and every one but those nearest to her, who ought by nature to have been most interested in her, was anxious to help her forward in her mental culture. Her family would have kept her back, and did so as far as they could; and had Mary Wollstonecraft been weaker and smaller than she was, the early tyranny she lived under would have crushed her. But to compensate for this she found friends and admirers wherever she turned; and if unrecognized at home, her worth was understood and acknowledged abroad.

About the same time, too, as her acquaintance with Mr. Clare, began her first passionate friendship, with a girl about two years older than herself— Fanny Blood, for many years the lode-star of Mary's heart. Fanny was a gentle, gifted, spiritual, but weak woman, whose wish ever went beyond her will, and whose sensitiveness suffered what her weakness had not the courage to end. The two were fairly types of character and intellect: Mary's power and force of nature in strong contrast to Fanny's timidity and gentleness, as the last in her brilliant education threw Mary Wollstonecraft, unlearned as she was, into the shadow of comparative ignorance. No one would have thought then that the accomplished and intellectual Fanny Blood would owe her rescue from oblivion solely to that wild girl, so frank and so untutored, who regarded her as a superior being, and who despaired of ever attaining to her intellectual station,—that undisciplined being whose mind was merely then a disordered skein of tangled thoughts, without connection and without purpose. This affection changed the whole current of Mary's life. She began to study in real earnest, stipulating for time and power to do so. But somehow matters did not go on very smoothly: so when she was about nineteen she determined to leave home and go out as companion to a Mrs. Dawson, a widow lady at Bath: a lady, moreover, of such temper and habits as to render her companion's life one of unmitigated hardship. No one could live with her. After a few weeks or months every one quitted her in despair. But Mary remained two years with her, gaining such influence and control as forced the lady into more considerate treatment of her. This fact proves how great was her moral power over others, even at that age, as indeed this moral power became afterward one of her chief characteristics.

After her mother's death (her illness broke up Mary's connection with Mrs. Dawson), she went to live with her friend Fanny; and soon after, her father's affairs becoming embarrassed, going from bad to worse, sweeping away all in the wreck, her own portion and her sisters' as well, and leaving them without any provision for the future as without any resources for the present, she determined on her means of livelihood. She was not the woman to sit idly with her hands folded helplessly in her lap, while ruin was around her that energy could repair. She formed her plans, which were that she, Fanny, and her two younger sisters should open a day-school at Newington Green,[1] which they did, their establishment soon getting a reputation, and "answering," as people say, perfectly. But after some time poor Fanny's health gave way, and she was ordered out to Lisbon for change of air. There she married a Mr. Hugh Skeys, in February 1785, to die of premature confinement in the autumn of the same year. During her illness, Mary went over to Lisbon to attend her, leaving her school and her connections to themselves, ready, as she ever was in life, to sacrifice all of self for friendship, love, or principle.

On her return home—to find her school much decreased and her connection wavering—she wrote her first work, *Thoughts on the Education of Daughters*, receiving for it her first literary payment, which she handed over to Fanny's father and mother, who wished to get over to Ireland. That was essentially Mary Wollstonecraft—that generous, noble act! After this she gave up the school and went to Ireland as governess to the daughters of Lord Kingsborough, staying there a year, and then quitting them, as it appears, on account of some change in their plans: a tour on the continent, in which she was to have been included, being postponed. At Bristol, where she was with Lord Kingsborough's family, she wrote her story, *Mary: a Fiction*. And then she came up to London, determined to begin a literary life in good earnest, and to make authorship her profession, if not her pride, partly urged thereto by her publisher, Mr. Johnson, whose kindness and friendliness formed an epoch of immeasurable importance in her life: for without him perhaps she would never have decided on literature as a profession, and might have gone on through her whole life as governess or school-mistress, content with personal influence and local superiority, instead of making herself a name that shall last as long as women are loved or as genius is honoured.

The life she had chosen was not, however, all for gain or self. She spent large sums on her family, educating her sisters as governesses and assisting her brothers to better their situations. Her father himself was by this time dependent on her: his affairs all so entangled and embarrassed that she took them into her own hands to arrange as she best might. Her personal

---

[1]   A neighborhood in North London.

expenses she cut down to the smallest possible amount, living always in the extreme of economy that she might lavish upon others, spending on the pleasures and well-being of her relatives whatever she could save from her own needs or enjoyments.

And now began the real life by which henceforth she was known; now she came out fairly before the world as a thinker and a writer; now for the first time she found her true intellectual sphere, and could measure herself with her equals.

All the best people of the time loved Mary Wollstonecraft. Who could have failed to do so? Beautiful, enthusiastic, true, sensitive, clever in intellect, commanding in mind, the best part of a man's nature united with the lovingness and loveliness of a woman's: who could have failed to love her? Not Dr. Price; not her own publisher, Mr. Johnson; not Mr. Bonnycastle, the mathematician; nor Dr. Fordyce; nor Fuseli.[1] These were all men of worth and note, and all acknowledged Mary Wollstonecraft's superiority and glorious nobility of soul. No light award in those days of woman's silken slavery and sugared degradation. Between Fuseli and herself indeed existed a very tender and a very true affection, which, however, did not advance her much in any way, filling her heart with regrets and tinging her mind with a sad and scornful scepticism that neither brought her happiness nor led her up to truth.

And now Mary's great work was written—*A Vindication of the Rights of Woman*—one of the boldest and bravest things ever published. Bolder then than now, when the idea of woman's equality has become so familiarized among us that America shows us even doctors, and lawyers, and clergymen, and orators, all women, and when the fact that women have minds and the right to use them is becoming slowly established among men. Mary Wollstonecraft then stood quite alone in her doctrine: the very class she had defended turning the most bitterly against her, and the oppressed whom she championed rending her to pieces as she stood fighting for them. As indeed was to be expected, being but natural, from those in whom long habits of slavery have eaten out all independence and all moral dignity, in whose hearts oppression has strangled the very instinct of justice. We have enough now of that slavish submission of Englishwomen which is not wifely duty so much as the obedience of the harem. It is a feeling wholly apart from that intelligent compliance with the will of the nobler, the ideal

---

[1]   Richard Price (1723–91), Presbyterian minister at Newington Green, leader of a group called the Rational Dissenters; Joseph Johnson (1738–1809), radical publisher; John Bonnycastle (1750?–1821), English mathematician and astronomer; James Fordyce (1720–96), author of "Sermons to Young Women" (1766); John Henry Fuseli (1741–1825), Swiss-born Romantic painter.

of which female slavery is the mournful reverse, and which exalts the one who is humbled. Mary Wollstonecraft broke lance against no such sacred temple as this, but simply against that degradation which would lead a woman to make herself the toy and plaything of men's passions. Who shall dare to say she was wrong?

Of her relations with Mr. Imlay[1] it is difficult to form a correct opinion. Not on account of the morality of the act, but on account of its ill success. She took his name, she loved him, she bore his child; but his love for her was transient, and evidently of a lower nature than hers: and so this greatest social experiment that could be made turned out ill, and the sorrow and the shame fell on her alone. She and Mr. Imlay lived together for about a year and a half, when by separation, by discontent, by inconstancy, by a thousand little nothings which weigh a man down on the side of selfishness, Mr. Imlay wished to free himself from the connection, which eventually he did, almost breaking Mary's heart in the trial. The fault in this severance was in his want of frankness. It might have been from an affectionate and timid fear to pain her; it might have been that he wished her to wean herself from him, and so sought to weaken her affections gradually; or it might have been from cowardice and the shame of having it known what a base part he was playing. Be that as it may, it is certain that for months—passing almost into years—he kept poor Mary on the most horrible rack humanity can know, until at last she firmly decided on ending the strife, and so broke off all relations, even of friendship, with Mr. Imlay: though ever retaining for him a warm and tender affection, and, woman-like, never suffering any expression of censure against him for her sake. It is certain that she loved him the most intensely of any one in life. Her early friendship for Fanny Blood, her gratitude toward Mr. Johnson, her platonic attachment for Fuseli, which made her so unhappy in its moonlight unreality, its mere vision of the bliss that might have been, and even her connection and marriage with Godwin: none of all these or of other affections had the same influence over her heart and life as this unhappy love for Imlay. It was the shattering of the crystal, the drying up of the well of life; it was the blighting of her honour, the ruin of her happiness. We doubt much if Mary Wollstonecraft ever really recovered from the moral shock of this desolation, or ever really loved or hoped as she had done before. The despair which made that noble heart seek suicide so resolutely as she did[2]

---

[1] Gilbert Imlay (1754–1828), American timber-merchant and author, father of Mary Wollstonecraft's first daughter Fanny (born 1794).

[2] In November 1795, Mary Wollstonecraft tried to drown herself from Putney Bridge after having been abandoned by Imlay.

could not have lightly passed away. Even as Godwin's wife, Mary must have sometimes regretted Imlay.

In 1797, she married Godwin,[1] after having lived with him openly before, unmarried. The world upon this was shocked. Mrs. Siddons and Mrs. Opie,[2] and others of the celebrated women of that day, withdrew themselves from her now, when, according to their code, she had made amends for her transgressions, and had become an "honest woman." As Mrs. Imlay, all the world knowing that no marriage ceremony had been performed, all the world had received and courted her. When yielding to the opinion she did not respect, she forsook her own faith and became the legal wife of Godwin, the world forsook her in return: a sharp punishment and an instructive lesson against all such tampering with conscience. In the month of September, 1797, Mary Wollstonecraft died, leaving behind her a little girl—afterward Mrs. Shelley—whose birth cost the mother's life.[3] Leaving also an imperishable name wherever courage and truth shall be revered and conscience held higher than conformity. She is one of our greatest women, because one of the first who stormed the citadel of selfishness and ignorance, because one of the bravest and one of the most complete. Hers was one of those great loving, generous souls that make no bargain between self and duty, that dare to follow out their own law and to walk by their own light, that refuse vicarious help and work out their salvation by their own strength, that appeal to God for judgment, not to man for approbation. She was one of the priestesses of the future; and men will yet gather constancy and truth from her example: so true it is that a good deed never dies out, but extends its influence as far as Humanity can reach.

Mary Wollstonecraft's whole life proved her character in its dutiful self-sacrifice and its strong independent will, in its noble adherence to principle and its brave assertion of unbiased judgment: so that when she was over-persuaded into that marriage with Godwin, against her former faith, she committed her greatest sin, and her only one of that kind, the resigning of her own opinion for that of the world's, which world-opinion she lost by the means she took to gain it, wherein was no injustice if some severity of sentence.

We have Mary Wollstonecrafts by the dozen among us in her abstract ability: how many in her moral courage? Yet we have the same fight to fight

---

1   William Godwin (1756–1836), English author and political philosopher, father of Mary Wollstonecraft's second daughter Mary (born 1797).
2   Sarah Kemble Siddons (1755–1831), English actress; Amelia Anderson Opie (1769–1853), English poet.
3   Mary Shelley (1797–1851), author of *Frankenstein* (1818).

that she had, and the same things remain undone that she would fain have forwarded with a helping hand. Who will take this stigma of cowardice and the slave's degradation from the women of England? Who will show that we have minds as subtle and wills as strong as Mary Wollstonecraft of the past? Who will prove that if they will our women shall be free and noble, as Godwin's wife would have made them, as Godwin's wife did make herself?

Whose voice will answer us from the distance, whose hand meet us in the darkness?

2. "Marriage Gaolers," *Household Words* (5 July 1856), pp. 583–85.

Gaolers are of various kinds. There are gaolers of criminal prisons—men of square heads and powerful shoulders, who carry colossal keys in their mighty hands, and look as if they lived over a gunpowder train with the match burning, and they knew it; gaolers of financial prisons, jovial and lynx-eyed, who pry sharply into feminine pockets and baskets, and direct trembling women to the six-in-ten and eight-in-four they came to see; gaolers of political prisons—of an apocryphal order these in England—whose romantic daughters file off chains at dead of night, drug guards with brandy and laudanum—a fine thing in cholera times—and, with a tear and a blessing, and lots of money stolen from the till, set the captive hero free to the infinite disgrace of their gaoler relative; and there are gaolers parochial and gaolers lunatic—nautical gaolers and scholastic gaolers; but the worst gaoler of all is the marital gaoler, as constituted by the laws of our illogical merrie old England.

An absolute lord is this marital gaoler. He holds the person, property, and reputation of his conjugal prisoner in as fast a gaol as ever was built of granite and iron. Society and law are the materials, unsubstantial enough, out of which he has built his house of duress; but in those airy cells lie more broken hearts than ever the sternest dungeon held. More injustice is committed there than in the vilest Austrian prison known. If the gaoler-marital be a decent fellow, and in love with his prisoner, things may go on smoothly enough. But if he be a man of coarse or fickle passions—if he be a man without conscientiousness or honour—if he be a man of violent temper, of depraved habits, of reckless life, he may ill-treat, ruin, and destroy his prisoner at his pleasure—all in the name of the law, and by virtue of his conjugal rights. The prisoner-wife is not recognized by the law; she is her gaoler's property, the same as his dog or his horse; with this difference, that he cannot openly sell her; and if he maim or murder her he is liable to punishment, as he would be to prosecution by the Cruelty to Animals Society, if he maimed or ill-treated his dog or his horse. As "the very legal being of the wife is suspended during the marriage, or at least incorporated and consolidated with that of the husband" (*vide* Blackstone),[1] it is therefore simply as a sentient animal, not as a wife, nor as a citizeness, that she can claim the protection of the laws; and then only in cases of personal and distinct brutality which threatens her life. The same protection, and only the same, as is granted to slaves in the United States—as is granted to all sentient and domesticated animals in most civilized communities. The prisoner-wife has no property. All that she possessed before her marriage, and all that she may earn, save, or inherit after her marriage, belongs to her husband. He may squander her fortune at the gaming-table, or among his mistresses; he may bequeath it to his illegitimate children, leaving his wife and her children to beggary; he may do with it as he will; the law makes him lord and gaoler, and places the poor trembling victim unreservedly in his hands. The like may he do with the earnings, the savings of his wife, during his incarceration, if he have committed a crime; during his desertion, if he have taken a fancy to desert her for some one else; during a separation, forced on him by her friends, to protect her from his brutality. Whatever be the cause which has thrown the wife on her own resources, and made her work and gain, he may swoop down like a bird of prey on the earnings gained by her own work while she was alone; he may seize them and carry them off unhindered, leaving her to the same terrible round of toil and spoliation, until one or the other may die. That this is not mere declamation, three authentic instances of the exercise of such marital rights are given in a certain admirable, wise, and witty pamphlet[2] recently published: of which we will say no more in the way of criticism than that it is worthy of SYDNEY SMITH.[3]

"A widow, with a small personal property and three young children, was induced, by a scoundrel lurking under the garb of a preacher, to marry her without a settlement. He then threw off the mask, treated her and her children most scandalously, and indulged in the most disgraceful drunkenness and debauchery. Still, his career was so short, that when he sunk under his excesses, the little property was not seriously impaired, and the poor woman though again in a state of pregnancy, was not in actual despair. In a few days she was driven to madness when she discovered that this man, shortly after the marriage, had bequeathed her little all to an illegitimate child of his own."

A second case given, is that of a young girl who married, somewhat

---

1   William Blackstone (1723–80), English jurist, author of *Commentaries on the Law of England*.
2   Remarks upon the Law of Marriage and Divorce, suggested by the Hon. Mrs. Norton's Letters to the Queen. Ridgeway, Piccadilly. [Linton's note]
3   The author of the "witty pamphlet" quoted by Linton was Caroline Sheridan Norton (1808–77), English writer of poetry and prose. Sydney Smith (1771–1845), English clergyman and essayist, champion of Catholic emancipation.

against her father's consent, a young man of indifferent character. "Her father died suddenly without having made a will or settlement of any kind: and very shortly after, the husband in a moment of drunken fury, committed a felonious assault on his unhappy wife. He was tried and convicted of the felony, and the property of the wretched wife, which, upon its descending to her, was instantly transferred by the law to him, became forfeited to the crown by reason of a felony of which she was not the perpetrator, but the victim."

In the third case, the husband of a very decent woman was convicted of a crime in his own family too horrible to particularise. He was sent to prison for three years. The wife removed to a distant part of the country, where, under an assumed name, she supported herself and her children in comfort, and was even enabled to save out of her earnings. One evening her husband came suddenly to the house, inflamed with drink, and burning with evil passions. He came in the name of the English law to claim his marital rights over her person and her earnings, to take his place in the family whose virtue he had outraged, and whose safety he had endangered. Convicted of such a horrible crime as he had been, he was none the less lord and master; the wife could none the more obtain a release from him and his vice. He was gaoler by right of English law; and she was his prisoner by the fiat of English bigotry.

But there is a difference in properties, the personal and the real: the first belongs to the husband, the second to the heir.

If a wife die without children, her houses and lands pass to her next male heir; but if she have a child, and that child be heard to cry but once, and both mother and babe then instantly expire, they belong to her husband for life, under the not very intelligible title of Tenant by the Courtesy of England Consummate. Should the babe live, the gaoler-marital is only Tenant by the Courtesy of England Inchoate, and has to give up possession on the boy's twenty-first birthday. The sheep, oxen, Sèvres china, kid gloves, satin shoes, lace collars, gold bracelets, breloques, chains, hair-pins, furniture, and pet dogs, constituting, among a thousand like articles, what is called personalty, belong unreservedly to the husband; who can pawn, sell, or give them away, the instant the clergyman has pronounced the marriage blessing. Now what do you say to these as perquisites of the gaoler marital?

Turning now from property to divorce—what do we find? A gaoler marital may entertain as many ladies light-of-love as he pleases. He may support them out of his wife's property, he may even endow them with that property after his death, and leave his lawful lady and her children to want and misery,— and the wife has no remedy. The relief of divorce was not instituted for her. Many have tried the question, and almost all have been thrown. In an infinite number of years, and out of millions of victims groaning for deliverance, only four have obtained divorce. Cruelty, infidelity, vice, crime, desertion, nothing that would seem to be a natural and common-sense breaking of the nuptial bond is allowed to stand as a legal severance, for her benefit. The wife must bear her chains to the grave, though they eat into her very soul; she must submit to every species of wrong and tyranny—the law has no shield for her! But when a gaoler wishes to get rid of a prisoner, it is quite another thing! It is in reality but an affair of money. If he can afford the various legal processes demanded by our wise laws, he can be free tomorrow,—be his wife the most virtuous lady in the land. If he chooses he can collude with some villain, whom he accuses of being his wife's lover. The man does not defend the action, and judgment is allowed to go by default. The villain is assessed in damages which he may pay with one hand and receive with the other. We say that all this may happen if a gaoler will; the law does not provide against such a possibility. The accused wife is not told of the time or manner of the trial. She is not supposed to appear as a witness, nor to defend herself by counsel. The action is not brought against her, but against the lover, for damage alleged to be done to the gaoler's property; the wife's existence, as wife or woman is ignored; she is only judged and assessed by her monetary value. This is the English law of divorce, and English gentlemen's feelings on conjugal infidelity. And then we ridicule the foreigner's belief that we sell our wives, because we do not take them to market with a halter round their necks,—at least, not when we are in good society,—and because we only receive money as a manly manner of compensation, when they have given their souls and love to another. The difference may be great in form; certainly the one mode is simpler than the other; but surely the spirit is identically the same!

This, then, is marriage: on the one side a gaoler, on the other a prisoner for life, a legal nonentity, classed with infants and idiots; or, if there should ever come liberty, coming only through that poor prisoner's hopeless ruin;—ruin she is powerless to avert, be she the most innocent of God's creatures. Neither property nor legal recognition, neither liberty nor protection has she, nothing but a man's fickle fancy, and a man's frail mercy between her and misery, between her and destruction. This is marriage as by the law of England. Let those who doubt it, and those who do not doubt it, consult the vigorous and manly writer, with a head as sound as his heart, whose pamphlet has supplied these notable illustrations.

3. "The Girl of the Period," *Saturday Review* 14 March 1868, pp. 339–40.

Time was when the stereotyped phrase, "a fair young English girl," meant the ideal of womanhood, to us, at least, of home birth and breeding. It meant a creature generous, capable, and modest; something franker than a Frenchwoman, more to be trusted than an Italian, as brave as an American but more refined, as domestic as a German and more graceful. It meant a girl who could be trusted alone if need be, because of the innate purity and dignity of her nature, but who was neither bold in bearing nor masculine in mind; a girl who, when she married, would be her husband's friend and companion, but never his rival; one who would consider their interests identical, and not hold him as just so much fair game for spoil; who would make his house his true home and place of rest, not a mere passage-place for vanity and ostentation to go through; a tender mother, an industrious housekeeper, a judicious mistress. We prided ourselves as a nation on our women. We thought we had the pick of creation in this fair young English girl of ours, and envied no other men their own. We admired the languid grace and subtle fire of the South; the docility and childlike affectionateness of the East seemed to us sweet and simple and restful; the vivacious sparkle of the trim and sprightly Parisienne was a pleasant little excitement when we met with it in its own domain; but our allegiance never wandered from our brown-haired girls at home, and our hearts were less vagrant than our fancies. This was in the old time, and when English girls were content to be what God and nature had made them. Of late years we have changed the pattern, and have given to the world a race of women as utterly unlike the old insular ideal as if we had created another nation altogether. The girl of the period, and the fair young English girl of the past, have nothing in common save ancestry and their mother-tongue; and even of this last the modern version makes almost a new language, through the copious additions it has received from the current slang of the day.

The girl of the period is a creature who dyes her hair and paints her face, as the first articles of her personal religion; whose sole idea of life is plenty of fun and luxury; and whose dress is the object of such thought and intellect as she possesses. Her main endeavour in this is to outvie her neighbours in the extravagance of fashion. No matter whether, as in the time of crinolines, she sacrificed decency, or, as now, in the time of trains, she sacrifices cleanliness; no matter either, whether she makes herself a nuisance and an inconvenience to every one she meets. The girl of the period has done away with such moral muffishness as consideration for others, or regard for counsel and rebuke. It was all very well in old-fashioned times, when fathers and mothers had some authority and were treated with respect, to be tutored and made to obey, but she is far too fast and flourishing to be stopped in mid-career by these slow old morals; and as she dresses to please herself, she does not care if she displeases every one else. Nothing is too extraordinary and nothing too exaggerated for her vitiated taste; and things which in themselves would be useful reforms if let alone become monstrosities worse than those which they have displaced so soon as she begins to manipulate and improve. If a sensible fashion lifts the gown out of the mud, she raises hers midway to her knee. If the absurd structure of wire and buckram, once called a bonnet, is modified to something that shall protect the wearer's face without putting out the eyes of her companion, she cuts hers down to four straws and a rosebud, or a tag of lace and a bunch of glass beads. If there is a reaction against an excess of Rowland's Macassar,[1] and hair shiny and sticky with grease is thought less nice than if left clean and healthily crisp, she dries and frizzes and sticks hers out on end like certain savages in Africa, or lets it wander down her back like Madge Wildfire's,[2] and thinks herself all the more beautiful the nearer she approaches in look to a maniac or a negress. With purity of taste she has lost also that far more precious purity and delicacy of perception which sometimes mean more than appears on the surface. What the *demi-monde* does in its frantic efforts to excite attention, she also does in imitation. If some fashionable *dévergondée en evidence*[3] is reported to have come out with her dress below her shoulder-blades, and a gold strap for all the sleeve thought necessary, the girl of the period follows suit next day; and then wonders that men sometimes mistake her for her prototype, or that mothers of girls not quite so far gone as herself refuse her as a companion for their daughters. She has blunted the fine edges of feeling so much that she cannot understand why she should be condemned for an imitation of form which does not include imitation of fact; she cannot be made to see that modesty of appearance and virtue ought to be insepa- rable, and that no good girl can afford to appear bad, under penalty of receiv- ing the contempt awarded to the bad.

This imitation of the *demi-monde* in dress leads to something in manner and feeling, not quite so pronounced perhaps, but far too like to be honourable to herself or satisfactory to her friends. It leads to slang, bold talk, and fastness; to the love of pleasure and indifference to duty; to the desire of money before either love or happiness; to uselessness at home, dissatisfaction with the monotony of ordinary life, and horror of all useful work; in a word, to the worst forms of luxury and selfishness, to the most fatal effects arising from want of high principle and absence of tender feel- ing. The girl of the period envies the queens of the *demi-monde* far more than she abhors them. She sees them gorgeously attired and sumptuously appointed, and she knows them to be flattered, fêted, and courted with a

---

[1]   An oily hair ointment.
[2]   A wildly dressed figure from Sir Walter Scott's novel *The Heart of Midlothian* (1818).
[3]   (French), shameless hussy.

certain disdainful admiration of which she catches only the admiration while she ignores the disdain. They have all for which her soul is hungering, and she never stops to reflect at what a price they have bought their gains, and what fearful moral penalties they pay for their sensuous pleasures. She sees only the coarse gilding on the base token, and shuts her eyes to the hideous figure in the midst, and the foul legend written round the edge. It is this envy of the pleasures, and indifference to the sins, of the *demimonde*, which is doing such infinite mischief to the modern girl. They brush too closely by each other, if not in actual deeds, yet in aims and feelings; for the luxury which is bought by vice with the one is the thing of all in life most passionately desired by the other, though she is not yet prepared to pay quite the same price. Unfortunately, she has already paid too much— all that once gave her distinctive national character. No one can say of the modern English girl that she is tender, loving, retiring, or domestic. The old fault so often found by keen-sighted Frenchwomen, that she was so fatally *romanesque*,[1] so prone to sacrifice appearances and social advantages for love, will never be set down to the girl of the period. Love indeed is the last thing she thinks of, and the least of the dangers besetting her. Love in a cottage, that seductive dream which used to vex the heart and disturb the calculations of prudent mothers, is now a myth of past ages. The legal barter of herself for so much money, representing so much dash, so much luxury and pleasure—that is her idea of marriage; the only idea worth entertaining. For all seriousness of thought respecting the duties or the consequences of marriage, she has not a trace. If children come, they find but a stepmother's cold welcome from her; and if her husband thinks that he has married anything that is to belong to him—a *tacens et placens uxor*[2] pledged to make him happy—the sooner he wakes from his hallucination and understands that he has simply married some one who will condescend to spend his money on herself, and who will shelter her indiscretions behind the shield of his name, the less severe will be his disappointment. She has married his house, his carriage, his balance at the banker's, his title; and he himself is just the inevitable condition clogging the wheel of her fortune; at best an adjunct, to be tolerated with more or less patience as may chance. For it is only the old-fashioned sort, not girls of the period *pur sang*,[3] that marry for love, or put the husband before the banker. But she does not marry easily. Men are afraid of her; and with reason. They may amuse themselves with her of an evening, but they do not take her readily for life.

---

[1] Romantic.
[2] (Latin), silent and pleasing wife.
[3] (French), pure-blooded.

Besides, after all her efforts, she is only a poor copy of the real thing; and the real thing is far more amusing than the copy, because it is real. Men can get that whenever they like; and when they go into their mothers' drawing-rooms, to see their sisters and their sisters' friends, they want something of quite different flavour. *Toujours perdrix*[1] is bad providing all the world over; but a continual weak imitation of *toujours perdrix* is worse. If we must have only one kind of thing, let us have it genuine; and the queens of St. John's Wood in their unblushing honesty, rather than their imitators and make-believes in Bayswater and Belgravia.[2] For, at whatever cost of shocked self-love or pained modesty it may be, it cannot be too plainly told to the modern English girl that the net result of her present manner of life is to assimilate her as nearly as possible to a class of women whom we must not call by their proper—or improper—name. And we are willing to believe that she has still some modesty of soul left hidden under all this effrontery of fashion, and that, if she could be made to see herself as she appears to the eyes of men, she would mend her ways before too late.

It is terribly significant of the present state of things when men are free to write as they do of the women of their own nation. Every word of censure flung against them is two-edged, and wounds those who condemn as much as those who are condemned; for surely it need hardly be said that men hold nothing so dear as the honour of their women, and that no one living would willingly lower the repute of his mother or his sisters. It is only when these have placed themselves beyond the pale of masculine respect that such things could be written as are written now; when they become again what they were once they will gather round them the love and homage and chivalrous devotion which were then an Englishwoman's natural inheritance. The marvel, in the present fashion of life among women, is how it holds its ground in spite of the disapprobation of men. It used to be an old-time notion that the sexes were made for each other, and that it was only natural for them to please each other, and to set themselves out for that end. But the girl of the period does not please men. She pleases them as little as she elevates them; and how little she does that, the class of women she has taken as her models of itself testifies. All men whose opinion is worth having prefer the simple and genuine girl of the past, with her tender little ways and pretty bashful modesties, to this loud and rampant modernization, with her false red hair and painted skin, talking slang as glibly as a man, and by preference leading the conversation to doubtful subjects. She thinks she is piquante and exciting when she thus makes

---

[1]   (French), forever fallen.
[2]   Fashionable London neighborhoods.

herself the bad copy of a worse original; and she will not see that though men laugh with her they do not respect her, though they flirt with her they do not marry her; she will not believe that she is not the kind of thing they want, and that she is acting against nature and her own interests when she disregards their advice and offends their taste. We do not see how she makes out her account, viewing her life from any side; but all we can do is to wait patiently until the national madness has passed, and our women have come back again to the old English ideal, once the most beautiful, the most modest, the most essentially womanly in the world.

4. "The Wild Women as Social Insurgents," *The Nineteenth Century* vol. XXX no. 176, October 1891, pp. 596–605.

We must change our ideals. The Desdemonas and Dorotheas, the Enids and Imogens, are all wrong. Milton's Eve is an anachronism; so is the Lady; so is Una; so are Christabel and Genevieve. Such women as Panthea and Alcestis, Cornelia and Lucretia, are as much out of date as the chiton and the peplum, [1] the bride's hair parted with a spear, or the worth of a woman reckoned by the flax she spun and the thread she wove, by the number of citizens she gave to the State, and the honour that reflected on her through the heroism of her sons. All this is past and done with—effete, rococo, dead. For the "*tacens et placens uxor*"[2] of old-time dreams we must acknowledge now as our Lady of Desire the masterful *domina* of real life—that loud and dictatorial person, insurgent and something more, who suffers no one's

---

[1] Desdemona is the innocent wronged wife of Othello in Shakespeare's *Othello* (1604–05). Dorothea is the heroine of the 1798 poem "Hermann and Dorothea" by Johann Wolfgang von Goethe (1749–1832). Enid is the loyal wife of Geraint in *The Idylls of the King* (1859) by Alfred, Lord Tennyson (1809–92). Imogen is the wife of Posthumus Leonatus in Shakespeare's *Cymbeline* (1609–10). John Milton's (1608–74) Eve, in Book VIII of his epic poem *Paradise Lost* (1667) tempts Adam to eat the forbidden fruit because "So dear I love him, that...without him live no life." The Lady dies for love of Sir Launcelot. Una is one of the major protagonists in *The Faerie Queene* (1596) by Edmund Spenser (1552–99); she represents Truth, which the Redcrosse Knight must find in order to be a true Christian. Christabel is the "gentle maid" victimized by Geraldine in the 1816 poem "Christabel" by Samuel Taylor Coleridge (1772–1834). Genevieve is the heroine of Coleridge's poem "Love" (1799). Panthea, as described by Xenophon (c. 444 BC–c. 357 BC), exemplified a noble woman's heroism and love for her husband. In Greek myth, Alcestis gave her life for her husband Admetus. Cornelia (fl. second century BC) was the higly cultured mother of Roman reformers Tiberius and Gaius Gracchus. Lucretia, as described by Titus Livy (59 BC–17 AD) killed herself after being raped in order to set an example for Rome and to eliminate (even unintentional) unchastity from her husband's home. The chiton and the peplum were garments worn by Ancient Greek women.

[2] (Latin), silent and pleasing wife.

opinion to influence her mind, no venerable law hallowed by time, nor custom consecrated by experience, to control her actions. Mistress of herself, the Wild Woman as a social insurgent preaches the "lesson of liberty" broadened into lawlessness and license. Unconsciously she exemplifies how beauty can degenerate into ugliness, and shows how the once fragrant flower, run to seed, is good for neither food nor ornament.

Her ideal of life for herself is absolute personal independence coupled with supreme power over men. She repudiates the doctrine of individual conformity for the sake of the general good; holding the self-restraint involved as an act of slavishness of which no woman worth her salt would be guilty. She makes between the sexes no distinctions, moral or aesthetic, nor even personal; but holds that what is lawful to the one is permissible to the other. Why should the world have parcelled out qualities or habits into two different sections, leaving only a few common to both alike? Why, for instance, should men have the fee-simple of courage, and women that of modesty? to men be given the right of the initiative—to women only that of selection? to men the freer indulgence of the senses—to women the chaster discipline of self-denial? The Wild Woman of modern life asks why; and she answers the question in her own way.

"*Rien n'est sacré pour un sapeur.*"[1] Nothing is forbidden to the Wild Woman as a social insurgent; for the one word that she cannot spell is, Fitness. Devoid of this sense of fitness, she does all manner of things which she thinks bestow on her the power, together with the privileges, of a man; not thinking that in obliterating the finer distinctions of sex she is obliterating the finer traits of civilization, and that every step made towards identity of habits is a step downwards in refinement and delicacy—wherein lies the essential core of civilization. She smokes after dinner with the men; in railway carriages; in public rooms—when she is allowed. She thinks she is thereby vindicating her independence and honouring her emancipated womanhood. Heaven bless her! Down in the North-country villages, and elsewhere, she will find her prototypes calmly smoking their black cutty-pipes, with no sense of shame about them. Why should they not? These ancient dames with "whiskin' beards about their mou's," withered and unsightly, worn out, and no longer women in desirableness or beauty—why should they not take to the habits of men? They do not disgust, because they no longer charm; but even in these places you do not find the younger women with cutty-pipes between their lips. Perhaps in the coal districts, where women work like men and with men, and are dressed as men, you will see pipes as well as hear blasphemies; but that is surely not an admirable

---

[1] (French), nothing is sacred to a drunkard.

state of things, and one can hardly say that the pit-brow women, excellent persons and good workers as they are in their own way, are exactly the glasses in which our fine ladies find their loveliest fashions—the moulds wherein they would do well to run their own forms. And when, after dinner, our young married women and husbandless girls, despising the old distinctions and trampling under foot the time-honoured conventions of former generations, "light up" with the men, they are simply assimilating themselves to this old Sally and that ancient Betty down in the dales and mountain hamlets; or to the stalwart cohort of pit-brow women for whom sex has no aesthetic distinctions. We grant the difference of method. A superbly dressed young woman, bust, arms, and shoulders bare, and gleaming white and warm beneath the subdued light of a luxurious dinner-table—a beautiful young creature, painted, dyed, and powdered according to the mode—her lips red with wine and moist with liqueur—she is really different from mumping old Betty in unwomanly rags smoking at her black cutty-pipe by the cottage door on the bleak fell-side. In the one lies an appeal to the passions of men; in the other is the death of all emotion. Nevertheless, the acts are the same, the circumstances which accompany them alone being different.

Free-traders in all that relates to sex, the Wild Women allow men no monopoly in sports, in games, in responsibilities. Beginning by "walking with the guns," they end by shooting with them; and some have made the moor a good training-ground for the jungle. As life is constituted, it is necessary to have butchers and sportsmen. The hunter's instinct keeps down the wild beasts, and those who go after big game do as much good to the world as those who slaughter home-bred beasts for the market. But in neither instance do we care to see a woman's hand. It may be merely a sentiment, and ridiculous at that; still, sentiment has its influence, legitimate enough when not too widely extended; and we confess that the image of a "butching" woman, nursing her infant child with hands red with the blood of an ox she has just poleaxed or of a lamb whose throat she has this instant cut, is one of unmitigated horror and moral incongruity. Precisely as horrible, as incongruous, is the image of a well-bred sportswoman whose bullet has crashed along the spine of a leopardess, who has knocked over a rabbit or brought down a partridge. The one may be a hard-fisted woman of the people, who had no inherent sensitiveness to overcome—a woman born and bred among the shambles and accustomed to the whole thing from childhood. The other may be a dainty-featured aristocrat, whose later development belies her early training; but the result is the same in both cases—the possession of an absolutely unwomanly instinct, an absolutely unwomanly indifference to death and suffering; which certain of the Wild Women of the present day cultivate as one of their protests against the limitations of sex. The viragoes[1] of all times have always had this same instinct, this same indifference. For nothing of all this is new in substance. What is new is the translation into the cultured classes of certain qualities and practices hitherto confined to the uncultured and—savages.

This desire to assimilate their lives to those of men runs through the whole day's work of the Wild Women. Not content with croquet and lawn tennis, the one of which affords ample opportunities for flirting—for the Wild Women are not always above that little pastime—and the other for exercise even more violent than is good for the average woman, they have taken to golf and cricket, where they are hindrances for the one part, and make themselves "sights" for the other. Men are not graceful when jumping, running, stooping, swinging their arms, and all the rest of it. They are fine, and give a sense of power that is perhaps more attractive than mere beauty; but, as schoolboys are not taught gymnastics after the manner of the young Greeks, to the rhythmic cadence of music, so that every movement may be rendered automatically graceful, they are often awkward enough when at play; and the harder the work the less there is of artistic beauty in the manner of it. But if men, with their narrower hips and broader shoulders, are less than classically lovely when they are putting out their physical powers, what are the women, whose broad hips give a wider step and less steady carriage in running, and whose arms, because of their narrower shoulders, do not lend themselves to beautiful curves when they are making a swinging stroke at golf or batting and bowling at cricket? The prettiest woman in the world loses her beauty when at these violent exercises. Hot and damp, mopping her flushed and streaming face with her handkerchief, she has lost that sense of repose, that delicate self-restraint, which belongs to the ideal woman. She is no longer dainty. She has thrown off her grace and abandoned all that makes her lovely for the uncomely roughness of pastimes wherein she cannot excel, and of which it was never intended she should be a partaker.

We have not yet heard of women polo-players; but that will come. In the absurd endeavour to be like men, these modern *homasses*[2] will leave nothing untried; and polo-playing, tent-pegging, and tilting at the quintain[3] are all sure to come in time. When weeds once begin to grow, no limits can be put to their extent unless they are stubbed up betimes.

---

[1] Women regarded as noisy, scolding, or domineering.

[2] This term originated in French 18th century writing about sexual transgression. Linton uses it here to refer to man-women or female men.

[3] A post or an object mounted on a post, used as a target in jousting exercises.

The Wild Women, in their character of social insurgents, are bound by none of the conventions which once regulated society. In them we see the odd social phenomenon of the voluntary descent of the higher to the lower forms of ways and works. "Unladylike" is a term that has ceased to be significant. Where "unwomanly" has died out we could scarcely expect this other to survive. The special must needs go with the generic; and we find it so with a vengeance! With other queer inversions the frantic desire of making money has invaded the whole class of Wild Women; and it does not mitigate their desire that, as things are, they have enough for all reasonable wants. Women who, a few years ago, would not have shaken hands with a dressmaker, still less have sat down to table with her, now open shops and set up in business on their own account—not because they are poor, which would be an honourable and sufficing reason enough, but because they are restless, dissatisfied, insurgent, and like nothing so much as to shock established prejudices and make the folk stare. It is such a satire on their inheritance of class distinction, on their superior education—perhaps very superior, stretching out to academical proportions! It is just the kind of topsy-turvydom that pleases them. They, with their long descent, grand name, and right to a coat-of-arms which represents past ages of renown,— they to come down into the market-place, shouldering out the meaner fry, who must work to live—taking from the legitimate traders the pick of their custom, and making their way by dint of social standing and personal influence—they to sell bonnets in place of buying them—to make money instead of spending it—what fun! What a grand idea it was to conceive, and grander still to execute! In this insurgent playing at shopkeeping by those who do not need to do so we see nothing grand nor beautiful, but much that is thoughtless and mean. Born of restlessness and idleness, these spasmodic make-believes after serious work are simply pastimes to the Wild Women who undertake them. There is nothing really solid in them, no more than there was of philanthropy in the fashionable craze for slumming which broke out like a fever a winter or two ago. Shopkeeping and slumming, and some other things too, are just the expression of that restlessness which makes of the modern Wild Woman a second Io,[1] driving her afield in search of strange pleasures and novel occupations, and leading her to drink of the muddiest waters so long as they are in new channels cut off from the old fountains. Nothing daunts this modern Io. No barriers restrain, no obstacles prevent. She appears on the public stage and executes dances which one would not like one's daughter to see, still less perform.

---

[1] After having been turned into a calf by Jupiter to escape Juno's wrath, Io is stung by a gadfly and flees wildly, ending up a queen in Africa.

She herself knows no shame in showing her skill—and her legs. Why should she? What free and independent spirit, in these later days, is willing to be bound by those musty principles of modesty which did well enough for our stupid old great-grandmothers—but for us? Other times, other manners; and womanly reticence is not of these last!

There is no reason why perfectly good and modest women should not be actresses. Rightly taken, acting is an art as noble as any other. But here, as elsewhere, are gradations and sections; and just as a wide line is drawn between the cancan and the minuet, so is there between the things which a modest woman may do on the stage and those which she may not. Not long ago that line was notoriously overstepped, and certain of our Wild Women pranced gaily from the safe precincts of the permissible into those wider regions of the more than doubtful, where, it is to be supposed, they enjoyed their questionable triumph—at least for the hour.

The spirit of the day is both vagrant and self-advertising, both bold and restless, contemptuous of law and disregarding restraint. We do not suppose that women are intrinsically less virtuous than they were at the time of Hogarth's "Last Stake;"[1] but they are more dissatisfied, less occupied, and infinitely less modest. All those old similes about modest violets and chaste lilies, flowers blooming unseen, and roses that "open their glowing bosoms" but to one love only—all these are as rococo as the Elizabethan ruff or Queen Anne's "laced head." Everyone who has a "gift" must make that gift public; and, so far from wrapping up talents in a napkin, pence are put out to interest, and the world is called on to admire the milling. The enormous amount of inferior work which is thrown on the market in all directions is one of the marvels of the time. Everything is exhibited. If a young lady can draw so far correctly as to give her cow four legs and not five, she sends her sketches to some newspaper, or more boldly transfers them on to a plate or pot, and exhibits them at some art refuge for the stage below mediocrity. It is heartbreaking when these inanities are sent by these poor young creatures who need the fortune they think they have in their "gift." It is contemptible when they are sent by the rich, distracted by vanity and idleness together. The love of art for its own sake, of intellectual work for the intellectual pleasure it brings, knows nothing of this insatiate vanity, this restless ambition to be classed among those who give to their work days where these others give hours. It is only the Wild Women who take these headers into artistic depths, where they flounder pitiably, neither dredging up unknown treasures, nor floating gaily in the sun on the

---

[1] "The Lady's Last Stake" was a satirical engraving by English artist William Hogarth (1697–1764), supposed to have influenced the pre-Raphaelite painter William Holman Hunt's series "The Awakening Conscience" (1854).

crest of the wave. When we think of the length of time it has taken to create all masterpieces—and, indeed, all good work of any kind, not necessarily masterpieces—it is food for wonder to see the jaunty ease with which the scarce-educated in an art throw off their productions, which then they fling out to the public as one tosses crumbs to the sparrows. But the Wild Women are never thorough. As artists, as literati, as tradeswomen, as philanthropists, it is all a mere touch-and-go kind of thing with them. The roots, which are first in importance in all growths, no matter what, are the last things they care to master. They would not be wild if they did.

About these Wild Women is always an unpleasant suggestion of the adventuress. Whatever their natural place and lineage, they are of the same family as those hotel heroines who forget to lock the chamber door—those confiding innocents of ripe years, who contract imperfect marriages—those pretty country blossoms who begin life modestly and creditably, and go on to flaunting notoriety and disgrace. One feels that it is only the accident of birth which differences these from those, and determines a certain stability of class. It is John Bradshaw[1] over again; but the "grace" is queerly bestowed. As a rule, these women have no scruples about money. They are notorious for never having small change; they get into debt with a facility as amazing in its want of conscience as its want of foresight; and then they take to strange ways for redeeming their credit and saving themselves from public exposure. If the secret history of some account-books could be written startling revelations would be made. Every now and then, indeed, things come to light which it would have been better to keep hidden; for close association with shady "promoters" and confessed blacklegs is not conducive to the honour of womanhood—at least as this honour was. Under the new *régime* blots do not count for so much. Every now and then, one, a trifle more shameless than her sisters, flourishes out openly before the world as an adept in a doubtful business—say, in the art of laying odds judiciously and hedging wisely. She is to be seen standing on her tub shouting with the best; and as little abashed by the unwomanliness of her "environment" as are her more mischievous compeers on the political stump. She knows that money is to be made as well as lost in the ring, and she does not see why, because she is a woman, she may not pick out plums with the rest.

If she has money enough—she is sure to call it "oof," so as to be in line with the verbal as well as the practical blackguardism of the day—she has

---

[1] John Bradshaw (1602–59) was elected president of the court for the trial of Charles I, in which Charles was sentenced to death. Although the judge should be neutral, there is little doubt that he was told what to do and say by the leading figures of the army, Oliver Cromwell and Henry Ireton. Thus, to use Linton's words, his "grace was queerly bestowed."

a stud of her own, and enters into all the details connected therewith with as much gusto as a village beldame enters into the life-events of her homely world. But while a foal is one of the most interesting things in life to one of these horsy Wild Women, a child is one of the least; and what young mother, with all the hopes and fears, the fervent love, the brilliant dreams, which lie about the cradle of her first-born, comes near in importance to that brood mare of racing renown, with her long-legged foal trotting by her side? The Wild Woman is never a delightful creature, take her how one will; but the horsy Wild Woman, full of stable slang and inverted instincts, can give points to the rest of her clan, and still be ahead of them all.

Sometimes our Wild Women break out as adventurous travelers; when they come home to write on what they have seen and done, books which have to be taken with salt by the spoonful, not only by the grain. Their bows are very large, and the string they draw preternaturally long. Experts contradict them, and the more experienced smile and shake their heads. But their own partisans uphold them; and that portion of the press where reason and manliness are suffocated by the sense of sex takes them as if they were so many problems of Euclid with Q.E.D. after "the end." How different these pseudo-heroines are from the quiet realities, such as Marianne North,[1] to name no other, who did marvels of which they never boasted, contented with showing the unanswerable results! They "covered down," they did not paint in high lights and exaggerated colours the various perils through which they had passed. The Wild Woman of the immediate day reverses the system. Under her manipulation a steep ascent is a sheer precipice, a crack in the road is a crevasse, a practicable bit of crag-climbing is a service of peril where each step is planted in the shadow of death; and hardships are encountered which exist only on paper and in the fertile imagination of the fair tourist. If, however, these hardships are real and not imaginary, the poor, wild vagrant returns broken and overstrained, and finds, when perhaps too late, that lovely woman may stoop to other folly besides that of listening to a dear loo'ed lad; and that, in her attempt to imitate, to rival, perhaps to surpass, man on his rightful ground she is not only destroying her distinctive charm of womanhood, but is perhaps digging her own grave, to be filled too surely as well as prematurely.

We are becoming a little surfeited with these Wild Women as globe-trotters and travelers. Their adventures, which for the most part are fictions based on a very small substratum of fact, have ceased to impress, partly because we have ceased to believe, and certainly ceased to respect. *Que diable allait-il faire dans cette galère?*[2] Who wanted them to run all these risks, supposing them to

---

[1] Marianne North (1830–90), English botanical painter.
[2] (French), what the devil are they doing out there?

be true? What good have they done by their days of starvation and nights of sleeplessness? their perils by land and sea? their chances of being devoured by wild beasts or stuck up by bushrangers? taken by brigands or insulted by rowdies of all nations? They have contributed nothing to our stock of knowledge, as Marianne North has done. They have solved no ethnological problem; brought to light no new treasures of nature; discovered no new field for British spades to till, no new markets for British manufactures to supply. They have done nothing but lose their beauty, if they had any; for what went out fresh and comely comes back haggard and weatherbeaten. It was quite unnecessary. They have lost, but the world has not gained; and that doctor's bill will make a hole in the publisher's cheque.

Ranged side by side with these vagrant Wild Women, globetrotting for the sake of a subsequent book of travels, and the *kudos* with the pence accruing, are those who spread themselves abroad as missionaries, and those—a small minority, certainly—who do not see why the army and the navy should be sealed against the sex. Among these female missionaries are some who are good, devoted, pure-hearted, self-sacrificing—all that women should be, all that the best women are, and ever have been, and ever will be. But also among them are the Wild Women—creatures impatient of restraint, bound by no law, insurgent to their finger-tips, and desirous of making all other women as restless and disoriented as themselves. Ignorant and unreasonable, they would carry into the sun-laden East the social conditions born of the icy winds of the North. They would introduce into the zenana[1] the circumstances of a Yorkshire home. In a country where jealousy is as strong as death, and stronger than love, they would incite the women to revolt against the rule of seclusion, which has been the law of the land for centuries before we were a nation at all. That rule has worked well for the country, inasmuch as the chastity of Hindu women and the purity of family life are notoriously intact. But our Wild Women swarm over into India as zenana missionaries, trying to make the Hindus as discontented, as restless, as unruly as themselves. The zenana would not suit us. The meekest little mouse among us would revolt at a state of things which does not press too heavily on those who have known nothing else and inherited no other traditions. But it does suit the people who have framed and who live under these laws; and we hold it to be an ethnological blunder, as well as a political misdemeanour, to send out these surging apostles of disobedience and discontent to carry revolt and confusion among our Indian fellow-subjects. It is part of the terrible restlessness with which this age is afflicted, part of the contempt for law in all its forms which certain women have adopted from certain men, themselves too

---

[1] Secluded women's quarters; harem.

effeminate, too little manly to be able to submit to discipline. These are the men who hound on the Wild Women to ever fresh extravagances. Those pestilent papers which are conducted by these rebels against law and order are responsible for a large amount of the folly which all true lovers of womanly beauty and virtue deplore and fight against. It is they who hold up to public admiration acts and sentiments which ought to be either sternly repressed as public faults or laughed down as absurdities.

Unlike the female doctors, who, we believe, undertake no proselytizing, and are content to merely heal the bodies while leaving alone the souls and lives of the "purdah-women,"[1] the zenana missionaries go out with the express purpose of teaching Christian theology and personal independence. We hold each to be an impertinence. Like the Jews, the Hindu men have ample means of judging of our Christianity, and what it has done for the world which professes it. They also have ample means of judging of the effects of our womanly independence, and what class of persons we turn out to roam about the world alone. If they prefer this to that, they have only to say so, and the reform will come from within, as it ought—as all reforms must, to be of value. If they do not, it is not for our Wild Women to carry the burden of their unrest into the quiet homes of the East; which homes, too, are further protected by the oath taken by the sovereign to respect the religion of these Eastern subjects. When we have taught the Hindu women to hunt and drive, play golf and cricket, dance the cancan on a public stage, make speeches in Parliament, cherish "dear boys" at five-o'clock tea, and do all that our Wild Women do, shall we have advanced matters very far? Shall we have made the home happier, the family purer, the women themselves more modest, more chaste? Had we not better cease to pull at ropes which move machinery of which we know neither the force nor the possible action? Why all this interference with others? Why not let the various peoples of the earth manage their domestic matters as they think fit? Are our Wild Women the ideal of female perfection? Heaven forbid! But to this distorted likeness they and their backers are doing their best to reduce all others.

Aggressive, disturbing, officious, unquiet, rebellious to authority and tyrannous to those whom they can subdue, we say emphatically that they are about the most unlovely specimens the sex has yet produced, and between the "purdah-woman" and the modern *homasses* we, for our own parts, prefer the former. At least the purdah-woman knows how to love. At least she has not forgotten the traditions of modesty as she has been taught them. But what about our half-naked girls and young wives, smoking and

---

1   Seclusion of women from public observation among Muslims and some Hindus, especially in India.

drinking with the men? our ramping platform orators? our unabashed self-advertisers? our betting women? our horse-breeders? our advocates of free love, and our contemners of maternal life and domestic duties?

The mind goes back over certain passages in history, and the imagination fastens on certain names which stand as types of womanly loveliness and love-worthiness. Side by side with them were the *homasses* of their day. Where there was a Countess of Salisbury, for whom not a man in the castle but would have died, cheerfully, gladly, rejoiced to carry his death as his tribute to her surpassing charm, there was also a Black Agnes, who did not disdain to insult her baffled foe, and who had none of the delightfulness which made the Countess of Salisbury so beloved—which made the even yet more distinctly heroic Jane de Montfort so prepotent over her followers.[1] Here stands Lady Rachel Russell; there the arch-virago old Bess of Hardwicke.[2] The one is our English version of Panthea, of Arria; the other is Xantippe in a coif and peaked stomacher.[3] On one canvas we have Lady Fanshawe; on the other, Lady Eldon[4]—all the same as now we have certain sweet and lovely women who honour their womanhood and fulfil its noblest ideals, and these Wild Women of blare and bluster, who are neither man nor woman—wanting in the well-knit power of the first and in the fragrant sweetness of the last.

Excrescences of the times, products of peace and idleness, of prosperity and over-population—would things be better if a great national disaster pruned our superfluities and left us nearer to the essential core of facts? Who knows! Storms shake off the nobler fruit but do not always beat down the ramping weeds. Still, human nature has the trick of pulling itself right in times of stress and strain. Perhaps, if called upon, even our Wild Women would cast off their ugly travesty and become what modesty and virtue designed them to be; and perhaps their male adorers would go back to the ranks of masculine self-respect, and leave off this base subservience to folly which now disfigures and unmans them. *Chi lo sa?*[5] It does no one harm to hope. This hope, then, let us cherish while we can and may.

---

[1] The Countess of Salisbury gets her noble reputation from the play (possibly by Shakespeare) *The Reign of King Edward the Third*. Black Agnes, wife of the Earl of March, is known by Scots as "Saviour of Dunbar Castle" for her role in foiling a siege attempt by the forces of the Earl of Salisbury in the 14th century.

[2] Lady Rachel Russell's second husband Lord William Russell was executed for high treason in 1683. "Old Bess of Hardwicke" was Elizabeth, Countess of Shrewsbury, to whose charge, in 1572, Mary Queen of Scots was committed. The countess treated the captive queen with great harshness.

[3] Xantippe, wife of the philosopher Socrates, was generally considered to be a shrew.

[4] Lady Fanshawe, wife of poet Sir Richard Fanshawe, and author of sentimental "Memoirs." Lady Eldon was known for attempting to smuggle French lace into England without paying the duty.

[5] (Italian), who knows?

Appendix C: The Rebel of the Family: The Life of Eliza Lynn Linton

Nancy Fix Anderson
Loyola University-New Orleans

When the venerable Victorian novelist Eliza Lynn Linton died in 1898, she was eulogized by her colleagues for her lifelong contribution to Victorian letters, praised as one who "lived the literary life through half a century, strenuously, industriously, and with unflinching honesty" (Low 107–08), a woman whose writings won the acclaim of "a bead-roll of illustrious men and women" (*Academy* 440). It was not her literary merit, however, that contemporaries most commented on—as she herself ruefully recognized, she was no George Eliot, but was rather a reliable productive writer whose novels achieved popularity but not great critical praise. What was most notable about Eliza Lynn Linton was the strong political and social fervor in her writings, which she used as a vehicle for what became her greatest passion—her opposition to greater freedom and rights for women. Insisting with increasing intensity in both her fiction and her periodical articles that women's place was in the home, subservient to superior male authority, she earned the reputation as the leading critic of the "modern woman" in late-Victorian England. As the sympathetic Walter Besant said in poetic tribute to her after her death, "She fought for Women; yet with women fought / The sexless tribe, the shrieking sisterhood ... / All womanly—brave woman!—was thy task / Thy life-long battle waged the life-long day!" (Besant 135).

What intrigued and puzzled many of Linton's contemporaries about her anti-feminism was that it contrasted so sharply with her own emancipated life style. An independent self-supporting woman of strong views who separated from her husband after a brief disastrous marriage in order to pursue her own career, Linton lived in such a way as to deny the very principles she so ardently espoused. An agnostic who argued that religious skepticism was a manly creed whereas the weaker female sex needed the support of religion, a moralist who warned against lesbianism in the women's movement but whose closest emotional relationships were with women, Linton was indeed, as one women's rights sympathizer said with frustration, leading "a vigorous campaign against such of her sisters as were following the example of industry and independence that she herself had set them" (Paston 505). It is this contradiction that makes Eliza Lynn Linton such an intriguing and important figure to scholars. An understanding of her life and writings challenges us to think beyond static ideological categories, and helps us better to appreciate the complex dynamics of Victorian women's history.

Eliza Lynn [later Linton] was born on 22 February 1822, into a conservative Anglican clerical family living in the Lake District.[1] The youngest of twelve children whose exhausted mother died shortly after Eliza's birth, she grew up feeling out of sorts with her family, and especially with her stern and emotionally remote father. It is always dangerous to take too literally a person's later autobiographical reconstruction of her childhood, but not only Linton's later reflections but also her writings in her youth clearly show her sense of alienation from her family. As she poignantly wrote in her autobiography, she felt "so isolated in the family, so out of harmony with them all, and by my own faults of temperament such a little Ishmaelite and outcast, that as much despair as can exist with childhood overwhelmed and possessed me" (*Christopher Kirkland* 1:60). Feeling keenly the lack of maternal love, the young Eliza Lynn expressed her anger at her unloving father by rebelling against all he stood for. She challenged Vicar Lynn's religious beliefs as well as his vocation by rejecting Christianity, and she defied his Toryism by espousing Whig and later radical and even what she labeled as communist views.

As a means of escape from her unhappy family situation as well as a way of gaining the attention and love she so craved, this self-styled "rebel of the family" determined that she would become a famous author. At age fifteen she boldly wrote to the publisher Richard Bentley, to ask if she could become a contributor to the *Bentley's Miscellany*. Voicing concern as to whether he "will think my *sex* a disadvantage or not," she told him frankly that she thought it was (21 Dec 1837 Bentley Collection). She asked him to respond anonymously, so that her family would not know what she was doing. If his response was positive, he should send to her house a Whig newspaper, and a Tory newspaper if he rejected the idea. Although that youthful venture did not end in success, she later succeeded in getting some poems published in the popular family magazine *Ainsworth's Magazine* in 1844. With her ambition fueled, at age twenty-two, an age when most young Victorian ladies sought to transfer from the shelter and protection of their father to that of a husband, Eliza Lynn made the gritty decision to leave the paternal home to make her way on her own as a writer in London.

The fact that Vicar Lynn agreed to this most unconventional action suggests that he was more understanding of his daughter's needs than she later remembered, or perhaps that he was merely relieved to have the probably annoying rebellious daughter out of the vicarage. He did provide her with a small allowance, and he arranged for his London lawyer to keep an

---

[1]   For biographies of Linton, see Anderson and Layard.

eye on her. Finding lodging in a boarding house, the aspiring young author plunged into deep research for an historical novel, a genre popular in the 1840s. Her determination and hard work led to fruition, for in 1847 she published *Azeth, the Egyptian*, a ponderous novel which nevertheless received generally positive reviews. This early success confirmed her ambition to become a professional writer.

Defying the conventions of respectable Victorian society by moving to London to live on her own and to forge a career, Eliza Lynn was, as she later described a fictional character clearly modeled on herself, "one of the vanguard of the independent women" (*Christopher Kirkland* 1:253). She mixed with the avant-garde literary society of mid-Victorian London, and formed a close friendship with the aging poet and Greek scholar Walter Savage Landor, to whom she looked as to a father—a father quite different from the emotionally cold, disapproving Vicar Lynn. Priding herself on being the renowned writer's "dear daughter," she was inspired to use classical Greece as the setting for her next historical novel, *Amymone*, which she published in 1848. The iconoclastic young author used this novel as a platform to challenge Victorian patriarchy, creating the eponymous character as a fierce defender of respectability and as a vicious critic of women's freedom. As Eliza Lynn editorialized, "Oh, what foe so bitter to her own sex as woman? So pitiless as she, so hard and stern?" (2:98–99). The hero of the novel is Aspasia, the freedom-loving consort of Pericles, a loving womanly woman who nevertheless "would have a more free and a more equal standing-place for women, and no longer see them the mere puppets which they now are, mindless and without will, living a formal life devoid of any higher intention than to give yet another slave to their husbands" (2:103). Despite its polemics, Landor's patronage helped create a favorable reception for *Amymone*.

Needing more income than the modest earnings from her novels provided, even supplemented as they were by the small allowance from her father, in 1848 Eliza Lynn secured a position as a staff member of the newspaper *Morning Chronicle*, becoming the first woman journalist to draw a fixed salary in England (Layard 59). During this time she became romantically involved with a man, an Irish Catholic doctor, Edward McDermot. In her private unpublished notebooks written in 1848 and 1849 are passionate poems to "E.D." In one of these she urges him to "come, buy my fresh strawberries, buy them my love! / And gather them quicker and quicker! / ... Thou shalt come to my side when the moon's in the sky / And I'll feed thee throughout the long night." And in another: "Kiss me when I'm sleeping, love, and kiss me when I'm waking / 'Tis the only fountain where my thirst of love is slaking ..." (Linton MSS). In her autobiography, she said they did not marry because he was a Catholic, and as a freethinker she could not accept his religion

(*Christopher Kirkland* 2:223). She must have nurtured the memory of this love, however, for in her will, written in old age, she bequeathed to McDermot several sentimental items including a gold pencil case with "amour" on the seal (Somerset House). He was apparently her only male love attachment; all her other deep emotional relationships would be with women.

Her despair over the failed relationship with McDermot was augmented by professional failure. Eliza Lynn's third novel, *Realities*, published in 1851, was so controversial that it brought down on her a firestorm of condemnation. This novel, set in contemporary England, had the inflammatory message of proclaiming not just women's political and social, but also sexual freedom. John Chapman, the prospective publisher, shocked by this manifesto of free love, demanded that Linton bowdlerize the manuscript by cutting certain objectionable passages, which he said were "addressed [to] and excited the sensual nature and were therefore injurious." He argued that as a publisher of books of free thought, he had to be very careful of moral issues (Haight 130–31). Eliza Lynn refused, and eventually got the book published elsewhere, but in expurgated form and at her own expense.

Bold in writing the book, Linton was nevertheless not prepared for the intense criticism she then received. It seemed to crush her spirit, and certainly sent her into a deep depression. She did not publish another novel for fourteen years. She was also dismissed from the *Morning Chronicle*, and had trouble finding other literary work. Linton eventually succeeded in getting a job in Paris as a correspondent to an English newspaper, and there found her life slowly reenergized. The major professional breakthrough came in 1853 when Charles Dickens engaged her to write for his journal *Household Words*. Linton became a regular contributor, writing in the 1850s and 1860s many pieces on topics such as divorce reform (a radical topic which the conservative but unhappily married Dickens could support), and diverse innocuous short stories. Dickens did warn his sub-editor W.H. Wills to screen carefully her contributions: "I don't know how it is that she gets so near the sexual side of things as to be a little dangerous to us at times." One of her stories in particular he urged Wills to examine "to see that there is no court bawdy in it" (14 October 1854 Henry Huntington MSS). Nevertheless, Dickens valued Eliza Lynn's talent and discipline, for, as she later proudly reported, he wrote next to her name in his list of contributors, "good for anything, and thoroughly reliable" (Autobiographical Essay).

Returning from Paris to England in 1854 to go to the Lake District to care for her dying father, Eliza Lynn developed a friendship with a fellow radical living nearby, the artisan engraver and publisher, William James Linton. She wrote several pieces for his revolutionary journal *The English Republic*, including a panegyric to Mary Wollstonecraft, praising the *Vindication of the*

Rights of Woman as "one of the boldest and bravest things ever published" (this volume, Appendix B, p. 406), even though at the same time she published an article in *Household Words* on "The Rights and Wrongs of Women," in which she argued in what would later become her hallmark tone that women's place was in the home. A woman, she argued, who is "too gifted, too intelligent, to find scope for her mind and heart" in domestic duties "is simply not a woman. She is a natural blunder, a mere unfinished sketch" (160).

The conflicting messages about women's role in society in part reflect Eliza Lynn's developing ability to adapt the tone of her articles to the journal for which she was writing. They probably also reflect her own conflicted feelings about women's role, as she, now in her early thirties, faced the loneliness that was part of her independent lifestyle. She was even then envisioning taking on a domestic life of her own. William James Linton's wife Emily,[1] the mother of a large young family, was fatally ill, and Eliza Lynn, herself a motherless child, made the decision that she would take the mother's place when Emily Linton died, a decision she says was made at the mother's request.

That this decision was ill-founded became apparent even before Emily Linton's death, as evidenced in painfully autobiographical stories Eliza Lynn published during this time in *Household Words*, where she describes self-sacrificing young women marrying widowers with small children; these stories show how much she was already regretting the decision. In one story, written in 1855, the year before Emily Linton died, the young woman is repelled by her future husband's touch: "Those restless burning fingers passing perpetually over her hand, irritated her beyond her self-command … When he held her, her teeth set hard and her nerves strung like cords. She felt sometimes as if she could have killed him when he touched her" ("Sentiment and Action" 343). In this story, the woman on her wedding day refuses to marry. Eliza Lynn did not make a similar choice. In 1858, the year after Emily Linton's death, Eliza Lynn and William James Linton married, not for better but for worse.

That the marriage was a disaster from the first was clearly revealed in a story Eliza Lynn (now Linton) published in the *National Magazine* the month after their wedding, in which she describes a young maid who goes through the woods looking for a stick, rejects all she sees, and finally as she is leaving the woods, picks up a crooked stick. Linton compares the maid to a young woman who rejects suitors until she finally ends up with a "crooked stick"

---

1 Emily Linton was the sister of William James Linton's deceased first wife, and therefore they could not have married legally in England. Either they went abroad to marry, or, as William James Linton's biographer F.B. Smith suggests, they never legally married (43).

(98–100). Their marriage was a union of complete opposites: Eliza was orderly, ambitious, practical, and William disorderly, careless, idealistic. Eliza was clearly the dominant personality, and, scorning her husband as weak, in her fictional autobiography, in which she reverses her own sex and that of others, she comfortably writes of her husband as a woman.

When they were first married, they lived in London in fashionable Bayswater, where the new Mrs. Linton tried to establish their home as a literary center. Frustrated by her husband's slovenly ways, his refusal to pursue his artistic career seriously, and his preoccupation with revolutionary activity, the increasingly conservative Eliza had the burden of supporting the family with her writing. She now used as her professional name "Mrs. Lynn Linton"—or "E. Lynn Linton," keeping her birth name in equal prominence with her married name as a means, as she said of one of her fictional autobiographical characters, of maintaining "cherished individualism" (*Lizzie Lorton* 137). To earn sufficient money she was compelled to write inconsequential potboiler pieces in such periodicals as the *National Magazine, Temple Bar*, and *Chambers' Journal*, as well as continuing as a contributor to *Household Words* and its successor *All the Year Round*. One noteworthy series of articles she did write during this time, significant in terms of her later career as a critic of women although little noticed at the time, were contributions from 1860–62 to the *London Review*, in which she critiqued the social behavior of modern women. She argued, as she had earlier in *Household Words*, for the primacy of women's domestic role, a theme that would gradually become the dominant motif in her writings.

After several unhappy years in London, William James Linton retreated with his children back to his Lake District home, while Eliza Lynn Linton stayed in London, visiting the family only in the summers. She tried to redirect her career back to her primary goal of writing fiction, and did succeed in the mid-1860s in publishing several moderately successful novels with ambivalent messages about the true role of women. The final break to the marriage came in 1866, when William James Linton decided to move to the United States. There was some question that his wife might come also, but that did not happen. They never divorced, ostensibly because there were no grounds of marital infidelity, a requirement for divorce in Victorian England. They never saw each other again, even though William James Linton came back to England several times. Despite the generally miserable marriage, which William James Linton's biographer F. B. Smith assumed had never been consummated (135), there must have been some affection between them, at least in the early days, for on one of William James Linton's trips back to England, he wrote her that, although he agreed they should never see each other again, he "would have been glad to hold you to my heart again, my lips on yours," but it was better to leave things as they were (Layard 270). In his autobiography, William James Linton mentioned his earlier two marriages, but not his last marriage to Eliza Lynn Linton.

Freed from the constraints of married life, Eliza Lynn Linton pursued her writing career with vigor and determination. She found the ideal forum to express her developing ideas on the proper status of women: the prestigious conservative *Saturday Review*. Still a radical freethinking icono-clast, she was nevertheless becoming increasingly conservative on the volatile topic of women's changing role in society and public life. When the young Eliza Lynn had set out on her own to pursue her ambitions, she was indeed a pathbreaker, with no organized movement to support her demands for self-determination. By the late 1860s, however, English women had begun to join together to work for change in women's lives, to provide better education, more employment opportunities, more equitable legal rights, and, for the first time in 1867, the right to vote. It would be expected that Linton, an early advocate of women's emancipation and herself an independent woman, would support the demands for greater freedom for women. Instead, in her *Saturday Review* essays, written from 1866 until the mid-1870s, she castigated women whose behavior deviated from her newly formed ideal of the domestic sheltered devoted wife and mother.

Developing themes she had set forth in her earlier articles in *Household Words* and *London Review*, Linton's *Saturday Review* articles received wide attention and provoked intense controversy. The most notorious was one of the earliest, "The Girl of the Period" (this volume, Appendix B, pp. 412-17), published in the March 14, 1868 issue, in which Linton suggests that young girls who wear makeup and have bold manners envy and imitate the *demi-monde*. Called "perhaps the most sensational middle article that the *Saturday Review* ever published" (Bevington 110), the article, published anonymously but soon identified as Linton's, added a new phrase to the late-Victorian lexi-con, with both defenders and critics of the "girl of the period" continuing the debate for many years.

Linton continued her attacks on women in subsequent *Saturday Review* articles, fervently criticizing not only those who sought social freedom, but even more so, women who demanded political rights and employment outside their natural domestic sphere. Condemning women's rights women as "shrieking sisters," "the epicene sex," and "grim females," she argued that the ideal woman lived in retirement, with "patience, self-sacrifice, tenderness, quietness," recognizing the natural superiority of men ("Ideal Women" 609–10). These essays, full of ambivalent messages and often stark misogyny, were popular enough so that later, in 1883, they were collected and reissued in book form as *The Girl of the Period and Other Social Essays*. Linton also published a collection of periodical essays on women in a volume entitled *Ourselves* (1869), although increasingly she separated her own identity from that of women, a sex she came to denigrate as weak, dependent, and irrational.

The anomaly of an independent woman condemning female independence infuriated many women because of its seeming hypocrisy. As one young woman who quarreled with Linton said, "Had not she herself, when a girl, rebelled in her own home, and gone to live in London alone in order to make a living? If she revolted in her girlhood, why make such a dead set against those of her own sex as followed the example she herself had set by breaking away from home influence?" (Cockran 172). Linton's response was usually that she had been wrong to seek independence and self-sufficiency, and that her life had been hard and unhappy. Nevertheless, as Emily Symonds pointed out after Linton's death, few would believe that Linton would have been happier "if she had remained in the bosom of an uncongenial family, condemned to the futile occupations of the young lady of her class, instead of going out into the world, and working at the profession that she loved." Moreover, if Linton was so unhappy, "why did she not renounce her own profession, close her books, return to her husband, and content herself with the domestic sphere?" (Paston 511).

That Linton herself was conflicted over women's nature and role in society was apparent in her fictional writings during this middle stage of her career, which often contained messages that contradicted the misogynistic tone of her periodical essays. Such novels as *Patricia Kemball* (1875) and *The World Well Lost* (1877) include strong female main characters, sympathetically drawn, although most of the novels ended with the women finding true happiness in the arms of a superior protecting man. Creating controversy not just on the woman question, Linton's most sensational novel during this time and probably the most controversial novel she ever wrote, was *The True History of Joshua Davidson, Christian and Communist* (1872), which dealt with the hypocrisies of religion. In it she suggests that if Jesus were reborn into Victorian England, he would be a communist. Her fictional Jesus ("Joshua Davidson") is stoned to death by the powers in the Church (the leader of whom is a vicar strikingly similar to her own vicar father). Since political and religious iconoclasms were safer than challenges to the moral code in Victorian England, *The True History of Joshua Davidson* was an immediate best seller.

By the mid-1870s, Linton had established herself as a respected and successful, if controversial, woman of letters. In 1876, however, she suddenly decided to leave England to live in Italy, not to return until 1884. Although the ostensible reason was to escape the fog and cold of London, probably the more compelling motivation was to escape the collapse of an emotional relationship with a young woman. Linton had had earlier intense relationships with women, including a passionate attachment to a neighbor in the Lake District not long before she left her paternal home, and another relationship with a young woman after her breakup with Edward McDermot. It is difficult to decipher the nature of these associations from Linton's autobiography, especially because of its selective sex reversals. They were, however, clearly with women, but it is unknown whether they included a physical sexual involvement or if they were only perhaps unrecognized highly charged homoerotic attachments. Clearly, however, although Linton's intellectual companions were mostly male, her closest emotional attachments were to women. In this latest relationship with a woman who Linton's contemporary biographer George Layard cryptically said "was one who was very dear to her, but was not worthy of her affection" (189),[1] the woman tried to blackmail Linton because of their physical contacts, which Linton (writing as the male Christopher Kirkland) insisted were purely innocent. As an escape, Linton went to Italy.

After this painful episode, Linton tended to form safer, more controlling maternal relationships with young women. She therefore took as her companion to Italy a young daughter of a family friend, Beatrice Sichel, describing their time together as "merry as a wedding bell" (*Christopher Kirkland* 3:241). In Italy they spent some time in Rome with the lesbian artistic community which included the prominent American sculptor Harriet Hosmer. During these travels Linton continued her regular literary production of novels and articles.

Linton's idyllic life of travel with Beatrice Sichel ended in 1880 when the young woman returned to England to marry. Even though Sichel remained close to Linton for the rest of her life, the loss of the young woman's close companionship was a heavy emotional blow to Linton, "quite as severe a trial to me as the breakup of my married life had been" (*Christopher Kirkland* 3:248). Reeling from this loss, Linton wrote her most intriguing and ambiguous novel on the woman question, *The Rebel of the Family* (1880). Linton's fictional rebel, Perdita, modeled on her memory of her own turbulent and emotionally desolate childhood, wants more out life than stultifying domesticity, and she needs to work in order to support herself. Portraying sympathetically Perdita's desire for meaningful work, Linton nevertheless has her get an unsatisfying job working in the Post Office. Perdita is attracted to a group of independent women's rights women, whose leader is the evil lesbian seductress, Bell Blount. Perdita is rescued from the temptations of women's rights and of lesbianism by a strong manly man. As one reviewer of this novel pointed out, its mixed messages make the reader think at one moment "that Mrs. Linton is disposed

---

[1] See also Linton *Christopher Kirkland* 3:229–30.

to applaud, at another to condemn, the unattractive if conscientious ways of the Rebel of the Family" (*Saturday Review* 20 November 1880:650).

Staying alone in Italy for several more years, Linton finally returned to England in 1884. Now at age 62, she launched her most emotionally demanding project, writing her autobiography. Casting it in fictional form with herself as a man "as a screen which takes off the sting of boldness and self-exposure" (Linton to George Bentley, 21 February 1885 Bentley Collection), Linton was probably also able through the sex reversal to express more accurately her own sense of identity as an independent ambitious self-determined person, qualities which in her patriarchal culture were considered attributes of male and not female personalities. To her dismay, *The Autobiography of Christopher Kirkland* was not a critical success, in part because of the confusion created by the sex reversals. As Layard pointed out, "to those who could read between the lines the effect was somewhat bizarre, while to those not in the secret the story was in parts incomprehensible" (p. vii).

Linton then turned her attention to what became the all-absorbing mission of her life: to stop the surging tide of advancing women from taking over places in the public world which she thought belonged rightly to the superior sex. Having earlier labeled women's rights women as "shrieking sisters," she now added such damning sobriquets as the "wild women," her impassioned sense of purpose intensifying as the New Women of the 1890s claimed even more social freedom and political power.

Linton's anti-feminist arguments, couched in misogynist rhetoric, warned of the disasters that would ensue if women were emancipated from the home. Home life would lose all peace, the political world would be tainted by the dominating emotion-ruled tyrants, and inevitably this gynecracy would cause the decline and fall of the British Empire. As evidence she wrote for *Fortnightly Review* a series of articles from 1887 to 1889 on the history of women, a history which she argued showed that a civilization's strength was in inverse proportion to the social freedoms of women. [Among the many rebuttals to her arguments were those of the women's suffrage leader Millicent Fawcett, who pointed out that countries like those in the Ottoman Empire, where women were secluded in zenanas, were weak powers (555–63)].

Linton also warned about the moral dangers of female emancipation. She opposed such new freedoms as bicycle riding, in fear of immoral results including women falling off their bicycles into the arms of strange men. Shocked by female sportswomen, mixed life-drawing art and medical classes, sex education for females, and other evidences to her of the breakdown of the moral order, she championed the work of her old nemesis, the mythical social censor Mrs. Grundy, who was, she said in the *New Review*, a useful drag on a wheel of a coach plunging downhill on a path to destruction (309).

Linton, who though self-educated had longed for a more formal disciplined schooling, condemned the movement for higher education for women. Having herself separated from her husband, she decried the judicial decisions that gave women greater freedom to leave unhappy or abusive marriages.

Unambiguous in her impassioned anti-feminist periodical articles, in her fictional writings Linton continued to reveal her ambivalence towards women's role in society. One of her last novels, *The One Too Many* (1894), for example, is the story of a young woman, Moira, whose widowed mother cannot support her and her younger sister. Moira wants to get a job to support herself, but her mother disallows that and forces her instead to marry an effete old man. Sweet submissive Moira is contrasted with four Girton girls, who are portrayed as cigarette-smoking degenerates who are either grim man-haters or seductive man-lovers. One of the Girton girls, however, is redeemable, and despite herself, falls in love and gets married, for "her Higher Education had not entirely rooted out, though it had warped, her woman's nature" (202). Moira, on the other hand, drowns herself, sinking "as the dead thing might, without a struggle to her doom" (358). Ironically, Linton dedicated this strange novel to "the sweet girls still among us" (n.p.) As a reviewer in the *Athenaeum* pointed out, the message of the book seems to be that "it is wiser to revolt than to submit" (342). The next year, Linton published an unambiguously and unequivocally anti-feminist novel, *In Haste and at Leisure*, in which she scathingly attacked the New Woman.

Linton's last novel, published posthumously, was an autobiographical fantasy, describing what her life might have been like if she had been born a physically attractive woman. *The Second Youth of Theodora Desanges* (1899) is the story of an old Lintonesque woman, Theodora, who is a strong opponent of women's rights. By a miracle Theodora is transformed into a beautiful alluring young woman, at whose feet men fall in passionate devotion. Although beautiful and young, Theodora nevertheless remains a fervent enemy of the New Woman.

Even though in the last years of her life her writings became increasingly shrill in their anti-feminist invectives, Eliza Lynn Linton remained a respected woman of letters and opinion. When Herbert Spencer wanted someone of note to publish a response to one of his critics, he called on his friend Mrs. Lynn Linton. Thomas Hardy valued her as a friend, and said that he could long thereafter remember the exact spot where he first read "The Girl of the Period." Algernon Swinburne praised her as the equal of Charlotte Brontë. In 1896, when women were first allowed to sit on the governing council of the Society of Authors, Linton was among the first elected. With such respected male colleagues maintaining her intellectual vigor and self-worth, her emotional life was nurtured in old age with her motherly attachment to the young novelist Beatrice Harraden, whose 1894 *Ships That Pass in the Night* was a critical success. An unlikely soulmate in that Harraden was a university graduate and women's rights advocate who later became a follower of Emmeline Pankhurst, Harraden described herself as "everything which my friend Mrs. Lynn Lynton [*sic*] hates. Yet she loves me" (Tooley 325).

Having escaped the rush of London in 1895 to move to the quieter life in Malvern, a spa town in the midlands of England, the aging Linton had characteristically returned to bustling London to attend a dinner of the Society of Authors as well as other events, when she caught bronchial pneumonia and died on 14 July 1898. Linton's death brought forth extravagant tributes to her long productive life as an eminent woman of letters. Not long after her death, however, her fame as well as her infamy faded, and her novels went out of print. Only her novels related to religion, *The Autobiography of Christopher Kirkland*, *The True History of Joshua Davidson*, and the 1879 *Under Which Lord?* have been reprinted, as part of the 1976 Garland *Novels of Faith and Doubt* series. In recent years, however, as feminist criticism has matured and has transcended limiting either/or mentalities, Linton in her rich ambiguities and complexities has become a figure of lively scholarly interest. This is a development which Linton, who even as a lonely motherless young girl defied convention and respectability to try to achieve the notice of the world, would welcome, although the attention is coming largely from feminist scholars whose philosophy she ostensibly condemned but in many ways inadvertently championed.

Works Cited

Academy, 25 May 1901: 440.

Anderson, Nancy Fix. *Woman against Women in Victorian England: A Life of Eliza Lynn Linton*. Bloomington: Indiana UP, 1987.

Athenaeum, 17 March 1894: 342.

Bentley Collection. University of Illinois Library. Urbana, Illinois.

Besant, Walter. "E. Lynn Linton." *Queen*, 23 July 1898: 135.

Bevington, Merle. *The Saturday Review, 1855–1868*. NY: Columbia UP, 1941.

Cockran, Henrietta. *Celebrities and I*. London: Hutchinson and Co., 1902.

Fawcett, Millicent. "The Enfranchisement of Women." *Fortnightly Review*, April 1889: 555–63.

Haight, Gordon. *George Eliot and John Chapman, with John Chapman's Diary*. New Haven: Yale UP, 1940.

Henry Huntington Library MSS. HM 18169. San Marino, California.

Layard, George Somes. *Mrs. Lynn Linton: Her Life, Letters, and Opinions*. London: Methuen and Co., 1901.

Linton, E. Lynn. *Amymone: A Romance in the Days of Pericles.* 3 vols. London: Richard Bentley, 1848.

———. Autobiographical Essay (unpublished). Harry Ransom Humanities Research Center. U. of Texas. Austin, Texas.

———. *The Autobiography of Christopher Kirkland.* 3 vols. London: Richard Bentley and Son, 1883.

———. "Crooked Sticks." *National Magazine,* June 1858: 98–100.

———. "Ideal Women." *Saturday Review,* 9 May 1868: 609–10.

———. *Lizzie Lorton of Greyrigg.* Amer. ed. New York: Harper and Brothers, 1866.

———. "Mary Wollstonecraft." *The English Republic,* 1854: 4: 418–24.

———. "Nearing the Rapids." *New Review,* March 1894: 302–10.

———. *The One Too Many.* London: Chatto and Windus, 1894.

———. "The Rights and Wrongs of Women." *Household Words,* 1 April 1854: 158–61.

———. "Sentiment and Action." *Household Words,* 10 November 1855: 337–45.

Linton, Eliza Lynn MSS. Keswick Museum. Keswick, Cumbria, England.

Low, Sidney. *Pall Mall Gazette,* quoted in *Academy,* 30 July 1898: 107–08.

Paston, George [Emily Symonds]. "A Censor of Modern Womanhood." *Fortnightly Review,* 1 September 1901: 505–19.

Saturday Review, 20 November 1880: 650.

Smith, F.B. *Radical Artisan: William James Linton, 1812–97.* Manchester: Manchester UP, 1973.

Somerset House, London. Will of Eliza Lynn Linton.

Tooley, Sarah. "Beatrice Harraden at Home." *Young Woman,* June 1897: 321–26.

Appendix D: Blending Journalism with Fiction: Eliza Lynn Linton and Her Rise to Fame as a Popular Novelist[1]

Andrea L. Broomfield
Johnson County Community College

Eliza Lynn Linton was not born with special talent for writing fiction. She learned her craft slowly and often painfully, and even later in her life after she had published over twenty novels, she still had not achieved unqualified fame for her work. William Loadon, the Lynn family lawyer, predicted correctly when he told her that only with effort could "some kind of a vertebrate organism ... be evolved out of the protoplastic pulp" (qtd. in Layard 47–48). That Linton was dissatisfied with the quality and reception of her fiction is evident in her correspondence and in her condemnations and *ad feminam* attacks on more successful women; George Eliot is the most famous example.[2] Her first years in London were particularly difficult as she struggled to stay afloat financially and to gain prominence in literary circles. While her first two novels, *Azeth, the Egyptian* (1847) and *Amymone: A Romance in the Days of Pericles* (1848), met with moderate success, her third novel, *Realities* (1851), was a failure that forced the author's self reckoning. At that point she turned primarily to journalism, and for the next thirteen years she practiced and perfected the art of punditry. This decision had manifold repercussions for her career: it cemented her reputation as Victorian England's most prominent antifeminist, she achieved lasting fame

---

[1] I gratefully acknowledge *Victorian Literature and Culture* for allowing me to use sections of my forthcoming article, "Much More Than An Antifeminist: Eliza Lynn Linton and the Rise of Victorian Popular Journalism," in this essay. I would also like to thank and acknowledge the University of Illinois for allowing me access to the Bentley Manuscript Collection at the University of Illinois Library.

[2] In the final chapter of *My Literary Life* (1899), Linton recalls with striking detail her first meeting with George Eliot, as well as her opinion of Eliot's rise to fame. At one point, she snidely notes that Eliot, before she had become "the Great Genius of her age," was "essentially under-bred and provincial," and that she "had an unwashed, unbrushed, unkempt look altogether" (95). Attacks such as these led Beatrice Harraden, in her prefatory remarks to *My Literary Life*, to write that it "is to be regretted ... that [Linton] is not here herself to tone down some of her more pungent remarks and criticisms, hastily thrown off in bitter moments such as come to us all" (6).

for her *Saturday Review* "Girl of the Period" (or G.O.P.) essays, she contributed first-hand to the evolution of popular journalism, and most importantly, she became a more popular and sought-after novelist as a result of regularly practicing journalism. While Linton has always enraged and provoked readers—now as well as then—she nonetheless achieved popular acclaim for the wit, style, originality, and panache that imbue her essays and her later novels. Her early years in London, however, were a time when her talents were too often mismatched with her objectives. Indeed, it took Linton several years to realize that her best hope of achieving fame and financial security lay with journalism rather than with fiction. This essay will trace the course of those early years in London, and it will suggest that Linton's decision to practice journalism on a full-time basis was largely responsible for reviving her fiction-writing career. *The Rebel of the Family* in particular attests to how adept she eventually became at blending the best features of her journalism with her fiction.

Given the restrictive and demoralizing nature of Eliza Lynn's home life, particularly as she describes it in her fictionalized autobiography, *The Autobiography of Christopher Kirkland* (1885), it is remarkable that she could envision herself becoming a writer at all. As a motherless girl growing up in an isolated part of the Lake District, Linton was bullied by her father to conform to the role of a demure and submissive lady. In *My Literary Life*, Linton recalled that while living at home, she was ordered "to have no opinion of [her] own, or if unfortunate enough to have one ... to keep it to [herself]" (36). Furthermore, Linton and her sisters were denied any formal education, and Vicar Lynn saw no reason to waste money on hiring a governess, given his opinion that a girl's education was a useless extravagance (Anderson 22–23; *The Autobiography of Christopher Kirkland* I:42–43). Left largely to herself, Linton used her access to the large family library and undertook her own education. She mastered several modern languages, achieved competency in Latin and Greek, and read widely in history, philosophy, and literature.

Linton's determination at age fifteen to become a novelist was possibly based more on social pressure for women writers to confine themselves to fiction, rather than on what her inclinations and talents best suited her for. Her passion for scholarship and writing, combined with her outspoken nature, might easily have led her toward some genre other than fiction had her family been more supportive, and had social circumstances been less restrictive for women in general. Young Eliza Lynn did have a desire to write stories; the practice amused her when she was lonely, cheered her when she was depressed, and allowed her to create more fulfilling and enriching conclusions to the mundane events that transpired in her life.[1] But as she grew older, writing fiction also became a means of channeling her increasing scholarly knowledge and penchant for research into a tangible product; later, it also became her pulpit. Journalism would have been the ideal vehicle for Linton's proclivities and interests at this stage in her life, but in the 1830s when she was coming of age, very few women had achieved any financial success in journalism, in large part because the respectable periodicals of the time were still largely controlled by elite men of letters who maintained that nonfiction was the domain of men (Tuchman 140–43). Hence, after Linton's father grudgingly permitted her to move to London, she spent months in the British Library conducting research into the culture of ancient Egypt in order to publish a novel. *Azeth, The Egyptian* testifies to her knowledge of ancient Egyptian life, but the quality of its story and characterization also indicates that Linton would not achieve lasting acclaim on the basis of her fiction writing alone.

Published at her own expense with Newby and Son in 1847, *Azeth the Egyptian* was by no means greeted with derision by reviewers or by the London literary establishment. Historical novels, the genre into which *Azeth* fell, had begun to fall out of favor by the late 1840s, but some reviewers commended Linton for breathing new life into the art form, while other reviewers saw the novel as promise of better work to come. The praise was almost always qualified; however, *Bentley's Miscellany* commended the author's passion, noting that the novel was "no piece of task-work on the part of the writer," but it also thought the novel "long, cumbrous, over-wrought" (248–49). In a similar vein, the *Athenæum* commented positively on the author's exuberant fancy, claiming that she was not "convulsive." However, it cautioned that some readers would "at once be repelled by the names of Amasis, and Psammetichus, and Sethos, and Nitocris"; nor would they "bestow a moment on the secrets of the Pyramids. Such [readers] will find 'Azeth' over-wrought, tedious—florid with a profusion of gorgeous colour, and deficient in that clearness of construction which gives force and progressive interest to the narration of adventure" (88). Significantly, most reviewers at this stage recognized that Linton's real talent lay in research and history. *The Athenæum* suggested that the novel's deficiencies resulted from the author having "too much, rather than too little learning" (88); the *New Monthly Magazine* commended the novel's historical accuracy as "satisfactory as any hitherto given of a very obscure epoch, and of transactions

---

[1] Nancy Fix Anderson discusses the psychodynamic dimension of Linton's fiction, and how Linton, as a young girl, would write stories to help her come to terms with the loss of her mother, to assuage her loneliness, and to work through her sexual confusion and/or longings. See in particular chapters 1 and 2 of Anderson's *Woman Against Women*.

extremely difficult to explain" (278); *Ainsworth's Magazine* thought the novel "a very careful and well-executed picture of ancient Egyptian life" (187). Such reviewers indicated that Linton's fiction writing career would not prosper unless she worked equally hard on plot and characterization.

Less explicit in the reviews, but nonetheless more troubling to Linton, was the underlying message that young ladies should not "dabble" in the history of ancient cultures; they should leave such research to men formally trained to conduct serious and disciplined inquiry into the past. To avoid the possibility of such criticism becoming more explicit and hence jeopardizing the start of her novel-writing career, Linton attached a preface to her next novel, *Amymone: A Romance in the Days of Pericles:* "In publishing another novel of the same character as the former, I feel that I am open to the charge of pedantry and presumption for choosing subjects beyond a woman's grasp. I can only offer, as excuse, my love for all classical life, and my fervent hope that this love may stand in the place of deeper knowledge" (v). *Amymone*, like *Azeth*, does indeed contain a compendium of information about an ancient culture's religious, political, social, and gender structures, all of which ostensibly serves as a colorful setting for the novel's story line.

Amymone mirrored Linton's own growing confusion as to what purpose her fiction should serve and how best to blend her various interests into a well-wrought, unified artistic product. On the surface, *Amymone's* plot is melodramatic. Murder, subterfuge, and hidden identity are key components to this story about an angry young woman, Amymone, who puts her husband up to murder in order that she and he might inherit an estate and the rights of Athenian citizenship. However, *Amymone* goes beyond melodrama to become in many instances a resource of information about Athenian laws, government, and social codes, as well as the author's first explicit, albeit contradictory, discussion of a woman's rights and duties. These three components—melodrama, encyclopedia of information, and polemic discussion of women's rights—do not work well together. They clash, and as a result, the novel seems quite amateurish, both to readers today as well as to reviewers and readers then.

Predictably, reviews of *Amymone* resembled those of *Azeth*, with many reviewers praising Linton's accurate depiction of life in classical Greece, but also commenting on the awkward nature of the plot. Walter Savage Landor, Linton's adopted "father" and mentor, complimented the work in *Fraser's* for its careful depiction of life in ancient Athens: "Bekker, in his Gallus, is not more correct in his representation of the Romans, than is this lady in the representation of the Athenians," he enthused (429). The *Spectator*, which was also reviewing *Azeth* as well as Linton's third novel, *Realities*, authoritatively dismissed the novel because it was burdened with history and obscure details. Neither *Azeth* nor *Amymone*, it concluded, "exhibit that imagination which is necessary to embody the spirit of the past, or that aptitude for a perception of the events of life which is necessary to form a story" (499). Although primarily positive (most likely because the novel was published by Bentley), *Bentley's Miscellany* objected that the novel was "too diffuse" (251). Probably many readers agreed with Charlotte Brontë's opinion that both *Azeth* and *Amymone* were "literally impossible to digest— they presented to my imagination Lytton Bulwer in petticoats—an overwhelming vision" (qtd. in Anderson 51).

Amymone's relatively low sale price of £100 for the manuscript, and its failure to ignite a wide audience's enthusiasm, convinced Linton that she would have to try harder if she were to compete with other rising mid-century novelists. She decided to heed George Henry Lewes's advice to "quit those remote regions of the antique world in which [your] thoughts hitherto have wandered too much at large, and, leaving Egypt to its mummies and antiquities, no less than Greece, with its temptations, like Sirens, to the young imagination, resolutely move amidst the thronging forms of modern life, and paint from *them*" (qtd. in Anderson 56).

Linton's third novel, aptly entitled *Realities*, was her attempt to move in this direction and was to be the pivotal work of her career. Keenly aware that *Jane Eyre* had taken London by storm, in spite of, or perhaps even because of, the daring risks that Charlotte Brontë took with her characterizations of Jane and Rochester, Linton was determined to take similar risks in her own work. Although she was willing to leave behind her interest in ancient culture, she was unwilling to give up her desire to preach to her audience. She promised Bentley, her prospective publisher, that *Realities* was to be "*strong*": "I confidently expect a success equal to Jane Eyre. This may sound vain, but I feel *sure* of it—" (Bentley Collection, n.d.).

At this juncture, Linton took a fateful step without apparent understanding of its positive consequences for her later career. She applied for a job at the *Morning Chronicle* in 1848 because she needed a steady salary to continue writing novels. Ironically, her decision did not appear to be based on a desire to push boundaries or to make a statement about middle-class women's capability for work outside the home; indeed, Linton seemed uninterested in the fact that her very application to the *Morning Chronicle* was a bold move that few other women in the 1840s would have dared attempt. She simply needed money, and she saw herself as capable of writing well and adhering to deadlines.

Cook, however, was amazed at the youth, not to mention the sex, of the applicant, and Linton's recounting of her first interview with Cook is worth repeating. The editor had been intrigued enough by the young woman's rather peculiar novels to request an interview, during which Linton recorded him as saying: "So! You are the little girl who has written that queer book [*Amymone*], and want to be one of the press-gang, are you? ... I say, though, youngster, you never wrote all that rubbish yourself! Some of your brothers helped you. You never scratched all those queer classics and mythology into your own numbskull without help. At your age it is impossible" (qtd. in Layard 57–58). After Linton assured Cook that she had indeed written *Azeth* and *Amymone* without assistance, he assigned her to write a report on a miners' strike. Giving her a set time, he ordered her to "take the side of the men; but—d'ye hear?—you are not to assassinate the masters. Leave them a leg to stand on, and don't make Adam Smith turn in his grave by any cursed theories smacking of socialism and the devil knows what" (qtd. in Layard 59). Upon writing to Cook's specifications, Linton was promptly hired. As a result, she became the first salaried woman journalist in England.

As a journalist with the *Morning Chronicle*, Linton spent her time reporting on fêtes, writing book reviews, and filling in for the theater reviewer when he was out of town (Layard 58). Although treated as a "Girl Friday," Linton's job exposed her fully to the diversity of London life, thus giving her a wealth of information to use in *Realities*. Whereas before, Linton had mined the British Library for sources on ancient Egypt and Greece, she now mined the city itself for information on nineteenth-century England. Her job gave her access to sights forbidden to sheltered ladies who never ventured into unfashionable districts, and given the raw anger and frustration that imbues *Realities*, Linton's exposure to such sights obviously offended her deeply. She, in turn, was determined to make sure that her readers would be angered by the injustices she depicted, and then inspired to push for reform.[1]

Realities attacks the *laissez-faire* capitalist system which brutalizes the underclass, and it also attacks the patriarchal status quo by delineating how the British government and legal system is ultimately responsible for wife abuse and neglect. While the novel is by no means stridently feminist, it does promote Linton's long-held beliefs that divorce should be legal in some instances, that married women should be allowed custody of their young children, and that they are entitled to their property and earnings if they are separated from their husbands (*Christopher Kirkland* III:2). Linton, thinly disguised as the narrator, often preaches to the reader about these

---

[1] That scenes in *Realities* came from Linton's work at the *Morning Chronicle* is evidenced when a review in *Bentley's Miscellany* notes that much of the material comes from "letters which have appeared from time to time in the Morning Chronicle, and which have aroused the public mind" (670).

issues, sometimes leaving the story itself to languish as a result. In one of the novel's many subplots, Jane, an impoverished sick woman whose sister must turn to prostitution in order to help save her from starvation, is a lightening rod for many such speeches. At the beginning of volume three, as Jane lies in her hovel, "pale, half-starved," in "pain and weariness, and apathetic ignorance," the narrator stops the action to elaborate on the system responsible for Jane's plight:

> When a system must be supported,
> individual sufferings are of no account. It is the
> same with laws and ethics. Grand principles are
> laid down—grand resolutions passed—the abstract
> right is demonstrated—and men are required to
> believe and perform. Yet all modifications of
> power—down to patent idiocy—are denied; and the
> weakling is given the work of the giant, the child
> is judged side by side with the hero. (III:2)

The narrator continues:

> We can raise a people into heroes or grind them into
> brutes as we will. We can elevate them mentally and
> morally by the laws of material improvement as easily
> as we have left them to deteriorate by vicious material
> combinations. There is no natural reason why the lowest
> of the people should not be educated into an equality
> with the present moral and intellectual condition of the
> gentry, as there was no natural reason which prevented
> the burgher class from rising out of the ranks of the
> serfdom of the past, or which will prevent them rising
> still higher in the future. Physical advantages in the
> daily lives of the poor will work moral advancement,
> and intellectual development will react on their social
> condition. In believing this, and in acting on it, we only
> believe the same truth as that which is demonstrated by
> an improved class of crops or an improved breed of
> cattle. (3–4)

And so on. These lengthy speeches, which at times become angry, plaintive, or even hopeless-sounding in tone, take up much of the novel. Extracted from the work, they work exceedingly well as sermons or social criticism, but as a part of a novel, they often appear overly long, distanced from the events and characters' lives, and even quite generic.

The plot's decidedly *un*realistic nature further jeopardizes the novel's artistic integrity. In it, young Clare de Saumarez runs away to London to escape her family's dictatorial attitudes and social conservatism. She takes to the stage, is seduced by her stage manager, then finds out that she is really the daughter of a de Saumarez servant. She is mentored by a clergyman who wishes to marry her, but she rejects him and ends up triumphantly married to a socialist named Perceval Glynn.

As an unmarried, middle-class woman who dared to incorporate graphic seduction scenes and defense of prostitutes into her novel, as well as a stridently socialist message, Linton set her novel up for a humiliating failure.[1] Published at her own expense by Saunders and Otley, *Realities* died a quick death, and perhaps because of stinging reviews of the book's subject matter, poorly executed plot, and the author's audacity, Linton was abruptly fired from her job at the *Morning Chronicle* the same year as the novel's publication.[2]

Abandoned by supporters, increasingly short of funds, and unable to find periodicals willing to publish her short fiction, Linton was left humiliated and depressed. But *Realities'* failure compelled Linton to reevaluate her career, her limitations as a novelist, and most importantly, what her legitimate talents actually were, and how they could be better used to help her achieve fame and financial security. In spite of having been fired from the *Morning Chronicle*, Linton evidently concluded that her passion for preaching and fact finding

---

[1] George Henry Lewes, in his influential essay, "The Lady Novelists," praised George Sand, Jane Austen, Charlotte Brontë, and Elizabeth Gaskell for their talent at realistically depicting the "feminine experience," but he notes that Lynn Linton's hostility in *Amymone* "against received notions" becomes in *Realities* "avowed, incessant, impetuous; it was a passionate and exaggerated protest against conventions, which failed of its intended effect because it was too exaggerated, too manifestly unjust." She "feels deeply, paints vividly what she feels, but she sees dimly" (77). The *Athenaeum* was more biting, claiming that none "of the conventionalisms against which [Lynn Linton] raves like a Pythoness are half so artificial ... as the respective stratagems and forbearances of her hero and heroine" (627). The *New Monthly Magazine* called Linton's portrayal of Vasty Vaughn's wife "hideous" (235). It went on to say: "Miss Lynn is a determined social reformer, and that our social system requires reform on many points which she attacks, there can be no doubt; but we shall be very much mistaken if the defective condition of our laws, and the ugly vices which she dissects with such an eager hand, are cured or mended by her novel" (235).

[2] Layard, relying on what Linton herself writes in the *Autobiography of Christopher Kirkland*, writes: "The year 1851 ... found Eliza Lynn severing her connection with the *Morning Chronicle*. What was the actual beginning of the breach between her and the editor is not altogether clear. It is enough to say that she suddenly failed to please" (77).

would fare better in journalism than in fiction, irrespective of the disadvantage that her sex posed in this particular literary situation. In 1854, Linton left for Paris to work as a correspondent for an English newspaper and to rebuild her career. Freed from the stigma of being a second-rate novelist who had written a scandalous work, freed from the tangles of personal relations and family problems, Linton was able in Paris to devote her attention to learning the unwritten rules of her chosen field. She first swallowed her pride and discarded her earlier, idealistic perceptions of the literary marketplace, and she began to gauge more accurately how audience approval drove sales and profits in the publishing industry, and hence, how audience determined a writer's salary range and popularity.

In an 1878 letter to one of her relatives, Linton shared some wisdom that she herself had accepted years earlier: "True success comes only by hard work, great courage in self-correction and the most earnest and intense determination to succeed, not thinking that every endeavour is already success" (qtd. in Layard 212). Linton's emphasis on succeeding and willingness to endure self-correction suggests that her objectives after *Realities* were no longer geared towards a radical alteration of the status quo, so much as a desire to remain financially afloat and to achieve fame and influence. She recognized as well the need to adapt to her profession's unsavory, Darwinist character and to master the rules of the game in order to compete with her colleagues—the majority of whom were male, and thus, in a better position to achieve success. In recalling her time working for the newspaper in Paris, she wrote:

> Here I entered on a new set of experiences, and
> broke fresh ground everywhere.... In the interests
> of his paper, each man wished to be first in the field
> and to have the practical monopoly of private
> information. Hence, brotherly kindness, and doing
> to others as you would be done by, did not obtain
> among men whose professional loyalty lay in misleading,
> tripping the heels of, and outstripping their
> competitors. (qtd. in Layard 77–78)

Lynn Linton wisely saved her own heel-tripping for professionally inclined women who either competed directly with her, or whose aspirations threatened the patriarchal status quo that she had decided it was most profitable to defend. Linton strategized to make professional women and "blue stockings" vulnerable to her well-aimed journalistic attacks on their "misplaced" priorities, while at the same time attempting to divert attention from her own ambitions in such a public sphere. Always ambivalent about women's rights, she had apparently little trouble taking an antifeminist approach to the woman-question debate that was beginning to grip Victorian England at mid-century. She also developed a number of personal trademarks that remained consistent in her prose, regardless of the range of periodicals for which she wrote: striking caricatures, short, authoritative sentences, catch phrases, shock tactics, provocative twists on old stereotypes—particularly of foreigners, society ladies, women's rights activists, and preachers—and reductive arguments all characterize her writing at this time. When her 1854 "Rights and Wrongs of Women" appeared in *Household Words*, it was evident that she had found an angle and a message that resonated not only with the editor, Charles Dickens, but more importantly, with a large, middle-class audience.

The exhortations, polemics, and long-winded, often digressive sermons that littered the pages of *Azeth*, *Amymone*, and *Realities* finally found a place in a growing periodicals industry that profited off readers' anxieties about changing gender roles, shifts in class identity, and continued urban and imperial expansion (Houghton 5). Recognizing that gender was a highly profitable subject to claim as her own, Linton quickly fine-tuned her ability to simultaneously outrage critics and delight admirers. Her name soon became known, and her ideas were debated throughout the press as well as in homes, at society balls, and in public debates. As the Victorian authority on women's wrongs, Linton was guaranteed a steady stream of requests for article submissions and speaking engagements—a popularity that her earlier fiction had never gained her.

When Linton published *Grasp Your Nettle* in 1865, her first novel since *Realities*, she evidently used the wisdom that she had gained in journalism and from her early failures to make her fiction more appealing, although it remained as provocative and controversial as ever. Rather than slow, pedantic narratives weighted down by abstract sermons or an overabundance of obscure information, instead of thinly developed characters acting in barely believable situations, Linton's later fiction sparkles with the same verve, wit, and topicality that colors her essays. *The Rebel of the Family* itself demonstrates how cleverly Linton applied to her fiction her journalistic trademarks of caricature and stereotype in order to engage all sorts of readers.

Linton's most famous essays are rife with memorable caricatures of women. Linton also insists in many of her essays that women can easily be grouped into "types": fashionable, demimonde, buttercup, epicene, grim, ideal, shrieking, wild, girls of the period, and so forth. Linton created many of these types and caricatures while writing for *Temple Bar* and for the *London Review* in the early 1860s, before she became famous overnight for her March 1868 *Saturday Review* essay, "The Girl of the Period." Her use of caricature was arguably the key to her fame—and to the controversy that accompanied it. While some of these reductive and oftentimes comic representations of women caused legitimate anger and consternation among many serious-thinking women and men, they became famous and even a part of social parlance. Indeed a "girl of the period" appears in Anthony Trollope's 1868 novel, *The Vicar of Bullhampton* (Anderson 120).

Most adept at her caricatures of women's rights activists, Linton had little trouble filling *Rebel of the Family* with characters who seem to be taken directly out of her periodical essays. When Perdita attends the West Hill Hall lecture series on women's rights and meets up with Leslie Crawford, she and the readers are exposed to Linton's parade of the Shrieking Sisterhood in all its floridity.

"A lady from America, with three Christian names before a doubled surname, making five in all, and a toilette from Paris that would have made the typical duchess envious" is the first on the platform (p. 186, this edition). Her "thin dry metallic voice and her intonation," along with her supreme confidence in her oratorical powers, meant that she "never lost her thread; never stopped for a word nor entangled herself in a phrase; never stuttered nor stammered nor went back over the ground already quartered, but spoke and spoke and spoke with the limpidity and fluidity of a torrent" (187). This type of character appears briefly in numerous G.O.P. essays, but she is fully developed in Linton's "The Epicene Sex" (August 1872). When the lady from America takes the platform in *Rebel of the Family*, she talks incessantly, but well. Indeed, the narrator notes, "her case-hardened self-sufficiency was as ugly as a physical deformity" (*Rebel* 187). In the "Epicene Sex," Linton berates this same type of woman, although in that context, she is portrayed as a "heavy British matron rearing her ample shoulders above the board, as she lays down the law on the duties of men towards women—especially sons-in-law—and the advantage to all concerned if wives are liberally dealt with in the matter of housekeeping money" (243). Whereas the lady from America rises to a public platform to deliver her pronouncement on the evils of men and the blessings of women, the matron in "The Epicene Sex" eagerly gets to her legs "after the cheese has been removed, to turn on a stream of verbal insipidity for a quarter of an hour at a stretch" (243).

Shortly after the lady from America makes her speech at the West Hill Hall, another recognizable Linton type takes the podium. She is a woman with "close-cropped hair, a Tyrolese hat with a cock's feather at the side, a shirt-collar and a shirt-front, a waistcoat and a short jacket. In everything outward she was like a man, save for whiskers—which however she simulated with a short kind of cheek-curl; and for moustaches—which were more than indicated" (188). As Deborah Meem points out in "Eliza Lynn Linton and the

Rise of Lesbian Consciousness" (1997), this type will soon be recognized by late Victorian readers as Havelock Ellis's congenital invert—a mannish lesbian. In 1880, however, she "can only be described as she appears" (Meem 550–51). Linton did much before Ellis, however, to make these women common-place caricatures in many of her essays. They appear as early as 1866 in "Fuss and Feathers," wearing spectacles and carrying alpaca umbrellas; they also "have big knuckles and bony shoulders, and a costume defiant of millinery laws, and a shibboleth defiant of ordinary prohibitions" (197–98).

Given her importance in the plot to *The Rebel of the Family*, Linton spends the most time caricaturing the women's suffrage leader, Bell Blount. Her large body, overbearing demeanor, brassy voice, bad manners, and sloppy housekeeping qualify her as a prototypical lesbian as well, stamped as she is with Linton's own unique set of attributes. When Bell proceeds to impose herself on Perdita after the Winstanley family has been invited to sit in Mr. Brocklebank's box at the theater, her description causes everyone, including readers, to feast on her with a horrid fascination:

> A woman of decidedly remarkable appearance presented
> herself. She was dressed in a satin gown of flaming
> scarlet; round her throat was a broad, heavy, silver
> dog-collar, and on her neck rows on rows of those
> green iridescent shells which are the apotheosis of the
> street-whelk. Her white hair, combed straight up from
> her face, fell down her back in youthful waves; and she
> had rings and brooches and bracelets and artificial
> flowers wherever they could be placed. (270)

The flaming satin gown is hardly original; readers are meant to see her in the same category as the prostitute. But a woman compared to a gastropod mollusk—a whelk— is cause for reflection. Bell, Linton implies, prowls the theater, the street, the lecture hall, searching for innocent girls to take into her home and bed, just as the mollusk preys on tiny bits of ocean life to take into its spiral shell. Throughout her essays that depict such women, Linton is ever resourceful and creative as she attempts to take well-established stereotypes of controversial or unpopular figures and give them a new edge. Indeed, variations of Bell appear in many of Linton's essays. In "La Femme Passée" (July 1868), we witness the washed-out society lady, who like Bell dresses her hair in youthful fashions in an attempt to look young and girlish. In "The Fashionable Woman" (August 1868), an "inexpressible air of haggard weariness creeps over her" from her dissipated lifestyle, and to appear wholesome, she "rushes off for help to paints and cosmetics, to stimulants and drugs, and attempts to restore the tarnished freshness of her beauty by the very means which further corrode it" (185). In "The Epicene Sex," Linton uncharitably describes her as a "hard, unblushing, unloving" woman whose "ideal of happiness lies in swagger and notoriety," who hates home life and who despises "home virtues," who has "no tender regard for men and no instinctive love for children" (243).

In all of these cases—the American lady, the mannish woman, and Bell Blount herself—Linton adeptly blends elements of her most successful journalism into her fiction. Certainly Linton was efficient. She recognized when a caricature would take hold of the popular imagination and result in animated discussions about the nature of women in general. John Douglas Cook, who had rehired Linton to write for the *Saturday Review* when he became its editor, recognized that the periodical's fame would hinge on how frequently people discussed and disseminated ideas that they had come across while reading it. Likewise, Linton understood that her striking, audacious caricatures must survive beyond the pages of her essays and novels if they too, were to keep her name and reputation in the public sphere.

While Linton's methods of achieving popularity and influence are just as questionable as those of any enterprising journalist's or novelist's (both then and now), her ability to gauge precisely what readers would buy and what editors would publish—and her ability to do so in spite of the significant hurdles that her sex posed in this male-dominated profession—is both remarkable and significant. Linton did in "The Girl of the Period" what several women's rights activists had had immense trouble doing: she popularized most of the tenets of the Woman Question. While her essays and New Woman novels often reduce the movement to relatively simplistic terms, Linton nonetheless introduced the debate "to the good society of English drawing rooms" (qtd. in Anderson 123). Particularly after Linton published "The Girl of the Period," several magazines and writers who had before been apathetic to the subject of women's rights (or to any subject pertaining to women, for that matter), began contributing to the debate that this one essay alone incited. *Macmillan's Magazine, Punch, Eclectic Review, St. Paul's Magazine, Tinsley's Magazine*, and *Victoria Magazine* immediately responded with essays that took varied and expansive approaches to the issues Linton raised. By taking the same arguments and incorporating them into her fiction, Linton perpetuated the discussion and more importantly, she widened its appeal by drawing in hundreds of fiction readers who might never have opened the *Saturday Review* or other such weeklies, let alone read about this debate in more obscure and specialized women's rights publications, such as *The Common Cause*. By taking advantage of the dynamic and changing nature of periodicals publishing in the late nineteenth century,

Linton not only achieved a name in journalism, but she was also able to discover how successfully her brand of journalism could translate into widely popular and topical novels—novels that continue to amuse, delight, outrage, and provoke readers today.

Works Cited

Anderson, Nancy Fix. *Woman Against Women in Victorian England: A Life of Eliza Lynn Linton.* Bloomington: Indiana UP, 1987.

"A Contrast" [of *Azeth* and *Amymone*]. *Bentley's Miscellany*, 26 (1848): 248–55.

Houghton, Walter. "Periodical Literature and the Articulate Classes." *The Victorian Periodical Press: Samplings and Soundings.* Eds. Joanne Shattock and Michael Wolff. Leicester: Leicester UP, 1982. 3–27.

Landor, Walter Savage. "Harold, and Amymone." *Fraser's Magazine* 38, (1848): 429–33.

Layard, George Somes. *Mrs. Lynn Linton: Her Life, Letters, and Opinions.* London: Methuen, 1901.

Lewes, George Henry. "The Lady Novelists." *Westminster Review*, 58 (1852): 70–77.

Linton, Eliza Lynn. *Amymone: A Romance in the Days of Pericles.* 3 vols. London: Richard Bentley, 1848.

———. *The Autobiography of Christopher Kirkland.* 3 vols. London: Bentley and Son, 1885.

———. "The Epicene Sex." *Saturday Review*, 24 August 1872: 242–43.

———. "Fashionable Women." *Saturday Review*, 8 August 1868: 184–85.

———. "Fuss and Feathers." *Temple Bar.* vol. 17 (1866): 192–99.

———. "The Girl of the Period." *Saturday Review*, 14 March 1868: 339–40.

———. "La Femme Passée." *Saturday Review*, 11 July 1868: 49–50.

———. *My Literary Life.* London: Hodder and Stroughton, 1899.

———. *Realities: A Tale.* 3 vols. London: Saunders and Otley, 1851.

———. *The Rebel of the Family.* 3 vols. 1880. Reprint (3 vols. in 1). London: Chatto and Windus, 1880.

———. "Rights and Wrongs of Women." *Household Words*, 1 April 1854: 257–60.

———. To Richard Bentley. n.d. Bentley Collection. University of Illinois Library. Urbana, Illinois.

Meem, Deborah T. "Eliza Lynn Linton and the Rise of Lesbian Consciousness." *Journal of the History of Sexuality*, 7 (1997): 537–60.

"Novels of the Day" [Rev. of *Realities*]. *Bentley's Miscellany*, 29 (1851): 669–70.

"Novels of the Day" [Rev. of *Realities*]. *New Monthly Magazine*, 92 (1851): 228–36.

Rev. of *Azeth, The Egyptian*. *Ainsworth's Magazine*, 11 (1847): 187–88.

Rev. of *Azeth, The Egyptian*. *Athenaeum*, 23 January 1847: 88–89.

Rev. of *Azeth, The Egyptian*. *New Monthly Magazine*, Feb., 1848: 278–82.

Rev. of *Azeth, Amymone*, and *Realities*. *Spectator*, 24 May 1851: 499.

Rev. of *Realities*. *Athenæum*, 14 June 1851: 626–27.

Tuchman, Gaye, with Nina E. Fortin. *Edging Women Out: Victorian Novelists, Publishers, and Social Change*. New Haven: Yale UP, 1989.

Appendix E: Eliza Lynn Linton as a New Woman Novelist

Constance Harsh
Colgate University

The early 1890s in Britain saw an extensive public discussion of the advanced "New Woman," who demanded freedoms of behavior and education that had been traditionally denied to her sex. Essayists, playwrights, and novelists found in her a figure of inspiration, contempt, or fun. Among those who denigrated the New Woman, Eliza Lynn Linton was one of the most impassioned. She was also perhaps the most experienced in anti-feminist rhetoric, having maintained a vociferous opposition to modern varieties of femininity since her first piece attacking "The Girl of the Period" in 1868. In 1891–92 she famously pursued a breed she called "the Wild Women" in the *Nineteenth Century*: "The Wild Women as Politicians," "The Wild Women as Social Insurgents," and "The Partisans of the Wild Women." These three pieces insistently warn that the twisted instincts of modern women have given them a lust for power that threatens to flatten the difference between the sexes. While they represent a minority, their potential influence is sufficiently pernicious to warrant "treat[ing] the[ir] preposterous claims [...] as if this little knot of noisy Maenads did really threaten the stability of society and the well-being of the race" ("Politicians" 79). These articles and other contemporary pieces helped establish Linton as one of the chief opponents of New Women. Her persistence (and doubtless the volume of her invective) led *Punch* to create a satirical counterpart, "Mrs. Shriek Shriekon," who concludes a litany of complaints by observing, "It's a bad world, my masters, and I'm never tired of saying so."[1]

Linton's essays are the best known of her later comments on the modern woman. But she also contributed to what has come to be called New Woman fiction, a loose genre that encompasses a large number of 1890s novels about advanced women. As early as 1880, Linton had made the proto-New Woman Perdita Winstanley the heroine of *The Rebel of the Family*. By the 1890s Linton's sympathy for female characters in search of a career had significantly diminished. Two of her novels from this decade, *The One Too Many* (1894) and *In Haste and at Leisure* (1895), feature alarmingly liberated

---

[1] Of course the word "shriek" evokes "The Shrieking Sisterhood," one of Linton's earlier names for women's rights activists (and the title of her article in the 12 May 1870 *Saturday Review*).

women who exemplify the dangers to which Linton's non-fictional work called attention. Overtly, they resemble other conservative New Woman novels in their skepticism about women's expanding social role. Indeed those recent critics who have examined the genre have paid attention to these novels, if at all, as simple expressions of Linton's notorious anti-feminist views.[1] Yet Linton's antifeminism was never uncomplicated even in her essays,[2] and the discursive nature of fiction provides many opportunities for her ambivalence about women's issues to emerge. This ambivalence shows itself most obviously through a device Linton repeatedly employed in her novels: the juxtaposition of an old-fashioned girl and an unconventional girl. Nancy Fix Anderson has seen an autobiographical significance in this pattern, which mirrors Eliza's early experience as an ungainly rebel rejected by her family in favor of her conventionally feminine sister Lucy (Anderson 14). Given this personal dimension, and given Linton's admiration for "vigorous pluck" (Harraden 125), the self-willed improper woman inevitably becomes a figure of some respect despite the narrative's nominal disapproval. But the ambiguity of this contraposition is simply the most visible token of Linton's own intellectual conflicts. Deeply convinced that mid-Victorian notions of good taste were essential to the survival of civilization, she was also committed to Social Darwinian notions of social change. Emotionally drawn to stasis and intellectually devoted to evolution, Linton depicts a world whose ostensible principles are repeatedly undermined by the experience of her characters. Through their very inconsistencies, the two novels make an unsettling but uniquely interesting contribution to the genre.

---

[1] Kate Flint briefly refers to *The One Too Many* as an example of anti-New Woman fiction (305, 307). Penny Boumelha, discussing "Women and the New Fiction 1880–1900," offers an interesting reading of the self-contradictory ideology of *The Rebel of the Family* (75–77), but does not mention the later two novels. Ann Ardis, who mentions *The One Too Many* in passing, pays some attention to *In Haste* as a conservative novel in which a New Woman learns true womanliness (96–98; some of the plot details are inaccurate). Jane Eldridge Miller, Sally Ledger, and Lyn Pykett are interested in Linton exclusively as a reactionary essayist.

[2] For instance, despite the largely hysterical tone of "The Judicial Shock to Marriage," Linton also offers a sober discussion of persistent problems in marriage laws, acknowledging the value of some nineteenth-century reform legislation. Beatrice Harraden observed at her death, "I have always thought she cared more for a liberal education for women than she herself realised" ("Mrs. Lynn Linton" 125). Moreover, as best I can tell Linton showed surprisingly little agitation about pro-New Woman novelists. In 1895, for example, "The Philistine's Coming Triumph" would have provided a perfect opportunity to excoriate George Egerton, Mona Caird, Sarah Grand, and their ilk, but Linton spends only half a paragraph on "certain books written by women for men and women" (40). As her earlier comments in "Candour in English Fiction" reveal, Linton was a moderate in her support for authors' right to free expression.

Unlike other, more ideologically single-minded New Woman novels, *The One Too Many* in particular makes a progressive argument through the flimsiness of the conservative polemic Linton constructs.

In both works, Linton's evident intention is to hold outrageous young women up to scorn. *In Haste*, the more heavy-handed of the two, focuses on Phoebe Barrington, an impressionable young egotist who smartens up her dress and becomes a women's rights orator at the behest of other members of the feminist Excelsior Club. The night of her most triumphant address, on the necessity of women's domination over men, Phoebe is dismayed by the return of her husband Sherrard. He wishes to resume their marriage, which their parents had suspended due to their youth; she turns him into the street. Here Linton echoes her own 1891 essay "The Judicial Shock to Marriage," which decries the Clitheroe decision[1] as an invitation for women's selfish whims to govern married life. Like the imaginary women of her essay, Phoebe refuses to be Sherrard's wife out of vanity but then returns to burden him with her upkeep once she has run out of more attractive options. In Linton's vision of modern English life, men are bound by a code of gentlemanly conduct, while women are, as Phoebe's big speech suggests, "fettered by no limitations of sex and controlled by no restrictions of conventional authority" (I:263). In contrast to his wife, Sherrard has truly matured; now a perfect English gentleman, he feels revulsion for his miscreant wife with her heavy makeup and bleached hair. His true mate would be the demure Edith Armytage, the minister's daughter who lives near the estate he has unexpectedly inherited. Sherrard takes up the life of an ideal squire in a perfect upper-class society in which women are tasteful and retiring and men rule wisely and honorably. Except for the presence of the Excelsiorites, who temporarily invade to electioneer for one of their male supporters, this corner of England is a paradise. By the end of the novel the Excelsior Club has fallen apart and Phoebe has renounced her feminist politics. Hoping wistfully to become a good wife and mother, she seeks a reconciliation with her husband, who dutifully agrees but will never again love her.

The One Too Many, dedicated "to the sweet girls still left among us who have no part in the new revolt but are content to be dutiful, innocent, and sheltered," pays equal attention to two women. Moira West, who is "the good dear girl of a quiet English home" (2), marries the priggish aesthete Launcelot Brabazon at the behest of her mother. Brabazon treats her dismissively, and eventually begins an extended flirtation with Girton-educated Julia Belcarro.

---

[1] *Regina* v. *Jackson*, the 1891 case that established "that a writ for the restitution of conjugal rights did not entitle a husband to detain his wife against her will" (Shanley 158; see also 177–83).

Honor and convention keep Moira apart from her soulmate George Armstrong, who is a fine athletic young Englishman. The novel contrasts the passively feminine Moira with the aggressively self-willed Effie Chegwin, a Girton girl who does ineffectual charity work among the poor and is given to slangy, smoke-filled conversations with her three college chums: man-crazy Julia, pessimistic Laura Prestbury, and man-hating Carrie Mason. Effie has fallen in love with young policeman James Hartley, and she tries to advance his career by pulling strings politically and by doing a little spying in the slums. When he is wounded in a struggle with Irish terrorists whom Effie has fingered, she nurses him herself. They confess their love, and despite the disgust of her friends and family they plan to marry. Moira, who lacks the assertiveness to rein in her husband or run off with George, drowns herself in despair.

While both novels are somewhat idiosyncratic examples of New Woman fiction, they fall within the typical range of the genre. The juxtaposition of an old and a new woman—Moira with Effie, and Phoebe with Edith—was used to great effect in George Gissing's *The Odd Women* (1893), as well as in Sarah Grand's *The Heavenly Twins* (1893) and Maggie Swan's obscure *A Neglected Privilege: The Story of a Modern Woman* (1896). It is true that most novels critical of the New Woman choose to focus on a single sympathetic but misguided protagonist whose ideas change after she experiences motherhood or true love. For example, the all-too-modern Gwen Waring in Iota's *A Yellow Aster* (1894) is a victim of bad parenting who marries without affection to satisfy her scientific curiosity. But her overly intellectual mother's regression to infancy on her deathbed shocks Gwen into love for her worthy husband and newborn child. Similarly, the heroine of Percival Pickering's *A Pliable Marriage* (1895) contracts a platonic marriage only to fall passionately in love with her husband. The protagonists of Mrs. Humphry Ward's *Marcella* (1894), Mrs. Burton Harrison's *A Bachelor Maid* (1894), and Horace Bleackley's *Une Culotte* (1894) pursue independent destinies for themselves only until they recognize their undying love for the faithful men they had spurned. Here Linton provides an instructive contrast. She has limited affection for the female creatures of her imagination, and little sense that reform might be possible for New Women—Phoebe Barrington of *In Haste* perhaps comes closest with her final wistfulness for the husband's love she has thrown away. Her particular employment of polar opposites, one feminine and one mannish, one compliant and one selfish, works against character development, since she sets up her characters as immutable principles of female nature. (In contrast, Gissing's Rhoda Nunn and Monica Widdowson undergo some change by encountering their complementary opposite.) Unlike the autobiographical fiction of Sarah Grand or George Egerton, Linton's work resists reader identification with her female protagonists. Her narrative voice hands down severe judgments, or at best bestows a lofty seal of approval. Anderson has shrewdly observed that, unlike other antifeminist women, Linton lacks any sense of fellow-feeling with her subjects: "The conventional women, however much they denigrated women, transmitted a sense of female identity, whereas Eliza always seemed to distance herself from her targets, and referred to women as 'they' rather than 'we'" (131).[1] So, in the strength of her hatred for New Women, Linton might seem to be an outlier among New Woman novelists. Still, Elizabeth Robins's *George Mandeville's Husband* (1894) and George Moore's *Celibates* (1895) share Linton's intense loathing for unworthy female protagonists. George Mandeville, a would-be George Eliot, is a heartless and physically disgusting woman who is responsible for the death of her saintly daughter; Mildred Lawson (in the first story of *Celibates*) is a spiritually empty, undersexed woman who longs vainly to be a genius. As with Phoebe Barrington, there is no redemption for Robins's or Moore's heroines; they are figures of contempt.[2] While Linton's attitude to her subject is atypical, it is certainly not unique.

Yet there seems to have been some general agreement among contemporary observers that Linton had become extreme in her essays and in her fiction. Anderson has noted that "Eliza's attacks [on the New Woman] were so distorted and unrealistic as to be ridiculous, and evoked reactive sympathy for her targets" (212). Even Linton's sympathetic first biographer would suggest that *In Haste* (which he finds generally wholesome) might have gone too far: "There is much in the book that is unpleasant and that jars like grit between the teeth [...]" (Layard 316). At her death, it is true, Walter Besant published a poem in *Queen* commending her anti-feminist struggle (Anderson 231). But an obituary article in the *Daily Telegraph*, while emphasizing her importance as an essayist, singled out *The One Too Many* for unfavorable notice for its problematic treatment of women's colleges: "[S]he betrayed a good deal of ignorance of their real conditions of existence, and perhaps may be held to have pushed the rights of caricature too far." Certainly college-educated women, including Linton's friend Beatrice Harraden, took offense (Layard 301–2). One of the outraged letters that poured into the offices of the *Lady's Pictorial* (where the novel was initially serialized) asked, "[C]an it be considered fair to depict purely imaginary and entirely offensive characters as embodying the results of

---

[1]   Deborah Meem has interestingly noted that Linton almost always employed a male persona in her writing, but briefly dropped the mask in an 1898 letter to her sister Lucy: "at last, six months before her death, the private female self is visible" (540). For the most part Linton clearly wished to conceal this self.

[2]   Miller reads "Mildred Lawson" differently, as "a condemnation of the Victorian feminine ideal" (24). Unlike Miller, I do not see Mildred as a victim of her "Victorian upbringing," but as a woman whose innate vanity is released by advanced ideas about women.

the training and teaching given at a well-known and existing institution?" (Layard 291). At the time of its initial publication, *The One Too Many* garnered mixed reviews. Readers acknowledged Linton's craftsmanship, and some called her novel "powerful and remarkable" or "delightful." But others criticized her exaggeration; George Saintsbury in the *Academy*, among others, recognized that her "two chief sets of characters [...] draw [...] an apparently opposed moral."[1] *In Haste* received much more negative assessments, and reviewers implied that Linton's passionate antifeminism was out of control. The *Bookman* gently theorized that "perhaps she hates too bitterly to be a good satirist and an effective censor" (176); the *Scotsman* more directly suggested that her novel was "a gross and truculent caricature, miles outside of all canons of art and ordinary good taste [...]." And the *Times* echoed *Punch*'s word choice: "There is such a fault as shrieking against shriekers [...]."[2]

If Linton received more pointed criticism, by and large, than the other novelists I have mentioned above, it is probably because of her affinity for wild exaggeration in the details that make up the texture of a realistic novel.[3] For many readers, these touches were evidently jarring; as we have seen, for college-educated women the specifics of *The One Too Many* were deeply offensive. But clearly even those not personally touched by any of her attacks found that Linton had violated "ordinary good taste." Here the reviews were identifying a crucial element of her literary approach. For Linton, ironically enough, is violating good taste to reveal the importance of good taste. Her obsession with ugliness of speech and dress reflects her conviction that a great deal is at stake in questions of aesthetics. Her penchant for overkill in making her point is clear in an early scene between Effie and her cousin George:

> "Well," said George, when he entered; "and how are you?"
> "Prime," said Effie; "how are you?"
> "All right," said George.
> "I see you are—fit as a fiddle," she returned. "Have one?" she added, handing him her cigarette case.

---

[1] For her craftsmanship, see especially reviews in the *Times* and *Academy*. The *Daily Telegraph* found the book "powerful and remarkable," while the *Scotsman* judged it to be "delightful." Criticisms of Linton's exaggeration can be found in *Academy* and *Spectator*, while the *Times*, *Athenæum*, and *Spectator* noted the novel's self-undermining quality.

[2] Negative reviews of *In Haste* also appeared in *Academy*, *Daily Telegraph*, *Athenæum*, and *Spectator*.

[3] There were of course popular novels even more vituperative and extravagant than Linton's. Marie Corelli's *The Sorrows of Satan* (1895) contains astonishingly melodramatic fulminations against New Woman novelists, some of them from the lips of Satan himself. But Corelli, to her fury, was not taken seriously by critics; Linton was.

"Thanks awfully," he answered; "but I prefer a cigar."

"So do I," said Effie; "and I have some glorious fellows."

Going to an inlaid cupboard on slender legs, which was her cigar store, she took out a light-brown bundle which she put up to her face as lovingly as another girl would have half-caressed, half-smelt a rose. "These are beauties," she said, laughing; "reserved for my special pals." (41–42)

The relentlessness of Effie's slang here is striking (no sentence of hers is free from it), and George's reliance on standard English strengthens the effect. In this as in much else, Linton seems not to know when she should quit. The antiheroine of In Haste sinks even lower than Effie as she speaks contemptuously of her absent husband to his mother: "Oh yes, I know he is awful spoons on me, and all that. But he will have to see things in a different light when he comes [...] And I don't care a twopenny damn—you know a twopenny damn is classical, and proved quite innocent—for that old oofbird he has got hold of" (I:234). But Phoebe's choice of costume for the night of her greatest oratorical success provides one of her greatest offenses against good taste. And Linton's description of her appearance, with its mixture of overwrought hatred and erotic excitement, offers a similarly over-the-top experience for readers:

Her gown was of soft, flesh-coloured silken stuff, fitting as perfectly as if it had been a second skin, so that you scarcely knew which was flesh and which was silken stuff, and where the one ended and the other began. Not an ornament of any kind broke the lines which this "liquefaction of her clothes" expressed as clearly as if she had been dressed in the North-girl's famous net. Arms, neck, and bust were bare, and gleaming white and warm in the strong yet artistically-shaded light thrown on to the platform. (I:259–60)

The description continues along the same lines with descriptions of the speaker's hair, eyes, mouth, and voice.

Even when Linton is not operating at highest pitch, she shows a persistent concern with her characters' sense of style. Although Effie Chegwin is not wholly without style—"She dressed well, if somewhat too close to masculine severity for perfect taste" (40), Linton notes that her great failure is an aesthetic one: "Not bold nor bad she had yet lost that ineffable something which gives womankind its essential charm, endows it with its special power, and throws over it, as it were, a veil of mystic beauty" (41). Moira, in contrast, is "the very perfection of a beautiful and refined, tender and undeviating womanhood [...]" (80). *In Haste* describes Mrs. Ada Norman, one of the more sympathetic Excelsiorites, as notably careless in her personal appearance: "Her flaxen hair was always falling loose from its random and undecided fastenings. Her bonnet was generally half off her head; her gowns were loose and fluffy [...]" (I:87). Yet even worse are her compatriots, who cultivate a tastelessly seductive beauty. "They were generally pretty and always supremely well dressed; and they looked of the kind to lead men astray by their personal witcheries, rather than to dominate them by their intellectual superiority or to elevate them by their spiritual supremacy" (I:71). Under their tutelage Phoebe becomes the overdressed, cosmetically enhanced, bleached-blonde vixen Linton loves to hate. And Edith Armytage stands in striking contrast as a quietly lovely woman who, unlike Phoebe, has not had her hair permed.

Linton would elsewhere associate emancipated women's aesthetic failures with a pernicious lessening in sex distinctions that would lead to female domination and male weakness. A column in the *St. James's Budget* from 1894 strikes the characteristic note:

The most salient characteristic of the New Woman is her want of good taste in her determined obliteration of all lines of distinction between herself and man. [...] The women are to be supreme [...]. The grand and active and virile virtues are to give place to the gentler and more negative. ("The New Woman")

Among the Excelsiorites of *In Haste*, one of the most contemptible to Linton is the Honourable Constance Casey, who "dressed so much like a man that once the duenna of the ladies' room of a certain railway station hastily ordered her out of the place, under the belief that she was one of the forbidden sex" (I:80).[1] The Girton girls of *The One Too Many*, we are repeatedly told, are like

---

[1] Constance Casey, who takes a notably amorous attitude to young women, is also the novel's most readily identifiable lesbian. She and the other Excelsiorites evoke an earlier Linton character, Bell Blount of *The Rebel of the Family*, a feminist separatist who has taken another woman as her wife; despite the unconventionality of Bell's life and beliefs, it is her loud clothing and aggressive manner that Linton most condemns. (In a characteristic detail, the novel insists upon Bell's lamentable absence of taste in interior design.) Meem has identified *In Haste*'s notion of New Women as a "third sex" as an indication of Linton's acquaintance with the literature of homosexuality. For Meem, the women of the Excelsior Club are protolesbians who must be vanquished because of Linton's troubled relationship with her own repressed lesbianism. In this novel and others, "only by tortured indirection can Linton own her desire" (559). I note below that Linton wishes to communicate revulsion from advanced women, but surely her description of Phoebe's outfit also communicates the author's own erotic fascination with showy women.

bad imitation men. "These four were in a sense like boys; and even Laura Prestbury might stand as the analogue of one of those 'mother's darlings' who are like pots that have gone astray in the baking" (53). Yet there is something else at work in the novels. Effie's use of slang does not make her resemble the men in *The One Too Many*; as I have observed, her indisputably manly cousin conspicuously avoids neologisms. And surely Phoebe's near-Godivan turn at the podium does not create any confusion about whether she is a man. Similarly, by and large Linton does not create men who have been emasculated by domineering women: men such as James Hartley, Armand Norris, and Captain Norman emerge from their association with advanced women with their masculine dignity intact. Curiously enough, Linton does little to dramatize the supposedly horrific consequences of women's emancipation; she puts forth a great deal of smoke with very little fire. Despite her professed concern with epicene creatures and cultural effeminacy, what ultimately seems most at stake in the question of taste is simply aesthetics. Through her extravagant exaggerations she wishes to create in her reader the same visceral revulsion she feels from women who violate her standards of tastefulness. Linton seems convinced that bad taste reveals a deeper failure, but does not conclusively demonstrate what that might be.

Linton herself seems at least subliminally aware that she is on shaky ground. Her characterization of Launcelot Brabazon in *The One Too Many* actively undermines her apparent equation of tasteful self-presentation and moral worth. Brabazon is from his introduction an example of aesthetic excess: "he was as careful of his personal appearance as the most notorious masher of them all; and he dressed with so much elegance—such a very opulence of regard for taste and fit—as might seem to mean the admiration of women. He curled his hair and waxed his moustache; used all the new appliances for his nails and hands [...]" (10). Admiring Moira for her style of beauty rather than her character, he makes her into a kind of doll as he selects the items for her trousseau. "He decided what colours she should wear; and certain fabrics were tabooed as certain fashions were forbidden" (73). In his attention to fashion, Linton sees an essential unmanliness that finds its clearest expression on their wedding day, when he uses their first moments alone to critique her appearance and when he makes a sexless response to her involuntary embrace during a thunderstorm: "Do not be foolish, my dear Moira [...]. You will crush your hat and ruffle your hair and make yourself unsightly" (98).

For Linton, Brabazon's concern with matters she considers the province of women impeaches his character as a man. Yet he is a more ambiguous figure than this over-nicety might suggest. He is, for one thing, as insistent on his right to rule his wife as any old-fashioned manly man. And he does in fact have the excellent taste that Linton values: the imitation Medici wedding-dress he commissions for Moira suits her superbly. Linton grants that at least one of his judgments is sound: "Effie offended all his ideas of good taste and fine breeding, in which, perhaps, he was not so far to blame [...]" (89). And his strictures on the morality of appearances, evidently meant to be the "nonsense" Moira deems it, fall fairly close to Linton's own ideas:

> "The proper choice of colours so as to be in harmony with the colouring of the person, and the proper fashion of a garment so as to be in harmony with its material, are questions of more importance than appear on the face of things," said Mr. Brabazon with his professorial air. "This sense of harmony, my dear Moira, runs through all life and is not confined to one thing only. In the proper choice of colour, and the proper adjustment of material with form, we see more than the educated artistry of taste—we see the evidence of moral perspicacity and spiritual refinement." (177)

Exaggerated as this is, it is not so different from Linton's conviction that the gaudy dress of the Excelsiorites betrays the meretriciousness of their souls. And, in an exceptionally interesting passage, Linton's narrative judgments blend almost seamlessly into Brabazon's judgment. The West and Chegwin families meet for the first time in years at a railway station.

> What a contrast [the two girls] made as they now stood together on the platform [...]! Moira, tall, fair, graceful, timid [...]; Effie, square in her forms, with crisp black hair and mannish movements, absolutely self-confident, absolutely fearless and unabashed, the bloom all gone both physically and morally, and in its place that unmistakable hardness with which experience touches the face and eyes, after it has moulded the heart and mind. Moira, apparently full of latent possibilities and undeveloped poetry; Effie, keen, observant, alive, alert, scientific, not poetic, [...] contemptuous of the past and eagerly rushing to meet the future [...].
>
> And then their dress—this, too, was as widely different as all the rest. Moira was dressed in some soft clinging stuff [...] [that] went to perfection with her golden hair [...]. While Effie—but to be sure she was in travelling costume, so that a certain severity was to be looked for and up to a given point was in good taste. But, Mr. Brabazon thought as he scanned the new arrivals [...] that even travel did not excuse that hideous little jockey-cap [...]. (79–80)

Here the narrator has made a comparison between the women that, if not wholly disparaging of Effie, is fairly critical. Brabazon is brought in at this point to two ends: to provide expert testimony on Effie's outfit, and to intensify the narrator's criticism. Admittedly an extreme aesthete, he has the license to offer the extremely negative remarks from which the narrator has conscientiously drawn back. (The break in the sentence after "While Effie—" is telling; the narrator is trying to be painfully fair.) Brabazon here is not so much, as he sometimes appears in his tyrannical dealings with Moira, the narrative's villain as its hatchet man. He is a pivotal figure for *The One Too Many*, embodying at once a domestic injustice Linton finds reprehensible and an aesthetic sensibility she endorses. His character helps destabilize Linton's argument for aesthetics. Ultimately his mistreatment of Moira is the most salient aspect of his character, and his commitment to good taste cannot help but compromise taste itself as a virtue.

Brabazon also plays a significant role as *The One Too Many* explores an issue that ultimately pits Linton's affinity for the status quo against her Social Darwinism. Linton's work shows an ongoing interest in the relationship between appearance and reality. One of her bugbears is "relative values," a relativism that she associates with the modern world and that holds that the appearance of a thing may not reflect its true nature. In conversation with Lady Oldenshaw, Julia Belcarro identifies "relative values" as one of her subjects at Girton; the sensible older woman, only partly understanding her, remarks meaningly that "the one thing no one can afford to neglect is appearances" (300).[1] With Brabazon this subject takes an intriguingly semiotic turn. While talking to Laura Prestbury and Julia Belcarro, he takes exception to Julia's use of the word "jolly," observing that superior people avoid such terms:

> "What does it signify?" drawled Laura; "words are only symbols at the best. If we say 'awfully jolly,' and you merely 'pleasant,' we both mean the same thing, and the special word used to express our thought does not count."
>
> "A charming piece of dialectics," said Mr. Brabazon; "but not touching the esoteric sense—not laying bare the core of the thought.

---

[1] Phoebe Barrington also seems to be an adherent of relativism. Her mother's last word, "bad," is a judgment on Phoebe, but Phoebe makes her own interpretation: "'Her mind was quite gone,' said Phoebe to the caretaker; and the caretaker, understanding relative values, said; 'Yes, quite gone, ma'am.' But she thought to herself—'clearer than it has ever been since I have had charge of her!'" (II:255).

There are more things in heaven and earth than our philosophy can
fathom, and the intrinsic power of words is one of them."

"Not intrinsic," said Laura; "only suggestive." (239)

This exchange indicates that one aspect of modern relativism is skepticism
about the relationship of sign and signifier. Brabazon again becomes a vehicle for Linton's ambivalence. On the one hand, his rejection of the doctrine
that symbol-systems are arbitrary fits well with Linton's distaste for slang. On
the other hand, even beyond his offensive pomposity, his mystification of "the
intrinsic power of words" clashes with her own resolutely agnostic materialism.

Linton reveals a similar anxiety about signs in her repeated reference to
James Hartley by his official police designation, "Policeman 300 X."
Presumably this number provides a degrading reminder of his lower-class
status—his position as a cog within a bureaucratic apparatus—and therefore
his unfitness to marry Effie. But Hartley's alias does not adequately define
him. The narrator assures us that he has "the double nature of heroism
brightened with poetic feeling. He was essentially a gentleman in all that
constitutes true gentlehood" (69). By giving James a noble character, Linton
both minimizes the disgrace of Effie's prospective union with him and calls
into question conventional notions of class status. Despite the ambiguous
autobiographical issues in this relationship,[1] Linton evidently means us to
feel that Effie is being foolish and willful in her choice. But her own signals

---

[1] It is suggestive to note resemblances between this marriage and Linton's own. Like Effie,
Linton married a Cumbrian man socially inferior to herself and had to deal with ostracism
from some of her friends. Conceivably Linton could be offering a cautionary tale based
on her own experience in a marriage of two temperamentally unsuited people. But if this
is the case, then it is unclear why Linton does not provide more signals that James and
Effie are personally (rather than socially) unsuited. On the other hand, one might argue
that Linton is implying that Effie's choice is one that an intelligent young woman might
reasonably make. If Linton is indeed conscious of the autobiographical echoes here, she
has not succeeded in making use of them to support any argument.

   The One Too Many also offers remarkable parallels to the even more strongly autobiographical Rebel of the Family. The later novel represents a reshuffling of many important
elements of the earlier novel: a rich, tyrannical middle-aged man who marries a much
younger woman (in Rebel, Benjamin Brocklebank); a heartless, socially conscious mother
(Mrs. Winstanley); a pretty girl with no moral courage (Eva Winstanley); and an advanced
young woman (Perdita Winstanley) who marries a noble working-class man (Leslie
Crawford) against her family's wishes. In Rebel, however, Linton shows a consistent sympathy for her awkward, democratic, essentially feminist heroine, who possesses virtues her
ignorantly conventional family cannot appreciate. By The One Too Many, of course, Linton
has shifted her political ground considerably to the right. Her displacement of familiar
issues from a progressive to a conservative context may help account for the ideological
incoherence of the later novel.

about this marriage are ambiguous; appearances here may have no value, and the ominous police number may in fact have no useful meaning.

It should be obvious why the issue of signs is so crucial to Linton's evaluation of New Women. If there is something timeless about a cultural sign, whether it be in language or dress or behavior, if it infallibly points to a particular psychological or moral state, then signs can be the basis for judgments of the individuals who employ them. Deviations from established convention can be legitimately castigated as antisocial or even immoral. So, for Linton to grant that signs are arbitrary or that manners change would be to undermine her condemnation of the Excelsiorites of *In Haste* and the Girton girls of *The One Too Many*. If women's behavior is not set in stone by some universal moral law, then the studies and word choice and even tobacco use of young women might represent harmless variations consistent with virtuous conduct. As a staunch opponent of change in women's roles, and as the woman Herbert Spencer termed an infallible "Grundyometer" (Anderson 197), Linton felt great devotion to old-fashioned manners. But Linton also felt the pull of evolutionary models of social development.

Occasionally Linton's writings suggest that manners and opinions inevitably change over time. In a letter to a great-niece in 1884, she asserted her preference for science over religious belief, observing that "the inner convictions of individuals [...] change with climate, creed, civilisation, age, education. But nature is ever the same, and the truths of science are eternal" (Layard 243). A *St. James's Budget* column entitled "Between Optimism and Despair" concludes with advice that she might have advantageously taken herself: "We must have changes in our orderings of society, as the earth itself changes with the years; and to welcome the coming and speed the parting—when inevitable—is better business than to hold on to dissolution [...]." Her recognition of social evolution inevitably compromises her insistence on the maintenance of conventional standards. In a letter to the editor of the *Daily Graphic*, she attempted, not altogether successfully, to reconcile the inconsistencies of her positions.

The illustration you gave on 2nd March of the lady footballers at play, is one to make all but the most advanced of the sexless men and unsexed women who head this disastrous movement pause in dismay at the lengths to which it has gone. Has, indeed, all sense of fitness [...] left these misguided girls and women [...]? Say that modesty is conditional to the age and country; still, the sentiment is intrinsic if the manifestations vary. The woman who violates the canons of modesty of her own times is as reprehensible as if those canons were as essential as the elementary crimes and obligations of organised society. The Spartan girls ran their races naked and were not ashamed. What was accepted then as blameless would be a police offence now. [...] These boy-girls [...] sin against the laws of modesty in force at the present day [...]. (Layard 149)

Linton's argument for the immodesty of women's football founders on her acknowledgment that notions of modesty are historically specific. If notions of modesty change over time, then there must inevitably be moments when one system gives way to another—when a person falls afoul of a dying standard but not a nascent standard. But here Linton does not face the possibility that her standards are simply outdated.

Linton does hint at such a recognition in a part of the Moira-Effie comparison not quoted above: "They were as it might have been the two symbols of the ideal womanhood cherished in the past but dying out in the present, and of the new creation rising strong and sturdy from the more delicate, more fragrant ashes" (80). Indeed, another column in the *St. James's Budget* developed this notion of the survival of the fittest still more explicitly:

> The New Woman [...] will strangle the Old Ideal of reticence and dutifulness and modesty, unless that Old Ideal be the stronger of the two. There has always been this fight and this surrender. The New Woman, with her selfishness and want of Conscience, is trying conclusions with the better forms of modern womanhood, just as these killed the household drudge who could do nothing but suckle fools and chronicle small beer [...]. Abstract justice exists on paper only; and the race *is* to the swift as the battle is to the strong. ("The Rex Nemorum")

Linton's sneaking suspicion that New Women are the fittest, the inevitable victors in the cultural struggle for survival, undercuts her strident arguments against changes in manners.

The One Too Many establishes this self-sabotage most effectively. The narrative identifies the nearest proponent of Linton's own views as a priggish tyrant who hounds his vulnerable wife to her suicide. Moira, the girl who best exemplifies Linton's feminine ideal, is, in her creator's own confession to a reader, "a weak, pathetic, crushed, and invertebrate creature" (Layard 294).[1] Effie, the

---

[1] "Invertebrate" and "mollusc" are favorite Lintonian terms of abuse. Beyond their obvious signification of squishiness, these words interestingly suggest evolutionarily lower forms of life. This quotation comes from a letter of January 1894 to Alyce Bagram. In the same letter, Linton ingenuously professes shock that anyone would have taken Moira as a model: "Because I inscribed the book to all nice girls, I had no thought that any one would take Moira to be one, but that they would take the Girton girls as the thing to avoid. I must say this—the incapacity for fair judgment in the ordinary woman is the most distressing thing about her" (Layard 294). Linton seems interestingly blind to what Anderson has called her fundamental "contempt" for the "womanly woman" (130).

Girton girl who embodies all that Linton deprecates—women's higher education, aggressiveness, mannish behavior—also represents much that she values—vitality, strength, and optimism. Effie earns the narrator's grudging respect for her kindness to Moira and her courage in carrying out her marriage to James Hartley, and about halfway through the novel, Linton even calls Effie "that not unamiable insurgent whom all people condemned and no one could help liking" (222). By the end of the novel Linton seems to have demonstrated that the two choices open to women in British society are rebellion or suicide. Under the circumstances, despite Moira's superior tastefulness, Effie cannot help but seem the superior role model for young women. Effie is fitter for life than Moira, and so she triumphs where Moira fails.

In Haste paints a rather different picture, in which New Womanhood is a less adaptive form of behavior. But again Linton fails to dramatize the victory of good taste; once again, her story's use of Social Darwinian ideas destabilizes her official program. For once, Linton has created a positive ideal in Sherrard, Phoebe's long-suffering husband. As a personification of just male power, unlike Launcelot Brabazon, he apparently offers an attractive alternative to Wild Womanhood. Yet even here Linton manages to create a subversive undercurrent to her ostensible message. Although the novel suggests that only women's vanity stands between themselves and happiness, there is a surprising moment at the very end of Volume I that offers an entirely different view of power relations between the sexes. In this short scene, a lower-class couple and a male friend walk home from hearing Phoebe's most successful oration. The woman, Carrie, has been inspired by the speech to assert the rights of women to freedom and self-expression. But her brutish husband Tom silences her with the threat of physical force. Linton explicates the scene with a mixture of fatalism and sympathy: "Now, vote or no vote, could poor Carrie have held her own against this *ultima ratio* of all life—this superiority of brute force and muscular strength? [...] These are the sorrows of life which must perforce be borne [...]. We cannot change the eternal law of life. Weakness must submit to strength [...]" (I:273–74). While this moralizing is consistent with her view that men are evolutionarily superior (Anderson 127), it is a dramatic shifting of ground within this particular novel. Acknowledging for once that men could mistreat women, Linton implicitly grants the possibility that the Excelsior women might have some legitimate grounds for their political positions. While denying the potential for improvement, she reveals the need for change.

This is the only glimpse of working-class life in this novel, and it reveals more than simply Linton's snobbishness. For Linton, lower-class men are not an entirely different species from gentlemen—gentlemen simply have more fully developed their capacity for self-control. Phoebe Barrington's moment of truth comes when she learns that Armand Norris, a man whom she had trusted as a feminist sympathizer, has schemed against her virtue. Linton comments on the feelings "a naturally 'sheltered woman'" has at such a moment:

> Then she feels her helplessness, and the need she and all her sex have of the protection of men from the brutality of men. Then she realizes the force of this so-called equality of the sexes, and the bitter results of trusting women to themselves for their own safety and defence-work. (III:250)

Linton's very next book, *Dulcie Everton*, elaborated on the importance of cultivation for suppressing the violence that seems to be innate in masculinity. Elaine, the heartless vamp who brings misery to the eponymous heroine, overreaches herself when she flirts with young poet Percy Merritt. As the narrator observes:

> The most dangerous person with whom a woman can [romantically intrigue] [...] is a man who, with strong passions, absolute sincerity and independent views, is not [...] a "gentleman." As he has never graduated in the school of conventional propriety, he refuses to be influenced by social considerations. [...] [H]e ignores the fine distinctions made by gentleman between the actions of men and those of women—between the necessities of the social law and those of elemental humanity—but lumps them all in one basket, and calls the amalgam the New Morality. He reduces all things to their rudiments [...]. (II:133–34)

Ultimately the rudimentary Percy, spurned by Elaine, kills both her and himself. Up to this point Elaine, like Phoebe, has been enormously successful in manipulating men with her sexual allure; but her success is not enduring. What *Dulcie Everton* and *In Haste and at Leisure* share is a lurking suspicion that no woman, however powerful, can ever overwhelm the potential force of male violence. As Linton moralizes about Carrie's feminist self-assertion, "With gentleness she might do better, as then his coarse temper [...] would have no outside cause of irritation" (I:273). Even one of her essays concludes with a comparable warning, appealing for once to the divine (with her, probably shorthand for the laws of nature): "after all, the strong right arm is the *ultima ratio*, and God will have it so; and when men found, as they would, that they were outnumbered, outvoted, and politically nullified, they would soon have recourse to that ultimate appeal—and the last state of women would be worse than their first" ("Politicians" 88). Unlike her usual brief for feminine submission, which argues on aesthetic and moral grounds, this is a pragmatic argument from fear. Phoebe must return to her husband because her choices in patriarchal society are so limited: his unloving civility is preferable to Norris's brutal exploitation. She does acquire some feeling for her husband and child. But her decision is hardly the result of any joyous rediscovery of feminine instinct; it is timid, half-unwilling submission to his superior strength.

Nominally *In Haste* is a straightforward celebration of the patriarchal squirearchy against which the Excelsior Club tastelessly fights. But, as in *The One Too Many*, Linton's belief in brute fitness creates confusion. She proclaims two opposed truths: modern women have successfully plotted to overpower men; women can never overpower men and so must resign themselves to subordinate status. Unlike *The One Too Many*, this novel does not foresee the victory of New Women, in part because Linton has appropriated Social Darwinism's faith in physical force without its sense of social change. But it does dramatize the dangers of that masculine power that Linton elsewhere idealizes. She has at least made intelligible the feminist political struggle that she disdains.

Linton's unique contribution to the New Woman novel lies in the continuous intellectual self-immolation that reveals the instability of her anti-feminist ideology. The inconsistency between Linton's life and her work has always been obvious. Herself an advanced woman in her youth, she was happy to burn the bridge she herself had crossed. It is hard to avoid the impression of consummate hypocrisy her writings sometimes give. But it seems to me that Linton's work provides proof that she was a woman at least partly unknown to herself. Her nominal loyalties are not in complete control of the operation of her imagination.[1] Wishing to support the old-fashioned girl in *The One Too Many*, she produced a compelling argument for rebellious New Womanhood. Seeking to blast the bad taste of women's rights orators, she demonstrated the irrelevance of taste and the tyranny of patriarchal power. From novel to novel there is even inconsistency in the use of her conflicting ideologies: the Social Darwinism that ensures Effie's success definitively quashes Phoebe's feminism. The constant here is Linton's ambivalence about power, which is at once fascinating and dangerous whether wielded by self-assertive women or tyrannical men.

There are certain advantages to Linton's self-sabotage for today's feminist reader. Unlike many of the New Woman novels, Linton has not created

---

[1]   Anderson notes that Linton "apparently made only one draft of her articles, with occasional scratch-outs and insertions" (139). Perhaps this method of writing allowed few opportunities for self-censorship that might have smoothed out inconsistencies.

propaganda: the argument for feminism keeps glinting through the smoke of her furious execrations. Novels such as *George Mandeville's Husband* (on the conservative side) or Mona Caird's *The Daughters of Danaus* (on the radical side) offer very little space for the active participation of the reader. Each novel's case is unimpeachable, providing little sense of how English society could be of two minds on the issue of women's rights. Each novel is ready-made for enthusiastic acceptance or rejection. Particularly in *The One Too Many*, Linton has created a self-subverting fiction that encourages readers to take an active role in disentangling the ostensible ideology from the manifest evidence set before them. To work through Linton's fiction is to understand the painful difficulties of cultural change. And to work through *The One Too Many* is to achieve a hard-won feminist victory. The only reactionary path through *The One Too Many* leads to Moira's suicide, an action taken in despair at the intractability of a world Effie has proven to be malleable. The only way to make the novel intelligible is to embrace advanced thinking, whatever tasteless talk and behavior may accompany it. *The One Too Many* winds up as a powerful endorsement of the New Woman, and impressive testimony to the unconscious feminism of a notorious antifeminist.

Works Cited

Anderson, Nancy Fix. *Woman against Women in Victorian England: A Life of Eliza Lynn Linton*. Bloomington: Indiana UP, 1987.

Ardis, Ann L. *New Women, New Novels: Feminism and Early Modernism*. New Brunswick: Rutgers UP, 1990.

Boumelha, Penny. *Thomas Hardy and Women: Sexual Ideology and Narrative Form*. 1982. Madison: U of Wisconsin P, 1985.

"Death of Mrs. Lynn Linton." *Daily Telegraph* 16 July 1898: 7. [Possibly by W.L. Courtney, as its judgment of *The One Too Many* resembles that of his column of 9 Feb. 1894.]

Flint, Kate. *The Woman Reader: 1837–1914*. Oxford: Clarendon, 1993.

Harraden, Beatrice. "Mrs. Lynn Linton." *Bookman* 14 (Aug. 1898): 124–25.

Layard, George Somes. *Mrs. Lynn Linton: Her Life, Letters, and Opinions*. London: Methuen, 1901.

Ledger, Sally. *The New Woman: Fiction and Feminism at the fin de siècle*. Manchester: Manchester UP, 1997.

Linton, Eliza Lynn. "Between Despair and Optimism." *St. James's Budget*, 19 Oct. 1894: 3.

———. "Candour in English Fiction. II." *New Review*, 2 (Jan. 1890): 10–14.

———. *Dulcie Everton*. 2 vols. London: Chatto & Windus, 1896.

———. *In Haste and at Leisure*. 3 vols. London: Heinemann, 1895.

———. "The Judicial Shock to Marriage." *Nineteenth Century*, 29 (May 1891): 691–700.

———. "The New Woman." *St. James's Budget*, 6 July 1894: 3.

———. *The One Too Many*. Chicago: F. Tennyson Neely, 1894.

———. "The Partisans of the Wild Women." *Nineteenth Century*, 31 (Apr. 1892): 455–64.

———. "The Philistine's Coming Triumph." *National Review*, 26 (Sept. 1895): 40–49.

———. "The Rex Nemorum." *St. James's Budget*, 10 Aug. 1894: 3.

———. "The Wild Women as Politicians." *Nineteenth Century*, 30 (July 1891): 79–88.

———. "The Wild Women as Social Insurgents." *Nineteenth Century*, 30 (Oct. 1891): 596–605.

Meem, Deborah T. "Eliza Lynn Linton and the Rise of Lesbian Consciousness." *Journal of the History of Sexuality*, 7 (1997): 537–60.

Miller, Jane Eldridge. *Rebel Women: Feminism, Modernism and the Edwardian Novel*. London: Virago, 1994.

Pykett, Lyn. *The 'Improper' Feminine: The Women's Sensation Novel and the New Woman Writing*. London: Routledge, 1992.

Rev. of *In Haste and at Leisure*. *Athenæum*, 30 Mar. 1895: 405.

Rev. of *In Haste and at Leisure*. *Bookman*, 8 (Sept. 1895): 175–76.

Rev. of *In Haste and at Leisure*. *Daily Telegraph*, 22 Mar. 1895: 6.

Rev. of *In Haste and at Leisure*. *Scotsman*, 11 Mar. 1895: 3.

Rev. of *In Haste and at Leisure*. *Spectator*, 27 Apr. 1895: 584.

Rev. of *In Haste and at Leisure*. *The Times*, 28 Sept. 1895: 11.

Rev. of *The One Too Many*. *Athenæum*, 17 Mar. 1894: 342.

Rev. of *The One Too Many*. *Daily Telegraph*, 9 Feb. 1894: 6.

Rev. of *The One Too Many*. *Scotsman*, 12 Feb. 1894: 3.

Rev. of *The One Too Many*. *Spectator*, 31 Mar. 1894: 443–44.

Rev. of *The One Too Many*. *The Times*, 27 Mar. 1894: 9.

Saintsbury, George. Rev. of *The One Too Many*. *Academy*, 14 Apr. 1894: 305.

Shanley, Mary Lyndon. *Feminism, Marriage, and the Law in Victorian England, 1850–1895*. Princeton: Princeton UP, 1989.

"That Advanced Woman!" *Punch*, 22 Sept. 1894: 142.

Wallace, William. Rev. of *In Haste and at Leisure*. *Academy*, 30 Mar. 1895: 273.

Appendix F: Eliza Lynn Linton and the Canon

Valerie Sanders
Hull University

> At best, Mrs Linton's novels can be read today only with clinical curiosity to see *how* she managed to capture a public in spite of a conspicuous lack of creative ability. (Colby 36)

Eliza Lynn Linton has remained something of a curious phenomenon in literary history. Like Harriet Martineau earlier in the century, she became a household name, largely through the notoriety of one series (the "Girl of the Period" articles which began in the *Saturday Review* in 1868); then, by the time of her death in 1898, people were already reviewing her achievements as if she were a relic from a bygone age. The *Athenaeum*, for example, agreed she was a successful essayist, but decided she had "no innate talent for fiction, for she was no judge nor observer of character, and she had no ability for creating lively personages"(132); "her work, says your critic, is forgotten; she leaves nothing that will endure," the *Pall Mall Gazette* summarized.[1] A century after her death, her novels are out of print, women's presses give her a wide berth, and feminist scholars recoil from her strident anti-feminism. Her apparently hostile views of women make her difficult to assimilate into a history of "forgotten, but worthy" nineteenth-century women writers, such as Margaret Oliphant, Mrs. Humphry Ward, or Charlotte M. Yonge, whose reputations are currently enjoying a revival.[2] Although each of these novelists has been associated with anti-feminist attitudes, their work is sufficiently ambiguous to permit of ideologically more congenial readings than Linton's, and there have been Virago reprints of several of their novels.[3] On the other hand, Linton's

---

[1]   The *Athenaeum*, 23 July 1898, p. 132; Sidney Low in the *Pall Mall Gazette* cited by *The Academy Supplement*, 30 July 1898, p. 108.

[2]   John Sutherland's acclaimed biography of Mrs. Humphry Ward, *Mrs. Humphrey Ward: Eminent Victorian, Pre-eminent Edwardian* (1990), revived interest in her, as did Elisabeth Jay's of Margaret Oliphant, *Mrs. Oliphant: A Literary Life*, (1995), both published by the Clarendon Press. My own *Eve's Renegades: Victorian Anti-Feminist Women Novelists* (London and Basingstoke: Macmillan, 1996) includes Linton in the group.

[3]   For instance, of Yonge's *The Daisy Chain* (1988) and *The Clever Woman of the Family* (1985); Oliphant's *Miss Marjoribanks* (1987), *The Rector and the Doctor's Family* (1986), *Salem Chapel* (1986), *Phoebe Junior* (1986), and *The Perpetual Curate* (1987), while Alan Sutton reprinted *The Curate in Charge* (1987). Ward's *Marcella* was published by Virago (1984) and Broadview (2002), while Penguin reissued *Helbeck of Bannisdale* (1983) and World's Classics *Robert Elsmere* (1987).

star is clearly rising. Nancy Fix Anderson's biography (1987) presented a more sympathetic picture of Linton's complex psychological history than had been available before; while the centenary of her death was marked by a special session at the 1998 Modern Language Association convention in San Francisco, of which this book is partly the outcome. The vexed question of *how* to read Linton's fiction, both on its own and in relation to her journalism, so as to identify what lies behind the sensationalism and stereotyping, is still a difficult one. The overall aim of this essay is to see why Linton has remained so stubbornly outside the feminist canon, and to make a case for her inclusion, while suggesting that her writing admits of a more ideologically conflicted reading than her critics have always been ready to recognize.

However one looks at it, Eliza Lynn Linton was certainly an extraordinary writer, whose vituperative anger with society and drive to find herself a role that matched her principles must be of consuming interest to feminist scholars. The motherless youngest of twelve children living miles away from London, the literary center of Victorian culture; then the young woman allowed a year's grace in the capital to prove herself as a writer; then the separated wife and childless stepmother preaching domestic virtue to her contemporaries; finally the scourge of her society, adopting daughter-substitutes, who then left her to marry: Linton never chose an easy path for herself or secured a comfortable position in society. The verdict on her now is that her violent anti-feminism was out of date even in her own lifetime, and that such talent as she had was for journalism, rather than fiction-writing. Moreover, Linton herself made no effort to be liked by her readers. "She says she has never striven for popularity, and has boldly put forth her opinions, without caring for the consequences," reported Helen Black, who interviewed her in her London flat towards the end of her life (8). Nor was she willing to modify anything she wrote for "The Girl of the Period" when it was reissued in 1883:"I neither soften nor retract a line of what I have said" (I, viii). She clung uncompromisingly to the increasingly problematic view that a public and professional life was incompatible with a woman's duties as wife and mother.

So what exactly is Linton's claim on modern readers, and how might her work be read a century after her death? As Barbara Herrnstein Smith has argued, the "endurance" of a text, and its admission into the literary canon, depend on a pattern of complex interactions which form the process of cultural selection. In her view, canonical works—that body of writing studied in schools and colleges, and kept in print by publishers, the works scholars continue to discuss and debate—are commonly celebrated for their "generally benign 'humanistic' values," especially if these can be detached from the temporal moment in which they were produced (47–49). But if entry into the "mainstream" canon (which historically has included few works by women) is usually governed by aesthetic considerations and notions of "universality" or "representativeness," admission to the women's version is no foregone conclusion either. Linton has struggled for acceptance even into what John Guillory has identified as "noncanonical canons" (9). While few women writers are as unequivocally pro-feminist as contemporary scholars would like them to be, few are as stridently anti-feminist as Linton: even in her own lifetime, her stand was considered too extreme, and it would be difficult to see her values as exactly "benign." Nor has Linton had many critical backers in this century. As Lillian Robinson has observed, individual elevations from minor to major status "tend to be achieved by successful critical promotion" (115), a process of which Linton was herself only too well aware. Like Margaret Oliphant, Linton felt overshadowed by her near-contemporary, George Eliot, whose reputation seemed to be boosted by George Henry Lewes and the circle of admirers who gradually overcame their moral disapproval of her living arrangements, and applauded her as the greatest living woman novelist.

Linton was clearly irritated by Eliot, whose reputation she assessed on more than one occasion. For *Temple Bar* in 1885 she discussed John Cross's *Life* of Eliot, concluding that she was "always admired, believed in, sympathised with, helped forward" (51). She was also "eminently the result of other men's teachings," and "had no strength of character," relying on her admirers for sympathy and love. Though she calls Eliot's nature "at once jealous and dependent" (521), Linton's review is patently self-referential throughout, and burning with jealousy of what she regarded as Eliot's inflated reputation. She concluded that when all the fuss had died down, Eliot's life would be seen as "a contradiction"—the dullness of her last books overshadowing the vitality of her first, and her philosophic sayings, for which she was so much admired, finally acknowledged to be "protoplasm without grit or fire" (524). Nor had her opinion softened by the time she came to write on her supposed rival for *Women Novelists of Queen Victoria's Reign* (1897), or once more for *My Literary Life* (1899). Eliot was, in her view, vastly over-valued, her writing ponderous, and her life and principles at cross-purposes. Nevertheless, Linton was not without some admiration of Eliot, and the areas of her work she singles out for praise are perhaps surprising.

Discussing *Silas Marner* and *Adam Bede*, for example, in *Women Novelists*, she felt the shame involved in sexual lapse had been exaggerated: "George Eliot undoubtedly made a chronological mistake in both stories by the amount of conscientious remorse felt by her young men, and the depth of social degradation implied in this slip of her young women" (79). Linton here implies that Eliot was projecting her own heavy but anachronistic moralism on to an earlier period of social history when such lapses would be taken more casually by those involved. She also felt that Eliot laid too much emphasis generally in her writing on "self-sacrifice for the general good, of conformity with established moral standards, while her life was in direct opposition to her words" (88). Unfashionably, on the other hand, Linton sees Lucy Deane as the real heroine of *The Mill on the Floss*, and a more sympathetic one than Maggie Tulliver: "Sweet little Lucy had more of the true heroism of a woman in her patient acceptance of sorrow and her generous forgiveness of the cause thereof, than could be found in all Maggie's struggles between passion and principle" (74). Linton's views here are contradictory and almost deliberately perverse, but they help explain her preference for patient heroines of principle (such as her own honest Patricia Kemball, who endures being misunderstood and unappreciated in a household of hypocrites) rather than tempestuous drama-queens (like her Lizzie Lorton, who rages against her stepmother and siblings, and pitches herself at a handsome newcomer to the area). Linton seems to take an obstinate delight in turning Eliot's writing inside out and praising the parts other readers find least palatable, while also daring to say the unsayable about the great goddess-novelist. What is perhaps most significant about Linton's appraisal of her rival, however, is her identification of contradictions about Eliot that were also present in her own writing: "And it was this endeavour to co-ordinate insurgency and conformity, self-will and self-sacrifice, that made the discord of which every candid student of her work, who knew her history, was conscious from the beginning" (88–89). Exactly the same could be said of Linton herself.

In writing about Eliot, Linton must have recognized the closeness of their experiences: their overcoming of provincial exclusion and entry into national journalism, their precarious position on the edge of London literary bohemianism, and their inability to find love within the respectable confines of marriage and family life. The crucial difference was that Eliot had entered the canon within Linton's own lifetime, while Linton herself knew that the same process of literary "natural selection" was already closing her out. By the 1860s, as Nicola Thompson has observed, "with the phenomenal popularity of the novel, and its dominance by female writers and readers, a division began to emerge between popular and 'serious' literature" (8). Linton's fiction hovered awkwardly somewhere between the two. Most reviewers felt her work was "above the average of novels," as the *Saturday Review* (374) described *Sowing the Wind* (1867), but they quickly recognized her tendency to exaggerate and sensationalize, characteristics associated with popular, as opposed to serious, novels (374). Moreover, the main part of her career came after Eliot, Gaskell and the Brontës: with Austen, forbidding role-models and rivals to all their successors later in the century. She was also competing with the new generation of "sensationalists," Wilkie Collins, Mary Elizabeth

Braddon, and Mrs. Henry Wood, and later with the rising "New Woman" novelists, Sarah Grand and Grant Allen. Thomas Hardy emerged as a formidable competitor in the 1870s and 1880s. During this period the traditional three-decker novel was declining, but Linton largely continued writing in this mode (*The True History of Joshua Davidson* is a notable exception: it sold well in its time, and was republished as recently as 1976 by Garland). Much of the padding in Linton's novels, which has prevented their reissue in the commercially-conscious "modern classics" market, ironically derives from the pressures of a publishing tradition already on its way out when she was still accommodating herself to it.

In fact, her main interest in writing was the identification of cultural stereotypes. Their absence in George Eliot's work she saw as a serious failing, claiming in the *Temple Bar* article that her rival "created no literary types. She drew with the hand of a master living, breathing men and women; but they are individual not generic" (514). A contradictory factor in the history of canon-formation is that we require novelists to produce literary characters who are both individuals *and* types: Linton, for her part, favoured types only—hence the unpopular recurrence of violent caricatures among her characters.

The case against Linton goes roughly as follows: her novels are long-winded and the plots far-fetched. They are full of improbable incidents and illustrate a reactionary view of male-female relations, by which female energy is generally suppressed, motherhood sanctified, and subordination to strong men approved. Her women characters either die from their rebellious excesses (as happens with Lizzie Lorton) or are tamed into submission (Perdita Winstanley). She uses elements of the "sensation" tradition (such as murders in *Lizzie Lorton* and *Patricia Kemball*), but without the suspense and mystery of a Wilkie Collins or Mary Elizabeth Braddon. Nor is she even original. Borrowings from *Jane Eyre*, in the form of concealed mad wives, appear in *The Rebel of the Family* (1880) and *Grasp Your Nettle* (1865), while Jasper Trelawney, hero of the latter, is clearly modelled on Brontë's Rochester. Feminists feel let down by her because in her youth she wrote positively about Mary Wollstonecraft, and in her second novel, *Amymone* (1848), spoke up for women's rights—albeit in the days of Pericles—only to turn against women when she was in a stronger position to help them.[1] In addition, an outmoded class snobbishness forms an unpalatable undercurrent to several plots. Girton graduate Effie Chegwin in *The One Too Many* (1894) is seen as coarse for wanting to marry a policeman, while in *Lizzie Lorton*, the murderer-hero is deplored more for his ungentlemanliness in accepting excessive praise for rescuing the clergyman from drowning, than for his manslaughter of a

---

[1]   "Mary Wollstonecraft," *The English Republic*, III (1854), 418–24.

mine-worker. As for Linton herself, the journals began to see her in increasingly comic terms. For George Paston in *The Fortnightly Review* she was "a modern Dame Partington, vainly endeavouring to sweep the Atlantic Ocean of feminine evolution out of her back kitchen" (505); while *The Tomahawk* caricatured her as a "Prurient Prude" painting a harmless "girl of the period" as a hard-faced, horned she-devil (*The Woman Question* 116–17).

In her late journalism of the 1880s and 90s, Linton sounds shriller than ever, predicting the apocalyptic decline of British values into complete social anarchy. Seeing women as given to all the worst extremes of behavior, she steadily opposed their access to higher education, despite feeling badly educated herself; she thought the vote would make women discontented with their home lives, she feared the weakening of empire, and by 1892, she claimed that the "partisans of the wild women" would "give the keys of our foreign possessions into the hands of Russia or of France." ("Partisans" 458). The key issue for Linton was maternity, which she regarded as woman's "*raison d'être*." As she puts it in her essay on "The Wild Women as Politicians," using one of her strongest images, "The cradle lies across the door of the polling-booth and bars the way to the senate" (80). Linton clung tenaciously to a "separate spheres" ideology long after most other social theorists of the day had begun to admit that if the custom had ever existed, it had long since disintegrated under pressure on behalf of needy middle-class single women. Harriet Martineau, for instance, had recognized the need for such women to have paid employment as far back as 1859.[1]

Linton's views might have seemed more acceptable to modern critics if she herself had been a comfortable part of the society she represented: a happily married wife and mother—which apart from Elizabeth Gaskell, few of the great Victorian women novelists actually were. But Linton knew how difficult it was for an intelligent, original woman to find someone decent to marry; she knew what it was like to need paid employment, or to long for the freedom of a professional life in London. One of her most appealing narratives is the story of her visit to the *Morning Chronicle* offices to seek work with John Douglas Cook, its editor:

> "So! you are the little girl who has written that queer book, and want to be one of the press-gang, are you?" he said, half smiling, and speaking in a jerky and unprepared manner, both singular and reassuring. I took him in his humour and smiled too. "Yes, I am the woman," I said. "Woman, you call yourself? I call you a whippersnapper." (Van Thal 25)

---

[1] "On Female Industry," *Edinburgh Review* 109 (April 1859), 151–73.

Linton's quiet, deflating dignity, which contrasts with Cook's sexist bluster, makes as good a feminist point as any fuller argument could do, and shows that she was far from being unaware of the humorous condescension women were shown in their attempts to find work. Indeed the most attractive part of Linton's fiction, for feminists, is her creation of feisty heroines who question society's presumptions about women with all the vigor used by Linton herself in her journalism to uphold the opposite viewpoint.

Perdita Winstanley, the eponymous "Rebel of the Family," is one of Linton's best: immature, certainly, in her political naivete, but determined to find work rather than enter a mercenary marriage, or become a social butterfly at home. Linton's identification with her is warm and thorough, fully recognizing the anomalies of her position as a "poor lady" who is "neither able to earn money nor live independently" (p. 36, this edition). Unlike many strong-minded Victorian heroines who talk about work but never do any, Perdita actually sits and passes the Post-Office Savings Bank examination, and accepts a job there, aware that her duties are dull and many of the women fitted for something better. Linton is unusual in showing what it was like for sensitive middle-class women to work at something other than teaching, and she knew the details of what was involved. In *Sowing the Wind* (1867), she concentrates on journalism (something her rival George Eliot knew well, but never let her heroines try professionally), teetering on the edge of caricature as she describes Jane Osborn, a twenty-one year-old who writes for the *Comet* newspaper:

> She was decidedly plain; but she had fine grey eyes, large, deep-set, and intelligent, and she had a profusion of rich auburn hair, which another turn of the scale would have dyed to red. Her skin was of a duck's-egg white, fine and soft but covered with freckles; her nose was blunt and positive; her lips wide, clumsy, and ill-defined; her hands were small and good but her nails were dirty; and her shoes were down at heel, with the stockings rumpled round her ankles. (I, 28)

Though much of this is standard caricature of the bluestocking, Linton seems reluctant to dehumanize Jane, letting the softness and intelligence of the woman counteract the bohemianism of the intellectual. Moreover, as so often with her vigorous heroines, Linton gives Jane an impassioned speech on the importance of her chosen profession and principles: "Ah, you may talk as you like, Isola!" she tells the weaker woman against whom Linton's independent-minded viragos are characteristically placed, "babies, and love, and the graces and prettinesses are all very fine, I dare say, but give me the real solid pleasure of work—a man's work—work that influences the world—work that is power!" (*Sowing*, III, 29). Though her "official" point in contrasting masculine women like Jane with feminine ones like Isola is to suggest that marriage and maternity are what every woman wants, one feels that her real passion goes into the argument for the pleasure of creative, independent work. Moreover, she is realist enough to know that other forms of survival need to be found. More than any other Victorian woman novelist, she documents the frustrations of being a young, active and healthy woman at home with nothing to do, and the satisfaction of being allowed a role, however small, in the working world.

Another eponymous Linton heroine, Lizzie Lorton, begins life as a kind of tempestuous Dorothea Brooke, longing for something worthwhile to do with her unused energy. Unlike, for instance, Charlotte Yonge, Linton has relatively few sick and ailing characters in her novels, though some of her women are languid with boredom. Her young heroines are typically fit and strong, in keeping with her view that women should be taught to swim, load and fire a gun, climb a ladder, and ride a horse (Layard 148). Both Lizzie and Patricia Kemball can also manage a small sailing boat, though Lizzie is too bored and frustrated most of the time to do more than rage:

> She rose in the morning indifferent to all her actual life, but with a sobbing desire towards something unknown and far distant—travel, danger, war, shipwreck, even death itself, if in a stirring cause and where her fervent being could be fulfilled in some great deed of heroism before the world. (23)

Much of what Lizzie proclaims is clearly childish and designed for effect—as when she says she could defend her castle, head a regiment, or kill someone (Linton's murderers are usually men, however, unlike Braddon's). She fancies herself as Charlotte Corday or Lady Hester Stanhope (236), and believes that when a woman loves a man, she should tell him so, to his face. Patricia Kemball, a later heroine, reads like a reformed version of Lizzie without the destructive instincts, but with the same largely unused energy. Linton this time sees her as a "Joan of Arc figure, a Spartan, like a maid of another race and time" (297). Neither woman finds a legitimate outlet for her vitality, in that sense prefiguring Hardy's Eustacia Vye in *The Return of the Native* (1878) (Lizzie even drowns like Eustacia): circumstances ensure that their destinies of death and marriage respectively are meted out to them without the need for much conscious effort of their own.

If Linton was repeatedly drawn to strong, vibrant types in her novels, she was equally scornful of exaggerated effeminacy, both in women and in men. She was also adept at mimicking the precepts of anti-feminists and making them look ridiculous, as she does with Jabez Hamley in *Patricia Kemball*. This crude younger man who has married Patricia's aunt "liked women who were timid and who screamed easily ... He had an idea too that they should take very short steps—pretty pit-a-pat useless kind of steps—in fact a Chinese woman's walk modified" (48–49). Linton hated fine-ladyism as much as she did its opposite, loud hoydenism, and mocked the feeble delicacy of its practitioners, such as Dora Drummond, Patricia's lisping and hypocritical companion, and Margaret Elcombe's Aunt Harriet, worldly and mealy-mouthed, in *Lizzie Lorton*. Most of these women are matched with equally effete men: Sydney Lowe, Dora's husband, for instance, is introduced as "one of the light-weight men ... with good points, such as small hands and feet, broad shoulders, narrow hips, and a waist that would have matched a French officer's" (87–88). As far as Linton was concerned, such people deserved one another: "These women—soft, fair, and false," she remarks acidly of Dora, "have ever been the women men love best" (337). Patricia, by contrast, is matched with the manly and honest Gordon Frere—as his name suggests, a good-hearted brother figure she has known since childhood. She will have nothing to do with the mercenary marriages that form an important part of this, and most of Linton's other novels.

For all her professed belief in marriage, Linton, who had failed abysmally at it herself, focused throughout her career on monstrous alliances that involve, as she puts it in one of her last novels, *The One Too Many* (1894), "the sacrifice of a victim and the purchase of a slave" (I, 248). Older men with ambiguous sexual appetites repeatedly try to snare younger women into miserable marriages. Perdita has the sense to turn down Mr. Brocklebank in *The Rebel of the Family*, but Isola, in *Sowing the Wind*, finds herself married to a would-be baby-murderer, while Moira West, in *The One Too Many*, is given little choice but to accept the appalling egotist Launcelot Brabazon or remain an "encumbrance" at home. "I'd sweep a crossing sooner than be his wife," Moira's friend, the Girton girl Effie Chegwin tells her, recommending the more dignified alternative of work as a shop girl, but Moira lacks the drive to escape (I, 238). Unintentionally, Linton finds herself among the anti-marriage novelists of the 1890s, depicting a society that has submitted itself entirely to mercenary considerations at the expense of personal contentment. Few of her characters are promised happy marriages: those who are, such as Perdita and Leslie Crawford, or Patricia Kemball and Gordon Frere, are those with the most conventional expectations—of healthy companionship and mutual regard. They also make their own matches, consciously going against the wishes of their families who wish them to marry solely for economic and social advancement.

It is hardly surprising that for much of her life Linton favoured divorce, though she did not seek one from her husband.[1]

Despite her conservatism, Linton employed radical tactics in her novels that still have the power to surprise us. If we accept that she was trying to do something other than produce novels in the classic realist mode, we may be able to judge her work rather differently. Her interest was in unveiling hypocrisy and pseudo-respectability, which she was best able to do by means of caricature and exaggeration. *The True History of Joshua Davidson* (1872) in rewriting the story of Jesus Christ in a nineteenth-century social setting, shows that professing Christians fail to realize that their religion, followed through to its logical conclusion, means practising communism: yet, "to live according to Christ in modern Christendom was, as we found out, to be the next thing to criminal, and at all events qualified for prison discipline" (165). The fact that Linton was an agnostic daughter of a clergyman, and grand-daughter of the Bishop of Carlisle, added another extraordinary twist to the novel's background. Linton was no apologist for Christianity; indeed, she asks at the end of her novel: "Is the Christian world all wrong, or is practical Christianity impossible?" (276)—yet it is the society of her day that she casti-gates more than the church. Once she had found her voice—dating perhaps from the "Girl of the Period" articles, her most resounding success—Linton left no sacred edifice of society unscathed. It was as if she was now unafraid of anything and able to state her views without regard for prudish recoiling. Indeed, the directness of Linton's style is one of the most attractive things about her, and makes her novels easy and rapid to read.

In the *Autobiography of Christopher Kirkland* (1885) she employed shock tactics of a different kind: writing her autobiography with most of the sexes inverted, so that the troubles of her own life become that of her male persona. Though this choice may have meant sacrificing the opportunity to make more of what were specifically *women's* difficulties in battling her way through life, Linton undoubtedly makes her readers consider the impact of gender on a life. Are the sexes as interchangeable as the novel implies, or is it in fact the opposite notion that the plot suggests? Seeing herself as a man, Linton exper-iments with the shape of a human life, and sees her own, as Christopher's, governed by a turbulent passion she had elsewhere identified as belonging to a woman's nature, rather than a man's. A misfit in society as well as in his family, Christopher travels via a succession of violent mood-swings, to a belief in altruism and the annihilation of self.

---

[1] See, for example, her essay on "Maternity" in *Freeshooting: Extracts from the Works of Mrs Lynn Linton* (London: Chatto & Windus, 1892), or "The marriage tie," *New Review* (February 1892).

The book embodies another set of contradictions: Christopher's narcissism, culminating in his commitment to altruism; his womanish frustrations offered unconvincingly as a man's; his rebelliousness tamed into submission; his passionate relationships crushed, his final state lonely and unsuccessful. Christopher's towering egotism contrasts with Linton's own shrinking presence in *My Literary Life* (1899), which sounds like a real autobiography, but instead offers reminiscences of others, with only the most fragmentary appearances by Linton herself as a shy inexperienced apprentice to "literary life," rather than a confident participant.

Linton is hard to pin down because apart from anything else, she clearly enjoyed role-play. One minute she is Christopher Kirkland, another (ironically enough) "a matron myself, with pleasant brown-haired girls."[1] In these and her other writings, Linton constantly ambushes the reader with daring tactics. Unpredictably direct, unfair to herself, more so to others, Linton says what she thinks, castigating a sick society with images that are patently distorted, characters that are openly preposterous. Her Launcelot Brabazons, Effie Chegwins, Mr. Brocklebanks, and Bell Blounts are like Punch and Judy characters with comically suggestive names and personalities to match. Yet to dismiss her characters as entirely unrelated to social realism would be to overlook their topicality—primary cause of her exclusion from the canon. Linton uses them as extensions of her journalism to cudgel a society that appalled her, and which she was powerless to change. In that respect, she was very far from being the pillar of the community that modern readers expect an anti-feminist to be, but a discordant outsider: kind-hearted to individuals, if several contemporary testimonies are to be trusted, but exasperated with men and women collectively. In her later writings—both novels and journalism—Linton found little about contemporary life to praise. In her view, men had become effeminate and women manly. She denied that women were morally superior to men, as generations of conduct book writers had tried to imply, and regretted that it was so difficult for men and women to be straightforwardly friends. Indeed, she saw women as natural rule-breakers who would become hysterical and irresponsible if they were allowed to enter political life. As Nancy Fix Anderson has observed, she "always seemed to distance herself from her targets, and referred to women as 'they' rather than 'we'" (131).[2] In this failure to identify herself with women, though she had experienced a whole gamut of experiences that were problematic for them (limited access to education, entry into the professional London literary world, late marriage, separation, childlessness, unpopularity) lies the clue to

---

[1] E. Lynn Linton, *Ourselves: Essays on Women* (London: G. Routledge and Sons, 1870), p. 4.

[2] A major exception to this generalization is the volume of essays, *Ourselves*.

Linton's anomalous position as a Victorian woman writer who has remained firmly outside the canon.

A woman reluctant to identify herself as a woman, Linton remains fascinating because she stops short of recognizing all the various anomalies of her role. Many of her novels are about people taking up intransigent positions—something she does herself in her journalism. Writing with increasing stridency, she preached humility and docility for women. She ran away from home and recommended women to stay there. She was jealous of George Eliot, and recognized the contradictions between Eliot's stated morality and her life; yet her own life was much the same in its failure to exemplify her own teachings. Ultimately, Linton has remained outside the canon because her work is eccentric and unique. Her preferences are unpopular, and she herself finds it impossible to uphold them consistently. Feminists read her novels for their rebels rather than their conformists, yet leave Perdita Winstanley at the point where she has ceased to be a determined worker and is about to become a patient wife. "Our whole state here is a compromise between antiquated laws and modern feeling," Linton acknowledges in *Ourselves* (229). Her fluctuating, unstable career is testimony of her lifelong struggle to document that compromise, and ultimately to live with it.

Works Cited

Anderson, Nancy Fix. *Woman Against Women in Victorian England: A Life of Eliza Lynn Linton*. Bloomington and Indianapolis: Indiana UP, 1987.

The Athenaeum. "Mrs Lynn Linton." (23 July 1898): 131–32.

Black, Helen C. *Notable Women Authors of the Day*. Glasgow: David Bruce & Son, 1893.

Colby, Vineta. *The Singular Anomaly: Women Novelists of the Nineteenth Century*. New York: New York UP, 1970.

Guillory, John. *Cultural Capital: The Problem of Literary Canon Formation*. London and Chicago: U of Chicago Press, 1993.

Helsinger, Elizabeth K. et. al. *The Woman Question: Society and Literature in Britain and America 1837–1883, Vol I, Defining Voices*. Chicago and London: U of Chicago Press, 1983.

Layard, George Somes. *Mrs Lynn Linton: Her Life, Letters and Opinions*. London: Methuen, 1901.

Linton, E. Lynn. *The Autobiography of Christopher Kirkland*. 3 vols. London: Richard Bentley & Son, 1885.

———. *Freeshooting: Extracts from the Works of Mrs Lynn Linton*. London: Chatto & Windus, 1892.

———. "George Eliot." *Temple Bar* 73 (1885): 512–24.

——. *The Girl of the Period and Other Social Essays.* 2 vols. London: Richard Bentley & Son, 1883.

——. *Grasp Your Nettle: A Novel.* 3 vols. London: Smith, Elder, 1865.

——. *Lizzie Lorton of Greyrigg.* 3 vols in 1. London: Tinsley Brothers, 1867.

——. "The Marriage Tie: Its Sanctity and Abuse." *The New Review*, 6 (1892): 218–28.

——. "Mary Wollstonecraft." *The English Republic*, III (1854): 418–24.

——. *My Literary Life.* London: Hodder & Stoughton, 1899.

——. *The One Too Many.* 3 vols. London: Chatto & Windus, 1894.

——. *Ourselves: Essays on Women.* London: G. Routledge & Sons, 1870.

——. "The Partisans of the Wild Women." *Nineteenth Century*, 31 (1892): 455–64.

——. *Patricia Kemball.* 3 vols in 1. London: Chatto & Windus, 1875.

——. *The Rebel of the Family.* 3 vols. London: Chatto & Windus, 1880.

——. *Sowing the Wind.* 3 vols. London: Tinsley Brothers, 1867.

——. *The True History of Joshua Davidson.* London: Strachan & Co, 1872.

——. "The Wild Women. No. I. As Politicians." *Nineteenth Century*, 30 (1891): 79–88.

Martineau, Harriet. "Female Industry." *Edinburgh Review*, 109 (1859): 151–73.

"Mrs Lynn Linton." *The Academy Supplement* (30 July 1898): 107–08.

Oliphant, Margaret, et al. ed., *Women Novelists of Queen Victoria's Reign: A Book of Appreciations.* London: Hurst & Blackett, 1897.

Paston, George. "A Censor of Modern Womanhood." *Fortnightly Review*, 70 (1901).

Robinson, Lillian S. "Treason Our Text: Feminist Challenges to the Literary Canon." *Feminisms: An Anthology of Literary Theory and Criticism.* Ed. Robyn R. Warhol and Diane Price Herndl. Revised edition: Basingstoke: Macmillan, 1997. 115–28.

Smith, Barbara Herrnstein, *Contingencies of Value: Alternative Perspectives for Critical Theory.* Cambridge, Mass., and London: Harvard UP, 1988.

"Sowing the Wind." *The Saturday Review*, 23 March 1867.

Thompson, Nicola Diane, ed. *Victorian Women Writers and the Woman Question.* Cambridge: Cambridge UP, 1999.

Van Thal, Herbert. *Eliza Lynn Linton: The Girl of the Period.* London: George Allen & Unwin, 1979.